A TREASURY OF MODERN MYSTERIES

Volume 1

AGATHA CHRISTIE • JOYCE CAROL OATES
GEORGE FOX • HARRY KEMELMAN
BILL PRONZINI • DOROTHY SALISBURY DAVIS
MARGERY ALLINGHAM • DAPHNE du MAURIER

A TREASURY OF MODERN MYSTERIES

DONALD E. WESTLAKE • ARTHUR PORGES
THOMAS KYD • ROSS MACDONALD
IRA LEVIN • GEORGES SIMENON
JOHN D. MacDONALD • JAMES HOLDING
STANLEY ELLIN • IAN FLEMING • TRUMAN CAPOTE

VOLUME I

DOUBLEDAY & COMPANY, INC.
Garden City, New York

Library of Congress Catalog Number 73–77298
Printed in the United States of America

INTRODUCTION

MYSTERIES are fun to read.

Anyone who doesn't accept that proposition can go find another book. Other kinds of fiction can be more provocative, more searching, more revealing of the human condition, but there comes a time when a reader simply wants a good story with a beginning, a middle, an end, set in an orderly world where reason and virtue and a little bit of luck almost always guarantee the triumph of the good guys.

Within the boundaries of the mystery field, there is plenty of room for variation on this theme. Purists define the genre narrowly, limiting mysteries to the classic form of detective story, the straight whodunit with a sleuth, a puzzle, and ingeniously planted clues. Top-flight stories have been and still are being written in this form. But we live in a permissive age, and rules are so flexible as to be nonexistent. Today the term "mystery" is applied to almost any suspense story, usually involving a crime, usually equipped with a solution. Beyond that, definitions should be referred to Lewis Carroll: "When I use a word," Humpty Dumpty said, "it means just what I choose it to mean—neither more nor less." So—this is a collection of mysteries, entertaining mysteries, I think, and (for an additional rationale) all modern in the sense that they are post World War II.

The golden age of the mystery story, like the golden age in any field, is usually assigned to the past. How far back it recedes may depend as much on the eye—and age—of the beholder as on the quality of the books at hand. Some readers favor the hard-boiled private-eye adventures epitomized by Dashiell Hammett and Raymond Chandler, or the locked rooms and house parties of the twenties, or the gaslit era of Sherlock Holmes, or the macabre tales of Poe, but I think a case can be made for today as a contemporary golden age. The present day, defined as the postwar era, not only has witnessed the flourishing of perennial favorites like Agatha Christie, Rex Stout, Ngaio Marsh, and Ellery Queen, but the emergence of Ross Macdonald, John Le Carré, John D. MacDonald, and Ed McBain. There are steady reliables like Richard Lockridge, Sara Woods, Dell Shannon, Patricia Moyes, and Michael Gilbert. And there's a new wave, with Dick Francis, Michael

Crichton, Donald E. Westlake, Ira Levin, Emma Lathen, Peter Dickinson, Nicholas Freeling, George Baxt, John Godey, Colin Watson, Bill Pronzini, Dorothy Uhnak, and Maj Sjöwall and Per Wahlöö. Eric Ambler is still turning out his polished tales of intrigue, Georges Simenon's Maigret continues to probe the psychological depths, Harry Kemelman's rabbi scores a triumph almost every day of the week, Frederick Forsyth ingeniously melts bold headlines into gripping fiction, and Truman Capote reaches for a whole new genre with the nonfiction novel.

Within the mystery and suspense field, any litany of major writers in this period must also include such departed masters as Josephine Tey (*The Daughter of Time* belongs on every ten-best list), Charlotte Armstrong, Margery Allingham, William Irish, Ian Fleming, and Erle Stanley Gardner.

Selecting a treasury of mysteries from this wealth of material is a game any devotee can play. This particular collection, from Agatha Christie to Truman Capote, spans an ocean and a generation for a whole world of good reading.

A word about the authors of the longer works:

In *Endless Night* the postwar Agatha Christie has written as deft, as surprising, as masterful a story as her 1926 classic, *The Murder of Roger Ackroyd.* Dame Agatha is credited with more than eighty books—novels, plays, and short stories—with sales surpassing 350,000,000. The Christie for Christmas phenomenon regularly brightens the holiday season, one of her plays, *The Mousetrap,* is still running in London after twenty years, and movies based on her books include *Witness for the Prosecution, And Then There Were None,* and the delightful Miss Marple series with Margaret Rutherford. Now in her eighties, Dame Agatha is an institution.

Ross Macdonald is the acknowledged heir of Dashiell Hammett and Raymond Chandler. It is no accident that Archer, the name of Sam Spade's partner in Hammett's *The Maltese Falcon,* is also the name of Macdonald's series hero. In *The Goodbye Look* (Chandler had one called *The Long Goodbye*), Macdonald's Lew Archer embarks on one of his typical quests for truth and justice in a southern California where the smog of modern living encroaches on both landscape and people. From his Santa Barbara base, Macdonald, under his real name, Kenneth Millar, is one of the more effective warriors in the battle against oil spills and pollution. Idealism obviously motivates both the author and his hero.

Has there been a more stunning debut in the mystery field than *A Kiss Before Dying*? Any first-time reader who isn't properly amazed by the major revelation halfway through this Ira Levin novel simply hasn't learned how to suspend his disbelief. A second reading—to see how Levin achieved this effect—can only increase your admiration for his technique. Levin has gone on to greater fame with *Rosemary's Baby* and *The Stepford Wives,* but *A Kiss Before Dying* is still his classic work.

Whether or not Truman Capote invented the nonfiction novel with *In Cold Blood,* he created a fascinating study of two psychotic personalities. It is a chilling glimpse of a nether world, made all the more horrifying by contrast with the everyday life of a rural Kansas with its ordinary likable people who were victims, pursuers, and finally executioners.

The novellas are as diverse as the full-length books. Joyce Carol Oates focuses her penetrating searchlight on Norman and the Killer, and in that stark light there is no place to hide. In "Cain's Mark," Bill Pronzini tells a simple story of revenge, justifiable revenge, perhaps, but debilitating just the same. To the romantic setting of Venice, Daphne du Maurier brings a touch of the occult, her own special blend of magic and suspense in "Don't Look Now." Calm professionalism marks "Stan the Killer," with Georges Simenon's Maigret moving surely toward yet another successful resolution. And finally Ian Fleming's all-conquering hero, James Bond, unmasks a Russian spy, making the world just a bit safer for all of us who indulge in mystery reading.

For their co-operation and assistance in putting this anthology together, my thanks to Gloria Levitas, a former member of the editorial staff of *Ellery Queen's Mystery Magazine,* and Lucia Staniels, associate editor of the Literary Guild.

Marie R. Reno
Editor, The Mystery Guild, 1966–73

CONTENTS

VOLUME 1

VOLUME 2

A TREASURY OF MODERN MYSTERIES

Volume 1

ENDLESS NIGHT

by Agatha Christie

BOOK ONE

1

In my end is my beginning. . . . That's a quotation I've often heard people say. It sounds all right—but what does it really mean?

Is there ever any particular spot where one can put one's finger and say, "It all began that day, at such a time and such a place, with such an incident"?

Did my story begin, perhaps, when I noticed the sale bill hanging on the wall of the George and Dragon announcing sale by auction of that valuable property "The Towers," and giving particulars of the acreage, the miles and furlongs, and the highly idealized portrait of The Towers as it might have been perhaps in its prime, anything from eighty to a hundred years ago.

I was doing nothing particular, just strolling along the main street of Kingston Bishop, a place of no importance whatever, killing time. I noticed the sale bill. Why? Fate up to its dirty work? Or dealing out its golden handshake of good fortune? You can look at it either way.

Or you could say, perhaps, that it all had its beginnings when I met Santonix, during the talks I had with him; I can close my eyes and see his flushed cheeks, the over-brilliant eyes, and the movement of the strong yet delicate hand that sketched and drew plans and elevations of houses. One house in particular, a beautiful house, a house that would be wonderful to own!

My longing for a house, a fine and beautiful house, such a house as I could never hope to have, flowered into life then. It was a happy fantasy shared between us, the house that Santonix would build for me—if he lasted long enough . . .

A house that in my dream I would live in with the girl that I loved, a house in which just like a child's silly fairy story we should live together "happy ever afterward." All pure fantasy, all nonsense, but it started that tide of longing in me—longing for something I was never likely to have.

Or if this is a love story—and it is a love story, I swear—then why not begin where I first caught sight of Ellie standing in the dark fir trees of Gipsy's Acre?

Gipsy's Acre. Yes, perhaps I'd better begin there, at the moment when I turned away from the sale board with a little shiver because a black cloud had come over the sun, and asked a question carelessly enough of one of the locals, who was clipping a hedge in a desultory fashion nearby.

"What's this house, The Towers, like?"

I can still see the queer face of the old man as he looked at me sideways and said,

"That's not what us calls it here. What sort of a name is that?" He snorted disapproval. "It's many a year now since folks lived in it and called it The Towers." He snorted again.

I asked him then what he called it, and again his eyes shifted away from me in his old wrinkled face in that queer way country folk have of not speaking to you direct, looking over your shoulder or round the corner, as it were, as though they saw something you didn't; and he said,

"It's called hereabouts Gipsy's Acre."

"Why is it called that?" I asked.

"Some sort of a tale. I dunno rightly. One says one thing, one says another." And then he went on, "Anyway, it's where the accidents take place."

"Car accidents?"

"All kinds of accidents. Car accidents mainly nowadays. It's a nasty corner there, you see."

"Well," I said, "if it's a nasty curve, I can well see there might be accidents."

"Rural council put up a danger sign, but it don't do no good, that don't. There are accidents just the same."

"Why Gipsy?" I asked him.

Again his eyes slipped past me and his answer was vague.

"Some tale or other. It was gipsies' land once, they say, and they were turned off, and they put a curse on it."

I laughed.

"Aye," he said, "you can laugh, but there's places as *is* cursed. You smart alecks in town don't know about them. But there's places as is cursed, all right, and there's a curse on this place. People got killed here in the quarry when they got the stone out to build. Old Geordie, he fell over the edge there one night and broke his neck."

"Drunk?" I suggested.

"He may have been. He liked his drop, he did. But there's many drunks as fall—nasty falls—but it don't do them no lasting harm. But Geordie, he got his neck broke. In there," he pointed up behind him to the pine-covered hill, "in Gipsy's Acre."

Yes, I suppose that's how it began. Not that I paid much attention to it at the time. I just happened to remember it. That's all. I think—that is, when I think properly—that I built it up a bit in my mind. I don't know if it was before or later that I asked if there were still any gipsies about there. He said there weren't many anywhere nowadays. The police were always moving them on, he said. I asked,

"Why doesn't anybody like gipsies?"

"They're a thieving lot," he said disapprovingly. Then he peered more closely at me. "Happen you've got gipsy blood yourself?" he suggested, looking hard at me.

I said not that I knew of. It's true; I do look a bit like a gipsy. Perhaps that's what fascinated me about the name of Gipsy's Acre. I thought to myself as I was standing there smiling back at him, amused by our conversation, that perhaps I had a bit of gipsy blood.

Gipsy's Acre. I went up the winding road that led out of the village and wound up through the dark trees and came at last to the top of the hill so that I could see out to sea and the ships. It was a marvelous view and I thought, just as one does think things, "I wonder how it would be if Gipsy's Acre was my acre?"—just like that. It was only a ridiculous thought. When I passed my hedge clipper again, he said,

"If you want gipsies, there's old Mrs. Lee, of course. The Major, he give her a cottage to live in."

"Who's the Major?" I asked.

He said in a shocked voice, "Major Phillpot, of course." He seemed quite upset that I should ask! I gathered that Major Phillpot was God locally. Mrs. Lee was some kind of dependent of his, I suppose, whom he'd provided for. The Phillpots seemed to have lived there all their lives and more or less to run the place.

As I wished my old boy good day and turned away, he said,

"She's got the last cottage at the end of the street. You'll see her outside, maybe. Doesn't like the inside of houses. Them as has got gipsy blood don't."

So there I was, wandering down the road, whistling and thinking about Gipsy's Acre. I'd almost forgotten what I'd been told when I saw a tall black-haired old woman staring at me over a garden hedge. I knew at once it must be Mrs. Lee. I stopped and spoke to her.

"I hear you can tell me all about Gipsy's Acre up there," I said.

She stared at me through a tangled fringe of black hair and she said,

"Don't have nought to do with it, young man. You listen to me. Forget about it. You're a good-looking lad. Nothing good comes out of Gipsy's Acre and never will."

"I see it's up for sale," I said.

"Aye, that's so, and more fool he who buys it."

"Who's likely to buy it?"

"There's a builder after it. More than one. It'll go cheap. You'll see."

"Why should it go cheap?" I asked curiously. "It's a fine site."

She wouldn't answer that.

"Supposing a builder buys it cheap; what will he do with it?"

She chuckled to herself. It was malicious, unpleasant laughter.

"Pull down the old ruined house and build, of course. Twenty–thirty houses, maybe—and all with a curse on them."

I ignored the last part of the sentence. I said, speaking before I could stop myself,

"That would be a shame. A great shame."

"Ah, you needn't worry. They'll get no joy of it, not those who buys and not those who lays the bricks and mortar. There'll be a foot that slips on the ladder, and there'll be the lorry that crashes with a load, and the slate that falls from the roof of a house and finds its mark. And the trees, too. Crashing, maybe, in a sudden gale. Ah, you'll see! There's none that'll get any good out of Gipsy's Acre. They'd do best to leave it alone. You'll see. You'll see." She nodded vigorously and then she repeated softly to herself, "*There's no luck for them as meddles with Gipsy's Acre*. There never has been."

I laughed. She spoke sharply.

"Don't laugh, young man. It comes to me as may be one of these days you'll laugh on the wrong side of your mouth. There's never been no luck there, not in the house nor yet in the land."

"What happened in the house?" I asked. "Why has it been empty so long? Why was it left to fall down?"

"The last people that lived there died, all of them."

"How did they die?" I asked out of curiosity.

"Best not to speak of it again. But no one cared to come and live in it afterward. It was left to molder and decay. It's forgot by now and best that it should be."

"But you could tell me the story," I said wheedlingly. "You know all about it."

"I don't gossip about Gipsy's Acre." Then she let her voice drop to a kind of phony beggar's whine. "I'll tell your fortune now, my pretty lad, if you like. Cross my palm with silver and I'll tell your fortune. You're one of those that'll go far one of these days."

"I don't believe nonsense about fortunetelling," I said, "and I haven't any silver. Not to spare, anyway."

She came nearer to me and went on in a wheedling voice. "Sixpence now. Sixpence now. I'll do it for sixpence. What's that? Nothing at all. I'll do it for sixpence because you're a handsome lad with a ready tongue and a way with you. It could be that you'll go far."

I fished a sixpence out of my pocket, not because I believed in any of her foolish superstitions but because for some reason I liked the old fraud even if I did see through her. She grabbed the coin from me and said,

"Give me your hand then. Both hands."

She took my hands in her withered claw and stared down at the open palms. She was silent for a minute or two, staring. Then she dropped my hands abruptly, almost pushing them away from her. She retreated a step and spoke harshly.

"If you know what's good for you, you'll get out of Gipsy's Acre here and now and you won't come back! That's the best advice I can give you. Don't come back."

"Why not? Why shouldn't I come back?"

"Because if you do, you'll come back to sorrow and loss and danger maybe. There's trouble, black trouble, waiting for you. Forget you ever saw this place. I'm warning you."

"Well, of all the—"

But she had turned away and was retreating to the cottage. She went in and slammed the door. I'm not superstitious. I believe in luck, of course, who doesn't? But not a lot of superstitious nonsense about ruined houses with curses on them. And yet I had an uneasy feeling that the sinister old creature had seen something in my hands. I looked down at my two palms spread out in front of me. What could anyone see in the palms of anyone's hands? Fortunetelling was arrant nonsense —just a trick to get money out of you—money out of your silly credulity. I looked up at the sky. The sun had gone in, the day seemed different now. A sort of shadow, a kind of menace. Just an approaching storm, I thought. The wind was beginning to blow, the backs of the leaves were showing on the trees. I whistled to keep my spirits up and walked along the road through the village.

I looked again at the pasted-up bill advertising the auction of The Towers. I even made a note of the date. I had never attended a property sale in my life, but I thought to myself that I'd come and attend this one. It would be interesting to see who bought The Towers—that is to say, interesting to see who became the owner of Gipsy's Acre. Yes, I think that's really where it all began. . . . A fantastic notion occurred to me. I'd come and pretend to myself that I was the man who was going to bid for Gipsy's Acre! I'd bid against the local builders! They'd drop out, disappointed in their hopes of buying it cheap. I'd buy it and I'd go to Rudolf Santonix and say, "Build me a house. I've bought the site for you." And I'd find a girl, a wonderful girl, and we'd live in it together happy ever after.

I often had dreams of that kind. Naturally they never came to anything, but they were fun. That's what I thought then. Fun! Fun, my God! If I'd only known!

2

IT WAS PURE chance that had brought me to the neighborhood of Gipsy's Acre that day. I was driving a hire car, taking some people down from London to attend a sale—a sale not of a house but of its contents. It was a big house just at the outskirts of the town, a particularly ugly one. I drove an elderly couple there who were interested, from what I could overhear of their conversation, in a collection of papier-mâché, whatever papier-mâché was. The only time I ever heard it mentioned before was by my mother in connection with washing-up bowls. She'd said that a papier-mâché washing-up bowl was far better than a plastic one any day! It seemed an odd thing for rich people to want to come down and buy a collection of the stuff.

However, I stored the fact away in my mind and I thought I would look in a dictionary or read up somewhere what papier-mâché really was. Something that people thought worthwhile to hire a car for, and go down to a country sale and bid for. I liked knowing about things. I was twenty-two years of age at that time and I had picked up a fair amount of knowledge one way and another. I knew a good deal about cars, was a fair mechanic and a careful driver. Once I'd worked with horses in Ireland. I nearly got entangled with a dope gang, but I got wise and quit in time. A job as a chauffeur to a classy car hire firm isn't bad at all. Good money to be made with tips. And not usually too strenuous. But the work itself was boring.

Once I'd gone fruit picking in summertime. That didn't pay much, but I enjoyed myself. I'd tried a lot of things. I'd been a waiter in a third-class hotel, life guard on a summer beach, I'd sold encyclopedias and vacuum cleaners and a few other things. I'd once done horticultural work in a botanical garden and had learned a little about flowers.

I never stuck to anything. Why should I? I'd found nearly everything I did interesting. Some things were harder work than others, but I didn't really mind that. I'm not really lazy. I suppose what I really am is restless. I want to go everywhere, see everything, do everything. I want to find something. Yes, that's it. I want to find something.

From the time I left school I wanted to find something, but I didn't yet know what that something was going to be. It was just something I was looking for in a vague, unsatisfied sort of way. It was somewhere. Sooner or later I'd know all about it. It might perhaps be a girl. . . . I like girls, but no girl I'd met so far had been important. . . . You liked them all right, but then you went on to the next one quite gladly. They were like the jobs I took. All right for a bit, and then you got fed up with them and you wanted to move on to the next one. I'd gone from one thing to another ever since I'd left school.

A lot of people disapproved of my way of life. I suppose they were what you might call my well-wishers. That was because they didn't understand the first thing about me. They wanted me to go steady with a nice girl, save money, get married to her and then settle down to a nice steady job. Day after day, year after year, world without end, amen. Not for yours truly! There must be something better than that. Not just all this tame security, the good old welfare state limping along in its half-baked way! Surely, I thought, in a world where man has been able to put satellites in the sky and where men talk big about visiting the stars, there must be something that rouses you, that makes your heart beat, that's worthwhile searching all over the world to find! One day, I remember, I was walking down Bond Street. It was during my waiter period and I was due on duty. I'd been strolling, looking at some shoes in a shop window. Very natty they were. Like they say in the advertisements in newspapers: *What smart men are wearing today* and there's usually a picture of the smart man in question. My word, he usually looks a twerp! Used to make me laugh, advertisements like that did.

I passed on from the shoes to the next window. It was a picture shop. Just three pictures in the window artily arranged with a drape of limp velvet in some neutral color arranged over a corner of a gilt frame. Cissy, if you know what I mean. I'm not much of a one for art. I dropped in to the National Gallery once out of curiosity. Fair gave me the pip, it did. Great big shiny colored pictures of battles in rocky glens, or emaciated saints getting themselves stuck with arrows. Portraits of simpering great ladies sitting smirking in silks and velvets and lace. I decided then and there that art wasn't for me. But the picture I was looking at now was somehow different. There were three pictures in the window. One a landscape, nice bit of country for what I call every day. One of a woman drawn in such a funny way, so much out of proportion, that you could hardly see she was a woman. I suppose that's what they call *art nouveau.* I don't know what it was about. The third picture was my picture. There wasn't really much to it, if you know what I mean. It was—how can I describe it? It was kind of simple. A lot of space in it and a few great widening circles all round each other, if you can put it that way. All in different colors —odd colors that you wouldn't expect. And here and there, there were sketchy bits of color that didn't seem to mean anything. Only somehow they did mean something! I'm no good at description. All I can say is that one wanted terribly to go on looking at it.

I just stood there, feeling queer, as though something very unusual had happened to me. Those fancy shoes now, I'd have liked them to wear. I mean I take quite a bit of trouble about my clothes. I like to dress well so as to make an impression, but I never seriously thought in my life of buying a pair of shoes in Bond Street. I know the kind of fancy prices they ask there—fifteen pounds a pair, those shoes might be. Handmade or something, they call it, making it more worthwhile, for some reason. Sheer waste of money that would be. A classy line in shoes, yes, but you can pay too much for class. I've got my head screwed on the right way.

But this picture, what would that cost, I wondered? Suppose I were to buy that picture? You're crazy, I said to myself. You don't go for pictures, not in a general way. That was true enough. But I wanted this picture. . . . I'd like it to be mine. I'd like to be able to hang it and sit and look at it as long as I liked and know that I owned it! Me! Buying pictures. It seemed a crazy idea. I took a look at the picture again. Me wanting that picture didn't make sense, and anyway, I probably couldn't afford it. Actually I was in funds at just that moment. A lucky tip on a horse. This picture would probably cost a packet. Twenty pounds? Twenty-five? Anyway, there would be no harm in asking. They couldn't eat me, could they? I went in, feeling rather aggressive and on the defensive.

The inside of the place was all very hushed and grand. There was a sort of muted atmosphere, with neutral color walls and a velvet settee on which you could sit and look at the pictures. A man who looked a little like the model for the perfectly dressed man in advertisements came and attended to me, speaking in a rather hushed voice to match the scenery. Funnily, he didn't look superior as they usually do in high-grade Bond Street shops. He listened to what I said and then he took the picture out of the window and displayed it for me against a wall, holding it there for me to look at as long as I wanted. It came to me then—in the way you sometimes know just exactly how things are, that the same rules didn't apply to pictures as they do about other things. Someone might come into a place like this dressed in shabby old clothes and a frayed shirt and turn out to be a millionaire who wanted to add to his collection. Or he could come in looking cheap and flashy, rather like me, perhaps, but somehow or other he'd got such a yen for a picture that he managed to get the money together by some kind of sharp practice.

"A very fine example of the artist's work," said the man who was holding the picture.

"How much?" I said briskly.

The answer took my breath away.

"Twenty-five thousand," he said in his gentle voice.

I'm quite good at keeping a poker face. I didn't show anything. At least I don't think I did. He added some name that sounded foreign. The artist's name, I suppose, and that it had just come on the market from a house in the country, where the people who lived there had had no idea what it was. I kept my end up and sighed.

"It's a lot of money, but it's worth it, I suppose," I said.

Twenty-five thousand pounds. What a laugh!

"Yes," he said, and sighed. "Yes, indeed." He lowered the picture very gently and carried it back to the window. He looked at me and smiled. "You have good taste," he said.

I felt that in some way he and I understood each other. I thanked him and went out into Bond Street.

3

I DON'T KNOW much about writing things down—not, I mean, in the way a proper writer would do. The bit about that picture I saw, for instance. It doesn't really have anything to do with anything. I mean, nothing came of it, it didn't lead to anything and yet I feel somehow that it is important, that it has a place somewhere. It was one of the things that happened to me that meant something. Just like Gipsy's Acre meant something to me. Like Santonix meant something to me.

I haven't really said much about him. He was an architect. Of course, you'll have gathered that. Architects are another thing I'd never had much to do with, though I knew a few things about the building trade. I came across Santonix in the course of my wanderings. It was when I was working as a chauffeur, driving the rich around places. Once or twice I drove abroad, twice to Germany—I knew a bit of German—and once or twice to France—I had a smattering of French, too—and once to Portugal. They were usually elderly people who had money and bad health in about equal quantities.

When you drive people like that around, you begin to think that money isn't so hot, after all. What with incipient heart attacks, lots of bottles of little pills you have to take all the time, and losing your temper over the food or the service in hotels. Most of the rich people I've known have been fairly miserable. They've got their worries, too. Taxation and investments. You hear them talking together or to friends. Worry! That's what's killing half of them. And their sex life's not so hot either. They've either got long-legged blonde sexy wives who are playing them up with boy friends somewhere, or they're married to the complaining kind of woman, hideous as hell, who keeps telling them where they get off. No. I'd rather be myself—Michael Rogers, seeing the world and getting off with good-looking girls when he feels like it!

Everything a bit hand-to-mouth, of course, but I put up with that. Life was good fun, and I'd been content to go on with life being fun. But I suppose I would have, in any case. That attitude goes with youth. When youth begins to pass, fun isn't fun any longer.

Behind it, I think, was always the other thing—wanting someone and something. . . . However, to go on with what I was saying, there was one old boy I used to drive down to the Riviera. He'd got a house being built there. He went down to look how it was getting on. Santonix was the architect. I don't really know what nationality Santonix was. English I thought at first, though it was a funny sort of name I'd never heard before. But I don't think he was English. Scandinavian of some kind, I guess. He was an ill man. I could see that at once. He was young and very fair and thin, with an odd face—a face that was askew somehow. The two sides of it didn't match. He could be quite bad-tempered to his clients. You'd have thought that since they were paying the money, that they'd call the tune and do the bullying. That wasn't so. Santonix bullied *them,* and he was always quite sure of himself although they weren't.

This particular old boy of mine was frothing with rage, I remember, as soon as he arrived and had seen how things were going. I used to catch snatches here and there when I was standing by ready to assist in my chauffeurly and handyman way. It was always on the cards that Mr. Constantine would have a heart attack or a stroke.

"You have not done as I said," he half screamed. "You have spent too much money. Much too much money. It is not as we agreed. It is going to cost me more than I thought!"

"You're absolutely right," said Santonix. "But the money's got to be spent."

"It shall not be spent! It shall not be spent. You have got to keep within the limits I laid down. You understand?"

"Then you won't get the kind of house you want," said Santonix. "I know what you want. The house I build you will be the house you want. I'm quite sure of that and you're quite sure of it, too. Don't give me any of your pettifogging middle-class economies. You want a house of quality and you're going to get it, and you'll boast about it to your friends and they'll envy you. I don't build a house for anyone, I've told you that. There's more to it than money. This house isn't going to be like other people's houses!"

"It is going to be terrible. Terrible."

"Oh, no, it isn't. The trouble with you is that you don't know what you want. Or at least so anyone might think. But you do know what you want really, only you can't bring it out into your mind. You can't see it clearly. But I know. That's the one thing I always know—what people are after and what they want. There's a feeling in you for quality. I'm going to give you quality."

He used to say things like that. And I'd stand by and listen. Somehow or other I could see for myself that this house that was being built there among pine trees looking over the sea wasn't going to be the usual house. Half of it didn't look out toward the sea in a conventional way. It looked inland, up to a certain curve of mountains, up to a glimpse of sky between hills. It was odd and unusual and very exciting.

Santonix used to talk to me sometimes when I was off duty. He said, "I only build houses for people I want to build for."

"Rich people, you mean?"

"They have to be rich or they couldn't pay for the houses. But it's not the money I'm going to make out of it I care about. My clients have to be rich because I want to make the kind of houses that cost money. The house only isn't enough, you see. It has to have the setting. That's just as important. It's like a ruby or an emerald. A beautiful stone is only a beautiful stone. It doesn't lead you anywhere further. It doesn't mean anything, it has no form or significance until it has its setting. And the setting has to have a beautiful jewel to be worthy of it. I take the setting, you see, out of the landscape, where it exists only in its own right. It has no meaning until there is my house sitting proudly like a jewel within its grasp." He looked at me and laughed. "You don't understand?"

"I suppose not," I said slowly, "and yet—in a way—I think I do. . . ."

"That may be." He looked at me curiously.

We came down to the Riviera again later. By then the house was nearly finished. I won't describe it because I couldn't do it properly, but it was—well—something special—and it was beautiful. I could see that. It was a house you'd be proud of, proud to show to people, proud to look at yourself, proud to be in with the right person, perhaps. And then suddenly one day Santonix said to me,

"I could build a house for you, you know. I'd know the kind of house you'd want."

I shook my head.

"I shouldn't know myself," I said honestly.

"Perhaps you wouldn't. I'd know for you." Then he added, "It's a thousand pities you haven't got the money."

"And never shall have," I said.

"You can't say that," said Santonix. "Born poor doesn't mean you've got to stay poor. Money's queer. It goes where it's wanted."

"I'm not sharp enough," I said.

"You're not ambitious enough. Ambition hasn't woken up in you, but it's there, you know."

"Oh, well," I said, "someday when I've woken up ambition and I've made money, then I'll come to you and say, 'Build me a house.'"

He sighed then. He said,

"I can't wait. . . . No, I can't afford to wait. I've only a short time to go now. One house—two houses more. Not more than that. One doesn't want to die young. . . . Sometimes one has to. . . . It doesn't really matter, I suppose."

"I'll have to wake up my ambition quick."

"No," said Santonix. "You're healthy, you're having fun. Don't change your way of life."

I said, "I couldn't if I tried."

I thought that was true then. I liked my way of life and I was having fun and there was never anything wrong with my health. I've driven a lot of people who've made money, who've worked hard, and who've got ulcers and coronary thrombosis and many other things as a result of working hard. I didn't want to work hard. I could do a job as well as another, but that was all there was to it. And I hadn't got ambition, or I didn't think I had ambition. Santonix had had ambition, I suppose. I could see that designing houses and building them, the planning of the drawing and something else that I couldn't quite get hold of, all that had taken it out of him. He hadn't been a strong man to begin with. I had a fanciful idea sometimes that he was killing himself before his time by the work he had put out to drive his ambition. I didn't want to work. It was as simple as that. I distrusted work, disliked it. I thought it was a very bad thing that the human race had unfortunately invented for itself.

I thought about Santonix quite often. He intrigued me almost more than anyone I knew. One of the oddest things in life, I think, is the things one remembers. One chooses to remember, I suppose. Something in one must choose. Santonix and his house were one of the things, and the picture in Bond Street and visiting that ruined house The Towers and hearing the story of Gipsy's Acre—all those were the things that I'd chosen to remember! Sometimes girls that I met, and journeys to the foreign places in the course of driving clients about. The clients were all the same—dull. They always stayed at the same kind of hotels and ate the same kind of unimaginative food.

I still had that queer feeling in me of waiting for something, waiting for something to be offered to me, or to happen to me, I don't quite know which way describes it best. I suppose really I was looking for a girl, the right sort of girl—by which I don't mean a nice, suitable girl to settle down with, which is what my mother would have meant or my Uncle Joshua or some of my friends. I didn't know at that time anything about love. All I knew about was sex. That was all anybody of my generation seemed to know about. We talked about it too much, I think, and heard too much about it and took it too seriously. We didn't know—any of my friends or myself—what it was really going to be when it happened. Love, I mean. We were young and virile and we looked the girls over we met and we appreciated their curves and their legs and the kind of eye they gave you, and you thought to yourself: "Will they or won't they? Should I be wasting my time?" And the more girls you made, the more you boasted and the finer fellow you were thought to be, and the finer fellow you thought yourself.

I'd no real idea that that wasn't all there was to it. I suppose it happens to everyone sooner or later and it happens suddenly. You don't think as you imagine you're going to think: "This might be the girl for me. . . . This is the girl who is going to be mine." At least, I didn't feel it that way. I didn't know that when it happened it would happen quite suddenly. That I would say: "That's the girl I belong to. I'm hers. I belong to her, utterly, for always." No. I never dreamed it would be like that. Didn't one of the old comedians say once—wasn't it one of his stock jokes?—"I've been in love once, and if I felt it coming on again, I tell you I'd emigrate." It was the same with me. If I had known, if I had only known what it could all come to mean, I'd have emigrated too! If I'd been wise, that is.

4

I HADN'T FORGOTTEN my plan of going to the auction.

There was three weeks to go. I'd had two more trips to the Continent—one to France and the other to Germany. It was when I was in Hamburg that things came to a crisis. For one thing, I took a violent dislike to the man and his wife I was driving. They represented everything I disliked most. They were rude, inconsiderate, unpleasant to look at, and I suppose they developed in me a feeling of being unable to stand this life of sycophancy any longer. I was careful, mind you. I thought I couldn't stand them another day, but I didn't tell them so. No good running yourself in bad with the firm that employs you. So I telephoned up their hotel, said I was ill, and I wired London saying the same thing. I said I might be in quarantine and it would be advisable if they sent out a driver to replace me. Nobody could blame me for that. They wouldn't care enough about me to make further inquiries, and they'd merely think that I was too feverish to send them any more news. Later, I'd turn up in London again, spinning them a yarn of how ill I'd been! But I didn't think I should do that. I was fed up with the driving racket.

That rebellion of mine was an important turning point in my life. Because of that and of other things, I turned up at the auction rooms on the appointed date.

"Unless sold before by private treaty" had been pasted across the original board. But it was still there, so it hadn't been sold by private treaty. I was so excited I hardly knew what I was doing.

As I say, I had never been to a public auction of property before. I was imbued with the idea that it would be exciting, but it wasn't exciting. Not in the least. It was one of the most moribund performances I have ever attended. It took place in a semi-gloomy atmosphere, and there were only about six or seven people there. The auctioneer was quite different from those auctioneers that I had seen presiding at furniture sales or things of that kind—men with facetious voices and very hearty and full of jokes. This one, in a dead and alive voice, praised the property and described the acreage and a few things like that and then he went half-heartedly into the bidding. Somebody made a bid of £5,000. The auctioneer gave a tired smile rather as one who hears a joke that isn't really funny. He made a few remarks and there were a few more bids. They were mostly country types standing around. Someone who looked like a farmer, someone who I guessed to be one of the competitive builders, a couple of lawyers, I think, one a man who looked as though he was a stranger from London, well dressed and professional-looking. I don't know if he made an actual bid; he may have done. If so, it was very quietly and done more by gesture. Anyway, the bidding petered to an end, the auctioneer announced in a melancholy voice that the reserve price had not been reached, and the thing broke up.

"That was a dull business," I said to one of the country-looking fellows whom I was next to as I went out.

"Much the same as usual," he said. "Been to many of these?"

"No," I said, "actually it's the first."

"Come out of curiosity, did you? I didn't notice you doing any bidding."

"No fear," I said. "I just wanted to see how it would go."

"Well, it's the way it runs very often. They just want to see who's interested, you know."

I looked at him inquiringly.

"Only three of 'em in it, I should say," said my friend. "Whetherby from Helminster. He's the builder, you know. Then Dakham and Coombe, bidding on behalf of some Liverpool firm, I understand, and a dark horse from London, too, I should say a lawyer. Of course there may be more in it than that, but those seemed the main ones to me. It'll go cheap. That's what everyone says."

"Because of the place's reputation?" I asked.

"Oh, you've heard about Gipsy's Acre, have you? That's only what the country people say. Rural council ought to have altered that road years ago—it's a death trap."

"But the place has got a bad reputation?"

"I tell you that's just superstition. Anyway, as I say, the real business'll happen now behind the scenes, you know. They'll go and make offers. I'd say the Liverpool people might get it. I don't think Whetherby'll go high enough. He likes buying cheap. Plenty of properties coming into the market nowadays for development. After all, it's not many people who could afford to buy the place, pull that ruined house down and put up another house there, could they?"

"Doesn't seem to happen very often nowadays," I said.

"Too difficult. What with taxation and one thing and another, and you can't get domestic help in the country. No, people would rather pay thousands for a luxury flat in a town nowadays up on the sixteenth floor of a modern building. Big unwieldy country houses are a drag in the market."

"But you could build a modern house," I argued. "Labor-saving."

"You could, but it's an expensive business, and people aren't so fond of living lonely."

"Some people might be," I said.

He laughed and we parted. I walked along frowning, puzzling to myself. My feet took me without my really noticing where I was going along the road between the trees and up, up to the curving road that led between the trees to the moorlands.

And so I came to the spot in the road where I first saw Ellie. As I said, she was standing just by a tall fir tree and she had the look, if I can so explain it, of someone who hadn't been there a moment before but had just materialized, as it were, out of the tree. She was wearing a sort of dark green tweed, and her hair was the soft brown color of an autumn leaf, and there was something a bit unsubstantial about her. I saw her and I stopped. She was looking at me, her lips just parted, looking slightly startled. I suppose I looked startled, too. I wanted to say something and I didn't quite know what to say. Then I said,

"Sorry. I—I didn't mean to startle you. I didn't know there was anyone here."

She said, and her voice was very soft and gentle, it might have been a little girl's voice but not quite. She said,

"It's quite all right. I mean, I didn't think anyone would be here either." She looked a little round her and said, "It—it's a lonely spot." And she shivered just a little.

There was rather a chilly wind that afternoon. But perhaps it wasn't the wind. I don't know. I came a step or two nearer.

"It is a sort of scary place rather, isn't it?" I said. "I mean, the house being a ruin the way it is."

"The Towers," she said thoughtfully. "That was the name of it, wasn't it, only—I mean, there don't seem to have been any towers."

"I expect that was just a name," I said. "People call their houses names like The Towers to make them sound grander than they are."

She laughed just a little. "I suppose that was it," she said. "This—perhaps you know, I'm not sure—this is the place that they're selling today or putting up for auction?"

"Yes," I said. "I've come from the auction now."

"Oh." She sounded startled. "Were you—are you—interested?"

"I'm not likely to buy a ruined house with a few hundred acres of woodland land," I said. "I'm not in that class."

"Was it sold?" she asked.

"No, it didn't come up to the reserve."

"Oh. I see." She sounded relieved.

"You didn't want to buy it either, did you?" I said.

"Oh, no," she said, "of course not." She sounded nervous about it.

I hesitated and then I blurted out the words that came to my lips.

"I'm pretending," I said. "I can't buy it, of course, because I haven't got any money, but I'm interested. I'd like to buy it. I want to buy it. Open your mouth and laugh at me if you like, but that's the way it is."

"But isn't it rather too decrepit, too—"

"Oh, yes," I said. "I don't mean I want it like it is now. I want to pull this down, cart it all away. It's an ugly house and I think it must have been a sad house. But this place isn't sad or ugly. It's beautiful. Look here. Come a little this way, through the trees. Look out at the view that way where it goes to the hills and the moors. D'you see? Clear away a vista here—and then you come this way—"

I took her by the arm and led her to a second point of the compass. If we were behaving unconventionally, she did not notice it. Anyway, it wasn't that kind of way I was holding her. I wanted to show her what I saw.

"Here," I said, "here you see where it sweeps down to the sea and where the rocks show out there. There's a town between us and that, but we can't see it because of the hills bulging out further down the slope. And then you can look a third way, to a vague foresty valley. Do you see now if you cut down trees and make big vistas and clear this space round the house, do you see what a beautiful house you could have here? You wouldn't site it where the old one is. You'd go about fifty—a hundred yards to the right, here. This is where you could have a house, a wonderful house. A house built by an architect who's a genius."

"Do you know any architects who are geniuses?" She sounded doubtful.

"I know one," I said.

Then I started telling her about Santonix. We sat down side by side on a fallen tree and I talked. Yes, I talked to that slender woodland girl whom I'd never seen before and I put all I had into what I was telling her. I told her the dream that one could build up.

"It won't happen," I said; "I know that. It couldn't happen. But think.

Think into it just like I'm thinking into it. There we'd cut the trees and there we'd open up, and we'd plant things, rhododendrons and azaleas, and my friend Santonix would come. He'd cough a good deal because I think he's dying of consumption or something, but he could do it. He could do it before he died. He could build the most wonderful house. You don't know what his houses are like. He builds them for very rich people, and they have to be people who want the right thing. I don't mean the right thing in the conventional sense. Things people who want a dream come true want. Something wonderful."

"I'd want a house like that," said Ellie. "You make me see it, feel it. . . . Yes, this would be a lovely place to live. Everything one has dreamed of come true. One could live here and be free, not hampered, not tied round by people pushing you into doing everything you don't want, keeping you from doing anything you do want. Oh, I am so sick of my life and the people who are round me and everything!"

That's the way it began, Ellie and I together. Me with my dream and she with her revolt against her life. We stopped talking and looked at each other.

"What's your name?" she said.

"Mike Rogers," I said. "Michael Rogers," I amended. "What's yours?"

"Fenella." She hesitated and then said, "Fenella Goodman," looking at me with a rather troubled expression.

This didn't seem to take us much farther, but we went on looking at each other. We both wanted to see each other again—but just for the moment we didn't know how to set about it.

5

WELL, THAT'S HOW it began between Ellie and myself. It didn't really go along so very quickly, I suppose, because we both had our secrets. Both had things we wanted to keep from the other, and so we couldn't tell each other as much about ourselves as we might have done, and that kept bringing us up sharp, as it were, against a kind of barrier. We couldn't bring things into the open and say, "When shall we meet again? Where can I find you? Where do you live?" Because, you see, if you ask the other person that, they'd expect you to tell the same.

Fenella looked apprehensive when she gave me her name. So much so that I thought for a moment that it mightn't be her real name. I almost thought that she might have made it up! But of course I knew that that was impossible. I'd given her my real name.

We didn't know quite how to take leave of each other that day. It was awkward. It had become cold and we wanted to wander down from The Towers—but what then? Rather awkwardly, I said tentatively,

"Are you staying round here?"

She said she was staying in Market Chadwell. That was a market town not very far away. It had, I knew, a large hotel, three-starred. She'd be staying there, I guessed. She said, with something of the same awkwardness, to me,

"Do you live here?"

"No," I said, "I don't live here. I'm only here for the day."

Then a rather awkward silence fell again. She gave a faint shiver. A cold little wind had come up.

"We'd better walk," I said, "and keep ourselves warm. Are you—have you got a car or are you going by bus or train?"

She said she'd left a car in the village.

"But I'll be quite all right," she said.

She seemed a little nervous. I thought perhaps she wanted to get rid of me but didn't quite know how to manage it. I said,

"We'll walk down, shall we, just as far as the village."

She gave me a quick grateful look then. We walked slowly down the winding road on which so many car accidents had happened. As we came round a corner, a figure stepped suddenly from beneath the shelter of the fir tree. It appeared so suddenly that Ellie gave a start and said "Oh!" It was the old woman I had seen the other day in her own cottage garden—Mrs. Lee. She looked a great deal wilder today, with a tangle of black hair blowing in the wind and a scarlet cloak round her shoulders; the commanding stance she took up made her look taller.

"And what would you be doing, my dears?" she said. "What brings you to Gipsy's Acre?"

"Oh," Ellie said, "we aren't trespassing, are we?"

"That's as may be. Gipsies' land this used to be. Gipsies' land and they drove us off it. You'll do no good here, and no good will come to you prowling about Gipsy's Acre."

There was no fight in Ellie; she wasn't that kind. She said gently and politely,

"I'm very sorry if we shouldn't have come here. I thought this place was being sold today."

"And bad luck it will be to anyone who buys it!" said the old woman. "You listen, my pretty, for you're pretty enough, bad luck will come to whoever buys it. There's a curse on this land, a curse put on it long ago, many years ago. You keep clear of it. Don't have nought to do with Gipsy's Acre. Death it will bring you, and danger. Go away home across the sea and don't come back to Gipsy's Acre. Don't say I didn't warn you."

With a faint spark of resentment Ellie said,

"We're doing no harm."

"Come now, Mrs. Lee," I said, "don't frighten this young lady."

I turned in an explanatory way to Ellie.

"Mrs. Lee lives in the village. She's got a cottage there. She tells fortunes and prophesies the future. All that, don't you, Mrs. Lee?" I spoke to her in a jocular way.

"I've got the gift," she said simply, drawing her gipsylike figure up straighter still. "I've got the gift. It's born in me. We all have it. I'll tell your fortune, young lady. Cross my palm with silver and I'll tell your fortune for you."

"I don't think I want my fortune told."

"It'd be a wise thing to do. Know something about the future. Know what to avoid, know what's coming to you if you don't take care. Come now, there's plenty of money in your pocket. Plenty of money. I know things it would be wise for you to know."

I believe the urge to have one's fortune told is almost invariable in women. I've noticed it before with girls I knew. I nearly always had to pay for them to go into the fortunetellers' booths if I took them to a fair. Ellie opened her bag and laid two half crowns in the old woman's hand.

"Ah, my pretty, that's right now. You hear what old Mother Lee will tell you."

Ellie drew off her glove and laid her small delicate palm in the old woman's hand. She looked down at it, muttering to herself. "What do I see now? What do I see?"

Suddenly she dropped Ellie's hand abruptly.

"I'd go away from here if I were you. Go—and don't come back! That's what I told you just now, and it's true. I've seen it again in your palm. Forget Gipsy's Acre, forget you ever saw it. And it's not just the ruined house up there; it's the land itself that's cursed."

"You've got a mania about that," I said roughly. "Anyway, the young lady has nothing to do with the land here. She's only here for a walk today; she's nothing to do with this neighborhood."

The old woman paid no attention to me. She said dourly,

"I'm telling you, my pretty. I'm warning you. You can have a happy life—but you must avoid danger. Don't come to a place where there's danger or where there's a curse. Go away where you're loved and taken care of and looked after. You've got to keep yourself safe. Remember that. Otherwise—otherwise—" she gave a short shiver—"I don't like to see it. I don't like to see what's in your hand."

Suddenly, with a queer, brisk gesture she pushed back the two half crowns into Ellie's palm, mumbling something we could hardly hear. It sounded like "It's cruel. It's cruel, what's going to happen." Turning, she stalked away at a rapid pace.

"What a—what a frightening woman," said Ellie.

"Pay no attention to her," I said gruffly. "I think she's half off her head anyway. She just wants to frighten you off. They've got a sort of feeling, I think, about this particular piece of land."

"Have there been accidents here? Have bad things happened?"

"Bound to be accidents. Look at the curve and the narrowness of the road. The town council ought to be shot for not doing something about it. Of course there'll be accidents here. There aren't enough signs warning you."

"Only accidents—or other things?"

"Look here," I said, "people like to collect disasters. There are plenty of disasters always to collect. That's the way stories build themselves up about a place."

"Is that one of the reasons why they say this property which is being sold will go cheap?"

"Well, it may be, I suppose. Locally, that is. But I don't suppose it'll be sold locally. I expect it'll be bought for developing. You're shivering," I said. "Don't shiver. Come on, we'll walk fast." I added, "Would you rather I left you before you got back into the town?"

"No. Of course not. Why should I?"

I made a desperate plunge.

"Look here," I said, "I shall be in Market Chadwell tomorrow. I—I suppose—I don't know whether you'll still be there . . . I mean, would there be any chance of—seeing you?" I shuffled my feet and turned my head away. I got rather red, I think. But if I didn't say something now, how was I going to go on with this?

"Oh, yes," she said, "I shan't be going back to London until the evening."

"Then perhaps—would you—I mean, I suppose it's rather cheek—"

"No, it isn't."

"Well, perhaps you'd come and have tea at a café—the Blue Dog, I think it's called. It's quite nice," I said. "It's—I mean, it's—" I couldn't get hold of the word I wanted and I used the word that I'd heard my mother use once or twice—"it's quite ladylike," I said anxiously.

Then Ellie laughed. I suppose it sounded rather peculiar nowadays.

"I'm sure it'll be very nice," she said. "Yes. I'll come. About half-past four. Will that be right?"

"I'll be there waiting for you," I said. "I—I'm glad." I didn't say what I was glad about.

We had come to the last turn of the road where the houses began.

"Good-by, then," I said, "till tomorrow. And—don't think again about what that old hag said. She just likes scaring people, I think. She's not all there," I added.

"Do you feel it's a frightening place?" Ellie asked.

"Gipsy's Acre? No, I don't," I said. I said it perhaps a trifle too decidedly, but I didn't think it was frightening. I thought as I'd thought before, that it was a beautiful place, a beautiful setting for a beautiful house. . . .

Well, that's how my first meeting with Ellie went. I was in Market Chadwell the next day waiting in the Blue Dog and she came. We had tea together and we talked. We still didn't say much about ourselves, nor about our lives, I mean. We talked mostly about things we thought, and felt; and then Ellie glanced at her wrist watch and said she must be going because her train to London left at five-thirty.

"I thought you had a car down here," I said.

She looked slightly embarrassed then and she said no, no, that hadn't been her car yesterday. She didn't say whose it had been. That shadow of embarrassment came over us again. I raised a finger to the waitress and paid the bill, then I said straight out to Ellie,

"Am I—am I ever going to see you again?"

She didn't look at me; she looked down at the table. She said,

"I shall be in London for another fortnight."

I said,

"Where? How?"

We made a date to meet in Regent's Park in three days' time. It was a fine day. We had some food in the open-air restaurant and we walked in Queen Mary's garden and we sat there in two deck chairs and we talked. From that time on we began to talk about ourselves. I'd had some good schooling, I told her, but otherwise I didn't amount to much. I told her about the jobs I'd had, some of them, at any rate, and how I'd never stuck to things and how I'd been restless and wandered about trying this and that. Funnily enough, she was entranced to hear all this.

"So different," she said, "so wonderfully different."

"Different from what?"

"From me."

"You're a rich girl?" I said.

"Yes," she said, "I'm a poor little rich girl."

She talked then in a fragmentary way about her background of riches, of stifling comfort, of boredom, of not really choosing your own friends, of never doing what you wanted—sometimes looking at people who seemed to be enjoying themselves, when she wasn't. Her mother had died when she was a baby and her father had married again. And then, not many years after, he had died, she said. I gathered she didn't care much for her stepmother. She'd lived mostly in America but also traveling abroad a fair amount.

It seemed fantastic to me, listening to her, that any girl in this age and time could live this sheltered, confined existence. True, she went to parties and entertainments, but it might have been fifty years ago, it seemed to me, from the way she talked. There didn't seem to be any intimacy, any fun! Her life was as different from mine as chalk from cheese. In a way it was fascinating to hear about it, but it sounded stultifying to me.

"You haven't really got any friends of your own then?" I said incredulously. "What about boy friends?"

"They're chosen for me," she said rather bitterly. "They're deadly dull."

"It's like being in prison," I said.

"That's what it seems like."

"And really no friends of your own?"

"I have now. I've got Greta."

"Who's Greta?" I said.

"She came first as an *au pair* girl—no, not quite that, perhaps. But anyway I'd had a French girl who lived with us for a year, for French, and then Greta came from Germany, for German. Greta was different. Everything was different once Greta came."

"You're very fond of her?" I asked.

"She helps me," said Ellie. "She's on my side. She arranges so that I can do things and go places. She'll tell lies for me. I couldn't have got away to come down to Gipsy's Acre if it hadn't been for Greta. She's keeping me company and looking after me in London while my stepmother's in Paris. I write two or three letters and if I go off anywhere, Greta posts them every three or four days so that they have a London postmark."

"Why did you want to go down to Gipsy's Acre, though?" I asked. "What for?"

She didn't answer at once.

"Greta and I arranged it," she said. "She's rather wonderful," she went on. She thinks of things, you know. She suggests ideas."

"What's this Greta look like?" I asked.

"Oh, Greta's beautiful," she said. "Tall and blonde. She can do anything."

"I don't think I'd like her," I said.

Ellie laughed.

"Oh, yes, you would. I'm sure you would. She's very clever, too."

"I don't like clever girls," I said. "And I don't like tall blonde girls. I like small girls with hair like autumn leaves."

"I believe you're jealous of Greta," said Ellie.

"Perhaps I am. You're very fond of her, aren't you?"

"Yes, I am very fond of her. She's made all the difference in my life."

"And it was she suggested you come down here. Why, I wonder? There's not much to see or do in this part of the world. I find it rather mysterious."

"It's our secret," said Ellie, and looked embarrassed.

"Yours and Greta's? Tell me."

She shook her head. "I must have some secrets of my own," she said.

"Does your Greta know you're meeting me?"

"She knows I'm meeting someone. That's all. She doesn't ask questions. She knows I'm happy."

After that there was a week when I didn't see Ellie. Her stepmother had come back from Paris, also someone whom she called Uncle Frank, and she explained almost casually that she was having a birthday, and that they were giving a big party for her in London.

"I shan't be able to get away," she said. "Not for the next week. But after that—after that, it'll be different."

"Why will it be different after that?"

"I shall be able to do what I like then."

"With Greta's help, as usual?" I said.

It used to make Ellie laugh the way I talked about Greta. She'd say, "You're so silly to be jealous of her. One day you must meet her. You'll like her."

"I don't like bossy girls," I said obstinately.

"Why do you think she's bossy?"

"By the way you talk about her. She's always busy arranging something."

"She's very efficient," said Ellie. "She arranges things very well. That's why my stepmother relies on her so much."

I asked what her Uncle Frank was like.

She said, "I don't know him really so very well. He was my father's sister's husband, not a real relation. I think he's always been rather a rolling stone and got into trouble once or twice. You know the way people talk about someone and sort of hint things."

"Not socially acceptable?" I asked. "Bad lot?"

"Oh, nothing really bad, I think, but he used to get into scrapes, I believe. Financial ones. And trustees and lawyers and people used to have to get him out of them. Pay up for things."

"That's it," I said. "He's the bad hat of the family. I expect I'd get on better with him than I would with the paragon Greta."

"He can make himself very agreeable when he likes," said Ellie. "He's good company."

"But you don't really like him?" I asked sharply.

"I think I do. . . . It's just that sometimes, oh, I can't explain it. I just feel I don't know what he's thinking or planning."

"One of our planners, is he?"

"I don't know what he's really like," said Ellie again.

She didn't ever suggest that I should meet any of her family. I wondered sometimes if I ought to say something about it myself. I didn't know how she felt about the subject. I asked her straight out at last.

"Look here, Ellie," I said, "do you think I ought to—meet your family, or would you rather I didn't?"

"I don't want you to meet them," she said at once.

"I know I'm not much—" I said.

"I don't mean it that way, not a bit! I mean they'd make a fuss. I can't stand a fuss."

"I sometimes feel," I said, "that this is rather a hole-and-corner business. It puts me in a rather bad light, don't you think?"

"I'm old enough to have my own friends," said Ellie. "I'm nearly twenty-one. When I am twenty-one, I can have my own friends and nobody can stop me. But now you see—well, as I say, there'd be a terrible fuss and they'd cart me off somewhere so that I couldn't meet you. There'd be—oh, do, do let's go on as we are now."

"Suits me if it suits you," I said. "I just didn't want to be, well, too underhand about everything."

"It's not being underhand. It's just having a friend one can talk to and say things to. It's someone one can—" she smiled suddenly—"one can make believe with. You don't know how wonderful that is."

Yes, there was a lot of that—make-believe! More and more our times together were to turn out that way. Sometimes it was me. More often it was Ellie who'd say, "Let's suppose that we've bought Gipsy's Acre and that we're building a house there."

I had told her a lot about Santonix and about the houses he'd built. I tried to describe to her the kind of houses they were and the way he thought about things. I don't think I described it very well, because I'm not good at describing things. Ellie, no doubt, had her own picture of the house—our house. We didn't say "our house," but we knew that's what we meant. . . .

So for over a week I wasn't to see Ellie. I had taken out what savings I had (there weren't many), and I'd bought her a little green shamrock ring made of some Irish bog stone. I'd given it to her for a birthday present and she'd loved it and looked very happy.

"It's beautiful," she said.

She didn't wear much jewelry and when she did, I had no doubt it was real diamonds and emeralds and things like that, but she liked my Irish green ring.

"It will be the birthday present I like best," she said.

Then I got a hurried note from her. She was going abroad with her family to the South of France immediately after her birthday.

"But don't worry," she wrote, "we shall be back again in two or three weeks' time, on our way to America this time. But anyway, we'll meet again then. I've got something special I want to talk to you about."

I felt restless and ill at ease not seeing Ellie and knowing she'd gone abroad to France. I had a bit of news about the Gipsy's Acre property, too. Apparently it had been sold by private treaty, but there wasn't much information about who'd bought it. Some firm of London solicitors apparently were named as the purchasers. I tried to get more information about it, but I couldn't. The firm in question were very cagey. Naturally I didn't approach the principals. I palled up to one of their clerks and so got a little vague information. It had been bought for a very rich client who was going to hold it as a good investment capable of appreciation when the land in that part of the country was becoming more developed.

It's very hard to find out about things when you're dealing with really exclusive firms. Everything is as much of a deadly secret as though they were M.I.5 or something! Everyone is always acting on behalf of someone else who can't be named or spoken of! Takeover bids aren't in it!

I got into a terrible state of restlessness. I stopped thinking about it all and I went and saw my mother.

I hadn't been to see her for a good long time.

6

MY MOTHER LIVED in the same street she had lived in for the last twenty years—a street of drab houses all highly respectable and devoid of any kind of beauty or interest. The front doorstep was nicely whitened and it looked just the same as usual. It was No. 46. I pressed the front doorbell. My mother opened the door and stood there looking at me. She looked just the same as usual, too. Tall and angular, gray hair parted in the middle, mouth like a rattrap, and eyes that were eternally suspicious. She looked hard as nails. But where I was concerned, there was a core of softness somewhere in her. She never showed it, not if she could help it, but I'd found out that it was there. She'd never stopped for a moment wanting me to be different, but her wishes were never going to come true. There was a perpetual state of stalemate between us.

"Oh," she said, "so it's you."

"Yes," I said, "it's me."

She drew back a little to let me pass, and I came into the house and went on past the sitting-room door and into the kitchen. She followed me and stood looking at me.

"It's been quite a long time," she said. "What have you been doing?"

I shrugged my shoulders.

"This and that," I said.

"Ah," said my mother, "as usual, eh?"

"As usual," I agreed.

"How many jobs have you had since I saw you last?"

I thought a minute. "Five," I said.

"I wish you'd grow up."

"I'm fully adult," I said. "I have chosen my way of life. How have things been with you?" I added.

"Also as usual," said my mother.

"Quite well and all that?"

"I've no time to waste being ill," said my mother. Then she said abruptly, "What have you come for?"

"Should I have come for anything in particular?"

"You usually do."

"I don't see why you should disapprove so strongly of my seeing the world," I said.

"Driving luxurious cars all over the Continent! Is that your idea of seeing the world?"

"Certainly."

"You won't make much of a success in that. Not if you throw up the job at a day's notice and go sick, dumping your clients in some heathen town."

"How did you know about that?"

"Your firm rang up. They wanted to know if I knew your address."

"What did they want me for?"

"They wanted to reemploy you, I suppose," said my mother. "I can't think why."

"Because I'm a good driver and the clients like me. Anyway, I couldn't help it if I went sick, could I?"

"I don't know," said my mother.

Her view clearly was that I could have helped it.

"Why didn't you report to them when you got back to England?"

"Because I had other fish to fry," I said.

She raised her eyebrows. "More notions in your head? More wild ideas? What jobs have you been doing since?"

"Petrol pump. Mechanic in a garage. Temporary clerk, washer-up in a sleazy night-club restaurant."

"Going down the hill, in fact," said my mother with a kind of grim satisfaction.

"Not at all," I said. "It's all part of the plan. My plan!"

She sighed. "What would you like, tea or coffee? I've got both."

I plumped for coffee. I've grown out of the tea drinking habit. We sat there with our cups in front of us and she took a homemade cake out of a tin and cut us each a slice.

"You're different," she said suddenly.

"Me, how?"

"I don't know, but you're different. What's happened?"

"Nothing's happened. What should have happened?"

"You're excited," she said.

"I'm going to rob a bank," I said.

She was not in the mood to be amused. She merely said,

"No, I'm not afraid of your doing that."

"Why not? Seems a very easy way of getting rich quickly nowadays."

"It would need too much work," she said. "And a lot of planning. More brain work than you'd like to have to do. Not safe enough, either."

"You think you know all about me," I said.

"No, I don't. I don't really know anything about you, because you and I are as different as chalk and cheese. But I know when you're up to something. You're up to something now. What is it, Micky. Is it a girl?"

"Why should you think it's a girl?"

"I've always known it would happen someday."

"What do you mean by 'someday'? I've had lots of girls."

"Not the way I mean. It's only been the way of a young man with nothing to do. You've kept your hand in with girls, but you've never been really serious till now."

"But you think I'm serious now?"

"Is it a girl, Micky?"

I didn't meet her eyes. I looked away and said, "In a way."

"What kind of a girl is she?"

"The right kind for me," I said.

"Are you going to bring her to see me?"

"No," I said.

"It's like that, is it?"

"No, it isn't. I don't want to hurt your feelings, but—"

"You're not hurting my feelings. You don't want me to see her in case I should say to you 'Don't.' Is that it?"

"I wouldn't pay any attention if you did."

"Maybe not, but it would shake you. It would shake you somewhere inside, because you take notice of what I say and think. There are things I've guessed about you—and maybe I've guessed right and you know it. I'm the only person in the world who can shake your confidence in yourself. Is this girl a bad lot who's got hold of you?"

"Bad lot?" I said, and laughed. "If you only saw her! You make me laugh."

"What do you want from me? You want something. You always do."

"I want some money," I said.

"You won't get it from me. What do you want it for—to spend on this girl?"

"No," I said, "I want to buy a first-class suit to get married in."

"You're going to marry her?"

"If she'll have me."

That shook her.

"If you'd only tell me something!" she said. "You've got it badly, I can see that. It's the thing I always feared, that you'd choose the wrong girl."

"Wrong girl! Hell!" I shouted. I was angry.

I went out of the house and I banged the door.

7

WHEN I GOT home, there was a telegram waiting for me—it had been sent from Antibes.

Meet me tomorrow four-thirty usual place.

Ellie was different. I saw it at once. We met as always in Regent's Park and at first we were a bit strange and awkward with each other. I had something I was going to say to her and I was in a bit of a state as to how to put it. I suppose any man is when he comes to the point of proposing marriage.

And she was strange about something, too. Perhaps she was considering the nicest and kindest way of saying No to me. But somehow I didn't think that. My whole belief in life was based on the fact that Ellie loved me. But there was a new independence about her, a new confidence in herself which I could hardly feel was simply because she was a year older. One more birthday can't make that difference to a girl. She and her family had been in the South of France and she told me a little about it. And then rather shyly she said,

"I—I saw that house there, the one you told me about. The one that architect friend of yours had built."

"What—Santonix?"

"Yes. We went there to lunch one day."

"How did you do that? Does your stepmother know the man who lives there?"

"Dmitri Constantine? Well—not exactly, but she met him and—well—Greta fixed it up for us to go there as a matter of fact."

"Greta again," I said, allowing the usual exasperation to come into my voice.

"I told you," she said, "Greta is very good at arranging things."

"Oh, all right. So she arranged that you and your stepmother—"

"And Uncle Frank," said Ellie.

"Quite a family party," I said, "and Greta, too, I suppose."

"Well, no, Greta didn't come because, well—" Ellie hesitated—"Cora, my stepmother, doesn't treat Greta exactly like that."

"She's not one of the family, she's a poor relation, is she?" I said. "Just the *au pair* girl, in fact. Greta must resent being treated that way sometimes."

"She's not an *au pair* girl; she's a kind of companion to me."

"A chaperon," I said, "a cicerone, a duenna, a governess. There are lots of words."

"Oh, do be quiet," said Ellie, "I want to tell you. I know now what you mean about your friend Santonix. It's a wonderful house. It's—it's quite different. I can see that if he built a house for us it would be a wonderful house."

She had used the words quite unconsciously. Us, she had said. She had gone to the Riviera and had made Greta arrange things so as to see the house I had described, because she wanted to visualize more clearly the house that we would, in the dream world we'd build for ourselves, have built for us by Rudolf Santonix.

"I'm glad you felt like that about it," I said.

She said: "What have you been doing?"

"Just my dull job," I said, "and I've been to a race meeting and I put some money on an outsider. Thirty to one. I put every penny I had on it and it won by a length. Who says my luck isn't in?"

"I'm glad you won," said Ellie, but she said it without excitement, because putting all you had in the world on an outsider, and the outsider winning, didn't mean anything in Ellie's world. Not the kind of thing it meant in mine.

"And I went to see my mother," I added.

"You've never spoken much of your mother."

"Why should I?" I said.

"Aren't you fond of her?"

I considered. "I don't know," I said. "Sometimes I don't think I am. After all, one grows up and—outgrows parents. Mothers and fathers."

"I think you do care about her," said Ellie. "You wouldn't be so uncertain when you talk about her otherwise."

"I'm afraid of her in a way," I said. "She knows me too well. She knows the worst of me, I mean."

"Somebody has to," said Ellie.

"What do you mean?"

"There's a saying by some great writer or other that no man is a hero to his valet. Perhaps everyone ought to have a valet. It must be so hard otherwise, always living up to people's good opinion of one."

"Well, you certainly have ideas, Ellie," I said. I took her hand. "Do you know all about me?" I said.

"I think so," said Ellie. She said it quite calmly and simply.

"I never told you much."

"You mean you never told me anything at all; you always clammed up. That's different. But I know quite well what you are like, you yourself."

"I wonder if you do," I said. I went on, "It sounds rather silly saying I love you. It seems too late for that, doesn't it? I mean, you've known about it a long time, practically from the beginning, haven't you?"

"Yes," said Ellie, "and you knew, too, didn't you, about me?"

"The thing is," I said, "what are we going to do about it? It's not going to be easy, Ellie. You know pretty well what I am, what I've done, the sort of life I've led. I went back to see my mother and the grim respectable little street she lives in. It's not the same world as yours, Ellie. I don't know that we can ever make them meet."

"You could take me to see your mother."

"Yes, I could," I said, "but I'd rather not. I expect that sounds very harsh to you, perhaps cruel, but you see we've got to lead a queer life together, you and I. It's not going to be the life that you've led and it's not going to be the life that I've led either. It's got to be a new life where we have a sort of meeting ground between my poverty and ignorance and your money and culture and social knowledge. My friends will think you're stuck-up and your friends will think I'm socially unpresentable. So what are we going to do?"

"I'll tell you," said Ellie, "exactly what we're going to do. We're going to live on Gipsy's Acre in a house—a dream house—that your friend Santonix will build for us. That's what we're going to do." She added, "We'll get married first. That's what you mean, isn't it?"

"Yes," I said, "that's what I mean. If you're sure it's all right for you."

"It's quite easy," said Ellie; "we can get married next week. I'm of age, you see. I can do what I like now. That makes all the difference. I think perhaps you're right about relations. I shan't tell my people and you won't tell your mother, not until it's all over and then they can throw fits and it won't matter."

"That's wonderful," I said, "wonderful, Ellie. But there's one thing. I hate telling you about it. We can't live at Gipsy's Acre, Ellie. Wherever we build our house, it can't be there because it's sold."

"I know it's sold," said Ellie. She was laughing. "You don't understand, Mike. I'm the person who's bought it."

8

I SAT THERE on the grass by the stream among the water flowers with the little paths and the stepping stones all round us. A good many other people were sitting round about us, but we didn't notice them or even see they were there, because we were like all the others—a young couple talking about their future. I stared at her and stared at her. I just couldn't speak.

"Mike," she said. "There's something, something I've got to tell you. Something about me, I mean."

"You don't need to," I said; "no need to tell me anything."

"Yes, but I must. I ought to have told you long ago, but I didn't want to because—because I thought it might drive you away. But it explains, in a way, about Gipsy's Acre."

"You bought it?" I said. "But how did you buy it?"

"Through lawyers," she said, "the usual way. It's a perfectly good investment, you know. The land will appreciate. My lawyers were quite happy about it."

It was odd suddenly to hear Ellie, the gentle and timid Ellie, speaking with such knowledge and confidence of the business world of buying and selling.

"You bought it for us?"

"Yes. I went to a lawyer of my own, not the family one. I told him what I wanted to do, I got him to look into it, I got everything set up and in train. There were two other people after it, but they were not really desperate and they wouldn't go very high. The important thing was that the whole thing had to be set up and arranged ready for me to sign as soon as I came of age. It's signed and finished."

"But you must have made some deposit or something beforehand. Had you enough money to do that?"

"No," said Ellie, "no, I hadn't control of much money beforehand, but of course there are people who will advance you money. And if you go to a new firm of legal advisers, they will want you to go on employing them for business deals once you've come into what money you're going to have, so they're willing to take the risk that you might drop down dead before your birthday comes."

"You sound so businesslike," I said, "you take my breath away!"

"Never mind business," said Ellie. "I've got to get back to what I'm telling you. In a way I've told it you already, but I don't suppose really you realize it."

"I don't want to know," I said. My voice rose, I was almost shouting. "Don't tell me anything. I don't want to know anything about what you've done or who you've been fond of or what has happened to you."

"It's nothing of that kind," she said. "I didn't realize that that was what you were fearing it might be. No, there's nothing of that kind. No sex secrets. There's nobody but you. The thing is that I'm—well—I'm rich."

"I know that," I said; "you've told me already."

"Yes," said Ellie with a faint smile, "and that's what you said to me, 'poor little rich girl.' But in a way it's more than that. My grandfather, you see, was enormously rich. Oil. Mostly oil. And other things. The wives he paid alimony to are dead, there was only my father and myself left because his two other sons were killed. One in Korea and one in a car accident. And so it was all left in a great big huge trust and when my father died suddenly, it all came to me. My father had made provision for my stepmother before, so she didn't get anything more. It was all mine. I'm—actually one of the richest women in America, Mike."

"Good Lord," I said. "I didn't know . . . Yes, you're right, I didn't know it was like that."

"I didn't want you to know. I didn't want to tell you. That was why I was afraid when I said my name—Fenella Goodman. We spell it G-u-t-e-m-a-n, and I thought you might know the name of Guteman, so I slurred over it and made it into Goodman."

"Yes," I said, "I've seen the name of Guteman vaguely. But I don't think I'd have recognized it even then. Lots of people are called names rather like that."

"That's why," she said, "I've been so hedged around all the time and fenced in and imprisoned. I've had detectives guarding me and young men being checked before they're allowed even to speak to me. Whenever I've made a friend, they've had to be quite sure it wasn't an unsuitable one. You don't know what a terrible, terrible prisoner's life it is! But now that's all over, and if you don't mind—"

"Of course I don't mind," I said; "we shall have lots of fun. In fact," I said, "you couldn't be too rich a girl for me!"

We both laughed. She said: "What I like about you is that you can be natural about things."

"Besides," I said, "I expect you pay a lot of tax on it, don't you? That's one of the few nice things about being like me. Any money I make goes into my pocket and nobody can take it away from me."

"We'll have our house," said Ellie, "our house on Gipsy's Acre." Just for a moment she gave a sudden little shiver.

"You're not cold, darling," I said. I looked up at the sunshine.

"No," she said.

It was really very hot. We'd been basking. It might almost have been the South of France.

"No," said Ellie, "it was just that—that woman, that gipsy that day."

"Oh, don't think of her," I said. "She was crazy anyway."

"Do you think she really thinks there's a curse on the land?"

"I think gipsies are like that. You know—always wanting to make a song and dance about some curse or something."

"Do you know much about gipsies?"

"Absolutely nothing," I said truthfully. "If you don't want Gipsy's Acre, Ellie, we'll buy a house somewhere else. On the top of a mountain in Wales, on the coast of Spain or an Italian hillside, and Santonix can build us a house there just as well."

"No," said Ellie, "that's how I want it to be. It's where I first saw you walking up the road, coming round the corner very suddenly, and then you saw me and stopped and stared at me. I'll never forget that."

"Nor will I," I said.

"So that's where it's going to be. And your friend Santonix will build it."

"I hope he's still alive," I said with an uneasy pang. "He was a sick man."

"Oh, yes," said Ellie, "he's alive. I went to see him."

"You went to see him?"

"Yes. When I was in the South of France. He was in a sanatorium there."

"Every minute, Ellie, you seem to be more and more amazing. The things you do and manage."

"He's rather a wonderful person, I think," said Ellie, "but rather frightening."

"Did he frighten you?"

"Yes, he frightened me very much for some reason."

"Did you talk to him about us?"

"Yes. Oh, yes, I told him all about us and about Gipsy's Acre and about the house. He told me then that we'd have to take a chance with him. He's a very ill man. He said he thought he still had the life left in him to go and see the site, to draw the plans, to visualize it and get it all sketched out. He said he wouldn't mind really if he died before the house was finished, but I told him," added Ellie, "that he mustn't die before the house was finished because I wanted him to see us live in it."

"What did he say to that?"

"He asked me if I knew what I was doing marrying you, and I said of course I did."

"And then?"

"He said he wondered if you knew what you were doing."

"I know, all right," I said.

"He said, 'You will always know where you're going, Miss Guteman.' He said, 'You'll be going always where you want to go and because it's your chosen way.'

"'But Mike,' he said, 'might take the wrong road. He hasn't grown up enough yet to know where he's going.'

"I said," said Ellie, "'he'll be quite safe with me.'"

She had superb self-confidence. I was angry, though, at what Santonix had said. He was like my mother. She always seemed to know more about me than I knew myself.

"I know where I'm going," I said. "I'm going the way I want to go and we're going it together."

"They've started pulling down the ruins of The Towers already," said Ellie.

She began to talk practically.

"It's to be a rush job as soon as the plans are finished. We must hurry. Santonix said so. Shall we be married next Tuesday?" said Ellie. "It's a nice day of the week."

"With nobody else there," I said.

"Except Greta," said Ellie.

"To hell with Greta," I said. "She's not coming to our wedding. You and I and nobody else. We can pull the necessary witnesses out of the street."

I really think, looking back, that that was the happiest day of my life. . . .

BOOK TWO

9

SO THAT WAS that, and Ellie and I got married. It sounds abrupt just putting it like that, but you see it was really just the way things happened. We decided to be married, and we got married.

It was part of the whole thing—not just an end to a romantic novel or a fairy story. "And so they got married and lived happily ever afterward." You can't, after all, make a big drama out of living happily ever afterward. We were married and we were both happy and it was really quite a time before anyone got on to us and began to make the usual difficulties and commotions, and we'd made up our mind to those.

The whole thing was really extraordinarily simple. In her desire for freedom Ellie had covered her tracks very cleverly up to now. The useful Greta had taken all the necessary steps and was always on guard behind her. And I had realized fairly soon that there was nobody really whose business it was to care terribly about Ellie and what she was doing. She had a stepmother who was engrossed in her own social life and love affairs. If Ellie didn't wish to accompany her to any particular spot on the globe, there was no need for Ellie to do so. She'd had all the proper governesses and lady's maids and scholastic advantages, and if she wanted to go to Europe, why not? If she chose to have her twenty-first birthday in London, again why not? Now that she had come into her vast fortune, she had the whip hand of her family in so far as spending her money went. If she'd wanted a villa on the Riviera or a castle on the Costa Brava or a yacht or any of those things, she had only to mention the fact and someone among the retinues that surround millionaires would put everything in hand immediately.

Greta, I gather, was regarded by her family as an admirable stooge. Competent, able to make all arrangements with the utmost efficiency, subservient, no doubt, and charming to the stepmother, the uncle and a few odd cousins who seemed to be knocking about. Ellie had no fewer than three lawyers at her command, from what she let fall every now and then. She was surrounded by a vast financial network of bankers and lawyers and the administrators of trust funds. It was a world that I just got glimpses of every now and then, mostly from things that Ellie let fall carelessly in the course of conversation. It didn't occur to her, naturally, that I wouldn't know about all those things. She had been brought up in the midst of them and she naturally concluded that the whole world knew what they were and how they worked and all the rest of it.

In fact, getting glimpses of the special peculiarities of each other's lives was unexpectedly what we enjoyed most in our early married life. To put it quite crudely—and I did put things crudely to myself, for that was the only way to get to terms with my new life—the poor don't really know how the rich live, and the rich don't know how the poor live, and to find out is really enchanting to both of them. Once I said uneasily,

"Look here, Ellie. Is there going to be an awful schemozzle over all this, over our marriage, I mean?"

Ellie considered without, I noticed, very much interest.

"Oh, yes," she said, "they'll probably be awful." And she added, "I hope you won't mind too much."

"I won't mind—why should I?—but you. Will they bully you over it?"

"I expect so," said Ellie, "but one needn't listen. The point is that they can't do anything."

"But they'll try?"

"Oh, yes," said Ellie. "They'll try." Then she added thoughtfully, "They'll probably try and buy you off."

"Buy me off?"

"Don't look so shocked," said Ellie, and she smiled a rather happy little girl's smile. "It isn't put exactly like that." Then she added, "They bought off Minnie Thompson's first, you know."

"Minnie Thompson? Is that the one they always call the oil heiress?"

"Yes, that's right. She ran off and married a life guard off the beach."

"Look here, Ellie," I said uneasily. "I was a life guard at Littlehampton once."

"Oh, were you? What fun! Permanently?"

"No, of course not. Just one summer, that's all."

"I wish you wouldn't worry," said Ellie.

"What happened about Minnie Thompson?"

"They had to go up to two hundred thousand dollars, I think," said Ellie. "He wouldn't take less. Minnie was man-mad and really a half-wit," she added.

"You take my breath away, Ellie," I said. "I've not only acquired a wife. I've got something I can trade for solid cash at any time."

"That's right," said Ellie. "Send for a high-powered lawyer and tell him you're willing to talk turkey. Then he fixes up the divorce and the amount of alimony," said Ellie, continuing my education. "My step-mother's been married four times," she added, "and she's made quite a lot out of it." And then she said, "Oh, Mike, don't look so shocked."

The funny thing is that I was shocked. I felt a priggish distaste for the corruption of modern society in its richer phases. There had been something so little-girl-like about Ellie, so simple, almost touching in her attitude, that I was astonished to find how well up she was in worldly affairs and how much she took for granted. And yet I knew that I was right about her fundamentally. I knew quite well the kind of creature that Ellie was. Her simplicity, her affection, her natural sweetness. That didn't mean she had to be ignorant of things. What she did know and took for granted was a fairly limited slice of humanity. She didn't know much about my world, the world of scrounging for jobs, of race course gangs and dope gangs, the rough-and-tumble dangers of life, the sharp-aleck flashy type that I knew so well from living among them all my life. She didn't know what it was to be brought up decent and respectable but always hard up for money, with a mother who worked her fingers to the bone in the name of respectability, determining that her son should do well in life. Every penny scrimped for and saved, and the bitterness when your gay carefree son threw away his chances or gambled his all on a good tip.

She enjoyed hearing about my life as much as I enjoyed hearing about hers. Both of us were exploring a foreign country.

Looking back, I see what a wonderfully happy life it was, those early days with Ellie. At the time I took them for granted, and so did she.

We were married in a registry office in Plymouth. Guteman is not an uncommon name. Nobody, reporters or otherwise, knew the Guteman heiress was in England. There had been vague paragraphs in papers occasionally, describing her as in Italy or on someone's yacht. We were married in the registrar's office, with his clerk and a middle-aged typist as witnesses. He gave us a serious little harangue on the serious responsibilities of married life, and wished us happiness. Then we went out, free and married. Mr. and Mrs. Michael Rogers! We spent a week in a seaside hotel and then we went abroad. We had a glorious three weeks traveling about wherever the fancy took us and no expense spared.

We went to Greece, and we went to Florence, and to Venice and lay on the Lido, then to the French Riviera and then to the Dolomites. Half the places I forget the names of now. We took planes or chartered a yacht or hired large and handsome cars. And while we enjoyed ourselves, Greta, I gathered from Ellie, was still on the home front doing her stuff.

Traveling about in her own way, sending letters and forwarding all the various post cards and letters that Ellie had left with her.

"There'll be a day of reckoning, of course," said Ellie. "They'll come down on us like a cloud of vultures. But we might as well enjoy ourselves until that happens."

"What about Greta?" I said. "Won't they be rather angry with her when they find out?"

"Oh, of course," said Ellie, "but Greta won't mind. She's tough."

"Mightn't it stop her getting another job?"

"Why should she get another job?" said Ellie. "She'll come and live with us."

"No!" I said.

"What do you mean, no, Mike?"

"We don't want anyone living with us," I said.

"Greta wouldn't be in the way," said Ellie, "and she'd be very useful. Really, I don't know what I'd do without her. I mean, she manages and arranges everything."

I frowned. "I don't think I'd like that. Besides, we want our own house—our dream house. After all, Ellie—we want it to ourselves."

"Yes," said Ellie, "I know what you mean. But all the same—" She hesitated. "I mean, it would be very hard on Greta not to have anywhere to live. After all, she's been with me, done everything for me for four years now. And look how she's helped me to get married and all that."

"I won't have her butting in between us all the time!"

"But she's not like that at all, Mike. You haven't even met her yet."

"No. No, I know I haven't, but—but it's nothing to do with, oh, with liking her or not. We want to be by ourselves, Ellie."

"Darling Mike," said Ellie softly.

We left it at that for the moment.

During the course of our travels we had met Santonix. That was in Greece. He had been in a small fisherman's cottage near the sea. I was startled by how ill he looked, much worse than when I had seen him a year ago. He greeted both Ellie and myself very warmly.

"So you've done it, you two," he said.

"Yes," said Ellie, "and now we're going to have our house built, aren't we?"

"I've got the drawings for you here, the plans," he said to me. "She's told you, hasn't she, how she came and ferreted me out and gave me her—commands," he said, choosing the word thoughtfully.

"Oh! not commands," said Ellie. "I just pleaded."

"You know we've bought the site?" I said.

"Ellie wired and told me. She sent me dozens of photographs."

"Of course you've got to come and see it first," said Ellie. "You mightn't like the site."

"I do like it."

"You can't really know till you've seen it."

"But I have seen it, child. I flew over five days ago. I met one of your hatchet-faced lawyers there—the English one."

"Mr. Crawford?"

"That's the man. In fact, operations have already started: clearing the ground, removing the ruins of the old house, foundations—drains—When you get back to England, I'll be there to meet you." He got out his plans then and we sat talking and looking at our house-to-be. There was even a rough water-color sketch of it as well as the architectural elevations and plans.

"Do you like it, Mike?"

I drew a deep breath.

"Yes," I said, "that's it. That's absolutely it."

"You used to talk about it enough, Mike. When I was in a fanciful mood, I used to think that piece of land had laid a spell upon you. You were a man in love with a house that you might never own, that you might never see, that might never even be built."

"But it's going to be built," said Ellie. "It's going to be built, isn't it?"

"If God or the devil wills it," said Santonix. "It doesn't depend on me."

"You're not any—any better?" I asked doubtfully.

"Get it into your thick head. I shall never be better. That's not on the cards."

"Nonsense," I said. "People are finding cures for things all the time. Doctors are gloomy brutes. They give people up for dead, and then the people laugh and cock a snook at them and live for another fifty years."

"I admire your optimism, Mike, but my malady isn't one of that kind. They take you to the hospital and give you a change of blood and back you come again with a little leeway of life, a little span of time gained. And so on, getting weaker each time."

"You are very brave," said Ellie.

"Oh, no, I'm not brave. When a thing is certain, there's nothing to be brave about. All you can do is to find your consolation."

"Building houses?"

"No, not that. You've less vitality all the time, you see, and therefore building houses becomes more difficult, not easier. The strength keeps giving out. No. But there are consolations. Sometimes very queer ones."

"I don't understand you," I said.

"No, you wouldn't, Mike. I don't know really that Ellie would. She might." He went on, speaking not so much to us as to himself. "Two things run together, side by side. Weakness and strength. The weakness of fading vitality and the strength of frustrated power. It doesn't matter, you see, what you do now! You're going to die anyway. So you can do anything you choose. There's nothing to deter you; there's nothing to hold you back. I could walk through the streets of Athens shooting down every man or woman whose face I didn't like. Think of that."

"The police could arrest you just the same," I pointed out.

"Of course they could. But what could they do? At the most take my life. Well, my life's going to be taken by a greater power than the law in a very short time. What else could they do? Send me to prison for twenty—thirty years? That's rather ironical, isn't it? There aren't twenty or thirty years for me to serve. Six months—one year—eighteen months at the utmost. There's nothing anyone can do to me. So in the span that's left to me I am king. I can do what I like. Sometimes it's a very heady thought. Only—only, you see, there's not much temptation because there's nothing particularly exotic or lawless that I want to do."

After we had left him, as we were driving back to Athens, Ellie said to me,

"He's an odd person. Sometimes, you know, I feel frightened of him."

"Frightened of Rudolf Santonix—why?"

"Because he isn't like other people and because he has a—I don't know—a ruthlessness and an arrogance about him somewhere. And I think that he was trying to tell us, really, that knowing he's going to die soon has increased his arrogance. Supposing," said Ellie, looking at me in an animated way, with almost a rapt and emotional expression on her face, "supposing he built us our lovely castle, our lovely house on the cliff's edge there in the pines, supposing we were coming to live in it. There he was on the doorstep and he welcomed us in and then—"

"Well, Ellie?"

"Then, supposing he came in after us, he slowly closed the doorway behind us, and sacrificed us there on the threshold. Cut our throats or something."

"You frighten me, Ellie. The things you think of!"

"The trouble with you and me, Mike, is that we don't live in the real world. We dream of fantastic things that may never happen."

"Don't think of sacrifices in connection with Gipsy's Acre."

"It's the name, I suppose, and the curse upon it."

"There isn't any curse," I shouted. "It's all nonsense. Forget it."

That was in Greece.

10

IT WAS, I think, the day after that. We were in Athens. Suddenly, on the steps of the Acropolis, Ellie ran into people that she knew. They had come ashore from one of the Hellenic cruises. A woman of about thirty-five detached herself from the group and rushed along the steps to Ellie exclaiming,

"Why, I never did. It's really you, Ellie Guteman? Well, what are you doing here? I'd no idea. Are you on a cruise?"

"No," said Ellie, "just staying here."

"My, but it's lovely to see you. How's Cora? Is she here?"

"No, Cora is at Salzburg, I believe."

"Well, well." The woman was looking at me and Ellie said quietly, "Let me introduce—Mr. Rogers, Mrs. Bennington."

"How d'you do. How long are you here for?"

"I'm leaving tomorrow," said Ellie.

"Oh, dear! My, I'll lose my party if I don't go, and I just don't want to miss a word of the lecture and the descriptions. They do hustle one a bit, you know. I'm just beat at the end of the day. Any chance of meeting you for a drink?"

"Not today," said Ellie; "we're going on an excursion."

Mrs. Bennington rushed off to rejoin her party. Ellie, who had been going with me up the steps of the Acropolis, turned round and moved down again.

"That rather settles things, doesn't it?" she said to me.

"What does it settle?"

Ellie did not answer for a minute or two and then she said with a sigh, "I must write tonight."

"Write to whom?"

"Oh, to Cora, and to Uncle Frank, I suppose, and Uncle Andrew."

"Who's Uncle Andrew? He's a new one."

"Andrew Lippincott. Not really an uncle. He's my principal guardian or trustee or whatever you call it. He's a lawyer—a very well-known one."

"What are you going to say?"

"I'm going to tell them I'm married. I couldn't say suddenly to Nora Bennington, 'Let me introduce my husband.' There would have been frightful shrieks and exclamations and 'I never heard you were married. Tell me all about it, darling,' et cetera, et cetera, et cetera. It's only fair that my stepmother and Uncle Frank and Uncle Andrew should be the first to know." She sighed. "Oh, well, we've had a lovely time up to now."

"What will they all say or do?" I asked.

"Make a fuss, I expect," said Ellie in her placid way. "It doesn't matter if they do, and they'll have sense enough to know that. We'll have to have a meeting, I expect. We could go to New York. Would you like that?" She looked at me inquiringly.

"No," I said, "I shouldn't like it in the least."

"Then they'll come to London, probably, or some of them will. I don't know if you'd like that any better."

"I shouldn't like any of it. I want to be with you and see our house going up brick by brick as soon as Santonix gets there."

"So we can," said Ellie. "After all, meetings with the family won't take long. Possibly just one big splendid row would do. Get it over in one. Either we fly over there or they fly over here."

"I thought you said your stepmother was at Salzburg."

"Oh, I just said that. It sounded odd to say I didn't know where she was. Yes," said Ellie with a sigh, "we'll go home and meet them all. Mike, I hope you won't mind too much."

"Mind what—your family?"

"Yes. You won't mind if they're nasty to you?"

"I suppose it's the price I have to pay for marrying you," I said. "I'll bear it."

"There's your mother," said Ellie thoughtfully.

"For heaven's sake, Ellie, you're not going to try and arrange a meeting between your stepmother in her frills and her furbelows and my mother from her back street. What do you think they'd ever have to say to each other?"

"If Cora was my own mother they might have quite a lot to say to each other," said Ellie. "I wish you wouldn't be so obsessed with class distinctions, Mike!"

"Me!" I said incredulously. "What's your American phrase—I come from the wrong side of the tracks, don't I?"

"You don't want to write it on a placard and pin it on yourself."

"I don't know the right clothes to wear," I said bitterly. "I don't know the right way to talk about things and I don't know anything really about pictures or art or music. I'm only just learning who to tip and how much to give."

"Don't you think, Mike, that that makes it all much more exciting for you? I think so."

"Anyway," I said, "you're not to drag my mother into your family party."

"I wasn't proposing to drag anyone into anything, but I think, Mike, I ought to go and see your mother when we go back to England."

"No," I said explosively.

She looked at me rather startled.

"Why not, Mike, though? I mean, apart from anything else, I mean it's just very rude not to. Have you told her you're married?"

"Not yet."

"Why not?"

I didn't answer.

"Wouldn't the simplest way be to tell her you're married and take me to see her when we get back to England?"

"No," I said again. It was not so explosive this time but it was still fairly well underlined.

"You don't want me to meet her," said Ellie slowly.

I didn't, of course. I suppose it was obvious enough, but the last thing I could do was to explain. I didn't see how I could explain.

"It wouldn't be the right thing to do," I said slowly. "You must see that. I'm sure it would lead to trouble."

"You think she wouldn't like me?"

"Nobody could help liking you, but it wouldn't be— Oh, I don't know how to put it. But she might be upset and confused. After all, well, I mean I've married out of my station. That's the old-fashioned term. She wouldn't like that."

Ellie shook her head slowly.

"Does anybody really think like that nowadays?"

"Of course they do. They do in your country, too."

"Yes," she said, "in a way that's true, but—if anyone makes good there—"

"You mean if a man makes a lot of money."

"Well, not only money."

"Yes," I said, "it's money. If a man makes a lot of money, he's admired and looked up to and it doesn't matter where he was born."

"Well, that's the same everywhere," said Ellie.

"Please, Ellie," I said. "Please don't go and see my mother."

"I still think it's unkind."

"No, it isn't. Can't you let me know what's best for my own mother? She'd be upset. I tell you she would."

"But you must tell her you've got married."

"All right," I said. "I'll do that."

It occurred to me it would be easier to write to my mother from abroad. That evening when Ellie was writing to Uncle Andrew and Uncle Frank and her stepmother Cora van Stuyvesant, I, too, was writing my own letter. It was quite short.

"Dear Mum," I wrote. "I ought to have told you before but I felt a bit awkward. I got married three weeks ago. It was all rather sudden. She's a very pretty girl and very sweet. She's got a lot of money, which makes things a bit awkward sometimes. We're going to build ourselves a house somewhere in the country. Just at present we're traveling around Europe. All the best. Yours, Mike."

The results of our evening's correspondence were somewhat varied. My mother let a week elapse before she sent a letter remarkably typical of her.

"Dear Mike. I was glad to get your letter. I hope you'll be very happy. Your affectionate mother."

As Ellie had prophesied, there was far more fuss on her side. We'd stirred up a regular hornet's nest of trouble. We were beset by reporters who wanted news of our romantic marriage, there were articles in the papers about the Guteman heiress and her romantic elopement, there were letters from bankers and lawyers. And finally official meetings were arranged. We met Santonix on the site of Gipsy's Acre and we looked at the plans there and discussed things, and then having seen things under way we came to London, took a suite at Claridge's and prepared, as they say in old-world books, to receive cavalry.

The first to arrive was Mr. Andrew P. Lippincott. He was an elderly man, dry and precise in appearance. He was long and lean, with suave and courteous manners. He was a Bostonian and from his voice I wouldn't have known he was an American. By arrangement through the telephone he called upon us in our suite at 12 o'clock. Ellie was nervous, I could tell, although she concealed it very well.

Mr. Lippincott kissed Ellie and extended a hand and a pleasant smile to me.

"Well, Ellie my dear, you are looking very well. Blooming, I might say."

"How are you, Uncle Andrew? How did you come? Did you fly?"

"No, I had a very pleasant trip across on the *Queen Mary*. And this is your husband?"

"This is Mike, yes."

I played up, or thought I did. "How are you, sir?" I said. Then I asked him if he'd have a drink, which he refused pleasantly. He sat down in an upright chair with gilt arms to it and looked, still smiling, from Ellie to me.

"Well," he said, "you young people have been giving us shocks. All very romantic, eh?"

"I'm sorry," said Ellie; "I really am sorry."

"Are you?" said Mr. Lippincott rather dryly.

"I thought it was the best way," said Ellie.

"I am not altogether of your opinion there, my dear."

"Uncle Andrew," Ellie said, "you know perfectly well that if I'd done it any other way, there would have been the most frightful fuss."

"Why should there have been such a frightful fuss?"

"You know what they'd have been like," said Ellie. "You, too," she added accusingly. She added, "I've had two letters from Cora. One yesterday and one this morning."

"You must discount a certain amount of agitation, my dear. It's only natural under the circumstances, don't you think?"

"It's my business who I get married to and how and where."

"You may think so, but you will find that the women of any family would rarely agree as to that."

"Really, I've saved everyone a lot of trouble."

"You may put it that way."

"But it's true, isn't it?"

"But you practiced, did you not, a good deal of deception, helped by someone who should have known better than to do what she did."

Ellie flushed.

"You mean Greta? She only did what I asked her to. Are they all very upset with her?"

"Naturally. Neither she nor you could expect anything else, could you? She was, remember, in a position of trust."

"I'm of age. I can do what I like."

"I am speaking of the period of time before you were of age. The deceptions began then, did they not?"

"You mustn't blame Ellie, sir," I said. "To begin with, I didn't know what was going on, and since all her relations are in another country, it wasn't easy for me to get in touch with them."

"I quite realize," said Mr. Lippincott, "that Greta posted certain letters and gave certain information to Mrs. Van Stuyvesant and to myself as she was requested to do by Ellie here, and made, if I may say so, a very competent job of it. You have met Greta Andersen, Michael? I may call you Michael, since you are Ellie's husband."

"Of course," I said, "call me Mike. No, I haven't met Miss Andersen—"

"Indeed? That seems to me surprising." He looked at me with a long thoughtful gaze. "I should have thought that she would have been present at your marriage."

"No, Greta wasn't there," said Ellie. She threw me a look of reproach and I shifted uncomfortably.

Mr. Lippincott's eyes were still resting on me thoughtfully. He made me uncomfortable. He seemed about to say something more, then changed his mind.

"I'm afraid," he said after a moment or two, "that you two, Michael and Ellie, will have to put up with a certain amount of reproaches and criticism from Ellie's family."

"I suppose they are going to descend on me in a bunch," said Ellie.

"Very probably," said Mr. Lippincott. "I've tried to pave the way," he added.

"You're on our side, Uncle Andrew?" said Ellie, smiling at him.

"You must hardly ask a prudent lawyer to go as far as that. I have learned that in life it is wise to accept what is a *fait accompli*. You two have fallen in love with each other and have got married and have, I understood you to say, Ellie, bought a piece of property in the south of England and are already started building a house on it. You propose, therefore, to live in this country?"

"We want to make our home here, yes. Do you object to our doing that?" I said with a touch of anger in my voice. "Ellie's married to me and she's a British subject now. So why shouldn't she live in England?"

"No reason at all. In fact, there is no reason why Fenella should not live in any country she chooses, or indeed have property in more than one country. The house in Nassau belongs to you, remember, Ellie."

"I always thought it was Cora's. She always has behaved as though it was."

"But the actual property rights are vested in you. You also have the house in Long Island whenever you care to visit it. You are the owner of a greal deal of oil-bearing property in the West." His voice was amiable, pleasant, but I had the feeling that the words were directed at me in some curious way. Was it his idea of trying to insinuate a wedge between me and Ellie? I was not sure. It didn't seem very sensible, rubbing it in to a man that his wife owned property all over the world and was fabulously rich. If anything, I should have thought that he would have played down Ellie's property rights and her money and all the rest of it. If I was a fortune hunter, as he obviously thought, that would be all the more grist to my mill. But I did realize that Mr. Lippincott was a subtle man. It would be hard at any time to know what he was driving at—what he had in his mind behind his even and pleasant manner. Was he trying in a way of his own to make me feel uncomfortable, to make me feel that I was going to be branded almost publicly as a fortune hunter? He said to Ellie,

"I've brought over a certain amount of legal stuff which you'll have to go through with me, Ellie. I shall want your signature to many of these things."

"Yes, of course, Uncle Andrew. Any time."

"As you say, any time. There's no hurry. I have other business in London, and I shall be over here for about ten days."

Ten days, I thought. That's a long time. I rather wished that Mr. Lippincott wasn't going to be here for ten days. He appeared friendly enough toward me, though, as you might say, indicating that he still reserved his judgment on certain points, but I wondered at that moment whether he was really my enemy. If he was, he would not be the kind of man to show his hand.

"Well," he went on, "now that we've all met and come to terms, as you might say, for the future, I would like to have a short interview with this husband of yours."

Ellie said, "You can talk to us both." She was up in arms. I put a hand on her arm.

"Now don't flare up, ducks; you're not a mother hen protecting a chicken." I propelled her gently to the door in the wall that led into the bedroom. "Uncle Andrew wants to size me up," I said. "He's well within his rights."

I pushed her gently through the double doors. I shut them both and came back into the room. It was a large, handsome sitting room. I came back and took a chair and faced Mr. Lippincott. "All right," I said. "Shoot."

"Thank you, Michael," he said. "First of all I want to assure you that I am not, as you may be thinking, your enemy in any way."

"Well," I said, "I'm glad to hear that." I didn't sound very sure about it.

"Let me speak frankly," said Mr. Lippincott, "more frankly than I could do before that dear child to whom I am guardian and of whom I am very fond. You may not yet appreciate it fully, Michael, but Ellie is a most unusually sweet and lovable girl."

"Don't you worry. I'm in love with her, all right."

"That is not at all the same thing," said Mr. Lippincott in his dry manner. "I hope that as well as being in love with her you can also appreciate what a really dear and in some ways very vulnerable person she is."

"I'll try," I said. "I don't think I'll have to try very hard. She's tops, Ellie is."

"So I will go on with what I was about to say. I shall put my cards on the table with the utmost frankness. You are not the kind of young man that I should have wished Ellie to marry. I should like her, as her family would have liked her, to marry someone of her own surroundings, of her own set–"

"A toff, in other words," I said.

"No, not only that. A similar background is, I think, to be desired as a basis for matrimony. And I am not referring to the snob attitude. After all, Herman Guteman, her grandfather, started life as a dock hand. He ended up as one of the richest men in America."

"For all you know I might do the same," I said. "I may end up one of the richest men in England."

"Everything is possible," said Mr. Lippincott. "Do you have ambitions that way?"

"It's not just the money," I said. "I'd like to–I'd like to get somewhere and do things and–" I hesitated, stopped.

"You have ambitions, shall we say? Well, that is a very good thing, I am sure."

"I'm starting at long odds," I said, "starting from scratch. I'm nothing and nobody and I won't pretend otherwise."

He nodded approval.

"Very frankly and handsomely said. I appreciate it. Now, Michael, I am no relation to Ellie, but I have acted as her guardian, I am a trustee, left so by her grandfather, of her affairs, I manage her fortune and her investments. And I assume, therefore, a certain responsibility for them. Therefore I want to know all that I can know about the husband she has chosen."

"Well," I said, "you can make inquiries about me, I suppose, and find out anything you like easily enough."

"Quite so," said Mr. Lippincott. "That would be one way of doing it. A wise precaution to take. But actually, Michael, I should like to know all that I can about you from your own lips. I should like to hear your own story of what your life has been up to now."

Of course I didn't like it. I expect he knew I wouldn't. Nobody in my position would like that. It's second nature to make the best of yourself. I'd made a point of that at school and onward, boasted about things a bit, said a few things, stretching the truth a bit. I wasn't ashamed of it. I think it's natural. I think it's the sort of thing that you've got to do if you want to get on. Make out a good case for yourself. People take you at your own valuation, and I didn't want to be like that chap in Dickens. They read it out on the television, and I must say it's a good yarn on its own. Uriah something his name was, always going about being humble and rubbing his hands, and actually planning and scheming behind that humility. I didn't want to be like that.

I was ready enough to boast a bit with the chaps I met or to put up a good case to a prospective employer. After all, you've got a best side and a worst side of yourself and it's no good showing the worst side and harping on it. No, I'd always done the best for myself describing my activities up to date. But I didn't fancy doing that sort of thing with Mr. Lippincott. He'd rather pooh-poohed the idea of making private inquiries about me, but I wasn't at all sure that he wouldn't do so, all the same. So I gave him the truth unvarnished, as you might say.

Squalid beginnings, the fact that my father had been a drunk, but that I'd had a good mother, that she'd slaved a good bit to help me get educated. I made no secret of the fact that I'd been a rolling stone, that I'd moved from one job to another. He was a good listener, encouraging, if you know what I mean. Every now and then, though, I realized how shrewd he was. Just little questions that he slipped in, or comments, some comment that I might have rushed in unguardedly either to admit or to deny.

Yes, I had a sort of feeling that I'd better be wary and on my toes.

And after ten minutes I was quite glad when he leaned back in his chair and the inquisition, if you could call it that, and it wasn't in the least like one, seemed to be over.

"You have an adventurous attitude to life, Mr. Rogers—Michael. Not a bad thing. Tell me more about this house that you and Ellie are building."

"Well," I said, "it's not far from a town called Market Chadwell."

"Yes," he said, "I know just where it is. As a matter of fact, I ran down to see it. Yesterday, to be exact."

That startled me a little. It showed he was a devious kind of fellow who got round to more things than you might think he would.

"It's a beautiful site," I said defensively, "and the house we're building is going to be a beautiful house. The architect's a chap called Santonix—Rudolf Santonix. I don't know if you've ever heard of him, but—"

"Oh, yes," said Mr. Lippincott, "he's quite a well-known name among architects."

"He's done work in the States, I believe."

"Yes, an architect of great promise and talent. Unfortunately I believe his health is not good."

"He thinks he's a dying man," I said, "but I don't believe it. I believe he'll get cured, get well again. Doctors—they'll say anything."

"I hope your optimism is justified. You are an optimist."

"I am about Santonix."

"I hope all you wish will come true. I may say that I think you and Ellie have made an extremely good purchase in the piece of property that you have bought."

I thought it was nice of the old boy to use the pronoun "you." It wasn't rubbing it in that Ellie had done the buying on her own.

"I have had a consultation with Mr. Crawford—"

"Crawford?" I frowned slightly.

"Mr. Crawford of Reece and Crawford, a firm of English solicitors. Mr. Crawford was the member of the firm who put the purchase in hand. It is a good firm of solicitors and I gather that this property was acquired at a cheap figure. I may say that I wondered slightly at that. I am familiar with the present prices of land in this country and I really felt rather at a loss to account for it. I think Mr. Crawford himself was surprised to get it at so low a figure. I wondered if you knew at all why this property happened to go so cheaply. Mr. Crawford did not advance any opinion on that. In fact he seemed slightly embarrassed when I put the question to him."

"Oh, well," I said, "it's got a curse on it."

"I beg your pardon, Michael. What did you say?"

"A curse, sir," I explained. "The gipsy's warning, that sort of thing. It is known locally as Gipsy's Acre."

"Ah. A story?"

"Yes. It seems rather confused and I don't know how much people have made up and how much is true. There was a murder or something long ago. A man and his wife and another man. Some story that the husband shot the other two and then shot himself. At least that's the verdict that was brought in. But all sorts of other stories go flying about. I don't think anyone really knows what happened. It was a good long time ago. It's changed hands about four or five times since, but nobody stays there long."

"Ah," said Mr. Lippincott appreciatively, "yes, quite a piece of English folklore." He looked at me curiously. "And you and Ellie are not afraid of the curse?" He said it lightly, with a slight smile.

"Of course not," I said. "Neither Ellie nor I would believe in any rubbish of that kind. Actually, it's a lucky thing, since because of it we got it cheap." When I said that, a sudden thought struck me. It was lucky in one sense, but I thought that with all Ellie's money and her property and all the rest of it, it couldn't matter to her very much whether she bought a piece of land cheap or at the top price. Then I thought, no, I was wrong. After all, she'd had a grandfather who came up from being a dock laborer to a millionaire. Anyone of that kind would always wish to buy cheap and sell dear.

"Well, I am not superstitious," said Mr. Lippincott, "and the view from your property is quite magnificent." He hesitated. "I only hope that when you come to move into your house to live there, that Ellie will not hear too many of these stories that are going about."

"I'll keep everything from her that I can," I said. "I don't suppose anybody will say anything to her."

"People in country villages are very fond of repeating stories of that kind," said Mr. Lippincott. "And Ellie, remember, is not as tough as you are, Michael. She can be influenced easily. Only in some ways. Which brings me—" he stopped without going on to say what he had been going to. He tapped on the table with one finger. "I'm going to speak to you now on a matter of some difficulty. You said just now that you had not met this Greta Andersen."

"No, as I said, I haven't met her yet."

"Odd. Very curious."

"Well?" I looked at him inquiringly.

"I should have thought you'd have been almost sure to have met her," he said slowly. "How much do you know about her?"

"I know that she's been with Ellie some time."

"She has been with Ellie since Ellie was seventeen. She has occupied a post of some responsibility and trust. She came first to the States in the capacity of secretary and companion. A kind of chaperon to Ellie when Mrs. Van Stuyvesant, her stepmother, was away from home, which I may say was a quite frequent occurrence." He spoke particularly dryly when he said this. "She is, I gather, a well-born girl with excellent references, half Swedish, half German. Ellie became, quite naturally, very much attached to her."

"So I gather," I said.

"In some ways Ellie was, I suppose, almost too much attached to her. You don't mind my saying that."

"No. Why should I mind? As a matter of fact, I've—well, I've thought so myself once or twice. Greta this and Greta that. I got—well, I know I've no business to, but I used to get fed-up sometimes."

"And yet she expressed no wish for you to meet Greta?"

"Well," I said, "it's rather difficult to explain. But I think, yes, I think she probably did suggest it in a mild way once or twice but, well, we were too taken up with having met each other. Besides, oh, well, I suppose I didn't really want to meet Greta. I didn't want to share Ellie with anyone."

"I see. Yes, I see. And Ellie did not suggest Greta being present at your wedding?"

"She did suggest it," I said.

"But—but you didn't want her to come. Why?"

"I don't know. I really don't know. I just felt that this Greta, this girl or woman I'd never met, she was always horning in on everything. You know, arranging Ellie's life for her. Sending post cards and letters and filling in for Ellie, arranging a whole itinerary and passing it on to the family. I felt that Ellie was dependent on Greta in a way, that she let Greta run her, that she wanted to do everything that Greta wanted. I—oh, I'm sorry, Mr. Lippincott, I oughtn't to be saying all these things perhaps. Say I was just plain jealous. Anyway, I blew up and I said I didn't want Greta at the wedding, that the wedding was ours, that it was just our business and nobody else's. And so we went along to the registrar's office and his clerk and the typist from his office were the two witnesses. I daresay it was mean of me to refuse to have Greta there, but I wanted to have Ellie to myself."

"I see. Yes, I see, and I think, if I may say so, that you were wise, Michael."

"You don't like Greta either," I said shrewdly.

"You can hardly use the word 'either,' Michael, if you have not even met her."

"No, I know but, well, I mean if you hear a lot about a person, you can form some sort of idea of them, some judgment of them. Oh, well, call it plain jealousy. Why don't *you* like Greta?"

"This is without prejudice," said Mr. Lippincott, "but you are Ellie's husband, Michael, and I have Ellie's happiness very much at heart. I don't think that the influence that Greta has over Ellie is a very desirable one. She takes too much upon herself."

"Do you think she'll try and make trouble between us?" I asked.

"I think," said Mr. Lippincott, "that I have no right to say anything of that kind."

He sat looking cautiously at me and blinking like a wrinkled old tortoise.

I didn't know quite what to say next. He spoke first, choosing his words with some care.

"There has been, then, no suggestion that Greta Andersen might take up her residence with you?"

"Not if I can help it," I said.

"Ah. So that is what you feel? The idea has been mooted."

"Ellie did say something of the kind. But we're newly married, Mr. Lippincott. We want our house—our new home—to ourselves. Of course she'll come and stay sometimes, I suppose. That'll only be natural."

"As you say, that would be only natural. But you realize, perhaps, that Greta is going to be in a somewhat difficult position as regards further employment. I mean, it is not a question of what Ellie thinks of her, but of what the people who engaged her and reposed trust in her feel."

"You mean that you or Mrs. Van What's-her-name won't recommend her for another post of the same kind?"

"They are hardly likely to do so except so far as to satisfy purely legal requirements."

"And you think that she'll want to come to England and live on Ellie."

"I don't want to prejudice you too much against her. After all, this is mostly in my mind. I dislike some of the things she has done and the way she has done them. I think that Ellie, who has a very generous heart, will be upset at having, shall we say, blighted Greta's prospects in many ways. She might impulsively insist on her coming to live with you."

"I don't think Ellie will insist," I said slowly. I sounded a little worried all the same, and I thought Lippincott noticed it. "But couldn't we—Ellie, I mean—couldn't Ellie pension her off?"

"We should not put it precisely like that," said Mr. Lippincott. "There is a suggestion of age about pensioning anyone off, and Greta is a young woman, and I may say a very handsome young woman. Beautiful, in fact," he added in a deprecating, disapproving voice. "She's very attractive to men, too."

"Well, perhaps she'll marry," I said. "If she's all that, why hasn't she got married before this?"

"There have been people attracted, I believe, but she has not considered them. I think, however, that your suggestion is a very sound one. I think it might be carried out in a way that would not hurt anyone's susceptibilities. It might seem quite a natural thing to do on Ellie's having attained her majority and having had her marriage helped on by Greta's good offices—settle a sum of money upon her in a fit of gratitude." Mr. Lippincott made the last two words sound as sour as lemon juice.

"Well, then, that's all right," I said cheerfully.

"Again I see that you are an optimist. Let us hope that Greta will accept what is offered to her."

"Why shouldn't she? She'd be mad if she didn't."

"I don't know," said Mr. Lippincott. "I should say it would be extraordinary if she did not accept, and they will remain on terms of friendship, of course."

"You think— What do you think?"

"I would like to see her influence over Ellie broken," said Mr. Lippincott. He got up. "You will, I hope, assist me and do everything you can to further that end?"

"You bet I will," I said. "The last thing I want is to have Greta in our pockets all the time."

"You might change your mind when you see her," said Mr. Lippincott.

"I don't think so," I said. "I don't like managing females, however efficient and even handsome they are."

"Thank you, Michael, for listening to me so patiently. I hope you will give me the pleasure of dining with me, both of you. Possibly next Tuesday evening? Cora van Stuyvesant and Frank Barton will probably be in London by that time."

"And I've got to meet them, I suppose?"

"Oh, yes, that will be quite inevitable." He smiled at me and this time his smile seemed more genuine than it had before. "You mustn't mind too much," he said. "Cora, I expect, will be very rude to you.

Frank will be merely tactless. Reuben won't be over just at present."

I didn't know who Reuben was—another relation, I supposed.

I went across to the connecting doors and opened them. "Come on, Ellie," I said, "the grilling is over."

She came back in the room and looked quickly from Lippincott to myself, then she went across and kissed him.

"Dear Uncle Andrew," she said. "I can see you've been nice to Michael."

"Well, my dear, if I weren't nice to your husband, you wouldn't have much use for me in the future, would you? I do reserve the right to give a few words of advice now and then. You're very young, you know, both of you."

"All right," said Ellie, "we'll listen patiently."

"Now, my dear, I'd like to have a word with you if I may."

"My turn to be odd man out," I said, and I too went into the bedroom.

I shut the two double doors ostentatiously, but I opened the inner one again after I got inside. I hadn't been as well brought up as Ellie, so I felt a bit anxious to find out how double-faced Mr. Lippincott might turn out to be. But actually there was nothing I need have listened to. He gave Ellie one or two wise words of advice. He said she must realize that I might find it difficult to be a poor man married to a rich wife, and then he went on to sound her about making a settlement on Greta. She agreed to it eagerly and said she'd been going to ask him that herself. He also suggested that she should make an additional settlement on Cora van Stuyvesant.

"There is no earthly need that you should do so," he said. "She has been very well provided for in the matter of alimony from several husbands. And she is, as you know, paid an income, though not a very big one, from the trust fund left by your grandfather."

"But you think I ought to give her more still?"

"I think there is no legal or moral obligation to do so. What I think is that you will find her far less tiresome and shall I say catty if you do so. I should make it in the form of an increased income, which you could revoke at any time. If you find that she has been spreading malicious rumors about Michael or yourself or your life together, the knowledge that you can do that will keep her tongue free of those more poisonous barbs that she so well knows how to plant."

"Cora has always hated me," said Ellie. "I've known that." She added rather shyly, "You do like Mike, don't you, Uncle Andrew?"

"I think he's an extremely attractive young man," said Mr. Lippincott. "And I can quite see how you came to marry him."

That, I suppose, was as good as I could expect. I wasn't really his type, and I knew it. I eased the door gently to and in a minute or two Ellie came to fetch me.

We were both standing saying good-by to Lippincott when there was a knock on the door and a page boy came in with a telegram. Ellie took it and opened it. She gave a little surprised cry of pleasure.

"It's Greta," she said; "she's arriving in London tonight and she'll be coming to see us tomorrow. How lovely." She looked at us both. "Isn't it?" she said.

She saw two sour faces and heard two polite voices saying, one: "Yes, indeed, my dear," the other one: "Of course."

11

I HAD BEEN out shopping the next morning and I arrived back at the hotel rather later than I had meant. I found Ellie sitting in the central lounge, and opposite her was a tall blonde young woman. In fact Greta. Both of them were talking nineteen to the dozen.

I'm never any hand at describing people, but I'll have a shot at describing Greta. To begin with, one couldn't deny that she was, as Ellie had said, very beautiful and also, as Mr. Lippincott had reluctantly admitted, very handsome. The two things are not exactly the same. If you say a woman is handsome, it does not mean that actually you yourself admire her. Mr. Lippincott, I gathered, had not admired Greta. All the same, when Greta walked across the lounge into a hotel or in a restaurant, men's heads turned to look at her. She was a Nordic type of blonde with pure gold corn-colored hair. She wore it piled high on her head in the fashion of the time, not falling straight down on each side of her face in the Chelsea tradition. She looked what she was—Swedish or north German. In fact, pin on a pair of wings and she could have gone to a fancy dress ball as a Valkyrie. Her eyes were a bright clear blue, and her contours were admirable. Let's admit it. She was something!

I came along to where they were sitting and joined them, greeting them both in what I hope was a natural, friendly manner, though I couldn't help feeling a bit awkward. I'm not always very good at acting a part. Ellie said immediately,

"At last, Mike, this is Greta."

I said I guessed it might be, in a rather facetious, not very happy manner. I said,

"I'm very glad to meet you at last, Greta."

Ellie said,

"As you know very well, if it hadn't been for Greta, we would never have been able to get married."

"All the same, we'd have managed it somehow," I said.

"Not if the family had come down on us like a ton of coals. They'd have broken it up somehow. Tell me, Greta, have they been very awful?" Ellie asked. "You haven't written or said anything to me about that."

"I know better," said Greta, "than to write to a happy couple when they're on their honeymoon."

"But were they very angry with you?"

"Of course! What do you imagine? But I was prepared for that, I can assure you."

"What have they said or done?"

"Everything they could," said Greta cheerfully. "Starting with the sack, naturally."

"Yes, I suppose that was inevitable. But—but what have you done? After all, they can't refuse to give you references."

"Of course they can. And after all, from their point of view I was placed in a position of trust and abused it shamefully." She added, "Enjoyed abusing it, too."

"But what are you doing now?"

"Oh, I've got a job ready to walk into."

"In New York?"

"No. Here in London. Secretarial."

"But are you all right?"

"Darling Ellie," said Greta, "how can I not be all right with that lovely check you sent me in anticipation of what was going to happen when the balloon went up."

Her English was very good, with hardly any trace of accent, though she used a lot of colloquial terms which sometimes didn't run quite right.

"I've seen a bit of the world, fixed myself up in London and bought a good many things as well."

"Mike and I have bought a lot of things, too," said Ellie, smiling at the recollection.

It was true. We'd done ourselves pretty well with our continental shopping. It was really wonderful that we had dollars to spend, no niggling treasury restrictions. Brocades and fabrics in Italy for the house. And we'd bought pictures, too, both in Italy and in Paris, paying what seemed fabulous sums for them. A whole world had opened up to me that I'd never dreamed would have come my way.

"You both look remarkably happy," said Greta.

"You haven't seen our house yet," said Ellie. "It's going to be wonderful. It's going to be just like we dreamed it would be, isn't it, Mike?"

"I have seen it," said Greta. "The first day I got back to England, I hired a car and drove down there."

"Well?" said Ellie.

I said Well? too.

"Well," said Greta consideringly. She shifted her head from side to side.

Ellie looked grief-stricken, horribly taken aback. But I wasn't taken in. I saw at once that Greta was having a bit of fun with us. If the thought just flashed across my mind for a moment that her kind of fun wasn't very kind, it hardly had time to take root. Greta burst out laughing, a high musical laugh that made people turn their heads and look at us.

"You should have seen your faces," she said, "especially yours, Ellie. I have to tease you just a little. It's a wonderful house, lovely. That man's a genius."

"Yes," I said, "he's something out of the ordinary. Wait till you meet him."

"I have met him," said Greta. "He was down there the day I went. Yes, he's an extraordinary person. Rather frightening, don't you think?"

"Frightening?" I said, surprised. "In what way?"

"Oh, I don't know. It's as though he looks through you and—well, sees right through to the other side. That's always disconcerting." Then she added, "He looks rather ill."

"He is ill. Very ill," I said.

"What a shame. What's the matter with him, tuberculosis, something like that?"

"No," I said, "I don't think it's tuberculosis. I think it's something to do with—oh, with blood."

"Oh, I see. Doctors can do almost anything nowadays, can't they, unless they kill you first while they're trying to cure you. But don't let's think of that. Let's think of the house. When will it be finished?"

"Quite soon, I should think, by the look of it. I'd never imagined a house could go up so quickly," I said.

"Oh," said Greta carelessly, "that's money. Double shifts and bonuses—all the rest of it. You don't really know yourself, Ellie, how wonderful it is to have all the money you have."

But I did know. I had been learning, learning a great deal in the last few weeks. I'd stepped as a result of marriage into an entirely different world, and it wasn't the sort of world I'd imagined it to be from the outside. So far in my life, a lucky double had been my highest knowledge of affluence. A whack of money coming in, and spending it as fast as I could on the biggest blow-out I could find. Crude, of course. The crudeness of my class. But Ellie's world was a different world. It wasn't what I should have thought it to be. Just more and more super luxury. It wasn't bigger bathrooms and larger houses and more electric light fittings and bigger meals and faster cars. It wasn't just spending for spending's sake and showing off to everyone in sight. Instead, it was curiously simple—the sort of simplicity that comes when you get beyond the point of splashing for splashing's sake. You don't want three yachts or four cars and you can't eat more than three meals a day, and if you buy a really top-price picture, you don't want more than perhaps one of them in a room. It's as simple as that. Whatever you have is just the best of its kind, not so much because it is the best but because there is no reason if you like or want any particular thing why you shouldn't have it. There is no moment when you say, "I'm afraid I can't afford that one." So in a strange way it makes sometimes for such a curious simplicity that I couldn't understand it. We were considering a French impressionist picture, a Cézanne, I think it was. I had to learn that name carefully. I always mixed it up with a tzigane, which I gather is a gipsy orchestra. And then as we walked along the streets of Venice, Ellie stopped to look at some pavement artists. On the whole they were doing some terrible pictures for tourists which all looked the same. Portraits with great rows of shining teeth and usually blonde hair falling down their necks.

And then she bought quite a tiny picture, just a picture of a little glimpse through to a canal. The man who had painted it appraised the look of us and she bought it for £6 by English exchange. The funny thing was that I knew quite well that Ellie had just the same longing for that £6 picture that she had for the Cézanne.

It was the same way one day in Paris. She'd said to me suddenly,

"What fun it would be—let's get a really nice crisp French loaf of bread and have that with butter and one of those cheeses wrapped up in leaves."

So we did, and Ellie, I think, enjoyed it more than the meal we'd had the night before which had come to about £20 English. At first I couldn't understand it; then I began to see. The awkward thing was that I could see now that being married to Ellie wasn't just fun and games. You have to do your homework, you have to learn how to go into a restaurant and the sort of things to order and the right tips, and when for some reason you gave more than usual. You have to memorize what you drink with certain foods. I had to do most of it by observation. I couldn't ask Ellie because that was one of the things she wouldn't have understood. She'd have said, "But, darling Mike, you can have anything you like. What does it matter if waiters think you ought to have one particular wine with one particular thing?" It wouldn't have mattered to her because she was born to it, but it mattered to me because I couldn't do just as I liked. I wasn't simple enough. Clothes, too. Ellie was more helpful there, for she could understand better. She just guided me to the right places and told me to let them have their head.

Of course I didn't look right and sound right yet. But that didn't matter much. I'd got the hang of it, enough so that I could pass muster with people like old Lippincott, and shortly, presumably, when Ellie's stepmother and uncles were around, but actually it wasn't going to matter in the future at all. When the house was finished and when we'd moved in, we were going to be far away from everybody. It could be our kingdom. I looked at Greta sitting opposite me. I wondered what she'd really thought of our house. Anyway, it was what I wanted. It satisfied me utterly. I wanted to drive down and go through a private path through the trees which led down to a small cove which would be our own beach which nobody could come to on the land side. It would be a thousand times better, I thought, plunging into the sea there. A thousand times better than a lido spread along a beach with hundreds of bodies lying there. I didn't want all the senseless rich things. I wanted—there were the words again, my own particular words—I want, I want . . . I could feel all the feeling surging up in me. I wanted a wonderful woman and a wonderful house like nobody else's house, and I wanted my wonderful house to be full of wonderful things—things that belonged to me. Everything would belong to me.

"He's thinking of our house," said Ellie.

It seemed that she had twice suggested to me that we should now go into the dining room. I looked at her affectionately.

Later in the day—it was that evening—when we were dressing to go out to dinner, Ellie said a little tentatively,

"Mike, you do—you do like Greta, don't you?"

"Of course I do," I said.

"I couldn't bear it if you didn't like her."

"But I do," I protested. "What makes you think I don't?"

"I'm not quite sure. I think it's the way you hardly look at her even when you're talking to her."

"Well, I suppose that's because—well, because I feel nervous."

"Nervous of Greta?"

"Yes, she's a bit awe-inspiring, you know."

And I told Ellie how I thought Greta looked rather like a Valkyrie.

"Not as stout as an operatic one," said Ellie, and laughed. We both laughed. I said,

"It's all very well for you because you've known her for years. But she is just a bit—well, I mean she's very efficient and practical and sophisticated." I struggled with a lot of words which didn't seem to be quite the right ones. I said suddenly, "I feel—I feel at a disadvantage with her."

"Oh, Mike!" Ellie was conscience-stricken. "I know we've got a lot of things to talk about. Old jokes and old things that happened and all that. I suppose—yes, I suppose it might make you feel rather shy. But you'll soon get to be friends. She likes you. She likes you very much. She told me so."

"Listen, Ellie, she'd probably tell you that anyway."

"Oh, no, she wouldn't. Greta's very outspoken. You heard her. Some of the things she said today."

It was true that Greta had not minced her words during luncheon. She had said, addressing me rather than Ellie,

"You must have thought it queer sometimes, the way I was backing Ellie up when I'd not even seen you. But I got so mad—so mad with the life that they were making her lead. All tied up in a cocoon with their money, their traditional ideas. She never had a chance to enjoy herself, go anywhere really by herself and do what she wanted. She wanted to rebel but she didn't know how. And so—yes, all right, I urged her on. I suggested she should look at properties in England. Then I said when she was twenty-one she could buy one of her own and say good-by to all that New York lot."

"Greta always has wonderful ideas," said Ellie. "She thinks of things I'd probably never have thought of myself."

What were those words Mr. Lippincott had said to me? "She has too much influence over Ellie." I wondered if it was true. Queerly enough, I didn't really think so. I felt that there was a core somewhere in Ellie that Greta, for all that she knew her so well, had never quite appreciated. Ellie, I was sure, would always accept any ideas that matched with the ideas she wanted to have herself. Greta had preached rebellion to Ellie, but Ellie herself wanted to rebel, only she was not sure how to do so. But I felt that Ellie, now that I was coming to know her better, was one of those very simple people who have unexpected reserves. I thought Ellie would be quite capable of taking a stand of her own if she wished to. The point was that she wouldn't very often wish to, and I thought then how difficult everyone was to understand. Even Ellie. Even Greta. Even perhaps my own mother. . . . The way she looked at me with fear in her eyes.

I wondered about Mr. Lippincott. I said, as we were peeling some outsize peaches,

"Mr. Lippincott seems to have taken our marriage very well, really. I was surprised."

"Mr. Lippincott," said Greta, "is an old fox."

"You always say so, Greta," said Ellie, "but I think he's rather a dear. Very strict and proper and all that."

"Well, go on thinking so if you like," said Greta. "Myself, I wouldn't trust him an inch."

"Not trust him!" said Ellie.

Greta shook her head. "I know. He's a pillar of respectability and trustworthiness. He's everything a trustee and a lawyer should be."

Ellie laughed and said, "Do you mean he's embezzled my fortune? Don't be silly, Greta. There are thousands of auditors and banks and check-ups and all that sort of thing."

"Oh, I expect he's all right, really," said Greta. "All the same, those are the people that do embezzle. The trustworthy ones. And then everyone says afterwards, 'I'd never have believed it of Mr. A or Mr. B. The last man in the world.' Yes, that's what they say. 'The last man in the world.'"

Ellie said thoughtfully that her Uncle Frank, she thought, was much more likely to go in for dishonest practices. She did not seem unduly worried or surprised by the idea.

"Oh, well, he looks like a crook," said Greta. "That handicaps him to start with. All that geniality and bonhomie. But he'll never be in a position to be a crook in a big way."

"Is he your mother's brother or your father's brother?" I asked. I hadn't had time to think much about Ellie's relations.

"He's my father's sister's husband," said Ellie. "She left him and married someone else and died about six or seven years ago. Uncle Frank has more or less stuck on with the family."

"There are three of them," said Greta kindly and helpfully. "Three leeches hanging round, as you might say. Ellie's actual uncles were killed, one in Korea and one in a car accident, so what she's got is a much-damaged stepmother, an Uncle Frank, an amiable hanger-on in the family home, and her cousin Reuben whom she calls uncle, but he's only a cousin, and Andrew Lippincott and Stanford Lloyd."

"Who is Stanford Lloyd?" I asked, bewildered.

"Oh, another sort of trustee, isn't he, Ellie? At any rate he manages your investments and things like that. Which can't really be very difficult, because when you've got as much money as Ellie has, it sort of makes more money all the time without her having to do much about it. Those are the main surrounding group," Greta added, "and I have no doubt that you will be meeting them fairly soon. They'll be over here to have a look at you."

I groaned and looked at Ellie. Ellie said very gently and sweetly, "Never mind, Mike; they'll go away again."

12

THEY DID COME over. None of them stayed very long. Not that time—not on a first visit. They came over to have a look at me. I found them difficult to understand because, of course, they were all American. They were types with which I was not well acquainted. Some of them were pleasant enough. Uncle Frank, for instance. I agreed with Greta about him. I wouldn't have trusted him a yard. I had come across the same type in England. He was a big man with a bit of a paunch and pouches under his eyes that gave him a dissipated look which was not far from the truth, I imagine. He had an eye for women, I thought, and even more of an eye for the main chance. He borrowed money from me once or twice, quite small sums just, as it were, something to tide him over for a day or two. I thought it was not so much that he needed the money but he wanted to test me out, to see if I lent money easily. It was rather worrying because I wasn't sure which was the best way to take it. Would it have been better to refuse point-blank and let him know I was a skinflint or was it better to assume an appearance of careless generosity, which I was very far from feeling? To hell with Uncle Frank, I thought.

Cora, Ellie's stepmother, was the one that interested me most. She was a woman of about forty, well turned out, with tinted hair and a rather gushing manner. She was all sweetness to Ellie.

"You mustn't mind those letters I wrote you, Ellie," she said. "You must admit that it came as a terrible shock, your marrying like that. So secretly. But of course I know it was Greta who put you up to it, doing it that way."

"You mustn't blame Greta," said Ellie. "I didn't mean to upset you all so much. I just thought that—well, the less fuss—"

"Well, of course, Ellie dear, you have something there. All the men of business were simply livid—Stanford Lloyd and Andrew Lippincott. I suppose they thought everyone would blame them for not looking after you better. And of course they'd no idea what Mike would be like. They didn't realize how charming he was going to be. I didn't myself." She smiled across at me, a very sweet smile and one of the falsest ones I'd ever seen! I thought to myself that if ever a woman hated a man, it was Cora who hated me. I thought her sweetness to Ellie was understandable enough. Andrew Lippincott had gone back to America and had, no doubt, given her a few words of caution. Ellie was selling some of her property in America, since she herself had definitely decided to live in England, but she was going to make a large allowance to Cora so that the latter could live where she chose. Nobody mentioned Cora's husband much. I gathered he'd already taken himself off to some other part of the world, and had not gone there alone. In all probability, I gathered, another divorce was pending. There wouldn't be much alimony out of this one. Cora's last marriage had been to a man a good many years younger than herself, with more attractions of a physical kind than cash.

Cora wanted that allowance. She was a woman of extravagant tastes. No doubt old Andrew Lippincott had hinted clearly enough that it could be discontinued any time if Ellie chose, or if Cora so far forgot herself as to criticize Ellie's new husband too virulently.

Cousin Reuben, or Uncle Reuben, did not make the journey. He wrote instead to Ellie a pleasant, noncommittal letter hoping she'd be very happy, but doubted if she would like living in England. "If you don't, Ellie, you come right back to the States. Don't think you won't get a welcome here, because you will. Certainly you will from your Uncle Reuben."

"He sounds rather nice," I said to Ellie.

"Yes," said Ellie meditatively. She wasn't, it seemed, quite so sure about it.

"Are you fond of any of them, Ellie?" I asked. "Or oughtn't I to ask you that?"

"Of course you can ask me anything." But she didn't answer for a moment or two, all the same. Then she said, with a sort of finality and decision, "No, I don't think I am. It seems odd, but I suppose it's because they don't really belong to me. Only by environment, not by relationship. They none of them are my flesh-and-blood relations. I loved my father, what I remembered of him. I think he was rather a weak man, and I think my grandfather was disappointed in him because he hadn't got much head for business. He didn't want to go into the business life. He liked going to Florida and fishing, that sort of thing. And then later he married Cora and I never cared for Cora much—or Cora for me, for that matter. My own mother, of course, I don't remember. I liked Uncle Henry and Uncle Joe. They were fun —in some ways more fun than my father was. He, I think, was in some ways a quiet and rather sad man. But the uncles enjoyed themselves. Uncle Joe was, I think, a bit wild, the kind that is wild just because they've got lots of money. Anyway, he was the one who got smashed up in the car, and the other one was killed fighting in the war. My grandfather was a sick man by that time, and it was a terrible blow to him that all his three sons were dead. He didn't like Cora and he didn't care much for any of his more distant relatives. Uncle Reuben, for instance. He said you could never tell what Reuben was up to. That's why he made arrangements to put his money in trust. A lot of it went to museums and hospitals. He left Cora well provided for, and his daughter's husband Uncle Frank."

"But most of it to you?"

"Yes. And I think that worried him a little bit. He did his best to get it looked after for me."

"By Uncle Andrew and by Mr. Stanford Lloyd. A lawyer and a banker."

"Yes. I suppose he didn't think I could look after it very well by myself. The odd thing is that he let me come into it at the age of twenty-one. He didn't keep it in trust till I was twenty-five, as lots of people do. I expect that was because I was a girl."

"That's odd," I said. "It would seem to me that it ought to be the other way round?"

Ellie shook her head. "No," she said, "I think my grandfather thought that young males were always wild and hit things up and that blondes with evil designs got hold of them. I think he thought it would be a good thing if they had plenty of time to sow their wild oats. That's your English saying, isn't it? But he said once to me, 'If a girl is going to have any sense at all, she'll have it at twenty-one. It won't make any difference making her wait four years longer. If she's going to be a fool, she'll be a fool then just as much.' He said, too," Ellie looked at me and smiled, "that he didn't think I was a fool. He said, 'You mayn't know very much about life, but you've got good sense, Ellie. Especially about people. I think you always will have.'"

"I don't suppose he would have liked me," I said thoughtfully.

Ellie has a lot of honesty. She didn't try and reassure me by saying anything but what was undoubtedly the truth.

"No," she said, "I think he'd have been rather horrified. To begin with, that is. He'd have had to get used to you."

"Poor Ellie," I said suddenly.

"Why do you say that?"

"I said it to you once before, do you remember?"

"Yes. You said poor little rich girl. You were quite right, too."

"I didn't mean it the same way this time," I said. "I didn't mean that you were poor because you were rich. I think I meant—" I hesitated. "You've too many people," I said, "at you. All round you. Too many people who want things from you but who don't really care for you. That's true, isn't it?"

"I think Uncle Andrew really cares for me," said Ellie a little doubtfully. "He's always been nice to me, sympathetic. The others—no, you're quite right. They only want things."

"They come and cadge off you, don't they? Borrow money off you, want favors. Want you to get them out of jams, that sort of thing. They're *at* you, *at* you, *at* you!"

"I suppose it's quite natural," said Ellie calmly, "but I've done with them all now. I'm coming to live here in England. I shan't see much of them."

She was wrong there, of course, but she hadn't grasped that fact yet. Stanford Lloyd came over later by himself. He brought a great many documents and papers and things for Ellie to sign and wanted her agreement on investments. He talked to her about investments and shares and property that she owned, and the disposal of trust funds. It was all double Dutch to me. I couldn't have helped her or advised her. I couldn't have stopped Stanford Lloyd from cheating her, either. I hoped he wasn't, but how could anyone ignorant like myself be sure?

There was something about Stanford Lloyd that was almost too good to be true. He was a banker, and he looked like a banker. He was rather a handsome man, though not young. He was very polite to me and thought dirt of me though he tried not to show it.

"Well," I said when he had finally taken his departure, "that's the last of the bunch."

"You didn't think much of any of them, did you?"

"I think your stepmother Cora is a double-faced bitch if I ever knew one. Sorry, Ellie, perhaps I oughtn't to say that."

"Why not, if that's what you think? I expect you're not far wrong."

"You must have been lonely, Ellie," I said.

"Yes, I was lonely. I knew girls of my own age. I went to a fashionable school but I was never really free. If I made friends with people, somehow or other they'd get me separated, push another girl at me instead. You know? Everything was governed by the social register. If I'd cared enough about anybody to make a fuss—but I never got far enough. There was never anybody I really cared for. Not until Greta came, and then everything was different. For the first time someone was really fond of me. It was wonderful." Her face softened.

"I wish," I said, as I turned away toward the window.

"What do you wish?"

"Oh, I don't know . . . I wish perhaps that you weren't—weren't quite so dependent on Greta. It's a bad thing to be as dependent as that on anyone."

"You don't like her, Mike," said Ellie.

"I do," I protested hurriedly. "Indeed I do. But you must realize, Ellie, that she is—well, she's quite a stranger to me. I suppose—let's face it—I'm a bit jealous of her. Jealous because she and you—well, I didn't understand before—how linked together you were."

"Don't be jealous. She's the only person who was good to me, who cared about me—till I met you."

"But you have met me," I said, "and you've married me." Then I said it again, what I'd said before, "And we're going to live together happily ever afterward."

13

I'M TRYING AS best I can, though that isn't saying much, to paint a picture of the people who came into our lives, that is to say, who came into my life because, of course, they were in Ellie's life already. Our mistake was that we thought they'd go out of Ellie's life. But they didn't. They'd no intention of doing so. However, we didn't know that then.

The English side of our life was the next thing that happened. Our house was finished, we had a telegram from Santonix. He'd asked us to keep away for about a week, then the telegram came. It said, "Come tomorrow."

We drove down there, and we arrived at sunset. Santonix heard the car and came out to meet us, standing in front of the house. When I saw our house finished, something inside me leaped up, leaped up as though to burst out of my skin! It was my house—and I'd got it at last! I held Ellie's arm very tight.

"Like it?" said Santonix.

"It's the tops," I said. A silly thing to say, but he knew what I meant.

"Yes," he said, "it's the best thing I've done. . . . It's cost you a mint of money and it's worth every penny of it! I've exceeded my estimates all round. Come on, Mike," he said, "pick her up and carry her over the threshold. That's the thing to do when you enter into possession with your bride!"

I flushed and then I picked up Ellie—she was quite a lightweight—and carried her, as Santonix had suggested, over the threshold. As I did so, I stumbled just a little and I saw Santonix frown.

"There you are," said Santonix, "be good to her, Mike. Take care of her. Don't let any harm happen to her. She can't take care of herself. She thinks she can."

"Why should any harm happen to me?" said Ellie.

"Because it's a bad world and there are bad people in it," said Santonix, "and there are some bad people round you, my girl. I know. I've seen one or two of them. Seen them down here. They came nosing around, sniffing around like the rats they are. Excuse my French, but somebody's got to say it."

"They won't bother us," said Ellie; "they've all gone back to the States."

"Maybe," said Santonix, "but it's only a few hours by plane, you know."

He put his hands on her shoulders. They were very thin now, very white-looking. He looked terribly ill.

"I'd look after you myself, child, if I could," he said, "but I can't. It won't be long now. You'll have to fend for yourself."

"Cut out the gipsy's warning, Santonix," I said, "and take us round the house. Every inch of it."

So we went round the house. Some of the rooms were still empty, but most of the things we'd bought, pictures and the furniture and the curtains, were there.

"We haven't got a name for it," said Ellie suddenly. "We can't call it The Towers; that was a ridiculous name. What was the other name for it that you told me once?" she said to me. "Gipsy's Acre, wasn't it?"

"We won't call it that," I said sharply. "I don't like that name."

"It'll always be called that hereabouts," said Santonix.

"They're a lot of silly superstitious people," I said.

And then we sat down on the terrace looking at the setting sun and the view, and we thought of names for the house. It was a kind of game. We started quite seriously and then we began to think of every silly name we possibly could. "Journey's End," "Heart's Delight" and names like boarding houses—"Seaview," "Fairholme," "The Pines." Then suddenly it grew dark and cold, and we went indoors. We didn't draw the curtains, just closed the windows. We'd brought down provisions with us. On the following day an expensively acquired domestic staff was coming.

"They'll probably hate it and say it's lonely and they'll all go away," said Ellie.

"And then you'll give them double the money to stay on," said Santonix.

"You think," said Ellie, "that everyone can be bought!" But she only said it laughingly.

We had brought *pâté en croûte* with us and French bread and large red prawns. We sat round the table laughing and eating and talking. Even Santonix looked strong and animated, and there was a kind of wild excitement in his eyes.

And then it happened suddenly. A stone crashed in through the window and dropped on the table. Smashed a glass too, and a sliver of glass slit Ellie's cheek. For a moment we sat paralyzed, then I sprang up, rushed to the window, unbolted it and went out on the terrace. There was no one to be seen. I came back into the room again.

I picked up a paper napkin and bent over Ellie, wiping away a little trickle of blood I saw coursing down her cheek.

"It's hurt you. . . . There, dear, it's nothing much. It's just a wee cut from a sliver of glass."

My eyes met those of Santonix.

"Why did anyone do it?" said Ellie. She looked bewildered.

"Boys," I said, "you know, young hooligans. They knew, perhaps, we were settling in. I daresay you were lucky that they only threw a stone. They might have had an air gun or something like that."

"But why should they do it to us? Why?"

"I don't know," I said. "Just beastliness."

Ellie got up suddenly. She said,

"I'm frightened. I'm afraid."

"We'll find out tomorrow," I said. "We don't know enough about the people round here."

"Is it because we're rich and they're poor?" said Ellie. She asked it not of me but of Santonix, as though he would know the answer to the question better than I did.

"No," said Santonix slowly, "I don't think it's that. . . ."

Ellie said,

"It's because they hate us. . . . Hate Mike and hate me. Why? Because we're happy?"

Again Santonix shook his head.

"No," Ellie said, as though she were agreeing with him, "no, it's something else. Something we don't know about. Gipsy's Acre. Anyone who lives here is going to be hated. Going to be persecuted. Perhaps they will succeed in the end in driving us away. . . ."

I poured out a glass of wine and gave it to her.

"Don't, Ellie," I begged her. "Don't say such things. Drink this. It's a nasty thing to happen, but it was only silliness, crude horseplay."

"I wonder," said Ellie, "I wonder . . ." She looked hard at me. "Somebody is trying to drive us away, Mike. To drive us away from the house we've built, the house we love."

"We won't let them drive us away," I said. I added, "I'll take care of you. Nothing shall hurt you."

She looked again at Santonix.

"You should know," she said; "you've been here while the house was building. Didn't anyone ever say anything to you? Come and throw stones—interfere with the building of the house?"

"One can imagine things," said Santonix.

"There were accidents, then?"

"There are always a few accidents in the building of a house. Nothing serious or tragic. A man falls off a ladder, someone drops a load on his foot, someone gets a splinter in his thumb and it goes septic."

"Nothing more than that? Nothing that might have been meant?"

"No," said Santonix, "*no*. I swear to you, no!"

Ellie turned to me.

"You remember that gipsy woman, Mike. How queer she was that day, how she warned me not to come here."

"She's just a bit crazy, a bit off her head."

"We've built on Gipsy's Acre," said Ellie. "We've done what she told us not to do." Then she stamped her foot. "I won't let them drive me away. I won't let anyone drive me away!"

"Nobody shall drive us away," I said. "We're going to be happy here."

We said it like a challenge to fate.

14

THAT'S HOW OUR life began at Gipsy's Acre. We didn't find another name for the house. That first evening fixed Gipsy's Acre in our heads.

"We'll call it Gipsy's Acre," said Ellie, "just to show! A kind of challenge, don't you think? It's our Acre, and to hell with the gipsy's warning."

She was her old gay self again the next day and soon we were busy getting ourselves settled in, and getting also to know the neighborhood and the neighbors. Ellie and I walked down to the cottage where the gipsy woman lived. I felt it would be a good thing if we found her digging in her garden. The only time Ellie had seen her before was when she told our fortunes. If Ellie saw she was just an ordinary old woman—digging up potatoes—but we didn't see her. The cottage was shut up. I asked if she were dead, but the neighbor I asked shook her head.

"She must have gone away," she said. "She goes away from time to time, you know. She's a gipsy, really. That's why she can't stay in houses. She wanders away and comes back again." She tapped her forehead. "Not quite right up there."

Presently she said, trying to mask curiosity, "You've come from the new house up there, haven't you? The one on the top of the hill that's just been built."

"That's right," I said. "We moved in last night."

"Wonderful-looking place it is," she said. "We've all been up to look at it while it was building. Makes a difference, doesn't it, seeing a house like that where all those gloomy trees used to be." She said to Ellie rather shyly, "You're an American lady, aren't you, so we heard?"

"Yes," said Ellie, "I'm American—or I was, but now I'm married to an Englishman, so I'm an Englishwoman."

"And you've come here to settle down and live, haven't you?"

We said we had.

"Well, I hope you'll like it, I'm sure." She sounded doubtful.

"Why shouldn't we?"

"Oh, well, it's lonely up there, you know. People don't always like living in a lonely place among a lot of trees."

"Gipsy's Acre," said Ellie.

"Ah, you know the local name, do you? But the house that was there before was called The Towers. I don't know why. It hadn't got any towers, at least not in my time."

"I think The Towers is a silly name," said Ellie. "I think we'll go on calling it Gipsy's Acre."

"We'll have to tell the post office if so," I said, "or we shan't get any letters."

"No, I suppose we shan't."

"Though when I come to think of it," I said, "would that matter, Ellie? Wouldn't it be much nicer if we didn't get any letters?"

"It might cause a lot of complications," said Ellie. "We shouldn't even get our bills."

"That would be a splendid idea," I said.

"No, it wouldn't," said Ellie. "Bailiffs would come in and camp there. Anyway," she said, "I wouldn't like not to get any letters. I'd want to hear from Greta."

"Never mind Greta," I said. "Let's go on exploring."

So we explored Kingston Bishop. It was a nice village, nice people in the shops. There was nothing sinister about the place. Our domestic help didn't take to it much, but we soon arranged that hired cars should take them into the nearest seaside town or into Market Chadwell on their days out. They were not enthusiastic about the location of the house, but it was not superstition that worried them. I pointed out to Ellie nobody could say the house was haunted because it had been just built.

"No," Ellie agreed, "it's not the house. There's nothing wrong with the house. It's outside. It's that road where it curves round through the trees and that bit of rather gloomy wood where that woman stood and made me jump so that day."

"Well, next year," I said, "we might cut down those trees and plant a lot of rhododendrons or something like that."

We went on making plans.

Greta came down and stayed with us for a weekend. She was enthusiastic about the house, and congratulated us on all our furnishings and pictures and color schemes. She was very tactful. After the weekend she said she wouldn't disturb the honeymooners any longer, and anyway she'd got to get back to her job.

Ellie enjoyed showing her the house. I could see how fond Ellie was of her. I tried to behave very sensibly and pleasantly, but I was glad when Greta went back to London, because her staying there had been a strain on me.

When we'd been there a couple of weeks, we were accepted locally and made the acquaintance of God. He came one afternoon to call upon us. Ellie and I were arguing about where we'd have a flower border when our correct, to me slightly phony-looking, manservant came out from the house to announce that Major Phillpot was in the drawing room. It was then that I said in a whisper to Ellie: "God!" Ellie asked me what I meant.

"Well, the locals treat him like that," I said.

So we went in and there was Major Phillpot. He was just a pleasant, nondescript man of close on sixty. He was wearing country clothes, rather shabby; he had gray hair going a little thin on top and a short bristly mustache. He apologized for his wife not being able to come and call on us. She was something of an invalid, he said. He sat down and chatted with us. Nothing he said was remarkable or particularly interesting. He had the knack of making people feel at their ease. He touched quite lightly on a variety of subjects. He didn't ask any direct questions, but he soon got it into his head where our particular interests lay. He talked to me about racing and to Ellie about making a garden and what things did well in this particular soil. He had been to the States once or twice. He found out that though Ellie didn't care much for race meetings, she was fond of riding. He told her that if she was going to keep horses, she could go up a particular track through the pine woods and she would come out on a good stretch of moor where she could have a good gallop. Then we came to the subject of our house and of the stories about Gipsy's Acre.

"I see you know the local name," he said, "and all the local superstitions, too, I expect."

"Gipsies' warnings in profusion," I said. "Far too many of them. Mostly old Mrs. Lee."

"Oh, dear," said Phillpot. "Poor old Esther. She's been a nuisance, has she?"

"Is she a bit dotty?" I asked.

"Not so much as she likes to make out. I feel more or less responsible for her. I settled her in that cottage," he said. "Not that she's grateful for it. I'm fond of the old thing, though she can be a nuisance sometimes."

"Fortunetelling?"

"No, not particularly. Why, has she told your fortune?"

"I don't know if you can call it a fortune," said Ellie. "It was more a warning to us against coming here."

"That seems rather odd to me." Major Phillpot's rather bristly eyebrows rose. "She's usually got rather a honeyed tongue in fortunes. Handsome stranger, marriage bells, six children and a heap of good fortune and money in your hand, pretty lady." He imitated rather unexpectedly the gipsy whine of her voice. "The gipsies used to camp here a lot when I was a boy," he said. "I suppose I got fond of them then, though they were a thieving lot, of course. But I've always been attracted to them. As long as you don't expect them to be law-abiding, they're all right. Many a tin mug of gipsy stew I've had as a schoolboy. We felt the family owed Mrs. Lee something; she saved the life of a brother of mine when he was a child. Fished him out of a pond when he'd gone through the ice."

I made a clumsy gesture and knocked a glass ashtray off a table. It smashed into fragments.

I picked up the pieces and Major Phillpot helped me.

"I expect Mrs. Lee's quite harmless, really," said Ellie. "I was very foolish to have been so scared."

"Scared, were you?" His eyebrows rose again. "It was as bad as that, was it?"

"I don't wonder she was afraid," I said quickly. "It was almost more like a threat than a warning."

"A threat!" He sounded rather incredulous.

"Well, it sounded that way to me. And then the first night we moved in here something else happened."

I told him about the stone crashing through the window.

"I'm afraid there are a good many young hooligans about nowadays," he said, "though we haven't got many of them round here—not nearly as bad as some places. Still, it happens, I'm sorry to say." He looked at Ellie. "I'm very sorry you were frightened. It was a beastly thing to happen, your first night moving in."

"Oh, I've got over it now," said Ellie. "It wasn't only that, it was—it was something else that happened not long afterward."

I told him about that, too. We had come down one morning and we had found a dead bird skewered through with a knife and a small piece of paper with it which said in an illiterate scrawl, "Get out of here if you know what's good for you."

Phillpot looked really angry then. He said, "You should have reported that to the police."

"We didn't want to," I said. "After all, that would only have put whoever it is even more against us."

"Well, that kind of thing has got to be stopped," said Phillpot. Suddenly he became the magistrate. "Otherwise, you know, people will go on with the thing. Think it's funny, I suppose. Only—only this sounds a bit more than fun. Nasty—malicious— It's not," he said, rather as though he was talking to himself, "it's not as though anyone round here could have a grudge against you—a grudge against either of you personally, I mean."

"No," I said, "it couldn't be that because we're both strangers here."

"I'll look into it," Phillpot said.

He got up to go, looking round him as he did.

"You know," he said, "I like this house of yours. I didn't think I should. I'm a bit of an old square, you know, what used to be called an old fogy. I like old houses and old buildings. I don't like all these matchbox factories that are going up all over the country. Big boxes. Like beehives. I like buildings with some ornament on them, some grace. But I like this house. It's plain and very modern, I suppose, but it's got shape and light. And when you look out from it you see things—well, in a different way from the way you've seen them before. It's interesting. Very interesting. Who designed it? An English architect or a foreigner?"

I told him about Santonix.

"Hm," he said, "I think I read about him somewhere. Would it have been in *House and Gardens*? Some photographs and things."

I said he was fairly well known.

"I'd like to meet him sometime, though I don't suppose I'd know what to say to him. I'm not artistic."

Then he asked us to settle a day to come and have lunch with him and his wife.

"You can see how you like my house," he said.

"It's an old house, I suppose?" I said.

"Built 1720. Nice period. The original house was Elizabethan. That was burnt down about 1700 and a new one built on the same spot."

"You've always lived here, then?" I said. I didn't mean him personally, of course, but he understood.

"Yes. We've been here since Elizabethan times. Sometimes prosperous, sometimes down and out, selling land when things have gone badly, buying it back when things went well. I'll be glad to show it to you both," he said and, looking at Ellie, he added with a smile, "Americans like old houses, I know. You're the one who probably won't think much of it," he said to me.

"I won't pretend I know much about old things," I said.

He stumped off then. In his car there was a spaniel waiting for him. It was a battered old car with the paint rubbed off, but I was getting my values by now. I knew that in this part of the world he was still God, all right, and he'd set the seal of his approval on us. I could see that. He liked Ellie. I was inclined to think that he'd liked me, too, although I'd noticed the appraising glances which he shot over me from time to time, as though he was making a quick snap judgment on something he hadn't come across before.

Ellie was putting splinters of glass carefully in the wastepaper basket when I came back into the drawing room.

"I'm sorry it's broken," she said regretfully. "I liked it."

"We can get another like it," I said. "It's modern."

"I know. What startled you, Mike?"

I considered for a moment.

"Something Phillpot said. It reminded me of something that happened when I was a kid. A pal of mine at school and I played truant and went out skating on a local pond. Ice wouldn't bear us, silly little asses that we were. He went through and was drowned before anyone could get him out."

"How horrible."

"Yes. I'd forgotten all about it until Phillpot mentioned that about his own brother."

"I like him, Mike. Don't you?"

"Yes, very much. I wonder what his wife is like?"

We went to lunch with the Phillpots early the following week. It was a white Georgian house, rather beautiful in its lines, though not particularly exciting. Inside, it was shabby but comfortable. There were pictures of what I took to be ancestors on the walls of the long dining room. Most of them were pretty bad, I thought, though they might have looked better if they had been cleaned. There was one of a fair-haired girl in pink satin that I rather took to. Major Phillpot smiled and said:

"You've picked one of our best. It's a Gainsborough, and a good one, though the subject of it caused a bit of trouble in her time. Strongly suspected of having poisoned her husband. May have been prejudice, because she was a foreigner. Gervase Phillpot picked her up abroad somewhere."

A few other neighbors had been invited to meet us—Dr. Shaw, an elderly man with a kindly but tired manner. He had to rush away before we had finished our meal. There was the Vicar, who was young and earnest, and a middle-aged woman with a bullying voice who bred corgis. And there was a tall, handsome, dark girl called Claudia Hardcastle, who seemed to live for horses, though hampered by having an allergy which gave her violent hay fever.

She and Ellie got on together rather well. Ellie adored riding and she, too, was troubled by an allergy.

"In the States it's mostly ragweed gives it to me," she said, "but horses, too, sometimes. It doesn't trouble me much nowadays because they have such wonderful things that doctors can give you for different kinds of allergies. I'll give you some of my capsules. They're bright orange. And if you remember to take one before you start out, you don't as much as sneeze once."

Claudia Hardcastle said that would be wonderful.

"Camels do it to me worse than horses," she said. "I was in Egypt last year—and the tears just streamed down my face all the way round the Pyramids."

Ellie said some people got it with cats.

"And pillows." They went on talking about allergies.

I sat next to Mrs. Phillpot, who was tall and willowy and talked exclusively about her health in the intervals of eating a hearty meal. She gave me a full account of all her various ailments and of how puzzled many eminent members of the medical profession had been by her case. Occasionally she made a social diversion and asked me what I did. I parried that one, and she made half-hearted efforts to find out whom I knew. I could have answered truthfully "Nobody," but I thought it would be well to refrain—especially as she wasn't a real snob and didn't really want to know. Mrs. Corgi, whose proper name I hadn't caught, was much more thorough in her queries, but I diverted her to the general iniquity and ignorance of vets! It was all quite pleasant and peaceful, if rather dull.

Later, as we were making a rather desultory tour of the garden, Claudia Hardcastle joined me.

She said rather abruptly, "I've heard about you—from my brother."

I looked surprised. I couldn't imagine it to be possible that I knew a brother of Claudia Hardcastle's.

"Are you sure?" I said.

She seemed amused.

"As a matter of fact, he built your house."

"Do you mean Santonix is your brother?"

"Half brother. I don't know him very well. We rarely meet."

"He's wonderful," I said.

"Some people think so, I know."

"Don't you?"

"I'm never sure. There are two sides to him. At one time he was going right down the hill . . . People wouldn't have anything to do with him. And then—he seemed to change. He began to succeed in his profession in the most extraordinary way. It was as though he was—" she paused for a word—"dedicated."

"I think he is—just that."

Then I asked her if she had seen our house.

"No—not since it was finished."

I told her she must come and see it.

"I shan't like it, I warn you. I don't like modern houses. Queen Anne is my favorite period."

She said she was going to put Ellie up for the golf club. And they were going to ride together. Ellie was going to buy a horse—perhaps more than one. She and Ellie seemed to have made friends.

When Phillpot was showing me his stables, he said a word or two about Claudia.

"Good rider to hounds," he said. "Pity she's mucked up her life."

"Has she?"

"Married a rich man years older than herself. An American. Name of Lloyd. It didn't take. Came apart almost at once. She went back to her own name. Don't think she'll every marry again. She's anti-man. Pity."

When we were driving home, Ellie said, "Dull—but nice. Nice people. We're going to be very happy here, aren't we, Mike?"

I said, "Yes, we are," and took my hand from the steering wheel and laid it over hers.

When we got back, I dropped Ellie at the house and put away the car in the garage.

As I walked back to the house, I heard the faint twanging of Ellie's guitar. She had a rather beautiful old Spanish guitar that must have been worth a lot of money. She used to sing to it in a soft, low, crooning voice. Very pleasant to hear. I didn't know what most of the songs were. American spirituals partly, I think, and some old Irish and Scottish ballads—sweet and rather sad. They weren't pop music or anything of that kind. Perhaps they were folk songs.

I went round by the terrace and paused by the window before going in.

Ellie was singing one of my favorites. I don't know what it was called. She was crooning the words softly to herself, bending her head down over the guitar and gently plucking the strings. It had a sweet-sad haunting little tune.

> Man was made for Joy and Woe
> And when this we rightly know
> Thro' the World we safely go . . .
>
> Every Night and every Morn
> Some to Misery are born.
> Every Morn and every Night
> Some are born to Sweet Delight,
> Some are born to Endless Night. . . .

She looked up and saw me.

"Why are you looking at me like that, Mike?"

"Like what?"

"You're looking at me as though you loved me."

"Of course I love you. How else should I be looking at you?"

"But what were you thinking just then?"

I answered slowly and truthfully, "I was thinking of you as I saw you first—standing by a dark fir tree." Yes, I'd been remembering that first moment of seeing Ellie, the surprise of it and the excitement . . .

Ellie smiled at me and sang softly,

> Every Morn and every Night
> Some are born to Sweet Delight,
> Some are born to Sweet Delight,
> Some are born to Endless Night.

One doesn't recognize in one's life the really important moments—not until it's too late.

That day when we'd been to lunch with the Phillpots and came back so happily to our home was such a moment. But I didn't know it then—not until afterward.

I said, "Sing the song about the fly." And she changed to a gay little dance tune and sang,

> Little Fly,
> Thy Summer's play
> My thoughtless hand
> Has brushed away.
>
> Am not I
> A fly like thee?
> Or art not thou
> A man like me?
>
> For I dance
> And drink, and sing
> Till some blind hand
> Shall brush my wing.
>
> If thought is life
> And strength and breath
> And the want
> Of thought is death;
>
> Then am I
> A happy fly
> If I live
> Or if I die.

Oh, Ellie—Ellie . . .

15

IT'S ASTONISHING IN this world how things don't turn out at all the way you expect them to!

We'd moved into our house and were living there and we'd got away from everyone just the way I'd meant and planned. Only, of course, we hadn't got away from everyone. Things crowded back upon us across the ocean and in other ways.

First of all there was Ellie's blasted stepmother. She sent letters and cables and asked Ellie to go and see estate agents. She'd been so fascinated, she said, by our house that she really must have a house of her own in England. She said she'd love to spend a couple of months every year in England. And hard on her last cable she arrived and had to be taken round the neighborhood with lots of orders to view. In the end she more or less settled on a house—a house about fifteen miles away from us. We didn't want her there; we hated the idea—but we couldn't tell her so. Or rather, what I really mean is even if we had told her so, it wouldn't have stopped her taking it if she'd wanted it. We couldn't order her not to come there. It was the last thing Ellie wanted. I knew that. However, while she was still awaiting a surveyor's report, some cables arrived.

Uncle Frank, it seemed, had got himself into a jam of some kind. Something crooked and fraudulent, I gathered, which would mean a big sum of money to get him out. More cables passed to and fro between Mr. Lippincott and Ellie. And then there turned out to be some trouble between Stanford Lloyd and Lippincott. There was a row about some of Ellie's investments. I had felt, in my ignorance and credulity, that people who were in America were a long way away. I'd never realized that Ellie's relations and business connections thought nothing of taking a plane over to England for twenty-four hours and then flying back again. First Stanford Lloyd flew over and back again. Then Andrew Lippincott flew over.

Ellie had to go up to London and meet them. I hadn't got the hang of these financial things. I think everybody was being fairly careful in what they said. But it was something to do with the settling up of the trusts on Ellie, and a kind of sinister suggestion that either Mr. Lippincott had delayed the matter or it was Stanford Lloyd who was holding up the accounting.

In a lull between these worries Ellie and I discovered our Folly. We hadn't really explored all our property yet (only the part just round the house). We used to follow up tracks through the woods and see where they led. One day we followed a sort of path that had been so overgrown that you couldn't really see where it was at first. But we tracked it out and in the end it came out at what Ellie said was a Folly —a sort of little white ridiculous temple-looking place. It was in fairly good condition, so we cleared it up and had it painted and we put a table and a few chairs in it and a divan and a corner cupboard in which we put china and glasses and some bottles. It was fun, really. Ellie said we'd have the path cleared and made easier to climb and I said no, it would be more fun if no one knew where it was except us. Ellie thought that was a romantic idea.

"We certainly won't let Cora know," I said, and Ellie agreed.

It was when we were coming down from there, not the first time but later, after Cora had gone away and we were hoping to be peaceful again, that Ellie, who was skipping along ahead of me, suddenly tripped over the root of a tree and fell and sprained her ankle.

Dr. Shaw came and said she'd taken a nasty sprain but that she'd be able to get about again all right in perhaps a week. Ellie sent for Greta then. I couldn't object. There was no one really to look after her properly—no woman, I mean. The servants we had were pretty useless, and anyway, Ellie wanted Greta. So Greta came.

She came and she was a great blessing, of course, to Ellie. And to me as far as that went. She arranged things and kept the household working properly. Our servants gave notice about now. They said it was too lonely—but really I think Cora had upset them. Greta put in advertisements and got another couple almost at once. She looked after Ellie's ankle, amused her, fetched things for her that she knew she liked, the kind of books and fruit and things like that—things I knew nothing about. And they seemed frightfully happy together. Ellie was certainly delighted to see Greta. And somehow or other Greta just didn't go away again. . . . She stopped on. Ellie said to me,

"You don't mind, do you, if Greta stays on for a bit?"

I said, "Oh, no. No, of course not."

"It's such a comfort having her," said Ellie. "You see, there are so many sort of female things we can do together. One's awfully lonely without another woman about."

Every day I noticed Greta was taking a bit more upon herself, giving orders, queening it over things. I pretended I liked having Greta there, but one day when Ellie was lying with her foot up inside the drawing room and Greta and I were out on the terrace, we suddenly got into a row together. I can't remember the exact words that started it. Something that Greta said, it annoyed me and I answered sharply back. And then we went on, hammer and tongs. Our voices rose. She let me have it, saying all the vicious, unkind things she could think of, and I pretty well gave her as good as I was getting. Told her she was a bossy, interfering female, that she'd far too much influence over Ellie, that I wasn't going to stand having Ellie bossed about the whole time. We shouted at each other and then suddenly Ellie came hobbling out on the terrace looking from one to the other of us, and I said,

"Darling, I'm sorry. I'm terribly sorry."

I went back into the house and settled Ellie on the sofa again. She said,

"I didn't realize. I didn't realize a bit that you—that you really hated having Greta here."

I soothed her and calmed her and said she mustn't take any notice, that I just lost my temper, that I was rather quarrelsome sometimes. I said all that was the matter was that I thought Greta was just a bit bossy. Perhaps that was natural enough because she'd been used to being so. And in the end I said I really liked Greta very much, it was just that I'd lost my temper because I'd been upset and worried. So it ended that I practically begged Greta to stay on.

It was quite a scene we'd had. I think quite a good many other people in the house had heard it as well. Our new manservant and his wife certainly did. When I get angry, I do shout. I daresay I really overdid it a bit. I'm like that.

Greta seemed to make a point of worrying a great deal about Ellie's health, saying she oughtn't to do this or that.

"She isn't really very strong, you know," she said to me.

"There's nothing wrong with Ellie," I said; "she's always perfectly well."

"No, she isn't, Mike. She's delicate."

When Dr. Shaw next came to have a look at Ellie's ankle and to tell her, by the way, that it was quite all right again, just bind it up if she was going to walk over rough ground, I said to him, I suppose in rather the foolish way that men do,

"She isn't delicate or anything, is she, Dr. Shaw?"

"Who says she's delicate?" Dr. Shaw was the kind of practitioner that is fairly rare nowadays and was, indeed, known locally as "Leave-it-to-Nature-Shaw."

"Nothing wrong with her as far as I can see," he said. "Anyone can sprain their ankle."

"I didn't mean her ankle. I wondered if she had a weak heart or anything like that."

He looked at me through the top of his spectacles. "Don't start imagining things, young man. What put it into your head? You're not the type that worries usually about women's ailments?"

"It was only what Miss Andersen said."

"Ah. Miss Andersen. What does she know about it? Not medically qualified, is she?"

"Oh, no," I said.

"Your wife's a woman of great wealth," he said, "according to local gossip, anyway. Of course some people just imagine all Americans are rich."

"She is wealthy," I said.

"Well, you must remember this. Rich women get the worst of it in many ways. Some doctor or other is always giving them powders and pills, stimulants or pep pills, or tranquilizers, things that on the whole they'd be better without. Now the village women are much healthier because nobody worries about their health in the same way."

"She does take some capsules or something," I said.

"I'll give her a check-up if you like. Might as well find out what muck she's been given. I can tell you, before now I've said to people, 'Chuck the whole lot in the wastepaper basket.'"

He spoke to Greta before he left. He said,

"Mr. Rogers asked me to give Mrs. Rogers a general check-up. I can't find anything much wrong with her. I think more exercises in the open air might do her good. What does she take in the way of medicines?"

"She has some tablets that she takes when she's tired, and some that she takes for sleeping if she wants them."

She and Dr. Shaw went and had a look at Ellie's prescriptions. Ellie was smiling a little.

"I don't take all these things, Dr. Shaw," she said. "Only the allergy capsules."

Shaw took a look at the capsules, read the prescription and said there was no harm in that, and passed on to a prescription for sleeping pills.

"Any trouble with sleeping?"

"Not living in the country. I don't think I've taken a single sleeping pill since I've been here."

"Well, that's a good thing." He patted her on the shoulder. "There's nothing wrong with you, my dear. Inclined to worry a bit sometimes, I should say. That's all. These capsules are mild enough. Lot of people take them nowadays and they don't do them any harm. Go on with them, but leave the sleeping pills alone."

"I don't know why I worried," I said to Ellie apologetically. "I suppose it was Greta."

"Oh," said Ellie, and laughed, "Greta fusses about me. She never takes any remedies herself." She said, "We'll have a turn-out, Mike, and throw most of these things away."

Ellie was getting on very friendly terms with most of our neighbors now. Claudia Hardcastle came over quite often, and she and Ellie went riding together occasionally. I didn't ride. I'd dealt with cars and mechanical things all my life. I didn't know the first thing about a horse in spite of mucking out stables in Ireland for a week or two once, but I thought to myself that sometime or other when we were in London I'd go to a posh riding stable and learn how to ride properly. I didn't want to start down here. People would laugh at me, very likely. I thought riding was perhaps good for Ellie. She seemed to enjoy it.

Greta encouraged her to ride, although Greta herself also knew nothing about horses.

Ellie and Claudia went together to a sale, and on Claudia's advice Ellie bought herself a horse, a chestnut called Conquer. I urged Ellie to be careful when she went out riding by herself, but she laughed at me.

"I've ridden since I was three years old," she said.

So she usually went for a ride about two or three times a week. Greta used to drive the car and go into Market Chadwell to do the shopping.

One day Greta said at lunchtime, "You and your gipsies! There was a terrible-looking old woman this morning. She stood in the middle of the road. I might have run over her. Just stood smack in front of the car. I had to pull up. Coming up the hill, too."

"Why, what did she want?"

Ellie was listening to us both, but she didn't say anything. I thought, though, that she looked rather worried.

"Damn cheek; she threatened me," said Greta.

"Threatened you?" I said sharply.

"Well, she told me to get out of here. She said, 'This is gipsy land here. Go back. Go back, the lot of you. Go back to where you came from if you wish to be safe.' And she lifted up her fist and shook it at me. She said, 'If I curse you,' she said, 'there'll be no good luck for you ever again. Buying our land and raising houses on our land. We don't want houses where tent dwellers should be.'"

Greta said a lot more. Ellie said to me afterward, frowning a little, "It all sounded most improbable, didn't you think so, Mike?"

"I think Greta was exaggerating a bit," I said.

"It didn't sound right somehow," said Ellie. "I wonder if Greta was making some of it up?"

I considered. "Why would she want to make things up?" Then I asked sharply, "You haven't seen our Esther lately, have you? Not when you are out riding?"

"The gipsy woman? No."

"You don't sound quite sure, Ellie," I said.

"I think I've caught glimpses of her," said Ellie. "You know, standing among the trees, peering out but never near enough for me to be sure."

But Ellie came back from a ride one day, white and shaking. The old woman had come out from in between the trees. Ellie had reined up and stopped to speak to her. She said the old woman was shaking her fist and muttering under her breath. Ellie said, "This time I was angry. I said to her,

" 'What do you want here? This land doesn't belong to you. It's our land and our house.' "

The old woman had said then,

"It'll never be your land and it'll never belong to you. I warned you once and I've warned you twice. I shan't warn you again. It won't be long now—I can tell you that. It's death I see. There behind your left shoulder. It's death standing by you, and it's death will have you. That horse you're riding has got one white foot. Don't you know that it's bad luck to ride a horse with one white foot? It's death I see and the grand house you've built falling in ruins!"

"This has got to be stopped," I said angrily.

Ellie didn't laugh it off this time. Both she and Greta looked upset. I went straight down to the village. I went first to Mrs. Lee's cottage. I hesitated for a moment but there was no light there and I went on to the police station. I knew the sergeant in charge—Sergeant Keene, a square, sensible man. He listened to me, then he said,

"I'm sorry you've had this trouble. She's a very old woman and she may be getting tiresome. We've never had much real trouble with her up to now. I'll speak to her and tell her to lay off."

"If you would," I said.

He hesitated a minute and then said,

"I don't like to suggest things—but as far as you know, Mr. Rogers, is there anyone around here who might—perhaps for some trivial cause—have it in for you or your wife?"

"I should think it most unlikely. Why?"

"Old Mrs. Lee has been flush of money lately—I don't know where it's coming from—"

"What are you suggesting?"

"It could be someone is paying her—someone who wants you out of here. There was an incident—a good many years ago. She took money from someone in the village—to frighten a neighbor away. Doing this same sort of stuff—threats—warnings—evil-eye business—Village people are superstitious. You'd be surprised at the number of villages in England that have got their private witch, so to speak. She got a warning then, and so far as I know she's never tried it on since—but it could be like that. She's fond of money— They'll do a lot for money—"

But I couldn't accept that idea. I pointed out to Keene that we were complete strangers here. "We've not had time to make enemies," I said.

I walked back to the house worried and perplexed. As I turned the corner of the terrace, I heard the faint sound of Ellie's guitar, and a tall figure, who had been standing by the window looking in, wheeled round and came toward me. For a moment I thought it was our gipsy, then I relaxed as I recognized Santonix.

"Oh," I said with a slight gasp, "it's you. Where have you sprung from? We've not heard from you for ages."

He didn't answer me directly. He just caught my arm and drew me away from the window.

"So she's here!" he said. "I'm not surprised. I thought she'd come sooner or later. Why did you let her? She's dangerous. You ought to know that."

"You mean Ellie?"

"No, no, not Ellie. The other one! What's her name? Greta."

I stared at him.

"Do you know what Greta's like, or don't you? She's come, hasn't she? Taken possession! You won't get rid of her now. She's come to stay."

"Ellie sprained her ankle," I said. "Greta came to look after her. She's —I suppose she's going soon."

"You don't know anything of the kind. She always meant to come. I knew that. I took her measure when she came down while the house was building."

"Ellie seems to want her," I muttered.

"Oh, yes, she's been with Ellie some time, hasn't she? She knows how to manage Ellie."

That was what Lippincott had said. I'd seen for myself lately how true it was.

"Do you want her here, Mike?"

"I can't throw her out of the house," I said irritably. "She's Ellie's old friend. Her best friend. What the hell can I do about it?"

"No," said Santonix, "I suppose you can't do anything, can you?"

He looked at me. It was a very strange glance. Santonix was a strange man. You never knew what his words really meant.

"Do you know where you're going, Mike?" he said. "Have you any idea? Sometimes I don't think you know anything at all."

"Of course I know," I said. "I'm doing what I want to. I'm going where I wanted."

"Are you? I wonder. I wonder if you really know what you want yourself. I'm afraid for you with Greta. She's stronger than you are, you know."

"I don't see how you make that out. It isn't a question of strength."

"Isn't it? I think it is. She's the strong kind, the kind that always gets her way. You didn't mean to have her here. That's what you said. But here she is, and I've been watching them. She and Ellie sitting together, at home together, chattering and settled in. What are you, Mike? The outsider? Or aren't you an outsider?"

"You're crazy, the things you say. What do you mean—I'm an outsider? I'm Ellie's husband, aren't I?"

"Are you Ellie's husband or is Ellie your wife?"

"You're daft," I said. "What's the difference?"

He sighed. Suddenly, his shoulders sagged as though vigor went out of him.

"I can't reach you," said Santonix. "I can't make you hear me. I can't make you understand. Sometimes I think you do understand, sometimes I think you don't know anything at all about yourself or anyone else."

"Look here," I said. "I'll take so much from you, Santonix. You're a wonderful architect—but—"

His face changed in the queer way it had.

"Yes," he said, "I'm a good architect. This house is the best thing I have done. I'm as near as possible satisfied with it. You wanted a house like this. And Ellie wanted a house like this, too, to live in with you. She's got it and you've got it. Send that other woman away, Mike, before it's too late."

"How can I upset Ellie?"

"That woman's got you where she wants you," said Santonix.

"Look here," I said, "I don't like Greta. She gets on my nerves. The other day I even had a frightful row with her. But none of it's as simple as you think."

"No, it won't be simple with her."

"Whoever called this place Gipsy's Acre and said it had a curse on it may have had something," I said angrily. "We've got gipsies who jump out from behind trees and shake fists at us and warn us that if we don't get out of here, some awful fate will happen to us. This place that ought to be good and beautiful."

They were queer words to say, those last ones. I said them as though it was somebody else saying them.

"Yes, it should be like that," said Santonix. "It should be. But it can't be, can it, if there is something evil possessing it?"

"You don't believe, surely, in—"

"There are many queer things I believe. . . . I know something about evil. Don't you realize, haven't you often felt, that I am partly evil myself? Always have been. That's why I know. I know when it's near me, although I don't always know exactly where it is. . . . I want the house I built purged of evil. You understand that?" His tone was menacing. "You understand that? It matters to me."

Then his whole manner changed.

"Come on," he said. "Don't let's talk a lot of nonsense. Let's come in and see Ellie."

So we went in through the window and Ellie greeted Santonix with enormous pleasure.

Santonix showed all his normal manner that evening. There were no more histrionics; he was his own self—charming, light-hearted. He talked mostly to Greta, giving her as it were the special benefit of his charm. And he had a lot of charm. Anyone would have sworn that he was impressed by her, that he liked her, that he was anxious to please her. It made me feel that Santonix was really a very dangerous man; there was a great deal more to him than I had ever glimpsed.

Greta always responded to admiration. She showed herself at her best. She could on occasions dim her beauty or else reveal it, and tonight she looked as beautiful as I'd ever seen her. Smiling at Santonix, listening to him as though spellbound. I wondered what lay behind his manner. You never knew with Santonix. Ellie said she hoped he was staying for several days, but he shook his head. He had to leave on the following day, he said.

"Are you building something now? Are you busy?"

He said no, he'd just come out of the hospital.

"They've patched me up once more," he said, "but it's probably for the last time."

"Patched you up? What do they do to you?"

"Drain the bad blood out of my body and put some good, fresh red blood in," he said.

"Oh." Ellie gave a little shudder.

"Don't worry," said Santonix, "it will never happen to you."

"But why has it got to happen to you?" said Ellie. "It's cruel."

"Not cruel, no," said Santonix. "I heard what you were singing just now.

> Man was made for Joy and Woe
> And when this we rightly know
> Thro' the World we safely go.

I go safely because I know why I'm here. And for you, Ellie,

> Every Morn and every Night
> Some are born to Sweet Delight.

That's you."

"I wish I could feel safe," said Ellie.

"Don't you feel safe?"

"I don't like to be threatened," said Ellie. "I don't like anyone to put a curse on me."

"You're talking about your gipsy?"

"Yes."

"Forget it," said Santonix. "Forget it for tonight. Let's be happy. Ellie—your health— Long life to you—and a quick and merciful end to me—and good luck to Mike here—" He stopped, his glass raised toward Greta.

"Yes?" said Greta. "And to me?"

"And to you, what's coming to you! Success, perhaps?" he added, half quizzically with an ironic question in his tone.

He went away next morning early.

"What a strange man he is," Ellie said. "I've never understood him."

"I never understand half of what he says," I answered.

"He knows things," said Ellie thoughtfully.

"You mean he knows the future?"

"No," said Ellie, "I didn't mean that. He knows people. I said it to you once before. He knows people better than they know themselves. Sometimes he hates them because of that, and sometimes he's sorry for them. He's not sorry for me, though," she added meditatively.

"Why should he be?" I demanded.

"Oh, because—" said Ellie.

16

IT WAS THE next day in the afternoon that as I was walking rather rapidly in the darkest part of the wood where the shade of the pine trees was more menacing than anywhere else, I saw the figure of a tall woman standing in the drive. I took a quick impulsive step off the path. I'd taken it for granted that she was our gipsy, but I stopped in sudden recoil when I saw who it actually was. It was my mother. She stood there tall and grim and gray-haired.

"Good Lord," I said, "you startled me, Mum. What are you doing here? Come to see us? We've asked you often enough, haven't we?"

We hadn't actually. I'd extended one rather lukewarm invitation, that was all. I'd put it, too, in a way which made it pretty sure that my mother wouldn't accept. I didn't want her here. I'd never wanted her here.

"You're right," she said. "I've come to see you at last. To see all's well with you. So this is the grand house you've built, and it is a grand house," she said, looking over my shoulder.

I thought I detected in her voice the disapproving acidity that I'd expected to find.

"Too grand for the likes of me, eh?" I said.

"I didn't say that, lad."

"But you thought it."

"It wasn't what you were born to, and no good comes from getting out of your station in life."

"Nobody'd ever get anywhere if they listened to you."

"Aye, I know that's what you say and think, but I don't know what good ambition's ever done to anybody. It's the kind of thing that turns to dead sea fruit in your mouth."

"Ah, for God's sake, don't croak," I said. "Come on. Come along up to see our grand house for yourself and turn up your nose at it. And come and see my grand wife, too, and turn up your nose at her if you dare."

"Your wife? I've seen her already."

"What do you mean, you've seen her already?" I demanded.

"So she didn't tell you, eh?"

"What?" I demanded.

"That she came to see me."

"She came to see you?" I asked, dumbfounded.

"Yes. There she was one day standing outside the door, ringing the bell and looking a little scared. She's a pretty lass and a sweet one for all the fine clothes she had on. She said, 'You're Mike's mother, aren't you?' and I said, 'Yes, and who are you?' and she said, 'I'm his wife.' She said, 'I had to come to see you. It didn't seem right that I shouldn't know Mike's mother. . . .' And I said, 'I bet he didn't want you to,' and she hesitated, and I said, 'You don't need to mind telling me that.

I know my boy and I know what he'd want or not want.' She said, 'You think—perhaps he's ashamed of you because he and you are poor and I'm rich, but it isn't like that at all. That isn't like him at all. It isn't. Really, it isn't.' I said again, 'You don't need to tell me, lass. I know what faults my boy has. That's not one of his faults. He's not ashamed of his mother and he's not ashamed of his beginnings.

"'He's not ashamed of me.' I said to her, 'He's afraid of me if anything. I know too much about him, you see.' And that seemed to amuse her. She said, 'I expect mothers always feel like that—that they know all about their sons. And I expect sons always feel embarrassed just because of that!'

"I said in a way that might be true enough. When you're young, you're always putting on an act to the world. I mind myself, when I was a child in my auntie's house. On the wall over my bed there was a great big eye in a gilt frame. It said, 'Thou God seest me.' Gave me the creeps, it did, all up my spine before I went to sleep."

"Ellie should have told me she'd been to see you," I said. "I don't see why she should keep it such a secret. She should have told me."

I was angry. I was very angry. I'd had no idea that Ellie would keep secrets like that from me.

"She was a little scared of what she'd done, maybe, but she'd no call to be frightened of you, my boy."

"Come on," I said, "come on and see our house."

I don't know whether she liked our house or not. I think not. She looked round the rooms and raised her eyebrows and then she went into the terrace room. Ellie and Greta were sitting there. They'd just come in from outside and Greta had a scarlet wool cloak half over her shoulders. My mother looked at them both. She just stood there for a moment as though rooted to the spot. Ellie jumped up and came forward and across the room.

"Oh, it's Mrs. Rogers," she said. Then turning to Greta, "It's Mike's mother come to see our house and us. Isn't that nice? This is my friend Greta Andersen."

And she held out both her hands and took Mum's, and Mum looked at her and then looked over her shoulder at Greta very hard.

"I see," she said to herself, "I see."

"What do you see?" asked Ellie.

"I wondered," said Mum. "I wondered what it would all be like here." She looked round her. "Yes, it's a fine house. Fine curtains and fine chairs and fine pictures."

"You must have some tea," said Ellie.

"You look as if you've finished tea."

"Tea's a thing that need never be finished," said Ellie. Then she said to Greta, "I won't ring the bell. Greta, will you go out to the kitchen and make a fresh pot of tea?"

"Of course, darling," said Greta, and went out of the room looking over her shoulder once in a sharp, almost scared way at my mother.

My mother sat down.

"Where's your luggage?" said Ellie. "Have you come to stay? I hope you have."

"No, lass, I won't stay. I'm going back by train in half an hour's time. I just wanted to look in on you." Then she added rather quickly, probably because she wished to get it out before Greta came back, "Now don't worry yourself, love. I told him how you came to see me and paid me a visit."

"I'm sorry, Mike, that I didn't tell you," said Ellie firmly, "only I thought perhaps I'd better not."

"She came out of the kindness of her heart, she did," said my mother. "She's a good girl you've married, Mike, and a pretty one. Yes, a very pretty one." Then she added half audibly, "I am sorry."

"Sorry," said Ellie, faintly puzzled.

"Sorry for thinking the things I did," said my mother, and added with a slight air of strain, "Well, as you say, mothers are like that. Always inclined to be suspicious of daughters-in-law. But when I saw you, I knew he'd been lucky. It seemed too good to be true to me, that it did."

"What impertinence," I said, but I smiled at her as I said it. "I always had excellent taste."

"You've always had expensive taste, that's what you mean," said my mother, and looked at the brocade curtains.

"I'm not really the worse for being an expensive taste," said Ellie, smiling at her.

"You make him save a bit of money from time to time," said Mum; "it'll be good for his character."

"I refuse to have my character improved," I said. "The advantage of taking a wife is that the wife thinks everything you do is perfect. Isn't that so, Ellie?"

Ellie was looking happy again now. She laughed and said, "You're above yourself, Mike! The conceit of you."

Greta came back then with the teapot. We'd been a little ill at ease and we were just getting over it. Somehow when Greta came back the strain came on again. My mother resisted all endeavors on Ellie's part to make her stay over, and Ellie didn't insist after a short while. She and I walked down together with my mother along the winding drive through the trees and to the gateway.

"What do you call it?" my mother asked abruptly.

Ellie said, "Gipsy's Acre."

"Ah," said my mother, "yes, you've got gipsies around here, haven't you?"

"How did you know that?" I asked.

"I saw one as I came up. She looked at me queer, she did."

"She's all right, really," I said, "a little half baked, that's all."

"Why do you say she's half baked? She'd a funny look to her when she looked at me. She's got a grievance against you of some kind?"

"I don't think it's real," said Ellie. "I think she's imagined it all. That we've done her out of her land or something like that."

"I expect she wants money," said my mother. "Gipsies are like that. Make a big song and dance sometimes of how they've been done down one way or another. But they soon stop when they get some money in their itching palms."

"You don't like gipsies," said Ellie.

"They're a thieving lot. They don't work steady and they don't keep their hands off what doesn't belong to them."

"Oh, well," Ellie said, "we—we don't worry any more now."

My mother said good-by and then added, "Who's the young lady that lives with you?"

Ellie explained how Greta had been with her for three years before she married and how but for Greta she would have had a miserable life.

"Greta's done everything to help us. She's a wonderful person," said Ellie. "I wouldn't know how to—how to get on without her."

"She's living with you or on a visit?"

"Oh, well," said Ellie. She avoided the question. "She—she's living with us at present because I sprained my ankle and had to have someone to look after me. But I'm all right again now."

"Married people do best alone together when they're starting," my mother said.

We stood by the gate watching my mother march away down the hill.

"She's got a very strong personality," said Ellie thoughtfully.

I was angry with Ellie, really very angry because she'd gone and found out my mother and visited her without telling me. But when she turned and stood looking at me with one eyebrow raised a little and the funny half-timid, half-satisfied little-girl smile on her face, I couldn't help relenting.

"What a deceitful little thing you are," I said.

"Well," said Ellie, "I've had to be sometimes, you see."

"That's like a Shakespeare play I once saw. They did it at a school I was at." I quoted rather self-consciously, "'She hath deceived her father and may deceive thee.'"

"What did you play—Othello?"

"No," I said, "I played the girl's father. That's why I remember that speech, I suppose. It's practically the only thing I had to say."

"'She hath deceived her father and may deceive thee,'" said Ellie thoughtfully. "I didn't ever deceive my father as far as I know. Perhaps I would have later."

"I don't suppose he would have taken very kindly to your marrying me," I said, "any more than your stepmother did."

"No," said Ellie, "I don't suppose he would. He was pretty conventional, I think." Then she gave that funny little-girl smile again. "So I suppose I'd have had to be like Desdemona and deceived my father and run away with you."

"Why did you want to see my mother so much, Ellie?" I asked curiously.

"It's not so much I wanted to see her," said Ellie, "but I felt terribly bad not doing anything about it. You haven't mentioned your mother very often, but I did gather that she's always done everything she could for you. Come to the rescue about things and worked very hard to get you extra schooling and things like that. And I thought it seemed so mean and purse-proud of me not to go near her."

"Well, it wouldn't have been your fault," I said; "it would have been mine."

"Yes," said Ellie. "I can understand that perhaps you didn't want me to go and see her."

"You think I've got an inferiority complex about my mother? That's not true at all, Ellie. I assure you it isn't. It wasn't that."

"No," said Ellie thoughtfully, "I know that now. It was because you didn't want her to do a lot of mother stuff."

"Mother stuff?" I queried.

"Well," said Ellie, "I can see that she's the kind of person who would know quite well what other people ought to do. I mean, she'd want you to go in for certain kinds of jobs."

"Quite right," I said. "Steady jobs. Settling down."

"It wouldn't have mattered very much now," said Ellie. "I daresay it was very good advice. But it wouldn't have been the right advice ever for you, Mike. You're not a settler-down. You don't want to be steady. You want to go and see things and do things—be on top of the world."

"I want to stay here in this house with you," I said.

"For a while, perhaps . . . And I think—I think you'll always want to come back here. And so shall I. I think we shall come here every year, and I think we shall be happier here than anywhere else. But you'll want to go places, too. You'll want to travel and see things and buy things. Perhaps think up new plans for doing the garden here. Perhaps we'll go and look at Italian gardens, Japanese gardens, landscape gardens of all kinds."

"You make life seem very exciting, Ellie," I said. "I'm sorry I was cross."

"Oh, I don't mind your being cross," said Ellie. "I'm not afraid of you." Then she added, with a frown, "Your mother didn't like Greta."

"A lot of people don't like Greta," I said.

"Including you."

"Now look here, Ellie, you're always saying that. It's not true. I was just a bit jealous of her at first, that was all. We get on very well now." And I added, "I think perhaps she makes people get rather on the defensive."

"Mr. Lippincott doesn't like her either, does he? He thinks she's got too much influence over me," said Ellie.

"Has she?"

"I wonder why you should ask that. Yes, I think perhaps she has. It's only natural. She's rather a dominant personality and I had to have someone I could trust in and rely on. Someone who'd stand up for me."

"And see you got your own way?" I asked her, laughing.

We went into the house arm in arm. For some reason it seemed dark that afternoon. I suppose because the sun had just left the terrace and left a feeling of darkness behind it. Ellie said,

"What's the matter, Mike?"

"I don't know," I said. "Just suddenly I felt as though someone were walking over my grave."

"A goose is walking over your grave. That's the real saying, isn't it?" said Ellie.

Greta wasn't about anywhere. The servants said she'd gone out for a walk.

Now that my mother knew all about my marriage and had seen Ellie, I did what I had really wanted to do for some time. I sent her a large check. I told her to move into a better house and to buy herself any additional furniture she wanted. Things like that. I had doubts, of course, as to whether she would accept it or not. It wasn't money that I'd worked for and I couldn't honestly pretend it was. As I had expected, she sent the check back torn in two, with a scrawled note. "I'll have nought to do with any of this," she wrote. "You'll never be different. I know that now. Heaven help you." I flung it down in front of Ellie.

"You see what my mother's like," I said. "I married a rich girl, and I'm living on my rich wife's money and the old battleax disapproves of it!"

"Don't worry," said Ellie. "Lots of people think that way. She'll get over it. She loves you very much, Mike," she added.

"Then why does she want to alter me all the time? Make me into her pattern. I'm myself. I'm not anybody else's pattern. I'm not my mother's little boy to be molded the way she likes. I'm myself. I'm an adult. I'm me!"

"You're you," said Ellie, "and I love you."

And then, perhaps to distract me, she said something rather disquieting.

"What do you think," she said, "of this new manservant of ours?"

I hadn't thought about him. What was there to think? If anything, I preferred him to our last one, who had not troubled to conceal his low opinion of my social status.

"He's all right," I said. "Why?"

"I just wondered whether he might be a security man."

"A security man? What do you mean?"

"A detective. I thought Uncle Andrew might have arranged it."

"Why should he?"

"Well—possible kidnaping, I suppose. In the States, you know, we usually had guards—especially in the country."

Another of the disadvantages of having money that I hadn't known about!

"What a beastly idea!"

"Oh, I don't know. . . . I suppose I'm used to it. What does it matter? One doesn't really notice."

"Is the wife in it, too?"

"She'd have to be, I think, though she cooks very well. I should think that Uncle Andrew, or perhaps Stanford Lloyd, whichever one of them thought of it, must have paid our last ones to leave, and had these two all lined up ready to take their place. It would have been quite easy."

"Without telling you?" I was still incredulous.

"They'd never dream of telling me. I might have kicked up a fuss. Anyway, I may be quite wrong about them," she went on dreamily.

"It's only that one gets a kind of feeling when one's been used to people of that kind always being around."

"Poor little rich girl," I said savagely.

Ellie did not mind at all.

"I suppose that does describe it rather well," she said.

"The things I'm learning about you all the time, Ellie," I said.

17

WHAT A MYSTERIOUS thing sleep is. You go to bed worrying about gipsies and secret enemies and detectives planted in your house and the possibilities of kidnaping and a hundred other things, and sleep whisks you away from it all. You travel very far and you don't know where you've been, but when you wake up, it's to a totally new world. No worries, no apprehensions. Instead, when I woke up on the 17th September, I was in a mood of boisterous excitement.

"A wonderful day," I said to myself with conviction. "This is going to be a wonderful day." I meant it. I was like those people in advertisements that offer to go anywhere and do anything. I went over plans in my head. I had arranged to meet Major Phillpot at a sale at a country house about fifteen miles away. They had some very nice stuff there and I'd already marked down two or three items in the catalogue. I was quite excited about the whole thing.

Phillpot was very knowledgeable about period furniture and silver and things of that kind, not because he was artistic—he was entirely a sporting man—but simply because he knew. His whole family was knowledgeable.

I looked over the catalogue at breakfast. Ellie had come down in a riding habit. She rode most mornings now—sometimes alone, sometimes with Claudia. She had the American habit of drinking coffee and a glass of orange juice and nothing much else for breakfast. My tastes now that I hadn't got to restrain them in any way were very much those of a Victorian squire! I liked lots of hot dishes on the sideboard. I ate kidneys this morning and sausages and bacon as well. Delicious.

"What are you doing, Greta?" I asked.

Greta said she was meeting Claudia Hardcastle at the station at Market Chadwell and they were going up to London to a white sale. I asked what a white sale was.

"Does there really have to be white in it?" I asked.

Greta looked scornful and said that a white sale meant a sale of household linen and blankets and towels and sheets, etc. There were some very good bargains at a special shop in Bond Street, of which she had been sent a catalogue.

I said to Ellie, "Well, if Greta is going to London for the day, why don't you drive in and meet us at the George in Bartington? The food there's very good, so old Phillpot said. He suggested you might come. One o'clock. You go through Market Chadwell and then you take a turning about three miles after that. It's signposted, I think."

"All right," said Ellie, "I'll be there."

I mounted her and she went off riding through the trees. Ellie loved riding. She rode up one of the winding tracks and came out on the downs and had a gallop before returning home. I left the smaller car for Ellie, as it was easier to park, and took the big Chrysler myself. I got to Bartington Manor just before the sale began. Phillpot was there already and had kept a place for me.

"Some quite nice stuff here," he said. "One or two good pictures. A Romney and a Reynolds. I don't know if you're interested?"

I shook my head. My taste at the moment was entirely for modern artists.

"Several dealers here," Phillpot went on, "a couple down from London. See that thin man over there with the pinched lips? That's Cressington. Pretty well known. Not brought your wife?"

"No," I said, "she's not awfully keen on sales. Anyway, I didn't particularly want her to come this morning."

"Oh? Why not?"

"There's going to be a surprise for Ellie," I said. "Did you notice Lot Forty-two?"

He took a glance at the catalogue and then looked across the room.

"Hm. That papier-mâché desk? Yes. Rather a beautiful little piece. One of the best examples of papier-mâché I've seen. Desk rather rare, too. Plenty of hand desks to stand on tables. But this is an early example. Never seen one quite like it before."

The little piece was inlaid with a design of Windsor Castle, and the sides of it had bouquets of roses and thistles and shamrock.

"Beautiful condition," said Phillpot. He looked at me curiously. "I shouldn't have thought it was your taste, but—"

"Oh, it isn't," I said. "It's a little too flowery and ladylike for me. But Ellie loves the stuff. It's her birthday next week and I want it as a present for her. A surprise. That's why I didn't want her to know I was bidding for it today. But I know there's nothing I could give her that she'd like more. She'll be really surprised."

We went in and took seats and the sale began. Actually, the piece I wanted was run up pretty high. Both the London dealers seemed keen on it, although one of them was so practiced and reserved about it that you could hardly notice the almost infinitesimal motion of his catalogue, which the auctioneer was observing closely. I bought a carved Chippendale chair as well, which I thought would look well in our hall, and some enormous brocade curtains in good condition.

"Well, you seem to have enjoyed yourself, all right," said Phillpot, rising to his feet when the auctioneer completed the morning's sale. "Want to come back this afternoon?"

I shook my head.

"No, there's nothing in the second half of the sale that I want. Mostly bedroom furniture and carpets and things like that."

"No, I didn't think you'd be interested. Well—" he looked at his watch—"we'd better be getting along. Is Ellie meeting us at the George?"

"Yes, she'll be there."

"And—er—Miss Andersen?"

"Oh, Greta's gone to London," I said. "She's gone to what they call a white sale. With Miss Hardcastle, I believe."

"Oh, yes, Claudia said something about it the other day. Prices of sheets and things are fantastic nowadays. Do you know what a linen pillow case costs? Thirty-five shillings. Used to buy 'em from six bob."

"You're very knowledgeable on household purchases," I said.

"Well, I hear my wife complaining about them." Phillpot smiled. "You're looking in the pink of condition, Mike. Happy as a sandboy."

"That's because I've got the papier-mâché desk," I said, "or, at any rate, that's partly it. I just woke up feeling happy this morning. You know those days when everything in the world seems right."

"Hm," said Phillpot, "be careful. That's what's known as being fey."

"Fey?" I said. "That's something Scottish, isn't it?"

"It comes before disaster, my boy," said Phillpot. "Better curb your exuberance."

"Oh, I don't believe those silly superstitions," I said.

"Nor in gipsies' prophecies, eh?"

"We haven't seen our gipsy lately," I said. "Well, not for a week at least."

"Perhaps she's away from the place," said Phillpot.

He asked me if I'd give him a lift in my car and I said I would.

"No use taking the two of them. You can drop me here on your way back, can't you? What about Ellie? Will she be bringing her car over?"

"Yes, she's bringing the little one."

"Hope the George will put on a good meal," said Major Phillpot. "I'm hungry."

"Did you buy anything?" I asked. "I was too excited to notice."

"Yes, you've got to keep your wits about you when you're bidding. Have to notice what the dealers are doing. No. I made a bid or two, but everything went far above my price."

I gathered that although Phillpot owned enormous quantities of land round about, his actual income did not amount to much. He was what you might describe as a poor man though a large landowner. Only by selling a good portion of his land would he have had money to spend, and he didn't want to sell his land. He loved it.

We got to the George and found a good many cars standing there already—possibly some of the people from the auction. I didn't see Ellie's, though. We went inside and I looked around for her, but she hadn't turned up yet. However, it was only just past one.

We went and had a drink at the bar while we were waiting for Ellie to arrive. The place was pretty crowded. I looked into the dining room, but they were still holding our table. There were a good many local faces that I knew, and sitting at a table by the window was a man whose face seemed familiar to me. I was sure I knew him but I couldn't remember when and where I'd met him. I didn't think he was a local. I was sure he was a stranger because his clothes didn't fit in with these parts. Of course I've knocked up against a great many people in my time and it is unlikely that I can remember them all easily. But this was a face, I thought, that I'd seen lately. I hadn't seen him at the sale as far as I could remember.

The presiding goddess of the George, rustling in her usual black silk of affected Edwardian style, which she always wore, came up to me and said,

"Will you be coming to your table soon, Mr. Rogers? There's one or two waiting."

"My wife will be here in a minute or two," I said.

I went back to rejoin Phillpot. I thought perhaps that Ellie might have had a puncture.

"We'd better go in," I said. "They seem getting rather upset about it. They've got quite a crowd today. I'm afraid," I added, "that Ellie isn't the most punctual of people."

"Ah," said Phillpot in his old-fashioned style, "the ladies make a point of keeping us waiting, don't they? All right, Mike, if that's all right by you. We'll go in and start lunch."

We went into the dining room, chose steak and kidney pie off the menu, and started.

"It's too bad of Ellie," I said, "to stand us up like this." I added that it was possibly because Greta was in London. "Ellie's very used, you know," I said, "to Greta helping her to keep appointments, reminding her of them, and getting her off in time and all that."

"Is she very dependent on Miss Andersen?"

"In that way, yes," I said.

We went on eating and passed from the steak and kidney pie to apple tart with a self-conscious piece of phony pastry on top of it.

"I wonder if she's forgotten all about it," I said suddenly.

"Perhaps you'd better ring up."

"Yes, I think I'd better."

I went out to the phone and rang. Mrs. Carson, the cook, answered.

"Oh, it's you, Mr. Rogers. Mrs. Rogers hasn't come home yet."

"What do you mean, hasn't come home? Home from where?"

"She hasn't come back from her ride yet."

"But that was after breakfast. She can't have been riding the whole morning."

"She didn't say anything different. I was expecting her back."

"Why didn't you ring up sooner and let me know about it?" I asked.

"Well, I wouldn't know where to get at you, you see. I didn't know where you'd gone."

I told her I was at the George at Bartington and gave her the number. She was to ring up the moment Ellie came in or she had news of her. Then I went back to join Phillpot. He saw from my face at once that something was wrong.

"Ellie hasn't come home," I said. "She went off riding this morning. She usually does most mornings, but it only lasts half an hour to an hour."

"Now don't worry before you need to, boy," he said kindly. "Your place is in a very lonely part, you know. Maybe her horse went lame and she might be walking it home. All that moorland and downs above the woods. There's nobody much in that part to send a message by or anything like that."

"If she decided to change her plans and ride over and see anyone, anything like that," I said, "she'd have rung here. She'd have left a message for us."

"Well, don't get het up yet," Phillpot said. "I think we'd better go now, right away, and see what we can find out."

As we went out to the car park, another car drove away. In it was the man I had noticed in the dining room and suddenly it came to me who it was. Stanford Lloyd or someone just like him. I wondered what he could be doing down here. Could he be coming to see us? If so, it was odd he hadn't let us know. In the car with him was a woman who had looked like Claudia Hardcastle, but surely she was in London with Greta, shopping. It all floored me rather . . .

As we drove away, Phillpot looked at me once or twice. I caught his eye once and said rather bitterly,

"All right. You said I was fey this morning."

"Well, don't think of that yet. She may have had a fall and sprained an ankle or something like that. She's a good horsewoman, though," he said. "I've seen her. I can't feel an accident is really likely."

I said, "Accidents can happen at any time."

We drove fast and came at last to the road over the downs above our property, looking about us as we went. Now and again we stopped to ask people. We stopped a man who was digging peat and there we got the first news.

"Seen a riderless horse I have," he said. "Two hours ago maybe or longer. I would-a caught it but it galloped off when I got near it. Didn't see anyone though."

"Best drive home," suggested Phillpot; "there may be news of her there."

We drove home but there was no news. We got hold of the groom and sent him off to ride over the moorland in search of Ellie. Phillpot telephoned his own house and sent a man from there, too. He and I went up a path together and through the wood, the one that Ellie often took, and came out on the downs there.

At first there was nothing to be seen. Then we walked along the edge of the wood near where some of the other paths came out and so—we found her. We saw what looked like a huddled heap of clothes. The horse had come back and was now standing cropping near that huddled heap. I began to run. Phillpot followed me faster than I'd have thought a man of his age could have kept up.

She was there—lying in a crumpled-up heap, her little white face turned up to the sky. I said,

"I can't—I can't—" and turned my face away.

Phillpot went and knelt down by her. He got up almost at once.

"We'll get hold of a doctor," he said. "Shaw. He's the nearest. But—I don't think it's any use, Mike."

"You mean—she's dead?"

"Yes," he said, "it's no good pretending anything else."

"Oh, God!" I said, and turned away. "I can't believe it. Not Ellie."

"Here, have this," said Phillpot.

He took a flask out of his pocket, unscrewed it and handed it to me. I took a good deep pull at it.

"Thanks," I said.

The groom came along then, and Phillpot sent him off to fetch Dr. Shaw.

18

SHAW CAME UP in a battered old Landrover—I suppose the car he used for going to visit isolated farms in bad weather. He barely looked at either of us. He went straight and bent over Ellie. Then he came over to us.

"She's been dead at least three or four hours," he said. "How did it happen?"

I told him how she'd gone off riding as usual after breakfast that morning.

"Has she had any accidents up to this time when she's been out riding?"

"No," I said, "she was a good rider."

"Yes, I know she's a good rider. I've seen her once or twice. She's ridden since she was a child, I understand. I wondered if she might have had some accident lately and that that might have affected her nerve a bit. If the horse had shied—"

"Why should the horse shy? It's a quiet brute—"

"There's nothing vicious about this particular horse," said Major Phillpot. "He's well behaved, not nervy. Has she broken any bones?"

"I haven't made a complete examination yet, but she doesn't seem physically injured in any way. There may be some internal injury. Might be shock, I suppose."

"But you can't die of shock," I said.

"People have died of shock before now. If she'd had a weak heart—"

"They said in America that she had a weak heart—some kind of weakness at least."

"Hm. I couldn't find much trace of it when I examined her. Still, we didn't have a cardiograph. Anyway, no point in going into that now. We shall know later. After the inquest."

He looked at me consideringly, then he patted me on the shoulder.

"You go home and go to bed," he said. "You're the one who's suffering from shock."

In the queer way people materialize out of nowhere in the country, we had three or four people standing by, by this time—one a hiker who had come along from the main road seeing our little group, one a rosy-faced woman who I think was going to a farm over a short cut, and an old road man. They were making exclamations and remarks.

"Poor young lady."

"So young, too. Thrown from her horse, was she?"

"Ah, well, you never know with horses."

"It's Mrs. Rogers, isn't it? The American lady from The Towers?"

It was not until everyone else had exclaimed in their astonished fashion that the aged road man spoke. He gave us information. Shaking his head, he said,

"I musta seen it happen. I musta seen it happen."

The doctor turned sharply on him.

"What did you see happen?"

"I saw a horse bolting across country."

"Did you see the lady fall?"

"No. No, I didn't. She were riding along the top of the woods when I saw her and after that I'd got me back turned and I was cutting the stones for the road. And then I heard hoofs and I looked up and there was the horse agalloping. I didn't think there'd been an accident. I thought the lady perhaps had got off and let go of the horse in some way. It wasn't coming toward me; it was going in the other direction."

"You didn't see the lady lying on the ground?"

"No, I don't see very well far. I saw the horse because it showed against the sky-line."

"Was she riding alone? Was there anyone with her, or near her?"

"Nobody near her. No. She was all alone. She rode not very far from me, past me, going along that way. She was bearing toward the woods, I think. No, I didn't see anyone at all except her and the horse."

"Might have been the gipsy what frightened her," said the rosy-faced woman.

I swung round.

"What gipsy? When?"

"Oh, must have been—well, it must have been three or four hours ago when I went down the road this morning. About quarter to ten maybe, I saw that gipsy woman. The one as lives in the cottage in the village. Least I think it was she. I wasn't near enough to be sure. But she's the only one as goes about hereabouts in a red cloak. She was walking up a path through the trees. Somebody told me as she'd said nasty things to the poor American young lady. Threatened her. Told her something bad would happen if she didn't get out of this place. Very threatening, I hear she was."

"The gipsy," I said. Then, bitterly, to myself, though out loud, "Gipsy's Acre. I wish I'd never seen the place."

BOOK THREE

19

IT'S EXTRAORDINARY HOW difficult it is for me to remember what happened after that—I mean, the sequence of it all. Up to then, you see, it's all clear in my mind. I was a little doubtful where to begin, that was all. But from then on it was as though a knife fell, cutting my life into two halves. What I went on to from the moment of Ellie's death seems to me now like something for which I was not prepared. A confusion of thrusting people and elements and happenings where I wasn't myself in control of anything any more. Things happened not to me, but all around me. That's what it seemed like.

Everybody was very kind to me. That seems the thing I remember best. I stumbled about and looked dazed and didn't know what to do. Greta, I remember, came into her element. She had that amazing power that women have to take charge of a situation and deal with it. Deal, I mean, with all the small unimportant details that someone has to see to. I would have been incapable of seeing to them.

I think the first thing I remembered clearly after they'd taken Ellie away and I'd got back to my house—our house—*the* house—was when Shaw came along and talked to me. I don't know how long after that was. He was quiet, kind, reasonable—just explaining things clearly and gently.

Arrangements. I remember his using the word arrangements. What a hateful word it is. All the things it stands for. All the things in life that have grand words. Love—sex—life—death—hate. Those aren't the things that govern existence at all. It's lots of other pettifogging, degrading things. Things you have to endure, things you never think about until they happen to you. Undertakers, arrangements for funerals. And servants coming into rooms and pulling the blinds down. Why should blinds be pulled down because Ellie was dead? Of all the stupid things!

That was why, I remember, I felt quite grateful to Dr. Shaw. He dealt with such things so kindly and sensibly, explaining gently why certain things had to be—talking rather slowly, I remember, so that he could be quite sure I was taking them in.

I didn't know what an inquest would be like. I'd never been to one. It seemed to me curiously unreal, amateurish. The coroner was a small fussy little man with pince-nez. I had to give evidence of identification, to describe the last time I had seen Ellie at the breakfast table, and her departure for her usual morning ride and the arrangement we had made to meet later for lunch. She had seemed, I said, exactly the same as usual, in perfectly good health.

Dr. Shaw's evidence was quiet, inconclusive. No serious injuries, a wrenched collar bone and bruises such as would result from a fall from the horse, not of a very serious nature, and inflicted at the time of death. She did not appear to have moved again after she had fallen. Death, he thought, had been practically instantaneous. There was no specific organic injury to have caused death, and he could give no other explanation of it than she had died from heart failure caused by shock. As far as I could make out from the medical language used, Ellie had died simply as the result of absence of breath—of asphyxia of some kind. Her organs were healthy, her stomach contents normal.

Greta, who also gave evidence, stressed rather more forcibly than she had done to Dr. Shaw before that Ellie had suffered from some form of heart malady three or four years ago. She had never heard anything definite mentioned, but Ellie's relations had occasionally said that her heart was weak and that she must take care not to overdo things. She had never heard anything more definite than that.

Then we came to the people who had seen or been in the vicinity at the time the accident happened. The old man who had been cutting peat was the first of them. He had seen the lady pass him; she'd been about fifty yards or so away. He knew who she was, though he'd never spoken to her. She was the lady from the new house.

"You knew her by sight?"

"No, not exactly by sight, but I knew the horse, sir. It's got a white fetlock. Used to belong to Mr. Carey over at Shettlegroom. I've never heard it's anything but quiet and well behaved, suitable for a lady to ride."

"Was the horse giving any trouble when you saw it? Playing up in any way?"

"No, it was quiet enough. It was a nice morning."

There had not been many people about, he said. He hadn't noticed many. That particular track across the moor wasn't much used except as a short cut occasionally to one of the farms. Another track crossed it about a mile further away. He'd seen one or two passers-by that morning, but not to notice—one man on a bicycle, another man walking. They were too far away for him to see who they were, and he hadn't noticed much, anyway. Earlier, he said, before he'd seen the lady riding, he'd seen old Mrs. Lee, or so he thought. She was coming up the track toward him, and then she turned off and went into the woods. She often walked across the moors and in and out of the woods.

The coroner asked why Mrs. Lee was not in court. He understood that she'd been summoned to attend. He was told, however, that Mrs. Lee had left the village some days ago—nobody knew exactly when. She had not left any address behind. It was not her habit to do so; she often went away and came back without notifying anyone, so there was nothing unusual about this. In fact one or two people said they thought she'd already left the village before the day the accident happened. The coroner asked the old man again.

"You think, however, that it was Mrs. Lee you saw?"

"Couldn't say, I'm sure. Wouldn't like to be certain. It was a tall woman and striding along, and had on a scarlet cloak like Mrs. Lee wears sometimes. But I didn't look particular. I was busy with what I was doing. Could have been she, it could have been someone else. Who's to say?"

As for the rest, he repeated very much what he had said to us. He'd seen the lady riding nearby, he'd often seen her riding before. He hadn't paid any particular attention. Only later did he see the horse galloping alone. It looked as though something had frightened it, he said. "At least, it could be that way." He couldn't tell what time that was. Might have been eleven, might have been earlier. He saw the horse much later, further away. It seemed to be returning toward the woods.

Then the coroner recalled me and asked me a few more questions about Mrs. Lee—Mrs. Esther Lee of Vine Cottage.

"You and your wife knew Mrs. Lee by sight?"

"Yes," I said, "quite well."

"Did you talk with her?"

"Yes, several times. Or rather," I added, "she talked to us."

"Did she at any time threaten you or your wife?"

I paused a moment or two.

"In a sense she did," I said slowly, "but I never thought—"

"You never thought what?"

"I never thought she really meant it," I said.

"Did she sound as though she had any particular grudge against your wife?"

"My wife said so once. She said she thought she had some special grudge against her, but she couldn't see why."

"Had you or your wife at any time ordered her off your land, threatened her, treated her roughly in any way?"

"Any aggression came from her side," I said.

"Did you ever have the impression that she was mentally unbalanced?"

I considered. "Yes," I said, "I did. I thought she had come to believe that the land on which we had built our house belonged to her, or belonged to her tribe or whatever they call themselves. She had a kind of obsession about it." I added slowly, "I think she was getting worse, more and more obsessed by the idea."

"I see. She never offered your wife physical violence at any time?"

"No," I said slowly, "I don't think it would be fair to say that. It was all—well, all a sort of gipsy's warning stuff. 'You'll have bad luck if you stay here.' 'There'll be a curse on you unless you go away.'"

"Did she mention the word death?"

"Yes, I think so. We didn't take her seriously. At least," I corrected myself, "I didn't."

"Do you think your wife did?"

"I'm afraid she did sometimes. The old woman, you know, could be rather alarming. I don't think she was really responsible for what she was saying or doing."

The proceedings ended with the coroner adjourning the inquest for a fortnight. Everything pointed to death being due to accidental causes, but there was not sufficient evidence to show what had caused the accident to occur. He would adjourn the proceedings until he had heard the evidence of Mrs. Esther Lee.

20

THE DAY AFTER the inquest I went to see Major Phillpot and I told him point-blank that I wanted his opinion. Someone whom the old peat-cutting man had taken to be Mrs. Esther Lee had been seen going up toward the woods that morning.

"You know the old woman," I said. "Do you actually think that she would have been capable of causing an accident by deliberate malice?"

"I can't really believe so, Mike," he said. "To do a thing like that you need a very strong motive—revenge for some personal injury caused to you. Something like that. And what has Ellie ever done to her? Nothing."

"It seems crazy, I know. Why was she constantly appearing in that queer way, threatening Ellie, telling her to go away? She seemed to have a grudge against her, but how could she have a grudge? She'd never met Ellie or seen her before. What was Ellie to her but a perfectly strange American? There's no past history, no link between them."

"I know, I know," said Phillpot. "I can't help feeling, Mike, that there's something here that we don't understand. I don't know how much your wife was over in England previous to her marriage. Did she ever live in this part of the world for any length of time?"

"No, I'm sure of that. It's all so difficult. I don't really know anything about Ellie. I mean, who she knew, where she went. We just—met." I checked myself and looked at him. I said, "You don't know how we came to meet, do you? No," I went on, "you wouldn't guess in a hundred years how we met." And suddenly, in spite of myself, I began to laugh. Then I pulled myself together. I could feel that I was very near hysteria.

I could see his kind patient face just waiting till I was myself again. He was a helpful man. There was no doubt of that.

"We met here," I said. "Here at Gipsy's Acre. I had been reading the notice board of the sale of The Towers and I walked up the road, up the hill, because I was curious about this place. And that's how I first saw her. She was standing there under a tree. I startled her—or perhaps it was she who startled me. Anyway, that's how it all began. That's how we came to live here in this damned, cursed, unlucky place."

"Have you felt that all along, that it would be unlucky?"

"No. Yes. No, I don't know, really. I've never admitted it. I've never wanted to admit it. But I think she knew. I think she's been frightened all along." Then I said slowly, "I think somebody deliberately wanted to frighten her."

He said rather sharply, "What do you mean by that? Who wanted to frighten her?"

"Presumably the gipsy woman. But somehow I'm not quite sure about it. . . . She used to lie in wait for Ellie, you know, tell her this place would bring her bad luck. Tell her she ought to go away from it."

"Tcha!" He spoke angrily. "I wish I'd been told more about that. I'd have spoken to old Esther. Told her she couldn't do things like that."

"Why did she?" I asked. "What made her?"

"Like so many people," said Phillpot, "she likes to make herself important. She likes either to give people warnings or else tell their fortunes and prophesy happy lives for them. She likes to pretend she knows the future."

"Supposing," I said slowly, "somebody gave her money. I've been told she's fond of money."

"Yes, she was very fond of money. If someone paid her—that's what you're suggesting? What put that idea into your head?"

"Sergeant Keene," I said. "I should never have thought of it myself."

"I see." He shook his head doubtfully.

"I can't believe," he said, "that she would deliberately try to frighten your wife to the extent of causing an accident."

"She mayn't have counted on a fatal accident. She might have done something to frighten the horse," I said, "let off a squib or flapped a sheet of white paper or something. Sometimes, you know, I did feel that she had some entirely personal grudge against Ellie, a grudge for some reason that I don't know about."

"That sounds very far-fetched."

"This place never belonged to her?" I asked. "The land, I mean."

"No. Gipsies may have been warned off this property probably more than once. Gipsies are always getting turned off places, but I doubt if they keep up a lifelong resentment about it."

"No," I said, "that would be far-fetched. But I do wonder if for some reason that we don't know about—she was???"

"A reason we don't know about—what reason?"

I reflected a moment or two.

"Everything I say will just sound fantastic. Let's say that, as Keene suggested, someone paid her to do the things she did. What did that someone want? Say they wanted to make us both go away from here. They concentrated on Ellie, not on me, because I wouldn't be scared in the way Ellie would be. They frightened her to get her—and through her both of us—to leave here. If so, there must be some reason for wanting the land to come on the market again. Somebody, shall we say, for some reason wants our land." I stopped.

"It's a logical suggestion," Phillpot said, "but I know of no reason why anyone should."

"Some important mineral deposit," I suggested, "that nobody knows about."

"Hm, I doubt it."

"Something like buried treasure. Oh, I know it sounds absurd. Or—well, say the proceeds of some big bank robbery."

Phillpot was still shaking his head but rather less vehemently now.

"The only other proposition," I said, "is to go one step farther back as you did just now—behind Mrs. Lee to the person who paid Mrs. Lee. That might be some unknown enemy of Ellie's."

"But you can't think of anyone it would be likely to be?"

"No. She didn't know anyone down here. That I'm sure of. She had no links with this place." I got up. "Thank you for listening to me," I said.

"I wish I could have been more helpful."

I went out of the door, fingering the thing that I was carrying in my pocket. Then, taking a sudden decision, I turned on my heel and went back into the room.

"There's something I'd like to show you," I said. "Actually, I was going to take it down to show to Sergeant Keene and see what he could make of it."

I dived into my pocket and brought out a stone round which was wrapped a crumpled bit of paper with printed writing on it.

"This was thrown through our breakfast window this morning," I said. "I heard the crash of the glass as I came down the stairs. A stone was thrown through the window once before when we first came here. I don't know if this is the same person or not."

I took off the wrapping paper and held it out to him. It was a dirty, coarse bit of paper. There was some printing on it in rather faint ink. Phillpot put on his spectacles and bent over the piece of paper. The message on it was quite short. All it said was, *It was a woman who killed your wife.*

Phillpot's eyebrows went up.

"Extraordinary," he said. "Was the first message you got printed?"

"I can't remember now. It was just a warning to go away from here. I can't even remember the exact wording of it now. Anyway, it seems pretty certain that that was hooligans. This doesn't seem quite the same."

"Do you think it was thrown in by someone who knew something?"

"Probably just a bit of silly cruel malice in the anonymous letter class. You get it, you know, a good deal in villages."

He handed it back to me.

"But I think your instinct was right," he said, "to take it to Sergeant Keene. He'll know more about these anonymous things than I should."

I found Sergeant Keene at the police station, and he was definitely interested.

"There's queer things going on here," he said.

"What do you think it means?" I asked.

"Hard to say. Might be just malice leading up to accusing some particular person."

"It might be just accusing Mrs. Lee, I suppose?"

"No, I don't think it would have been put that way. It might be—I'd like to think it was—it might be that someone saw or heard something—heard a noise or a cry or the horse bolted right past someone, and they saw or met a woman soon afterward. But it sounds as though it was a different woman from the gipsy, because everyone thinks the gipsy's mixed up in this anyway. So this sounds as though another, an entirely different woman was meant."

"What about the gipsy?" I said. "Have you had news of her, found her?"

He shook his head slowly.

"We know some of the places she used to go when she left here. East Anglia, that way. She'd friends there among the gipsy clan. She's not been there, they say, but they'd say that anyway. They clam up, you know. She's fairly well known by sight in those parts, but nobody's seen her. All the same, I don't think she's as far away as East Anglia."

There was something peculiar about the way he said the words.

"I don't quite understand," I said.

"Look at it this way. She's scared. She's got good reason to be. She's been threatening your wife, frightening her, and now, say, she caused an accident and your wife died. The police'll be after her. She knows that, so she'll go to earth, as you might say. She'll put as big a distance between herself and us as she possibly can. But she won't want to show herself. She'd be afraid of public transport."

"But you'll find her? She's a woman of striking appearance."

"Ah, yes, we shall find her eventually. These things take a little time. That is, if it was that way."

"But you think it was some other way."

"Well, you know what I've wondered all along. Whether somebody was paying her to say the things she did."

"Then she might be even more anxious to get away," I said.

"But somebody else would be anxious, too. You've got to think of that, Mr. Rogers."

"You mean," I said slowly, "the person who paid her."

"Yes."

"Supposing it was a—a woman who paid her."

"And supposing somebody has some idea of that. And so they start sending anonymous messages. That woman would be scared, too. She needn't have meant this to happen, you know. However much she got that gipsy woman to frighten your wife away from this place, she wouldn't have meant it to result in Mrs. Rogers' death."

"No," I said. "Death wasn't meant. It was just to frighten us—to frighten my wife and to frighten me into leaving here."

"And now who's going to be frightened? The woman who caused the accident. And that's Mrs. Esther Lee. And so she's going to come clean, isn't she? Say it wasn't really her doing. She'll admit even that she was paid money to do it. And she'll mention a name. She'll say who paid her. And somebody wouldn't like that, would they, Mr. Rogers?"

"You mean this unknown woman that we've more or less postulated without even knowing there's any such person?"

"Man or woman, say someone paid her. Well, that someone would want her silenced pretty quickly, wouldn't they?"

"You're thinking she might be dead?"

"It's a possibility, isn't it?" said Keene. Then he made what seemed quite an abrupt change of subject. "You know that kind of Folly place, Mr. Rogers, that you've got up at the top of your woods?"

"Yes," I said, "what of it? My wife and I had it repaired and fixed up a bit. We used to go up there occasionally but not very often. Not lately certainly. Why?"

"Well, we've been hunting about, you know. We looked into this Folly. It wasn't locked."

"No," I said, "we never bothered to lock it. There was nothing of value in there, just a few odd bits of furniture."

"We thought it possible old Mrs. Lee had been using it, but we found no traces of her. We did find this, though. I was going to show it to you anyway." He opened a drawer and took out a small delicate gold-chased lighter. It was a woman's lighter and it had an initial on it in diamonds—the letter C. "It wouldn't be your wife's, would it?"

"Not with the initial C. No, it's not Ellie's," I said. "She hadn't anything of that kind. And it's not Miss Andersen's either. Her name is Greta."

"It was up there where somebody had dropped it. It's a classy bit of goods—cost money."

"C," I said, repeating the initial thoughtfully. "I can't think of anyone who's been with us whose initial is C except Cora," I said. "That's my wife's stepmother. Mrs. Van Stuyvesant, but I really can't see her scrambling up to the Folly along that very overgrown path. And anyway, she hasn't been staying with us for quite a long time. About a month. I don't think I've ever seen her using this lighter. Perhaps I wouldn't notice anyway," I said. "Miss Andersen might know."

"Well, take it up with you and show it to her."

"I will. But if so, if it's Cora's, it seems odd that we've never seen it when we've been in the Folly lately. There's not much stuff there. You'd notice something like this lying on the floor—it was on the floor?"

"Yes, quite near the divan. Of course anybody might use that Folly. It's a handy place, you know, for a couple of lovers to meet any time. The locals I'm talking about. But they wouldn't be likely to have a thing of this kind."

"There's Claudia Hardcastle," I said, "but I doubt if she'd have anything as fancy as this. And what would she be doing in the Folly?"

"She's quite a friend of your wife's, isn't she?"

"Yes," I said, "I think she's Ellie's best friend down here."

"Ah," said Sergeant Keene.

I looked at him rather hard. "You don't think Claudia Hardcastle was a—an enemy of Ellie's, do you? That would be absurd."

"Doesn't seem any reason why she should be, I agree, but you never know with ladies."

"I suppose—" I began, and then stopped because what I was going to say would seem perhaps rather odd.

"Yes, Mr. Rogers?"

"I believe that Claudia Hardcastle was originally married to an American—an American named Lloyd. Actually that's the name of my wife's principal trustee in America—Stanford Lloyd. But there must be hundreds of Lloyds and anyway, it would only be a coincidence if it was the same person. And what would it have to do with all this?"

"It doesn't seem likely. But then—" he stopped.

"The funny thing is that I thought I saw Stanford Lloyd down here on the day of—the accident—having lunch in the George at Bartington—"

"He didn't come to see you?"

I shook my head.

"He was with someone who looked rather like Miss Hardcastle. But probably it was just a mistake on my part. You know, I suppose, that it was her brother who built our house?"

"Does she take an interest in the house?"

"No," I said, "I don't think she likes her brother's type of architecture." Then I got up. "Well, I won't take any more of your time. Try and find the gipsy."

"We shan't stop looking, I can tell you that. Coroner wants her, too."

I said good-by and went out of the police station. In the queer way that so often happens when you suddenly meet someone you've been talking about, Claudia Hardcastle came out of the post office just as I was passing it. We both stopped. She said with that slight embarrassment that you have when you meet someone that's been recently bereaved,

"I'm so terribly sorry, Mike, about Ellie. I won't say any more. It's beastly when people say things to you. But I have just—just to say that."

"I know," I said. "You were very nice to Ellie. You made her feel at home here. I've been grateful."

"There was one thing I wanted to ask you and I thought perhaps I'd better do it now before you go to America. I hear you're going quite soon."

"As soon as I can. I've got a lot to see to there."

"It was only—if you were putting your house on the market, I thought it might be a thing you'd set in motion before you went away. . . . And if so—if so, I'd rather like to have the first refusal of it."

I stared at her. This really did surprise me. It was the last thing I'd expected.

"You mean you'd like to buy it? I thought you didn't even care for that type of architecture?"

"My brother Rudolf said to me that it was the best thing he'd done. I daresay he knows. I expect you'll want a very large price for it, but I could pay it. Yes, I'd like to have it."

I couldn't help thinking it was odd. She'd never shown the faintest appreciation of our house when she'd come to it. I wondered as I'd wondered once or twice before what her links with her half-brother really were. Had she really a great devotion to him? Sometimes I'd almost thought that she disliked him, perhaps hated him. She spoke of him certainly in a very odd way. But whatever her actual emotions were, he meant something to her—meant something important. I shook my head slowly.

"I can see that you might think I'd want to sell the place and leave here because of Ellie's death," I said. "But actually that's not so at all. We lived here and were happy, and this is the place I shall remember her best. I shan't sell Gipsy's Acre—not for any consideration! You can be quite sure of that."

Our eyes met. It was like a kind of tussle between us. Then hers dropped.

I took my courage in both hands and spoke.

"It's no business of mine, but you were married once. Was the name of your husband Stanford Lloyd?"

She looked at me for a moment without speaking. Then she said abruptly,

"Yes," and turned away.

21

CONFUSION— THAT'S ALL I can remember when I look back. Newspapermen asking questions—wanting interviews—masses of letters and telegrams—Greta coping with them—

The first really startling thing was that Ellie's family were not, as we had supposed, in America. It was quite a shock to find that most of them were actually in England. It was understandable, perhaps, that Cora van Stuyvesant should be. She was a very restless woman, always dashing across to Europe—to Italy, to Paris, to London and back again to America—to Palm Beach, out West to the ranch; here, there and everywhere. On the actual day of Ellie's death she had been not more than fifty miles away, still pursuing her whim of having a house in England. She had rushed over to stay in London for two or three days and gone to fresh house agents for fresh orders to view and had been touring round the country seeing half a dozen on that particular day.

Stanford Lloyd, it turned out, had flown over in the same plane for a business meeting in London. These people learned of Ellie's death, not from the cables which we had dispatched to the United States, but from the public press.

An ugly wrangle developed about where Ellie should be buried. I had assumed it was only natural that she'd be buried here where she had died—here where she and I had lived.

But Ellie's family objected violently to this. They wanted the body in due course brought to America to be buried with her forebears—where her grandfather and her father, her mother and others had been laid to rest. I suppose it was natural, really, when one comes to think of it.

Andrew Lippincott came down to talk to me about it. He put the matter in a reasonable way.

"She never left any directions as to where she wished to be buried," he pointed out to me.

"Why should she?" I demanded hotly. "How old was she—twenty-one? You don't think at twenty-one you're going to die. You don't start thinking then the way you want to be buried. If we'd ever thought about it, we'd assume we'd be buried together somewhere even if we didn't die at the same time. But who thinks of death in the middle of life?"

"A very just observation," said Mr. Lippincott. Then he said, "I'm afraid you'll also have to come to America, you know. There's a great deal of business interests you'll have to look into."

"What sort of business? What have I got to do with business?"

"You could have a great deal to do with it," he said. "Don't you realize that you're the principal beneficiary under the will?"

"You mean because I'm Ellie's next of kin or something?"

"No. Under her will."

"I didn't know she ever made a will."

"Oh, yes," said Mr. Lippincott. "Ellie was quite a businesslike young woman. She'd had to be, you know. She'd lived in the middle of that kind of thing. She made a will on coming of age and almost immediately after she was married. It was lodged with her lawyer in London with a request that one copy should be sent to me." He hesitated and then said, "If you do come to the States, which I advise, I also think that you should place your affairs in the hands of some reputable lawyer there."

"Why?"

"Because in the case of a vast fortune, large quantities of real estate, stocks, controlling interests in varying industries, you will need technical advice."

"I'm not qualified to deal with things like that," I said. "Really, I'm not."

"I quite understand," said Mr. Lippincott.

"Couldn't I place the whole thing in your hands?"

"You could do so."

"Well, then, why don't I?"

"All the same, I think you should be separately represented. I am already acting for some members of the family, and a conflict of interests might arise. If you will leave it in my hands, I will see that your interests are safeguarded by your being represented by a thoroughly able attorney."

"Thank you," I said, "you're very kind."

"If I may be slightly indiscreet—" he looked a little uncomfortable—it pleased me rather thinking of Lippincott being indiscreet.

"Yes?" I said.

"I should advise you to be very careful of anything you sign. Any business documents. Before you sign anything, read it thoroughly and carefully."

"Would the kind of document you're talking about mean anything to me if I do read it?"

"If it is not all clear to you, you will then hand it over to your legal adviser."

"Are you warning me against somebody or something?" I said, with a suddenly aroused interest.

"That is not at all a proper question for me to answer," said Mr. Lippincott. "I will go this far. Where large sums of money are concerned, it is advisable to trust nobody."

So he was warning me against someone, but he wasn't going to give me any names. I could see that. Was it against Cora? Or had he had suspicions—perhaps suspicions of some long standing—of Stanford Lloyd, that florid banker so full of bonhomie, so rich and carefree, who had recently been over here "on business"? Might it be Uncle Frank who might approach me with some plausible documents? I had a sudden vision of myself, a poor innocent boob, swimming in a lake surrounded by evilly disposed crocodiles, all smiling false smiles of amity.

"The world," said Mr. Lippincott, "is a very evil place."

It was perhaps a stupid thing to say, but quite suddenly I asked him a question.

"Does Ellie's death benefit anyone?" I asked.

He looked at me sharply.

"That's a very curious question. Why do you ask that?"

"I don't know," I said, "it just came into my head."

"It benefits you," he said.

"Of course," I said. "I take that for granted. I really meant—does it benefit anyone else?"

Mr. Lippincott was silent for quite a long time.

"If you mean," he said, "does Fenella's will benefit certain other people in the way of legacies, that is so in a minor degree. Some old servants, an old governess, one or two charities, but nothing of any particular moment. There's a legacy to Miss Andersen, but not a large one, for she has already, as you probably know, settled a very considerable sum on Miss Andersen."

I nodded. Ellie had told me she was doing that.

"You were her husband. She had no other near relations. But I take it that your question did not mean specifically that."

"I don't know quite what I meant by it," I said. "But somehow or other, you've succeeded, Mr. Lippincott, in making me feel suspicious—suspicious of I don't know whom or why. Only—well, suspicious. I don't understand finance," I added.

"No, that is quite apparent. Let me say only that I have no exact knowledge, no exact suspicions of any kind. At someone's death there is usually an accounting of their affairs. This may take place quickly or it may be delayed for a period of many years."

"What you really mean," I said, "is that some of the others quite likely might put a few fast ones over and ball up things generally. Get me perhaps to sign releases—whatever you call the things."

"If Fenella's affairs were not, shall we say, in the healthy state they ought to be, then—yes, possibly her premature death might be, shall we say, fortunate for someone—we will name no names—someone perhaps who could cover his traces more easily if he had a fairly simple person, if I may say so, like yourself to deal with. I will go that far, but I do not wish to speak further on the matter. It would not be equitable to do so."

There was a simple funeral service held in the little church. If I could have stayed away, I would have done so. I hated all those people who were staring at me lining up outside the church. Curious eyes. Greta pulled me through things. I don't think I'd realized until now what a strong, reliable character she was. She made the arrangements, ordered flowers, arranged everything. I understood better now how Ellie had come to depend upon Greta as she had done. There aren't many Gretas in the world.

The people in the church were mostly our neighbors—some, even, that we had hardly known. But I noticed one face that I had seen before, but which I could not at the moment place. When I got back to the house, Carson told me there was someone in the drawing room waiting to see me.

"I can't see anyone today. Send him away. You shouldn't have let him in!"

"Excuse me, sir. He said he was a relation."

"A relation?"

Suddenly I remembered the man I'd seen in the church.

Carson was handing me a card.

It meant nothing to me for a moment. Mr. William R. Pardoe. I turned it over and shook my head. Then I handed it to Greta.

"Do you know by any chance who this is?" I said. "His face seemed familiar, but I couldn't place it. Perhaps it's one of Ellie's friends."

Greta took it from me and looked at it. Then she said,

"Of course."

"Who is it?"

"Uncle Reuben. You remember. Ellie's cousin. She's spoken of him to you, surely?"

I remembered then why the face had seemed familiar to me. Ellie had had several photographs in her sitting room of her various relations carelessly placed about the room. That was why the face had been familiar to me. I had seen it so far only in a photograph.

"I'll come," I said.

I went out of the room and into the drawing room. Mr. Pardoe rose to his feet and said,

"Michael Rogers? You may not know my name, but your wife was my cousin. She called me Uncle Reuben always, but we haven't met, I know. This is the first time I've been over since your marriage."

"Of course I know who you are," I said.

I don't know quite how to describe Reuben Pardoe. He was a big burly man with a large face, wide and rather absent-looking, as though he were thinking of something else. Yet after you had talked to him for a few moments, you got the feeling that he was more on the ball than you would have thought.

"I don't need to tell you how shocked and grieved I was to hear of Ellie's death," he said.

"Let's skip that," I said. "I'm not up to talking about it."

"No, no, I can understand that."

He had a certain sympathetic personality and yet there was something about him that made me vaguely uneasy. I said, as Greta entered,

"You know Miss Andersen?"

"Of course," he said. "How are you, Greta?"

"Not too bad," said Greta. "How long have you been over?"

"Just a week or two. Touring around."

"I have seen you before," I said. On an impulse I went on. "I saw you the other day."

"Really? Where?"

"At an auction sale at a place called Bartington Manor."

"I remember now," he said, "yes, yes, I think I remember your face. You were with a man about sixty with a brown mustache."

"Yes," I said. "A Major Phillpot."

"You seemed in good spirits," he said, "both of you."

"Never better," I said, and repeated with the strange wonder that I always felt, "Never better."

"Of course—at that time you didn't know what had happened. That was the date of the accident, wasn't it?"

"We were expecting," I said, "Ellie to join us for lunch."

"Tragic," said Uncle Reuben. "Really tragic . . ."

"I had no idea," I said, "that you were in England. I don't think Ellie had any idea either?" I paused, waiting for what he would tell me.

"No," he said, "I hadn't written. In fact, I didn't know how much time I should have over here, but actually I'd concluded my business earlier than I thought and I was wondering if after the sale I'd have the time to drive over and see you."

"You came over from the States on business?" I asked.

"Well, partly yes and partly no. Cora wanted some advice from me on one or two matters. One concerning this house she's thinking of buying."

It was then that he told me that Cora was in England. Again I said,

"We didn't know that even."

"She was actually staying not far from here that day," he said.

"Near here? Was she in a hotel?"

"No, she was staying with a friend."

"I didn't know she had any friends in this part of the world."

"A woman called—now what was her name?—Hard-something. Hardcastle."

"Claudia Hardcastle?" I was surprised.

"Yes. She was quite a friend of Cora's. Cora knew her when she was in the States. Didn't you know?"

"I know very little," I said. "Very little about the family."

I looked at Greta.

"Did you know that Cora knew Claudia Hardcastle?"

"I don't think I ever heard her speak of her," said Greta. "So that's why Claudia didn't turn up that day."

"Of course," I said, "she was going with you by train to London. You were to meet at Market Chadwell station—"

"Yes—and she wasn't there. She rang up the house just after I'd left. Said some American visitor was turning up unexpectedly and she couldn't leave home."

"I wonder," I said, "if the American visitor could have been Cora."

"Obviously," said Reuben Pardoe. He shook his head. "It all seems so confused," he said. He went on, "I understand the inquest was adjourned."

"Yes," I said.

He drained his cup and got up.

"I won't stay to worry you any more," he said. "If there's anything I can do, I'm staying at the Majestic Hotel in Market Chadwell."

I said I was afraid there wasn't anything he could do, and thanked him. When he had gone away, Greta said,

"What does he want, I wonder? Why did he come over?" And then sharply, "I wish they'd all go back where they belong."

22

THERE WAS NOTHING more for me to do at Gipsy's Acre. I left Greta in charge of the house while I sailed to New York to wind up things there and to take part in what I felt with some dread was going to be the most ghastly gold-plated obsequies for Ellie.

"You're going into the jungle," Greta warned me. "Look after yourself. Don't let them skin you alive."

She was right about that. It was the jungle. I felt it when I got there. I didn't know about jungles—not that kind of jungle. I was out of my depth, and I knew it. I wasn't the hunter; I was the hunted. There were people all around me in the undergrowth gunning for me. Sometimes,

I expect, I imagined things. Sometimes my suspicions were justified. I remember going to the lawyer supplied for me by Mr. Lippincott (a most urbane man who treated me rather as a general practitioner might have done in the medical profession). I had been advised to get rid of certain mining properties to which the title deeds were not too clear.

He asked me who had told me so, and I said it was Stanford Lloyd.

"Well, we must look into it," he said. "A man like Mr. Lloyd ought to know."

He said to me afterward,

"There's nothing wrong with your title deeds, and there is certainly no point in your selling the land in a hurry, as he seems to have advised you. Hang on to it."

I had the feeling then that I'd been right—everybody was gunning for me. They all knew I was a simpleton when it came to finance.

The funeral was splendid and, I thought, quite horrible. Gold-plated, as I had surmised. At the cemetery, masses of flowers, the cemetery itself like a public park and all the trimmings of wealthy mourning expressed in monumental marble. Ellie would have hated it, I was sure of that. But I suppose her family had a certain right to her.

Four days after my arrival in New York, I had news from Kingston Bishop.

The body of old Mrs. Lee had been found in the disused quarry on the far side of the hill. She had been dead some days. There had been accidents there before, and it had been said that the place ought to be fenced in—but nothing had been done. A verdict of accidental death had been brought in, and a further recommendation to the council to fence the place off. In Mrs. Lee's cottage a sum of three hundred pounds had been found hidden under the floor boards, all in one-pound notes.

Major Phillpot had added in a postscript, "I'm sure you will be sorry to hear that Claudia Hardcastle was thrown from her horse and killed out hunting yesterday."

Claudia—killed? I couldn't believe it! It gave me a very nasty jolt. Two people—within a fortnight, killed in a riding accident. It seemed like an almost impossible coincidence.

I don't want to dwell on that time I spent in New York. I was a stranger in an alien atmosphere. I felt all the time that I had to be wary of what I said and what I did. The Ellie that I had known, the Ellie that had belonged peculiarly to me, was not there. I saw her now only as an American girl, heiress to a great fortune, surrounded by friends and connections and distant relatives, one of a family that had lived there for five generations. She had come from there as a comet might have come, visiting my territory.

Now she had gone back to be buried with her own folk, to where her own home was. I was glad to have it that way. I shouldn't have been easy feeling her there in the prim little cemetery at the foot of the pine woods just outside the village. No, I shouldn't have been easy.

"Go back where you belong, Ellie," I said to myself.

Now and again that haunting little tune of the song she used to sing to her guitar came into my mind. I remembered her fingers gently twanging the strings.

Every Morn and every Night
Some are born to Sweet Delight

and I thought, "That was true of you. You were born to Sweet Delight. You had Sweet Delight there at Gipsy's Acre. Only it didn't last very long. Now it's over. You've come back to where perhaps there wasn't much delight, where you weren't happy. But you're at home here, anyway. You're among your own folk."

I wondered suddenly where I should be when the time came for me to die. Gipsy's Acre? It could be. My mother would come and see me laid in my grave—if she wasn't dead already. But I couldn't think of my mother being dead. I could think more easily of death for myself. Yes, she'd come and see me buried. Perhaps the sternness of her face wouldn't relax. I took my thoughts away from her. I didn't want to think of her. I didn't want to go near her or see her.

That last isn't quite true. It wasn't a question of seeing her. It was always with my mother a question of her seeing me, of her eyes looking through me, of an anxiety that swept out like a miasma embracing me. I thought, "Mothers are the devil! Why have they got to brood over their children? Why do they feel they know all about their children? They don't. They don't! She ought to be proud of me, happy for me, happy for the wonderful life that I've achieved. She ought—" Then I wrenched my thoughts away from her again.

How long was I over in the States? I can't even remember. It seemed an age of walking warily, of being watched by people with false smiles and enmity in their eyes. I said to myself every day, "I've got to get through this. I've got to get through this—and then—" Those were the two words I used. Used in my own mind, I mean. I used them every day several times. And then— They were the two words of the future. I used them in the same way that I had once used those other two words—I want . . .

Everyone went out of their way to be nice to me because I was rich! Under the terms of Ellie's will, I was an extremely rich man. It felt very odd. I had investments I didn't understand—shares, stocks, property. And I didn't know in the least what to do with them all.

The day before I went back to England, I had a long conversation with Mr. Lippincott. I always thought of him like that in my mind—as Mr. Lippincott. He'd never become Uncle Andrew to me. I told him that I thought of withdrawing the charge of my investments from Stanford Lloyd.

"Indeed!" His grizzled eyebrows rose. He looked at me with his shrewd eyes and his poker face and I wondered what exactly his "indeed" meant.

"Do you think it's all right to do that?" I asked anxiously.

"You have reasons, I presume?"

"No," I said, "I haven't got reasons. A feeling, that's all. I suppose I can say anything to you?"

"The communication will be privileged, naturally."

"All right," I said. "I just feel that he's a crook!"

"Ah." Mr. Lippincott looked interested. "Yes, I should say your instinct was possibly sound."

So I knew then that I was right. Stanford Lloyd had been playing hanky-panky with Ellie's bonds and investments and all the rest of it. I signed a power of attorney and gave it to Andrew Lippincott.

"You're willing," I said, "to accept it?"

"As far as financial matters are concerned," said Mr. Lippincott, "you can trust me absolutely. I will do my best for you in that respect. I don't think you will have any reason to complain of my stewardship."

I wondered exactly what he meant by that. He meant something. I think he meant that he didn't like me, had never liked me, but financially he would do his best for me because I had been Ellie's husband. I signed all necessary papers. He asked me how I was going back to England. Flying? I said no, I wasn't flying, I was going by sea. "I've got to have a little time to myself," I said. "I think a sea voyage will do me good."

"And you are going back to take up your residence—where?"

"Gipsy's Acre," I said.

"Ah. You propose to live there."

"Yes," I said.

"I thought perhaps you might have put it on the market for sale."

"No," I said, and the no came out rather stronger than I meant. I wasn't going to part with Gipsy's Acre. Gipsy's Acre had been part of my dream—the dream that I'd cherished since I'd been a callow boy.

"Is anybody looking after it while you have been away in the States?"

I said that I'd left Greta Andersen in charge.

"Ah," said Mr. Lippincott, "yes. Greta."

He meant something in the way he said "Greta" but I didn't take him up on it. If he disliked her, he disliked her. He always had. It left an awkward pause, then I changed my mind. I felt that I'd got to say something.

"She was very good to Ellie," I said. "She nursed her when she was ill. She came and lived with us and looked after Ellie. I—I can't be grateful enough to her. I'd like you to understand that. You don't know what she's been like. You don't know how she helped and did everything after Ellie was killed. I don't know what I'd have done without her."

"Quite so, quite so," said Mr. Lippincott. He sounded drier than you could possibly imagine.

"So you see I owe her a lot."

"A very competent girl," said Mr. Lippincott.

I got up and said good-by and I thanked him.

"You have nothing for which to thank me," said Mr. Lippincott, dry as ever.

He added, "I wrote you a short letter. I have sent it by air mail to Gipsy's Acre. If you are going by sea, you will probably find it waiting there on arrival." Then he said, "Have a good voyage."

So that was that.

When I got back to my hotel, I found a cable. It asked me to come to a hospital in California. It said a friend of mine, Rudolf Santonix, had asked for me, he had not long to live and he wished to see me before he died.

I changed my passage to a later boat and flew to San Francisco. He wasn't dead yet, but he was sinking very fast. They doubted, they said, if he would recover consciousness before he died, but he had asked for me very urgently. I sat there in that hospital room watching him, watching what looked like a shell of the man I knew. He'd always looked ill, he'd always had a kind of queer transparency about him, a delicacy, a frailness. He lay now looking a deadly, waxen figure. I sat there thinking, "I wish he'd speak to me. I wish he'd say something. Just something before he dies."

I felt so alone, so horribly alone. I'd escaped from enemies now, I'd got to a friend—my only friend, really. He was the only person who knew anything about me, except Mum, but I didn't want to think of Mum.

Once or twice I spoke to a nurse, asked her if there wasn't anything they could do, but she shook her head and said noncommittally,

"He might recover consciousness or might not."

I sat there. And then at last he stirred and sighed. The nurse raised him up very gently. He looked at me but I didn't know whether he recognized me or not. He was just looking at me as though he looked past me and beyond me. Then suddenly a difference came into his eyes. I thought, "He does know me; he does see me." He said something very faintly, and I bent over the bed so as to catch it. But they didn't seem words that had any meaning. Then his body had a sudden spasm and twitch, and he threw his head back and shouted out,

"You damned fool. . . . Why didn't you go the other way?"

Then he just collapsed and died.

I don't know what he meant—or even if he knew himself what he was saying.

So that was the last I saw of Santonix. I wonder if he'd have heard me if I had said anything to him? I'd like to have told him once more that the house he'd built me was the best thing I had in the world—the thing that mattered most to me. Funny that a house could mean that. I suppose it was a sort of symbolism about it. Something you want. Something you want so much that you don't quite know what it is. But he'd known what it was and he'd given it to me. And I'd got it. And I was going home to it.

Going home. That's all I could think about when I got on the boat—that and a deadly tiredness at first. . . . And then a rising tide of happiness oozing up, as it were, from the depths. . . . I was going home. I was going home . . .

> Home is the sailor, home from the sea
> And the hunter home from the hill . . .

23

YES, THAT WAS what I was doing. It was all over now. The last of the fight, the last of the struggle. The last phase of the journey.

It seemed so long ago to the time of my restless youth. The days of "I want, I want." But it wasn't long. Less than a year. . . .

I went over it all—lying there in my bunk and thinking.

Meeting Ellie—our times in Regent's Park—our marriage in the registrar's office. The house—Santonix building it—the house completed.

Mine, all mine. I was me—me—me as I wanted to be—as I'd always wanted to be. I'd got everything I'd wanted, and I was going home to it.

Before I left New York, I'd written one letter and sent it off by air mail to get there ahead of me. I'd written to Phillpot. Somehow I felt that Phillpot would understand, though others mightn't.

It was easier to write than to tell him. Anyway, he'd got to know. Everyone had got to know. Some people probably wouldn't understand, but I thought he would. He'd seen for himself how close Ellie and Greta had been, how Ellie had depended on Greta. I thought he'd realize how I'd come to depend upon her also, how it would be impossible for me to live alone in the house where I'd lived with Ellie unless there was someone there to help me. I don't know if I put it very well. I did my best.

"I'd like you," I wrote, "to be the first one to know. You've been so kind to us, and I think you'll be the only person to understand. I can't face living all alone at Gipsy's Acre. I've been thinking all the time I've been in America and I've decided that as soon as I get home, I'm going to ask Greta to marry me. She's the only person I can really talk to about Ellie, you see. She'll understand. Perhaps she won't marry me, but I think she will. . . . It will make everything as though there were the three of us together still."

I wrote the letter three times before I could get it to express just what I wanted to say. Phillpot ought to get it two days before my return.

I came up on deck as we were approaching England. I looked out as the land came nearer. I thought, "I wish Santonix was with me." I did wish it. I wished he could know how everything was all coming true—everything I'd planned—everything I'd thought—everything I'd wanted.

I'd shaken off America, I'd shaken off the crooks and the sycophants and all the whole lot of them whom I hated and whom I was pretty sure hated me and looked down on me for being so low-class! I was coming back in triumph. I was coming back to the pine trees and the curling, dangerous road that made its way up through Gipsy's Acre to the house on the hilltop. My house! I was coming back to the two things I wanted. My house—the house that I'd dreamed of, that I'd planned, that I'd wanted above everything. That and a wonderful woman. . . . I'd known always that I'd meet one day a wonderful woman. I had met her. I'd seen her and she'd seen me. We'd come together. A wonderful woman. I'd known the moment I saw her that

I belonged to her, belonged to her absolutely and for always. I was hers. And now—at last—I was going to her.

Nobody saw me arrive at Kingston Bishop. It was almost dark and I came by train and I walked from the station, taking a roundabout side road. I didn't want to meet any of the people in the village. Not that night. . . .

The sun had set when I came up the road to Gipsy's Acre. I'd told Greta the time I'd arrive. She was up there in the house waiting for me. At last! We'd done with subterfuges now and all the pretenses—the pretense of disliking her—I thought now, laughing to myself, of the part I'd played, a part I'd played carefully right from the beginning. Disliking Greta, not wanting her to come and stay with Ellie. Yes, I'd been very careful. Everyone must have been taken in by that pretense. I remembered the quarrel we'd faked up so that Ellie should overhear it.

Greta had known me for what I was the first moment we met. We'd never had any silly illusions about each other. She had the same kind of mind, the same kind of desires as I had. We wanted the world, nothing less! We wanted to be on top of the world. We wanted to fulfill every ambition. We wanted to have everything, deny ourselves nothing. I remembered how I'd poured out my heart to her when I first met her in Hamburg, telling my frenzied desire for things. I hadn't got to conceal my inordinate greed for life from Greta. She has the same greed herself. She said,

"For all you want out of life, you've got to have money."

"Yes," I said, "and I don't see how I'm going to get it."

"No," said Greta, "you won't get it by hard work. You're not the kind."

"Work!" I said. "I'd have to work for years! I don't want to wait. I don't want to be middle-aged." I said, "You know the story about that chap Schliemann, how he worked, toiled, and made a fortune so that he could have his life's dream come true and go to Troy and dig it up and find the graves of Troy. He got his dream, but he had to wait till he was forty. But I don't want to wait till I'm a middle-aged man. Old. One foot in the grave. I want it now when I'm young and strong. You do too, don't you?" I said.

"Yes. And I know the way you can do it. It's easy. I wonder you haven't thought of it already. You can get girls easily enough, can't you? I can see that. I can feel it."

"Do you think I care about girls—or ever have really? There's only one girl I want," I said. "You. And you know that. I belong to you. I knew it the moment I saw you. I knew always that I'd meet someone like you. And I have. I belong to you."

"Yes," said Greta, "I think you do."

"We both want the same things out of life," I said.

"I tell you it's easy," said Greta. "Easy. All you've got to do is to marry a rich girl—one of the richest girls in the world. I can put you in the way of doing that."

"Don't be fantastic," I said.

"It's not fantastic; it'll be easy."

"No," I said, "that's no good to me. I don't want to be the husband of a rich wife. She'll buy me things and we'll do things and she'll keep me in a golden cage, but that's not what I want. I don't want to be a tied-up slave."

"You needn't be. It's the sort of thing that needn't last for long. Just long enough. Wives do die, you know."

I stared at her.

"Now you're shocked," she said.

"No," I said, "I'm not shocked."

"I thought you wouldn't be. I thought perhaps already—?" She looked at me inquiringly, but I wasn't going to answer that. I had still some self-preservation left. There are some secrets one doesn't want anyone to know. Not that they were much in the way of secrets, but I didn't like to think of them. I didn't like to think of the first one. Silly, though. Puerile. Nothing that mattered. I had had a boy's passion for a classy wrist watch that a boy—a friend of mine at school—had been given. I wanted it. I wanted it badly. It had cost a lot of money. A rich godfather had given it to him. Yes, I wanted that, but I didn't think I'd ever have a chance of getting it. Then there was the day we went skating together. The ice wasn't strong enough to bear. Not that we thought of it beforehand. It just happened. The ice cracked. I skated across to him. He was hanging on. He had gone through a hole and he was hanging onto the ice which was cutting his hands. I went across to pull him out, of course, but just as I got there, I saw the glint of the wrist watch. I thought, "Supposing he goes under and drowns." I thought how easy it would be. . . .

It seemed almost unconsciously, I think, that I unfastened the strap, grabbed the watch and pushed his head under instead of trying to pull him out. . . . Just held his head under. He couldn't struggle much; he was under the ice. People saw and came toward us. They thought I was trying to pull him out! They got him out in due course, with some difficulty. They tried artificial respiration on him, but it was too late. I hid my treasure away in a special place where I kept things now and then—things I didn't want Mum to see because she'd ask me where I got them. She came across that watch one day when she was fooling about with my socks. Asked me if that wasn't Pete's watch? I said of course it wasn't—it was one I'd swapped with a boy at school.

I was always nervous with Mum—I always felt she knew too much about me. I was nervous with her when she found the watch. She suspected, I think. She couldn't know, of course. Nobody knew. But she used to look at me—in a funny way. Everybody thought I'd tried to rescue Pete. I don't think she ever thought so. I think she knew. She didn't want to know, but her trouble was that she knew too much about me. I felt a bit guilty myself sometimes, but it wore off fairly soon.

And then later on, when I was in camp—it was during our military training time—chap called Ed and I had been to a sort of gambling place. I'd had no luck at all, lost everything I had, but Ed had won a packet. He changed his chips, and he and I were coming home and he was stuffed up with notes. His pockets were bulged with them. Then a couple of toughs came round the corner and went for us. They were pretty handy with the flick knives they'd got. I got a cut in the arm, but Ed got a proper sort of stab. He went down under it. Then there was a noise of people coming. The toughs hooked it. I could see that if I was quick . . . I was quick! My reflexes are pretty good—I wrapped a handkerchief round my hand and I pulled out the knife from Ed's wound and I stuck the knife in again a couple of times in better places. He gave a gasp and passed out. I was scared, of course—scared for a second or two, and then I knew it was going to be all right. So I felt—well—naturally I felt proud of myself for thinking and acting quick! I thought, "Poor old Ed; he always was a fool." It took me no time at all to transfer those notes to my own pocket! Nothing like having quick reflexes, seizing your opportunity. The trouble is the opportunities don't come very often. Some people, I suppose, get scared when they know they've killed someone. But I wasn't scared. Not this time.

Mind you, it's not a thing you want to do too often. Not unless it might be really worth your while. I don't know how Greta sensed that about me. But she'd known. I don't mean that she'd known that I'd actually killed a couple of people. But I think she knew the idea of killing wouldn't shock me or upset me. I said,

"What's all this fantastic story, Greta?"

She said, "I am in a position to help you. I can bring you in touch with one of the richest girls in America. I more or less look after her. I live with her. I have a lot of influence over her."

"Do you think she'd look at someone like me?" I said. I didn't believe it for a moment. Why should a rich girl, who could have her pick of any attractive, sexy man she liked, go for me?

"You've got a lot of sex appeal," said Greta. "Girls go for you, don't they?"

I grinned and said I didn't do too badly.

"She's never had that kind of thing. She's been looked after too well. The only young men she's been allowed to meet are conventional kinds—bankers' sons, tycoons' sons. She's groomed to make a good marriage in the moneyed class. They're terrified of her meeting handsome foreigners who might be after her money. But naturally she's keener on people like that. They'd be new to her, something she's never seen before. You've got to make a big play for her. You've got to fall in love with her at first sight and sweep her off her feet! It'll be easy enough. She's never had anyone to make a real sexy approach to her. You could do it."

"I could try," I said doubtfully.

"We could set it up," said Greta.

"Her family would step in and stop it."

"No, they wouldn't," said Greta. "They wouldn't know anything about it. Not until it was too late. Not until you'd got married secretly."

"So that's your idea?"

So we talked about it. We planned. Not in detail, mind you. Greta went back to America, but she kept in touch with me. I went on with various jobs. I'd told her about Gipsy's Acre and that I wanted it, and she said that was just fine for setting up a romantic story. We laid our plans so that my meeting with Ellie would take place there. Greta would work Ellie up about having a house in England and getting away from her family as soon as she came of age.

Oh, yes, we set it up. Greta was a great planner. I don't think I could have planned it, but I knew I could play my part all right. I'd always enjoyed playing a part. And so that's how it happened. That's how I met Ellie.

It was fun, all of it. Mad fun because, of course, there was always a risk—there was always a danger that it wouldn't come off. The thing that made me really nervous were the times that I had to meet Greta. I had to be sure, you see, that I never gave myself away by looking at Greta. I tried not to look at her. We agreed it was best that I should take a dislike to her, pretend jealousy of her. I carried that out all right. I remember the day she came down to stay. We staged a quarrel—a quarrel that Ellie could hear. I don't know whether we overdid it a bit. I don't think so. Sometimes I was nervous that Ellie might guess or something, but I don't think she did. I don't know. I don't know, really. I never did know about Ellie.

It was very easy to make love to Ellie. She was very sweet. Yes, she was really sweet. Just sometimes I was afraid of her because she did things without telling me. And she knew things that I never dreamt she knew. But she loved me. Yes, she loved me. Sometimes—I think I loved her too. . . .

I don't mean it was ever like Greta. Greta was the woman I belonged to. She was sex personified. I was mad for her, and I had to hold myself in. Ellie was something different. I enjoyed living with her, you know. Yes, that sounds very queer now I think back to it. I enjoyed living with her very much.

I'm putting this down now because this is what I was thinking that evening when I arrived back from America. When I arrived back on top of the world, having got all I'd longed for in spite of the risks, in spite of the dangers, in spite of having done a pretty good murder, though I say it myself!

Yes, it was a bit tricky, I thought once or twice, but nobody could tell, not the way we'd done it. Now the risks were over, the dangers were over, and here I was coming up to Gipsy's Acre—coming as I'd come up it that day after I'd first seen the poster on the walls and gone up to look at the ruins of the old house. Coming up and rounding the bend—

And then—it was then I saw her. I mean it was then I saw Ellie. Just as I came round the corner of the road in the dangerous place where the accidents happened. She was there in the same place just where she'd been before, standing in the shadow of the fir tree. Just as she'd stood, when she'd started a little as she saw me and I'd started, seeing her. There we'd looked at each other first and I'd come up and spoken to her, played the part of the young man who's fallen suddenly in love. Played it jolly well, too! Oh, I tell you I'm a fine actor!

But I hadn't expected to see her now. . . . I mean, I couldn't see her now, could I? But I was seeing her. . . . She was looking—looking straight at me. Only—there was something that frightened me—something that frightened me very much. It was, you see, just as though she didn't see me—I mean I knew she couldn't really be there. I knew she was dead—but I saw her. She was dead and her body was buried in the cemetery in the U.S.A. But all the same, she was standing under the fir tree and she was looking at me. No, not at me. She was looking as though she expected to see me, and there was love in her face—the same love that I had seen one day—one day when she'd been plucking the strings of her guitar—that day when she'd said to me, "What were you thinking of?" and I said, "Why do you ask me?" and she said, "You were looking at me as though you loved me." I'd said something silly like "Of course I love you."

I stopped dead. I stopped dead there in the road. I was shaking. I said out loud,

"Ellie."

She didn't move; she just stayed there looking . . . looking straight through me. That's what frightened me because I knew if I thought for a minute, I'd know why she didn't see me, and I didn't want to know. No, I didn't want to know that. I was quite sure that I didn't want to know that. Looking straight at the place where I was—not seeing me. I ran then. I ran like a coward up the rest of the road to where the lights were shining in my house, until I pulled myself out of the silly panic that I was in. This was my triumph. I'd got home. I was the hunter home from the hills, back to my house, back to the other thing that I'd wanted more than anything in the world, to the wonderful woman whom I belonged to body and soul.

And now we'd get married and we'd live in the House. We'd get all we'd played for! We'd won— Won hands down!

The door wasn't latched. I went in, stamping my feet, and through the open door of the library. And there was Greta standing by the window waiting for me. She was glorious. She was the most glorious and the most lovely thing I'd ever seen. She was like a Brunnehilde, a super Valkyrie with shining golden hair. She smelt and looked and tasted of sex. We'd denied ourselves so long except for occasional brief meetings up in the Folly.

I came straight into her arms, a sailor home from the sea to where he belonged. Yes, it was one of the most wonderful moments of my life.

Presently we came down to earth. I sat down and she shoved a small pile of letters toward me. I picked out almost automatically one with an American stamp. It was the air mail letter from Lippincott. I wondered what he'd put in it, why he'd had to write me a letter?

"Well," said Greta with a deep, satisfied sigh, "we've made it."

"V-day all right," I said.

We both laughed, laughed wildly. There was champagne on the table. I opened it and we drank to each other.

"This place is wonderful," I said, looking round. "It's more beautiful than I remember it. Santonix— But I haven't told you. Santonix is dead."

"Oh, dear," said Greta, "what a pity. So he really was ill?"

"Of course he was ill. I never wanted to think so. I went and saw him when he was dying."

Greta gave a little shiver.

"I shouldn't like to do that. Did he say anything?"

"Not really. He said I was a damned fool—I ought to have gone the other way."

"What did he mean—what way?"

"I don't know what he meant," I said. "I suppose he was delirious. Didn't know what he was talking about."

"Well, this house is a fine monument to his memory," said Greta. "I think we'll stick on to it, don't you?"

I stared at her. "Of course. Do you think I'm going to live anywhere else?"

"We can't live here all the time," said Greta. "Not all the year round. Buried in a hole like this village?"

"But it's where I want to live—it's where I always meant to live."

"Yes, of course. But after all, Mike, we've got all the money in the world. We can go anywhere! We can go all over the Continent—we'll go on safari in Africa. We'll have adventures. We'll go and look for things—exciting pictures. We'll go to the Angkor Vat. Don't you want to have an adventurous life?"

"Well, I suppose so . . . But we'll always come back here, won't we?"

I had a queer feeling—a queer feeling that something had gone wrong somewhere. That's all I'd ever thought of. My house and Greta. I hadn't wanted anything else. But she did. I saw that. She was just beginning. Beginning to want things. Beginning to know she could have them. I had a sudden cruel foreboding. I began to shiver.

"What's the matter with you, Mike? You're shivering. Have you caught a cold or something?"

"It's not that," I said.

"What's happened, Mike?"

"I saw Ellie," I said.

"What do you mean, you saw Ellie?"

"As I was walking up the road, I turned the corner and there she was, standing under a fir tree, looking at—I mean looking toward me."

Greta stared.

"Don't be ridiculous. You—you imagined things."

"Perhaps one does imagine things. This is Gipsy's Acre, after all. Ellie was there, all right, looking—looking quite happy. Just like herself, as though she'd—she'd always been there and was always going to be there."

"Mike!" Greta took hold of my shoulder. She shook me. "Mike, don't say things like that. Had you been drinking before you got here?"

"No, I waited till I got here to you. I knew you'd have champagne waiting for us."

"Well, let's forget Ellie and drink to ourselves."

"It was Ellie," I said obstinately.

"Of course it wasn't Ellie! It was just a trick of the light—something like that."

"It was Ellie, and she was standing there. She was looking—looking for me and at me. But she couldn't see me. Greta, she couldn't see me." My voice rose. "And I know why. I know why she couldn't see me."

"What do you mean?"

It was then that I whispered for the first time under my breath,

"Because that wasn't me. I wasn't there. There was nothing for her to see but Endless Night." Then I shouted out in a panic-stricken voice, "Some are born to Sweet Delight, some are born to Sweet Delight and some are born to Endless Night. Me, Greta, me.

"Do you remember, Greta," I said, "how she sat on that sofa? She used to play that song on her guitar, singing it in her gentle voice. You must remember.

"'*Every Night and every Morn,*'" I sang it under my breath, "'*Some to Misery are born. Every Morn and every Night some are born to Sweet Delight.*' That's Ellie, Greta. She was born to sweet delight. '*Some are born to Sweet Delight, Some are born to Endless Night.*' That's what Mum knew about me. She knew I was born to endless night. I hadn't got there yet. And Santonix knew. He knew I was heading that way. But it mightn't have happened. There was just a moment, just one moment, the time Ellie sang that song. I could have been quite happy, couldn't I, really, married to Ellie? I could have gone on being married to Ellie."

"No, you couldn't," said Greta. "I never thought you were the type of person who lost your nerve, Mike." She shook me roughly by the shoulder again. "Wake up."

I stared at her.

"I'm sorry, Greta. What have I been saying?"

"I suppose they got you down over there in the States. But you did all right, didn't you? I mean, all the investments are all right?"

"Everything's fixed," I said. "Everything's fixed for our future. Our glorious, glorious future."

"You speak very queerly. I'd like to know what Lippincott says in his letter."

I pulled his letter toward me and opened it. There was nothing inside except a cutting from a paper—not a new cutting. It was old and rather rubbed. I stared down at it. It was a picture of a street. I recognized the street, with rather a grand building in the background. It was a street in Hamburg with some people coming toward the photographer—two people in the forefront walking arm in arm. They were Greta and myself. So Lippincott had known. He'd known all along that I already knew Greta. Somebody must have sent him this cutting sometime, probably with no nefarious intention. Just amused perhaps to recognize Miss Greta Andersen walking along the streets of Hamburg. He had known I knew Greta and I remembered how particularly he had asked me whether I had met or not met Greta Andersen. I had denied it, of course, but he'd known I was lying. It must have begun his suspicion of me.

I was suddenly afraid of Lippincott. He couldn't suspect, of course, that I'd killed Ellie. He suspected something, though. Perhaps he suspected even that.

"Look," I said to Greta, "he knew we knew each other. He's known it all along. I've always hated that old fox and he's always hated you," I said. "When he knows that we're going to marry, he'll suspect." But then I knew that Lippincott had certainly suspected that Greta and I were going to marry, he suspected that we knew each other, he suspected perhaps that we were lovers.

"Mike, will you stop being a panic-stricken rabbit. Yes, that's what I said—a panic-stricken rabbit. I admired you. I've always admired you. But now you're falling to pieces. You're afraid of everyone."

"Don't say that to me."

"Well, it's true."

"*Endless night.*"

I couldn't think of anything else to say. I was still wondering just what it meant. Endless night. It meant blackness. It meant that I wasn't there to be seen. I could see the dead, but the dead couldn't see me although I was living. They couldn't see me because I wasn't really there. The man who loved Ellie wasn't really there. He'd entered of his own accord into endless night. I bent my head lower toward the ground.

"*Endless night,*" I said again.

"Stop saying that," Greta screamed. "Stand up! Be a man, Mike. Don't give in to this absurd superstitious fancy."

"How can I help it?" I said. "I've sold my soul to Gipsy's Acre, haven't I? Gipsy's Acre's never been safe. It's never been safe for anyone. It wasn't safe for Ellie and it isn't safe for me. Perhaps it isn't safe for you."

"What do you mean?"

I got up. I went toward her. I loved her. Yes, I loved her still with a last tense sexual desire. But love, hate, desire—aren't they all the same? Three in one and one in three. I could never have hated Ellie, but I hated Greta. I enjoyed hating her. I hated her with all my heart and with a leaping joyous wish—I couldn't wait for the safe ways, I didn't want to wait for them. I came nearer to her.

"You filthy bitch!" I said. "You hateful, glorious, golden-haired bitch. You're not safe, Greta. You're not safe from me. Do you understand? I've learned to enjoy—to enjoy killing people. I was excited the day that I knew Ellie had gone out with that horse to her death. I enjoyed myself all the morning because of killing, but I've never got near enough to killing until now. This is different. I want more than just knowing that someone's going to die because of a capsule they swallowed at breakfast time. I want more than pushing an old woman over a quarry. I want to use my hands."

Greta was afraid now. She, whom I'd belonged to ever since I met her that day in Hamburg, met her and gone to pretend illness, to throw up my job, to stay there with her. Yes, I'd belonged to her then, body and soul. I didn't belong to her now. I was myself. I was coming into another kind of kingdom to the one I'd dreamed of.

She was afraid. I loved seeing her afraid and I fastened my hands round her neck. Yes, even now when I am sitting here writing down all about myself (which, mind you, is a very happy thing to do)—to write all about yourself and what you've been through and what you felt and thought and how you deceived everyone—yes, it's wonderful to do. Yes, I was wonderfully happy when I killed Greta. . . .

24

THERE ISN'T REALLY very much to say after that. I mean, things came to a climax there. One forgets, I suppose, that there can't be anything better to follow—that you've had it all. I just sat there for a long time. I don't know when they came. I don't know whether they all came at once. . . . They couldn't have been there all along, because they wouldn't have let me kill Greta. I noticed that God was there first. I don't mean God. I'm confused. I mean Major Phillpot. I'd liked him always; he'd been very nice to me. He was rather like God in some ways, I think—I mean if God had been a human being and not something supernatural—up in the sky somewhere. He was a very fair man—

very fair and kind. He looked after things and people. Tried to do his best for people.

I don't know how much he'd known about me. I remember the curious way he looked at me that morning in the sale room when he said that I was "fey." I wonder why he thought I happened to be fey that day?

Then when we were there with that little crumpled heap on the ground that was Ellie in her riding habit. . . . I wonder if he knew then or had some idea that I'd had something to do with it?

After Greta's death, as I say, I just sat there in my chair, staring down at my champagne glass. It was empty. Everything was very empty—very empty indeed. There was just one light that we'd switched on, Greta and I, but it was in the corner. It didn't give much light, and the sun—I think the sun must have set a long time ago. I just sat there and wondered what was going to happen next with a sort of dull wonder.

Then, I suppose, the people began coming. Perhaps a lot of people came at once. They came very quietly, if so, or else I wasn't hearing or noticing anybody.

Perhaps if Santonix had been there, he would have told me what to do. Santonix was dead. He'd gone a different way to my way, so he wouldn't be any help. Nobody really would be any help.

After a bit I noticed Dr. Shaw. He was so quiet I hardly knew he was there at first. He was sitting quite near me, just waiting for something. After a while I thought he was waiting for me to speak. I said to him,

"I've come home."

There were one or two other people moving somewhere behind him. They seemed to be waiting—to be waiting for something that he was going to do.

"Greta's dead," I said. "I killed her. I expect you'd better take the body away, hadn't you?"

Somebody somewhere let off a flash bulb. It must have been a police photographer photographing the body. Dr. Shaw turned his head and said sharply,

"Not yet."

He turned his head round back to me again. I leaned toward him and said,

"I saw Ellie tonight."

"Did you? Where?"

"Outside standing under a fir tree. It was the place I first saw her, you know." I paused a moment and then said, "She didn't see me. . . .

She couldn't see me because I wasn't there." And after a while I said, "That upset me. It upset me very much."

Dr. Shaw said, "It was in the capsule, wasn't it? Cyanide in that capsule? That's what you gave Ellie that morning?"

"It was for her hay fever," I said; "she always took a capsule as a preventive against her allergy when she went riding. Greta and I fixed up one or two of the capsules with wasp stuff from the garden shed and joined them together again. We did it up in the Folly. Smart, wasn't it?" And I laughed. It was an odd sort of laugh. I heard it myself. It was more like a queer little giggle. I said, "You'd examined all the things she took, hadn't you, when you came to see her ankle? Sleeping pills, the allergy capsules, and they were all quite all right, weren't they? No harm in any of them."

"No harm," said Dr. Shaw. "They were quite innocent."

"That was rather clever, really, wasn't it?" I said.

"You've been quite clever, yes, but not clever enough."

"All the same, I don't see how you found out."

"We found out when there was a second death—the death you didn't mean to happen."

"Claudia Hardcastle?"

"Yes. She died the same way as Ellie did. She fell from her horse in the hunting field. Claudia was a healthy girl, too, but she just fell from her horse and died. The time wasn't so long there, you see. They picked her up almost at once and there was still the smell of cyanide to go by. If she'd lain in the open air like Ellie for a couple of hours, there'd have been nothing—nothing to smell, nothing to find. I don't see how Claudia got the capsule, though. Unless you'd left one behind in the Folly. Claudia used to go to the Folly sometimes. Her fingerprints were there and she dropped a lighter there."

"We must have been careless. Filling them was rather tricky."

Then I said,

"You suspected I had something to do with Ellie's death, didn't you? All of you?" I looked round at the shadowy figures. "Perhaps all of you."

"Very often one knows. But I wasn't sure whether we'd be able to do anything about it."

"You ought to caution me," I said reprovingly.

"I'm not a police officer," said Dr. Shaw.

"What are you then?"

"I'm a doctor."

"I don't need a doctor," I said.

"That remains to be seen."

I looked at Phillpot then, and I said,

"What are you doing? Come here to judge me, to preside at my trial?"

"I'm only a justice of the peace," he said. "I'm here as a friend."

"A friend of mine?" That startled me.

"A friend of Ellie's," he said.

I didn't understand. None of it made sense to me, but I couldn't help feeling rather important. All of them there! Police and doctors, Shaw and Phillpot, who was a busy man in his way. The whole thing was very complicated. I began to lose count of things. I was very tired, you see. I used to get tired suddenly and go to sleep . . .

And all the coming and going. People came to see me,—all sorts of people. Lawyers, a solicitor, I think, and another kind of lawyer with him and doctors. Several doctors. They bothered me and I didn't want to answer them.

One of them kept asking me if there was anything I wanted. I said there was. I said there was only one thing I wanted. I said I wanted a ball pen and a lot of paper. I wanted, you see, to write down all about it, how it all came to happen. I wanted to tell them what I'd felt, what I'd thought. The more I thought about myself, the more interesting I thought it would be to everybody. Because I was interesting. I was a really interesting person and I'd done interesting things.

The doctors—one doctor, anyway—seemed to think it was a good idea. I said,

"You always let people make a statement, so why can't I write my statement out? Someday, perhaps, everybody can read it."

They let me do it. I couldn't write very long on end. I used to get tired. Somebody used a phrase like "diminished responsibility," and somebody else disagreed. All sorts of things you hear. Sometimes they don't think you're even listening. Then I had to appear in court and I wanted them to fetch me my best suit because I had to make a good figure there. It seemed they had had detectives watching me for some time. Those new servants. I think they'd been engaged or put on my trail by Lippincott. They found out too many things about me and Greta. Funny, after she was dead, I never thought of Greta much. . . . After I'd killed her, she didn't seem to matter any more.

I tried to bring back the splendid triumphant feeling that I'd had when I strangled her. But even that was gone away. . . .

They brought my mother to see me quite suddenly one day. There she was looking at me from the doorway. She didn't look as anxious as she used to look. I think all she looked now was sad. She hadn't much to say and nor had I. All she said was,

"I tried, Mike. I tried very hard to keep you safe. I failed. I was always afraid that I should fail."

I said, "All right, Mum, it wasn't your fault. I chose to go the way I wanted."

And I thought suddenly, "That's what Santonix said. He was afraid for me, too. He hadn't been able to do anything either. Nobody could have done anything—except perhaps I myself. . . . I don't know. I'm not sure. But every now and then I remember—I remember that day when Ellie said to me, "What are you thinking of when you look at me like that?" and I said, "Like what?" She said, "As though you loved me." I suppose in a way I did love her. I could have loved her. She was so sweet, Ellie. Sweet delight . . .

I suppose the trouble with me was that I wanted things too much, always. Wanted them, too, the easy way, the greedy way.

That first time, that first day I came to Gipsy's Acre and met Ellie. As we were going down the road again, we met Esther. It put it into my head that day, the warning she gave Ellie, put it in my head to pay her. I knew she was the kind would do anything for money. I'd pay her. She'd start warning Ellie and frightening her, making her feel that she was in danger. I thought it might make it seem more possible then that Ellie had died from shock. That first day, I know now, I'm sure of it, Esther was really frightened. She was really frightened for Ellie. She warned her, warned her to go away, to have nothing to do with Gipsy's Acre. She was warning her, of course, to have nothing to do with me. I didn't understand that. Ellie didn't understand either.

Was it me Ellie was afraid of? I think it must have been, though she didn't know it herself. She knew there was something threatening her, she knew there was danger. Santonix knew the evil in me, too, just like my mother. Perhaps all three of them knew. Ellie knew but she didn't mind, she never minded. It's odd, very odd. I know now. We were very happy together. Yes, very happy. I wish I'd known then that we were happy. . . . I had my chance. Perhaps everyone has a chance. I—turned my back on it.

It seems odd, doesn't it, that Greta doesn't matter at all?

And even my beautiful house doesn't matter.

Only Ellie . . . And Ellie can never find me again—Endless Night . . . That's the end of my story.

In my end is my beginning—that's what people are always saying. But what does it mean?

And just where does my story begin? I must try and think. . . .

NORMAN AND THE KILLER

by Joyce Carol Oates

BECAUSE HE WAS an ordinary man, whose reflection in mirrors and in incidental windows could have belonged to anyone, Norman had never thought of himself as involved in anything that could attract attention. He had no interest in going to see accidents or fires or other disasters because he would be pushed around by the crowd and would not complain, and because he had no heart to peer in, there, at the very center of the jostling, to see the exposed bleeding flesh suddenly catapulted out of the usual channels of life. Because he was a gentle man, a shy man, no longer exactly young, whose life had attached itself gently to his family, he was surprised at the professional hardness with which he was able to meet customers in the clothing store he managed, and at the violence of the love he was suffering through for a woman his brother-in-law had introduced him to. In his youth he had read much and was able to appreciate the spiritual hardness of the heroes of great fiction, who seemed to him to walk upon ropes stretched over nothing, dazzling and performing endlessly, without fear of death. Their absolution of their humanity made them heroes and for this Norman envied them but could not believe in them; they told him nothing about himself.

The young woman's name was Ellen and she too had read much in her youth, which her dark opaque eyes suggested had been an extension of the life she now led, sternly bleak and self-satisfied, a loneliness that had to be respected because it had been her own choice. She had been married for several years, in her early twenties, but of this Norman did not allow himself to think. He often frightened himself at the anxiety he felt for her: his desperation to protect her from whatever startled her eyes, whatever drew her mind away from him as if he were no more than an accidental accomplice to the caprices of her memory, calculated to remind her always of other evenings, other years. Yet he knew he had no right to that desperation, for she did not belong to him. At times he disliked her for her power over him, but most of the time, during the long identical days at the store, his love for this woman—whom he did not really know—was so absurdly great as to overwhelm him, threaten him with an obscure, inexplicable violence, something that might have been building up in him through the years while he had lived at home, a child grown into a man without anyone really noticing. Waking each morning in his old room, in the old house, he would smell resentfully the odors of breakfast being cooked downstairs and would think that, if he did not marry Ellen, he would wake to this every morning for the rest of his life.

One afternoon they drove out of the city to a summer playhouse. The drive took two hours, and Norman was pleased at Ellen's friendliness. She spoke of the playhouse, some actors she knew, and this made him think idly that she was to him like the women he had been seeing in movies all his life: ethereal and majestic, following a script he did not know, could not anticipate, yet smiling out of the very graciousness of their own near-beauty, welcoming his admiration while not exactly acknowledging it. She wore white; the self-conscious pose of her profile distracted him from the road. She was talking now of her job. Norman thought of marrying her, of living with her, but at this his face flinched, for it seemed impossible that this should ever be; his very reflection, glancing down at him out of the rear-view mirror, the dusty reflection of a rather heavy, polite, stern face, with wisps of damp dark hair curled down on his forehead, caught his eye as if he were sharing a secret with it, a secret of perplexed failure. "I may have to leave this job, after six years," she said. He glanced over at her. "There are complications," she said.

He turned into a filling station to get gas. He did not want to ask her about these complications, but he knew she was anxious to continue. In the bright glare from the sun she looked younger than she was; her youth had always seemed to Norman like a weapon. They waited for the man to put in the gas. "Always complications, involvements," she said. "Personal relationships start off so cleanly but then become too involved. Even business relationships. . . ." She smirked at something, some memory; for a moment her face was unfamiliar, her nose sharp, her eyes darker with the intensity of a bemused unpleasant thought. Norman, unhappy, turned to pay the station attendant. He peered up at a man his own age, of moderate height, dressed in greasy clothes; the man's face was smeared with dirt and perspiration. "Hot day," said the man, with a smirk something like Ellen's.

Norman, staring at him, felt his heart begin to pound absurdly. The man's face was familiar, unmistakable. For an instant they stared at each other. The man licked his lips, a stout strong man yet a little startled by Norman's look, and turned away. Norman stared at his back. He wanted to open the door and get out, do something. Beside him Ellen was talking, he could not understand her. Finally she touched his arm. "Is something wrong?" she said. "I think I know that man," he said. As soon as he said this something seemed to assure him: he did not know the man, it was impossible, it did not matter. Nothing mattered. "Know him from where?" Ellen said. "I don't know, nothing. It doesn't matter," he said.

The man returned with Norman's change. Norman tried not to look at him, for the intensity of his feeling had alarmed him: he thought of his uncle, now institutionalized, who had been committed at last by his patient wife, an ordinary man who could not stop talking. In that instant, as he first looked at the attendant's face, Norman felt a kinship with that other, lost man, whom he had not thought of for ten years. . . . But he did look at the station attendant's face after all. The man was smiling without enthusiasm, a smile that stretched his lips to show discolored teeth, leaving the rest of his face indifferent. He had a rather plump face, he had obviously gained weight, Norman saw, but still, out of that heavy, dirt-streaked face, another face confronted him, unmistakable. It was the face of a boy, maybe seventeen. "Here y'are, thank you," the man said. He had a dirty rag over one shoulder. It was strange, Norman thought, fumbling for the ignition, that the man had not offered to clean his windshield.

He drove away. His heart was pounding furiously. "Why didn't you ask him if he knew you?" Ellen said. "It seems to mean a lot to you." She sounded resentful, but he knew that if he were to continue she would lose interest. "No, nothing. A mistake," Norman said. Yet his mind flashed and dazzled him: he knew the face, of course, he might have been shuffling through a deck of cards to come to it, through a handful of old snapshots, waiting patiently for it to turn up. "You're driving rather fast," Ellen said. He slowed down. He glanced at his watch and was surprised to see that it was so early. A great block of time seemed to have passed, jerked away from him. Back at the garage, was the man staring after this car, his smile abandoned? Norman looked fiercely at the countryside. He shut his mind, pushed everything away. Aside. He would not think, he would not remember.

They had dinner at a country inn near the theater. It was dim and pretentious, but he saw that Ellen enjoyed it. In her white silk dress and dark necklace she looked clean, harshly clean and young, her shoulders poised against an unfamiliar background of rough-hewn wooden walls decorated with old wrought-iron objects Norman could not have identified. Yet Norman heard himself say, "Did you say you had a brother?" Yes, she had said. Why did he ask that? Why at this moment? She had a brother who lived in Europe, what did it matter? She was always antagonistic about families, friends, any relationships that belonged to the past. Norman wanted to touch her hand, not to comfort her but to ask for help. The darkness of his mind was released, flowing steadily, unhurriedly, and out of that flood of old faces his heartbeat anticipated the anguish of his revelation. "Excuse me," he said, standing. He caught her glance: she was thinking that he behaved strangely, he could not be trusted. He went to the men's room. There, his back against the tiled wall, he rubbed his eyes and waited until the turmoil ceased. He remembered the face now. He knew he had remembered it at once. Now it came clearly, a boy's face, dirty and hard, and rearing behind it a gray March morning, an indifferent mottled sky. "My God," Norman said aloud. He wanted to rush back to Ellen as if he had something joyous to tell her. But his legs were weak; he reached out to get his balance. Or he would go to a telephone. He would telephone the police. And his father—but his father was dead, had been dead for years. He felt strangely peaceful; something might have been decided. When he returned to their table, where this attractive young woman awaited him, concerned for him, he felt his fingers twitch as if he wanted to reach out to embrace her, to have her draw him to her so that he would no longer need to think.

One Saturday afternoon when he was fifteen Norman and his brother Jack were coming home from a movie. It was about four-thirty: late winter, the day already ending, a chill bleak wind. The Technicolor of the movie had dazzled Norman's eyes, so that the warehouses they passed now seemed to him unsubstantial and deceptive, not remnants of a world but anticipations of a fuller, greater world he would grow into. Invisible behind the vision of that movie had been flights of music, but here there was no music, only their hurrying footsteps. Jack, at seventeen, was not much taller than Norman, both were small for their ages, with meek, dark defensive faces. There were other boys Norman preferred to be with—even his younger brother—but Jack never made friends easily, shrugged away the long days spent at the high school with a disdainful closed expression, so that only after his death did Norman find out, from other people, that Jack was considered a little strange—not slow, exactly, because he had always been good at mathematics, but not quite quick enough, not right enough, somehow inferior.

They went down by the river, Jack's idea, and here the wind was stronger. An odor of something rotting was in the air. Norman and his brother wore jackets that were alike, the same size, made of material like canvas, a dull faded green. Sitting at the end of one of the old docks was a middle-aged man in the same kind of jacket. He did not look around, he might have been asleep or drunk. "What's he doing out here, he don't have a fish pole," Jack said resentfully. They walked past the dock. Norman shared Jack's resentment, because it seemed to him something was wrong, something adult was out of place, and if this was so, then everything might be out of place. The familiar waterfront had become, in the poor light, parched with heavy clouds that gave to everything a strange lightless glare that hurt Norman's eyes. Jack, as if to comfort him, talked of what they would have for supper that night—he had smelled the spaghetti sauce cooking before they left. But Norman was watching something ahead—movement back by the unloading platform of one of the old warehouses, a giant monstrosity that had been abandoned for years. An immense exhaustion touched him suddenly, for this world was so banal a betrayal of the world of that movie, so unimaginative a failure, that he could not respond to it. A few more years, he thought, and his life would change: he did not yet know just how it would change. He would not be like Jack, begging to quit school, his side of the room cluttered with auto racing magazines. And he thought, glancing at Jack's worried face, that he could not admire him as an older brother, for Jack was not big or strong enough. He did not like Jack because Jack did not bully him; he pitied Jack because Jack at seventeen had to wear the same jacket he wore at fifteen, and the two of them, bored with each other, were doomed to be brothers forever and could do nothing about it.

"There's some guys," Jack said. Norman saw three boys on the dock ahead. Something was tilting, falling over. It was a hollow metal cylinder that was buoyed up for a moment on the water, then sank. "Do you know them?" Norman said. "Are they in your class?" "No, not them bastards," Jack said. As a child, Norman had always taken his responses from other people, and now, at fifteen, he felt Jack's sudden stiffened look pass over him at once. They kept on walking, Jack a little ahead. The three boys were laughing at something, their snatches of words incomprehensible and harsh, as if they spoke a foreign language. One, in a soiled flannel shirt, was lighting a cigarette. They were about Jack's age. As Jack and Norman approached they grew quiet, staring out at the water. Jack was looking straight ahead, but Norman could not help but glance at the boys—absolutely ordinary faces with identical blank, cautious expressions, their hair much too long. They stood with their legs apart, as if posing. The boy in the flannel shirt lit his cigarette and tossed the match out into the water. Jack and Norman passed by, were by them, and Norman felt his legs want to run—he did not know why—but Jack did not hurry. Norman's breathing had quickened. Nothing had happened, no one had said a word, yet just before he was hit something in him shouted at the back of Jack's head: You fool! You goddamn fool for getting us into this!

A board struck Norman on the right shoulder and he spun around, gaping. He saw the three faces lunge at him, serious and quiet. Then the pain exploded again, this time on his chest, and he felt himself falling, falling back into nothing; then he struck the water hard. It swelled upon him and he sank into its frigid softness with his eyes opened in terror at the sky. His arms jerked, his legs threshed, but caught at nothing. It seemed queer to him that the water was cold and hard, yet could not support him. . . . Then he came to the surface, choking. Someone yelled, "Get that one!" and Norman tried to fling himself backward, anywhere. He did not know yet that Jack was in the water too. Something struck the water beside his head, he did not know what, and disappeared at once. Through the film before his eyes he saw one of the boys striking at the water by the dock with a long piece of rusty metal, his face hard and deliberate, as if he were chopping wood and counting the strokes. Norman pressed backward, out and backward, his heart pounding so violently that he could not see. Someone shouted—a word Norman did not recognize—and it seemed that in the freezing water words were shattered and had no meaning, did not matter, nothing mattered.

When he woke, it was with reluctance. Immediately the air assaulted him: he lay on his back against something hard, faces were peering down at him. Adults. He had been brought back. In curious alarm they stared at him and he at them; then he began to vomit. Someone held him. His body convulsed as if struggling against an invisible enemy, writhing and fleeing. They spoke to him, there was a siren somewhere, even a woman's voice, and though he could now understand their words he felt himself an intruder, someone returned from the dead who has no business overhearing anything. It was said later that he called for Jack at once, but he never remembered this. They had answered by assuring him that Jack was all right, he was already in the ambulance, but of course this was a lie.

During the play he could not sit still. He perspired heavily. Onstage, the actors moved through their lines without hesitation, pert and skillful, but Norman understood nothing. He might have been drowning again, drowning in air and words of another language, remote even from the woman who sat beside him. At intermission they went outside and he could tell from her silence that she was not pleased. They stared out together at a flower garden, some design of grass and flowers murky in the twilight but heavy with meaning, deliberate and plotted. "Would you like to go home?" Ellen said softly. As if guilty, Norman could not meet her eyes. He heard her words but could not make sense of them, for he was staring once again through that cold film at the boys up on the dock—secure and dry—the faces of two of them raw and blurred, but the other face now clear. He recognized it. "Why don't we go home," Ellen said, touching his arm. Norman knew that if he broke down before her he would lose her, of course; her sympathy could not be trusted. "No, I'm all right," he said, almost angrily. "It's nothing."

He stayed at her apartment for only a few minutes. She was tired and distracted and apologetic, and she seemed not to see how he wanted to remain with her, he would have talked of anything, done anything, if only she would protect him against the violence of the past—After he left her he went to a bar for a while and then, dizzy and sickened, he went home. In bed old fragments of prayers taunted his mind, and now and then it seemed to him quite clear that he had made a mistake, that he was perhaps losing his mind. He would do nothing. He would not give in. In the morning he would wake as usual to the pleasant smells from the kitchen below, he would go to the store and call Ellen, he would never drive out to that part of the country again.

But he was unable to call her. He started to dial her number several times, but always something came up and he was relieved to put back the receiver. Once he caught himself walking somewhere very deliberately—to his desk in the back office. He opened one of the drawers and glanced in at the pistol there, half covered with papers. Trembling, he hid it with papers. He stood there, staring down at the drawer for a while. No one came in, nothing happened. The ordinariness of everything, the refusal of life to change at all, baffled and angered him. He felt nauseous but nothing happened. In the rest room, watching himself suspiciously in the mirror, he believed shakily that his reflection was that of a guilty man.

After the store closed he drove out to the country. The drive took less time than it had the other day. While he drove he thought of nothing, not even Ellen, who ought to have been sitting beside him. . . . If he returned to the gas station and saw the man again, and if he could assure himself that it was not the same man he wanted, then perhaps he would call Ellen from the station; he would do that. But as he neared the small junction where the garage was supposed to be, he found himself looking shrewdly around, at houses, down lanes, down side roads. He passed the garage. No one was outside. A shabby garage with dented Coke signs and signs with scrawled numbers on them advertising gas prices, and other signs advertising cigarettes and spark plugs. The drive was just dirt and gravel, not paved. They did little business, he thought, and this was good. Several miles farther he turned down a side road and drove slowly along: country without houses, wild fields unowned by people, woods gone wild. When he saw a shanty by the edge of a woods, half a mile back from the road, he stopped the car and got out.

The shanty was deserted. It was roofed with tar paper and its wood had turned black. Inside there were newspapers on the ground, an old dented pan, some rags, a few tiny ant hills. Weeds blossomed everywhere. Norman tried to imagine what use the shanty had had, who might have built it. It seemed to him a mystery: built, abandoned, now ready for him and his brother's killer.

When he drove back he stopped at the garage for gas. The man who serviced him was not the killer, but Norman saw that there was another man inside, drinking soda pop. "What time do you people close?" Norman said. "Stay open till ten, summer," the man said. Norman hardly glanced at him. His eyes kept moving back to the open door of the garage. "That's all, thanks," he said, smiling. It was the first time he had smiled since having first seen that man.

He called Ellen from his home. At once his voice became anxious and apologetic, and her silence tormented him. "I know, I know what you said that time about not wanting to get involved with people you can't trust," he said hopelessly, "and how you don't want—you don't—" He fell silent. The vision of her that her silence evoked in him was transparent and unfamiliar; was she going to say nothing? How long had they known each other? "I am going to see you again, aren't I?" Norman said. "Yes, of course," she said faintly. "But I think you should get some rest or see a doctor. You don't seem yourself. . . ." "No, there's nothing wrong with me," Norman said sharply. She did not reply, as if startled. "When can I see you? Tomorrow?" Norman said. "No, not tomorrow, I forgot— I have something—" "What are you doing?" she said. "I'm sorry, I just can't make it then. The day after tomorrow?" Norman said. "Can I call you?" "Of course you can call me," she said meekly and coldly. Norman felt in that instant her strange hatred for him, for the force that drew him from her and before which he was so helpless; his eyes smarted with tears. "I'll call you, then," he said. He had the idea as he hung up that perhaps he would never see her again, and yet he could do nothing about it.

The next evening he drove out to the country again. Signs, barns, houses, side roads had become familiar. On the floor of the back seat were a small bag of groceries and two blankets and an old kerosene lamp he had found in the attic. It was nearly ten o'clock when he approached the garage. His heart was thudding dangerously, yet it did not upset him. He knew his body would not fail him, he could drive it as he drove the car. It was when he did not make himself think of the killer, when, out of disgust or fear, he tried to think of other things, that he felt the overwhelming guilt that had become for him the most extraordinary emotion he had ever felt. Now, prepared, everything ready and planned, he felt no guilt at all. With his car headlights off, he parked down the road from the garage, watching. Bushes screened him partly. There was his man—dragging a carton of empty soda pop bottles inside the garage. Norman waited. He had never before felt quite so free: the immensity of freedom to act and to act entirely without consequence. He wondered if that man and the two boys with him had experienced this same sweet suffocating freedom that afternoon sixteen years ago. . . . The garage darkened. Norman had no trouble making out the killer, who was taller than the other man and walked with heavy plodding steps as if he were overcome by the heat or by exhaustion. There was something self-righteous in that walk, Norman saw. The men went to their cars, the car doors slammed shut almost simultaneously, the other man drove off. The killer paused to light a cigarette. He tossed the match onto the gravel and Norman's lips jerked into a grin of recognition.

He stepped on the gas pedal and was able to head off the man's car just as it was about to turn onto the road. Norman leaned across the seat and waved into the glaring headlights. The man yelled, "What do you want? We're closed." But Norman had already gotten out of the car. "Something's wrong with my car, it's an emergency," he said. The man swore. His car engine roared and the car rocked impatiently back on the gravel as the man twisted the steering wheel. "You, wait," Norman said. "Not so fast." He took the gun out of his pocket and approached the man's open window. Behind the headlights he was helpless now, his face sagging at the sight of the gun as if he expected it. Norman's heart thudded viciously and he heard his own words as if from a distance. "I want to talk to you. I don't want to hurt you. You just get in this other car." The man did not move. Norman could hear him swallow. "Did you recognize me the other day?" he said. The man's eyes were fascinated by the gun. "There's no money in there," he said hoarsely. "Just some dollar bills. We made—we made a goddamned four dollars today—" "I don't want money," Norman said. "Get out. Get in my car." The man moved jerkily, then paused. Everything was still except for the noises of the insects. "You don't want any money?" the man said after a moment.

Norman sat beside him and the man drove. They went along slowly, down the dirt road, jerking and bouncing in the ruts. "They're waiting for me at home," the man said cautiously. "My wife and kids." Norman said nothing. When they reached the shanty—he had left a rag near the ditch for a marker—he had the man turn off the road and drive down an old cow lane and into the woods. The car churned and became entangled in underbrush. "Look, I don't know what you want," the man said, bowed over the steering wheel, "but I—I— Why don't you get somebody else for it, not me— My wife is—" "I'm not going to hurt you," Norman said. He was a little embarrassed at the man's fear: he had supposed the man would be the same as he had been sixteen years ago, cold and deliberate, without emotion. "I just want to talk with you," he said. "I want to get the truth from you. Where were you about sixteen years ago?"

He watched the man's damp face. It was an ugly, confused face, and yet its younger image had not been ugly, exactly. "I don't—I don't know," the man muttered. "Please try to remember," Norman said. "What's your name?" "Cameron," he said at once. "Anyone around here would know me— Look, what do you want? I don't know you. With that gun there—" "I'm not going to hurt you," Norman said softly. "Just tell me where you were sixteen years ago." "We come up from Kentucky, first me then my mother and father," he said. Again he swallowed clumsily. "I was maybe twenty then. I don't know. Look, I think you want some other man, I mean, it looks to me you got some other man in mind—" "You never came up from Kentucky," Norman said. "Or if you did you were younger than that." "I don't know how old I was," the man said, "maybe I was younger—" His face rippled nervously. "You remember me, don't you?" Norman said. "You knew me the other day, too, didn't you?" "What other day?" the man said. In his heavy face this new, nervous rigidity contrasted ludicrously with the lazy slabs of flesh close about his jaws. He looked as if he were trying to shake himself free of the weight of his flesh. "I only want to talk to you, then the police will take care of it," Norman said. "Take care of what?" the man said at once. "You know what," Norman said. The man stared across at him. He supposes I am crazy, Norman thought. "So you don't admit it? That you remember me?" he said. He might have been speaking to a customer in the store, prodding and herding him on to a purchase, some clothing Norman himself looked at but did not see, had no interest in seeing because he had already seen it too many times before. "I'm not going to force anything out of you," Norman said. "I give you my word on that. We're going to have a long talk, nothing hurried. Because I've been waiting sixteen years—" "What's this sixteen years?" the man said. His voice was trembling and raw, a voice Norman had not yet heard from him. There was a certain edginess there too, a recklessness that made Norman draw back so he could watch the man more carefully. Nothing was going to go wrong. He had control. While insects swirled about the headlights and tapped against the windshield Norman felt strength course through him as if it were a sign, a gift, something supernatural. "Sixteen years ago you killed my brother," he said. "Sixteen years ago last March." "Killed your brother!" said the man. He made a whistling noise. "Look, mister, I never killed nobody. I told you before—it looked like you were after somebody else, something you said— You got the wrong guy here, believe me. I never killed nobody. Who was your brother? Am I supposed to know you? Were you in the Army with me or something?" Norman let him talk. The man's words tumbled from him as if stunned with shock; they meant nothing. Finally he stopped. The insects flicked themselves lightly against the car windows and disappeared. "Turn off the lights," Norman said. He had his flashlight ready. "What do you want?" said the man. "What are you going to do?" "Turn them off. All right, now get out. Get out," Norman said. "What are you going to do?" said the man. "Are you going to—going to— You said something about the police, why don't you call them or something? I mean, they got these things on record, could look it up and see when it was—they keep a record of all these things, mister, that would clear it all up— Because I never killed nobody, not even in the Army when we was overseas, and not even by accident or anything— Was your brother in the Army?" "Get out of the car," said Norman. "Then where are we going?" the man said, gripping the steering wheel. "What are you going to do to me?" "I want to talk to you," Norman said. "You're crazy!" the man whispered.

They went in the shanty, Norman behind the man. Norman put the things down and shone the flashlight around from corner to corner. "What place is this?" the man said. "What are you going to do?" His teeth had begun to chatter; Norman was astonished. "Please sit down," he said. Cobwebs hung dustily from the ceiling. In the glare of the flashlight the weeds were stark and vivid, casting brittle shadows that froze in a complex, teethlike structure against the bottoms of the walls.

The man sat, slowly, groping about. He looked gross and foolish sitting in the weeds, his fat stomach straining against his belt. About his forehead dark strands of hair were plastered as if arranged by hand. Norman crouched against the opposite wall. "I want the truth from you," he whispered. "The truth." The man's lips began to move, but he said nothing. "Try to remember," Norman said. "You killed a boy and he's dead, his life was ended in a few minutes, and now you're here with me and alive, you've got to see the difference between the two— He'd be just bones now, everything rotted away if you dug him up, and you're sitting here alive. He was seventeen when you killed him." The man brushed weeds away from him as if they were insects, in terror; then he stopped abruptly. "I think you do remember me," Norman said. I was with him that day. You and the other two boys—"

"Other two?"

"Other two boys. All three of you. You pushed us in the river and wouldn't let us out. You hit Jack with something—when they found him his face was all slashed. I saw it myself. It was you and two other boys. I know your face."

The man began to shake his head. "My wife is waiting for me," he said faintly, "I can't talk too long. . . ."

"Where are the other two? Did they leave the city?"

"Mister, I got to go home— They're—"

"Shut up about that!" Norman cried. He waited until his anger died down. "I just want the truth. A boy is dead and you killed him and you're going to tell the truth before you leave here!"

"Mister, I never killed nobody—"

"But I saw you. I saw *you.* I saw your face."

"It wasn't me, it was somebody else."

"It was you."

"I got all kinds of cousins and guys that look like me—"

"Living up here?"

"Sure, around here, in the city too—"

"You said you were from Kentucky."

The man paused. His teeth chattered and he stared at Norman as if a flash of pain had overcome him. Then he said, "I am. They come up too."

"You all came up? When was this?"

"A while ago, I don't know—"

"You're lying," Norman said. "Goddamn filthy liar."

"I'm not lying!"

The man's lips twisted up into a terrified angry grimace. Norman felt his own lips twitch as if in imitation. "I want justice, nothing but justice," Norman whispered. He was shining the flashlight on the man's heaving chest so that the fainter halo of light illuminated the man's face, startling shadows upward from his nose and lips and the deep sockets of his eyes. "I've given up things to get here tonight," Norman said. "I'm going to get an answer from you, going to get justice. We must have justice." He might have marveled at what he said, at his strange talent, for where in the long tedious days at the store and in the evenings at home had he learned such things? Yet he felt the truth of what he was saying. It was true. He had been sent here, he could not turn away from it now if he wanted to. For this man he had given up Ellen, he would never break free and into her world now, he had given her up, killed her in himself. "There are things that have to be finished up, made even," Norman said. "If I turned you over to the police without a confession it wouldn't do any good. Nobody would care. Nobody knows about it any more except me and my family and you. . . . Are you going to tell me the truth?"

The man sat staring down at his thick legs, motionless.

"You and two other kids, one Saturday afternoon," Norman said softly. "On the docks. You knocked us both in the water and wouldn't let us out. You hit Jack, cut up his face. His eye was cut. My brother drowned but I, I didn't, a man sitting down aways came over and got me. You read about it in the papers probably. You and them. You kept on reading it till it was forgotten. Nobody cared. And even me, I suppose I forgot it too. . . . Now are you going to tell me the truth?"

After several hours the man was sitting in the same position. Norman had lit the kerosene lamp and was sitting with his back against the wall, watching the man cautiously. When he asked the man about telling the truth, sometimes he answered and sometimes he did not. When he said nothing Norman had to fight down an impulse to strike him. He had to control his anger. "You son of a bitch," the man whispered. "Going to shoot me anyway, why not now?"

"I just want the truth," Norman said. "I want it written down and signed. Your confession."

"My confession . . ."

"On paper. Signed with your name."

"Then what?"

"I told you what."

"Then you're going to shoot me, aren't you?"

"No. I told you."

"Should I write it on paper or what? Do you have some?"

"Then you did do it?"

The man squinted. "Didn't you say you saw me?"

"Yes, I saw you."

"Then I must of done it."

"Do you admit it?"

The man's face looked paralyzed. "Do you?" Norman said, leaning forward. The bovine stupidity of that face—which he felt he had been staring at for years, hating—was suddenly too much for him. He slashed the back of the gun against the man's knee, for no reason, without really knowing what he had done. The blow did not hurt, the man seemed only baffled by it. Norman's face burned. "You made me do that," he said accusingly. "I didn't mean to—I didn't plan— You made me do it."

"Going to shoot me, why not now?" the man said dully.

"Nobody's going to shoot you, for Christ's sake," Norman said. "Will you just tell the truth for once? Will you stop lying?"

"My wife—"

"To hell with that!"

"My wife can tell you. Lots of people could, but you don't care. You want to kill me."

The man hid his face in his hands. Norman could still see part of his anguished teeth. "No," Norman said. "I only want justice." But the word "justice" struck him suddenly as a puzzle: what was he talking about? It evoked in his mind an uncertain image of a courthouse with a flag flying over it, not a picture of any court in town but one out of a movie or a book. The image vanished. Norman sat up. His head had begun to pound, he had not eaten that day, he cared about nothing except this man. "I don't need sleep," he said without pride. "I can keep going until I get the truth from you. I've waited sixteen years now."

"Sixteen years," the man whispered. His hands came away from his face and in that instant Norman saw unmistakably a flash of something like recognition. A droplet of perspiration tumbled down the man's face, from his forehead to his chin and then to his wet shirt front, as if stunned by this recognition.

"Are you going to admit it?" Norman said.

"I'm not admitting anything!"

Norman's hand, holding the gun, jerked as if it had come alive. "What the hell do you mean?" he said. "A minute ago—"

"I'm not admitting anything!"

Norman waited until his heartbeat slowed. He felt on the precipice of terrible danger. Then he drew his knees up and watched the man silently. The emptiness in his stomach was turning into a kind of strength. While the kerosene lamp flickered indifferently, a cluster of moths and insects reeling about it, Norman and the man faced each other for a period of time. Norman was really not conscious of time passing; he might have been enchanted. "My brother and I were very close," he said softly. "He did things for me, stuck up for me. He looked like me only he was a lot bigger . . . he was going to go to college. Then one day you killed him. Just like that. For no reason." Norman wondered if the man was listening. "Why did you do it? For no reason, nothing, not even for money, just nothing. . . . Something in a murderer's brain must pinch him and make him do it, and everything is ruined. Lives are ruined. Nothing can be right and balanced again until justice is won—the injured party has to have justice. Do you understand that? Nothing can be right, for years, for lifetimes, until that first crime is punished. Or else we'd all be animals. The crime keeps on and on unless it's punished. Somebody like me gets caught in the middle and can't have his own life. Here I have to ruin myself to make it right and never had any choice—" The man's eyes were fascinated by Norman's face; he could not look away. When it began to get light Norman turned off the kerosene lamp. The man, slouched across from him in the weeds, looked rumpled and sick and aged. He really was not Norman's age after all, but quite a bit older. "Here," said Norman. He took an orange out of the grocery bag and tossed it at the man. It struck his knee and fell to the ground. The man seemed not to notice. "Eat that. You need to eat," Norman said. The man pushed the orange away vaguely, yet still without seeming to notice it. Norman wondered if something was wrong. The night had passed quickly for him, yet at the same time something had happened that had cemented him irreparably to this shanty, to this damp ground, to the man's rumpled body; surely it was the same way with the killer. This was something Norman could understand, after all. The woman he had loved—and he could not quite summon up her face—had been in another world where nothing was simple, nothing could be depended upon. Perhaps he had really feared and hated that world. But here, with the man obedient before him, he had only one other thing to keep in mind for both of them: that day in March. Nothing more. He did not need to think of anything further.

The man jerked his head up as if someone had called him. "Eat that orange," Norman said. "That's good for you." The man shook his head slowly. "I said eat it," said Norman. Muscles tensed in his jaw. He waited. The man did not move. "Eat that orange," said Norman, "or I'll kill you." The man's hand dropped and closed over the orange, as if the hand were part of a machine clumsily manipulated. He picked it up and peered at it. "Eat," said Norman. "Eat." The man brought the orange slowly up to his mouth. "Take off the skin first," Norman said. The man hesitated. "I can't eat it," he whispered. Norman saw tears in his eyes. "Take off the skin first," Norman said more gently. He watched the man peel the orange. Juice trickled down his big hands and fell onto his trousers and onto the bent weeds. "Now eat it," said Norman.

When the man finished, Norman said, "Are you ready now to confess?" The man made a sound something like a sob. He wiped his mouth; he stared down at nothing. Norman's heart beat so violently that his arms had begun to tremble. For an instant he felt faint; black spots appeared before his eyes, like insects. But he forced himself to say, evenly, "Are you ready to confess?"

"I never did it," the man whispered.

"But you did. You did something. You killed somebody."

"What?"

"You killed–" Norman paused. "Nothing. That wasn't– Never mind that."

"Look, I never– I never hurt–"

"Stop lying!" Norman cried. "Do you want to make me hurt you? Is that it? Want to bring me down to your level, a goddamn filthy animal? I waited sixteen years to get the truth from you–"

"What do you want me to do?" the man said. He lifted his sticky palms in a gesture of helplessness. "Where's the paper? What should I write? You said you'd let me go then–"

"I said what?"

"Said the police would have a record of it–"

"I never said that," Norman whispered.

"Yes, you said it, I heard you. We would go from here to the police and they would have some record. Have it written down. In a file. That's how they do it."

"Look, I don't want to do this to you," Norman said. "I don't want to be here. I have my own life, my own life, and here I am, over thirty already, and haven't done anything–haven't started yet–wasting my time with his troubles, and you sit and whine about yourself! You! You gave yourself up to me the day you killed him and there's nothing you can do about it."

"I got proof I wasn't up here–nowhere near here–"

"Like hell."

"We can go out and–"

"Don't you move," Norman said. His eyes throbbed. His vision itself seemed to throb with outrage and dismay. Only now had he begun to realize that this man had tried to kill him too. Had wanted him to drown. At one time that groveling man had stood safe on a dock and wanted him to drown. . . . There was the same face, Norman saw suddenly, as if by magic that young face asserted itself again within the older flabby face.

"If—if you got some paper or something—"

"You'd write it wrong," Norman said.

"No, I'll write it, then you check it, then I'll sign it—"

Norman laughed tonelessly. "You must think I'm crazy," he said.

"What?"

"Who'd believe what you wrote? When you had a gun pointed at you! How can I prove you did it, how can I prove anything? You have me trapped now like you did *then*—I could be drowning out in the water, it's the same thing, I feel like I'm drowning here, there's nothing I can do to get you—to get justice—" Norman's voice had become feverish. His hatred now was impersonal and ubiquitous: he hated without any object, without any catalyst. Even his brother's memory had become an annoyance.

"But what are you going to do?" the man said, licking his lips. "I think they'd believe a note," he said softly.

"They wouldn't. Not a jury."

"If I confessed it out loud to them—"

"No."

"If I said how I remembered it, who was with me, what you two looked like—"

"No, not even then."

"If I—if I got in touch with one of those two guys, and he said—"

"You're lying."

Stunned, baffled, the man stared at him. It seemed to Norman obvious that he was lying now, that he really could not remember anything but was only pretending, as if to make Norman feel better. It was not the lie Norman hated him for but his talent at not remembering: why had Norman not this talent, why had he been cursed with remembering when he had tried so long to forget?

"All right. You can go," Norman said.

The man did not move. "What?"

"You can go. Go."

"You mean leave here?"

His legs moved, experimentally, but he did not get up. He was squinting at Norman. "You want me to go home?"

"Go home to your wife."

"Yes, all right," the man said. He got up slowly. His legs must have ached. Each of his movements was queer and gentle, as if he were still in a dream and feared overturning something fragile. "Yes," he whispered. The man tried not to look at Norman. He moved slowly, even his eyes moved slowly to the door, and it was finally his gesture of absurd fastidiousness—he paused to brush dirt and orange peels off his trousers—that overwhelmed Norman.

"You bastard, you killer!" Norman cried. "Going to walk out like that! It's in the newspapers every day how they kill people and walk out, nothing ever happens, nobody gets punished, nothing gets put right, and people like myself have to live under the shadow of it! Killers! What the hell do I care if you did it or not? If it wasn't you it was somebody else— Or even if nobody did it, if it was an accident or if I never even had a brother named Jack or anything—"

"Named Jack?" said the man.

Norman pulled the trigger. The shot was much louder than he had expected. When he opened his eyes the shanty was empty. He crawled to the doorway and looked out—there the man was, running, through the mist. He aimed the gun again and fired. The man stumbled, fell against a tree with his arms out in an embrace. Still on his knees, Norman fired again. "Everything I did for him," he sobbed, "everything ruined—my life ruined— He wouldn't give a damn anyway, that's how it always is. What do they care? I bring her home money every week, she forgets to say thanks, why should she say thanks? There's always more where that came from. Dirty bastards, killers, a whole world of killers, and that one there sitting all night long telling lies in front of me—as if I didn't know him right away!"

Something in him seemed to collapse. The earth beneath him tilted suddenly, and he felt spiky grass against his face; everything was dizzy, confused. His fingers grasped at the earth as if he believed his weight was not enough to hold him down and keep him from being sucked up into the depths of the morning sky. Minutes passed, Norman waited to regain his strength. "You there," he said bitterly. "Hey, you." The man did not answer. He must have been lying where he fell. Norman made a face, thinking of the day ahead, the airless routine: months, years of ordinary life, so sane and so remote from this field. He closed his eyes and felt his strength course slowly back into his body. Yet still he felt the numbed, beatific emptiness of one who no longer doubts that he possesses the truth, and for whom life will have forever lost its joy.

KESSLER, THE INSIDE MAN

by George Fox

THE CHANCES ARE I never would have joined the gang that stuck up the Le Ricot gambling casino if those bastards back in the States hadn't turned me down for a fourth Guggenheim. To many people, of course, even this wouldn't be justification. Considering the stresses I was under at the time, I found it sufficient.

Exploration of motive was the farthest thing from my mind when, on the evening of August 27, I climbed the floodlit marble steps of the casino. Not for an instant did I ask myself: Why are you, Monroe Kessler, once described as the most promising of the younger American poets, doing this? I wasn't even brooding about the dangerous minutes ahead. I could think of nothing except the tightness of my dinner jacket. I'd never worn one until three weeks before, but even at the tailor's I'd realized it didn't fit. Stavros, the scarred Greek criminal genius who planned the robbery, had insisted the garment was just right. "A rich American always buys formal clothes too small," he had said. "He figures that by the time he actually has to wear them he will have lost at least fifteen pounds. I know what I'm talking about. I spent one year, three months, two days in your country."

Like many masters of detail, Stavros tended to be short-sighted. The jacket's tightness had been annoying on the previous nights I'd visited the casino, but with a .32 automatic beneath my left armpit and a tear-gas grenade beneath my right, I felt like one of those net bags stuffed with walnuts. I stopped to examine myself in the huge gold-framed mirror that dominated the foyer, saw the same not-quite-fat shape I'd never grown used to; extra bulges weren't conspicuous. I studied my eyes for traces of nervousness but they were as noncommittally blue and heavy-pouched as ever. The *Saturday Review*'s comments on my first book popped into my mind: *Kessler's verse displays an inner tension that transcends his occasionally commonplace idioms. Unlike most academic poets, he has the courage to be banal if it suits his purposes.*

Stavros had used similar terms while describing his qualifications for the perfect inside man. I tried to be afraid, wondering why I wasn't, imagining pistol blasts and blaring klaxons and the clerical voices of detectives. Fear went off in my gut like a Roman candle. I winced at the cliché and the struggle to frame a better simile calmed me.

I went over to the barred cashier's window and bought three thousand francs' worth of plaques. The cashier rolled the bills, crammed them into a hollow brass cylinder, which he placed in a pneumatic tube. I started a little when the cylinder began its whisking journey to a steel-walled room on the second floor, where my cash would join the three quarters of a million dollars that poured into the casino on an average summer evening. The tear-gas grenade I carried was a perfect duplicate, externally, of the house's money cartridges. At eleven forty-one—forty-eight minutes away—I would order the cashier at gunpoint to shoot it up to the vault. After that, Stavros and the others would take over. By rough figuring, they were now half a mile out on the Mediterranean, approaching the seaward side of the casino aboard four two-man submarines.

Entering the main salon, I was struck again with mild disbelief at the sight of the elegantly dressed figures around me. I had lived in Europe for years but the trip to Le Ricot was my first close contact with wealthy Continentals. I had been shocked to learn that they really were the sour-fleshed grotesques of the Antonioni films. You can't accept anything so preposterous at first, but once you do you know where you're at.

I went to the roulette tables because the game required so little concentration. Gambling had never interested me. Even at childhood contests like fish, my luck had been bad. I laid a five-hundred-franc plaque on the red 22 square just before the croupier spun the wheel, then glanced over the bowed heads of the other bettors at the open balcony doors. That was the way Stavros' gunmen would come.

"*Rouge vingt-deux*," the croupier intoned. I didn't connect his words with me until he said in English, "You have won seventeen thousand francs, m'sieu."

I nodded toward the plaques he had heaped on the red 22 square and said, "Let it ride." For the first time since coming to Le Ricot, I'd made a decent profit on a bet. Maybe it was a sign that the rest of the evening would go well.

Again the wheel revolved, like a combination lock running amok. . . .

There isn't much point in going too far into my life before Stavros found me. It was a common pattern: M.A. from Columbia; marriage to a graduate student in sociology; teaching English in order to gain time for writing; three children; publication of my first book of verse, *Simon's Abacus Is Broken*, at the age of twenty-six; a grant to broaden my horizons by travel abroad; two more grants; refusal of a fourth; departure of wife and kids for the States, wife tearfully declaring on the gangplank: "We'll be waiting for you when you come to your senses." I couldn't go home. In the beginning I told myself it was the prospect of again teaching freshman composition, but that wasn't true. The fact was that during my five years in Paris I hadn't even had a good time. Foundations always issue monthly allotments exactly one dollar and twenty-two cents below the good-time level. I'm not sure why I expected to enjoy myself more without any money at all. I didn't, of course. But I still couldn't go home.

Occasionally, after spending one of the small checks my father in Brooklyn sometimes sent, I'd lie in my room on the Rue du Bac and dream about rich women with insatiable lusts for slightly overweight thirty-three-year-old poets. I was involved in one of these reveries when Stavros knocked. "How do you do, Mr. Kessler," he said in his gnarled growl of a voice when I opened the door. "I am coming in." Although I'd never seen him before in my life, I stepped out of the way. Genghis Khan would have stepped out of the way. Stavros wasn't much taller than myself but his stocky, broad-shouldered frame, clad in a black, Milan-cut suit, seemed to be wrapped around a core of suppressed power, like the casing of a hand grenade. His brown face was so ridged, scarred and pockmarked that it resembled a relief map of Serbia and his eyes were the caked gray of a fireplace scuttle that hadn't been washed for six months.

"Do you know who you are, Mr. Kessler?" he said, sitting in the room's only comfortable chair. "You are the son of a New York City sweater tycoon. You are not very smart, but your younger brother is even more stupid, so you are a vice-president of your father's company. You are in Europe for the second time, on a month's vacation. The first time was right after you graduated from college. You have slept with two Parisian whores and not enjoyed it and you wish you had brought your wife after all."

"My father is a seasonally unemployed carousel operator," I said, edging toward the door.

"What did the title of your book mean? I read it three times and there is no Simon and no abacus in any of the poems."

"It represents the collapse of—"

Shrugging, he cut me off: "Only as the son of the sweater tycoon do you interest me. For two years I have been searching for such a man. Thousands of them come to France each summer but they all have money. You do not, but you would like some. And how, I ask, is a poet who looks like the son of a sweater tycoon to get money?"

"Steal it," I said with a nervous laugh.

"Correct," he said, standing up. "Now we go."

"Where?"

"For the test. I believe in you, Mr. Kessler, but there must be a test."

Enchanted, I went with him. I'd realized almost immediately that he was a master criminal. He simply couldn't be anything else. A black Mercedes, a chauffeur behind the wheel, was double-parked outside. We got into the back and the limousine roared off. During the brief drive, Stavros told me that I had been selected to play a key role in a monumental robbery. "Later you will have the details," he said. "I shall tell you this much: your share will be nearly one-hundred thousand dollars. But first the test."

The test turned out to be holding up a small *boulangerie* in the Bastille district. Stavros gave me a handkerchief mask and an automatic pistol and waited in the car. It was easy. The proprietor, a little man with a Hitler moustache, handed over his cashbox, which contained less than a hundred francs, as soon as he saw the gun in my hand. Then he fainted. "Excellent," Stavros said, patting my shoulder as the Mercedes raced through the narrow street. "The job I have in mind for you will be only a little harder—and much more profitable. You can keep what you got from the baker."

A week later, equipped with a new wardrobe, plenty of cash, a rented Porsche and a forged U.S. passport identifying me as Leroy Tannenbaum from Great Neck, Long Island, I checked into the only hotel in Le Ricot, a coastal village east of Cannes. Dotting the jagged corniche hills around it were the summer villas of many of Europe's wealthiest families. Its small, unpublicized casino attracted the most moneyed bettors in the world.

Stavros hadn't said so but I'd guessed it was our target. "Lie on the beach, have a good time, gamble in the evenings," he'd told me in Paris, "but don't risk too much. The sons of sweater tycoons don't risk too much anymore. Somebody told them it was vulgar. I understand these things. Let them all get used to you, but not too used to you. Girls will be around. Have nothing to do with them. Women's memories are too good. When the time comes, I will give you further instructions."

There were girls all right, the kind of girls the fellows who write for the quarterlies ridicule. They slid over the beach in their bikinis, all with the same slightly curved bellies and impertinent navels and large but controlled breasts, their faces bearing identical small noses and fine chins, eyes masked by the same huge sunglasses. They were all exactly alike and my desire for them was agonizing. One of the worst things about being poor is that you have to settle for women with distinctive personalities. A lithe redhead tormented me in particular. She seemed always to hover on the edge of my vision like a loose eyelash—two beach umbrellas down, four spaces ahead in the line at the movies. I often felt like going up to her—she was the only girl at the resort who had no visible male protector—and saying, "My name is Leroy Tannenbaum and my father is a sweater tycoon." But I never did. Besides my fear of Stavros, I doubted that it would work.

Stavros contacted me on my twelfth day at Le Ricot. "Villa Demain," his familiar growling voice said over the phone. "Drive approximately seven and three-tenths kilometers west on Route Nationale Sept. You will pass an Esso station. Turn left at the first dirt road after it. The villa is on the sea. I will expect you at five twenty."

The room looked like a military command post, its walls covered with maps, pictures and charts, including huge blowups of the Le Ricot casino, an eighteenth-century château. "Our goal, of course," Stavros said. He gave me the tear-gas grenade disguised as a casino money cartridge and described its function. "At exactly eleven forty-one P.M. on the twenty-seventh, you will go to the ground-floor cashier's cage to turn in your plaques. The cashier normally would write a chit and propel it to the second-floor vault in a change cartridge. You will activate the grenade and make sure that it goes instead. The vault door can be opened only from within. I have tested a prototype of this grenade many times. The fumes will flush out the men in the vault within seconds. I will be waiting in the hall when the door opens."

"But the foyer is loaded with guards," I said. "How are you going to get past them and up the stairs? And how am I going to pull a gun on the cashier without being spotted?"

"At eleven forty and thirty seconds, seven men with automatic weapons will enter the casino by way of the seaward terrace. They—and myself—are coming ashore in four two-man submarines I rented very inexpensively at the skin-diving center in Cannes. The foyer guards will, of course, rush to combat them, leaving both of us clear paths to perform our missions. I have done much study for this project. It will earn us the equivalent of three quarters of a million American dollars. The second largest share will go to you."

"Why? I seem to have the least dangerous job."

"But with the greatest risk afterward. The other men and myself are known to every policeman in Europe. We will be masked. You will not. However, the chance of arrest is slighter than you might think. You have no criminal record and physically you are a type of American the insects at places like Le Ricot make a deliberate point of ignoring. You were declared invisible the day you arrived. You have been growing more invisible every day since. The police will get descriptions of you that could fit ten thousand tourists."

The implicit insult irritated me, even though I knew he was right.

"There is one other thing in your favor," Stavros went on. "I am the only member of the gang who knows who you are—or even what you look like. You will leave the casino when the raid is barely underway. Even if the rest of us are captured before the rendezvous, none of the others will be able to identify you. Some of them, I fear, would show little strength of character under police questioning."

Stavros spent the next hour and a half drilling me again and again on my role in the stickup. It was a great plan, all right. He even had a power yacht, the fastest on the Mediterranean, standing by for our getaway to Italy. I'm sure everything would have worked out fine if I hadn't gotten lucky at roulette. . . .

"*Rouge vingt-deux*," the croupier said the second time in a row. He shoved 210,000 francs' worth of plaques onto my square. A silence fell over the chattering men and women around the table. Every face turned toward me. I did some quick figuring in my head, realized I'd won nearly $40,000 on two spins of the wheel. It had happened so quickly that, at first, I merely uttered a small obligatory chuckle. Then a cable tightened in my left cheek, producing a massive twitch that threatened to join my ear and the corner of my mouth. "Well, what do you know about that," I said. I wasn't thinking about the money, not yet. If it had been cash instead of ivory-colored plastic rectangles, I probably would have. It was the eyes that rattled me—the envious or what-will-he-do-now eyes of the other players, the flat eyes of the croupier. I wasn't invisible now.

I couldn't quit while I was ahead. If I cashed in my plaques, I'd have no reason to go to the foyer cage later. I couldn't just sit back and make small bets, wait out the thirty-two minutes until the stickup. With $40,000 in winnings in front of me, I'd be under the constant gaze of the plainclothes security men stationed around the floor. There was only one answer—lose quickly.

The croupier's hand hovered above the wheel. "Does m'sieu wish to continue?" he asked.

I lit a cigaret, feeling a little sick, and said: "Leave it on red 22."

A murmur went through the assembled gamblers. The crowd around the table had tripled in the past minute and a half. My French was never too good but I caught the gist of the whispered comments: "The fat little American is crazy!"

They were still muttering when I felt a delicate tug at my sleeve. I glanced down and saw purple-veined fingers digging into the cloth. They belonged to a tiny, ancient woman with a toucan nose, on which perched diamond-framed pince-nez. "Pay no attention to them," she said in a British-accented voice that sounded as though it were being filtered through a bale of mosquito netting. "You're going to win. I saw the same thing happen at Antibes in June of 1907. That was the summer my sister came down with dysentery. Oh, it was thrilling. No one talked about anything else all season. You're going to win too. You'll see."

It was the old woman who started it, really. In a few words she gave me the nugget of mystic belief that sustains every gambler: hope that the laws of the universe could, every once in a while, go berserk. Red 22 might come up again. If it did, I'd win more than half a million dollars. And suddenly I saw it as real money, not a bothersome abstraction. Sweat burst through my skin like sulphuric acid penetrating muslin. The croupier spun the wheel, sending the ball on its third journey.

"I tried everything." The old woman's words, sifting up my right sleeve, were at once shrill and barely audible, like the death cry of a canary that had just had its throat cut with an ax. "I wrapped her in damp sheets for hours at a time and gave her calf rubs. We didn't know about Kaopectate then. I was the younger sister. It was hard. I wanted to be on the promenade, but I stayed with her. Perhaps it happened because we stopped over in Paris. The water there is notorious—"

The ball stopped on red 22.

"—and you can't even imagine the sounds that came out of the bathroom. . . ."

The laws of the universe had gone berserk. At the table, no one reacted at all, as if by practically cleaning out the house I'd overstepped the bounds of good taste. Anger banished the triumphant dizziness that went through me on seeing the mountain of additional plaques, more than eleven million francs' worth. I hoped Stavros' gunmen would have to kill a few people when they attacked. . . .

It was the first time in minutes that I'd thought about the raid. The full meaning of what had happened hit me: Stavros had predicted a maximum haul of three quarters of a million dollars and I'd already won more than half a million, every penny of it legal. In approximately twenty-four minutes I was going to risk my life to help steal my own money!

"Play is temporarily suspended," the croupier said. The only face more ashen in the room must have been my own.

"I said all along you'd win," the old woman clucked.

The crowd opened before me as I walked toward the bar, trying to figure a way out of my dilemma. If only I could contact Stavros, make a deal. But that was impossible. I ordered a Dubonnet on the rocks, looked at my watch: eleven twenty-two. The tear-gas grenade under my right arm felt as heavy as a tombstone. I could take the money and run for it, I thought. Stavros' gullied face appeared between me and the possibility like a chrome-steel wall. He'd find me no matter where I tried to hide. I was attempting to force imaginary pictures of his vengeance from my mind when a silk-gowned woman sat on the next stool and said softly: "Hello, my name is Inez."

It was the redhead from the beach, the unattainable girl who had haunted me for weeks. Our eyes met—hers were the lustrous off-green of a piece of ginger-ale bottle worn smooth by seawater—and I fully appreciated what half a million dollars could mean to a man. I was about to answer her when the casino *chef de jeu* approached. "If m'sieu will accept a check in the event he wins further," he said, "we will continue play."

Realizing at last what I had to do, I barely heard the man's unctuous voice. "I am the only member of the gang who knows who you are or even what you look like," Stavros had said. I'd have to kill him when he came through the casino door. Even if the police caught me later, I wouldn't be in any real trouble, not for shooting an armed stickup man.

"Don't believe in pushing my luck," I told the *chef de jeu*, sliding off the barstool. "Would you have my plaques taken to the cashier. And tell them to speed things up. Have a plane to catch." I turned to Inez and smiled. "Thank you," I said.

It was almost eleven thirty. On the way to the foyer, I dropped my gas grenade into a potted dwarf hibiscus. I remained by the cashier's cage while half-a-dozen attendants in footmen's uniforms paraded up with the trays holding my plaques. Directly before me was the front entrance; to my left, the broad staircase to the second floor. I wasn't afraid. I felt rather righteous, the way any man would who was about to protect his property from thieves. The fact that I liked Stavros was disquieting, but I shoved it out of my mind. What choice did I have?

The cashier took nearly three minutes to total my winnings on an adding machine, write a chit and shoot it to the vault through the pneumatic tube. Twenty seconds later a cylinder returned. The cashier took a wad of ten-thousand-franc notes from it, placed the money on the counter. A second cartridge clattered into the tray.

"My God," I cried, "they aren't going to send my cash down in those things, are they? It'll take half the night."

"Such is the customary procedure," said the *chef de jeu,* who had followed me to the foyer.

"Definitely won't do. You hustle some fellows up there and bring it all down at once. I told you I was in a hurry."

The *chef de jeu* shrugged. "All right. But it is a great deal of money, m'sieu. Perhaps a check . . ."

"No," I said firmly. To this day I'm not sure why I insisted on cash. Possibly because I couldn't shake the notion, after weeks of conditioning, that I was robbing the place.

The cashier went upstairs, flanked by two uniformed guards. It was now eleven thirty-four; almost seven minutes to go. Pretending to hunt for cigarets, I reached inside my jacket and flicked off the safety on my automatic. At eleven thirty-eight they reappeared at the head of the stairs, both guards carrying large suitcases. "The valises have been here since 1937," the *chef de jeu* said with a sigh. "They were never needed before. Do you wish the money counted in your presence?"

"Not necessary."

"We will, naturally, have the guards accompany you to—"

"I can take care of myself," I said, abruptly wondering if I really could. After all, how many academic poets have ever had to shoot it out with master criminals?

"The price of the valises has been deducted. They are two hundred francs each."

"Fine." My eyes were fixed on the second hand of my watch. When it swept past eleven forty, I turned toward the casino entrance—and saw Inez, the young redhead, standing just inside the door, probably waiting for another crack at me. The guards, breathing hard, put down the suitcases. Get away from there, I wanted to shout at the girl.

It was too late. The sounds of breaking glass, feminine screams and sub-machine-gun fire poured from the main salon. Stavros' men had arrived. In under five seconds the foyer was almost cleared. The guards drew their revolvers and ran into the salon, the *chef de jeu* on their heels; a handful of bettors standing near the gilt mirror fled outside; the cashier scrambled into his cage and threw himself on the floor. The only visible figures were myself and Inez, who hadn't budged from her post by the door, a peculiar, intense look in her green eyes. I pulled out my automatic.

Then there was Stavros, his stocky body encased from head to toe in a rubber frogman's suit, a gas mask hiding his face. Holding a machine pistol close to his chest, he charged past the girl and ran up the stairs, leaving damp footprints on the carpeting. "Stavros, he's got the money," Inez called after him. "The American won all the money!"

Her warning so stunned me that I momentarily forgot about the gun in my hand. No wonder I'd seen the bitch everywhere I went. She'd been spying for the Greek; despite his fine words, he hadn't trusted me all the way.

I raised my automatic, waited for Stavros to turn. But he kept going, unable to hear her through the skintight frogman's hood. She shouted his name again, in a shriek that carried over the tumult in the next room. This time he got it. He twisted about, brought the machine pistol into firing position—and lost his footing, bouncing down the stairs on his rump, legs straight out in front of him. The machine pistol flew from his hands.

I couldn't shoot, not with his dignity shattered like that. Maybe I wouldn't have been able to anyway. Instead, I hefted the suitcases and ran. An attendant had brought my rented sports car around to the front of the building before the raid. I threw the suitcases in the back, jumped into the driver's seat and hit the gas.

I hid out in a Cannes hotel. Stavros found me there late the next morning, two hours after my visit to the American Express office. I was sitting on the edge of the bed when he came through the door. Except for aiming a Mauser at my midsection, he didn't seem especially angry. His ash-gray eyes were almost sad. Inez, wearing bell-bottom slacks, peered over his shoulder. "Raise your hands, Monroe," he commanded.

I obeyed, pain stabbing up my right arm. The hand at the end of it looked like a knotted claw. I gritted my teeth and succeeded in opening the fingers, dropping a ball-point pen to the floor.

"Only Inez and I got away," Stavros said. "Only us. Where is the money?"

I nodded behind me. The bed was covered by hundreds of blue-jacketed booklets. "Right here. Five hundred and eleven thousand, two hundred and ninety-six dollars in traveler's checks. And I've signed every damned one of them with my right name. Go ahead and shoot."

He knew I had him. By now my killing at Le Ricot was headline news in every French newspaper and it wouldn't take the reporters long to trace my identity through American Express. If I were murdered or vanished mysteriously, the checks would be impossible to cash, even with the most expertly forged countersignatures.

Stavros put his gun away and sat next to me on the bed. "I do not really blame you for what happened." He sighed as he looked again at the booklets. "Even I would have been tempted."

"I'm honestly sorry," I said. "But it *was* my money, most of it. Giving up half a million for a chance at one hundred thousand just didn't make sense. And I want to do the right thing. After all, you staked me. I'll give you a third, okay?"

He placed his hand on my shoulder. "You are very generous," he said, "but I will need it all."

"No," I said.

"There are things you do not understand." Stavros' blunt fingers tightened slightly on my shoulder. "Do you know how old I am?"

I looked into his battered face. "Fifty?"

"I am seventy-three years old, Monroe."

Across the room, I heard Inez gasp. I guess he'd had her fooled too.

He continued as if he had not heard Inez. "I am seventy-three and all of my savings went into this enterprise. I was going to retire on the profits, take a sight-seeing tour around the world, then settle down in Greece. One third of your winnings will not be enough. I come from a long-lived family. My mother was one hundred and seven when she died. I do not want to be penniless when I am one hundred and seven. I would rather go to the police and tell them: 'It was I, Stavros, who planned the Le Ricot robbery. And my young American friend Monroe Kessler was the inside man.' A casino guard was killed last night, so they will put us in prison for a very long time. . . . Do you believe that I speak the truth?"

"Yes," I said. His hand once again tightened on my shoulder and his fingers began digging in so deeply I was afraid the bone might splinter. "I believe it. . . ."

We're in Valparaíso, Chile, now. Stavros likes Valparaíso, says he may stay another six months. Actually, it isn't too bad. I have a comfortable room off the kitchen and, except for driving Stavros around, my only duty is signing and cashing traveler's checks. It's been two and a half years and he's only spent thirty thousand dollars, so I suppose the money will last quite a while. Inez pulled out last September, while we were touring Newfoundland. I miss her. She used to sneak into my room occasionally after Stavros was asleep. I don't think she ever quite got over the shock of learning his real age.

I'm sure I could murder Stavros now without hesitation. I probably would if it wasn't for Faizal. He's a seven-foot-tall Algerian who joined us right after we left Cannes. Absolutely loyal to the Greek. Every once in a while I tell Stavros that I'd gladly sign over all the checks to him but he just laughs and says he happens to like my company. In point of fact, I think that he's too cheap to hire a regular chauffeur. Faizal can't drive.

Stavros sometimes lets me send a few poems to the States. My agent is very enthusiastic about my recent work. "I've never mentioned it before," he wrote back once, "but I felt your early stuff failed to catch the underlying despair of life in the twentieth century. But at the rate you're going lately, you ought to have a National Book Award under your belt before you're forty."

For all that I know, he may be right.

THE NINE MILE WALK

by Harry Kemelman

I HAD MADE an ass of myself in a speech I had given at the Good Government Association dinner, and Nicky Welt had cornered me at breakfast at the Blue Moon, where we both ate occasionally, for the pleasure of rubbing it in. I had made the mistake of departing from my prepared speech to criticize a statement my predecessor in the office of County Attorney had made to the press. I had drawn a number of inferences from his statement and had thus left myself open to a rebuttal which he had promptly made and which had the effect of making me appear intellectually dishonest. I was new to this political game, having but a few months before left the Law School faculty to become the Reform Party candidate for County Attorney. I said as much in extenuation, but Nicholas Welt, who could never drop his pedagogical manner (he was Snowdon Professor of English Language and Literature), replied in much the same tone that he would dismiss a request from a sophomore for an extension on a term paper, "That's no excuse."

Although he is only two or three years older than I, in his late forties, he always treats me like a schoolmaster hectoring a stupid pupil. And I, perhaps because he looks so much older with his white hair and lined, gnomelike face, suffer it.

"They were perfectly logical inferences," I pleaded.

"My dear boy," he purred, "although human intercourse is well-nigh impossible without inference, most inferences are usually wrong. The percentage of error is particularly high in the legal profession where the intention is not to discover what the speaker wishes to convey, but rather what he wishes to conceal."

I picked up my check and eased out from behind the table.

"I suppose you are referring to cross-examination of witnesses in court. Well, there's always an opposing counsel who will object if the inference is illogical."

"Who said anything about logic?" he retorted. "An inference can be logical and still not be true."

He followed me down the aisle to the cashier's booth. I paid my check and waited impatiently while he searched in an old-fashioned change purse, fishing out coins one by one and placing them on the counter beside his check, only to discover that the total was insufficient. He slid them back into his purse and with a tiny sigh extracted a bill from another compartment of the purse and handed it to the cashier.

"Give me any sentence of ten or twelve words," he said, "and I'll build you a logical chain of inferences that you never dreamed of when you framed the sentence."

Other customers were coming in, and since the space in front of the cashier's booth was small, I decided to wait outside until Nicky completed his transaction with the cashier. I remember being mildly amused at the idea that he probably thought I was still at his elbow and was going right ahead with his discourse.

When he joined me on the sidewalk I said, "A nine mile walk is no joke, especially in the rain."

"No, I shouldn't think it would be," he agreed absently. Then he stopped in his stride and looked at me sharply. "What the devil are you talking about?"

"It's a sentence and it has eleven words," I insisted. And I repeated the sentence, ticking off the words on my fingers.

"What about it?"

"You said that given a sentence of ten or twelve words—"

"Oh, yes." He looked at me suspiciously. "Where did you get it?"

"It just popped into my head. Come on now, build your inferences."

"You're serious about this?" he asked, his little blue eyes glittering with amusement. "You really want me to?"

It was just like him to issue a challenge and then to appear amused when I accepted it. And it made me angry.

"Put up or shut up," I said.

"All right," he said mildly. "No need to be huffy. I'll play. Hm-m, let me see, how did the sentence go? 'A nine mile walk is no joke, especially in the rain.' Not much to go on there."

"It's more than ten words," I rejoined.

"Very well." His voice became crisp as he mentally squared off to the problem. "First inference: the speaker is aggrieved."

"I'll grant that," I said, "although it hardly seems to be an inference. It's really implicit in the statement."

He nodded impatiently. "Next inference: the rain was unforeseen, otherwise he would have said, 'A nine mile walk in the rain is no joke,' instead of using the 'especially' phrase as an afterthought."

"I'll allow that," I said, "although it's pretty obvious."

"First inferences should be obvious," said Nicky tartly.

I let it go at that. He seemed to be floundering and I didn't want to rub it in.

"Next inference: the speaker is not an athlete or an outdoors man."

"You'll have to explain that one," I said.

"It's the 'especially' phrase again," he said. "The speaker does not say that a nine mile walk in the rain is no joke, but merely the walk—just the distance, mind you—is no joke. Now, nine miles is not such a terribly long distance. You walk more than half that in eighteen holes of golf—and golf is an old man's game," he added slyly. *I* play golf.

"Well, that would be all right under ordinary circumstances," I said, "but there are other possibilities. The speaker might be a soldier in the jungle, in which case nine miles would be a pretty good hike, rain or no rain."

"Yes," and Nicky was sarcastic, "and the speaker might be one-legged. For that matter, the speaker might be a graduate student writing a Ph.D. thesis on humor and starting by listing all the things that are not funny. See here, I'll have to make a couple of assumptions before I continue."

"How do you mean?" I asked, suspiciously.

"Remember, I'm taking this sentence *in vacuo*, as it were. I don't know who said it or what the occasion was. Normally a sentence belongs in the framework of a situation."

"I see. What assumptions do you want to make?"

"For one thing, I want to assume that the intention was not frivolous, that the speaker is referring to a walk that was actually taken, and that the purpose of the walk was not to win a bet or something of that sort."

"That seems reasonable enough," I said.

"And I also want to assume that the locale of the walk is here."

"You mean here in Fairfield?"

"Not necessarily. I mean in this general section of the country."

"Fair enough."

"Then, if you grant those assumptions, you'll have to accept my last inference that the speaker is no athlete or outdoors man."

"Well, all right, go on."

"Then my next inference is that the walk was taken very late at night or very early in the morning—say, between midnight and five or six in the morning."

"How do you figure that one?" I asked.

"Consider the distance, nine miles. We're in a fairly well-populated section. Take any road and you'll find a community of some sort in less than nine miles. Hadley is five miles away, Hadley Falls is seven and a half, Goreton is eleven, but East Goreton is only eight and you strike East Goreton before you come to Goreton. There is local train service along the Goreton road and bus service along the others. All the highways are pretty well traveled. Would anyone have to walk nine miles in a rain unless it were late at night when no buses or trains were running and when the few automobiles that were out would hesitate to pick up a stranger on the highway?"

"He might not have wanted to be seen," I suggested.

Nicky smiled pityingly. "You think he would be less noticeable trudging along the highway than he would be riding in a public conveyance where everyone is usually absorbed in his newspaper?"

"Well, I won't press the point," I said brusquely.

"Then try this one: he was walking toward a town rather than away from one."

I nodded. "It is more likely, I suppose. If he were in a town, he could probably arrange for some sort of transportation. Is that the basis for your inference?"

"Partly that," said Nicky, "but there is also an inference to be drawn from the distance. Remember, it's a *nine* mile walk and nine is one of the exact numbers."

"I'm afraid I don't understand."

That exasperated schoolteacher-look appeared on Nicky's face again. "Suppose you say, 'I took a ten mile walk' or 'a hundred mile drive'; I would assume that you actually walked anywhere from eight to a dozen miles, or that you rode between ninety and a hundred and ten miles. In other words, *ten* and *hundred* are round numbers. You might have walked *exactly* ten miles or just as likely you might have walked *approximately* ten miles. But when you speak of walking *nine* miles, I have a right to assume that you have named an exact figure. Now, we are far more likely to know the distance of the city from a given point than we are to know the distance of a given point from the city. That is, ask anyone in the city how far out Farmer Brown lives, and if he knows him, he will say, 'Three or four miles.' But ask Farmer Brown how far he lives from the city and he will tell you, 'Three and six-tenths miles—measured it on my speedometer many a time.'"

"It's weak, Nicky," I said.

"But in conjunction with your own suggestion that he could have arranged transportation if he had been in a city—"

"Yes, that would do it," I said. "I'll pass it. Any more?"

"I've just begun to hit my stride," he boasted. "My next inference is that he was going to a definite destination and that he had to be there at a particular time. It was not a case of going off to get help because his car broke down or his wife was going to have a baby or somebody was trying to break into his house."

"Oh, come now," I said, "the car breaking down is really the most likely situation. He could have known the exact distance from having checked the mileage just as he was leaving the town."

Nicky shook his head. "Rather than walk nine miles in the rain, he would have curled up on the back seat and gone to sleep, or at least stayed by his car and tried to flag another motorist. Remember, it's nine miles. What would be the least it would take him to hike it?"

"Four hours," I offered.

He nodded. "Certainly no less, considering the rain. We've agreed that it happened very late at night or very early in the morning. Suppose he had his breakdown at one o'clock in the morning. It would be five o'clock before he would arrive. That's daybreak. You begin to see a lot of cars on the road. The buses start just a little later. In fact, the first buses hit Fairfield around five-thirty. Besides, if he were going for help, he would not have to go all the way to town—only as far as the nearest telephone. No, he had a definite appointment, and it was in a town, and it was for some time before five-thirty."

"Then why couldn't he have got there earlier and waited?" I asked. "He could have taken the last bus, arrived around one o'clock, and waited until his appointment. He walks nine miles in the rain instead, and you said he was no athlete."

We had arrived at the Municipal Building where my office is. Normally, any arguments begun at the Blue Moon ended at the entrance to the Municipal Building. But I was interested in Nicky's demonstration and I suggested that he come up for a few minutes.

When we were seated I said, "How about it, Nicky, why couldn't he have arrived early and waited?"

"He could have," Nicky retorted. "But since he did not, we must assume that he was either detained until after the last bus left, or that he had to wait where he was for a signal of some sort, perhaps a telephone call."

"Then according to you, he had an appointment some time between midnight and five-thirty—"

"We can draw it much finer than that. Remember, it takes him four hours to walk the distance. The last bus stops at twelve-thirty A.M. If he doesn't take that, but starts at the same time, he won't arrive at his destination until four-thirty. On the other hand, if he takes the first bus in the morning, he will arrive around five-thirty. That would mean that his appointment was for some time between four-thirty and five-thirty."

"You mean that if his appointment was earlier than four-thirty, he would have taken the last night bus, and if it was later than five-thirty, he would have taken the first morning bus?"

"Precisely. And another thing: if he was waiting for a signal or a phone call, it must have come not much later than one o'clock."

"Yes, I see that," I said. "If his appointment is around five o'clock and it takes him four hours to walk the distance, he'd have to start around one."

He nodded, silent and thoughtful. For some queer reason I could not explain, I did not feel like interrupting his thoughts. On the wall was a large map of the county and I walked over to it and began to study it.

"You're right, Nicky," I remarked over my shoulder, "there's no place as far as nine miles away from Fairfield that doesn't hit another town first. Fairfield is right in the middle of a bunch of smaller towns."

He joined me at the map. "It doesn't have to be Fairfield, you know," he said quietly. "It was probably one of the outlying towns he had to reach. Try Hadley."

"Why Hadley? What would anyone want in Hadley at five o'clock in the morning?"

"The Washington Flyer stops there to take on water about that time," he said quietly.

"That's right, too," I said. "I've heard that train many a night when I couldn't sleep. I'd hear it pulling in and then a minute or two later I'd hear the clock on the Methodist Church banging out five." I went back to my desk for a timetable. "The Flyer leaves Washington at twelve forty-seven A.M. and gets into Boston at eight A.M."

Nicky was still at the map measuring distances with a pencil.

"Exactly nine miles from Hadley is the Old Sumter Inn," he announced.

"Old Sumter Inn," I echoed. "But that upsets the whole theory. You can arrange for transportation there as easily as you can in a town."

He shook his head. "The cars are kept in an enclosure and you have to get an attendant to check you through the gate. The attendant would remember anyone taking out his car at a strange hour. It's a pretty conservative place. He could have waited in his room until he got a call from Washington about someone on the Flyer—maybe the number of the car and the berth. Then he could just slip out of the hotel and walk to Hadley."

I stared at him, hypnotized.

"It wouldn't be difficult to slip aboard while the train was taking on water, and then if he knew the car number and the berth—"

"Nicky," I said portentously, "as the Reform District Attorney who campaigned on an economy program, I am going to waste the taxpayers' money and call Boston long distance. It's ridiculous, it's insane —but I'm going to do it!"

His little blue eyes glittered and he moistened his lips with the tip of his tongue.

"Go ahead," he said hoarsely.

I replaced the telephone in its cradle.

"Nicky," I said, "this is probably the most remarkable coincidence in the history of criminal investigation: *a man was found murdered in his berth on last night's twelve-forty-seven from Washington!* He'd been dead about three hours, which would make it exactly right for Hadley."

"I thought it was something like that," said Nicky. "But you're wrong about its being a coincidence. It can't be. Where did you get that sentence?"

"It was just a sentence. It simply popped into my head."

"It couldn't have! It's not the sort of sentence that pops into one's head. If you had taught composition as long as I have, you'd know that when you ask someone for a sentence of ten words or so, you get an ordinary statement such as 'I like milk'—with the other words made up by a modifying clause like, 'because it is good for my health.' The sentence you offered related to a *particular situation.*"

"But I tell you I talked to no one this morning. And I was alone with you at the Blue Moon."

"You weren't with me all the time I paid my check," he said sharply. "Did you meet anyone while you were waiting on the sidewalk for me to come out of the Blue Moon?"

I shook my head. "I was outside for less than a minute before you joined me. You see, a couple of men came in while you were digging out your change and one of them bumped me, so I thought I'd wait—"

"Did you ever see them before?"

"Who?"

"The two men who came in," he said, the note of exasperation creeping into his voice again.

"Why, no—they weren't anyone I knew."

"Were they talking?"

"I guess so. Yes, they were. Quite absorbed in their conversation, as a matter of fact—otherwise, they would have noticed me and I would not have been bumped."

"Not many strangers come into the Blue Moon," he remarked.

"Do you think it was they?" I asked eagerly. "I think I'd know them again if I saw them."

Nicky's eyes narrowed. "It's possible. There had to be two—one to trail the victim in Washington and ascertain his berth number, the other to wait here and do the job. The Washington man would be likely to come down here afterwards. If there was theft as well as murder, it would be to divide the spoils. If it was just murder, he would probably have to come down to pay off his confederate."

I reached for the telephone.

"We've been gone less than half an hour," Nicky went on. "They were just coming in and service is slow at the Blue Moon. The one who walked all the way to Hadley must certainly be hungry and the other probably drove all night from Washington."

"Call me immediately if you make an arrest," I said into the phone and hung up.

Neither of us spoke a word while we waited. We paced the floor, avoiding each other almost as though we had done something we were ashamed of.

The telephone rang at last. I picked it up and listened. Then I said, "O. K." and turned to Nicky.

"One of them tried to escape through the kitchen but Winn had someone stationed at the back and they got him."

"That would seem to prove it," said Nicky with a frosty little smile.

I nodded agreement.

He glanced at his watch. "Gracious," he exclaimed, "I wanted to make an early start on my work this morning, and here I've already wasted all this time talking with you."

I let him get to the door. "Oh, Nicky," I called, "what was it you set out to prove?"

"That a chain of inferences could be logical and still not be true," he said.

"Oh."

"What are you laughing at?" he asked snappishly. And then he laughed too.

CAIN'S MARK

by Bill Pronzini

THE FIRST THING Cain did when he arrived in San Francisco was to steal a car.

He stepped off the through Portland bus at the Seventh Street Terminal, carrying a blue airline overnight bag; it was a few minutes after midnight. He walked through the terminal, without haste, turning south to Mission Street and then east along there to a shadowed, unattended parking lot between Sixth and Seventh. He prowled among the scattered few cars still parked there until he found a dark blue, late-model sedan which satisfied him. From the pocket of his tan overcoat he took a thin piece of stiff, oddly shaped wire and bent to the door lock. Moments later, he slipped in beneath the wheel, placing the overnight bag on the seat beside him. He probed the ignition slot with the wire, and after a few moments more the sedan's engine began rumbling softly. The entire operation had taken perhaps two minutes; if anyone had been watching, it would simply have looked like he was entering his own car with his own set of keys.

Cain put the sedan in gear, switched on the headlights, and drove out of the lot, crossing the double yellow lines illegally to turn west on Mission. He picked up Bayshore Freeway South at Tenth and Bryant, eight blocks away. Traffic was light at this hour, but Cain remained in the center of the three lanes, maintaining a moderate speed.

Some twenty minutes later, he left the freeway at the Poplar Street exit in San Mateo. He drove through the dark, quiet, deserted streets, crossed El Camino Real, and entered the prosperous, well-landscaped community of Hillsborough. On Devaney Way, Cain made a left turn and went three blocks. In the middle of the fourth, he eased the sedan to the curb in front of a sprawling, two-story red-brick home with ornate grillwork balconies. On the left side of the house, just ahead of where Cain had parked, was a crushed, white-gravel drive, bordered on both sides by a six-foot hedge. He could not see the front door of the home because the hedge extended down to parallel the street in front, broken only by a grillwork gate to the rear of where he was parked. But he could see the open, empty garage clearly; a pale, hooded light burned over the door.

Cain shut off the headlights, but left the engine running. It was an extremely quiet engine, and he had to strain to hear it himself; he was sure no one in the red-brick house—or in any of the adjacent or facing houses—could hear it. He set the parking brake, and then slid across the seat to the passenger side. He wound down the window there, then lifted the blue overnight bag onto his lap and zippered it open and took the large-caliber automatic from inside.

He held the automatic on his right thigh and looked at the luminescent dial of his wristwatch. One-ten. Cain slid down in the seat until his eyes were on a level with the sill of the open window.

At twenty-seven minutes past one, headlights appeared on Devaney Way, coming toward him. Cain drifted lower on the seat. A red directional signal, indicating a left turn, came on below the headlamps as the car—a cream-colored Cadillac—approached. Cain nodded once in the darkness, his fingers tightening around the butt of the automatic on his thigh.

The Cadillac turned smoothly onto the white-gravel drive, red stop lights winking. Cain watched as the driver—the lone occupant—maneuvered the car into the open garage. Cain, ears straining, heard the faint slam of a car door moments later.

He raised up on the seat, placing his arm on the window sill, the automatic extended toward the garage. A shadowed figure emerged from inside, stopped, and there was a faint whirring sound as the automatic garage door began to slide down slowly. Then the man turned and Cain could see him clearly in the pale light from above the door.

He squeezed the trigger on the automatic three times, rapidly, sighting along the barrel; the explosions shattered the nocturnal quiet with reverberating sound. Each of the three shots went exactly where Cain had intended them to go: into the garage wall above and slightly to the left of the man there.

The man threw himself to the white-gravel drive, rolling swiftly toward the green hedge on his right. Cain dropped the automatic into the overnight bag, slid over under the wheel; with his left hand he released the parking brake, with his right he dropped the automatic transmission into Drive. The rear tires on the sedan screamed violently against the pavement, as Cain's foot bore down on the accelerator. He had time for one quick glance in the direction of the garage; the man lay partially hidden in the shadow of the hedge, head raised slightly, looking toward him. And then the sedan was moving away, gathering speed. In his rear-view mirror, Cain could see lights being flicked on in neighboring houses. He took the first corner, left, and when he had cleared the intersection he switched on his headlights. Two more blocks and a right turn, and Cain reduced his speed to the legal limit of twenty-five.

Just short of half-an-hour later, he re-entered the San Francisco city and county limits. He exited the Bayshore Freeway at Army Street, turning right off there on Harrison, and parked the sedan in front of a warehouse driveway. He got out then, taking the overnight bag, and walked quickly up three blocks to Mission Street; he caught, almost immediately, a Municipal Railway Bus downtown.

He left the muni at Sixth and walked up to cross Market. On the corner of Taylor and Geary, he entered the Graceling Hotel, registered under the name of Philip Storm, and was given a room on the third floor. Inside the room, he removed the gun from the bag, oiled and cleaned it, and reloaded the clip from a box of shells. When he finished, he replaced the automatic in the bag, put it under the bed, and lay down on top of the sheets.

It was almost dawn before he finally slept.

The man who had been shot at in Hillsborough was named James Agenrood.

Following the shooting, he sat in his mahogany-paneled, book-lined study. He was alone; his wife, who had been badly frightened, had taken several sleeping pills and finally gone to bed.

Agenrood poured brandy from a crystal decanter into an expensive snifter and tasted it without his usual enjoyment of the imported liquor. He had regained his composure, but his nerves were still greatly agitated.

He tasted the brandy again, and then slid the telephone toward him across the desk, dialed a number. It rang several times; finally, a sleepy voice said, "Hello?"

"Len?"

"Yes?"

"Jim."

"This is a hell of a time of night to be calling anybody, Jim," the sleepy voice said irritably.

Agenrood took a measured breath. "Somebody tried to kill me tonight," he said slowly.

"*What!*"

"Yes. About an hour ago."

There was silence for a moment, and then the voice, which was no longer sleepy, said, "Do you have any idea who it was?"

"No."

"Professional?"

"I'd say so. He seemed to know my habits, that I always go to the Club on Wednesday nights, and that I usually get home around one-thirty. He was waiting out on the street."

"Just one man?"

"I think so."

"Did you get a look at him?"

"It was too dark."

"How about the car?"

"Dark sedan, maybe last year's," Agenrood said. "I saw part of the license plate. DRD."

"Did you call the police?"

"No, of course not."

"I'll get somebody on it right away."

"I'd appreciate it, Len."

"Listen, Jim, whoever it was isn't affiliated with us. You know your standing with the National Office."

"I didn't think he was."

"Just so you know."

"Thanks, Len."

"I'll drop by your office tomorrow."

"All right."

"And Jim . . . be careful, will you?"

Agenrood laughed, but there was no trace of humor in his gray eyes. "I'll do that, don't worry."

He cradled the receiver, lifting the decanter of brandy again; he poured another drink—his fifth since the shooting. He sat staring into the snifter. His face, in the pale light from his desk lamp, was an inscrutable mask etched of solid stone.

Cain awoke at eleven the next morning, dressed leisurely, and then called room service and ordered a pot of coffee and some buttered toast. When it arrived, he carried it to the small writing desk. In one of its drawers he found notepaper and plain white envelopes and several soft-lead pencils.

He printed a short, two-paragraph missive on one of the pieces of paper, folded it carefully, and slipped it into an envelope. He addressed the envelope, sealed it, finished his breakfast, put on his overcoat, and went out to the elevator.

In a drugstore two blocks from the Graceling Hotel, Cain bought an eight-cent stamp. There was a mailbox on the opposite corner, and he dropped the envelope in there after noting on the front the times which mail was picked up there.

Before returning to the Graceling, Cain bought a newspaper from one of the sidewalk vendors. In his room, he read it carefully. There was no mention of the episode in Hillsborough. Cain had not expected that there would be; for one thing it had happened well past midnight, too late for the morning editions; for another, and more importantly, he knew that Agenrood would not have called in the police. But he read the paper thoroughly just the same.

He lay on his bed, thinking, for the remainder of the afternoon. At five o'clock, he went out to a nearby restaurant and ate a light supper. On the way back from there, he stopped at a parking garage which had a telephone booth. He inserted a dime and dialed a number from memory. A man's voice answered.

"Hello?"

Cain did not say anything.

"Hello?" the voice repeated.

Cain held the receiver away from his ear.

"Hello? Hello? Who is this?"

Cain hung up and left the garage.

The distinguished-looking man who sat in James Agenrood's private office at Consolidated Trades, Incorporated, tamped the dottle from his briar pipe and said, "Let's have a look at this note, Jim."

Wordlessly, Agenrood passed a folded sheet of paper across his marble-topped desk. The distinguished man picked it up, unfolded it, and read:

Agenrood:

What happened Wednesday night can happen again, if there is a need for it. And if there is, you can be very sure a garage wall will not be my primary target.

Stay by your phone this weekend.

The distinguished man folded the paper again and laid it carefully on Agenrood's desk. "No signature," he said.

"Did you expect there to be one?"

"Easy, Jim."

"I'm all right."

The distinguished man refilled his pipe. "What do you think he means?"

"It's obvious, isn't it?"

"Maybe."

"He wasn't trying to kill me the other night at all. He's not a professional assassin."

"Unless he's free-lancing."

"That's possible, I suppose," Agenrood said. "In any case, he knows a lot about me. I don't know how, but he's got my private telephone number at home."

"He called you?"

"Yes."

"When?"

"Last night."

"What did he say?"

"Nothing. Nothing at all. I could hear him breathing on the other end of the line, and then he hung up."

"How do you know it was him?"

"It was him," Agenrood said.

"You haven't talked to the police, have you?"

"I'm not a fool, Len."

"I didn't mean to imply that," the distinguished man, Len, said. "I've put Reilly and Pordenza on it. They're good men."

"Sure."

"They learned that a dark blue sedan was abandoned in the Mission District some time Wednesday night. It had been stolen earlier in the evening from a downtown parking lot. First three letters on the plate were DRD. It looks like that was the one he used."

"That bases him in San Francisco," Agenrood said. "The envelope this note came in was postmarked there."

Len nodded.

Agenrood said, "Did Reilly and Pordenza learn anything else?"

"No."

"Well, whoever he is, he's got to be known to the National Office," Agenrood said. "Only somebody within the Circle could find out as much about me as he seems to know."

Len rubbed his nose with an index finger. "Can you think of anybody who has a grudge against you? Anybody you pushed, no matter how lightly, at one time or another?"

"None that would try anything like this."

"Give me their names anyway."

Agenrood wrote several names on a sheet of paper from his desk and gave the list to Len. He glanced at it briefly and tucked it into the pocket of his olive silk suit. "Are you staying home this weekend?"

"What else can I do?"

"I can put a couple of men on your house in case he tries something."

"No, Len," Agenrood said. "How would that look?"

Len nodded slowly. "Yes, I see what you mean."

"I don't think he'll do anything until after he talks to me," Agenrood said. "I'll be all right."

"If he calls, you let me know right away."

"I will."

Len stood. "Try not to worry, will you? We'll find him before long."

Agenrood did not speak. The two men went to the door. When Len had gone, Agenrood closed the door and stood looking at it for a long moment.

"I hope so," he said finally, in a whispering voice. "I sincerely hope so."

On Saturday night, shortly past eight, Cain left the Graceling Hotel for the first time since Thursday evening. There was an icy wind off the bay, blowing ethereal wisps of fog overhead; he walked quickly. On Pine Street, near Powell, he entered a quiet, dark cocktail lounge. He ordered a draft beer from the red-vested barman, and then carried it with him into the rear of the lounge to where a public telephone booth stood between the rest room doors.

Inside the booth, Cain set the glass on the little shelf beneath the phone and dialed the same memorized number that he had on Thursday night.

Presently, there was a soft click and a man's voice said guardedly, "Yes?"

"Agenrood?"

A brief pause. "Yes?"

"Did you receive my note?"

Another pause, longer this time. Then, "I received it."

"Did you understand it?"

"I think I did."

"Good," Cain said. "I thought you would."

"Just who are you?"

"You don't really expect me to tell you that, do you?"

"All right, then. How much do you want?"

"Two hundred thousand dollars."

Cain heard Agenrood suck in his breath sharply.

"Did you hear me, Agenrood?"

"I heard you."

"Well?"

"I don't keep that kind of money."

"But you can get it readily enough."

"Suppose I don't agree?"

"What do *you* think?"

"You're making a very large mistake," Agenrood said. "I represent—"

"I know who you represent."

"Then you're a fool."

"Two hundred thousand dollars," Cain said.

"If I pay it, you won't live to spend it."

"If you don't," Cain said, "you won't *live*. Period."

There was a long silence.

"Well, Agenrood?"

"I'll have to think it over."

Cain smiled. "You do that."

"How can I get in touch with you?"

Cain continued to smile. "Stay by your phone, Agenrood," he said, and replaced the receiver gently.

James Agenrood paced the wine-colored carpet in his study nervously. He said, "He called about eight tonight, Len."

The distinguished man stood holding a snifter of brandy by Agenrood's desk. His features were grim. "And?"

"He wants two hundred thousand dollars."

Len said, "My God!"

"He's deadly serious. It was plain in his voice."

"What are you going to do?"

"I don't know," Agenrood said. "That's why I asked you to come by."

Len rolled the brandy snifter between his hands. "If you pay him," he said slowly, "it won't be the last time. If he knows you're worried, worried enough to come up with the money once, he'll be back. Again and again."

"Yes. I was thinking the same thing."

"I'd like to say Reilly and Pordenza have something further," Len said. "Or that somebody on that list you gave me checks out as possible."

"But there's nothing, is there?"

"Nothing at all."

"Then I've got to pay him," Agenrood said. "Either that, or—" He left it there, moistening his lips.

Len walked across to the wine-colored drapes covering a large picture window. He stood with his back to Agenrood. After a time he said, "That would be very dangerous, Jim."

"I know."

"You're established now, both here and with the National Office. And you're important to us, Jim. Very important. I think you realize what I mean. If something went wrong . . ."

"I know that, too," Agenrood said.

Len turned and met Agenrood's eyes. "I don't advise that alternative," he said quietly.

"Do you think I like the idea of it any better? But it doesn't look like I have much choice, does it?"

Len did not say anything.

"Will you help me, Len?" Agenrood asked.

"I don't know."

"I've never asked you for a favor before."

"No, you haven't."

"I want two men, that's all."

The distinguished man worried his lower lip. "How do you know he'll leave himself open? He's done the rest of it very shrewdly."

"If he doesn't, I can arrange it."

"Are you sure?"

"No," Agenrood said. "I'm not sure."

"When is he supposed to contact you again?"

"He didn't say. I don't think it will be too long, though."

"I see."

The two men stood quietly for several minutes. Agenrood said then, "More brandy, Len?"

"Yes."

Agenrood poured more brandy for each of them. They stood drinking in silence. Finally, Len said, "All right, Jim. *If* you can arrange a quiet place, out of the way. *If* you can do that."

Agenrood inclined his head and, wordlessly, they continued to stand drinking their brandy in the dark study.

The telephone booth in the lobby of the San Francisco Hilton Hotel smelled strongly of lime-scented after-shave lotion. Cain did not like the smell, but he kept the door shut tightly nonetheless. He said into the receiver, "What's your decision, Agenrood?"

"All right," Agenrood said. "I don't have any other alternative, do I?"

"You're a wise man," Cain told him. "When can you have the money?"

"By Tuesday."

"Fine."

"How do you want to pick it up?"

"You bring it to me. Personally."

"There's no need for that."

"There's a need for it," Cain said shortly.

There was a long silence, and then Agenrood said, "Whatever you say."

"If you don't come yourself, I'll know it."

"I'll come myself."

Cain nodded in the booth.

Agenrood said, "Where do I go?"

"Are you familiar with the Coast Highway, just south of Rockaway Beach?"

"Yes."

"There's a Standard station on the highway there that has gone out of business," Cain said. "Loy Brophy's is the name of it. Park in there, by the pumps, at midnight Tuesday. When you see headlights swing in off the highway, and they blink off and then back on again, follow the car. Have you got all that, Agenrood?"

"Yes. Is that all?"

"Just one more thing."

"Yes?"

"Make sure you're alone."

Cain left the Hilton Hotel. A block away, he hailed a taxicab and told the driver where he wanted to go. The driver looked at him curiously for a moment, and then shrugged expansively and edged out into the light Sunday afternoon traffic. Cain settled back against the rear seat, lit a cigarette, and thought out carefully what he was going to say when he arrived at his destination.

James Agenrood said, "That's all of it, Len. Just as he told it to me on the telephone."

The distinguished man shifted in his chair. He took the briar pipe from his suit pocket and looked at it for a moment. "It sounds like he's covering himself from all angles."

"Not quite."

"No," Len agreed. "Not quite."

"He won't be able to see inside my car unless he pulls right up next to me at the pumps. And even if he does that, it will be dark enough in the back seat to hide anybody down on the floorboards. He'd have to get out and walk right up to the car, and he's not going to do that, not there on the highway. He's got some other place in mind."

"Suppose that other place is one that's well-lighted, with a lot of people around?"

"I don't think so, Len," Agenrood said. "If that was his idea, he wouldn't have set it up for Rockaway Beach; that's a pretty dark and sparsely populated area. And he wouldn't go through all that business about blinking his headlights off and on, and then leaving with me following him."

Len nodded thoughtfully. "Maybe you're right."

"I think I am."

"Why do you suppose he wants you to bring the money personally? You'll see his face that way."

"I don't know," Agenrood admitted. "He has to be a little crazy to try something like this in the first place, and there's no way of telling what could be going through his mind. Maybe it's just a precaution against a trap and he's covering himself the way you said."

"Maybe," Len said. "And maybe he intends, once he has the money, to finish what he started Wednesday night."

"Yes," Agenrood said, taking a breath. "But it doesn't really matter, does it? If that's what he plans to do, he won't have the chance."

"I don't like it. It's damned risky."

"No riskier than turning him down, and then having to look over my shoulder every time I go out for a package of cigarettes until you locate him. *If* you locate him."

Len filled his pipe. When he had gotten it lighted, he said, "Reilly and Pordenza?"

"I know Pordenza. He's very capable."

"So is Reilly."

"All right, then."

"He told you he'd know if you didn't come yourself?"

"That's what he said."

"He might plan on watching your house, then."

"I thought of that."

"But we can't do anything there."

"No."

"How do we get Reilly and Pordenza into your car?"

"They can come across the rear of my property and slip in through the back entrance to the garage. I'll have the garage door closed, and if he's out on the street somewhere he won't be able to see inside. They can get in and out of sight before I come out."

"That sounds okay."

"I guess that's it, then."

"Yes, that's it. But listen, Jim, I don't want to lose you, and neither does the National Office. Go easy Tuesday night."

"I plan on doing just that," Agenrood said. "Everything is going to turn out just fine."

"I hope so. Because if there's any trouble, I can't help you, Jim. As much as the National Office likes you, they won't go to bat for you if there's a foul-up."

"I'm aware of that."

"Good luck, then."

Agenrood smiled faintly. "And good hunting?"

"Yes," Len said tonelessly, expressionlessly. "And good hunting."

At twenty minutes past nine on Tuesday night, Cain left the Graceling Hotel and walked to the corner of Taylor and Eddy streets. There, he entered a gray stone building; over the building's entrance was a yellow-and-black sign that read: RIGHT-WAY RENT-A-CAR—$5 PER DAY, 5¢ PER MILE.

It was five minutes till ten when Cain emerged from an adjacent parking facility, driving a new, light brown, two-door hardtop. He had had no difficulties.

The luminescent dial of Cain's wristwatch read ten-forty when he parked the hardtop less than half a block beyond James Agenrood's red brick home on Devaney Way in Hillsborough. He eased his body down on the seat, remaining beneath the wheel; he adjusted the rear-view mirror until he could see clearly Agenrood's garage, and the pale light that burned above its electronic door. He was not worried about being seen there, or of anything happening to him so near Agenrood's home; but he kept his right hand on the automatic in the pocket of his overcoat just the same.

Agenrood came out at eleven-thirteen; Cain saw his face clearly in the garage light. He was alone. He disappeared into the garage, and moments later the cream-colored Cadillac began to glide backward to the street. Headlights washed over the hardtop, but Cain was low enough on the seat so that he was sure Agenrood could not see him. The Cadillac swept past, and through the windshield now he watched it turn the corner at the first intersection and then vanish from sight.

Cain remained where he was for five minutes, timing it by his watch.

Then he straightened on the seat, and started the hardtop and drove off in the direction Agenrood had taken.

Cain turned off Sharp Park Road, south onto the Coast Highway, at twenty minutes before twelve. He drove through Pacifica and Rockaway Beach; the Pacific Ocean lay smooth and hushed and cold on his right, like a great limitless pool of quicksilver in the shine from the three-quarter moon overhead.

He began to slow down when he saw the black-shadowed shape of the closed Standard station ahead of him. He came parallel to it and then made a left-hand turn across the highway and swung up onto the square of asphalt in front of the station. The cream-colored Cadillac sat dark and silent by the forward pumps. Cain touched the headlight switch, shutting the beams off; immediately, he flicked them back on again. He drove across to the opposite side of the asphalt square, waited there to allow a large truck to pass, and then swung out onto the Coast Highway again, resuming a southerly direction.

He looked up into his rear-view mirror and saw Agenrood come out of the Standard station and fall in behind him.

Inside the cream-colored Cadillac, one of the two men hunched down on the floor of the back seat—Pordenza—said, "Where do you think he's heading?"

James Agenrood's hands were slick on the steering wheel. "I don't know," he answered.

"Well, I hope he gets there damned quick," Pordenza said. "I've got a charley horse in my leg."

"Just stay out of sight."

"Don't worry, Mr. Agenrood."

"We know what we're doing," Reilly put in quietly.

Agenrood watched the crimson lights two hundred yards ahead of him. A fine sheen of perspiration beaded his wide forehead. They continued for another mile, and then the left directional signal on the hardtop winked on; the car began to reduce its speed.

Agenrood said, "He's going to turn."

"Where?" Pordenza asked.

"There's a narrow dirt road up ahead. It winds up into the hills, to some private homes scattered across the tops."

"Anything between the highway and those homes?"

"No."

"That's it," Reilly said.

The hardtop turned onto the dirt road. Agenrood followed. They began to climb steadily; the road twisted an irregular path, with several dog-legs and a sharp curve now and then. High wisps of fog began to shred in Agenrood's headlights, and he could see that at the crests of the hills, where the private homes were, it was thick and blanketing.

The hardtop came around one of the dog-legs and its stop lights went on, flashing blood-red in the gray-black night. Agenrood said, "There's a turnout up ahead. I think he's going in there."

The hardtop edged into the turnout, parallel to the upper end, where a slope was grown thickly with bushes and scrub cypress. "He's stopping," Agenrood said.

"Pull up behind him," Pordenza directed from the floor of the back seat. "Leave a car's length between you."

Agenrood complied. When he saw the headlights on the hardtop go out, he shut his own off. It was dark then, but the moonlight—though dimmed now and then by the tendrils of fog—bathed the turnout with sufficient light to see by.

"What's he doing?" Pordenza asked.

"Just sitting there."

"When he gets out of the car, let him get clear of it by a few steps. Not too many. Then let us know."

Agenrood could hear faint stirrings in the back seat. He knew Reilly and Pordenza had moved one to each of the rear doors. They were waiting there now, with one hand on the door handles and the other wrapped around their guns.

"When we go," Reilly breathed from the back seat, "you get down on the front seat. Just in case."

"All right," Agenrood said, and the sweat on him was oily and cold now, flowing wetly along his body.

Cain sat very still beneath the wheel of the hardtop, his eyes lifted to the rear view mirror. There was no movement from inside the Cadillac; at least, none that he could see.

With his right hand, he took the automatic from the pocket of his overcoat and held it tightly in his fingers. He put his left hand on the door latch, and then took a long, deep breath, released it, and opened the door and stepped out onto the dusty surface of the turnout. He held the automatic low and slightly behind him, so that it was hidden from Agenrood's view by his leg.

Cain's muscles tensed, grew rigid. His eyes, unblinking, never left the Cadillac. He took one step away from the car, another, a third step toward the Cadillac.

Three things happened simultaneously.

There was a hoarse, muffled cry from inside the Cadillac; Agenrood's body disappeared, falling sideways; the rear doors of the Cadillac flew open and two men came out, very fast, guns extended in their hands.

Cain threw himself to the ground, rolled, once, twice, came up on his knees, bracing himself. Twin flashes of orange light came from either side of the Cadillac; the two explosions were so close together the sound of them became one. Dust splashed up to one side of Cain; at the same instant, he felt a jarring impact high on the left side of his chest, a quick cut of pain, and then the area went numb. But he did not lose his balance, and his eyes were clear. The automatic bucked twice, loudly, in his hand. He saw the man on the driver's side of the Cadillac whirl and fall, crying out.

The second man ducked behind the fender on the passenger side. Cain tried to turn his body there and couldn't; his entire left side was without feeling now. The man on the passenger side rose up cautiously, extending his gun, aiming, and then three rapid shots sounded from the scrub cypress on the slope. The second man stood up briefly, pirouetted, and vanished from sight.

The automatic dropped from Cain's fingers and he let his body sag forward until he lay huddled in the cold dust. He heard the whirring whine of the Cadillac's starter; then there were several shouts and the sound of running feet. A door was wrenched open. The Cadillac became silent again.

Cain tried to smile, but he was unable to move his facial muscles. He closed his eyes. A single pair of running feet approached him, and he felt a hand on his shoulder and heard somebody speaking to him. He could not understand the words.

Blackness began to unfold behind his eyes, and then there were no more sounds at all.

The private hospital room in Pacifica had greenish walls and smelled of ether and antiseptic and, faintly, of the day nurse's rosewater perfume. Cain sat propped up by several pillows on the single bed; his chest was bare, and the upper half of it was swathed in bandages.

There were two other men in the room. One was tall and had a long, thin neck that resembled nothing so much as a giraffe's; the other was short and studious-appearing, and wore a very large pair of horn-rimmed glasses. They sat on two white metal chairs at the foot of the bed.

The studious-appearing man said, "You're a damned fool, Cain. You know that, don't you?"

"Am I?" Cain said briefly. He was looking out of the window; it was a warm, clear day and he could see the Pacific Ocean, glass-smooth in the distance.

The studious man opened a leather briefcase on his lap and removed a single sheet of paper; it was filled with neat lines of typing, single-spaced. The man looked at Cain, and then looked back at the paper. "Do you know what this is?"

"No," Cain said.

"It's a report on one Steven Cain," the studious man told him. "A very comprehensive report we had compiled."

Cain continued to look out of the window.

"It says you were a Colonel in the Marines during the Second World War, twice decorated for valor on Leyte and Okinawa. It says that you graduated at the top of your class at the University of California, where you majored in Law Enforcement following the War. It says that you joined the San Francisco Police Force in 1949 and while you were a patrolman in the Mission District you once captured single-handedly four men in the act of robbing a factory payroll. It says that you were the youngest man in San Francisco police history to be promoted to the Detective Squad, and the second youngest to make Division Lieutenant." The studious man paused, looking up at Cain again. "There's more, a lot more. It's a very impressive record you've got, Cain."

Cain did not answer.

"Impressive enough to indicate a very acute intelligence," the studious man said. "But I don't see any sign of intelligence in this crazy stunt you pulled off here. I don't see anything at all of the man this report covers."

Again, Cain did not answer.

"It was because of your daughter, wasn't it, Cain?" the man with the long neck said suddenly, speaking for the first time. "Because of what happened to Doreen?"

Cain brought his eyes away from the window and let them rest on the man with the long neck. He kept his lips pressed tightly together.

"It's all there in the report," the man with the long neck told him. "About how you raised the girl after your wife died twelve years ago, about how you were devoted to her. And it's in there, too, about how she was run down and killed by a car on an afternoon eight months ago when she was coming home from high school; how a patrol car nearby saw the hit-and-run and chased the car and caught it a few blocks away; how the driver pulled a gun when they approached and one of the officers was forced to shoot him in self-defense, killing him instantly; how that driver upon later identification was found to be a twenty-three-year-old drug addict and a convicted felon; and how they found almost half a kilo of heroin under the dashboard of the car and maybe the other half in the kid . . ."

"That's enough!" Cain was leaning forward on the bed, oblivious to the sharp pain that the sudden movement had caused in his chest; his jaw was set grimly and his eyes were flashing.

The man with the long neck seemed not to hear him. "For all intents and purposes, you went just a little crazy when you heard the news, Cain. You needed somebody to strike out at, somebody to blame for your daughter's death. The kid was dead, so it had to be somebody else. That somebody else was James Agenrood. You let all your hate build for him, for the man you were sure was the Organization's San Francisco-area head of narcotics distribution.

"You began a one-man crusade to get Agenrood; at first, you went through official channels and the newspapers agreed to play down the investigation—which was why Agenrood never knew your name. You dug up or bought or intimidated every scrap of knowledge available on Agenrood. But at the end of it all, you hadn't uncovered a thing on him that could put him away; he was, officially, a respectable citizen, President of Consolidated Trades, Inc., and untouchable. You just couldn't let go of it, though. Getting Agenrood became an obsession; you neglected your official duties in the pursuit of it. The Commissioner had to call you in finally and order you to cease. But you refused, and he had no alternative but to suspend you indefinitely. A week later, you resigned. Shortly after that, you moved to Portland to live with a married sister and everybody here was both sorry and maybe a little glad to see you go because they thought that, finally, you were through with it.

"But you weren't through, were you, Cain? You had to get Agenrood, one way or another. You couldn't commit murder; you'd been an honest, dedicated cop too long to resort to that. So you went up to Portland and thought it all out, looking for another way, and then you came up with your idea. You came back here last Wednesday and stole a car to make the fake attempt on Agenrood's life look professional. You knew that he would never pay the kind of money you asked him for; you knew that there was only one other thing he could do. Hit you in the head, as they say. You made sure he would be there when it was tried, and then you contacted us. You were well aware that the government was as eager to get something on Agenrood as you were, and you told us just enough to get us interested—but not enough so that we knew what you were planning—and so that we would agree to send a couple of men up to that road to wait. And it worked out okay, at least to your way of thinking. We've got Agenrood on a charge of conspiracy to commit murder, among other things; he's through with the Organization, because they won't take the chance of becoming involved by jumping to his defense. So you got him, Cain. You got your revenge, all right."

Cain had slumped back against the pillows. But his jaw remained grim. He did not say anything.

"But was it worth it?" the man with the long neck went on finally. "Was it really worth it, Cain? Was it worth the prison sentence you're facing on a list of charges that range from car theft to carrying a concealed weapon? What the hell have you actually gained by all this? Why didn't you let us handle it? We'd have gotten Agenrood sooner or later. We always get them sooner or later."

The man with the long neck stopped speaking then, and it became very quiet in the room. After a long time, Cain said, "Maybe you would have gotten him, and maybe you wouldn't. I couldn't take the chance, don't you see? Agenrood killed my daughter, just as sure as if he had put a gun to her head and pulled the trigger. I had to be the one; it was up to me. I had to get him for Doreen. Don't you understand that?"

The two men looked at Cain, and then at one another. The room was silent again for several minutes. Then the two men stood, wordlessly, and walked to the door. They turned there, and their eyes returned to the bed.

"Don't you?" Cain said to them, very softly.

"Yes," the studious man answered, just as softly. He put his hand on the knob and opened the door. "Yes, Cain, we understand."

Cain, lying in the bed, staring at the closed door after they had gone, wondered if they really understood at all. But after a while, when he had been alone for some time, he decided that it did not matter, one way or the other.

THE PURPLE IS EVERYTHING

by Dorothy Salisbury Davis

YOU ARE LIKELY to say, reading about Mary Gardner, that you knew her, or that you once knew someone like her. And well you may have, for while her kind is not legion it endures and sometimes against great popular odds.

You will see Mary Gardner—or someone like her—at the symphony, in the art galleries, at the theater, always well-dressed if not quite fashionable, sometimes alone, sometimes in the company of other women all of whom have an aura, not of sameness, but of mutuality. Each of them has made—well, if not a good life for herself, at least the best possible life it was in her power to make.

Mary Gardner was living at the time in a large East Coast city. In her late thirties, she was a tall lean woman, unmarried, quietly feminine, gentle, even a little hesitant in manner but definite in her tastes. Mary was a designer in a well-known wallpaper house. Her salary allowed her to buy good clothes, to live alone in a pleasant apartment within walking distance of her work, and to go regularly to the theater and the Philharmonic. As often as she went to the successful plays, she attended little theater and the experimental stage. She was not among those who believed that a play had to say something. She was interested in "the submerged values." This taste prevailed also in her approach to the visual arts—a boon surely in the wallpaper business whose customers for the most part prefer their walls to be seen but not heard.

In those days Mary was in the habit of going during her lunch hour—or sometimes when she needed to get away from the drawing board—to the Institute of Modern Art which was less than a city block from her office. She had fallen in love with a small, early Monet titled "Trees Near L'Havre," and when in love Mary was a person of searching devotion. Almost daily she discovered new voices in the woodland scene, trees and sky reflected in a shimmering pool—with more depths in the sky, she felt, than in the water.

The more she thought about this observation the more convinced she became that the gallery had hung the picture upside down. She evolved a theory about the signature: it was hastily done by the artist, she decided, long after he had finished the painting and perhaps at a time when the light of day was fading. She would have spoken to a museum authority about it—if she had known a museum authority.

Mary received permission from the Institute to sketch within its halls and often stood before the Monet for an hour, sketchbook in hand. By putting a few strokes on paper she felt herself conspicuously inconspicuous among the transient viewers and the guards. She would not for anything have presumed to copy the painting and she was fiercely resentful of the occasional art student who did.

So deep was Mary in her contemplation of Claude Monet's wooded scene that on the morning of the famous museum fire, when she first smelled the smoke, she thought it came from inside the picture itself. She was instantly furious, and by an old association she indicted a whole genre of people—the careless American tourist in a foreign land. She was not so far away from reality, however, that she did not realize almost at once there was actually a fire in the building.

Voices cried out alarms in the corridors and men suddenly were running. Guards dragged limp hoses along the floor and dropped them—where they lay like great withered snakes over which people leaped as in some tribal rite. Blue smoke layered the ceiling and then began to fall in angled swatches—like theatrical scrims gone awry. In the far distance fire sirens wailed.

Mary Gardner watched, rooted and muted, as men and women, visitors like herself, hastened past bearing framed pictures in their arms; and in one case two men carried between them a huge Chagall night scene in which the little creatures seemed to be jumping on and off the canvas, having an uproarious time in transit. A woman took the Rouault from the wall beside the Monet and hurried with it after the bearers of the Chagall.

Still Mary hesitated. That duty should compel her to touch where conscience had so long forbidden it—this conflict increased her confusion. Another thrust of smoke into the room made the issue plainly the picture's survival, if not indeed her own. In desperate haste she tried to lift the Monet from the wall, but it would not yield.

She strove, pulling with her full strength—such strength that when the wire broke, she was catapulted backward and fell over the viewer's bench, crashing her head into the painting. Since the canvas was mounted on board, the only misfortune—aside from her bruised head which mattered not at all—was that the picture had jarred loose from its frame. By then Mary cared little for the frame. She caught up the painting, hugged it to her, and groped her way to the gallery door.

She reached the smoke-bogged corridor at the instant the water pressure brought the hoses violently to life. Jets of water spurted from every connection. Mary shielded the picture with her body until she could edge it within the raincoat she had worn against the morning drizzle.

She hurried along the corridor, the last apparently of the volunteer rescuers. The guards were sealing off the wing of the building, closing the fire prevention door. They showed little patience with her protests, shunting her down the stairs. By the time she reached the lobby the police had cordoned off civilians. Imperious as well as impervious, a policeman escorted her into the crowd, and in the crowd, having no use of her arms—they were still locked around the picture—she was shoved and jostled toward the door and there pitilessly jettisoned into the street. On the sidewalk she had no hope at all of finding anyone in that surging, gaping mob on whom she could safely bestow her art treasure.

People screamed and shouted that they could see the flames. Mary did not look back. She hastened homeward, walking proud and fierce, thinking that the city was after all a jungle. She hugged the picture to her, her raincoat its only shield but her life a ready forfeit for its safety.

It had been in her mind to telephone the Institute office at once. But in her own apartment, the painting propped up against cushions on the sofa, she reasoned that until the fire was extinguished she had no hope of talking with anyone there. She called her own office and pleaded a sudden illness—something she had eaten at lunch though she had not had a bite since breakfast.

The walls of her apartment were hung with what she called her "potpourri": costume prints and color lithographs—all, she had been proud to say, limited editions or artists' prints. She had sometimes thought of buying paintings, but plainly she could not afford her own tastes. On impulse now, she took down an Italian lithograph and removed the glass and mat from the wooden frame. The Monet fit quite well. And to her particular delight she could now hang it right side up. As though with a will of its own, the painting claimed the place on her wall most favored by the light of day.

There is no way of describing Mary's pleasure in the company she kept that afternoon. She would not have taken her eyes from the picture at all except for the joy that was renewed at each returning. Reluctantly she turned on the radio at five o'clock so that she might learn more of the fire at the Institute. It had been extensive and destructive—an entire wing of the building was gutted.

She listened with the remote and somewhat smug solicitude that one bestows on other people's tragedies to the enumeration of the paintings which had been destroyed. The mention of "Trees Near L'Havre" startled her. A full moment later she realized the explicit meaning of the announcer's words. She turned off the radio and sat a long time in the flood of silence.

Then she said aloud tentatively, "You are a thief, Mary Gardner," and after a bit repeated, "Oh, yes. You are a thief." But she did not mind at all. Nothing so portentous had ever been said about her before, even by herself.

She ate her dinner from a tray before the painting, having with it a bottle of French wine. Many times that night she went from her bed to the living-room door until she seemed to have slept between so many wakenings. At last she did sleep.

But the first light of morning fell on Mary's conscience as early as upon the painting. After one brief visit to the living room she made her plans with the care of a religious novice well aware of the devil's constancy. She dressed more severely than was her fashion, needing herringbone for backbone—the ridiculous phrase kept running through her mind at breakfast. In final appraisal of herself in the hall mirror she thought she looked like the headmistress of an English girls' school, which she supposed satisfactory to the task before her.

Just before she left the apartment, she spent one last moment alone with the Monet. Afterward, wherever, however the Institute chose to hang it, she might hope to feel that a little part of it was forever hers.

On the street she bought a newspaper and confirmed the listing of "Trees Near L'Havre." Although that wing of the Institute had been destroyed, many of its paintings had been carried to safety by way of the second-floor corridor.

Part of the street in front of the Institute was still cordoned off when she reached it, congesting the flow of morning traffic. The police on duty were no less brusque than those whom Mary had encountered the day before. She was seized by the impulse to postpone her mission—an almost irresistible temptation, especially when she was barred from entering the museum unless she could show a pass such as had been issued to all authorized personnel.

"Of course I'm not authorized," she exclaimed. "If I were I shouldn't be out here."

The policeman directed her to the sergeant in charge. He was at the moment disputing with the fire insurance representative as to how much of the street could be used for the salvage operation. "The business of this street is business," the sergeant said, "and that's my business."

Mary waited until the insurance man stalked into the building. He did not need a pass, she noticed. "Excuse me, officer, I have a painting—"

"Lady . . ." He drew the long breath of patience. "Yes, ma'am?"

"Yesterday during the fire a painting was supposedly destroyed—a lovely small Monet called—"

"Was there now?" the sergeant interrupted. Lovely small Monets really touched him.

Mary was becoming flustered in spite of herself. "It's listed in this morning's paper as having been destroyed. But it wasn't. I have it at home."

The policeman looked at her for the first time with a certain compassion. "On your living-room wall, no doubt," he said with deep knowingness.

"Yes, as a matter of fact."

He took her gently but firmly by the arm. "I tell you what you do. You go along to police headquarters on Fifty-seventh Street. You know where that is, don't you? Just tell them all about it like a good girl." He propelled her into the crowd and there released her. Then he raised his voice: "Keep moving! You'll see it all on the television."

Mary had no intention of going to police headquarters where, she presumed, men concerned with armed robbery, mayhem, and worse were even less likely to understand the subtlety of her problem. She went to her office and throughout the morning tried periodically to reach the museum curator's office by telephone. On each of her calls either the switchboard was tied up or his line was busy for longer than she could wait.

Finally she hit on the idea of asking for the Institute's Public Relations Department, and to someone there, obviously distracted—Mary could hear parts of three conversations going on at the same time—she explained how during the fire she had saved Monet's "Trees Near L'Havre."

"Near where, madam?" the voice asked.

"L'Havre." Mary spelled it. "By Monet," she added.

"Is that two words or one?" the voice asked.

"Please transfer me to the curator's office," Mary said and ran her fingers up and down the lapel of her herringbone suit.

Mary thought it a wise precaution to meet the Institute's representative in the apartment lobby, where she first asked to see his credentials. He identified himself as the man to whom she had given her name and address on the phone. Mary signaled for the elevator and thought about his identification: Robert Attlebury III. She had seen his name on the museum roster: Curator of . . . she could not remember.

He looked every inch the curator, standing erect and remote while the elevator bore them slowly upward. A curator perhaps, but she would not have called him a connoisseur. One with his face and disposition would always taste and spit out, she thought. She could imagine his scorn of things he found distasteful, and instinctively she knew herself to be distasteful to him.

Not that it really mattered what he felt about her. She was nobody. But how must the young unknown artist feel standing with his work before such superciliousness? Or had he a different mien and manner for people of his own kind? In that case she would have given a great deal for the commonest of his courtesies.

"Everything seems so extraordinary—in retrospect," Mary said to brook the silence of their seemingly endless ascent.

"How fortunate for you," he said, and Mary thought, perhaps it was.

When they reached the door of her apartment, she paused before turning the key. "Shouldn't you have brought a guard—or someone?"

He looked down on her as from Olympus. "I am someone."

Mary resolved to say nothing more. She opened the door and left it open. He preceded her and moved across the foyer into the living room and stood before the Monet. His rude directness oddly comforted her: he did, after all, care about painting. She ought not to judge men, she thought, from her limited experience of them.

He gazed at the Monet for a few moments, then he tilted his head ever so slightly from one side to the other. Mary's heart began to beat erratically. For months she had wanted to discuss with someone who really knew about such things her theory of what was reflection and what was reality in "Trees Near L'Havre." But now that her chance was at hand she could not find the words.

Still, she had to say something—something . . . casual. "The frame is mine," she said, "but for the picture's protection you may take it. I can get it the next time I'm at the museum."

Surprisingly, he laughed. "It may be the better part at that," he said.

"I beg your pardon?"

He actually looked at her. "Your story is ingenious, madam, but then it was warranted by the occasion."

"I simply do not understand what you are saying," Mary said.

"I have seen better copies than this one," he said. "It's too bad your ingenuity isn't matched by a better imitation."

Mary was too stunned to speak. He was about to go. "But . . . it's signed," Mary blurted out, and feebly tried to direct his attention to the name in the upper corner.

"Which makes it forgery, doesn't it?" he said almost solicitously.

His preciseness, his imperturbability in the light of the horrendous thing he was saying, etched detail into the nightmare.

"That's not my problem!" Mary cried, giving voice to words she did not mean, saying what amounted to a betrayal of the painting she so loved.

"Oh, but it is. Indeed it is, and I may say a serious problem if I were to pursue it."

"Please do pursue it!" Mary cried.

Again he smiled, just a little. "That is not the Institute's way of dealing with these things."

"You do not *like* Monet," Mary challenged desperately, for he had started toward the door.

"That's rather beside the point, isn't it?"

"You don't *know* Monet. You can't! Not possibly!"

"How could I dislike him if I didn't know him? Let me tell you something about Monet." He turned back to the picture and trailed a finger over one vivid area. "In Monet the purple is everything."

"The purple?" Mary said.

"You're beginning to see it yourself now, aren't you?" His tone verged on the pedagogic.

Mary closed her eyes and said, "I only know how this painting came to be here."

"I infinitely prefer not to be made your confidant in that matter," he said. "Now I have rather more important matters to take care of." And again he started toward the door.

Mary hastened to block his escape. "It doesn't matter what you think of Monet, or of me, or of anything. You've got to take that painting back to the museum."

"And be made a laughingstock when the hoax is discovered?" He set an arm as stiff as a brass rail between them and moved out of the apartment.

Mary followed him to the elevator, now quite beside herself. "I shall go to the newspapers!" she cried.

"I think you might regret it."

"Now I know. I understand!" Mary saw the elevator door open. "You were glad to think the Monet had been destroyed in the fire."

"Savage!" he said.

Then the door closed between them.

In time Mary persuaded—and it wasn't easy—certain experts, even an art critic, to come and examine "her" Monet. It was a more expensive undertaking than she could afford—all of them seemed to expect refreshments, including expensive liquors. Her friends fell in with "Mary's hoax," as they came to call her story, and she was much admired in an ever-widening and increasingly esoteric circle for her unwavering account of how she had come into possession of a "genuine Monet." Despite the virtue of simplicity, a trait since childhood, she found herself using words in symbolic combinations—the language of the company she now kept—and people far wiser than she would say of her: "How perceptive!" or "What insight!"—and then pour themselves another drink.

One day her employer, the great man himself, who prior to her "acquisition" had not known whether she lived in propriety or in sin, arrived at her apartment at cocktail time bringing with him a famous art historian.

The expert smiled happily over his second Scotch while Mary told again the story of the fire at the Institute and how she had simply walked home with the painting because she could not find anyone to whom to give it. While she talked, his knowing eyes wandered from her face to the painting, to his glass, to the painting, and back to her face again.

"Oh, I could believe it," he said when she had finished. "It's the sort of mad adventure that actually could happen." He set his glass down carefully where she could see that it was empty. "I suppose you know that there has never been an official complete catalogue of Monet's work?"

"No," she said, and refilled his glass.

"It's so, unfortunately. And the sad truth is that quite a number of museums today are hanging paintings under his name that are really unauthenticated."

"And mine?" Mary said, lifting a chin she tried vainly to keep from quivering.

Her guest smiled. "*Must* you know?"

For a time after that Mary tried to avoid looking at the Monet. It was not that she liked it less, but that now she somehow liked herself less in its company. What had happened, she realized, was that, like the experts, she now saw not the painting, but herself.

This was an extraordinary bit of self-discovery for one who had never had to deal severely with her own psyche. Till now, so far as Mary was concerned, the chief function of a mirror had been to determine the angle of a hat. But the discovery of the flaw does not in itself effect a cure; often it aggravates the condition. So with Mary.

She spent less and less time at home, and it was to be said for some of her new-found friends that they thought it only fair to reciprocate for having enjoyed the hospitality of so enigmatically clever a hostess. How often had she as a girl been counseled by parent and teacher to get out more, to see more people. Well, Mary was at last getting out more. And in the homes of people who had felt free to comment on her home and its possessions, she too felt free to comment. The more odd her comment—the nastier, she would once have said of it—the more popular she became. Oh, yes. Mary was seeing more people, lots more people.

In fact, her insurance agent—who was in the habit of just dropping in to make his quarterly collection—had to get up early one Saturday morning to make sure he caught her at home.

It was a clear sharp day, and the hour at which the Monet was most luminous. The man sat staring at it, fascinated. Mary was amused, remembering how hurt he always was that his clients failed to hang his company calendar in prominence. While she was gone from the room to get her checkbook, he got up and touched the surface of the painting.

"Ever think of taking out insurance on that picture?" he asked when she returned. "Do you mind if I ask how much it's worth?"

"It cost me . . . a great deal," Mary said, and was at once annoyed with both him and herself.

"I tell you what," the agent said. "I have a friend who appraises these objects of art for some of the big galleries, you know? Do you mind if I bring him round and see what he thinks it's worth?"

"No, I don't mind," Mary said in utter resignation.

And so the appraiser came and looked carefully at the painting. He hedged about putting a value on it. He wasn't the last word on these nineteenth-century impressionists and he wanted to think it over. But that afternoon he returned just as Mary was about to go out, and with him came a bearded gentleman who spoke not once to Mary or to the appraiser, but chatted constantly with himself while he scrutinized the painting. Then with a "tsk, tsk, tsk," he took the painting from the wall, examined the back, and rehung it—but reversing it, top to bottom.

Mary felt the old flutter interrupt her heartbeat, but it passed quickly.

Even walking out of her house the bearded gentleman did not speak to her; she might have been invisible. It was the appraiser who murmured his thanks but not a word of explanation. Since the expert had not drunk her whiskey, Mary supposed the amenities were not required of him.

She was prepared to forget him as she had the others—it was easy now to forget them all; but when she came home to change between matinee and cocktails, another visitor was waiting. She noticed him in the lobby and realized, seeing the doorman say a word to him just as the elevator door closed off her view, that his business was with her. The next trip of the elevator brought him to her door.

"I've come about the painting, Miss Gardner," he said, and offered his card. She had opened the door only as far as the latch chain permitted. He was a representative of the Continental Assurance Company, Limited.

She slipped off the latch chain.

Courteous and formal behind his double-breasted suit, he waited for Mary to seat herself. He sat down neatly opposite her, facing the painting, for she sat beneath it, erect, and she hoped, formidable.

"Lovely," he said, gazing at the Monet. Then he wrenched his eyes from it. "But I'm not an expert," he added and gently cleared his throat. He was chagrined, she thought, to have allowed himself even so brief a luxury of the heart.

"But is it authenticated?" She said it much as she would once have thought but not said, Fie on you!

"Sufficient to my company's requirements," he said. "But don't misunderstand—we are not proposing to make any inquiries. We are always satisfied in such delicate negotiations just to have the painting back."

Mary did not misunderstand, but she certainly did not understand either.

He took from his inside pocket a piece of paper which he placed on the coffee table and with the tapering fingers of an artist—or a banker—or a pickpocket—he gently maneuvered it to where Mary could see that he was proffering a certified check.

He did not look at her and therefore missed the spasm she felt contorting her mouth. "The day of the fire," she thought, but the words never passed her lips.

She took up the check in her hand: $20,000.

"May I use your phone, Miss Gardner?"

Mary nodded and went into the kitchen where she again looked at the check. It was a great deal of money, she thought wryly, to be offered in compensation for a few months' care of a friend.

She heard her visitor's voice as he spoke into the telephone—an expert now, to judge by his tone. A few minutes later she heard the front door close. When she went back into the living room both her visitor and the Monet were gone . . .

Some time later Mary attended the opening of the new wing of the Institute. She recognized a number of people she had not known before and whom, she supposed, she was not likely to know much longer.

They had hung the Monet upside down again.

Mary thought of it after she got home, and as though two rights must surely right a possible wrong, she turned the check upside down while she burned it over the kitchen sink.

THE VILLA *MARIE CELESTE*

by Margery Allingham

THE NEWSPAPERS WERE calling the McGill house in Chestnut Grove 'the villa *Marie Celeste*' before Chief Inspector Charles Luke noticed the similarity between the two mysteries, and that so shook him that he telephoned Albert Campion and asked him to come over.

They met in the Sun, a discreet pub in the suburban High Street, and stood talking in the small bar-parlour which was deserted at that time of day just after opening in the evening.

"The two stories *are* alike," Luke said, picking up his drink. He was at the height of his career then, a dark, muscular cockney, high cheek-boned and packed with energy and as usual he talked nineteen to the dozen, forcing home his points with characteristic gestures of his long hands. "I read the rehash of the *Marie Celeste* in the *Courier* this morning and it took me to the fair. Except that she was a ship and twenty-nine Chestnut Grove is a semidetached suburban house, the two desertion stories are virtually the same, even to the half-eaten breakfast left on the table in each case. It's uncanny, Campion."

The quiet, fair man in the horn rims stood listening affably as was his habit. As usual he looked vague and probably ineffectual: in the shadier corners of Europe it was said of him that no one ever took him seriously until just about two hours too late. At the moment he appeared faintly amused. The thumping force of Luke's enthusiasm always tickled him.

"You think you know what has happened to the McGill couple, then?" he ventured.

"The hell I do!" The policeman opened his small black eyes to their widest extent. "I tell you it's the same tale as the classic mystery of the *Marie Celeste*. They've gone like a stain under a bleach. One minute they were having breakfast together, like every other married couple for miles and the next they were gone, sunk without trace."

Mr Campion hesitated. He looked a trifle embarrassed. "As I recall the story of the *Marie Celeste* it had the simple charm of the utterly incredible," he said at last. "Let's see, she was a brig brought into Gib by a prize crew of innocent sailor-men, who had a wonderful tale to tell. According to them she was sighted in mid-ocean with all her sails set, her decks clean, her lockers tidy but not a soul on board. The details were fascinating. There were three cups of tea on the captain's table still warm to the touch, in his cabin. There was a cat asleep in the galley and a chicken ready for stewing in a pot on the stove." He sighed gently. "Quite beautiful," he said, "but witnesses also swore that with no one at the wheel she was still dead on course and that seemed a little much to the court of inquiry, who after kicking it about as long as they could, finally made the absolute minimum award."

Luke glanced at him sharply.

"That wasn't the *Courier*'s angle last night," he said. "They called it the 'world's favourite unsolved mystery'."

"So they did!" Mr Campion was laughing. "Because nobody wants a prosaic explanation of fraud and greed. The mystery of the *Marie Celeste* is just the prime example of the story which really is a bit too good to spoil, don't you think?"

"I don't know. It's not an idea which occurred to me," Luke sounded slightly irritated. "I was merely quoting the main outlines of the two tales: eighteen seventy-two and the *Marie Celeste* is a bit before my time. On the other hand, twenty-nine Chestnut Grove is definitely my business and you can take it from me no witness is being allowed to use his imagination in this inquiry. Just give your mind to the details, Campion. . . ." He set his tumbler down on the bar and began ticking off each item on his fingers.

"Consider the couple," he said. "They sound normal enough. Peter McGill was twenty-eight and his wife Maureen a year younger. They'd been married three years and got on well together. For the first two years they had to board with his mother while they were waiting for a house. That didn't work out too well so they rented a couple of rooms from Maureen's married sister. That lasted for six months and they got the offer of this house in Chestnut Grove."

"Any money troubles?" Mr Campion inquired.

"No." The Chief clearly thought the fact remarkable. "Peter seems to be the one lad in the family who had nothing to grumble about. His firm—they're locksmiths in Aldgate; he's in the office—are very pleased with him. His reputation is that he keeps within his income and he's recently had a raise. I saw the senior partner this morning and he's genuinely worried, poor old boy. He liked the young man and had nothing but praise for him."

"What about the girl?"

"She's another good type. Steady, reliable, kept on at her job as a typist until a few months ago when her husband decided she should retire to enjoy the new house and maybe raise a family. She certainly did her housework. The place is like a new pin now and they've been gone six days."

For the first time Mr Campion's eyes darkened with interest.

"Forgive me," he said, "but the police seem to have come into this disappearance very quickly. Surely six days is no time for a couple to be missing. What are you looking for, Charles? A body?"

Luke shrugged. "Not officially," he said, "but one doesn't have to have a nasty mind to wonder. We came into the inquiry quickly because the alarm was given quickly. The circumstances were extraordinary and the family got the wind up. That's the explanation of that." He paused and stood for a moment hesitating. "Come along and have a look," he said, and his restless personality was a live thing in the confined space. "We'll come back and have the other half of this drink after you've seen the set-up—I've got something really recherché here. I want you in on it."

Mr Campion, as obliging as ever, followed him out into the network of trim little streets lined with bandbox villas each set in a nest of flower garden. Luke was still talking.

"It's just down the end here and along to the right," he said, nodding towards the end of the avenue. "I'll give you the outline as we go. On the twelfth of June last Bertram Heskith, a somewhat overbright specimen who is the husband of Maureen's elder sister—the one they lodged with two doors down the road before number twenty-nine became available—dropped round to see them as he usually did just before eight in the morning. He came in at the back door which was standing open and found a half-eaten breakfast for two on the table in the smart new kitchen. No one was about so he pulled up a chair and sat down to wait." Luke's long hands were busy as he talked and Mr Campion could almost see the bright little room with the built-in furniture and the pot of flowers on the window ledge.

"Bertram is a toy salesman and one of a large family," Luke went on. "He's out of a job at the moment but is not despondent. He's a talkative man, a fraction too big for his clothes now and he likes his noggin but he's sharp enough. He'd have noticed at once if there had been anything at all unusual to see. As it was he poured himself a cup of tea out of the pot under the cosy and sat there waiting, reading the newspaper which he found lying open on the floor by Peter McGill's chair. Finally it occurred to him that the house was very quiet and he put his head round the door and shouted up the stairs. When he got no reply he went up and found the bed unmade, the bathroom still warm and wet with steam and Maureen's everyday hat and coat lying on a chair with her familiar brown handbag upon it. Bertram came down, examined the rest of the house and went on out into the garden. Maureen had been doing the laundry before breakfast. There was linen, almost dry, on the line and a basket lying on the green under it but that was all. The little rectangle of land was quite empty."

As his deep voice ceased he gave Campion a sidelong glance.

"And that my lad is that," he said. "Neither Peter nor Maureen have been seen since. When they didn't show up Bertram consulted the rest of the family and after waiting for two days they went to the police."

"Really?" Mr Campion was fascinated despite himself. "Is that all you've got?"

"Not quite, but the rest is hardly helpful," Luke sounded almost gratified. "Wherever they are they're not in the house or garden. If they walked out they did it without being seen which is more of a feat than you'd expect because they had interested relatives and friends all round them and the only things that anyone is sure they took with them are a couple of clean linen sheets. 'Fine winding sheets' one lady called them."

Mr Campion's brows rose behind his big spectacles.

"That's a delicate touch," he said. "I take it there is no suggestion of foul play? It's always possible, of course."

"Foul play is becoming positively common in London, I don't know what the old town is up to," Luke said gloomily, "but this set-up sounds healthy and happy enough. The McGills seem to have been pleasant normal young people and yet there are one or two little items which make you wonder. As far as we can find out Peter was not on his usual train to the city that morning but we have one witness, a third cousin of his, who says she followed him up the street from his house to the corner just as she often did on weekday mornings. At the top she went one way and she assumed that he went the other as usual but no one else seems to have seen him and she's probably mistaken. Well now, here we are. Stand here for a minute."

He had paused on the pavement of a narrow residential street, shady with plane trees and lined with pairs of pleasant little houses, stone-dashed and bay-windowed, in a style which is now a little out of fashion.

"The next gate along here belongs to the Heskiths'," he went on, lowering his voice a tone or so. "We'll walk rather quickly past there because we don't want any more help from Bertram at the moment. He's a good enough chap but he sees himself as the watchdog of his sister-in-law's property and the way he follows me round makes me self-conscious. His house is number twenty-five—the odd numbers are on this side—twenty-nine is two doors along. Now number thirty-one which is actually adjoined to twenty-nine on the other side is closed. The old lady who owns it is in hospital; but in thirty-three there live two sisters, who are aunts of Peter's. They moved there soon after the young couple. One is a widow." Luke sketched a portly juglike silhouette with his hands, "and the other is a spinster who looks like two yards of pump-water. Both are very interested in their nephew and his wife but whereas the widow is prepared to take a more or less benevolent view of her young relations, the spinster, Miss Dove, is apt to be critical. She told me Maureen didn't know how to lay out the money and I think that from time to time she'd had a few words with the girl on the subject. I heard about the 'fine linen sheets' from her. Apparently she'd told Maureen off about buying anything so expensive but the young bride had saved up for them and she'd got them." He sighed. "Women are like that," he said. "They get a yen for something and they want it and that's all there is to it. Miss Dove says she watched Maureen hanging them out on the line early in the morning of the day she vanished. There's one upstairs window in her house from which she can just see part of the garden at twenty-nine if she stands on a chair and clings to the sash." He grinned. "She happened to be doing just that at about half past six on the day the McGills disappeared and she insists she saw them hanging there. She recognized them by the crochet on the top edge. They're certainly not in the house now. Miss Dove hints delicately that I should search Bertram's home for them."

Mr Campion's pale eyes had narrowed and his mouth was smiling.

"It's a peach of a story," he murmured. "A sort of circumstantial history of the utterly impossible. The whole thing just can't have happened. How very odd, Charles. Did anyone else see Maureen that morning? Could she have walked out of the front door and come up the street with the linen over her arm unnoticed? I am not asking would she but could she?"

"No." The Chief made no bones about it. "Even had she wanted to, which is unlikely, it's virtually impossible. There are the cousins opposite, you see. They live in the house with the red geraniums over there directly in front of number twenty-nine. They are some sort of distant relatives of Peter's. A father, mother, five marriageable daughters—it was one of them who says she followed Peter up the road that morning. Also there's an old Irish granny who sits up in bed in the window of the front room all day. She's not very reliable—for instance she can't remember if Peter came out of the house at his usual time that day—but she would have noticed if Maureen had done so. No one saw Maureen that morning except Miss Dove, who, as I told you, watched her hanging linen on the line. The paper comes early; the milkman heard her washing machine from the scullery door when he left his bottles but he did not see her."

"What about the postman?"

"He's no help. He's a new man on the round and can't even remember if he called at twenty-nine. It's a long street and, as he says, the houses are all alike. He gets to twenty-nine about seven-twenty-five and seldom meets anybody at that door. He wouldn't know the McGills if he saw them, anyhow. Come on in, Campion, take a look round and see what you think."

Mr Campion followed his friend down the road and up a narrow garden path to where a uniformed man stood on guard before the front door. He was aware of a flutter behind the curtains in the house opposite as they appeared and a tall thin woman with a determinedly blank expression walked down the path of the next house but one and bowed to Luke meaningly as she paused at her gate for an instant before going back.

"Miss Dove," said Luke unnecessarily, as he opened the door. Number twenty-nine had few surprises for Mr Campion. It was almost exactly as he had imagined it. The furniture in the hall and front room was new and sparse, leaving plenty of room for future acquisitions but the kitchen-dining-room was well lived in and conveyed a distinct personality. Someone without much money, who had yet liked nice things, had lived there. He or she, and he suspected it was a she, had been generous, too, despite her economies, if the 'charitable' calendars and the packets of gipsy pegs bought at the door were any guide. The breakfast-table had been left as Bertram Heskith had found it and his cup was still there beside a third plate.

The thin man wandered through the house without comment, Luke at his heels. The scene was just as stated. There was no sign of hurried flight, no evidence of packing, no hint of violence. The dwelling was not so much untidy as in the process of being used. There was a pair of man's pyjamas on the stool in the bathroom and a towel hung over the basin to dry. The woman's handbag on the coat on a chair in the bedroom contained the usual miscellany, and two pounds three shillings, some coppers and a set of keys. Mr Campion looked at everything, the clothes hanging neatly in the cupboard, the dead flowers still in the vases but the only item which appeared to hold his attention was the wedding group which he found in a silver frame on the dressing-table. He stood before it for a long time, apparently fascinated, yet it was not a remarkable picture. As is occasionally the case in such photographs the two central figures were the least dominant characters in the entire group of vigorous, laughing guests. Maureen timid and gentle, with a slender figure and big dark eyes, looked positively scared of her own bridesmaids while Peter, although solid and with a determined chin, had a panic-stricken look about him which contrasted with the cheerful assured grin of the best man.

"That's Heskith," said Luke. "You can see the sort of chap he is—not one of nature's great outstanding success types but not the man to go imagining things. When he says he felt the two were there that morning, perfectly normal and happy as usual, I believe him."

"No Miss Dove here?" said Campion still looking at the group.

"No. That's her sister though deputizing for the bride's mother. And that's the girl from opposite, the one who thinks she saw Peter go up the road." Luke put a forefinger over the face of the third bridesmaid. "There's another sister here and the rest are cousins. I understand the pic doesn't do the bride justice. Everybody says she was a good-natured pretty girl. . . ." He corrected himself. "Is, I mean."

"The bridegroom looks a reasonable type to me," murmured Mr Campion. "A little apprehensive, perhaps."

"I wonder." Luke spoke thoughtfully. "The Heskiths had another photo of him and perhaps it's more marked in that, but don't you think there's a sort of ruthlessness in that face, Campion? It's not quite recklessness, more like decision. I knew a sergeant in the war with a face like that. He was mild enough in the ordinary way but once something shook him he acted fast and pulled no punches whatever. Well, that's neither here nor there. Come and inspect the linen line, and then, Heaven help you, you'll know just about as much as I do."

He led the way out to the back and stood for a moment on the concrete path which ran under the kitchen window separating the house from the small rectangle of shorn grass which was all there was of a garden.

A high rose hedge, carefully trained on rustic fencing, separated it from the neighbours on the right; at the bottom there was a garden shed and a few fruit trees and, on the left, greenery in the neglected garden of the old lady who was in hospital had grown up high so that a green wall screened the lawn from all but the prying eyes of Miss

Dove, who, even at that moment, Mr Campion suspected, was standing on a chair and clinging to a sash to peer at them.

Luke indicated the empty line slung across the green. "I had the linen brought in," he said. "The Heskiths were worrying and there seemed no earthly point in leaving it out to rot."

"What's in the shed?"

"A spade and fork and a hand-mower," said the Chief promptly. "Come and look. The floor is beaten earth and if it's been disturbed in thirty years I'll eat my ticket. I suppose we'll have to fetch it up in the end but we'll be wasting our time."

Mr Campion went over and glanced into the tarred wooden hut. It was tidy and dusty and the floor was dry and hard. Outside a dilapidated pair of steps leaned against the six-foot brick wall which marked the boundary.

Mr Campion tried them gingerly. They held, but not as it were with any real assurance, and he climbed up to look over the wall to the narrow path which separated it from the tarred fence of the rear garden of a house in the next street.

"That's an odd right of way," Luke said. "It leads down between the two residential roads. These suburban places are not very matey, you know. Half the time one street doesn't know the next. Chestnut Grove is classier than Philpott Avenue which runs parallel with it."

Mr Campion descended, dusting his hands. He was grinning and his eyes were dancing.

"I wonder if anybody there noticed her," he said. "She must have been carrying the sheets, you know."

The Chief turned round slowly and stared at him.

"You're not suggesting that she simply walked down here over the wall and out! In the clothes she'd been washing in? It's crazy. Why should she? Did her husband go with her?"

"No. I think he went down Chestnut Grove as usual, doubled back down this path as soon as he came to the other end of it near the station, picked up his wife and went off with her through Philpott Avenue to the bus stop. They'd only got to get to the Broadway to find a cab, you see."

Luke's dark face still wore an expression of complete incredulity. "But for Pete's sake *why?*" he demanded. "Why clear out in the middle of breakfast on a wash-day morning? Why take the sheets? Young couples can do the most unlikely things but there are limits. They didn't take their savings bank books you know. There's not much in them but they're still there in the writing desk in the front room. What are you getting at, Campion?"

The thin man walked slowly back on to the patch of grass.

"I expect the sheets were dry and she'd folded them into the basket before breakfast," he began slowly. "As she ran out of the house they were lying there and she couldn't resist taking them with her. The husband must have been irritated with her when he saw her with them but people are like that. When they're running from a fire they save the oddest things."

"But she wasn't running from a fire."

"Wasn't she!" Mr Campion laughed. "There were several devouring flames all round them just then I should have thought. Listen, Charles. If the postman called he reached the house at seven-twenty-five. I think he did call and with an ordinary plain business envelope which was too commonplace for him to remember. It would be the plainest of plain envelopes. Well, who was due at seven-thirty?"

"Bert Heskith. I told you."

"Exactly. So there were five minutes in which to escape. Five minutes for a determined, resourceful man like Peter McGill to act promptly. His wife was generous and easy going, remember, and so, thanks to that decision which you yourself noticed in his face, he rose to the occasion. He had only five minutes, Charles, to escape all those powerful personalities with their jolly, avid faces, whom we saw in the wedding group. They were all living remarkably close to him, ringing him round as it were, so that it was a ticklish business to elude them. He went the front way so that the kindly watchful eye would see him as usual and not be alarmed. There wasn't time to take anything at all and it was only because Maureen flying through the back garden to escape the back way saw the sheets in the basket and couldn't resist her treasures that they salvaged them. She wasn't quite so ruthless as Peter. She had to take something from the old life however glistening were the prospects for—" He broke off abruptly. Chief Inspector Luke, with dawning comprehension in his eyes, was already half-way to the gate on the way to the nearest police telephone box.

Mr Campion was in his own sitting-room in Bottle Street, Piccadilly, later that evening when Luke called. He came in jauntily, his black eyes dancing with amusement.

"It wasn't the Irish Sweep but the Football Pools," he said. "I got the details out of the promoters. They've been wondering what to do ever since the story broke. They're in touch with the McGills, of course, but Peter had taken every precaution to ensure secrecy and is insisting on his rights. He must have known his wife's tender heart and have made up his mind what he'd do if ever a really big win came off. The moment he got the letter telling him of his luck he put the plan into practice." He paused and shook his head admiringly. "I hand it to him," he said. "Seventy-five thousand pounds is like a nice fat chicken, plenty and more for two but only a taste for the whole of a very big family."

"What will you do?"

"Us? The police? Oh, officially we're baffled. We shall retire gracefully. It's not our business." He sat down and raised the glass his host handed to him.

"Here's to the mystery of the Villa *Marie Celeste*," he said. "I had a blind spot for it. It foxed me completely. Good luck to them, though. You know, Campion, you had a point when you said that the really insoluble mystery is the one which no one can bring himself to spoil. What put you on to it?"

"I suspect the charm of relatives who call at seven-thirty in the morning," said Mr Campion simply.

DON'T LOOK NOW

by Daphne du Maurier

"DON'T LOOK NOW," John said to his wife, "but there are a couple of old girls two tables away who are trying to hypnotise me."

Laura, quick on cue, made an elaborate pretence of yawning, then tilted her head as though searching the skies for a nonexistent aircraft.

"Right behind you," he added. "That's why you can't turn round at once—it would be much too obvious."

Laura played the oldest trick in the world and dropped her napkin, then bent to scrabble for it under her feet, sending a shooting glance over her left shoulder as she straightened once again. She sucked in her cheeks, the first tell-tale sign of suppressed hysteria, and lowered her head.

"They're not old girls at all," she said. "They're male twins in drag."

Her voice broke ominously, the prelude to uncontrolled laughter, and John quickly poured some more chianti into her glass.

"Pretend to choke," he said, "then they won't notice. You know what it is, they're criminals doing the sights of Europe, changing sex at each stop. Twin sisters here on Torcello. Twin brothers tomorrow in Venice, or even tonight, parading arm-in-arm across the Piazza San Marco. Just a matter of switching clothes and wigs."

"Jewel thieves or murderers?" asked Laura.

"Oh, murderers, definitely. But why, I ask myself, have they picked on me?"

The waiter made a diversion by bringing coffee and bearing away the fruit, which gave Laura time to banish hysteria and regain control.

"I can't think," she said, "why we didn't notice them when we arrived. They stand out to high heaven. One couldn't fail."

"That gang of Americans masked them," said John, "and the bearded man with a monocle who looked like a spy. It wasn't until they all went just now that I saw the twins. Oh God, the one with the shock of white hair has got her eye on me again."

Laura took the powder compact from her bag and held it in front of her face, the mirror acting as a reflector.

"I think it's me they're looking at, not you," she said. "Thank heaven I left my pearls with the manager at the hotel." She paused, dabbing the sides of her nose with powder. "The thing is," she said after a moment, "we've got them wrong. They're neither murderers nor thieves. They're a couple of pathetic old retired schoolmistresses on holiday, who've saved up all their lives to visit Venice. They come from some place with a name like Walabanga in Australia. And they're called Tilly and Tiny."

Her voice, for the first time since they had come away, took on the old bubbling quality he loved, and the worried frown between her brows had vanished. At last, he thought, at last she's beginning to get over it. If I can keep this going, if we can pick up the familiar routine of jokes shared on holiday and at home, the ridiculous fantasies about people at other tables, or staying in the hotel, or wandering in art galleries and churches, then everything will fall into place, life will become as it was before, the wound will heal, she will forget.

"You know," said Laura, "that really was a very good lunch. I did enjoy it."

Thank God, he thought, thank God. . . . Then he leant forward, speaking low in a conspirator's whisper. "One of them is going to the loo," he said. "Do you suppose he, or she, is going to change her wig?"

"Don't say anything," Laura murmured. "I'll follow her and find out. She may have a suitcase tucked away there, and she's going to switch clothes."

She began to hum under her breath, the signal, to her husband, of content. The ghost was temporarily laid, and all because of the familiar holiday game, abandoned too long, and now, through mere chance, blissfully recaptured.

"Is she on her way?" asked Laura.

"About to pass our table now," he told her.

Seen on her own, the woman was not so remarkable. Tall, angular, aquiline features, with the close-cropped hair which was fashionably called Eton crop, he seemed to remember, in his mother's day, and about her person the stamp of that particular generation. She would be in her middle sixties, he supposed, the masculine shirt with collar and tie, sports jacket, grey tweed skirt coming to mid-calf. Grey stockings and laced black shoes. He had seen the type on golf-courses and at dog-shows—invariably showing not sporting breeds but pugs—and if you came across them at a party in somebody's house they were quicker on the draw with a cigarette-lighter than he was himself, a mere male, with pocket-matches. The general belief that they kept house with a more feminine, fluffy companion was not always true. Frequently they boasted, and adored, a golfing husband. No, the striking point about this particular individual was that there were two of them. Identical twins cast in the same mould. The only difference was that the other one had whiter hair.

"Supposing," murmured Laura, "when I find myself in the toilette beside her she starts to strip?"

"Depends on what is revealed," John answered. "If she's hermaphrodite, make a bolt for it. She might have a hypodermic syringe concealed and want to knock you out before you reach the door."

Laura sucked in her cheeks once more and began to shake. Then, squaring her shoulders, she rose to her feet. "I simply must not laugh," she said, "and whatever you do, don't look at me when I come back, especially if we come out together." She picked up her bag and strolled self-consciously away from the table in pursuit of her prey.

John poured the dregs of the chianti into his glass and lit a cigarette. The sun blazed down upon the little garden of the restaurant. The Americans had left, and the monocled man, and the family party at the far end. All was peace. The identical twin was sitting back in her chair with her eyes closed. Thank heaven, he thought, for this moment at any rate, when relaxation was possible, and Laura had been launched upon her foolish, harmless game. The holiday could yet turn into the cure she needed, blotting out, if only temporarily, the numb despair that had seized her since the child died.

"She'll get over it," the doctor said. "They all get over it, in time. And you have the boy."

"I know," John had said, "but the girl meant everything. She always did, right from the start, I don't know why. I suppose it was the difference in age. A boy of school age, and a tough one at that, is someone in his own right. Not a baby of five. Laura literally adored her. Johnnie and I were nowhere."

"Give her time," repeated the doctor, "give her time. And anyway, you're both young still. There'll be others. Another daughter."

So easy to talk. . . . How replace the life of a loved lost child with a dream? He knew Laura too well. Another child, another girl, would have her own qualities, a separate identity, she might even induce hostility because of this very fact. A usurper in the cradle, in the cot, that had been Christine's. A chubby, flaxen replica of Johnnie, not the little waxen dark-haired sprite that had gone.

He looked up, over his glass of wine, and the woman was staring at him again. It was not the casual, idle glance of someone at a nearby table, waiting for her companion to return, but something deeper, more intent, the prominent, light blue eyes oddly penetrating, giving him a sudden feeling of discomfort. Damn the woman! All right, bloody stare, if you must. Two can play at that game. He blew a cloud of cigarette smoke into the air and smiled at her, he hoped offensively. She did not register. The blue eyes continued to hold his, so that finally he was obliged to look away himself, extinguish his cigarette, glance over his shoulder for the waiter and call for the bill. Settling for this, and fumbling with the change, with a few casual remarks about the excellence of the meal, brought composure, but a prickly feeling on his scalp remained, and an odd sensation of unease. Then it went, as abruptly as it had started, and stealing a furtive glance at the other table he saw that her eyes were closed again, and she was sleeping, or dozing, as she had done before. The waiter disappeared. All was still.

Laura, he thought, glancing at his watch, is being a hell of a time. Ten minutes at least. Something to tease her about, anyway. He began to plan the form the joke would take. How the old dolly had stripped to her smalls, suggesting that Laura should do likewise. And then the manager had burst in upon them both, exclaiming in horror, the reputation of the restaurant damaged, the hint that unpleasant consequences might follow unless . . . The whole exercise turning out to be a plant, an exercise in blackmail. He and Laura and the twins taken in a police launch back to Venice for questioning. Quarter of an hour . . . Oh, come on, come on . . .

There was a crunch of feet on the gravel. Laura's twin walked slowly past, alone. She crossed over to her table and stood there a moment, her tall, angular figure interposing itself between John and her sister. She was saying something, but he couldn't catch the words. What was the accent, though—Scottish? Then she bent, offering an arm to the seated twin, and they moved away together across the garden to the break in the little hedge beyond, the twin who had stared at John leaning on her sister's arm. Here was the difference again. She was not quite so tall, and she stooped more—perhaps she was arthritic. They disappeared out of sight, and John, becoming impatient, got up and was about to walk back into the hotel when Laura emerged.

"Well, I must say, you took your time," he began, then stopped, because of the expression on her face.

"What's the matter, what's happened?" he asked.

He could tell at once there was something wrong. Almost as if she were in a state of shock. She blundered towards the table he had just vacated and sat down. He drew up a chair beside her, taking her hand.

"Darling, what is it? Tell me–are you ill?"

She shook her head, and then turned and looked at him. The dazed expression he had noticed at first had given way to one of dawning confidence, almost of exaltation.

"It's quite wonderful," she said slowly, "the most wonderful thing that could possibly be. You see, she isn't dead, she's still with us. That's why they kept staring at us, those two sisters. They could see Christine."

Oh God, he thought. It's what I've been dreading. She's going off her head. What do I do? How do I cope?

"Laura, sweet," he began, forcing a smile, "look, shall we go? I've paid the bill, we can go and look at the cathedral and stroll around, and then it will be time to take off in that launch again for Venice."

She wasn't listening, or at any rate the words didn't penetrate.

"John, love," she said, "I've got to tell you what happened. I followed her, as we planned, into the *toilette* place. She was combing her hair and I went into the loo, and then came out and washed my hands in the basin. She was washing hers in the next basin. Suddenly she turned and said to me, in a strong Scots accent, 'Don't be unhappy any more. My sister has seen your little girl. She was sitting between you and your husband, laughing.' Darling, I thought I was going to faint. I nearly did. Luckily, there was a chair, and I sat down, and the woman bent over me and patted my head. I'm not sure of her exact words, but she said something about the moment of truth and joy being as sharp as a sword, but not to be afraid, all was well, but the sister's vision had been so strong they knew I had to be told, and that Christine wanted it. Oh John, don't look like that. I swear I'm not making it up, this is what she told me, it's all true."

The desperate urgency in her voice made his heart sicken. He had to play along with her, agree, soothe, do anything to bring back some sense of calm.

"Laura, darling, of course I believe you," he said, "only it's a sort of shock, and I'm upset because you're upset . . ."

"But I'm not upset," she interrupted. "I'm happy, so happy that I can't put the feeling into words. You know what it's been like all these weeks, at home and everywhere we've been on holiday, though I tried to hide it from you. Now it's lifted, because I know, I just know, that the woman was right. Oh Lord, how awful of me, but I've forgotten their name–she did tell me. You see, the thing is that she's a retired doctor, they come from Edinburgh, and the one who saw Christine went blind a few years ago. Although she's studied the occult all her life and been very psychic, it's only since going blind that she has really seen things, like a medium. They've had the most wonderful experiences. But to describe Christine as the blind one did to her sister, even down to the little blue-and-white dress with the puff sleeves that she wore at her birthday party, and to say she was smiling happily . . . Oh darling, it's made me so happy I think I'm going to cry."

No hysteria. Nothing wild. She took a tissue from her bag and blew her nose, smiling at him. "I'm all right, you see, you don't have to worry. Neither of us need worry about anything any more. Give me a cigarette."

He took one from his packet and lighted it for her. She sounded normal, herself again. She wasn't trembling. And if this sudden belief was going to keep her happy he couldn't possibly begrudge it. But . . . but . . . he wished, all the same, it hadn't happened. There was something uncanny about thought-reading, about telepathy. Scientists couldn't account for it, nobody could, and this is what must have happened just now between Laura and the sisters. So the one who had been staring at him was blind. That accounted for the fixed gaze. Which somehow was unpleasant in itself, creepy. Oh hell, he thought, I wish we hadn't come here for lunch. Just chance, a flick of a coin between this, Torcello, and driving to Padua, and we had to choose Torcello.

"You didn't arrange to meet them again or anything, did you?" he asked, trying to sound casual.

"No, darling, why should I?" Laura answered. "I mean, there was nothing more they could tell me. The sister had had her wonderful vision, and that was that. Anyway, they're moving on. Funnily enough, it's rather like our original game. They *are* going round the world before returning to Scotland. Only I said Australia, didn't I? The old dears . . . anything less like murderers and jewel thieves!"

She had quite recovered. She stood up and looked about her. "Come on," she said. "Having come to Torcello we must see the cathedral."

They made their way from the restaurant across the open piazza, where the stalls had been set up with scarves and trinkets and postcards, and so along the path to the cathedral. One of the ferry-boats had just decanted a crowd of sight-seers, many of whom had already found their way into Santa Maria Assunta. Laura, undaunted, asked her husband for the guidebook, and, as had always been her custom in happier days, started to walk slowly through the cathedral, studying mosaics, columns, panels from left to right, while John, less interested, because of his concern at what had just happened, followed close behind, keeping a weather eye alert for the twin sisters. There was no sign of them. Perhaps they had gone into the Church of Santa Fosca close-by. A sudden encounter would be embarrassing, quite apart from the effect it might have upon Laura. But the anonymous, shuffling tourists, intent upon culture, could not harm her, although from his own point of view they made artistic appreciation impossible. He could not concentrate, the cold clear beauty of what he saw left him untouched, and when Laura touched his sleeve, pointing to the mosaic of the Virgin and Child standing above the frieze of the Apostles, he nodded in sympathy yet saw nothing, the long, sad face of the Virgin infinitely remote, and turning on sudden impulse stared back over the heads of the tourists towards the door, where frescoes of the blessed and the damned gave themselves to judgement.

The twins were standing there, the blind one still holding on to her sister's arm, her sightless eyes fixed firmly upon him. He felt himself held, unable to move, and an impending sense of doom, of tragedy, came upon him. His whole being sagged, as it were, in apathy, and he thought, This is the end, there is no escape, no future. Then both sisters turned and went out of the cathedral and the sensation vanished, leaving indignation in its wake, and rising anger. How dare those two old fools practice their mediumistic tricks on him? It was fraudulent, unhealthy; this was probably the way they lived, touring the world making everyone they met uncomfortable. Give them half a chance and they would have got money out of Laura—anything.

He felt her tugging at his sleeve again. "Isn't she beautiful? So happy, so serene."

"Who? What?" he asked.

"The Madonna," she answered. "She has a magic quality. It goes right through to one. Don't you feel it too?"

"I suppose so. I don't know. There are too many people around."

She looked up at him, astonished. "What's that got to do with it? How funny you are. Well, all right, let's get away from them. I want to buy some postcards anyway." Disappointed, she sensed his lack of interest, and began to thread her way through the crowd of tourists to the door.

"Come on," he said abruptly, once they were outside, "there's plenty of time for postcards, let's explore a bit," and he struck off from the path, which would have taken them back to the centre where the little houses were, and the stalls, and the drifting crowd of people, to a narrow way amongst uncultivated ground, beyond which he could see a sort of cutting, or canal. The sight of water, limpid, pale, was a soothing contrast to the fierce sun above their heads.

"I don't think this leads anywhere much," said Laura. "It's a bit muddy, too, one can't sit. Besides, there are more things the guide-book says we ought to see."

"Oh, forget the book," he said impatiently, and, pulling her down beside him on the bank above the cutting, put his arms round her. "It's the wrong time of day for sight-seeing. Look, there's a rat swimming there the other side." He picked up a stone and threw it in the water, and the animal sank, or somehow disappeared, and nothing was left but bubbles.

"Don't," said Laura. "It's cruel, poor thing," and then suddenly, putting her hand on his knee, "Do you think Christine is sitting here beside us?"

He did not answer at once. What was there to say? Would it be like this forever?

"I expect so," he said slowly, "if you feel she is."

The point was, remembering Christine before the onset of the fatal meningitis, she would have been running along the bank excitedly, throwing off her shoes, wanting to paddle, giving Laura a fit of apprehension. "Sweetheart, take care, come back . . ."

"The woman said she was looking so happy, sitting beside us, smiling," said Laura. She got up, brushing her dress, her mood changed to restlessness. "Come on, let's go back," she said.

He followed her with a sinking heart. He knew she did not really want to buy postcards or see what remained to be seen; she wanted to go in search of the women again, not necessarily to talk, just to be near them. When they came to the open place by the stalls he noticed that the crowd of tourists had thinned, there were only a few stragglers left, and the sisters were not amongst them. They must have joined the main body who had come to Torcello by the ferry-service. A wave of relief seized him.

"Look, there's a mass of postcards at the second stall," he said quickly, "and some eye-catching head-scarves. Let me buy you a head-scarf."

"Darling, I've so many!" she protested. "Don't waste your lire."

"It isn't a waste. I'm in a buying mood. What about a basket? You know we never have enough baskets. Or some lace. How about lace?"

She allowed herself, laughing, to be dragged to the stall. While he rumpled through the goods spread out before them, and chatted up the smiling woman who was selling her wares, his ferociously bad Italian making her smile the more, he knew it would give the body of tourists more time to walk to the landing-stage and catch the ferry-service, and the twin sisters would be out of sight and out of their life.

"Never," said Laura, some twenty minutes later, "has so much junk been piled into so small a basket," her bubbling laugh reassuring him that all was well, he needn't worry any more, the evil hour had passed. The launch from the Cipriani that had brought them from Venice was waiting by the landing-stage. The passengers who had arrived with them, the Americans, the man with the monocle, were already assembled. Earlier, before setting out, he had thought the price for lunch and transport, there and back, decidedly steep. Now he grudged none of it, except that the outing to Torcello itself had been one of the major errors of this particular holiday in Venice. They stepped down into the launch, finding a place in the open, and the boat chugged away down the canal and into the lagoon. The ordinary ferry had gone before, steaming towards Murano, while their own craft headed past San Francesco del Deserto and so back direct to Venice.

He put his arm around her once more, holding her close, and this time she responded, smiling up at him, her head on his shoulder.

"It's been a lovely day," she said. "I shall never forget it, never. You know, darling, now at last I can begin to enjoy our holiday."

He wanted to shout with relief. It's going to be all right, he decided, let her believe what she likes, it doesn't matter, it makes her happy. The beauty of Venice rose before them, sharply outlined against the glowing sky, and there was still so much to see, wandering there together, that might now be perfect because of her change of mood, the shadow having lifted, and aloud he began to discuss the evening to come, where they would dine—not the restaurant they usually went to, near the Venice Theatre, but somewhere different, somewhere new.

"Yes, but it must be cheap," she said, falling in with his mood, "because we've already spent so much today."

Their hotel by the Grand Canal had a welcoming, comforting air. The clerk smiled as he handed over their key. The bedroom was familiar, like home, with Laura's things arranged neatly on the dressing-table, but with it the little festive atmosphere of strangeness, of excitement, that only a holiday bedroom brings. This is ours for the moment, but no more. While we are in it we bring it life. When we have gone it no longer exists, it fades into anonymity. He turned on both taps in the bathroom, the water gushing into the bath, the steam rising. Now, he thought afterwards, now at last is the moment to make love, and he went back into the bedroom, and she understood, and opened her arms and smiled. Such blessed relief after all those weeks of restraint.

"The thing is," she said later, fixing her ear-rings before the looking-glass, "I'm not really terribly hungry. Shall we just be dull and eat in the dining-room here?"

"God, no!" he exclaimed. "With all those rather dreary couples at the other tables? I'm ravenous. I'm also gay. I want to get rather sloshed."

"Not bright lights and music, surely?"

"No, no . . . some small, dark, intimate cave, rather sinister, full of lovers with other people's wives."

"H'm," sniffed Laura, "we all know what *that* means. You'll spot some Italian lovely of sixteen and smirk at her through dinner, while I'm stuck high and dry with a beastly man's broad back."

They went out laughing into the warm soft night, and the magic was about them everywhere. "Let's walk," he said, "let's walk and work up an appetite for our gigantic meal," and inevitably they found themselves by the Molo and the lapping gondolas dancing upon the water, the lights everywhere blending with the darkness. There were other couples strolling for the same sake of aimless enjoyment, backwards, forwards, purposeless, and the inevitable sailors in groups, noisy, gesticulating, and dark-eyed girls whispering, clicking on high heels.

"The trouble is," said Laura, "walking in Venice becomes compulsive once you start. Just over the next bridge, you say, and then the next one beckons. I'm sure there are no restaurants down here, we're almost at those public gardens where they hold the Biennale. Let's turn back. I know there's a restaurant somewhere near the Church of San Zaccaria, there's a little alley-way leading to it."

"Tell you what," said John, "if we go down here by the Arsenal, and cross that bridge at the end and head left, we'll come upon San Zaccaria from the other side. We did it the other morning."

"Yes, but it was daylight then. We may lose our way, it's not very well lit."

"Don't fuss. I have an instinct for these things."

They turned down the Fondamenta del l'Arsenale and crossed the little bridge short of the Arsenal itself, and so on past the Church of San Martino. There were two canals ahead, one bearing right, the other left, with narrow streets beside them. John hesitated. Which one was it they had walked beside the day before?

"You see," protested Laura, "we shall be lost, just as I said."

"Nonsense," replied John firmly. "It's the left-hand one, I remember the little bridge."

The canal was narrow, the houses on either side seemed to close in upon it, and in the daytime, with the sun's reflection on the water and the windows of the houses open, bedding upon the balconies, a canary singing in a cage, there had been an impression of warmth, of secluded shelter. Now, ill-lit, in darkness, the windows of the houses shuttered, the water dank, the scene appeared altogether different, neglected, poor, and the long narrow boats moored to the slippery steps of cellar entrances looked like coffins.

"I swear I don't remember this bridge," said Laura, pausing, and holding on to the rail, "and I don't like the look of that alley-way beyond."

"There's a lamp halfway up," John told her. "I know exactly where we are, not far from the Greek quarter."

They crossed the bridge, and were about to plunge into the alley-way, when they heard the cry. It came, surely, from one of the houses on the opposite side, but which one it was impossible to say. With the shutters closed, each of them seemed dead. They turned, and stared in the direction from which the sound had come.

"What was it?" whispered Laura.

"Some drunk or other," said John briefly, "come on."

Less like a drunk than someone being strangled, and the choking cry suppressed as the grip held firm.

"We ought to call the police," said Laura.

"Oh, for heaven's sake," said John. Where did she think she was—Piccadilly?

"Well, I'm off, it's sinister," she replied, and began to hurry away up the twisting alley-way. John hesitated, his eye caught by a small figure which suddenly crept from a cellar entrance below one of the opposite houses, and then jumped into a narrow boat below. It was a child, a little girl—she couldn't have been more than five or six—wearing a short coat over her minute skirt, a pixie hood covering her head. There were four boats moored, line upon line, and she proceeded to jump from one to the other with surprising agility, intent, it would seem, upon escape. Once her foot slipped and he caught his breath, for she was within a few feet of the water, losing balance; then she recovered, and hopped on to the furthest boat. Bending, she tugged at the rope, which had the effect of swinging the boat's after-end across the canal, almost touching the opposite side and another cellar entrance, about thirty feet from the spot where John stood watching her. Then the child jumped again, landing upon the cellar steps, and vanished into the house, the boat swinging back into mid-canal behind her. The whole episode could not have taken more than four minutes. Then he heard the quick patter of feet. Laura had returned. She had seen none of it, for which he felt unspeakably thankful. The sight of a child, a little girl, in what must have been near danger, her fear that the scene he had just witnessed was in some way a sequel to the alarming cry, might have had a disastrous effect on her overwrought nerves.

"What are you doing?" she called. "I daren't go on without you. The wretched alley branches in two directions."

"Sorry," he told her, "I'm coming."

He took her arm and they walked briskly along the alley, John with an apparent confidence he did not possess.

"There were no more cries, were there?" she asked.

"No," he said, "no, nothing. I tell you, it was some drunk."

The alley led to a deserted campo behind a church, not a church he knew, and he led the way across, along another street and over a further bridge.

"Wait a minute," he said, "I think we take this right-hand turning. It will lead us into the Greek quarter, the Church of San Georgio is somewhere over there."

She did not answer. She was beginning to lose faith. The place was like a maze. They might circle round and round forever, and then find themselves back again, near the bridge where they had heard the cry. Doggedly he led her on, and then, surprisingly, with relief, he saw people walking in the lighted street ahead, there was a spire of a church, the surroundings became familiar.

"There, I told you," he said, "that's San Zaccaria, we've found it all right. Your restaurant can't be far away." And anyway, there would be other restaurants, somewhere to eat, at least here was the cheering glitter of lights, of movement, canals beside which people walked, the atmosphere of tourism. The letters RISTORANTE in blue lights, shone like a beacon down a left-hand alley.

"Is this your place?" he asked.

"God knows," she said. "Who cares? Let's feed there anyway."

And so into the sudden blast of heated air and hum of voices, the smell of pasta, wine, waiters, jostling customers, laughter. "For two? This way, please." Why, he thought, was one's British nationality always so obvious? A cramped little table and an enormous menu scribbled in an indecipherable mauve ink, with the waiter hovering, expecting the order forthwith.

"Two very large Camparis, with soda," John said. "*Then* we'll study the menu."

He was not going to be rushed. He handed the bill of fare to Laura and looked about him. Mostly Italians—that meant the food would be good. Then he saw them. At the opposite side of the room. The twin sisters. They must have come into the restaurant hard upon

Laura and his own arrival, for they were only now sitting down, shedding their coats, the waiter hovering beside the table. John was seized with the irrational thought that this was no coincidence. The sisters had noticed them both, in the street outside, and had followed them in. Why, in the name of hell, should they have picked on this particular spot, in the whole of Venice, unless . . . unless Laura herself, at Torcello, had suggested a further encounter, or the sister had suggested it to her? A small restaurant near the Church of San Zaccaria, we go there sometimes for dinner. It was Laura, before the walk, who had mentioned San Zaccaria . . .

She was still intent upon the menu, she had not seen the sisters, but any moment now she would have chosen what she wanted to eat, and then she would raise her head and look across the room. If only the drinks would come. If only the waiter would bring the drinks, it would give Laura something to do.

"You know, I was thinking," he said quickly, "we really ought to go to the garage tomorrow and get the car, and do that drive to Padua. We could lunch in Padua, see the cathedral and touch St. Anthony's tomb and look at the Giotto frescoes, and come back by way of those various villas along the Brenta that the guidebook recommends so highly."

It was no use, though. She was looking up, across the restaurant, and she gave a little gasp of surprise. It was genuine. He could swear it was genuine.

"Look," she said, "how extraordinary! How really amazing!"

"What?" he said sharply.

"Why, there they are. My wonderful old twins. They've seen us, what's more. They're staring this way." She waved her hand, radiant, delighted. The sister she had spoken to at Torcello bowed and smiled. False old bitch, he thought. I know they followed us.

"Oh, darling, I must go and speak to them," she said impulsively, "just to tell them how happy I've been all day, thanks to them."

"Oh, for heaven's sake," he said. "Look, here are the drinks. And we haven't ordered yet. Surely you can wait until later, until we've eaten?"

"I won't be a moment," she said, "and anyway I want scampi, nothing first. I told you I wasn't hungry."

She got up, and, brushing past the waiter with the drinks, crossed the room. She might have been greeting the loved friends of years. He watched her bend over the table, shake them both by the hand, and because there was a vacant chair at their table she drew it up and sat down, talking, smiling. Nor did the sisters seem surprised, at least not the one she knew, who nodded and talked back, while the blind sister remained impassive.

All right, thought John savagely, then I *will* get sloshed, and he proceeded to down his Campari and soda and order another, while he pointed out something quite unintelligible on the menu as his own choice, but remembered scampi for Laura. "And a bottle of soave," he added, "with ice."

The evening was ruined anyway. What was to have been an intimate and happy celebration would now be heavy-laden with spiritualistic visions, poor little dead Christine sharing the table with them, which was so damned stupid when in earthly life she would have been tucked up hours ago in bed. The bitter taste of his Campari suited his mood of sudden self-pity, and all the while he watched the group at the table in the opposite corner, Laura apparently listening while the more active sister held forth and the blind one sat silent, her formidable sightless eyes turned in his direction.

She's phoney, he thought, she's not blind at all. They're both of them frauds, and they could be males in drag after all, just as we pretended at Torcello, and they're after Laura.

He began on his second Campari and soda. The two drinks, taken on an empty stomach, had an instant effect. Vision became blurred. And still Laura went on sitting at the other table, putting in a question now and again, while the active sister talked. The waiter appeared with the scampi, and a companion beside him to serve John's own order, which was totally unrecognisable, heaped with a livid sauce.

"The signora does not come?" enquired the first waiter, and John shook his head grimly, pointing an unsteady finger across the room.

"Tell the signora," he said carefully, "her scampi will get cold."

He stared down at the offering placed before him, and prodded it delicately with a fork. The pallid sauce dissolved, revealing two enormous slices, rounds, of what appeared to be boiled pork, bedecked with garlic. He forked a portion to his mouth and chewed, and yes, it was pork, steamy, rich, the spicy sauce having turned it curiously sweet. He laid down his fork, pushing the plate away, and became aware of Laura, returning across the room and sitting beside him. She did not say anything, which was just as well, he thought, because he was too near nausea to answer. It wasn't just the drink, but reaction from the whole nightmare day. She began to eat her scampi, still not uttering. She did not seem to notice he was not eating. The waiter, hovering at his elbow, anxious, seemed aware that John's choice was somehow an error, and discreetly removed the plate. "Bring me a green salad," murmured John, and even then Laura did not register surprise, or, as she might have done in more normal circumstances, accuse him of having had too much to drink. Finally, when she had finished her scampi, and was sipping her wine, which John had waved away, to nibble at his salad in small mouthfuls like a sick rabbit, she began to speak.

"Darling," she said, "I know you won't believe it, and it's rather frightening in a way, but after they left the restaurant in Torcello the sisters went to the cathedral, as we did, although we didn't see them in that crowd, and the blind one had another vision. She said Christine was trying to tell her something about us, that we should be in danger if we stayed in Venice. Christine wanted us to go away as soon as possible."

So that's it, he thought. They think they can run our lives for us. This is to be our problem from henceforth. Do we eat? Do we get up? Do we go to bed? We must get in touch with the twin sisters. They will direct us.

"Well?" she said. "Why don't you say something?"

"Because," he answered, "you are perfectly right, I don't believe it. Quite frankly, I judge your old sisters as being a couple of freaks, if nothing else. They're obviously unbalanced, and I'm sorry if this hurts you, but the fact is they've found a sucker in you."

"You're being unfair," said Laura. "They are genuine, I know it. I just know it. They were completely sincere in what they said."

"All right. Granted. They're sincere. But that doesn't make them well-balanced. Honestly, darling, you meet that old girl for ten minutes in a loo, she tells you she sees Christine sitting beside us, well, anyone with a gift for telepathy could read your unconscious mind in an instant, and then, pleased with her success, as any old psychic expert would be, she flings a further mood of ecstasy and wants to boot us out of Venice. Well, I'm sorry, but to hell with it."

The room was no longer reeling. Anger had sobered him. If it would not put Laura to shame he would get up and cross to their table, and tell the old fools where they could get off.

"I knew you would take it like this," said Laura unhappily. "I told them you would. They said not to worry. As long as we left Venice tomorrow everything would come all right."

"Oh, for God's sake," said John. He changed his mind and poured himself a glass of wine.

"After all," Laura went on, "we have really seen the cream of Venice. I don't mind going on somewhere else. And if we stayed—I know it sounds silly, but I should have a nasty nagging sort of feeling inside me, and I should keep thinking of darling Christine being unhappy and trying to tell us to go."

"Right," said John with ominous calm, "that settles it. Go we will. I suggest we clear off to the hotel straight away and warn the reception we're leaving in the morning. Have you had enough to eat?"

"Oh, dear," sighed Laura, "don't take it like that. Look, why not come over and meet them, and then they can explain about the vision to you? Perhaps you would take it seriously then. Especially as you are the one it most concerns. Christine is more worried over you than me. And the extraordinary thing is that the blind sister says you're psychic and don't know it. You are somehow *en rapport* with the unknown, and I'm not."

"Well, that's final," said John. "I'm psychic, am I? Fine. My psychic intuition tells me to get out of this restaurant now, at once, and we can decide what we do about leaving Venice when we are back at the hotel."

He signalled to the waiter for the bill and they waited for it, not speaking to each other, Laura unhappy, fiddling with her bag, while John, glancing furtively at the twins' table, noticed that they were tucking into plates piled high with spaghetti, in very unpsychic fashion. The bill disposed of, John pushed back his chair.

"Right. Are you ready?" he asked.

"I'm going to say goodbye to them first," said Laura, her mouth set sulkily, reminding him instantly, with a pang, of their poor lost child.

"Just as you like," he replied, and walked ahead of her, out of the restaurant without a backward glance.

The soft humidity of the evening, so pleasant to walk about in earlier, had turned to rain. The strolling tourists had melted away. One or two people hurried by under umbrellas. This is what the inhabitants who live here see, he thought. This is the true life. Empty streets by night, and the dank stillness of a stagnant canal beneath shuttered houses. The rest is a bright façade put on for show, glittering by sunlight.

Laura joined him and they walked away together in silence, and emerging presently behind the ducal palace came out into the Piazza San Marco. The rain was heavy now, and they sought shelter, still walking, with the few remaining stragglers under the colonnades. The orchestras had packed up for the evening. The tables were bare. Chairs had been turned upside down.

The experts are right, he thought. Venice is sinking. The whole city is slowly dying. One day the tourists will travel here by boat to peer down into the waters, and they will see pillars and columns and marble far, far beneath them, slime and mud uncovering for brief moments a lost underworld of stone. Their heels made a ringing sound on the pavement and the rain splashed from the gutterings above. A fine ending to an evening that had started with brave hope, with innocence.

When they came to their hotel Laura made straight for the lift, and John turned to the desk to ask the night-porter for the key. The man handed him a telegram at the same time. John stared at it a moment. Laura was already in the lift. Then he opened the envelope and read the message. It was from the headmaster of Johnnie's preparatory school.

> *Johnnie under observation suspected*
> *appendicitis in city hospital here.*
> *No cause for alarm but surgeon thought*
> *wise advise you.*
>
> *Charles Hill*

He read the message twice, then walked slowly towards the lift, where Laura was waiting for him. He gave her the telegram. "This came when we were out," he said. "Not awfully good news." He pressed the lift button as she read the telegram. The lift stopped at the second floor, and they got out.

"Well, this decides it, doesn't it?" she said. "Here is the proof. We have to leave Venice because we're going home. It's Johnnie who's in danger, not us. This is what Christine was trying to tell the twins."

The first thing John did the following morning was to put a call through to the headmaster at the preparatory school. Then he gave notice of their departure to the reception manager, and they packed while they waited for the call. Neither of them referred to the events of the preceding day, it was not necessary. John knew the arrival of the telegram and the foreboding of danger from the sisters was coincidence, nothing more, but it was pointless to start an argument about it. Laura was convinced otherwise, but intuitively she knew it was best to keep her feelings to herself. During breakfast they discussed ways and means of getting home. It should be possible to get themselves, and the car, on to the special car train that ran from Milan through to Calais, since it was early in the season. In any event, the headmaster had said there was no urgency.

The call from England came while John was in the bathroom. Laura answered it. He came into the bedroom a few minutes later. She was still speaking, but he could tell from the expression in her eyes that she was anxious.

"It's Mrs. Hill," she said. "Mr. Hill is in class. She says they reported from the hospital that Johnnie had a restless night, and the surgeon may have to operate, but he doesn't want to unless it's absolutely necessary. They've taken X-rays and the appendix is in a tricky position, it's not awfully straightforward."

"Here, give it to me," he said.

The soothing but slightly guarded voice of the headmaster's wife came down the receiver. "I'm so sorry this may spoil your plans," she said, "but both Charles and I felt you ought to be told, and that you might feel rather easier if you were on the spot. Johnnie is very plucky, but of course he has some fever. That isn't unusual, the surgeon says, in the circumstances. Sometimes an appendix can get displaced, it appears, and this makes it more complicated. He's going to decide about operating this evening."

"Yes, of course, we quite understand," said John.

"Please do tell your wife not to worry too much," she went on. "The hospital is excellent, a very nice staff, and we have every confidence in the surgeon."

"Yes," said John, "yes," and then broke off because Laura was making gestures beside him.

"If we can't get the car on the train, I can fly," she said. "They're sure to be able to find me a seat on a plane. Then at least one of us would be there this evening."

He nodded agreement. "Thank you so much, Mrs. Hill," he said, "we'll manage to get back all right. Yes, I'm sure Johnnie is in good hands. Thank your husband for us. Goodbye."

He replaced the receiver and looked round him at the tumbled beds, suitcases on the floor, tissue-paper strewn. Baskets, maps, books, coats, everything they had brought with them in the car. "Oh God," he said, "what a bloody mess. All this junk." The telephone rang again. It was the hall porter to say he had succeeded in booking a sleeper for them both, and a place for the car, on the following night.

"Look," said Laura, who had seized the telephone, "could you book one seat on the midday plane from Venice to London today, for me? It's imperative one of us gets home this evening. My husband could follow with the car tomorrow."

"Here, hang on," interrupted John. "No need for panic stations. Surely twenty-four hours wouldn't make all that difference?"

Anxiety had drained the colour from her face. She turned to him, distraught.

"It mightn't to you, but it does to me," she said. "I've lost one child, I'm not going to lose another."

"All right, darling, all right . . ." He put his hand out to her, but she brushed it off, impatiently, and continued giving directions to the porter. He turned back to his packing. No use saying anything. Better for it to be as she wished. They could, of course, both go by air, and then when all was well, and Johnnie better, he could come back and fetch the car, driving home through France as they had come. Rather a sweat, though, and a hell of an expense. Bad enough Laura going by air and himself with the car on the train from Milan.

"We could, if you like, both fly," he began tentatively, explaining the sudden idea, but she would have none of it. "That really *would* be absurd," she said impatiently. "As long as I'm there this evening, and you follow by train, it's all that matters. Besides, we shall need the car, going backwards and forwards to the hospital. And our luggage. We couldn't go off and just leave all this here."

No, he saw her point. A silly idea. It was only, well, he was as worried about Johnnie as she was, though he wasn't going to say so.

"I'm going downstairs to stand over the porter," said Laura. "They always make more effort if one is actually on the spot. Everything I want tonight is packed. I shall only need my overnight case. You can bring everything else in the car." She hadn't been out of the bedroom five minutes before the telephone rang. It was Laura. "Darling," she said, "it couldn't have worked out better. The porter has got me on a charter flight that leaves Venice in less than an hour. A special motor-launch takes the party direct from San Marco, in about ten minutes. Some passenger on the charter flight had cancelled. I shall be at Gatwick in less than four hours."

"I'll be down right away," he told her.

He joined her by the reception desk. She no longer looked anxious and drawn, but full of purpose. She was on her way. He kept wishing they were going together. He couldn't bear to stay on in Venice after she had gone, but the thought of driving to Milan, spending a dreary night in a hotel there alone, the endless dragging day which would follow, and the long hours in the train the next night, filled him with intolerable depression, quite apart from the anxiety about Johnnie. They walked along to the San Marco landing-stage, the Molo bright and glittering after the rain, a little breeze blowing, the postcards and scarves and tourist souvenirs fluttering on the stalls, the tourists themselves out in force, strolling, contented, the happy day before them.

"I'll ring you tonight from Milan," he told her. "The Hills will give you a bed, I suppose. And if you're at the hospital they'll let me have the latest news. That must be your charter party. You're welcome to them!"

The passengers descending from the landing-stage down into the waiting launch were carrying hand-luggage with Union Jack tags upon them. They were mostly middle-aged, with what appeared to be two Methodist ministers in charge. One of them advanced towards Laura, holding out his hand, showing a gleaming row of dentures when he smiled. "You must be the lady joining us for the homeward flight," he said. "Welcome aboard, and to the Union of Fellowship. We are all delighted to make your acquaintance. Sorry we hadn't a seat for hubby too."

Laura turned swiftly and kissed John, a tremor at the corner of her mouth betraying inward laughter. "Do you think they'll break into hymns?" she whispered. "Take care of yourself, hubby. Call me tonight."

The pilot sounded a curious little toot upon his horn, and in a moment Laura had climbed down the steps into the launch and was standing amongst the crowd of passengers, waving her hand, her scarlet coat a gay patch of colour amongst the more sober suiting of her companions. The launch tooted again and moved away from the landing-stage, and he stood there watching it, a sense of immense loss filling his heart. Then he turned and walked away, back to the hotel, the bright day all about him desolate, unseen.

There was nothing, he thought, as he looked about him presently in the hotel bedroom, so melancholy as a vacated room, especially when the recent signs of occupation were still visible about him. Laura's suitcases on the bed, a second coat she had left behind. Traces of powder on the dressing-table. A tissue, with a lipstick smear, thrown in the wastepaper basket. Even an old tooth-paste tube squeezed dry, lying on the glass shelf above the wash-basin. Sounds of the heedless traffic on the Grand Canal came as always from the open window, but Laura wasn't there any more to listen to it, or to watch from the small balcony. The pleasure had gone. Feeling had gone.

John finished packing, and, leaving all the baggage ready to be collected, he went downstairs to pay the bill. The reception clerk was welcoming new arrivals. People were sitting on the terrace overlooking the Grand Canal reading newspapers, the pleasant day waiting to be planned.

John decided to have an early lunch, here on the hotel terrace, on familiar ground, and then have the porter carry the baggage to one of the ferries that steamed between San Marco and the Porta Roma, where the car was garaged. The fiasco meal of the night before had left him empty, and he was ready for the trolley of hors d'oeuvres when they brought it to him, around midday. Even here, though, there was change. The head-waiter, their especial friend, was off-duty, and the table where they usually sat was occupied by new arrivals, a honeymoon couple, he told himself sourly, observing the gaiety, the smiles, while he had been shown to a small single table behind a tub of flowers.

She's airborne now, John thought, she's on her way, and he tried to picture Laura seated between the Methodist ministers, telling them, no doubt, about Johnnie ill in hospital, and heaven knows what else besides. Well, the twin sisters anyway could rest in psychic peace. Their wishes would have been fulfilled.

Lunch over, there was no point in lingering with a cup of coffee on the terrace. His desire was to get away as soon as possible, fetch the car, and be en route for Milan. He made his farewells at the reception desk, and, escorted by a porter who had piled his baggage on to a wheeled trolley, he made his way once more to the landing-stage of San Marco. As he stepped on to the steam-ferry, his luggage heaped beside him, a crowd of jostling people all about him, he had one momentary pang to be leaving Venice. When, if ever, he wondered, would they come again? Next year . . . in three years . . . Glimpsed first on honeymoon, nearly ten years ago, and then a second visit, *en passant,* before a cruise, and now this last abortive ten days that had ended so abruptly.

The water glittered in the sunshine, buildings shone, tourists in dark glasses paraded up and down the rapidly receding Molo; already the terrace of their hotel was out of sight as the ferry churned its way up the Grand Canal. So many impressions to seize and hold, familiar loved façades, balconies, windows, water lapping the cellar steps of decaying palaces, the little red house where d'Annunzio lived, with its garden—our house, Laura called it, pretending it was theirs—and too soon the ferry would be turning left on the direct route to the Piazzale Roma, so missing the best of the Canal, the Rialto, the farther palaces.

Another ferry was heading downstream to pass them, filled with passengers, and for a brief foolish moment he wished he could change places, be amongst the happy tourists bound for Venice and all he had left behind him. Then he saw her. Laura, in her scarlet coat, the twin sisters by her side, the active sister with her hand on Laura's arm, talking earnestly, and Laura herself, her hair blowing in the wind, gesticulating, on her face a look of distress. He stared, astounded, too astonished to shout, to wave, and anyway they would never have heard or seen him, for his own ferry had already passed and was heading in the opposite direction.

What the hell had happened? There must have been a hold-up with the charter flight and it had never taken off, but in that case why had Laura not telephoned him at the hotel? And what were those damned sisters doing? Had she run into them at the airport? Was it coincidence?

And why did she look so anxious? He could think of no explanation. Perhaps the flight had been cancelled. Laura, of course, would go straight to the hotel, expecting to find him there, intending, doubtless, to drive with him after all to Milan and take the train the following night. What a blasted mix-up. The only thing to do was to telephone the hotel immediately his ferry reached the Piazzale Roma and tell her to wait, he would return and fetch her. As for the damned interfering sisters, they could get stuffed.

The usual stampede ensued when the ferry arrived at the landing-stage. He had to find a porter to collect his baggage, and then wait while he discovered a telephone. The fiddling with change, the hunt for the number, delayed him still more. He succeeded at last in getting through, and luckily the reception clerk he knew was still at the desk.

"Look, there's been some frightful muddle," he began, and explained how Laura was even now on her way back to the hotel—he had seen her with two friends on one of the ferry-services. Would the reception clerk explain and tell her to wait? He would be back by the next available service to collect her. "In any event, detain her," he said. "I'll be as quick as I can." The reception clerk understood perfectly and John rang off.

Thank heaven Laura hadn't turned up before he had put through his call, or they would have told her he was on his way to Milan. The porter was still waiting with the baggage, and it seemed simplest to walk with him to the garage, hand everything over to the chap in charge of the office there, and ask him to keep it for an hour, when he would be returning with his wife to pick up the car. Then he went back to the landing-station to await the next ferry to Venice. The minutes dragged, and he kept wondering all the time what had gone wrong at the airport and why in heaven's name Laura hadn't telephoned. No use conjecturing. She would tell him the whole story at the hotel. One thing was certain. He would not allow themselves to be saddled with the sisters and become involved with their affairs. He could imagine Laura saying that they also had missed a flight, and could they have a lift to Milan?

Finally the ferry chugged alongside the landing-stage and he stepped aboard. What an anticlimax, thrashing back past the familiar sights to which he had bidden a nostalgic farewell such a short while ago! He didn't even look about him this time, he was so intent on reaching his destination. In San Marco there were more people than ever, the afternoon crowds walking shoulder to shoulder, every one of them on pleasure bent.

He came to the hotel, and pushed his way through the swing-door, expecting to see Laura, and possibly the sisters, waiting in the lounge on the left-hand side of the entrance. She was not there. He went to the desk. The reception clerk he had spoken to on the telephone was standing there, talking to the manager.

"Has my wife arrived?" John asked.

"No, sir, not yet."

"What an extraordinary thing. Are you sure?"

"Absolutely certain, sir. I have been here ever since you telephoned me at a quarter to two. I have not left the desk."

"I just don't understand it. She was on one of the vaporettos passing by the Accademia. She would have landed at San Marco about five minutes later and come on here."

The clerk seemed nonplussed. "I don't know what to say. The signora was with friends, did you say?"

"Yes. Well, acquaintances. Two ladies we had met at Torcello yesterday. I was astonished to see her with them on the vaporetto, and of course I assumed that the flight had been cancelled, and she had somehow met up with them at the airport and decided to return here with them, to catch me before I left."

Oh hell, what was Laura doing? It was after three. A matter of moments from San Marco landing-stage to the hotel.

"Perhaps the signora went with her friends to their hotel instead. Do you know where they are staying?"

"No," said John, "I haven't the slightest idea. What's more I don't even know the names of the two ladies. They were sisters, twins, in fact—looked exactly alike. But, anyway, why go to their hotel and not here?"

The swing-door opened but it wasn't Laura. Two people staying in the hotel.

The manager broke into the conversation, "I tell you what I will do," he said. "I will telephone the airport and check about the flight. Then at least we will get somewhere." He smiled apologetically. It was not usual for arrangements to go wrong.

"Yes, do that," said John. "We may as well know what happened there."

He lit a cigarette and began to pace up and down the entrance hall. What a bloody mix-up. And how unlike Laura, who knew he would be setting off for Milan directly after lunch—indeed, for all she knew he might have gone before. But surely, in that case, she would have telephoned at once, on arrival at the airport, had take-off been cancelled? The manager was ages telephoning, he had to be put through on some other line, and his Italian was too rapid for John to follow the conversation. Finally he replaced the receiver.

"It is more mysterious than ever, sir," he said. "The charter flight was not delayed, it took off on schedule with a full complement of passengers. As far as they could tell me, there was no hitch. The signora must simply have changed her mind." His smile was more apologetic than ever.

"Changed her mind," John repeated. "But why on earth should she do that? She was so anxious to be home tonight."

The manager shrugged. "You know how ladies can be, sir," he said. "Your wife may have thought that after all she would prefer to take the train to Milan with you. I do assure you, though, that the charter party was most respectable, and it was a Caravelle aircraft, perfectly safe."

"Yes, yes," said John impatiently, "I don't blame your arrangements in the slightest. I just can't understand what induced her to change her mind, unless it was meeting with these two ladies."

The manager was silent. He could not think of anything to say. The reception clerk was equally concerned. "It is possible," he ventured, "that you made a mistake, and it was not the signora that you saw on the vaporetto?"

"Oh no," replied John, "it was my wife, I assure you. She was wearing her red coat, she was hatless, just as she left here. I saw her as plainly as I can see you. I would swear to it in a court of law."

"It is unfortunate," said the manager, "that we do not know the name of the two ladies, or the hotel where they were staying. You say you met these ladies at Torcello yesterday?"

"Yes . . . but only briefly. They weren't staying there. At least, I am certain they were not. We saw them at dinner in Venice later, as it happens."

"Excuse me . . ." Guests were arriving with luggage to check in, the clerk was obliged to attend to them. John turned in desperation to the manager. "Do you think it would be any good telephoning the hotel in Torcello in case the people there knew the name of the ladies, or where they were staying in Venice?"

"We can try," replied the manager. "It is a small hope, but we can try."

John resumed his anxious pacing, all the while watching the swing-door, hoping, praying, that he would catch sight of the red coat and Laura would enter. Once again there followed what seemed an interminable telephone conversation between the manager and someone at the hotel in Torcello.

"Tell them two sisters," said John, "two elderly ladies dressed in grey, both exactly alike. One lady was blind," he added. The manager nodded. He was obviously giving a detailed description. Yet when he hung up he shook his head. "The manager at Torcello says he remembers the two ladies well," he told John, "but they were only there for lunch. He never learnt their names."

"Well, that's that. There's nothing to do now but wait."

John lit his third cigarette and went out on to the terrace, to resume his pacing there. He stared out across the canal, searching the heads of the people on passing steamers, motorboats, even drifting gondolas. The minutes ticked by on his watch, and there was no sign of Laura. A terrible foreboding nagged at him that somehow this was prearranged, that Laura had never intended to catch the aircraft, that last night in the restaurant she had made an assignation with the sisters. Oh God, he thought, that's impossible, I'm going paranoiac . . . Yet why, why? No, more likely the encounter at the airport was fortuitous, and for some incredible reason they had persuaded Laura not to board the aircraft, even prevented her from doing so, trotting out one of their psychic visions, that the aircraft would crash, that she must return with them to Venice. And Laura, in her sensitive state, felt they must be right, swallowed it all without question.

But granted all these possibilities, why had she not come to the hotel? What was she doing? Four o'clock, half-past four, the sun no longer dappling the water. He went back to the reception desk.

"I just can't hang around," he said. "Even if she does turn up, we shall never make Milan this evening. I might see her walking with these ladies, in the Piazza San Marco, anywhere. If she arrives while I'm out, will you explain?"

The clerk was full of concern. "Indeed, yes," he said. "It is very worrying for you, sir. Would it perhaps be prudent if we booked you in here tonight?"

John gestured, helplessly. "Perhaps, yes, I don't know. Maybe . . ."

He went out of the swing-door and began to walk towards the Piazza San Marco. He looked into every shop up and down the colonnades, crossed the piazza a dozen times, threaded his way between the tables in front of Florian's, in front of Quadri's, knowing that Laura's red coat and the distinct appearance of the twin sisters could easily be spotted, even amongst this milling crowd, but there was no sign of them. He joined the crowd of shoppers in the Merceria, shoulder to shoulder with idlers, thrusters, window-gazers, knowing instinctively that it was useless, they wouldn't be here. Why should Laura have deliberately missed her flight to return to Venice for such a purpose? And even if she had done so, for some reason beyond his imagining, she would surely have come first to the hotel to find him.

The only thing left to him was to try to track down the sisters. Their hotel could be anywhere amongst the hundreds of hotels and pensions scattered through Venice, or even across the other side at the Zattere, or farther again on the Giudecca. These last possibilities seemed remote. More likely they were staying in a small hotel or pension somewhere near San Zaccaria handy to the restaurant where they had dined last night. The blind one would surely not go far afield in the evening. He had been a fool not to have thought of this before, and he turned back and walked quickly away from the brightly lighted shopping district towards the narrower, more cramped quarter where they had dined last evening. He found the restaurant without difficulty, but they were not yet open for dinner, and the waiter preparing tables was not the one who had served them. John asked to see the *patrone*, and the waiter disappeared to the back regions, returning after a moment or two with the somewhat dishevelled-looking proprietor in shirt-sleeves, caught in a slack moment, not in full *tenue*.

"I had dinner here last night," John explained. "There were two ladies sitting at that table there in the corner." He pointed to it.

"You wish to book that table for this evening?" asked the proprietor.

"No," said John. "No, there were two ladies there last night, two sisters, *due sorelle*, twins, *gemelle*"—what was the right word for twins? "Do you remember? Two ladies, *sorelle, vecchie* . . ."

"Ah," said the man, "si, si, signore, *la povera* signorina." He put his hands to his eyes to feign blindness. "Yes, I remember."

"Do you know their names?" asked John. "Where they were staying? I am very anxious to trace them."

The proprietor spread out his hands in a gesture of regret. "I am ver' sorry, signore, I do not know the names of the signorine, they have been here once, twice perhaps, for dinner, they do not say where they were staying. Perhaps if you come again tonight they might be here? Would you like to book a table?"

He pointed around him, suggesting a whole choice of tables that might appeal to a prospective diner, but John shook his head.

"Thank you, no. I may be dining elsewhere. I am sorry to have troubled you. If the signorine should come"—he paused—"possibly I may return later," he added. "I am not sure."

The proprietor bowed, and walked with him to the entrance. "In Venice the whole world meets," he said smiling. "It is possible the signore will find his friends tonight. *Arrivederci*, signore."

Friends? John walked out into the street. More likely kidnappers . . .

Anxiety had turned to fear, to panic. Something had gone terribly wrong. Those women had got hold of Laura, played upon her suggestibility, induced her to go with them, either to their hotel or elsewhere. Should he find the Consulate? Where was it? What would he say when he got there? He began walking without purpose, finding himself, as they had done the night before, in streets he did not know, and suddenly came upon a tall building with the word QUESTURA above it. This is it, he thought. I don't care, something has happened, I'm going inside. There were a number of police in uniform coming and going, the place at any rate was active, and, addressing himself to one of them behind a glass-partition, he asked if there was anyone who spoke English. The man pointed to a flight of stairs and John went up, entering a door on the right where he saw that another couple were sitting, waiting, and with relief he recognised them as fellow-countrymen, tourists, obviously a man and his wife, in some sort of predicament.

"Come and sit down," said the man. "We've waited half-an-hour but they can't be much longer. What a country! They wouldn't leave us like this at home."

John took the proffered cigarette and found a chair beside them.

"What's your trouble?" he asked.

"My wife had her handbag pinched in one of those shops in the Merceria," said the man. "She simply put it down one moment to look at something, and you'd hardly credit it, the next moment it had gone. I say it was a sneak thief, she insists it was the girl behind the counter. But who's to say? These Ities are all alike. Anyway, I'm certain we shan't get it back. What have you lost?"

"Suitcase stolen," John lied rapidly. "Had some important papers in it."

How could he say he had lost his wife? He couldn't even begin . . .

The man nodded in sympathy. "As I said, these Ities are all alike. Old Musso knew how to deal with them. Too many Communists around these days. The trouble is, they're not going to bother with our troubles much, not with this murderer at large. They're all out looking for him."

"Murderer? What murderer?" asked John.

"Don't tell me you've not heard about it?" The man stared at him in surprise. "Venice has talked of nothing else. It's been in all the papers, on the radio, and even in the English papers too. A grizzly business. One woman found with her throat slit last week—a tourist too—and some old chap discovered with the same sort of knife wound this morning. They seem to think it must be a maniac because there doesn't seem to be any motive. Nasty thing to happen in Venice in the tourist season."

"My wife and I never bother with the newspapers when we're on holiday," said John. "And we're neither of us much given to gossip in the hotel."

"Very wise of you," laughed the man. "It might have spoilt your holiday, especially if your wife is nervous. Oh well, we're off tomorrow anyway. Can't say we mind, do we, dear?" He turned to his wife. "Venice has gone downhill since we were here last. And now this loss of the handbag really is the limit."

The door of the inner room opened, and a senior police officer asked John's companion and his wife to pass through.

"I bet we don't get any satisfaction," murmured the tourist, winking at John, and he and his wife went into the inner room. The door closed behind them. John stubbed out his cigarette and lighted another. A strange feeling of unreality possessed him. He asked himself what he was doing here, what was the use of it? Laura was no longer in Venice but had disappeared, perhaps forever, with those diabolical sisters. She would never be traced. And just as the two of them had made up a fantastic story about the twins, when they first spotted them in Torcello, so, with nightmare logic, the fiction would have basis in fact: the women were in reality disguised crooks, men with criminal intent who lured unsuspecting persons to some appalling fate. They might even be the murderers for whom the police sought. Who would ever suspect two elderly women of respectable appearance, living quietly in some second-rate pension or hotel? He stubbed out his cigarette, unfinished.

This, he thought, is really the start of paranoia. This is the way people go off their heads. He glanced at his watch. It was half-past six. Better pack this in, this futile quest here in police headquarters, and keep to the single link of sanity remaining. Return to the hotel, put a call through to the prep school in England, and ask about the latest news of Johnnie. He had not thought about poor Johnnie since sighting Laura on the vaporetto.

Too late, though. The inner door opened, the couple were ushered out.

"Usual clap-trap," said the husband sotto voce to John. "They'll do what they can. Not much hope. So many foreigners in Venice, all of 'em thieves! The locals all above reproach. Wouldn't pay 'em to steal from customers. Well, I wish you better luck."

He nodded, his wife smiled and bowed, and they had gone. John followed the police officer into the inner room.

Formalities began. Name, address, passport. Length of stay in Venice, etc., etc. Then the questions, and John, the sweat beginning to appear on his forehead, launched into his interminable story. The first encounter with the sisters, the meeting at the restaurant, Laura's state of suggestibility because of the death of their child, the telegram about Johnnie, the decision to take the chartered flight, her departure, and her sudden inexplicable return. When he had finished he felt as exhausted as if he had driven three hundred miles nonstop after a severe bout of flu. His interrogator spoke excellent English with a strong Italian accent.

"You say," he began, "that your wife was suffering the aftereffects of shock. This had been noticeable during your stay here in Venice?"

"Well, yes," John replied, "she had really been quite ill. The holiday didn't seem to be doing her much good. It was only when she met these two women at Torcello yesterday that her mood changed. The strain seemed to have gone. She was ready, I suppose, to snatch at every straw, and this belief that our little girl was watching over her had somehow restored her to what appeared normality."

"It would be natural," said the police officer, "in the circumstances. But no doubt the telegram last night was a further shock to you both?"

"Indeed, yes. That was the reason we decided to return home."

"No argument between you? No difference of opinion?"

"None. We were in complete agreement. My one regret was that I could not go with my wife on this charter flight."

The police officer nodded. "It could well be that your wife had a sudden attack of amnesia and meeting the two ladies served as a link, she clung to them for support. You have described them with great accuracy, and I think they should not be too difficult to trace. Meanwhile, I suggest you should return to your hotel, and we will get in touch with you as soon as we have news."

At least, John thought, they believed his story. They did not consider him a crank who had made the whole thing up and was merely wasting their time.

"You appreciate," he said, "I am extremely anxious. These women may have some criminal design upon my wife. One has heard of such things . . ."

The police officer smiled for the first time. "Please don't concern yourself," he said. "I am sure there will be some satisfactory explanation."

All very well, thought John, but in heaven's name, what?

"I'm sorry," he said, "to have taken up so much of your time.

Especially as I gather the police have their hands full hunting down a murderer who is still at large."

He spoke deliberately. No harm in letting the fellow know that for all any of them could tell there might be some connection between Laura's disappearance and this other hideous affair.

"Ah, that," said the police officer, rising to his feet. "We hope to have the murderer under lock and key very soon."

His tone of confidence was reassuring. Murderers, missing wives, lost handbags were all under control. They shook hands, and John was ushered out of the door and so downstairs. Perhaps, he thought, as he walked slowly back to the hotel, the fellow was right. Laura had suffered a sudden attack of amnesia, and the sisters happened to be at the airport and had brought her back to Venice, to their own hotel, because Laura couldn't remember where she and John had been staying. Perhaps they were even now trying to track down his hotel. Anyway, he could do nothing more. The police had everything in hand, and, please God, would come up with the solution. All he wanted to do right now was to collapse upon a bed with a stiff whisky, and then put through a call to Johnnie's school.

The page took him up in the lift to a modest room on the fourth floor at the rear of the hotel. Bare, impersonal, the shutters closed, with a smell of cooking wafting up from a courtyard down below.

"Ask them to send me up a double whisky, will you?" he said to the boy, "and a ginger-ale," and when he was alone he plunged his face under the cold tap in the wash-basin, relieved to find that the minute portion of visitor's soap afforded some measure of comfort. He flung off his shoes, hung his coat over the back of a chair, and threw himself down on the bed. Somebody's radio was blasting forth an old popular song, now several seasons out-of-date, that had been one of Laura's favourites a couple of years ago. "I love you, baby . . ." They had taped it and used to play it back in the car. He reached out for the telephone, and asked the exchange to put through the call to England. Then he closed his eyes, and all the while the insistent voice persisted, "I love you, baby . . . I can't get you out of my mind."

Presently there was a tap at the door. It was the waiter with his drink. Too little ice, such meagre comfort, but what desperate need. He gulped it down without the ginger-ale, and in a few moments the ever-nagging pain was eased, numbed, bringing, if only momentarily, a sense of calm. The telephone rang, and now, he thought, bracing himself for ultimate disaster, the final shock, Johnnie probably dying, or already dead. In which case nothing remained. Let Venice be engulfed . . .

The exchange told him that connection had been made, and in a moment he heard the voice of Mrs. Hill at the other end of the line. They must have warned her that the call came from Venice, for she knew instantly who was speaking.

"Hullo?" she cried. "Oh, I am so glad you rang. All is well. Johnnie has had his operation, the surgeon decided to do it at midday rather than wait, and it was completely successful. Johnnie is going to be all right. So you don't have to worry any more, and will have a peaceful night."

"Thank God," he answered.

"I know," she said, "we are all so relieved. Now I'll get off the line and you can speak to your wife."

John sat up on the bed, stunned. What the hell did she mean? Then he heard Laura's voice, cool and clear.

"Darling? Darling, are you there?"

He could not answer. He felt the hand holding the receiver go clammy cold with sweat. "I'm here," he whispered.

"It's not a very good line," she said, "but never mind. As Mrs. Hill told you, all is well. Such a nice surgeon, and a very sweet Sister on Johnnie's floor, and I really am happy about the way it's turned out. I came straight down here after landing at Gatwick—the flight O.K., by the way, but such a funny crowd, it'll make you hysterical when I tell you about them—and I went to the hospital, and Johnnie was coming round. Very dopey, of course, but so pleased to see me. And the Hills are being wonderful, I've got their spare-room, and it's only a short taxi-drive into the town and the hospital. I shall go to bed as soon as we've had dinner, because I'm a bit fagged, what with the flight and the anxiety. How was the drive to Milan? And where are you staying?"

John did not recognise the voice that answered as his own. It was the automatic response of some computer.

"I'm not in Milan," he said, "I'm still in Venice."

"Still in Venice? What on earth for? Wouldn't the car start?"

"I can't explain," he said. "There was a stupid sort of mix-up . . ."

He felt suddenly so exhausted that he nearly dropped the receiver, and, shame upon shame, he could feel tears pricking behind his eyes.

"What sort of mix-up?" Her voice was suspicious, almost hostile. "You weren't in a crash?"

"No . . . no . . . nothing like that."

A moment's silence, and then she said, "Your voice sounds very slurred. Don't tell me you went and got pissed."

Oh Christ . . . if she only knew! He was probably going to pass out any moment, but not from the whisky.

"I thought," he said slowly, "I thought I saw you, in a vaporetto, with those two sisters."

What was the point of going on? It was hopeless trying to explain.

"How could you have seen me with the sisters?" she said. "You knew I'd gone to the airport. Really, darling, you are an idiot. You seem to have got those two poor old dears on the brain. I hope you didn't say anything to Mrs. Hill just now."

"No."

"Well, what are you going to do? You'll catch the train at Milan tomorrow, won't you?"

"Yes, of course," he told her.

"I still don't understand what kept you in Venice," she said. "It all sounds a bit odd to me. However . . . thank God Johnnie is going to be all right and I'm here."

"Yes," he said, "yes."

He could hear the distant boom-boom sound of a gong from the headmaster's hall.

"You had better go," he said. "My regards to the Hills, and my love to Johnnie."

"Well, take care of yourself, darling, and for goodness sake don't miss the train tomorrow, and drive carefully."

The telephone clicked and she had gone. He poured the remaining drop of whisky into his empty glass, and, sousing it with ginger-ale, drank it down at a gulp. He got up, crossed the room, threw open the shutters, and leant out of the window. He felt light-headed. His sense of relief, enormous, overwhelming, was somehow tempered with a curious feeling of unreality, almost as though the voice speaking from England had not been Laura's after all but a fake, and she was still in Venice, hidden in some furtive pension with the two sisters.

The point was, he *had* seen all three of them on the vaporetto. It was not another woman in a red coat. The women *had* been there, with Laura. So what was the explanation? That he was going off his head? Or something more sinister? The sisters, possessing psychic powers of formidable strength, had seen him as their two ferries had passed, and in some inexplicable fashion had made him believe Laura was with them. But why, and to what end? No, it didn't make sense. The only explanation was that he had been mistaken, the whole episode an hallucination. In which case he needed psychoanalysis, just as Johnnie had needed a surgeon.

And what did he do now? Go downstairs and tell the management he had been at fault and had just spoken to his wife, who had arrived in England safe and sound from her charter flight? He put on his shoes and ran his fingers through his hair. He glanced at his watch. It was ten minutes to eight. If he nipped into the bar and had a quick drink it would be easier to face the manager and admit what had happened. Then, perhaps, they would get in touch with the police. Profuse apologies all round for putting everyone to enormous trouble.

He made his way to the ground floor and went straight to the bar, feeling self-conscious, a marked man, half-imagining everyone would look at him, thinking, *There's the fellow with the missing wife.* Luckily the bar was full and there wasn't a face he knew. Even the chap behind the bar was an underling who hadn't served him before. He downed his whisky and glanced over his shoulder to the reception hall. The desk was momentarily empty. He could see the manager's back framed in the doorway of an inner room, talking to someone within. On impulse, coward-like, he crossed the hall and passed through the swing-door to the street outside.

I'll have some dinner, he decided, and then go back and face them. I'll feel more like it once I've some food inside me.

He went to the restaurant nearby where he and Laura had dined once or twice. Nothing mattered any more, because she was safe. The nightmare lay behind him. He could enjoy his dinner, despite her absence, and think of her sitting down with the Hills to a dull, quiet evening, early to bed, and on the following morning going to the hospital to sit with Johnnie. Johnnie was safe too. No more worries, only the awkward explanations and apologies to the manager at the hotel.

There was a pleasant anonymity sitting down at a corner table alone in the little restaurant, ordering *vitello allo* Marsala and half a bottle of Merlot. He took his time, enjoying his food but eating in a kind of haze, a sense of unreality still with him, while the conversation of his nearest neighbours had the same soothing effect as background music.

When they rose and left, he saw by the clock on the wall that it was nearly half-past nine. No use delaying matters any further. He drank his coffee, lighted a cigarette, and paid his bill. After all, he thought, as he walked back to the hotel, the manager would be greatly relieved to know that all was well.

When he pushed through the swing-door, the first thing he noticed was a man in police uniform, standing talking to the manager at the desk. The reception clerk was there too. They turned as John approached, and the manager's face lighted up with relief.

"*Eccolo!*" he exclaimed, "I was certain the signore would not be far away. Things are moving, signore. The two ladies have been traced, and they very kindly agreed to accompany the police to the Questura. If you will go there at once, this *agente di polizia* will escort you."

John flushed. "I have given everyone a lot of trouble," he said. "I meant to tell you before going out to dinner, but you were not at the desk. The fact is that I have contacted my wife. She did make the flight to London after all, and I spoke to her on the telephone. It was all a great mistake."

The manager looked bewildered. "The signora is in London?" he repeated. He broke off, and exchanged a rapid conversation in Italian with the policeman. "It seems that the ladies maintain they did not go out for the day, except for a little shopping in the morning," he said, turning back to John. "Then who was it the signore saw on the vaporetto?"

John shook his head. "A very extraordinary mistake on my part which I still don't understand," he said. "Obviously, I did not see either my wife or the two ladies. I really am extremely sorry."

More rapid conversation in Italian. John noticed the clerk watching him with a curious expression in his eyes. The manager was obviously apologising on John's behalf to the policeman, who looked annoyed and gave tongue to this effect, his voice increasing in volume, to the manager's concern. The whole business had undoubtedly given enormous trouble to a great many people, not least the two unfortunate sisters.

"Look," said John, interrupting the flow, "will you tell the *agente* I will go with him to headquarters and apologise in person both to the police officer and to the ladies?"

The manager looked relieved. "If the signore would take the trouble," he said. "Naturally, the ladies were much distressed when a policeman interrogated them at their hotel, and they offered to accompany him to the Questura only because they were so distressed about the signora."

John felt more and more uncomfortable. Laura must never learn any of this. She would be outraged. He wondered if there were some penalty for giving the police misleading information involving a third party. His error began, in retrospect, to take on criminal proportions.

He crossed the Piazza San Marco, now thronged with after-dinner strollers and spectators at the cafes, all three orchestras going full blast in harmonious rivalry, while his companion kept a discreet two paces to his left and never uttered a word.

They arrived at the police station and mounted the stairs to the same inner room where he had been before. He saw immediately that it was not the officer he knew but another who sat behind the desk, a sallow-faced individual with a sour expression, while the two sisters, obviously upset—the active one in particular—were seated on chairs nearby, some underling in uniform standing behind them. John's escort went at once to the police officer, speaking in rapid Italian, while John himself, after a moment's hesitation, advanced towards the sisters.

"There has been a terrible mistake," he said. "I don't know how to apologise to you both. It's all my fault, mine entirely, the police are not to blame."

The active sister made as though to rise, her mouth twitching nervously, but he restrained her.

"We don't understand," she said, the Scots inflection strong. "We said goodnight to your wife last night at dinner, and we have not seen her since. The police came to our pension more than an hour ago and told us your wife was missing and you had filed a complaint against us. My sister is not very strong. She was considerably disturbed."

"A mistake. A frightful mistake," he repeated.

He turned towards the desk. The police officer was addressing him, his English very inferior to that of the previous interrogator. He had John's earlier statement on the desk in front of him, and tapped it with a pencil.

"So?" he queried. "This document all lies? You not speaka the truth?"

"I believed it to be true at the time," said John. "I could have sworn in a court of law that I saw my wife with these two ladies on a vaporetto in the Grand Canal this afternoon. Now I realise I was mistaken."

"We have not been near the Grand Canal all day," protested the sister, "not even on foot. We made a few purchases in the Merceria this morning, and remained indoors all afternoon. My sister was a little unwell. I have told the police officer this a dozen times, and the people at the pension would corroborate our story. He refused to listen."

"And the signora?" rapped the police officer angrily. "What happen to the signora?"

"The signora, my wife, is safe in England," explained John patiently. "I talked to her on the telephone just after seven. She did join the charter flight from the airport, and is now staying with friends."

"Then who you see on the vaporetto in the red coat?" asked the furious police officer. "And if not these signorine here, then what signorine?"

"My eyes deceived me," said John, aware that his English was likewise becoming strained. "I think I see my wife and these ladies but not, it was not so. My wife in aircraft, these ladies in pension all the time."

It was like talking stage Chinese. In a moment he would be bowing and putting his hands in his sleeves.

The police officer raised his eyes to heaven and thumped the table. "So all this work for nothing," he said. "Hotels and pensiones searched for the signorine and a missing signora *inglese,* when here we have plenty, plenty other things to do. You maka a mistake. You have perhaps too much vino at *mezzo giorno* and you see hundred signore in red coats in hundred vaporetti." He stood up, rumpling the papers on the desk. "And you, signorine," he said, "you wish to make complaint against this person?" He was addressing the active sister.

"Oh no," she said, "no, indeed. I quite see it was all a mistake. Our only wish is to return at once to our pension."

The police officer grunted. Then he pointed at John. "You very lucky man," he said. "These signorine could file complaint against you—very serious matter."

"I'm sure," began John, "I'll do anything in my power . . ."

"Please don't think of it," exclaimed the sister, horrified. "We would not hear of such a thing." It was her turn to apologise to the police officer. "I hope we need not take up any more of your valuable time," she said.

He waved a hand of dismissal and spoke in Italian to the underling. "This man walk with you to the pension," he said. "*Buona sera,* signorine," and, ignoring John, he sat down again at his desk.

"I'll come with you," said John. "I want to explain exactly what happened."

They trooped down the stairs and out of the building, the blind sister leaning on her twin's arm, and once outside she turned her sightless eyes to John.

"You saw us," she said, "and your wife too. But not today. You saw us in the future."

Her voice was softer than her sister's, slower, she seemed to have some slight impediment in her speech.

"I don't follow," replied John, bewildered.

He turned to the active sister and she shook her head at him, frowning, and put her fingers on her lips.

"Come along, dear," she said to her twin. "You know you're very tired, and I want to get you home." Then, sotto voce to John, "She's psychic. Your wife told you, I believe, but I don't want her to go into trance here in the street."

God forbid, thought John, and the little procession began to move slowly along the street, away from police headquarters, a canal to the left of them. Progress was slow, because of the blind sister, and there were two bridges to cross over two canals. John was completely lost after the first turning, but it couldn't have mattered less. Their police escort was with them, and anyway, the sisters knew where they were going.

"I must explain," said John softly. "My wife would never forgive me if I didn't," and as they walked he went over the whole inexplicable story once again, beginning with the telegram received the night before and the conversation with Mrs. Hill, the decision to return to England the following day, Laura by air, and John himself by car and train. It no longer sounded as dramatic as it had done when he had made his statement to the police officer, when, possibly because of his conviction of something uncanny, the description of the two vaporettos passing one another in the middle of the Grand Canal had held a sinister quality, suggesting abduction on the part of the sisters, the pair of them holding a bewildered Laura captive. Now that neither of the women had any further menace for him he spoke more naturally, yet with great sincerity, feeling for the first time that they were somehow both in sympathy with him and would understand.

"You see," he explained, in a final endeavour to make amends for having gone to the police in the first place, "I truly believed I had seen you with Laura, and I thought . . ." he hesitated, because this had been the police officer's suggestion and not his, "I thought that perhaps Laura had some sudden loss of memory, had met you at the airport, and you had brought her back to Venice to wherever you were staying."

They had crossed a large campo and were approaching a house at one end of it, with a sign PENSIONE above the door. Their escort paused at the entrance.

"Is this it?" asked John.

"Yes," said the sister. "I know it is nothing much from the outside, but it is clean and comfortable, and was recommended by friends." She turned to the escort. "*Grazie,*" she said to him, "*grazie tanto.*"

The man nodded briefly, wished them "*Buona notte,*" and disappeared across the campo.

"Will you come in?" asked the sister. "I am sure we can find you some coffee, or perhaps you prefer tea?"

"No, really," John thanked her, "I must get back to the hotel. I'm making an early start in the morning. I just want to make quite sure you do understand what happened, and that you forgive me."

"There is nothing to forgive," she replied. "It is one of the many examples of second sight that my sister and I have experienced time and time again, and I should very much like to record it for our files, if you permit it."

"Well, as to that, of course," he told her, "but I myself find it hard to understand. It has never happened to me before."

"Not consciously, perhaps," she said, "but so many things happen to us of which we are not aware. My sister felt you had psychic understanding. She told your wife. She also told your wife, last night in the restaurant, that you were to experience trouble, that you should leave Venice. Well, don't you believe now that the telegram was proof of this? Your son was ill, possibly dangerously ill, and so it was necessary for you to return home immediately. Heaven be praised your wife flew home to be by his side."

"Yes, indeed," said John, "but why should I see her on the vaporetto with you and your sister when she was actually on her way to England?"

"Thought transference, perhaps," she answered. "Your wife may have been thinking about us. We gave her our address, should you wish to get in touch with us. We shall be here another ten days. And she knows that we would pass on any message that my sister might have from your little one in the spirit world."

"Yes," said John awkwardly, "yes, I see. It's very good of you." He had a sudden rather unkind picture of the two sisters putting on headphones in their bedroom, listening for a coded message from poor Christine. "Look, this is our address in London," he said. "I know Laura will be pleased to hear from you."

He scribbled their address on a sheet torn from his pocket-diary, even, as a bonus thrown in, the telephone number, and handed it to her. He could imagine the outcome. Laura springing it on him one evening that the "old dears" were passing through London on their way to Scotland, and the least they could do was to offer them hospitality, even the spare-room for the night. Then a séance in the living-room, tambourines appearing out of thin air.

"Well, I must be off," he said, "goodnight, and apologies, once again, for all that has happened this evening." He shook hands with the first sister, then turned to her blind twin. "I hope," he said, "that you are not too tired."

The sightless eyes were disconcerting. She held his hand fast and would not let it go. "The child," she said, speaking in an odd staccato voice, "the child . . . I can see the child . . ." and then, to his dismay, a bead of froth appeared at the corner of her mouth, her head jerked back, and she half-collapsed in her sister's arms.

"We must get her inside," said the sister hurriedly. "It's all right, she's not ill, it's the beginning of a trance state."

Between them they helped the twin, who had gone rigid, into the house, and sat her down on the nearest chair, the sister supporting her. A woman came running from some inner room. There was a strong smell of spaghetti from the back regions. "Don't worry," said the sister, "the signorina and I can manage. I think you had better go. Sometimes she is sick after these turns."

"I'm most frightfully sorry . . ." John began, but the sister had already turned her back, and with the signorina was bending over her twin, from whom peculiar choking sounds were proceeding. He was obviously in the way, and after a final gesture of courtesy, "Is there anything I can do?" which received no reply, he turned on his heel and began walking across the square. He looked back once, and saw they had closed the door.

What a finale to the evening! And all his fault. Poor old girls, first dragged to police headquarters and put through an interrogation, and then a psychic fit on top of it all. More likely epilepsy. Not much of a life for the active sister, but she seemed to take it in her stride. An additional hazard, though, if it happened in a restaurant or in the street. And not particularly welcome under his and Laura's roof should the sisters ever find themselves beneath it, which he prayed would never happen.

Meanwhile, where the devil was he? The campo, with the inevitable church at one end, was quite deserted. He could not remember which way they had come from police headquarters, there had seemed to be so many turnings. Wait a minute, the church itself had a familiar appearance. He drew nearer to it, looking for the name which was sometimes on notices at the entrance. San Giovanni in Bragora, that rang a bell. He and Laura had gone inside one morning to look at a painting by Cima da Conegliano. Surely it was only a stone's throw from the Riva degli Schiavoni and the open wide waters of the San Marco lagoon, with all the bright lights of civilisation and the strolling tourists? He remembered taking a small turning from the Schiavoni and they had arrived at the church. Wasn't there the alley-way ahead? He plunged along it, but halfway down he hesitated. It didn't seem right, although it was familiar for some unknown reason.

Then he realised that it was not the alley they had taken the morning they visited the church, but the one they had walked along the previous evening, only he was approaching it from the opposite direction. Yes, that was it, in which case it would be quicker to go on and cross the little bridge over the narrow canal, and he would find the

Arsenal on his left and the street leading down to the Riva degli Schiavoni to his right. Simpler than retracing his steps and getting lost once more in the maze of back streets.

He had almost reached the end of the alley, and the bridge was in sight, when he saw the child. It was the same little girl with the pixie hood who had leapt between the tethered boats the preceding night and vanished up the cellar steps of one of the houses. This time she was running from the direction of the church on the other side, making for the bridge. She was running as if her life depended on it, and in a moment he saw why. A man was in pursuit, who, when she glanced backwards for a moment, still running, flattened himself against a wall, believing himself unobserved. The child came on, scampering across the bridge, and John, fearful of alarming her further, backed into an open doorway that led into a small court.

He remembered the drunken yell of the night before which had come from one of the houses near where the man was hiding now. This is it, he thought, the fellow's after her again, and with a flash of intuition he connected the two events, the child's terror then and now, and the murders reported in the newspapers, supposedly the work of some madman. It could be coincidence, a child running from a drunken relative, and yet, and yet . . . His heart began thumping in his chest, instinct warning him to run himself, now, at once, back along the alley the way he had come, but what about the child? What was going to happen to the child?

Then he heard her running steps. She hurtled through the open doorway into the court in which he stood, not seeing him, making for the rear of the house that flanked it, where steps led presumably to a back entrance. She was sobbing as she ran, not the ordinary cry of a frightened child but a panic-stricken intake of breath of a helpless being in despair. Were there parents in the house who would protect her, whom he could warn? He hesitated a moment, then followed her down the steps and through the door at the bottom, which had burst open at the touch of her hands as she hurled herself against it.

"It's all right," he called. "I won't let him hurt you, it's all right," cursing his lack of Italian, but possibly an English voice might reassure her. But it was no use—she ran sobbing up another flight of stairs, which were spiral, twisting, leading to the floor above, and already it was too late for him to retreat. He could hear sounds of the pursuer in the courtyard behind, someone shouting in Italian, a dog barking. This is it, he thought, we're in it together, the child and I. Unless we can bolt some inner door above he'll get us both.

He ran up the stairs after the child, who had darted into a room leading off a small landing, and followed her inside and slammed the door, and, merciful heaven, there was a bolt which he rammed into its socket. The child was crouching by the open window. If he shouted for help, someone would surely hear, someone would surely come before the man in pursuit threw himself against the door and it gave, because there was no one but themselves, no parents, the room was bare except for a mattress on an old bed, and a heap of rags in one corner.

"It's all right," he panted, "it's all right," and held out his hand, trying to smile.

The child struggled to her feet and stood before him, the pixie hood falling from her head on to the floor. He stared at her, incredulity turning to horror, to fear. It was not a child at all but a little thickset woman dwarf, about three feet high, with a great square adult head too big for her body, grey locks hanging shoulder-length, and she wasn't sobbing any more, she was grinning at him, nodding her head up and down.

Then he heard the footsteps on the landing outside and the hammering on the door, and a barking dog, and not one voice but several voices, shouting, "Open up! Police!" The creature fumbled in her sleeve, drawing a knife, and as she threw it at him with hideous strength, piercing his throat, he stumbled and fell, the sticky mess covering his protecting hands. And he saw the vaporetto with Laura and the two sisters steaming down the Grand Canal, not today, not tomorrow, but the day after that, and he knew why they were together and for what sad purpose they had come. The creature was gibbering in its corner. The hammering and the voices and the barking dog grew fainter, and, Oh, God, he thought, what a bloody silly way to die . . .

NEVER SHAKE A FAMILY TREE

by Donald E. Westlake

ACTUALLY, I WAS never so surprised in my life, and I was seventy-three my last birthday and eleven times a grandmother and twice a great-grandmother. But never in my life did I see the like, and that's the truth. It all began with my interest in genealogy, which I got from Mrs. Ernestine Simpson, a widow I met at Bay Arbor, in Florida, when I went there three summers ago. I certainly didn't like Florida—far too expensive, if you ask me, and far too bright, and with just too many mosquitoes and other insects to be believed—but I wouldn't say the trip was a total loss, since it did interest me in genealogical research, which is certainly a wonderful hobby, as well as being very valuable, what with one thing and another.

Actually, my genealogical researches have been valuable in more ways than one, since they have also been instrumental in my meeting some very pleasant ladies and gentlemen, although some of them only by postal, and of course it was through this hobby that I met Mr. Gerald Fowlkes in the first place.

But I'm getting far ahead of my story, and ought to begin at the beginning, except that I'm blessed if I know where the beginning actually is. In one way of looking at things, the beginning is my introduction to genealogy through Mrs. Ernestine Simpson, who has since passed on, but in another way the beginning is really almost two hundred years ago, and in still another way the story doesn't really begin until the first time I came across the name of Euphemia Barber.

Well. Actually, I suppose, I ought to begin by explaining just what genealogical research is. It is the study of one's family tree. One checks marriage and birth and death records, searches old family Bibles and talks to various members of one's family, and one gradually builds up a family tree, showing who fathered whom and what year, and when so-and-so got married, and when so-and-so died, and so on. It's really fascinating work, and there are any number of amateur genealogical societies throughout the country, and when one has one's family tree built up for as far as one wants—seven generations, or nine generations, or however long one wants—then it is possible to write this all up in a folder and bequeath it to the local library, and then there is a *record* of one's family for all time to come, and I for one think that's important and valuable to have even if my youngest boy, Tom, does laugh at it and says it's just a silly hobby. Well, it *isn't* a silly hobby. After all, I found evidence of murder that way, didn't I?

So, actually, I suppose the whole thing really begins when I first came across the name of Euphemia Barber. Euphemia Barber was John Anderson's second wife. John Anderson was born in Goochland County, Virginia, in 1754. He married Ethel Rita Mary Rayborn in 1777, just around the time of the Revolution, and they had seven children, which wasn't at all strange for that time, though large families have, I notice, gone out of style today, and I for one think it's a shame.

At any rate, it was John and Ethel Anderson's third child, a girl named Prudence, who is in my direct line on my mother's father's side, so of course I had them in my family tree. But then, in going through Appomattox County records—Goochland County being now a part of Appomattox, and no longer a separate county of its own—I came across the name of Euphemia Barber. It seems that Ethel Anderson died in 1793, in giving birth to her eighth child—who also died—and three years later, 1796, John Anderson remarried, this time marrying a widow named Euphemia Barber. At that time he was forty-two years of age, and her age was given as thirty-nine.

Of course, Euphemia Barber was not at all in my direct line, being John Anderson's second wife, but I was interested to some extent in her pedigree as well, wanting to add her parents' names and her place of birth to my family chart, and also because there were some Barbers fairly distantly related on my father's mother's side, and I was wondering if this Euphemia might be kin to them. But the records were very incomplete, and all I could learn was that Euphemia Barber was not a native of Virginia, and had apparently only been in the area for a year or two when she married John Anderson. Shortly after John's death in 1798, two years after their marriage, she sold the Anderson farm, which was apparently a somewhat prosperous location, and moved away again. So that I had neither birth nor death records on her, nor any record of her first husband, whose last name had apparently been Barber, but only the one lone record of her marriage to my great-great-great-great-great-grandfather on my mother's father's side.

Actually, there was no reason for me to pursue the question further, since Euphemia Barber wasn't in my direct line anyway, but I had worked diligently and, I think, well, on my family tree, and had it almost complete back nine generations, and there was really very little left to do with it, so I was glad to do some tracking down.

Which is why I included Euphemia Barber in my next entry in the *Genealogical Exchange*. Now, I suppose I ought to explain what the *Genealogical Exchange* is. There are any number of people throughout the country who are amateur genealogists, concerned primarily with their own family trees, but of course family trees do interlock, and any one of these people is liable to know about just the one record which has been eluding some other searcher for months. And so there are magazines devoted to the exchanging of such information, for nominal fees. In the last few years I had picked up all sorts of valuable leads in this way. And so my entry in the summer issue of the *Genealogical Exchange* read:

> BUCKLEY, Mrs. Henrietta Rhodes, 119 A Newbury St., Boston, Mass. Xch data on Rhodes, Anderson, Richards, Pryor, Marshall, Lord. Want any info Euphemia Barber, m. John Anderson, Va. 1796.

Well. The *Genealogical Exchange* had been helpful to me in the past, but I never received anywhere near the response caused by Euphemia Barber. And the first response of all came from Mr. Gerald Fowlkes.

It was a scant two days after I received my own copy of the summer issue of the *Exchange*. I was still poring over it myself, looking for people who might be linked to various branches of my family tree, when the telephone rang. Actually, I suppose I was somewhat irked at being taken from my studies, and perhaps I sounded a bit impatient when I answered the phone.

If so, the gentleman at the other end gave no sign of it. His voice was most pleasant, quite deep and masculine, and he said, "May I speak, please, with Mrs. Henrietta Buckley?"

"This is Mrs. Buckley," I told him.

"Ah," he said. "Forgive my telephoning, please, Mrs. Buckley. We have never met. But I noticed your entry in the current issue of the *Genealogical Exchange*—"

"Oh?" I was immediately excited, all thought of impatience gone. This was surely the fastest reply I'd ever had to date!

"Yes," he said. "I noticed the reference to Euphemia Barber. I do believe that may be the Euphemia Stover who married Jason Barber in Savannah, Georgia, in 1791. Jason Barber is my direct line, on my mother's side. Jason and Euphemia had only the one child, Abner, and I am descended from him."

"Well," I said. "You certainly do seem to have complete information."

"Oh, yes," he said. "My own family chart is almost complete. For twelve generations, that is. I'm not sure whether I'll try to go back farther than that or not. The English records before 1600 are so incomplete, you know."

"Yes, of course," I said. I was, I admit, taken aback. Twelve generations! Surely that was the most ambitious family tree I had ever heard of, though I had read sometimes of people who had carried particular branches back as many as fifteen generations. But to actually be speaking to a person who had traced his entire family back twelve generations!

"Perhaps," he said, "it would be possible for us to meet, and I could give you the information I have on Euphemia Barber. There are also some Marshalls in one branch of my family; perhaps I can be of help to you there, as well." He laughed, a deep and pleasant sound, which reminded me of my late husband, Edward, when he was most particularly pleased. "And, of course," he said, "there is always the chance that you may have some information on the Marshalls which can help me."

"I think that would be very nice," I said, and so I invited him to come to the apartment the very next afternoon.

At one point the next day, perhaps half an hour before Gerald Fowlkes was to arrive, I stopped my fluttering around to take stock of myself and to realize that if ever there were an indication of second childhood taking over, my thoughts and actions preparatory to Mr. Fowlkes' arrival were certainly it. I had been rushing hither and thither, dusting, rearranging, polishing, pausing incessantly to look in the mirror and touch my hair with fluttering fingers, all as though I were a flighty teen-ager before her very first date. "Henrietta," I told myself sharply, "you are seventy-three years old, and all that nonsense is well behind you now. Eleven times a grandmother, and just look at how you carry on!"

But poor Edward had been dead and gone these past nine years, my brothers and sisters were all in their graves, and as for my children, all but Tom, the youngest, were thousands of miles away, living their own lives—as of course they should—and only occasionally remembering to write a duty letter to Mother. And I am much too aware of the dangers of the clinging mother to force my presence too often upon

Tom and his family. So I am very much alone, except of course for my friends in the various church activities and for those I have met, albeit only by postal, through my genealogical research.

So it *was* pleasant to be visited by a charming gentleman caller, and particularly so when that gentleman shared my own particular interests.

And Mr. Gerald Fowlkes, on his arrival, was surely no disappointment. He looked to be no more than fifty-five years of age, though he swore to sixty-two, and had a fine shock of gray hair above a strong and kindly face. He dressed very well, with that combination of expense and breeding so little found these days, when the well-bred seem invariably to be poor and the well-to-do seem invariably to be horribly plebeian. His manner was refined and gentlemanly, what we used to call courtly, and he had some very nice things to say about the appearance of my living room.

Actually, I make no unusual claims as a housekeeper. Living alone, and with quite a comfortable income having been left me by Edward, it is no problem at all to choose tasteful furnishings and keep them neat. (Besides, I had scrubbed the apartment from top to bottom in preparation for Mr. Fowlkes' visit.)

He had brought his pedigree along, and what a really beautiful job he had done. Pedigree charts, photostats of all sorts of records, a running history typed very neatly on bond paper and inserted in a loose-leaf notebook—all in all, the kind of careful, planned, well-thought-out perfection so unsuccessfully striven for by all amateur genealogists.

From Mr. Fowlkes, I got the missing information on Euphemia Barber. She was born in 1765, in Salem, Massachusetts, the fourth child of seven born to John and Alicia Stover. She married Jason Barber in Savannah in 1791. Jason, a well-to-do merchant, passed on in 1794, shortly after the birth of their first child, Abner. Abner was brought up by his paternal grandparents, and Euphemia moved away from Savannah. As I already knew, she had then gone to Virginia, where she had married John Anderson. After that, Mr. Fowlkes had no record of her, until her death in Cincinnati, Ohio, in 1852. She was buried as Euphemia Stover Barber, apparently not having used the Anderson name after John Anderson's death.

This done, we went on to compare family histories and discover an Alan Marshall of Liverpool, England, around 1680, common to both trees. I was able to give Mr. Fowlkes Alan Marshall's birth date. And then the specific purpose of our meeting was finished. I offered tea and cakes, it then being four-thirty in the afternoon, and Mr. Fowlkes graciously accepted.

Before leaving, Mr. Fowlkes asked me to accompany him to a concert on Friday evening, and I very readily agreed. And so began the strangest three months of my entire life.

It didn't take me long to realize that I was being courted. Actually, I couldn't believe it at first. After all, at *my* age! But I myself did know some very nice couples who had married late in life—a widow and a widower, both lonely, sharing interests, and deciding to lighten their remaining years together—and looked at in that light it wasn't at all as ridiculous as it may appear at first.

Actually, I had expected my son Tom to laugh at the idea, and to dislike Mr. Fowlkes instantly upon meeting him. I suppose various fictional works that I have read had given me this expectation. So I was most pleasantly surprised when Tom and Mr. Fowlkes got along famously together from their very first meeting, and even more surprised when Tom came to me and told me Mr. Fowlkes had asked him if he would have any objection to his, Mr. Fowlkes', asking for my hand in matrimony. Tom said he had no objection at all, but actually thought it a wonderful idea, for he knew that both Mr. Fowlkes and myself were rather lonely, with nothing but our genealogical hobbies to occupy our minds.

As to Mr. Fowlkes' background, he very early gave me his entire history. He came from a fairly well-to-do family in upstate New York, and was himself now retired from his business, which had been a stock brokerage in Albany. He was a widower these last six years and his first marriage had not been blessed with any children, so that he was completely alone in the world.

The next three months were certainly active ones. Mr. Fowlkes—Gerald—squired me everywhere, to concerts and to museums and even, after we had come to know one another well enough, to the theater. He was at all times most polite and thoughtful, and there was scarcely a day went by but what we were together.

During this entire time, of course, my own genealogical researches came to an absolute standstill. I was much too busy, and my mind was much too full of Gerald, for me to concern myself with family members who were long since gone to their rewards. Promising leads from the *Genealogical Exchange* were not followed up for I didn't write a single letter. And though I did receive many in the *Exchange*, they all went unopened into a cubbyhole in my desk. And so the matter stayed, while the courtship progressed.

After three months Gerald at last proposed. "I am not a young man,

Henrietta," he said. "Nor a particularly handsome man"—though he most certainly was very handsome, indeed—"nor even a very rich man, although I do have sufficient for my declining years. And I have little to offer you, Henrietta, save my own self, whatever poor companionship I can give you, and the assurance that I will be ever at your side."

What a beautiful proposal! After being nine years a widow, and never expecting even in fanciful daydreams to be once more a wife, what a beautiful proposal and from what a charming gentleman!

I agreed at once, of course, and telephoned Tom the good news that very minute. Tom and his wife, Estelle, had a dinner party for us, and then we made our plans. We would be married three weeks hence. A short time? Yes, of course, it was, but there was really no reason to wait. And we would be honeymooning in Washington, D.C., where my oldest boy, Roger, has quite a responsible position with the State Department. After which we would return to Boston and take up our residence in a lovely old home on Beacon Hill, which was then for sale and which we would jointly purchase.

Ah, the plans! The preparations! How newly filled were my so-recently empty days!

I spent most of the last week closing my apartment on Newbury Street. The furnishings would be moved to our new home by Tom, while Gerald and I were in Washington. But, of course, there was ever so much packing to be done, and I got at it with a will.

And so at last I came to my desk, and my genealogical researches lying as I had left them. I sat down at the desk, somewhat weary, for it was late afternoon and I had been hard at work since sunup, and I decided to spend a short while getting my papers into order before packing them away. And so I opened the mail which had accumulated over the last three months.

There were twenty-three letters. Twelve asked for information on various family names mentioned in my entry in the *Exchange,* five offered to give me information, and six concerned Euphemia Barber. It was, after all, Euphemia Barber who had brought Gerald and me together in the first place, and so I took time out to read these letters.

And so came the shock. I read the six letters, and then I simply sat limp at the desk, staring into space, and watched the monstrous pattern as it grew in my mind. For there was no question of the truth, no question at all.

Consider: Before starting the letters, this is what I knew of Euphemia Barber: She had been born Euphemia Stover in Salem, Massachusetts, in 1765. In 1791 she married Jason Barber, a widower of Savannah, Georgia. Jason died two years later, in 1793, of a stomach upset. Three years later Euphemia appeared in Virginia and married John Anderson, also a widower. John Anderson died two years thereafter, in 1798, of stomach upset. In both cases Euphemia sold her late husband's property and moved on.

And here is what the letters added to that, in chronological order:

From Mrs. Winnie Mae Cuthbert, Dallas, Texas: Euphemia Barber, in 1800, two years after John Anderson's death, appeared in Harrisburg, Pennsylvania, and married one Andrew Cuthbert, a widower and a prosperous feed merchant. Andrew died in 1801, of a stomach upset. The widow sold his store, and moved on.

From Miss Ethel Sutton, Louisville, Kentucky: Euphemia Barber, in 1804, married Samuel Nicholson of Louisville, a widower and a well-to-do tobacco farmer. Samuel Nicholson passed on in 1807, of a stomach upset. The widow sold his farm, and moved on.

From Mrs. Isabelle Padgett, Concord, California: In 1808 Euphemia Barber married Thomas Norton, then Mayor of Dover, New Jersey, and a widower. In 1809 Thomas Norton died of a stomach upset.

From Mrs. Luella Miller, Bicknell, Utah: Euphemia Barber married Jonas Miller, a wealthy shipowner of Portsmouth, New Hampshire, a widower, in 1811. The same year Jonas Miller died of a stomach upset. The widow sold his property, and moved on.

From Mrs. Lola Hopkins, Vancouver, Washington: In 1813, in southern Indiana, Euphemia Barber married Edward Hopkins, a widower and a farmer. Edward Hopkins died in 1816, of a stomach upset. The widow sold the farm, and moved on.

From Mr. Roy Cumbie, Kansas City, Missouri: In 1819 Euphemia Barber married Stanley Thatcher of Kansas City, Missouri, a river barge owner and a widower. Stanley Thatcher died, of a stomach upset, in 1821. The widow sold his property, and moved on.

The evidence was clear, and complete. The intervals of time without dates could mean that there had been other widowers who had succumbed to Euphemia Barber's fatal charms, and whose descendants did not number among themselves an amateur genealogist. Who could tell just how many husbands Euphemia had murdered? For murder it quite clearly was, brutal murder, for profit. I had evidence of eight murders, and who knew but what there were eight more, or eighteen more? Who could tell, at this late date, just how many times Euphemia Barber had murdered for profit, and had never been caught?

Such a woman is inconceivable. Her husbands were always widowers, sure to be lonely, sure to be susceptible to a wily woman. She preyed on widowers, and left them all a widow.

Gerald.

The thought came to me, and I pushed it firmly away. It couldn't possibly be true; it couldn't possibly have a single grain of truth.

But what did I know of Gerald Fowlkes, other than what he had told me? And wasn't I a widow, lonely and susceptible? And wasn't I financially well off?

Like father, like son, they say. Could it be also, like great-great-great-great-great-grandmother, like great-great-great-great-great-grandson?

What a thought! It came to me that there must be any number of widows in the country, like myself, who were interested in tracing their family trees. Women who had a bit of money and leisure, whose children were grown and gone out into the world to live their own lives, and who filled some of the empty hours with the hobby of genealogy. An unscrupulous man, preying on well-to-do widows, could find no better introduction than a common interest in genealogy.

What a terrible thought to have about Gerald! And yet I couldn't push it from my mind, and at last I decided that the only thing I could possibly do was try to substantiate the autobiography he had given me, for if he had told the truth about himself, then he could surely not be a beast of the type I was imagining.

A stockbroker, he had claimed to have been, in Albany, New York. I at once telephoned an old friend of my first husband's who was himself a Boston stockbroker, and asked him if it would be possible for him to find out if there had been, at any time in the last fifteen or twenty years, an Albany stockbroker named Gerald Fowlkes. He said he could do so with ease, using some sort of directory he had, and would call me back. He did so, with the shattering news that no such individual was listed!

Still I refused to believe. Donning my coat and hat, I left the apartment at once and went directly to the telephone company, where, after an incredible number of white lies concerning genealogical research, I at last persuaded someone to search for an old Albany, New York, telephone book. I knew that the main office of the company kept books for other major cities, as a convenience for the public, but I wasn't sure they would have any from past years. Nor was the clerk I talked to, but at last she did go and search, and came back finally with the 1946 telephone book from Albany, dusty and somewhat ripped, but still intact, with both the normal listings and the yellow pages.

No Gerald Fowlkes was listed in the white pages, or in the yellow pages under Stocks & Bonds.

So. It was true. And I could see exactly what Gerald's method was. Whenever he was ready to find another victim, he searched one or another of the genealogical magazines until he found someone who shared one of his own past relations. He then proceeded to effect a meeting with that person, found out quickly enough whether or not the intended victim was a widow, of the proper age range, and with the properly large bank account, and then the courtship began.

I imagined that this was the first time he had made the mistake of using Euphemia Barber as the go-between. And I doubted that he even realized he was following in Euphemia's footsteps. Certainly, none of the six people who had written to me about Euphemia could possibly guess, knowing only of the one marriage and death, what Euphemia's role in life had actually been.

And what was I to do now? In the taxi, on the way back to my apartment, I sat huddled in a corner, and tried to think.

For this *was* a severe shock, and a terrible disappointment. And how could I face Tom, or my other children, or any of my friends, to whom I had already written the glad news of my impending marriage? And how could I return to the drabness of my days before Gerald had come to bring me gaiety and companionship and courtly grace?

Could I even call the police? I was sufficiently convinced myself, but could I possibly convince anyone else?

All at once, I made my decision. And, having made it, I immediately felt ten years younger, ten pounds lighter, and quite a bit less foolish. For, I might as well admit, in addition to everything else, this had been a terrible blow to my pride.

But the decision was made, and I returned to my apartment cheerful and happy.

And so we were married.

Married? Of course. Why not?

Because he will try to murder me? Well, of course, he *will* try to murder me. As a matter of fact, he has already tried, half a dozen times.

But Gerald is working at a terrible disadvantage. For he cannot murder me in any way that looks like murder. It must appear to be a natural death, or, at the very worst, an accident. Which means that he must be devious, and he must plot and plan, and never come at me openly to do me in.

And there is the source of his disadvantage. For I am forewarned, and forewarned is forearmed.

But what, really, do I have to lose? At seventy-three, how many days on this earth do I have left? And how *rich* life is these days! How rich compared to my life before Gerald came into it! Spiced with the thrill of danger, the excitement of cat and mouse, the intricate moves and countermoves of the most fascinating game of all.

And, of course, a pleasant and charming husband. Gerald *has* to be pleasant and charming. He can never disagree with me, at least not very forcefully, for he can't afford the danger of my leaving him. Nor can he afford to believe that I suspect him. I have never spoken of the matter to him, and so far as he is concerned I know nothing. We go to concerts and museums and the theater together. Gerald is attentive and gentlemanly, quite the best sort of companion at all times.

Of course, I can't allow him to feed me breakfast in bed, as he would so love to do. No, I told him, I was an old-fashioned woman, and believed that cooking was a woman's job, and so I won't let him near the kitchen. Poor Gerald!

And we don't take trips, no matter how much he suggests them.

And we've closed off the second story of our home, since I pointed out that the first floor was certainly spacious enough for just the two of us, and I felt I was getting a little old for climbing stairs. He could do nothing, of course, but agree.

And, in the meantime, I have found another hobby, though of course Gerald knows nothing of it. Through discreet inquiries, and careful perusal of past issues of the various genealogical magazines, and the use of the family names in Gerald's family tree, I am gradually compiling another sort of tree. Not a family tree, no. One might facetiously call it a hanging tree. It is a list of Gerald's wives. It is in with my genealogical files, which I have willed to the Boston library. Should Gerald manage to catch me after all, what a surprise is in store for the librarian who sorts out those files of mine! Not as big a surprise as the one in store for Gerald, of course.

Ah, here comes Gerald now, in the automobile he bought last week. He's going to ask me again to go for a ride with him.

But I shan't go.

THE REASON

by Arthur Porges

JAN VAN METER was very rich. He could trace his family back through New Amsterdam to fifteenth-century Holland. Obviously, Fred Clement thought, such a man didn't have to accept any casual police investigation as final.

"I'm certain that it was murder, and not suicide," van Meter said, his pale blue eyes glowing with conscious power. They had an odd surface sheen like that of polished stone, and stabbed into Clement's mild brown ones.

He doesn't think I look like much, the insurance detective reflected, with secret amusement. The old boy can't see that if I had as openly strong a personality as De Gaulle, for example, the little confidences that make my cases work out so well would never be forthcoming. Clement was a small, round man, with cheerful, soft eyes; his clothes were of good quality, but just sufficiently rumpled to give most people a fellow-feeling towards him never accorded the impeccable.

"The main reason the police call it suicide," Clement pointed out, "is that he put the gun-muzzle in his mouth. Now, if it were murder—"

"I've read the report," van Meter said, cutting him short, not so much in rudeness as in a businessman's sense of the value of time. "You can forget it. Bill would not, and did not, kill himself. No van Meter has ever done such a thing. He had no possible reason. He was successful, had a lovely wife and two fine children. Believe me, he was a happy man." He jabbed the detective again with his pale stare. "Midwestern Mutual tells me you're their crack investigator. I give you carte blanche. I want the swine who killed my boy. The sky is your limit on expenses; and when you find him—and you will, if it takes years, so don't expect to get off the hook—there will be a sizeable bonus above your salary."

"All right," Clement said mildly. "I'll investigate. And as long as I'm here, perhaps you could tell me something about your son: his habits, personality. You know what's useful, I'm sure."

"I'm ready to cooperate one hundred per cent. There were no skeletons in Bill's closet. And any in mine," he added, with a touch of grim humor, "are pretty dusty old bones by now."

"You said Bill was happy. Can you be sure of that?"

"Absolutely. He was always a cheerful, outgoing boy: good-natured. Something of a prankster, in his younger days, but never malicious.

"He married his childhood sweetheart, Moira Drake, had an excellent position as president of Shorwood Valley Bank; taught Sunday school classes, enjoyed hunting and fishing, owned a fine home in Sapphire Bay—why shouldn't he be happy? And his health was perfect; never sick a day. He was only thirty-seven, with a whole life to live. Would such a person, relaxing and perfectly normal on a Sunday morning, suddenly kill himself? Without even leaving a note, when his wife steps out for a few minutes? Police report—nonsense!"

Clement left the van Meter estate in a thoughtful mood. Nobody knew better than he that our society is one of masks and masquerades: that many a seemingly happy and successful person was like one of those fungus-blighted tropical trees—solid and healthy-looking, but ready to collapse at a blow, shattering to rotten powder. And yet, so far, William van Meter could not be considered a masquerader. On the other hand, very little evidence was in.

Clement's next stop was at the exclusive Sapphire Bay housing development. It was one of those oceanfront organizations run like a corporation, and very selective in its admissions. All the homes were strictly one acre minimum, and none valued under $75,000 which, by a curious coincidence, happened to be William van Meter's yearly salary.

If Clement hadn't carried a letter from the elder van Meter, he might never have got past the gate from the highway, which had its own guardhouse and a man in uniform presiding there. The detective's beat-up compact clearly was out of place on the immaculate private road which wound up and around giving one breathtaking view after another of the Atlantic, a rich turquoise color that sunny morning.

At nearly the highest point, in a magnificent home on five landscaped acres, Clement found Bill's widow. Five minutes in her presence convinced the investigator that if van Meter was a suicide, the motive had nothing to do with his wife. She was not beautiful, but she had a sweet graciousness that went to the core of her being. Her mouth was just too large for her narrow face, but showed tenderness, good-humor, and generosity. When she spoke, Clement noted that her voice struck the pure middle note with all the richness of a silver bell, yet with no metallic overtones. No man, he thought, could ever tire of that verbal melody, even if the woman spoke inanely, which was clearly not the case. Deeply feminine, she had the unequivocal frankness of a lady: somebody of so unquestioned a position that no pretenses were called for or even dreamed of. Quietly, she told him about her husband's last morning.

"He was lying on the sofa, reading the Sunday paper. I had been in the kitchen, and remembered that I promised to stop at Sally's—Sally Maitland, our neighbor—and give her a recipe. I told Bill I was going, that I'd be back in ten minutes. He said—" her voice shook briefly—"'I grudge every minute, Kitten,' and laughed. He had a wonderful, merry laugh, like a little boy without a care, who's watching a circus clown for the first time. We'd been married twelve years, but every day—several times a day—he told me how much he loved me, and what our marriage meant to him. I don't understand," she added, almost in a whisper, "how anybody can talk suicide. Bill had a conscience bigger than himself. He would never do such a thing to his children and me." She sat there in silence, apparently forgetting her visitor.

"You went to the Maitlands'," Clement prompted her softly.

"I'm sorry—I left you for a minute. Yes, I went out. And while I was there—it couldn't have been more than twenty minutes—we heard this popping sound. It was just like Bill's little .22, but I didn't recognize it at all; I didn't dream he'd be suddenly shooting, on a Sunday morning, and around the house. He took it down to the water once in a while, but never near the house. He hated to annoy people, and was very careful about guns always.

"But when I got back—by the kitchen door; and the radio playing some dreadful teen-age music—I'd left it on for news, but forgot that when I remembered about Sally and the recipe—when I got back, and looked in on B-Bill . . ." She was crying now.

"You needn't say any more—about that," Clement said.

She wiped her eyes.

"I'm s-sorry. Each time I think I'm under control again . . . but it's still only three weeks, you see. And it's so hard to believe somebody you love is gone—forever."

Gently, Clement led her to talk about Bill's past; he was soon able to infer that her husband, unlike some, didn't conceal much of his early life.

The family had lived in the east, but Bill had been sent to an outstanding and exclusive prep-school in California, Coleridge Academy. He had stayed there, except for vacation visits back to New York, until almost seventeen. Then, anxious to have him nearer home, his parents had enrolled the boy in the Wallingford School, a Maryland institution.

Clement's sympathetic manner, which stemmed as much from his character as his years of experience in dealing with the bereaved, enabled him to get a full account from the widow. It certainly seemed, he thought, as the slow, lovely voice sang on, that they'd had an ideal marriage. If Bill wore a mask, it was a completely new sort in the detective's world. When a man romped with his kids, constantly brought his wife flowers and little surprise gifts, was adored by every child in the community, and always sang—loudly and off-key—in the shower, you had to conclude that as in Beerbohm's famous story, the individual (if ever actually different inside) had changed to fit the false face, and was no longer a mummer.

Well, Clement told himself on leaving, I still haven't left home plate; not even a solid foul to my credit as a batter.

His next call was one of a series made on van Meter's neighbors in Sapphire Bay. Thanks to his letter from Bill's father, and a few phone calls from his widow, people were willing to cooperate. Here again, the verdict was unanimous. Everybody loved Bill van Meter: he was jolly, kind, helpful, wonderful with kids, and, in short, the perfect fellow to have next door. Nothing was too much trouble if it would make things easier for a friend.

Even the community's one malcontent (although the term was much too strong, Clement felt), Louis Busoni, who made it clear that he had a grievance against Sapphire Bay, expressed his approval of Bill. The others, Busoni hinted, backed off a little, more from his foreign name, perhaps, than anything in his character, which couldn't be faulted, since he was not only a distinguished wine manufacturer, but a collateral descendant of the musician. A Busoni, he implied delicately, had no reason to feel inferior to any Cary, Lee, or Fish. But Bill van Meter and his wife had often visited the Busonis.

"He loved my little Tina," Busoni said. "And she—she's beautiful! So beautiful at eight! What she gonna be at eighteen, I don't know! She was crazy about Bill. And Bill's wife—a wonderful lady, like a great princess, but so kind."

As he drove out through the gate, exchanging friendly waves with the guard (who had melted at the elder van Meter's signature on a pass), Clement began to wonder if it was really suicide. Maybe the old boy had something. A guy fixed like Bill was the last person in the world to make the big jump.

He decided to see Jan van Meter again; make a no-progress report, so to speak. Naturally, it was unacceptable.

"Everything you tell me," the old man said coldly, "confirms my own beliefs—that Bill was murdered. I don't know, and can't imagine why, or how the killer got the gun in his mouth. Knowing my son, I'd say it must have been somebody he knew and liked—somebody, maybe, who told him it was a joke. Bill enjoyed such things. Or used to. He was a lot more mature at thirty-seven, naturally, than at seventeen."

"If it was suicide," Clement said, "then the roots must go farther back. With your permission, I'd like to check into his early life—at the school here, and maybe even the one back in California."

"You have carte blanche," van Meter reminded him. "But I don't think you'll find any murderers at either Wallingford or Coleridge Academy."

"I'd like to agree with you on murder," Clement said. "But you know Sapphire Bay. Bill was alone for about twenty minutes. It has been proved that nobody came near the place. Some kids were playing nearby; a Mrs. Walton was watering across the street; even in back, a gardener was doing some work that morning. What with all those, and the guarded gates, no stranger could have come near Bill, as far as we —the police and I—know. Only Mrs. van Meter. And if you said she could possibly be guilty, I'd have to stick my neck out, knowing how often we misjudge people, and deny it. After seeing and talking to Bill's wife, I can't go for that one loophole."

"I should hope not," van Meter said, stiff with indignation. "If you had suggested such a thing, I'd have had you thrown out of this house. Moira a murderer, and of Bill! I say again, they were still in love, and happy as mere humans can ever be."

Since Clement had no answer to this, he didn't offer one. As long as the old man was willing to foot the bill, the detective had no objection to further investigation; but the lines must be his own. The murder theory was still cobweb frail, more air than substance, but suicide seemed equally improbable. That left accidental death. But how a man put a gun muzzle into his mouth, directly against the roof, and pressed the trigger—all inadvertently—was something Clement couldn't explain. However, years of insurance work had taught him that nothing was too bizarre to happen to or among human beings, and so he kept an open mind about Bill van Meter's strange death.

The pickings were lean at the Wallingford School in Maryland. Bill had enrolled there, fresh from Coleridge, when almost seventeen, and had left to attend Princeton at eighteen. That was in 1945.

The headmaster of Wallingford, a tweedy chap with an English accent, remembered Bill, and rather to Clement's annoyance, thought highly of him. The unanimity of opinion was no help. (Who ever heard of a guy without an enemy?)

"Very likeable young fellow; wellbred, but not stuffy. Always merry"—that word again, the detective thought, wryly—"but never mean or cruel; at least, by intention."

"How about accidentally?" Clement pounded.

"I can't recall any case. Once, I think, he dyed an old lady's dog with a harmless vegetable stain—bright purple. But when he heard that she cried, and thought they'd hurt the brute—actually it was pacified with hamburger, I believe, and would have been happy to be victimized daily—he sent her candy and apologies; so that later she became quite fond of Bill."

"Oh, brother!" Clement breathed. "This guy can't be for real; he makes Schweitzer look like the Marquis de Sade."

"Not at all," was the chilly reply. "The boy had a Puritan's conscience under the fun-loving nature of a—a—" He seemed at a loss for a comparison, so Clement supplied it.

"A Henry the Eighth?"

The headmaster's mouth twitched under its neat moustache.

"Not too good a try," he said dryly. "Henry's humor was both brutal and coarse. Quite the opposite of young van Meter's."

So that was that: another fat zero.

It seemed a waste of his client's money, but Clement decided to go west and learn what, if anything, Coleridge had to offer. But first he did some checking at Princeton, learning (without surprise) that everybody there loved Bill van Meter. Even more amazing was the fact that in spite of his money, good looks, and athletic ability (which led to a violent and unrelenting pursuit by all females old enough to wear nylons, and not too senile for hope), the boy dated only his childhood sweetheart, Moira Drake, and later married her on his twenty-fifth birthday, when he was three years out of college, and rapidly rising at the bank.

"Incredible," the detective muttered, studying his notes on the plane west. "Nobody killed Bill van Meter. He was an angel on loan, and Somebody Up There recalled him!"

The headmaster of Coleridge Academy was dead, but his wife was still alive and able to supply a few more facts, all equally bland and useless for Clement's purposes. He heard again the word "merry," and winced. But when she mentioned Bill's best friend, Larry Keith, the detective's attention sharpened.

"Where can I find him?" he asked. "Do you know?"

She didn't, of course; Keith had left a year after Bill; but there were records at school. . . .

There were good records, but out of date. However, this sort of thing was routine, so it took Clement only forty-eight hours to track Larry Keith down; he was a CPA, and quite successful.

"I've been rather out of touch with Bill," he told the detective somberly. "I couldn't believe it when I heard . . . Bill van Meter a suicide. It just doesn't add up. He was such a jolly fellow, if you know what I mean. Loved being alive; got along with everybody. We had a wonderful time as kids. Did one crazy thing after another, but never hurt anybody. The things I could tell you!"

He told quite a few, most of them far from new: the chamber pot on the flagpole; the huge purple shorts on General Wayne's bronze horse; the detergent in the Memorial Fountain—any school paper could supply such a list.

Baffled again, Clement went back east for another consultation with Jan van Meter.

"I knew very well you'd find nothing at either school," the old man said. "Bill didn't kill himself. But you had to satisfy yourself; I don't mind that. Now, however, it's time you changed course and began looking for a killer."

"I'll get to that," Clement said calmly. "But there are one or two things to check—pretty far out, I admit, but possibly related." He didn't explain, and van Meter didn't care to ask. He'd said carte blanche, and usually meant what he said.

The detective found out from Moira van Meter what paper Bill had been reading that morning. He went to the morgue, and scrutinized the issue, line by line. Nothing seemed relevant. Nobody had threatened to "tell all." No skeletons, presumably, had been hauled from closets via newsprint that morning. He'd already verified that Bill had not received a phone call while Moira was out those few minutes. Clement was stopped cold: blind alley, dead center.

He went over his notes again, thinking wryly of the Crofts saga about Inspector French, that bland and competent fellow, not unlike himself, who always re-read his notes when stumped.

There was only one thing left to check, however unpromising. Moira had mentioned leaving the radio on. It was barely possible that Bill, lounging in the next room, had heard something. God only knew what a happy man could hear over the air on a lazy Sunday that would make him put a gun-barrel in his mouth and blow off the top of his head, unmindful of the effect on beloved wife and children, but an investigator must be thorough. One fact overlooked could be it. You must never forget that, Clement knew.

He had to question Moira again; luckily, she listened to the same newscaster every Sunday morning; he was an acid-tongued and witty fellow.

Clement got a transcript of his talk. Not a word of it seemed to apply to Bill's action; all international and political comment, venomous, witty—remote from Sapphire Bay.

The investigator went back to his notes, fuming. Nothing there; the field had been reaped to the limit. All right, he told himself: think, man. You're missing something.

Then it came to him—one last angle. The newscaster hadn't quite begun when Moira left. There was an earlier program, a short one of the human interest variety. It should be looked into. Bill could have heard that, too, if listening.

So Clement returned to the station, got that transcript. It read:

> Good morning, ladies and gentlemen, this is Joe Satterfield with The Human Angle. I've cancelled my original story for today to bring you an exclusive from the Far West, the little community, almost a ghost town, of Gold Creek, California.
>
> A few days ago, some kids, playing soldier and hacking tall weeds with wooden swords, spotted the ruins of an old car. A little later, getting closer, they also found to their horror, a human skeleton inside.
>
> Twenty-four years ago, a salesman named Sam Kolitz was hurrying back from his customers in the east—back to his home in San Francisco. He was really rushing, and I'll tell you why in a minute. It's the pitiful topper to this heartbreaking story.
>
> But, near Gold Creek, the highway was blocked by an accident, a big oil truck jackknifed. Sam Kolitz couldn't wait, and learned about a little-used side road that met the highway farther north. He took it, and vanished for almost a quarter of a century.
>
> Do you know what day it was? They were able to tell from papers and receipts in the car. It was December 6, 1941. That's right, a Saturday: the one before Pearl Harbor.
>
> And how could a car with a man inside be lost all that time? It's a matter of crazy coincidences. When the blockage was cleared up, very few used the side road. Snow came early, and it was

heavy. The war drove casual motorists off the highways, and Gold Creek, the only town near the buried car, lost much of its population to the war plants.

Then there were mud-slides, and finally a huge mass of milk thistle—a terrible weed with murderous spines—sprung up to bar any approach to Sam Kolitz' tomb.

And there's another mystery: why all the bits and strands of rusted wire tangled in the rusty car? Was this salesman, a poor man of forty, robbed and tied with wire—left to die, after he pulled off that side road, perhaps for a nap, which he so badly needed?

Here's the topper. Sam Kolitz was hurrying home because he'd been telegraphed that his little daughter, Linda, nine, was dying. They never got to see each other. Linda died in February.

So far, we've been unable to locate Mrs. Kolitz; nobody knows if she's still alive. The disappearance of her husband shattered the poor woman, and she moved away.

Think of the tragedy. This salesman, trying to make it home, driving day and night. Blocked by an accident, he takes what he hopes will be a shortcut, or at least a way around. He's very tired, so he pulls off that dirt road for a nap. And then—and then, what? A killer? A madman? Or did Sam Kolitz take his own life, unable to go home to face his dying child? Or did he die of natural causes, perhaps in his sleep? Ah, but if any of these, why so much wire, thin, tough stuff, in and around the old car?

I wonder if we'll ever know the true story of Sam Kolitz, who vanished the day before Pearl Harbor, and was found this week, near the little town of Gold Creek, California.

This has been Joe Satterfield with The Human Angle. See you next Sunday.

Fred Clement whistled softly when he read this. Was there a tie-in? It didn't seem likely. Bill van Meter the callous slayer of a harmless salesman. Quite impossible. But wasn't Coleridge Academy near Gold Creek? Surely somebody there had mentioned the town.

Then a thought came to him, a dreadful vision. Feeling ill, he grabbed a jet, and headed west again. He had to have another talk with Larry Keith.

Keith seemed puzzled to see him again so soon, but quite cordial. Clement wasn't sure how to open the discussion. Did Keith know anything? It didn't look that way. He was ruddy, relaxed, cheerful; no little demon of guilt in his rather bulging grey eyes. A man would have to show some signs of soul-damage, *if* he knew.

After some meaningless questions about Bill's life at Coleridge, the detective yawned ostentatiously, and as if bringing up a minor matter of the most casual interest, said: "Mrs. van Meter—Bill's wife—mentioned one prank you forgot to tell me about. Something about a man in a car, near Gold Creek. That's pretty close to Coleridge, isn't it?"

"Car?" Keith repeated blankly. "I don't remember anything like—say!" He grinned broadly, eyes lighting up. "You know, I'd forgotten that one for years. Damned if it wasn't the day before Pearl Harbor. We had plenty to think about on Sunday, and never did check back as planned. But it was a lulu, all right; only Bill van Meter ever came up with such ideas. I wonder if Moira got it straight; it's too good to spoil."

"I'd like to hear your version," Clement said, a cold grue beginning to seize him. "Sounded very funny, what little she remembered." The hunch was right, he thought.

"Well, it was Saturday, and we had the afternoon off. It was a couple miles from school, I guess. Anyhow, we'd found this big spool of wire that must have fallen off a truck from one of the defense plants—stuff for England, maybe. It was real good steel, a kind of heavy piano wire, and plenty of it, too.

"Some kids would have sold it for a few bucks, but Bill was loaded, you know, and my folks weren't poor, either. So we took it along; we were just rambling around; it was pretty wild country then.

"Well, we spotted this jalopy pulled well off the old dirt road behind a clump of eucalyptus trees, and moved in real easy like for a look. There was a guy asleep in the back seat; some kind of a salesman, I think; there were sample cases. He was a fat, greasy-looking type, and needed a shave. Snoring like the devil. He was really dead to the world; drunk, maybe; or just pooped. Anyhow, that's when old Bill got this idea. We had all that wire, and so, very quietly, he begins to tie the car shut—no kidding! He wrapped one coil after another around, over, and through, with knots, loops, and tangles until it looked like a fish-net. You should have seen the job he did! I swear no opening big enough for a snake.

"'When he wakes up,' Bill says—the guy was still sleeping like the dead, and snoring real loud; must have had adenoids or something. Funny how I still remember that. And about him needing a shave so bad. 'When he wakes up,' Bill says, 'he'll get quite a shock.'

"'Sure,' I said. 'But all he has to do is lower a window and start yelling. Somebody will come along and get him out.'

"Bill said that was too easy, and would spoil the effect; so he jams all the windows by pushing little twigs and stuff into the cracks at the bottom—like wedges, you know. That old car was some sight when he got through, believe me.

"Then Bill said maybe it was a pretty low trick at that; not much traffic there, and the dope might be stuck for hours—overnight even—and lose dough. And so, to even things up for the fat peddler, he puts a twenty under the wiper. He was like that, Bill was, full of fun, great imagination, but never out to really hurt anybody, you understand. He figured the guy would be happy to make a double sawbuck from the joke. In those days, that was money. He'd have to sell a hell of a lot of neckties or whatever he had in his cases to net that much dough." Keith chuckled. "Wish we could have seen it. Man, without help he'd still be there! That wire is murder; you can't break it, or cut it with a knife. Only strong nippers can chop up such stuff."

Clement gulped, swallowing a sour spray that came up from his stomach. "You didn't read the papers about three weeks ago, when Bill kill—died?"

"What papers?" He goggled at the detective with prominent grey eyes. "Three weeks ago I was in Hawaii. Sure, I read the papers there, some of them. Why? Something on Bill?"

"Nothing," Clement said. "I was thinking about a different point; it doesn't matter."

Keith was obviously in the clear, and not just covering up. A body near Gold Creek would hardly be played up away from California. A paragraph here and there, at most, in a few mid-western or eastern papers. So Keith still didn't know the payoff of that 1941 prank of two teenagers; and Clement had no desire at all to enlighten him. Two deaths were enough, even twenty-four years apart. Not that this fellow was the sort to commit suicide over a joke that went sour; there was complacency in the bulging eyes, a sleek smugness about his whole person that ruled out such an act. And he was only a follower, to be fair.

Clement made a quick exit, in no mood for further talk. He was hardened to his job, and had seen some unpleasant things, and worse people, but this was a bad business. Sam Kolitz, the fat, probably flabby salesman, with bum feet, dead tired on his run home to a dying child, awakening from a much needed nap to find himself inexplicably wired in, as if some great metal spider had wrapped the car with her steel silk.

At first, there would be astonishment, doubt that he was really awake, and not still dreaming. Then annoyance at precious time wasted by some clown of a practical joker. And—the detective found himself actually shuddering—the beginning of fear as the tempered piano wire resisted all his efforts to make an opening. Apparently there was not even a knife in the car; not that one would help. No ordinary blade would work on such stuff. As Keith had said, it took heavy professional nippers. He'd try the windows, then, planning to yell until somebody heard him and got the needed tools. But all the windows were jammed. It's not easy to break such glass. Maybe he did manage it with something from the glove compartment, or a shoe; but then what? The wire was still there, a tight, small-meshed net; he couldn't break that with a shoe. No, all Sam Kolitz could do was shout. And keep shouting until his voice went.

Then the man must have panicked—but Clement didn't care to pursue the thought. Later, there was heavy snow to cover the car, muffle any cries, chill the life out of the scared salesman. Nobody came by, perhaps for weeks; gas was rationed, the road little used. Then the terrific thistles—Clement had seen them eight feet high; had once laughed at their odd scientific name: Sillybum. They were impossible to touch or get through, with needles only this side of cactus.

And now, years later, kids hacking with wooden swords; a ruined car with a grinning skull at one window; bony fingers still extended to claw futilely at the wire, finally rusted to pieces.

No wonder that Bill, with a Calvinistic conscience sharpened by responsibilities and maturity, was so abruptly and deeply soul-sick on learning what he'd done to a man hurrying home to a dying child—and Bill loved kids; no wonder, then, that Bill van Meter had to end himself on the spot, forgetting his wife, his own children, everything but the need to erase the searing vision of Sam Kolitz clawing vainly at a cocoon of piano wire.

"And, oh my Lord," Clement muttered, as his jet hissed eastwards. "What can I tell the van Meters—and Moira?"

Was it best, he wondered, to let Bill's death be blamed on an unknown killer, a madman? Or to hope that the family would be consoled to learn that because of a giant conscience he had taken his own life as some kind of amends for a boyish prank believed to be quite harmless? One carried out twenty-four years ago by a kid only distantly related to a family man of thirty-seven. It was a difficult decision to face.

COTTAGE FOR AUGUST

by Thomas Kyd

PROFESSOR HINMAN (MATHEMATICS) joined his colleagues in the Wurzhaus booth, and signaled for a sandwich and beer.

"You, too, I presume," said Professor Parks (English), "have looked on Beauty bare."

"True," said Professor Hinman, "but less frequently than I should wish."

There was an approving chuckle from Professor Mendel (Romance Languages).

"The phrase," said Parks, "was originally applied to Euclid. I wasn't thinking of you as lover-manqué."

Mendel defrothed his mustache with a paper napkin. "It's an odd thing. At faculty meetings we twitter. In class we drone. Here we talk like professors. Probably it's the beer."

"We've been discussing absolutes," explained Parks. "What would you say? Is it possible to produce samples of pure beauty, pure love, pure evil, and so on?—like samples of pure sulphur or copper?"

Hinman looked thirstily toward the counter. He was slight and unimposing, but people liked to hear his opinions. "There's no such thing as pure sulphur or copper. We call things *chemically* pure when they meet certain practical tests. I should say we might treat your absolutes in somewhat the same way."

"Precisely," said Parks. He tapped a column in his *Times*. "And here's 'chemically' pure evil. It meets any test."

"Test? What test?" This from Professor Katz (Social Sciences). He lifted his thin, dedicated shoulders.

"Katz has been telling us," said Parks, "that this incident reported in the *Times* should be thought of as an explosion of social tension. Three New York urchins attacked a Columbia freshman for his pocket money—exactly one dollar and fifty-five cents. Then they calmly clubbed him to death."

"I didn't say it was pretty!" Katz's voice rose several decibels. "It's hideous, it's terrifying. But so is the sight of a python swallowing a sheep."

Hinman received his beer with thanks, and took a reflective sip. "You mean that clubbing a Columbia freshman is only natural?"

"In a sense, yes—for those particular boys. You've seen Morningside Heights, and how its grandeur rises on the edge of Harlem. Just take a look sometime from below on 116th Street."

"I have. When I taught there, I used to forget the switch on the subway at 96th."

"Those boys weren't just clubbing another boy. They were clubbing the University and the Heights. In a way, they were clubbing their own ignorance and confusion."

"But they took the dollar fifty-five."

"Plus," said Mendel fairly, "one nickel-plated wrist watch."

Hinman worked on his sandwich for a moment.

"I think Katz has a point."

Parks sighed. "Here we go! You science people can analyze good and evil out of existence."

"Not at all," said Hinman. He nodded at the paper. "That's evil, but not *pure* evil—not so long as there's an explanation, even a bad explanation like Katz's."

Parks was silent, suspecting a trick.

"My point's simple enough," Hinman went on. "How can you have pure evil so long as you can imagine worse? What if that freshman had been clubbed by a fellow-freshman? The evil of the act would have been less divisible by Katz's social factor, or any other factor. Pure evil should be indivisible."

Mendel nodded. "I get it—a moving scale, determined by the increasing stature of the evil doer and the decreasing size of his prize. It would be purer evil if he had been clubbed by a freshman, still purer if he had been clubbed by a sophomore, and so on up the line—until he's clubbed by the Dean for half a buck, or by the Provost just for fun."

Parks' expression showed that he considered this levity in poor taste, but Hinman put it to use.

"Killing for fun, or for no reason at all, takes us out of the realm of evil into that of mental disease. The motive must be inadequate but understandable. Katz could put this better than I can, but how's this for a test? It approaches pure evil if some fortunate and intelligent human being, of recognizably normal tastes, is willing to deprive another human being of life for the sake of a petty personal convenience."

They thought this over a moment, then Mendel spoke with unusual seriousness. "I don't like your word 'willing.' Last summer I worked at the Huntington Library, and rented one of the little twin villas they have out there, perched on the edge of a canyon. Everything was fine except that the old lady next door had a queer little cough. It was like popping bubble-gum, and it came every fifteen seconds on the second. Our two places had a common drive along the ledge of the canyon, and soon I was calculating the chances of her car plunging over. My God, gentlemen, she was just a nice little old lady, but in my mind I was murdering her every day!"

"But you took no action."

"The devil I didn't! I began pestering her with warnings about that drive as much as she pestered me with her cough. Bad conscience."

Even Parks grinned, and Hinman nodded affectionately. "You're in the clear, Mendel. I think evil impulses must be what is meant by 'Original Sin.' Acting on them in reverse is 'Salvation by Grace.'"

He paused in sudden recollection. Then he spoke in a new tone.

"Still, a mere thought *can* be a sample of pure evil. So can an act of omission. Do you men have two o'clock classes?"

"Why?" asked Katz, glancing at his watch.

"I have an experience to tell you about. Mendel's story reminded me of it. An encounter with pure evil. I think it meets the test."

Their reply was to order more beer.

"I warn you this is unpleasant—so much so that my mind had almost plowed it under. Then a moment ago it came through clear again, as if it had happened yesterday. You're sure you want to hear it?"

They nodded.

"It was seven years ago, during the summer of 1949. That was my first year here, and the only time I've taught the summer session. It was hot, even for Cambridge, and Martha and the children almost perished. We had a top-floor apartment on Walker Street. It came to a boil when the sun hit the roof, and kept simmering all night long. We had been spending summers at a South Jersey beach, and scarcely knew what hot spells meant. The two girls were eight and nine. They and Martha just panted, and looked at me reproachfully. The boy cried. He was two, and had prickly heat that had become infected."

Parks, who was a bachelor, stirred uneasily. Hinman reassured him. "This isn't a tale of domestic squalor. That part's already over . . . At the beginning of August I knew we couldn't take it any longer, but the session had the full month more to run. I had to wait until the week's classes were over; then on a Saturday, August third, I made an expedition to Cape Anne. Martha had a doctor's appointment for the baby, so I couldn't use the car. I arrived on the earliest train, and began phoning real estate offices from the Gloucester station. If I could rent a cottage for August, the family could get out of Walker Street, and I could come up weekends.

"My chances, I knew, were dim. The heat had been driving people to the shore in droves, and this was past the mid-season rental period. My best bet, I had been told, was Annisquam, since it was slightly off the tourist track. I kept dropping nickels in the phone, and kept being told that I was wasting my time. The last office on my list gave me the usual answer, but with one slight addition. I might try the Annisquam antique dealer, a man named Mr. Potts. I called up Mr. Potts. There was no answer, but I got a taxi to his shop and finally tracked him down.

"Potts looked like a kindly old Uncle. He was a typical Yankee trader—all homespun simplicity on the outside, and solid granite inside. He might have something, but then again he might not—he wasn't exactly sure. When he learned I was a professor, he seemed more inclined to think he might have something. He had a nephew at the University. Did I know him? I didn't, but we discussed his nephew at considerable length. There we sat among his dusty antiques, me eyeing him like a spaniel.

"At last he came to the point. Actually there *was* an empty cottage, a nice one at a reasonable figure, but in a sort of way it was already rented. A young couple had left a deposit in early June, but they hadn't appeared on August first to pay the balance and take possession. Time was a-passing by, and it didn't seem exactly right to take the risk that they wouldn't show up, and thus make the owner take a loss. I agreed fervently that it didn't seem right at all. But on the other hand, he said, it didn't seem right to risk arrangements with a brand-new person either—unless that person paid cash on the nail.

"I fairly lunged for my wallet. I hadn't seen the cottage, but I paid the rental in full. I also paid the telephone deposit, ditto gas, ditto electricity, ditto water. I also signed a number of documents in triplicate. When we were through, never had rights of occupancy been more firmly secured—nor the cash considerations.

"Potts then drove me to the cottage. It wasn't simply nice, it was perfect. It was completely isolated at the edge of a big estate on a crescent of water called Sapphire Cove. It faced west, so that you would get the sunsets over the vast blue sweep of Ipswich Bay. Most wonderful of all, it was at least thirty degrees cooler than Walker Street, and within twenty feet of deep water.

"The granite in Potts had receded the moment the money changed hands. He showed me around like a friendly neighbor—four airy bedrooms, a neat kitchen, a huge living room, even a little country garden. We walked out to the water."

Hinman drew out a pencil and reached for a paper napkin.

"This is the part you must follow carefully. Here's the porch of the cottage. You walk over twenty feet of lawn, and you're on this level outcropping of brown rock. Ten feet below—just a nice dive—is the surface of the water, about twelve feet deep and so clear you can see bottom. Alongside the rock is a tier of natural stone steps, leading to a bit of steep shingle with a rowboat beached on its edge. You get the picture? In ten seconds a person on the rock could get to that boat, and in ten more seconds could be out in the water. From the cottage itself the operation might take ten to fifteen seconds more."

They nodded their understanding.

"When I asked Potts what the water was like, I got the usual New England joke. He winked and said it was 'bracing.' He also said there was a beach at the far end of the cove that would be safer bathing for the children. Since my girls were like little seals, I told him I wasn't worried. Then he went off in his car."

Parks interrupted. "You mean Potts isn't the villain of this piece?"

"Lord, no! Just a man who rented me a cottage."

Mendel protested. "Look, Hinman. In the annals of evil the miscreant is supposed to appear early and often. You're the only character left."

A curious look flickered over Hinman's face. He seemed about to say something, then switched to something else. "Two more 'characters' as you call them are about to appear. Just let me go on. I went back to the cottage to wait for Martha and the children. I had called her as soon as the deal was closed. The plan was for her to drive up and inquire for Potts' antique shop, then he would guide her to the cottage. She was due to arrive about two o'clock. I decided to make up some of the sleep I had been losing, and stretched out on the porch swing.

"It was after one when I woke up, and of course I was feeling logey. When it dawned on me where I was, the thought of that water out front came to me like a blessing. I stripped to my underpants and stepped out to the rock. But before I could dive, I heard a motor and watched a car rounding the drive. It wasn't Martha."

"Enter the miscreants," whispered Mendel.

"It was a Mr. and Mrs. Durham." Hinman paused, concentrating. "I wish I could make you see them. We've spoken of fortunate, intelligent people. Add youth—they were still in their twenties or very early thirties—complete ease of manner and remarkable good looks. He was built like a decathlon competitor, and had the appropriately crisp light hair and classic features. She was a quite lovely brunette, with a stunning figure. Her shorts and striped basque shirt let you see her perfect tan, and let you guess at all the rest."

Mendel murmured appreciatively. "Noble man and nubile lady. I see them—or at least her."

Hinman's failure to respond to this sally was the measure of his present dead-seriousness. His mood communicated itself to them, and they stirred a little uneasily.

"They were quite cultivated people and expert dispensers of charm—as I realized the moment they joined me on the rock. Sorry to inconvenience me, they said after introducing themselves, but they had just arrived, and Mr. Potts had sent them to explain. By the way, it turned out that this wasn't so—the visit was their own idea. Explain what? I asked, although I had already guessed. On the drive was their sports car, top down, and back seat piled high with luggage, including golf bags and painting easels. Their explanation came with easy fluency. They were the couple who had originally rented the cottage. They had arrived a few days after the beginning of their month because this was the first weekend and Mr. Durham's vacation had just begun.

"I realized I had a mean situation on my hands. In a sense, of course, they were in the right. All ten points of the law were with me, but that scarcely canceled their claim. If a third party had been considering who should have that cottage—the Hinmans or the Durhams—his decision would depend entirely on whether he was their friend or ours."

It was Katz's turn to interrupt. "You say Potts isn't the villain of this piece. I'm not so sure. What about his purely mercenary ethics—minimize your own risks regardless of the other fellow's?"

Hinman waited patiently until Katz had finished. Then he held out his two palms like the pans of a set of scales. "There were two factors that governed my reaction. I'll try to describe them as objectively as I can. First of all, the Durhams' approach was wrong. If they had been just a little shy and uncertain, discouraged but desperately hopeful, I might still have held on to the cottage as a family obligation, but I would have felt bad about it. But they didn't act that way. They were almost jolly about it. They either felt, or pretended to feel, complete assurance that I would just move over. They may have been using this technique—getting something by taking it for granted that it would be given—or they may just have been acting in character. Their whole attitude suggested that they were used to having their way. The world was their oyster, and bits of shell like myself could be casually flicked away. Behind their superficial graciousness, you could detect the hard core of egotism and the absolute conviction of superiority.

"The other factor is less creditable to myself. I was *feeling* their superiority and resenting it like the devil. There they were in all their handsome elegance, and there was I in my underpants. They were tanned, and I was the color of a flounder's belly. He was big and I was small. She was fresh as morning, and Martha, after a month in Cambridge, was looking as if she had been through a mangle. In the back of their car were golf clubs and easels, not babies with prickly heat. Need I say more?

"I was scrupulously polite, but I am sure I wasn't quite able to keep surliness out of my voice. My dealings, I said, had been with Mr. Potts, not with them. I had rented and paid for the cottage in good faith. My wife and children were on their way now. We needed the cottage, we had it, and we intended to keep it. I added that I was sorry and was sure Mr. Potts would return their deposit.

"One thing about my remarks, they were conclusive. Their effect upon Mr. and Mrs. Durham was remarkable. They didn't argue and they didn't scowl. Of course they didn't smile any longer either. Their faces simply became inanimate. It was as if they had suddenly turned into superlatively well-formed zombies. They still looked at me, but it was obvious that they no longer saw me. I felt extremely uncomfortable, especially since they made no move to leave. It's hard for a man to take even passive hostility from a beautiful woman, however little he may admire her, and I wanted an end of it. I mumbled a few more words of regret, made the obvious point that I had come out to swim, and then dived off the rock.

"Now this is bound to sound like an anticlimax. The moment I hit the water I understood why Annisquam was so cool. It was refrigerated by Ipswich Bay. I have felt cold water before—at Cape Cod and occasionally in South Jersey—but never anything like this. The July temperature in Massachusetts that year must have averaged ninety, but the water in that cove was nearer forty-five. I struck out in a hurry, hoping to warm up by activity. When I was about fifty yards offshore, I realized this was a mistake. I wasn't getting warm, I was getting numb. As I turned to hustle back to the rock, it occurred to me for the first time that it was just as well that someone was on it. The Durhams were there all right, in exactly their former positions, still silently watching me."

Hinman paused as he drank the last of his beer.

"Have any of you ever had a stomach cramp?"

They shook their heads.

"But you've had a leg cramp?"

They nodded.

"Well, just imagine the same kind of thing extending from your groin to your solar plexus and right through to your spine. Your body becomes one knot of pain, and your legs seem to disappear. I had intimations on the way in, while the Durhams were still above my line of vision, but the thing struck squarely after I had come under the lee of the rock—when I was only eight or ten feet from safety. I went under, but I flailed my arms and came up again. I let out a scream for help. Now you may not think I would be conscious of this, but I was—my scream sounded dreadful, hoarse and animal-like. One other thing about it: it was loud—loud enough to be heard on the rock, in the cottage, anywhere above that cove. Then I went under again.

"You've heard of the mental processes of drowning men—the flashing pictures of past events, and so on. With me everything was strictly contemporary and, believe it or not, there was room in a corner of my mind for embarrassment. I was going to be fished out by the Durhams. How could I hang onto the cottage after that? When I came up the second time, my eyes went to the boat on the shingle. The Durhams weren't there. I didn't yell again. The truth came to me like revelation. They weren't going to be there.

"I'll have to take this up now from Martha's angle. After she got my call, she still had to take the baby to the doctor, and to stock up at the supermarket since I would have the car in Cambridge during the week. But with relief from the heat in sight, the two girls were cooperative and even the baby was less irritable. By eleven thirty she was packed up and away, and by one thirty she was in Potts' antique shop in Annisquam. They chatted a little, then he got in the car to guide her to the cottage.

"They were both surprised to see the Durhams sitting on the porch steps. Mr. Potts had told her of the mix-up, but had assured her there was nothing to worry about. They hadn't kept to their contract, so the cottage was ours. Still the sight of them rising politely as the car pulled up was rather disturbing. But both proved to be models of graciousness and charm. They helped unload the children and kept up a light banter about coming in second best for the prize. Where was I? I had gone in the water about fifteen minutes ago and was probably swimming around in the cove. They were wondering if it would be all right if they took a dip themselves before leaving.

"Then Martha saw me. As I emerged up those stone steps and weaved toward the cottage, I must have looked like a walking bundle of seaweed, but she said that all she could see were my black eyesockets in my dead-white face. That, and the fact that I wasn't even looking at her. I was looking at the Durhams.

"Rage is supposed to release adrenaline. Maybe that's what got me ashore. I had gone under again after I saw there was to be no rescue, and somehow I must have scrabbled my way to the slope. I remember dragging myself out along the gunwale of the boat. The cramp left the moment I was on the shingle, almost like a leg cramp when you step out of bed. But then I got sick. I retched everything out of my stomach, then lay exhausted on the stones. After five to ten minutes I heard the car pull up and the sound of voices.

"As Martha noticed, I didn't even see her. I didn't see Potts or the children. I saw only the Durhams. He had seen me as soon as Martha, and watched my approach with a complete poker-face—he was leaning nonchalantly against the rail of the porch. She was kneeling at the steps, her back toward me, playing with my little boy. I stopped behind her and said 'Mrs. Durham.' She looked up over her shoulder, and I caught her expression. What do you suppose it was?"

Katz and Mendel shook their heads. Parks cleared his throat to speak, then decided against it.

"Well, what would you think? Fear? Guilt? Shame?"

They waited.

"No," said Hinman, "none of those things. Just disappointment. Just plain, ordinary disappointment."

His listeners lifted their empty glasses to their lips like synchronized marionettes.

"I told her to take her hands off the child and get up. Then I told both of them to start moving. I lost control as they climbed into their car and I began to yell 'Murderers' at them. I kept it up until they had backed out of the drive, then I passed out. It was all right. I met my classes on Monday."

Hinman had known all three of his listeners for at least five years. Now they sat immobile, avoiding his eyes and each other's.

"Well, that's the story. I don't want you to comment on it because I know the spot you're in. You can't quite believe it. For one thing the setting is all wrong—atmospherically impossible. A summer rental at Annisquam. Popsicles and sand-in-the-shoes—of course. Pure evil—no. Furthermore, my facts may not be quite so reliable as I think they are.

What if the Durhams didn't realize I was in trouble in that water?"

Hinman rubbed his hand over his eyes.

"In that case, you still have your sample of pure evil. Imagine *them* telling this story to *their* friends—about that ghastly little reptile who swiped their cottage from under their nose, then accused them of wanting to let him drown and his children become orphans. How could any human being think such a thing of other human beings! And all over what? Over nothing—over a cottage for August!"

THE GOODBYE LOOK

by Ross Macdonald

1

THE LAWYER, WHOSE name was John Truttwell, kept me waiting in the outer room of his offices. It gave the room a chance to work me over gently. The armchair I was sitting in was covered in soft green leather. Oil paintings of the region, landscapes and seascapes, hung on the walls around me like subtle advertisements.

The young pink-haired receptionist turned from the switchboard. The heavy dark lines accenting her eyes made her look like a prisoner peering out through bars.

"I'm sorry Mr. Truttwell's running so late. It's that daughter of his," the girl said rather obscurely. "He should let her go ahead and make her own mistakes. The way I have."

"Oh?"

"I'm really a model. I'm just filling in at this job because my second husband ran out on me. Are you really a detective?"

I said I was.

"My husband is a photographer. I'd give a good deal to know who—where he's living."

"Forget it. It wouldn't be worth it."

"You could be right. He's a lousy photographer. Some very good judges told me that his pictures never did me justice."

It was mercy she needed, I thought.

A tall man in his late fifties appeared in the open doorway. High-shouldered and elegantly dressed, he was handsome and seemed to know it. His thick white hair was carefully arranged on his head, as carefully arranged as his expression.

"Mr. Archer? I'm John Truttwell." He shook my hand with restrained enthusiasm and moved me along the corridor to his office. "I have to thank you for coming down from Los Angeles so promptly, and I apologize for keeping you waiting. Here I'm supposed to be semi-retired but I've never had so many things on my mind."

Truttwell wasn't as disorganized as he sounded. Through the flow of language his rather sad cold eyes were looking me over carefully. He ushered me into his office and placed me in a brown-leather chair facing him across his desk.

A little sunlight filtered through the heavily draped windows, but the room was lit by artificial light. In its diffused whiteness Truttwell himself looked rather artificial, like a carefully made wax image wired for sound. On a wall shelf above his right shoulder was a framed picture of a clear-eyed blonde girl who I supposed was his daughter.

"On the phone you mentioned a Mr. and Mrs. Lawrence Chalmers."

"So I did."

"What's their problem?"

"I'll get to that in a minute or two," Truttwell said. "I want to make it clear at the beginning that Larry and Irene Chalmers are friends of mine. We live across from each other on Pacific Street. I've known Larry all my life, and so did our parents before us. I learned a good deal of my law from Larry's father, the judge. And my late wife was very close to Larry's mother."

Truttwell seemed proud of the connection in a slightly unreal way. His left hand drifted softly over his side hair, as if he was fingering an heirloom. His eyes and voice were faintly drowsy with the past.

"The point I'm making," he said, "is that the Chalmerses are valuable people—personally valuable to me. I want you to handle them with great care."

The atmosphere of the office was teeming with social pressures. I tried to dispel one or two of them. "Like antiques?"

"Somewhat, but they're not old. I think of the two of them as objects of art, the point of which is that they don't have to be useful." Truttwell paused, and then went on as if struck by a new thought. "The fact is Larry hasn't accomplished much since the war. Of course he's made a great deal of money, but even that was handed to him on a silver platter. His mother left him a substantial nest egg, and the bull market blew it up into millions."

There was an undertone of envy in Truttwell's voice, suggesting that his feelings about the Chalmers couple were complicated and not entirely worshipful. I let myself react to the nagging undertone:

"Am I supposed to be impressed?"

Truttwell gave me a startled look, as if I'd made an obscene noise, or allowed myself to hear one. "I can see I haven't succeeded in making my point. Larry Chalmers's grandfather fought in the Civil War, then came to California and married a Spanish land-grant heiress. Larry was a war hero himself, but he doesn't talk about it. In our instant society that makes him the closest thing we have to an aristocrat." He listened to the sound of the sentence as though he had used it before.

"What about Mrs. Chalmers?"

"Nobody would describe Irene as an aristocrat. But," he added with unexpected zest, "she's a hell of a good-looking woman. Which is all a woman really has to be."

"You still haven't mentioned what their problem is."

"That's partly because it's not entirely clear to me." Truttwell picked up a sheet of yellow foolscap from his desk and frowned over the scrawlings on it. "I'm hoping they'll speak more freely to a stranger. As Irene laid out the situation to me, they had a burglary at their house while they were away on a long weekend in Palm Springs. It was a rather peculiar burglary. According to her, only one thing of value was taken—an old gold box that was kept in the study safe. I've seen that safe—Judge Chalmers had it put in back in the twenties—and it would be hard to crack."

"Have Mr. and Mrs. Chalmers notified the police?"

"No, and they don't plan to."

"Do they have servants?"

"They have a Spanish houseman who lives out. But they've had the same man for over twenty years. Besides, he drove them to Palm Springs." He paused, and shook his white head. "Still it does have the feel of an inside job, doesn't it?"

"Do you suspect the servant, Mr. Truttwell?"

"I'd rather not tell you whom or what I suspect. You'll work better without too many preconceptions. Well as I know Irene and Larry, they're very private people, and I don't pretend to understand their lives."

"Have they any children?"

"One son, Nicholas," he said in a neutral tone.

"How old is he?"

"Twenty-three or -four. He's due to graduate from the university this month."

"In January?"

"That's right. Nick missed a semester in his freshman year. He left school without telling anyone, and dropped out of sight completely for several months."

"Are his parents having trouble with him now?"

"I wouldn't put it that strongly."

"Could he have done this burglary?"

Truttwell was slow in replying. Judging by the changes in his eyes, he was trying out various answers mentally: they ranged from prosecution to defense.

"Nick could have done it," he said finally. "But he'd have no reason to steal a gold box from his mother."

"I can think of several possible reasons. Is he interested in women?"

Truttwell said rather stiffly: "Yes, he is. He happens to be engaged to my daughter Betty."

"Sorry."

"Not at all. You could hardly be expected to know that. But do be careful what you say to the Chalmerses. They're accustomed to leading a very quiet life, and I'm afraid this business has really upset them. The way they feel about their precious house, it's as if a temple had been violated."

He crumpled the yellow foolscap in his hands and threw it into a wastebasket. The impatient gesture gave the impression that he would be glad to be rid of Mr. and Mrs. Chalmers and their problems, including their son.

2

PACIFIC STREET ROSE like a slope in purgatory from the poor lower town to a hilltop section of fine old homes. The Chalmerses' California Spanish mansion must have been fifty or sixty years old, but its white walls were immaculate in the late-morning sun.

I crossed the walled courtyard and knocked on the iron-bound front door. A dark-suited servant with a face that belonged in a Spanish monastery opened the door and took my name and left me standing in the reception hall. It was an enormous two-storied room that made me feel small and then, in reaction, large and self-assertive.

I could see into the great white cave of the living room. Its walls were brilliant with modern paintings. Its doorway was equipped with black wrought-iron gates, shoulder high, which gave the place a museum atmosphere.

This was partly dispelled by the dark-haired woman who came in from the garden to greet me. She was carrying a pair of clippers and a clear red Olé rose. She laid the clippers down on a hall table but kept the rose, which exactly matched the color of her mouth.

Her smile was bright and anxious. "Somehow I expected you to be older."

"I'm older than I look."

"But I asked John Truttwell to get me the head of the agency."

"I'm a one-man agency. I co-opt other detectives when I need them."

She frowned. "It sounds like a shoestring operation to me. Not like the Pinkertons."

"I'm not big business, if that's what you want."

"It isn't. But I want somebody good, really good. Are you experienced in dealing with—well—" Her free hand indicated first herself and then her surroundings—"people like me?"

"I don't know you well enough to answer that."

"But *you're* the one we're talking about."

"I assume Mr. Truttwell recommended me, and told you I was experienced."

"I have a right to ask my own questions, don't I?"

Her tone was both assertive and lacking in self-assurance. It was the tone of a handsome woman who had married money and social standing and never could forget that she might just as easily lose these things.

"Go ahead and ask questions, Mrs. Chalmers."

She caught my gaze and held it, as if she were trying to read my mind. Her eyes were black and intense and impervious.

"All I really want to know is this. If you find the Florentine box—I assume John Truttwell told you about the gold box?"

"He said that one was missing."

She nodded. "Assuming you find it, and find out who took it, is that as far as it goes? I mean, you won't march off to the authorities and tell them all about it?"

"No. Unless they're already involved?"

"They aren't, and they're not going to be," she said. "I want this whole thing kept quiet. I wasn't even going to tell John Truttwell about the box, but he wormed it out of me. However, him I trust. I think."

"And me you think you don't?"

I smiled, and she decided to respond. She tapped me on the cheek with her red rose, then dropped it on the tile floor as if it had served its purpose. "Come into the study. We can talk privately there."

She led me up a short flight of steps to a richly carved oak door. Before she closed it behind us I could see the servant in the reception hall picking up after her, first the clippers, then the rose.

The study was an austere room with dark beams supporting the slanting white ceiling. The single small window, barred on the outside, made it resemble a prison cell. As if the prisoner had been looking for a way out, there were shelves of old law books against one wall.

On the facing wall hung a large picture which appeared to be an oil painting of Pacific Point in the old days, done in primitive perspective. A seventeenth-century sailing vessel lay in the harbor inside the curve of the point; beside it naked brown Indians lounged on the beach; over their heads Spanish soldiers marched like an army in the sky.

Mrs. Chalmers seated me in an old calf-covered swivel chair in front of a closed roll-top desk.

"These pieces don't go with the rest of the furniture," she said as if it mattered. "But this was my father-in-law's desk, and that chair you're sitting in was the one he used in court. He was a judge."

"So Mr. Truttwell told me."

"Yes, John Truttwell knew him. I never did. He died a long time ago, when Lawrence was just a small boy. But my husband still worships the ground his father walked on."

"I'm looking forward to meeting your husband. Is he at home?"

"I'm afraid not. He went to see the doctor. This burglary business has him all upset." She added: "I wouldn't want you to talk to him, anyway."

"Does he know I'm here?"

She moved away from me, leaning over a black oak refectory table. She fumbled a cigarette from a silver box and lit it with a matching table lighter. The cigarette, which she puffed on furiously, laid down a blue smokescreen between us.

"Lawrence didn't think it was a good idea to use a private detective. I decided to go ahead with you anyway."

"Why did he object?"

"My husband likes his privacy. And this box that was stolen—well, it was a gift to his mother from an admirer of hers. I'm not supposed to know that, but I do." Her smile was crooked. "In addition to which, his mother used it to keep his letters in."

"The admirer's letters?"

"My husband's letters. Larry wrote her a lot of letters during the war, and she kept them in the box. The letters are missing, too—not that they're of any great value, except maybe to Larry."

"Is the box valuable?"

"I think it is. It's covered with gold, and very carefully made. It was made in Florence during the Renaissance." She stumbled on the word, but got it out. "It has a picture on the lid, of two lovers."

"Insured?"

She shook her head, and crossed her legs. "It hardly seemed necessary. We never took it out of the safe. It never occurred to us that the safe could be broken into."

I asked to be allowed to see the safe. Mrs. Chalmers took down the primitive painting of the Indians and the Spanish soldiers. Where it had hung a large cylindrical safe was set deep in the wall. She turned the dial several times and opened it. Looking over her shoulder, I could see that the safe was about the diameter of a sixteen-inch gun and just as empty.

"Where's your jewelry, Mrs. Chalmers?"

"I don't have much, it never has interested me. What I do have, I keep in a case in my room. I took the case along with me to Palm Springs. We were there when the gold box was taken."

"How long has it been missing?"

"Let me see now, this is Tuesday. I put it in the safe Thursday night. Next morning we went to the desert. It must have been stolen after we left, so that makes four days, or less. I looked in the safe last night when we got home, and it was gone."

"What made you look in the safe last night?"

"I don't know. I really don't," she added, making it sound like a lie.

"Did you have some idea that it might be stolen?"

"No. Certainly not."

"What about the servant?"

"Emilio didn't take it. I can vouch for him, absolutely."

"Was anything taken besides the box?"

She considered the question. "I don't think so. Except the letters, of course, the famous letters."

"Were they important?"

"They were important to my husband, as I said. And of course to his mother. But she's been dead a long time, since the end of the war. I never met her myself." She sounded a little worried, as if she'd been denied a maternal blessing, and still felt defrauded.

"Why would a burglar take them?"

"Don't ask me. Probably because they were in the box." She made a face. "If you do find them, don't bother to bring them back. I've already heard them, or most of them."

"Heard them?"

"My husband used to read them aloud to Nick."

"Where is your son?"

"Why?"

"I'd like to talk to him."

"You can't." She was frowning again. Behind her beautiful mask there was a spoiled girl, I thought, like a fakir huddled in the statue of a god. "I wish John Truttwell had sent me someone else. Anyone else."

"What did I do wrong?"

"You ask too many questions. You're prying into our family affairs, and I've already told you more than I should."

"You can trust me." Immediately I regretted saying it.

"Can I really?"

"Other people have." I could hear an unfortunate selling note in my voice. I wanted to stay with the woman and her peculiar little case: she had the kind of beauty that made you want to explore its history. "And I'm sure Mr. Truttwell would advise you not to hold back with me. When a lawyer hires me I have the same privilege of silence as he does."

"Exactly what does that mean?"

"It means I can't be forced to talk about what I find out. Not even a Grand Jury with contempt powers can make me."

"I see." She had caught me off base, trying to sell myself, and now in a certain sense she could buy me; not with money, necessarily. "If you promise to be absolutely close-mouthed, even with John Truttwell, I'll tell you something. This may not be an ordinary burglary."

"Do you suspect it was an inside job? There's no sign that the safe was forced."

"Lawrence pointed that out. It's why he didn't want you brought into the case. He didn't even want me to tell John Truttwell."

"Who does he think stole the box?"

"He hasn't said. I'm afraid he suspects Nick, though."

"Has Nick been in trouble before?"

"Not this kind of trouble." The woman's voice had dropped almost out of hearing. Her whole body had slumped, as if the thought of her son was a palpable weight inside of her.

"What kind of trouble has he had?"

"Emotional problems so called. He turned against Lawrence and me for no good reason. He ran away when he was nineteen. It took the Pinkertons months to find him. It cost us thousands of dollars."

"Where was he?"

"Working his way around the country. Actually, his psychiatrist said it did him some good. He's settled down to his studies since. He's even got himself a girl." She spoke with some pride, or hope, but her eyes were somber.

"And you don't think he stole your box?"

"No, I don't." She tilted up her chin. "You wouldn't be here if I thought so."

"Can he open the safe?"

"I doubt it. We've never given him the combination."

"I noticed you've got it memorized. Do you have it written down anywhere?"

"Yes."

She opened the bottom right-hand drawer of the desk, pulled it all the way out and turned it over, dumping the yellow bank statements it contained. Taped to the bottom of the drawer was a slip of paper bearing a series of typewritten numbers. The tape was yellow and cracked with age, and the paper was so worn that the figures on it were barely decipherable.

"That's easy enough to find," I said. "Is your son in need of money?"

"I can't imagine what for. We give him six or seven hundred a month, more if he needs it."

"You mentioned a girl."

"He's engaged to Betty Truttwell, who is not exactly a gold digger."

"No other girls or women in his life?"

"No." But her answer was slow and dubious.

"How does he feel about the box?"

"Nick?" Her clear forehead wrinkled, as if my question had taken her by surprise. "As a matter of fact, he used to be interested in it when he was little. I used to let him and Betty play with it. We used–they used to pretend that it was Pandora's box. Magic, you know?"

She laughed a little. Her whole body was dreaming of the past. Then her eyes changed again. Her mind came up to their surface, hard and scared. She said in a thinner voice:

"Maybe I shouldn't have built it up so much. But I still can't believe he took it. Nick has usually been honest with us."

"Have you asked him if he took it?"

"No. We haven't seen him since we got back from the desert. He has his own apartment near the university, and he's taking his final exams."

"I'd like to talk to him, at least get a yes or no. Since he is under suspicion–"

"Just don't tell him his father suspects him. They've been getting along so well these last couple of years, I'd hate to see it spoiled."

I promised her to be tactful. Without any further persuasion she gave me Nick Chalmers's phone number and his address in the university community. She wrote them on a slip of paper in a childish unformed hand. Then she glanced at her watch.

"This has taken longer than I thought. My husband will be coming home for lunch."

She was flushed and brilliant-eyed, as if she was terminating an assignation. She hurried me out to the reception hall, where the dark-suited servant was standing with a blank respectful face. He opened the front door, and Mrs. Chalmers practically pushed me out.

A middle-aged man in a fine tweed suit got out of a black Rolls Royce in front of the house. He crossed the courtyard with a kind of military precision, as if each step he took, each movement of his arms, was separately controlled by orders sent down from on high. The eyes in his lean brown face had a kind of bright blue innocence. The lower part of his face was conventionalized by a square-cut, clipped brown mustache.

His pale gaze drifted past me. "What's going on here, Irene?"

"Nothing. I mean—" She drew in her breath. "This is the insurance man. He came about the burglary."

"You sent for him?"

"Yes." She gave me a shame-faced look. She was lying openly and asking me to go along with it.

"That was rather a silly thing to do," her husband said. "The Florentine box wasn't insured, at least not to my knowledge." He looked at me in polite inquiry.

"No," I said in a wooden voice.

I was angry with the woman. She had wrecked my rapport with her, and any possible rapport with her husband.

"Then we won't keep you further," he said to me. "I apologize for Mrs. Chalmers's blunder. I'm sorry your time has been wasted."

Chalmers moved toward me smiling patiently under his mustache. I stepped to one side. He edged past me in the deep doorway, taking care not to brush against me. I was a commoner, and it might be catching.

3

I STOPPED AT a gas station on the way to the university, and called Nick's apartment from an outdoor pay phone. A girl's voice answered:

"Nicholas Chalmers's residence."

"Is Mr. Chalmers there?"

"No he is not." She spoke with a professional lilt. "This is his answering service."

"How can I get in touch with him? It's important."

"I don't know *where* he is." An unprofessional note of anxiety had entered her voice. "Is this connected with his missing his exams?"

"It may very well be," I said in an open-ended way. "Are you a friend of Nick's?"

"Yes I am. Actually I'm not his answering service. I'm his fiancée."

"Miss Truttwell?"

"Do I know you?"

"Not yet. Are you in Nick's apartment?"

"Yes. Are you a counselor?"

"Roughly speaking, yes. My name is Archer. Will you wait there in the apartment for me, Miss Truttwell? And if Nick turns up, will you ask him to wait for me, too?"

She said she would. "I'll do anything that will help Nick." The implication seemed to be that he needed all the help he could get.

The university stood on a mesa a few miles out of town, beyond the airport. From a distance its incomplete oval of new buildings looked ancient and mysterious as Stonehenge. It was the third week in January, and I gathered that the midyear exams were in progress. The students I saw as I circled the campus had a driven preoccupied air.

I'd been there before, but not for several years. The student body had multiplied in the meantime, and the community attached to the campus had turned into a city of apartment buildings. It was strange, after Los Angeles, to drive through a city where everyone was young.

Nick lived in a five-storied building which called itself the Cambridge Arms. I rode the self-service elevator to the fifth floor and found the door of his apartment, which was number 51.

The girl opened the door before I knocked. Her eyes flickered when she saw it was only me. She had clean straight yellow hair that brushed the shoulders of her dark slacks suit. She looked about twenty.

"No Nick?" I said.

"I'm afraid not. You're Mr. Archer?"

"Yes."

She gave me a quick probing look, and I realized she was older than I'd thought. "Are you really a counselor, Mr. Archer?"

"I said roughly speaking. I've done a lot of counseling in an amateur sort of way."

"What do you do in a professional sort of way?"

Her voice wasn't unfriendly. But her eyes were honest and sensitive, ready to be affronted. I didn't want that to happen. She was the nicest thing I'd come across in some time.

"I'm afraid if I tell you, Miss Truttwell, you won't talk to me."

"You're a policeman, aren't you?"

"I used to be. I'm a private investigator."

"Then you're perfectly right. I don't want to talk to you."

She was showing signs of alarm. Her eyes and nostrils were dilated. Her face had a kind of sheen or glare on it. She said:

"Did Nick's parents send you here to talk to me?"

"How could they have? You're not supposed to be here. Since we are talking, by the way, we might as well do it inside."

After some hesitation, she stepped back and let me in. The living room was furnished in expensive but dull good taste. It looked like the kind of furniture the Chalmerses might have bought for their son without consulting him.

The whole room gave the impression that Nick had kept himself hidden from it. There were no pictures on the walls. The only personal things of any kind were the books in the modular bookcase, and most of these were textbooks, in politics, law, psychology, and psychiatry.

I turned to the girl. "Nick doesn't leave much evidence of himself lying around."

"No. He's a very secret boy–man."

"Boy or man?"

"He may be trying to make up his mind about that."

"Just how old is he, Miss Truttwell?"

"He just turned twenty-three last month—December 14. He's graduating half a year late because he missed a semester a few years ago. That is, he'll graduate if they let him make up his exams. He's missed three out of four now."

"Why?"

"It's not a school problem. Nick's quite brilliant," she said as though I'd denied it. "He's a whizz in poli sci, which is his major, and he's planning to study law next year." Her voice was a little unreal, like that of a girl reciting a dream or trying to recall a hope.

"What kind of a problem is it, Miss Truttwell?"

"A life problem, as they call it." She took a step toward me and stood with her hands hanging loose, palms facing me. "All of a sudden he quit caring."

"About you?"

"If that was all, I could stand it. But he cut loose from everything. His whole life has changed in the last few days."

"Drugs?"

"No. I don't think so. Nick knows how dangerous they are."

"Sometimes that's an attraction."

"I know, I know what you mean."

"Has he discussed it with you?"

She seemed confused for a second. "Discussed what?"

"The change in his life in the last few days."

"Not really. You see, there's another woman involved. An older woman." The girl was wan with jealousy.

"He must be out of his mind," I said by way of complimenting her.

She took it literally. "I know. He's been doing things he couldn't do if he were completely sane."

"Tell me about the things he's been doing."

She gave me a look, the longest one so far. "I *can't* tell you. I don't even know you."

"Your father does."

"Really?"

"Call him up if you don't believe me."

Her gaze wandered to the telephone, which stood on an end table by the chesterfield, then came back to my face. "That means you are working for the Chalmerses. They're Dad's clients."

I didn't answer her.

"What did Nick's parents hire you to do?"

"No comment. We're wasting time. You and I both want to see Nick get back inside his skin. We need each other's help."

"How can I help?"

I felt I was reaching her. "You obviously want to talk to someone. Tell me what Nick's been up to."

I was still standing like an unwanted guest. I sat down on the chesterfield. The girl approached it carefully, perching on one arm beyond my reach.

"If I do, you won't repeat it to his parents?"

"No. What have you got against his parents?"

"Nothing, really. They're nice people, I've known them all my life as friends and neighbors. But Mr. Chalmers is pretty hard on Nick; they're such different types, you know. Nick is very critical of the war, for example, and Mr. Chalmers considers that unpatriotic. He served with distinction in the last war, and it's made him kind of rigid in his thinking."

"What did he do in the war?"

"He was a naval pilot when he was younger than Nick is now. He thinks Nick is a terrible rebel." She paused. "He isn't really. I admit he was pretty wild-eyed at one time. That was several years ago, before Nick settled down to study. He was doing so well until last week. Then everything went smash."

I waited. Tentative as a bird, she slid off the arm of the chesterfield and plopped down beside me. She made a sour face and shut her eyes tight, holding back tears. In a minute she went on:

"I think that woman is at the bottom of it. I know what that makes me. But how can I help being jealous? He dropped me like a hotcake and took up with a woman old enough to be his mother. She's even married."

"How do you know that?"

"He introduced her to me as Mrs. Trask. I'm pretty sure she's from out of town—there are no Trasks in the phone book."

"He introduced you?"

"I forced him to. I saw them together in the Lido Restaurant. I went to their table and stayed there until Nick introduced me to her and the other man. His name was Sidney Harrow. He's a bill collector from San Diego."

"Did he tell you that?"

"Not exactly. I found out."

"You're quite a finder-outer."

"Yes," she said, "I am. Ordinarily I don't believe in snooping." She gave me a half-smile. "But there are times when snooping is called for. So when Mr. Harrow wasn't looking I picked up his parking ticket, which was lying on the table beside his plate. I took it out to the Lido parking lot and got the attendant to show me which was his car. It was a junky old convertible, with the back window torn out. The rest was easy. I got his name and address from the car registration in the front and put in a call to his place in San Diego, which turned out to be a collection agency. They said he was on his vacation. Some vacation."

"How do you know he isn't?"

"I haven't finished." For the first time she was impatient, carried along by her story. "It was Thursday noon when I met them in the restaurant. I saw the old convertible again on Friday night. It was parked in front of the Chalmerses' house. We live diagonally across the street and I can see their house from the window of my workroom. Just to make sure that it was Mr. Harrow's car, I went over there to check on the registration. This was about nine o'clock Friday night.

"It was his, all right. He must have heard me close the car door. He came rushing out of the Chalmerses' house and asked me what I was doing there. I asked him what he was doing. Then he slapped my face and started to twist my arm. I must have let out some kind of a noise, because Nick came out of the house and knocked Mr. Harrow down. Mr. Harrow got a revolver out of his car and I thought for a minute he was going to shoot Nick. They had a funny look on both their faces, as if they were both going to die. As if they really *wanted* to kill each other and be killed."

I knew that goodbye look. I had seen it in the war, and too many times since the war.

"But the woman," the girl said, "came out of the house and stopped them. She told Mr. Harrow to get into his car. Then she got in and they drove away. Nick said that he was sorry, but he couldn't talk to me right then. He went into the house and closed the door and locked it."

"How do you know he locked it?"

"I tried to get in. His parents were away, in Palm Springs, and he was terribly upset. Don't ask me why. I don't understand it at all, except that that woman is after him."

"Do you know that?"

"She's that kind of woman. She's a phony blonde with a big red sloppy mouth and poisonous eyes. I can't understand why he would flip over her."

"What makes you think he has?"

"The way she talked to him, as if she owned him." She spoke with her face and the front of her body averted.

"Have you told your father about this woman?"

She shook her head. "He knows I'm having trouble with Nick. But I can't tell him what it is. It makes Nick look so bad."

"And you want to marry Nick."

"I've waited for a long time." She turned and faced me. I could feel the pressure of her cool insistence, like water against a dam. "I intend to marry him, whether my father wants me to or not. I'd naturally prefer to have his approval."

"But he's opposed to Nick?"

Her face thinned. "He'd be opposed to any man whom I wanted to marry. My mother was killed in 1945. She was younger then than I am now," she added in faint surprise. "Father never remarried, for my sake. I wish for my sake he had."

She spoke with the measured emphasis of a young woman who had suffered.

"How old are you, Betty?"

"Twenty-five."

"How long is it since you've seen Nick?"

"Not since Friday night, at his house."

"And you've been waiting for him here since then?"

"Part of the time. Dad would worry himself sick if I didn't come home at night. Incidentally, Nick hasn't slept in his own bed since I started waiting for him here."

"When was that?"

"Saturday afternoon." She added with a seasick look: "If he wants to sleep with her, let him."

At this point the telephone rang. She rose quickly and answered it. After listening for a moment she spoke rather grimly into the receiver:

"This is Mr. Chalmers' answering service . . . No, I don't know where he is . . . Mr. Chalmers does not provide me with that information."

She listened again. From where I sat I could hear a woman's emotional voice on the line, but I couldn't make out her words. Betty repeated them: "'Mr. Chalmers is to stay away from the Montevista Inn.' I see. Your husband has followed you there. Shall I tell him that? . . . All right."

She put the receiver down, very gently, as if it was packed with high explosives. The blood mounted from her neck and suffused her face in a flush of pure emotion.

"That was Mrs. Trask."

"I was wondering. I gather she's at the Montevista Inn."

"Yes. So is her husband."

"I may pay them a visit."

She rose abruptly. "I'm going home. I'm not going to wait here any longer. It's humiliating."

We went down together in the elevator. In its automatic intimacy she said:

"I've spilled all my secrets. How do you make people do it?"

"I don't. People like to talk about what's hurting them. It takes the edge off the pain sometimes."

"Yes, I believe it does."

"May I ask you one more painful question?"

"This seems to be the day for them."

"How was your mother killed?"

"By a car, right in front of our house on Pacific Street."

"Who was driving?"

"Nobody knows, least of all me. I was just a small baby."

"Hit-run?"

She nodded. The doors slid open at the ground floor, terminating our intimacy. We went out together to the parking lot. I watched her drive off in a red two-seater, burning rubber as she turned into the street.

4

MONTEVISTA LAY ON the sea just south of Pacific Point. It was a rustic residential community for woodland types who could afford to live anywhere.

I left the freeway and drove up an oak-grown hill to the Montevista Inn. From its parking lot the rooftops below seemed to be floating in a flood of greenery. I asked the young man in the office for Mrs. Trask. He directed me to Cottage Seven, on the far side of the pool.

A bronze dolphin spouted water at one end of the big old-fashioned pool. Beyond it a flagstone path meandered through live oaks toward a white stucco cottage. A red-shafted flicker took off from one of the trees and crossed a span of sky, wings opening and closing like a fan lined with vivid red.

It was a nice place to be, except for the sound of the voices from the cottage. The woman's voice was mocking. The man's was sad and monotonous. He was saying:

"It isn't so funny, Jean. You can wreck your life just so many times. And my life, it's my life, too. Finally you reach a point where you can't put it back together. You should learn a lesson from what happened to your father."

"Leave my father out of this."

"How can I? I called your mother in Pasadena last night, and she says you're still looking for him. It's a wild-goose chase, Jean. He's probably been dead for years."

"No! Daddy's alive. And this time I'm going to find him."

"So he can ditch you again?"

"He never ditched me."

"That's the way I heard it from your mother. He ditched you both and took off with a piece of skirt."

"He did not." Her voice was rising. "You mustn't say such things about my father."

"I can say them if they're true."

"I won't listen!" she cried. "Get out of here. Leave me alone."

"I will not. You're coming home to San Diego with me and put up a decent front. You owe me that much after twenty years."

The woman was silent for a moment. The sounds of the place lapped in like gentle waves: a towhee foraging in the underbrush, a kinglet rattling. Her voice, when she spoke again, was calmer and more serious:

"I'm sorry, George, I truly am, but you might as well give up. I've heard everything you're saying so often, it just goes by like wind."

"You always came back before," he said with a note of hopefulness in his voice.

"This time I'm not."

"You have to, Jean."

His voice had thinned. Its hopefulness had twisted into a kind of threat. I began to move around the side of the cottage.

"Don't you dare touch me," she said.

"I have a legal right to. You're my wife."

He was saying and doing all the wrong things. I knew, because I'd said and done them in my time. The woman let out a small scream, which sounded as if she was tuning up for a bigger one.

I looked around the corner of the cottage, where the flagstone path ran into a patio. The man had pinned the woman in his arms and was kissing the side of her blond head. She had turned her face away, in my direction. Her eyes were chilly, as if her husband's kisses were freezing cold.

"Let go of me, George. We have company."

He released her and backed away, red-faced and wet-eyed. He was a large middle-aged man who moved awkwardly, as if he was the intruder instead of me.

"This is my wife," he said, more in self-excuse than introduction. "What was she yelling about?"

"It's all right," the woman said. "He wasn't hurting me. But you better leave now, George, before something does happen."

"I have to talk to you some more." He reached out a thick red hand toward her. The gesture was both menacing and touching, like something done by Frankenstein's innocent monster.

"You'd only get stirred up again."

"But I've got a right to plead my case. You can't cut me off without a hearing. I'm not a criminal like your father was. But even a criminal gets his day in court. You've got to give me a hearing."

He was getting very excited, and it was the kind of spinning excitement that could change to violence if it came up tails.

"You better go, Mr. Trask."

His wild wet gaze roved to me. I showed him an old Special Deputy badge I carried. He examined it closely, as if it was a curio.

"Very well, I'll go." He turned and walked away, pausing at the corner of the building to call back: "I'm not going very far."

The woman turned to me, sighing. Her hair had been disarranged, and she was fixing it with nervous fingers. It was done in a fluffy doll-like fashion that didn't go with her forty years or so. But in spite of Betty's description of her, she wasn't a bad-looking woman. She had a good figure under her blouse, and a handsome, heavy face.

She also had a quality that bothered me, a certain doubt and dimness about the eyes, as if she had lost her way a long time ago.

"That was good timing," she said to me. "You never know what George is going to do."

"Or anybody else."

"Are you the security man around here?"

"I'm filling in."

She looked me up and down, like a woman practicing to be a divorcée. "I owe you a drink. Do you like Scotch?"

"On the rocks, please."

"I have some ice. My name is Jean Trask, by the way."

I told her my name. She took me into the living room of the cottage and left me there while she went into the kitchen. Around the walls of the room a series of English hunting prints followed some red-coated hunters and their hounds over hills and through valleys to the death of the fox.

Ostensibly studying the prints, I circled the room to the open door of the bedroom and looked in. On the nearest of the two beds a woman's blue weekend case lay open, and the gold box was in it. On its painted lid a man and a woman in skimpy antique clothes disported themselves.

I was tempted to walk in and take the box, but John Truttwell wouldn't have liked that. Even without him, I'd probably have let the thing lie. I was beginning to sense that the theft of the box was just a physical accident of the case. Any magic it possessed, black or white or gold, was soaked up from the people who handled it.

But I took two steps into the bedroom and lifted the heavy lid of the box. It was empty. I heard Mrs. Trask crossing the living room, and I retreated in her direction. She slammed the bedroom door.

"We won't be using that room."

"What a pity."

She gave me a startled look, as if she was unaware of her own rough candor. Then she shoved a lowball glass at me. "Here."

She went into the kitchen and returned with a dark-brown drink for herself. As soon as she had taken a swallow or two, her eyes turned moist and bright and her color rose. She was a drinker, I thought, and I was there essentially because she didn't want to drink alone.

She knocked her drink back in a hurry and made herself another, while I nursed mine. She sat down in an armchair facing me across a coffee table. I was almost enjoying myself. The room was large and tranquil, and through the open front door I could hear quail muttering and puttering.

I had to spoil it. "I was admiring your gold box. Is it Florentine?"

"I suppose it is," she said, offhandedly.

"Don't you know? It looks quite valuable."

"Really? Are you an expert?"

"No. I was thinking in terms of security. I wouldn't leave it lying around like that."

"Thanks for your advice," she said unthankfully. She was quiet for a minute, sipping her drink. "I didn't mean to be rude just now; I have things on my mind." She leaned toward me in a show of interest. "Have you been in the security business long?"

"Over twenty years, counting my time with the police."

"You used to be a policeman?"

"That's right."

"Perhaps you can help me. I'm involved in a kind of nasty situation. I don't feel up to explaining it all right now, but I hired a man named Sidney Harrow to come here with me. He claimed to be a private detective but it turned out his main experience is repossessing cars. He's a fast man with a tow bar. Also he's dangerous." She finished her drink, and shivered.

"How do you know he's dangerous?"

"He almost killed my boyfriend. He's a fast man with a gun, too."

"You also have a boyfriend?"

"I call him my boyfriend," she said with a half-smile. "Actually we're more like brother and sister, or father and daughter—I mean mother and son." Her smile turned to a simper.

"What's his name?"

"That has no bearing on what I'm telling you. The point is that Sidney Harrow nearly shot him the other night."

"Where did this happen?"

"Right out in front of my boyfriend's house. I realized then that Sidney was a wild man, and he's been no use to me since. He has the picture and stuff but he's not doing anything with them. I'm afraid to go and ask for it back."

"And you want me to?"

"Maybe. I'm not committing myself yet." She spoke with the foolish wisdom of a woman who had no feeling for men and would always make the wrong decisions about them.

"What should Sidney be doing with the picture and stuff?"

"Finding out facts," she said carefully. "That's what I hired him to do. But I made the mistake of giving him some money and all he does is sit in his motel room and drink. I haven't even heard from him in two days."

"Which motel?"

"The Sunset, on the beach."

"How did you get involved with Sidney Harrow?"

"I'm not *involved* with him. A man I know brought him to the house last week and he seemed so lively and alert, just the man I was looking for." As if to renew the promise of that occasion, she raised her glass and drained the last few drops, coaxing them with her tongue. "He reminded me of my father when he was a young man."

For a moment she seemed at ease in the double memory. But her feelings were very shifty, and she couldn't hold this one long. I could see her quick-remembered happiness dying in her eyes.

She rose and started for the kitchen, then stopped abruptly, as if she'd come up against invisible glass. "I'm drinking too much," she said. "And I'm talking too much."

She left her glass in the kitchen and came back and stood over me. Her unhappy eyes regarded me suspiciously, as if I was the source of the unhappiness.

"Please get out of here, will you? Forget what I said to you, eh?"

I thanked her for the drink and drove downhill to the Ocean Boulevard and along it to the Sunset Motor Motel.

5

IT WAS ONE of the older buildings on the Pacific Point waterfront, two-storied and solidly constructed of red brick. In the harbor across the boulevard, sailboats lay in their slips like birds with their wings folded. A few Capris and Seashells were scudding down the channel before the January wind.

I parked in front of the motor hotel and went into the office. The gray-haired woman behind the desk gave me a bland experienced glance that took in my age and weight, my probable income and credit rating, and whether I was married.

She said she was Mrs. Delong. When I asked for Sidney Harrow, I could see my credit rating slip in the ledger of her eyes.

"Mr. Harrow has left us."

"When?"

"Last night. In the course of the night."

"Without paying his bill?"

Her look sharpened. "You know Mr. Harrow, do you?"

"Just by reputation."

"Do you know where I can get in touch with him? He gave us a San Diego business address. But he only worked parttime for them, they said, and they wouldn't assume any responsibility or give me his home address—if he has a home." She paused for breath. "If I knew where he lived I could get the police after him."

"I may be able to help you."

"How is that?" she said with some suspicion.

"I'm a private detective, and I'm looking for Harrow, too. Has his room been cleaned?"

"Not yet. He left his Do Not Disturb card out, which he did most of the time anyway. It was just a little while ago I noticed his car was gone and used my master key. You want to look over the room?"

"It might be a good idea. While we think of it, Mrs. Delong, what's his car license number?"

She looked it up in her file. "KIT 994. It's an old convertible, tan-colored, with the back window torn out. What's Harrow wanted for?"

"I don't know yet."

"Are you sure you're a detective?"

I showed her my photostat, and it satisfied her. She made a careful note of my name and address, and handed me the key to Harrow's room. "It's number twenty-one on the second floor at the back."

I climbed the outside stairs and went along the alley toward the rear. The windows of number twenty-one were closely draped. I unlocked the door and opened it. The room was dim, and sour with old smoke. I opened the drapes and let the light sluice in.

The bed had apparently not been slept in. The spread was rumpled, though, and several pillows were squashed against the headboard. A half-empty fifth of rye stood on the bedside table on top of a girlie magazine. I was a little surprised that Harrow had left behind a bottle with whisky in it.

He had also left, in the bathroom cabinet, a toothbrush and a tube of toothpaste, a three-dollar razor, a jar of hair grease, and a spray can of a spicy scent called Swingeroo. It looked as if Harrow had planned to come back, or had left in a great hurry.

The second possibility seemed more likely when I found an unmatched shoe in the darkest corner of the closet. It was a new pointed black Italian shoe for the left foot. Along with the shoe for the right foot it would have been worth at least twenty-five dollars. But I couldn't find the right shoe anywhere in the room.

In the course of looking for it I did find, on the high shelf of the closet under spare blankets, a brown envelope containing a small-size graduation picture. The smiling young man in the picture resembled Irene Chalmers and was probably, I decided, her son Nick.

My guess was pretty well confirmed when I found the Chalmerses' address, 2124 Pacific Street, penciled on the back of the envelope. I slid the picture back into the envelope and put it in my inside pocket and took it away with me.

After reporting the general situation to Mrs. Delong, I crossed the street to the harbor. The boats caught in the maze of floating docks rocked and smacked the water. I felt like getting into one of them and sailing out to sea.

My brief dip into Sidney Harrow's life had left a strain on my nerves. Perhaps it reminded me too strongly of my own life. Depression threatened me like a sour smoke drifting in behind my eyes.

The ocean wind blew it away, as it nearly always could. I walked the length of the harbor and crossed the asphalt desert of the parking lots toward the beach. The waves were collapsing like walls there, and I felt like a man escaping from his life.

You can't, of course. An old tan Ford convertible with a torn-out rear window was waiting for me at the end of my short walk. It was parked by itself in a drift of sand at the far edge of the asphalt. I looked in through the rear window and saw the dead man huddled on the back seat with dark blood masking his face.

I could smell whisky and the spicy odor of Swingeroo. The doors of the convertible weren't locked, and I could see the keys in the ignition. I was tempted to use them to open the trunk.

Instead I did the right thing, for prudential reasons. I was outside of Los Angeles County, and the local police had a very strong sense of territory. I found the nearest telephone, in a bait and tackle shop at the foot of the breakwater, and called the police. Then I went back to the convertible to wait for them.

The wind spat sand in my face and the sea had a shaggy green threatening look. High above it, gulls and terns were wheeling like a complex mobile suspended from the sky. A city police car crossed the parking lot and skidded to a stop beside me.

Two uniformed officers got out. They looked at me, at the dead man in the car, at me again. They were young men, with few discernible differences except that one was dark, one fair. Both had heavy shoulders and jaws, unmoved eyes, conspicuous guns in their holsters, and hands ready.

"Who is he?" said the blue-eyed one.

"I don't know."

"Who are you?"

I told them my name, and handed over my identification.

"You're a private detective?"

"That's right."

"But you don't know who this is in the car?"

I hesitated. If I told them it was Sidney Harrow, as I guessed, I'd have to explain how I found that out and would probably end up telling them everything I knew.

"No," I said.

"How did you happen to find him?"

"I was passing by."

"Passing by to where?"

"The beach. I was going to take a walk on the beach."

"That's a funny place to take a walk on a day like this," said the fair one.

I was ready to agree. The place had changed. The dead man had bled it of life and color. The men in uniform had changed its meaning. It was a dreary official kind of place with a cold draft blowing.

"Where you from?" the dark one asked me.

"Los Angeles. My address is on my photostat. I want it back, by the way."

"You'll get it back when we're finished with you. You got a car, or you come to town by public carrier?"

"Car."

"Where is your car?"

It hit me then, in a reaction that had been delayed by the shock of finding Harrow, if that's who he was. My car was parked in front of the Sunset Motor Hotel. Whether I told them about it or not, the police would find it there. They'd talk to Mrs. Delong and learn that I'd been on Harrow's trail.

That was what happened. I told them where my car was, and before long I was in an interrogation room in police headquarters being questioned by two sergeants. I asked several times for a lawyer, specifically the lawyer who had brought me to town.

They got up and left me alone in the room. It was an airless cubicle whose dirty gray plaster walls had been scribbled with names. I passed the time reading the inscriptions. Duke the Dude from Dallas had been there on a bum rap. Joe Hespeler had been there, and Handy Andy Oliphant, and Fast Phil Larrabee.

The sergeants came back and regretted to say that they hadn't been able to get in touch with Truttwell. But they wouldn't let me try to phone him myself. In a way this breach of my rights encouraged me: it meant that I wasn't a serious suspect.

They were on a fishing expedition, hoping I'd done their work for them. I sat and let them do some of mine. The dead man was Sidney Harrow, without much question: his thumbprint matched the thumbprint on his driver's license. He'd been shot in the head, once, and been dead for at least twelve hours. That placed the time of death no later than last midnight, when I had been at home in my apartment in West Los Angeles.

I explained this to the sergeants. They weren't interested. They wanted to know what I was doing in their county, and what my interest in Harrow was. They wheedled and begged and coaxed and pleaded and threatened me and made jokes. It gave me a queer feeling, which I didn't mention to them, that I had indeed inherited Sidney Harrow's life.

6

A MAN IN plain dark clothes came quietly into the room. Both the sergeants stood up, and he dismissed them. He had clipped gray hair, eyes that were hard and sober on either side of a scarred and broken nose. His mouth was chewed and ravaged by lifelong doubt and suspicion, and it kept working now. He sat down facing me across the table.

"I'm Lackland, Captain of Detectives. I hear you been giving our boys a bad time."

"I thought it was the other way around."

His eyes searched my face. "I don't see any marks on you."

"I have a right to a lawyer."

"We have a right to your cooperation. Try bucking us and you could end up flat on your rear end without a license."

"That reminds me, I want my photostat back."

Instead, he took a manila envelope out of his inside pocket and opened it. Among other things it contained a snapshot, or a piece of snapshot, which Lackland pushed across the table to me.

It was a picture of a man in his forties. He had fair thinning hair, bold eyes, a wry mouth. He looked like a poet who had missed his calling and had had to settle for grosser satisfactions.

His picture had been cut from a larger picture which had included other people. I could see girls' dresses on either side of him, but not the girls. The thing looked like a blown-up snapshot at least twenty years old.

"Know him?" Captain Lackland said.

"No."

He thrust his scarred face toward me like a warning of what my face might become. "You're sure about that, are you?"

"I'm sure." There was no use mentioning my unsupported guess that this was a picture Jean Trask had given Harrow, and that it was a picture of her father.

He leaned toward me again. "Come on now, Mr. Archer, help us out. Why was Sidney Harrow carrying this?" His forefinger jabbed at the blown-up snapshot.

"I don't know."

"You must have some idea. Why were *you* interested in Harrow?"

"I have to talk to John Truttwell. After that I may be able to say something."

Lackland got up and left the room. In about ten minutes he came back accompanied by Truttwell. The lawyer looked at me with concern.

"I understand you've been here for some time, Archer. You should have got in touch with me before." He turned to Lackland. "I'll talk to Mr. Archer in private. He's employed by me in a confidential capacity."

Lackland retreated slowly. Truttwell sat down across from me. "Why are they holding you, anyway?"

"A part-time bill collector named Sidney Harrow was shot last night. Lackland knows I was following Harrow. He doesn't know that Harrow was one of several people involved in the theft of the gold box."

Truttwell was startled. "You've found that out already?"

"It wasn't hard. This is the sloppiest burglary in history. The woman who has the box now keeps it lying around in plain view."

"Who is she?"

"Her married name is Jean Trask. Who she really is is another question. Apparently Nick stole the box and gave it to her. Which is why I can't talk freely, to Lackland or anyone else."

"I should certainly say you can't. Are you sure about all this?"

"Unless I've been having delusions." I stood up. "Can't we finish this outside?"

"Of course. Wait here for a minute."

Truttwell went out, closing the door behind him. He came back smiling and handed me the photostat of my license. "You're sprung. Oliver Lackland's a fairly reasonable man."

In the narrow corridor that led to the parking lot, I ran the gauntlet of Lackland and his sergeants. They nodded at me, too many times for comfort.

I told Truttwell what had happened as we drove across town in his Cadillac. He turned up Pacific Street.

"Where are we going?"

"To my house. You made quite an impression on Betty. She wants to ask your advice."

"What about?"

"It's probably something to do with Nick. He's all she thinks about." Truttwell added after a long pause: "Betty seems to believe I'm prejudiced against him. That's really not the case. But I don't want her to make any unnecessary mistakes. She's the only daughter I have."

"She told me she's twenty-five."

"Betty's very young for her age, though. Very young and vulnerable."

"Superficially, maybe. She struck me as a resourceful woman."

Truttwell gave me a look of pleased surprise. "I'm glad you think so. I brought her up by myself, and it's been quite a responsibility." After another pause he added: "My wife died when Betty was only a few months old."

"She told me her mother was killed by a hit-run driver."

"Yes, that's true." Truttwell's voice was almost inaudible.

"Was the driver ever caught?"

"I'm afraid not. The Highway Patrol found the car, near San Diego, but it was a stolen car. Strangely enough, whoever it was had made an attempt to burglarize the Chalmerses' house. My wife apparently saw them enter the house and scared them out of there. They ran her down when they made their getaway."

He gave me a bleak look which resisted further questions. We drove in silence the rest of the way to his house, which was diagonally across the street from the Chalmerses' Spanish mansion. He dropped me at the curb, said he had a client waiting, and drove away.

The architecture on upper Pacific Street was traditional but eclectic. Truttwell's house was a white colonial one, with green shutters upstairs and down.

I knocked on the green front door. It was answered by a gray little woman in a housekeeper's dim quasi-uniform. The formal lines which bracketed her mouth softened when I told her who I was.

"Yes. Miss Truttwell is expecting you." She led me up a curving stair to the door of a front room. "Mr. Archer is here to see you."

"Thanks, Mrs. Glover."

"Can I get you anything, dear?"

"No thanks."

Betty delayed her appearance till Mrs. Glover had gone. I could see why. Her eyes were swollen and her color was bad. She held her body tensely, like a kicked animal expecting to be kicked again.

She stood back to let me enter the room, and closed the door behind me. It was a young woman's study, bright with chintz and Chagall, its shelves loaded with books. She faced me standing up, with her back to the windows overlooking the street.

"I've heard from Nicholas." She indicated the orange telephone on the worktable. "You won't tell Father, will you?"

"He already suspects it, Betty."

"But you won't tell him anything more?"

"Don't you trust your father?"

"About anything else, yes. But you mustn't tell him what I'm going to tell you."

"I'll do my best, that's all I can promise. Is Nick in trouble?"

"Yes." She hung her head, and her bright hair curtained her face. "I think he intends to kill himself. I don't want to live, either, if he does."

"Did he say why?"

"He's done something terrible, he says."

"Like kill a man?"

She flung her hair back and looked at me with blazing dislike. "How can you say such a thing?"

"Sidney Harrow was shot on the waterfront last night. Did Nick mention him?"

"Of course not."

"What *did* he say?"

She was quiet for a minute, remembering. Then she recited slowly: "That he didn't deserve to live. That he'd let me down, and let his parents down, and he couldn't face any of us again. Then he said goodbye to me—a final goodbye." A hiccup of grief shook her.

"How long ago did he make the call?"

She looked at the orange phone, and then at her watch. "About an hour. It seems like forever, though."

She moved vaguely past me to the other side of the room and took a framed photograph down from a wall bracket. I moved up behind her and looked at it over her shoulder. It was a larger copy of the photograph in my pocket, which I had found in the closet of Harrow's motel room. I noticed now that in spite of his smiling mouth, the young man in the picture had somber eyes.

"I take it that's Nick," I said.

"Yes. It's his graduation picture."

She replaced it on its bracket, with a faintly ritual air, and went to the front windows. I followed her. She was looking out across the street toward the closed white front of the Chalmers house.

"I don't know what to do."

"We've got to find him," I said. "Did he say where he was calling from?"

"No, he didn't."

"Or anything else at all?"

"I don't remember anything else."

"Did he say what suicide method he had in mind?"

She hid her face behind her hair again and answered in a hushed voice: "He didn't say, this time."

"You mean he's gone through this routine before?"

"Not really. And you mustn't speak of it in that way. He's terribly serious."

"So am I." But I was angry at the boy for what he had done and was doing to the girl. "What did he do or say the other times?"

"He often talked about suicide when he got depressed. I don't mean that he threatened to do it. But he talked about ways and means. He never held anything back from me."

"Maybe it's time he started."

"You sound like Father. You're both prejudiced against him."

"Suicide is a cruel business, Betty."

"Not if you love the person. A depressed person can't help the way he feels."

I didn't argue any further. "You were going to tell me how he planned to do it."

"It wasn't a *plan*. He was simply talking. He said a gun was too messy, and pills were uncertain. The cleanest way would be to swim out to sea. But the thing that really haunted him, he said, was the thought of the rope."

"Hanging?"

"He told me he'd thought of hanging himself ever since he was a child."

"Where did he get that idea?"

"I don't know. But his grandfather was a Superior Court judge, and some people in town considered him a hanging judge—one who liked to sentence people to death. It may have influenced Nick, in a negative way. I've read of stranger things in history."

"Did Nick ever mention the hanging judge in the family?"

She nodded.

"And suicide?"

"Many times."

"That's quite a courtship he's been treating you to."

"I'm not complaining. I love Nick, and I want to be of some use to him."

I was beginning to understand the girl, and the more I understood the better I liked her. She had a serviceability that I had noticed before in widowers' daughters.

"Think back to his telephone call," I said. "Did he give any indication of where he was?"

"I don't remember any."

"Give it some time. Go and sit by the telephone."

She sat in a chair beside the table, with one hand on the instrument as if to keep it quiet.

"I could hear noises in the background."

"What kind of noises?"

"Wait a minute." She raised her hand for silence, and sat listening. "Children's voices, and splashing. Pool noises. I think he must have called me from the public booth at the Tennis Club."

7

THOUGH I'D VISITED the Tennis Club before, the woman at the front desk was strange to me. But she knew Betty Truttwell, and greeted her warmly.

"We never see you any more, Miss Truttwell."

"I've been terribly busy. Has Nick been here today?"

The woman answered with some reluctance: "As a matter of fact, he has been. He came in an hour or so ago, and went into the bar for a while. He wasn't looking too well when he came out."

"Do you mean that he was drunk?"

"I'm afraid he was, Miss Truttwell, since you asked me. The woman with him, the blonde, was under the weather, too. After they left I gave Marco a piece of my mind. But he said he only served them two drinks each. He said the woman was tight when they arrived, and Mr. Chalmers can't handle liquor."

"He never could," Betty agreed. "Who was the woman?"

"I forget her name—he's brought her in once before." She consulted the guest register which lay on the desk in front of her. "'Jean Swain.'"

"Not Jean Trask?" I said.

"It looks like 'Swain' to me."

She pushed the register toward me, indicating with her red fingertips where Nick had signed the woman's name and his own. It looked like 'Swain' to me, too. Her home address was given as San Diego. "Is she a fairly large blonde with a good figure, fortyish?"

"That's her. A good figure," she added, "if you like the fleshy type." She herself was very thin.

Betty and I walked toward the bar along the gallery that overlooked the pool. The children were still making pool noises. A few adults were stretched out on long chairs in corners, catching the thin warmth of the January sun.

The bar was empty except for a couple of men prolonging their lunch. The bartender and I exchanged nods of recognition. Marco was a short, quick, dark man in a red waistcoat. He admitted gloomily that Nick had been there.

"Matter of fact, I asked him to leave."

"Did he have a lot to drink?"

"Not here he didn't. I served him two single shots of bourbon, you can't make a federal case out of that. What happened, did he wreck his car?"

"I hope not. I'm trying to catch up with him before he wrecks anything. Do you know where he went?"

"No, but I'll tell you one thing, he was in a hell of a mood. When I wouldn't give him a third drink, he wanted to put up a fight. I had to show him my pool cue." Marco reached under the bar and showed it to us: the sawed-off butt of a heavy cue about two feet long. "I hated to pull it on a member, you know, but he was carrying a gun and I wanted him out of here, fast. Anyone else, I would have called the sheriff."

"He had a gun?" Betty said in a small, high voice.

"Yeah, it was in the pocket of his jacket. He kept it out of sight but you can't hide a big heavy gun like that." He leaned across the bar and peered into Betty's eyes. "What's the matter with him, anyway, Miss Truttwell? He never acted like this before."

"He's in trouble," she said.

"Does the dame have anything to do with his trouble? The blond dame? She drinks like she's got a hollow leg. She shouldn't be making him drink."

"Do you know who she is, Marco?"

"No. But she looks like trouble to me. I don't know what he thinks he's doing with *her.*"

Betty started for the door, then turned back to Marco again. "Why didn't you take the gun away from him?"

"I don't fool around with guns, Miss. That isn't my department."

We went out to Betty's two-seater in the parking lot. The club was on a cove of the Pacific, and I caught a whiff of the sea. It was a raw and rueful smell, conjuring up the place where I had found Sidney Harrow.

Betty and I were both silent and thoughtful as she drove up the long hill to the Montevista Inn. The young man in the office remembered me.

"You're just in time if you want to see Mrs. Trask. She's getting ready to leave."

"Did she say why?"

"I think she's had bad news. It must be serious, because she didn't even put up an argument when I had to charge her for an extra day. They usually put up an argument."

I made my way through the oak grove and tapped on the screen door of the stucco cottage.

The inner door was open, and Jean Trask answered from the bedroom: "My bags are ready, if you want to carry them out."

I crossed the living room and entered the bedroom. The woman was sitting at the dressing table, shakily applying lipstick.

Our eyes met in the mirror. Her hand wandered, describing a red clown mouth around her real one. She turned and got up clumsily, upsetting her stool.

"They sent you for my bags?"

"No. But I'll be glad to carry them." I picked up her matched blue bags. They were light enough.

"Put them down," she said. "Who are you anyway?"

She was ready to be afraid of anyone for any reason—so full of fear that some of it slopped over into me. Her huge red mouth alarmed me. Chilly laughter convulsed my stomach.

"I asked about you at the office," she said. "They told me they don't have a security guard. So what are you doing here?"

"At the moment I'm looking for Nick Chalmers. We don't have to beat around the bush. You must know he's in serious emotional trouble."

She answered as if she was glad to have someone to talk to: "He certainly is. He's talking about suicide. I thought a couple of drinks would do him good. They only made him worse."

"Where is he now?"

"I made him promise to go home and sleep it off. He said he would."

"Home to his apartment?"

"I guess so."

"You're pretty vague, Mrs. Trask."

"I try to keep myself that way. It's less painful," she added wryly.

"How did you get so interested in Nick?"

"It's none of your business. And I'm not taking any static from you."

Her voice rose as she gained confidence in her own anger. But a steady trill of fear ran through it.

"What are you so afraid of, Mrs. Trask?"

"Sidney Harrow got himself zapped last night." Her voice was rough with self-concern. "You must know that."

"How do *you* happen to know it?"

"Nick told me. I'm sorry I ever opened this can of worms."

"Did he kill Sidney?"

"I don't think he knows—that's how far off base he is. And I'm not waiting around to find out."

"Where are you going?"

She refused to tell me.

I went back to Betty and told her what I had learned, or part of it. We decided to go out to the university community in separate cars. My car was where it was supposed to be, in front of the Sunset Motor Motel. There was a parking ticket under the windshield wiper.

I tried to follow Betty's red two-seater, but she drove too fast for me, close to ninety on the straightaway. She was waiting for me when I reached the parking lot of the Cambridge Arms.

She ran toward me. "He's here. At least that's his car."

She pointed at a blue sports car standing beside her red one. I went and touched the hood. The engine was hot. The key was in the ignition.

"You stay down here," I said.

"No. If he makes trouble—I mean he won't if I'm there."

"That's a thought."

We went up together in the elevator. Betty knocked on Nick's door and called his name. "This is Betty."

There was a long waiting silence. Betty knocked again. Abruptly the door was pulled open. She took an involuntary step into the room, and ended up with her face against Nick's chest. He held her with one hand and with the other he pointed a heavy revolver at my stomach.

I couldn't see his eyes, which were hidden by dark wrap-around glasses. In contrast, his face was very pale. His hair was uncombed and hung down over his forehead. His white shirt was dirty. My mind recorded these things as if they might add up to my last sight of the world. I felt resentment more than fear. I hated the idea of dying for no good reason at the hands of a mixed-up overgrown boy I didn't even know.

"Drop it," I said routinely.

"I don't take orders from you."

"Come on now, Nick," Betty said.

She moved closer to him, trying to use her body to distract him. Her right arm slid around his waist, and she pressed one thigh forward between his legs. She raised her left arm as if she was going to loop it around his neck. Instead she brought it sharply down on his gun arm.

The revolver was pointing at the floor now. I dove for it and wrenched it out of his hand.

"Damn you!" he said. "Damn you both!"

A boy with a high voice or a girl with a low one came out of the apartment across the hall. "What's going on?"

"Initiation," I said.

Nick tore himself loose from Betty and swung at my face. I shifted and let his fist go by. I lowered my head and bulled him backward into his living room. Betty shut the door and leaned on it. Her color was high. She was breathing through her mouth.

Nick came at me again. I went under his fists and hit him solidly in the solar plexus. He lay down gasping for breath.

I spun the cylinder of his revolver. One shell had been fired. It was a Colt .45. I got out my black notebook and made a record of its number.

Betty moved between us. "You didn't have to hurt him."

"Yes I did. But he'll get over it."

She kneeled beside him and touched his face with her hand. He rolled away from her. The sounds he made fighting for breath gradually subsided. He sat up with his back against the chesterfield.

I sat on my heels facing him, and showed him his revolver. "Where did you get this, Nick?"

"I don't have to answer that. You can't make me incriminate myself."

His voice had a queer inhuman tone, as if it was being played back on tape. I couldn't tell what the tone meant. His eyes were effectively masked by the wrap-around glasses.

"I'm not a policeman, Nick, if that's what you think."

"I don't care what you are."

I tried again. "I'm a private detective working on your side. But I'm not quite clear what your side is. Do you want to talk about it?"

He shook his head like a child in a tantrum, whipping it rapidly from side to side until his hair blurred out. Betty said in a pained voice: "Please don't do that, Nicholas. You'll hurt your neck."

She smoothed his hair with her fingers. He sat perfectly still.

"Let me look at you," she said.

She took off his dark glasses. He grabbed for them, but she held them out of his reach. His eyes were black and glistening like asphalt squeezed from a crevice. They seemed to be leading a strange life of their own, with an inward look and an outward look alternating anxiety and aggression. I could understand why he wore the glasses to hide his sad changing eyes.

He covered his eyes with his hands and peered between his fingers.

"Please don't do that, Nick." The girl was kneeling beside him again. "What happened? Please tell me what happened."

"No. You wouldn't love me any more."

"Nothing could stop me loving you."

"Even if I killed somebody?" he said between his hands.

"Did you kill somebody?" I said.

He nodded slowly, once, keeping his head down and his face hidden.

"With this revolver?"

His head jerked downward in the affirmative.

Betty said: "He's in no condition to talk. You mustn't force him."

"I think he wants to get it off his chest. Why do you suppose he phoned you from the club?"

"To say goodbye."

"This is better than saying goodbye. Isn't it?"

She answered soberly: "I don't know. I don't know how much I can stand."

I turned to Nick again. "Where did you get the revolver?"

"It was in his car."

"Sidney Harrow's car?"

He dropped his hands from his face. His eyes were puzzled and fearful. "Yes. It was in his car."

"Did you shoot him in his car?"

His whole face clenched like a frightened baby's getting ready to cry. "I don't remember." He struck himself on the forehead with his fist. Then he struck himself in the mouth, hard.

"You're tormenting him," the girl said. "Can't you see he's sick?"

"Stop mothering him. He already has a mother."

His head came up in a startled movement. "You mustn't tell my mother. Or my father. Dad will kill me."

I made no promises. His parents would have to be told. "You were going to tell me where the shooting occurred, Nick."

"Yes. I remember now. We went to the hobo jungle back of Ocean Boulevard. Someone had left a fire burning and we sat by the coals. He wanted me to do a bad thing." His voice was naïve, like a child's. "I took his gun and shot him."

He made another scowling baby-face, so tight that it hid his eyes. He began to sob and moan, but no tears came. It was hard to watch his dry crying.

Betty put her arms around him. I said across the rhythms of his noise: "He's had breakdowns before, hasn't he?"

"Not like this."

"Did he stay at home, or was he hospitalized?"

"Home." She spoke to Nick. "Will you come home with me?"

He said something that might have been yes. I called the Chalmerses' number and got the servant, Emilio. He brought Irene Chalmers to the phone.

"This is Archer. I'm with your son in his apartment. He's not in a good way, and I'm bringing him home."

"Is he hurt?"

"He's mentally hurt, and talking about suicide."

"I'll get in touch with his psychiatrist," she said. "Dr. Smitheram."

"Is your husband there?"

"He's in the garden. Do you want to talk to him?"

"It isn't necessary. But you'd better prepare him for this."

"Can you handle Nick?"

"I think so. I have Betty Truttwell with me."

Before we left the apartment I called the Bureau of Criminal Investigation in Sacramento. I gave the number of the revolver to a man I knew named Roy Snyder. He said he'd try to check the name of the original owner. When we went down to my car I put the revolver in the trunk, locked in an evidence case.

8

WE RODE IN my car, with Betty driving and Nick on the front seat between us. He didn't speak or move until we stopped in front of his parents' house. Then he begged me not to make him go in.

I had to use a little force to get him out of the car. With one hand on his arm, and Betty walking on his far side, I marched him across the courtyard. He moved with deep reluctance, as if we planned to stand him up against the white wall and execute him.

His mother came out before we reached the front door. "Nick? Are you all right?"

"I'm okay," he said in his tape-recorder tone.

As we moved into the reception hall she said to me: "Do you *have* to talk to my husband?"

"Yes I do. I asked you to prepare him."

"I just couldn't do it," she said. "You'll have to tell him yourself. He's in the garden."

"What about the psychiatrist?"

"Dr. Smitheram had a patient with him, but he'll be here in a little while."

"You'd better call John Truttwell, too," I said. "This thing has legal angles."

I left Nick with the two women in the living room. Betty was solemn and quiet, as if Irene Chalmers's dark beauty cast a shadow over her.

Chalmers was in the walled garden, working among the plants. In clean, sun-faded Levis he looked thin, almost fragile. He was digging vigorously with a spade around some bushes which had been cut back for the winter and looked like dead thorny stumps.

He glanced up sharply at me, then slowly straightened, striking his spade upright in the earth. Greek and Roman statues stood around like nudists pitted by years of inclement weather.

Chalmers said rather severely: "I thought it was understood that the Florentine box was not insured."

"I wouldn't know about that, Mr. Chalmers. I'm not in the insurance business."

He got a little pale and tense. "I understood you to say you were."

"It was your wife's idea. I'm a private detective. John Truttwell called me in on your wife's behalf."

"Then he can damn well call you off again." Chalmers did a mental double take. "You mean my wife went to Truttwell behind my back?"

"It wasn't such a bad idea. I know you're concerned about your son, and I just brought him home. He's been running around with a gun, talking very loosely about suicide and murder."

I filled Chalmers in on what had been said and done. He was appalled. "Nick must be out of his mind."

"He is to a certain extent," I said. "But I don't think he was lying."

"You believe he committed a murder?"

"A man named Sidney Harrow is dead. There was bad blood between him and Nick. And Nick has admitted shooting him."

Chalmers swayed slightly and leaned on his spade, head down. There was a bald spot on the crown of his head, with a little hair brushed over it as if to mask his vulnerability. The moral beatings that people took from their children, I was thinking, were the hardest to endure and the hardest to escape.

But Chalmers wasn't thinking of himself. "Poor Nick. He was doing so well. What's happened to him?"

"Maybe Dr. Smitheram can tell you. It seems to have started with the gold box. Apparently Nick took it from your safe and gave it to a woman named Jean Trask."

"I never heard of her. What would she want with my mother's gold box?"

"I don't know. It seems important to her."

"Have you talked to this Trask woman?"

"Yes, I have."

"What did she do with my letters to my mother?"

"I don't know. I looked in the box, but it was empty."

"Why didn't you ask her?"

"She's a difficult woman to deal with. And more important things kept coming up."

Chalmers bit his mustache in chagrin. "Such as?"

"I learned that she hired Sidney Harrow to come to Pacific Point. Apparently they were searching for her father."

Chalmers gave me a puzzled look which wandered across the garden and over the wall to the sky. "What has all this got to do with us?"

"It isn't clear, I'm afraid. I have a suggestion, subject to John Truttwell's approval. And yours, of course. It might be a good idea to turn the gun over to the police and let them make ballistics tests."

"You mean give up without a fight?"

"Let's take this a step at a time, Mr. Chalmers. If it turns out that Nick's gun didn't kill Harrow, his confession is probably fantasy. If it did kill Harrow, we can decide then what to do next."

"We'll take it up with John Truttwell. I don't seem to be thinking too clearly." Chalmers put his fingers to his forehead.

"It still wouldn't be hopeless," I said, "even if Nick did kill him. I believe there may have been mitigating circumstances."

"How so?"

"Harrow had been throwing his weight around. He threatened Nick with a gun, possibly the same gun. This happened in front of your house the other night, when the box was stolen."

Chalmers gave me a doubtful look. "I don't see how you can possibly know that."

"I have an eyewitness." But I didn't name her.

"Do you have the gun with you?"

"It's in the trunk of my car. I'll show it to you."

We went through a screened lanai into the house and down a corridor to the reception hall. Nick and his mother and Betty were sitting in a stiff little group on a sofa in the living room, like people at a party that had died some time ago. Nick had put on his dark glasses again, like a black bandage over his eyes.

Chalmers went into the living room and stood in front of him looking down as if from a great height. "Is it true that you shot a man?"

Nick nodded dully. "I'm sorry. I didn't want to come home. I meant to kill myself."

"That's cowardly talk," Chalmers said. "You've got to act like a man."

"Yes, Dad," he said without hope.

"We'll do everything we can for you. Don't despair. Promise me that, Nick."

"I promise, Dad. I'm sorry."

Chalmers turned with a kind of military abruptness and came back to me. His face was stoical. Both he and Nick must have been aware that no real communication had taken place.

We went out the front door. On the sidewalk Chalmers looked down at his gardening clothes self-consciously.

"I hate to appear like this in public," he said, as if the neighbors might be watching him.

I opened the trunk of my car and showed him the revolver without removing it from the evidence case. "Have you ever seen it before?"

"No. As a matter of fact Nick never owned a gun. He's always detested the whole business of guns."

"Why?"

"I suppose he got it by osmosis from me. My father taught me to hunt when I was a boy. But the war destroyed my pleasure in hunting."

"I hear you had quite a lot of war experience."

"Who told you that?"

"John Truttwell."

"I wish John would keep his own counsel. And mine. I prefer not to talk about my part in the war." He looked down at the revolver with a kind of sad contempt, as if it symbolized all the forms of violence. "Do you really think we should entrust this gun to John?"

"What do you suggest?"

"I know what I'd *like* to do. Bury it ten feet deep and forget about it."

"We'd only have to dig it up again."

"I suppose you're right," he said.

Truttwell's Cadillac came into view, far down Pacific Street. He parked it in front of his own house and came across the street at a half-trot. He absorbed the bad news about Nick as if his mind had been tuned in to receive it.

"And this is the gun. It's loaded." I handed him the case with the key in the lock. "You better take charge of it until we decide what to do. I have a query in on its original ownership."

"Good." He turned to Chalmers. "Where's Nick?"

"In the house. We're expecting Dr. Smitheram."

Truttwell laid his hand on Chalmers's bony shoulder. "Too bad you and Irene have to go through it again."

"Please. We won't discuss it." Chalmers pulled away from Truttwell's hand. He turned abruptly and marched in his stoical way toward the front door.

I followed Truttwell across the street to his house. In his study, he locked the evidence case in a fireproof steel cabinet. I said:

"I'm glad to get that off my hands. I didn't want Lackland to catch me with it."

"Do you think I should turn it over to him today?"

"Let's see what Sacramento says about ownership. What did you mean, by the way, about Chalmers going through it all again? Has Nick been in this kind of trouble before?"

Truttwell took his time about answering. "It depends on what you mean by this kind of trouble. He's never been mixed up in a homicide before, at least not to my knowledge. But he's had one or two episodes —isn't that what the psychiatrists call them? A few years ago he ran away, and it took a nationwide search to bring him home."

"Was he on the hippie kick?"

"Not really. Actually he was trying to support himself. When the Pinkertons finally tracked him down on the east coast, he was working as a busboy in a restaurant. We managed to persuade him that he should come home and finish his education."

"How does he feel about his parents?"

"He's very close to his mother," Truttwell said dryly, "if that's desirable. I think he idolizes his father, but feels he can't measure up. Which is exactly how Larry Chalmers felt about his own father, the Judge. I suppose these patterns have to go on repeating themselves."

"You mentioned more than one episode," I prompted him.

"So I did." He sat down facing me. "It goes much further back, fourteen or fifteen years, and it may be the root of Nick's trouble. Dr. Smitheram seems to think so. But beyond a certain point he won't discuss it with me."

"What happened?"

"That's what Smitheram won't discuss. I think Nick was picked up by some sort of sexual psychopath. His family got him back in a hurry, but not before Nick was frightened out of his wits. He was only eight years old at the time. You can understand why nobody likes to talk about it."

I wanted to ask Truttwell some more questions, but the housekeeper tapped on the study door and opened it. "I heard you come in, Mr. Truttwell. Is there anything I can get you?"

"No thanks, Mrs. Glover. I'm going right out again. Where's Betty, by the way?"

"I don't know, sir." But the woman looked at me, rather accusingly.

"She's at the Chalmers house," I said.

Truttwell got to his feet, his entire body making an angry gesture. "I don't like that at all."

"It couldn't be helped. She was with me when I took Nick. She handled herself very well. And handled him."

Truttwell struck his thigh with his fist. "I didn't bring her up to be nurse to a psycho."

The housekeeper had a terrified expression. She withdrew and closed the door without any sound.

"I'm going over there and bring her home," Truttwell said. "She's wasted her entire girlhood on that weakling."

"She doesn't seem to think it was all waste."

"So you're on *his* side?" He sounded like a rival.

"No. I'm on Betty's side, and probably yours. This is a hell of a time to force a decision on her."

Truttwell got the message after a moment's thought. "You're right, of course."

9

BEFORE HE LEFT the house, Truttwell filled a pipe and lit it with a kitchen match. I stayed behind in his study to make a phone call to

Roy Snyder in Sacramento. It was five minutes to five by my watch, and I was just in time to catch Snyder before he quit for the night.

"Archer again. Do you have any information on the ownership of the Colt?"

"Yes, I do. It was bought new by a Pasadena man named Rawlinson. Samuel Rawlinson." Snyder spelled out the surname. "He made the purchase in September of 1941, and at the same time he got a permit to carry it from the Pasadena police. The permit was allowed to lapse in 1945. That's all I have."

"What reason did Rawlinson give for carrying a gun?"

"Business protection. He was the president of a bank," Snyder added dryly. "The Pasadena Occidental Bank."

I thanked him and dialed Pasadena Information. The Pasadena Occidental Bank was not listed, but Samuel Rawlinson was.

I put in a person-to-person call to Rawlinson. A woman answered. Her voice was rough and warm.

"I'm sorry," she explained to the operator. "It's hard for Mr. Rawlinson to come to the phone. Arthritis."

"I'll talk to her," I said.

"Go ahead, sir," the operator said.

"This is Lew Archer. Who am I talking to?"

"Mrs. Shepherd. I look after Mr. Rawlinson."

"Is he ill?"

"He's old," she said. "We all get old."

"You're so right, Mrs. Shepherd. I'm trying to trace possession of a gun which Mr. Rawlinson bought in 1941. A .45 Colt revolver. Will you ask him what he did with it?"

"I'll ask him."

She left the phone for a minute or two. It was a noisy line, and I could hear distant babblings, scraps of conversation fading just before I could grasp their meaning.

"He wants to know who you are," Mrs. Shepherd said. "And what right you have to ask him about any gun." She added apologetically: "I'm only quoting what Mr. Rawlinson said. He's a stickler."

"So am I. Tell him I'm a detective. The gun may or may not have been used last night to commit a crime."

"Where?"

"In Pacific Point."

"He used to spend his summers there," she said. "I'll ask him again." She went away and came back. "I'm sorry, Mr. Archer, he won't talk.

But he says if you want to come here and explain what it's all about, he'll discuss it with you."

"When?"

"This evening if you want. He never goes out evenings. The number is 245 on Locust Street."

I said I'd be there as soon as I could make it.

I was in my car, ready to go, when I realized I couldn't leave just yet. A black Cadillac convertible with a medical caduceus was parked just ahead of me. I wanted to have a word with Dr. Smitheram.

The front door of the Chalmers house was standing open, as if its security had been breached. I walked into the reception hall. Truttwell stood with his back to me, arguing with a large balding man who had to be the psychiatrist. Lawrence and Irene Chalmers were on the fringes of the argument.

"The hospital is contraindicated," Truttwell was saying. "We can't be sure what the boy will say, and hospitals are always full of leaks."

"My clinic isn't," the large man said.

"Possibly, just possibly, it isn't. Even so, if you or one of your employees were asked a question in court, you'd have to answer it. Unlike the legal profession—"

The doctor interrupted Truttwell: "Has Nick committed a crime of some sort?"

"I'm not going to answer that question."

"How can I look after a patient without information?"

"You have plenty of information, more than I have." Truttwell's voice seemed to buzz with an old resentment. "You've sat on that information for fifteen years."

"At least you recognize," Smitheram said, "that I haven't gone running to the police with it."

"Would the police be interested, doctor?"

"I'm not going to answer that question."

The two men faced each other in a quiet fury. Lawrence Chalmers tried to say something to them but they paid no attention.

His wife moved toward me, and drew me to one side. Her eyes were dull and unsurprised, as if she'd been hit by something that she'd seen coming from a long way off.

"Dr. Smitheram wants to take Nick to his clinic. What do you think we should do?"

"I agree with Mr. Truttwell. Your son needs legal security as well as medical."

"Why?" she said bluntly.

"He killed a man last night, he says, and he's been talking about it quite freely."

I paused to let the fact sink in. She handled it almost as if she'd been expecting it. "Who is the man?"

"Sidney Harrow is his name. He was involved in the theft of your Florentine box. So was Nick, apparently."

"Nick was?"

"I'm afraid so. With all these things on his mind, I don't think you should put him in any kind of clinic or hospital. Hospitals are always full of leaks, as Truttwell says. Couldn't you keep him at home?"

"Who would watch him?"

"You and your husband."

She glanced at her husband, appraisingly. "Maybe. I don't know if Larry is up to it. It doesn't show but he's terribly emotional, especially where Nick is concerned." She moved closer, letting me feel the influence of her body. "Would you, Mr. Archer?"

"Would I what?"

"Stand watch over Nick tonight?"

"No." The word came out hard and definite.

"We're paying your salary, you know."

"And I've been earning it. But I'm not a psychiatric nurse."

"I'm sorry I asked you."

There was a sting in her words. She turned her back on me and moved away. I decided I'd better get out of town before she had me fired. I went and told John Truttwell where I was going and why.

Truttwell's argument with the doctor had cooled down. He introduced me to Smitheram, who gave me a soft handclasp and a hard look. There was a troubled intelligence in his eyes.

I said: "I'd like to ask you some questions about Nick."

"This isn't the time or the place."

"I realize that, doctor. I'll see you at your office tomorrow."

"If you insist. Now if you'll excuse me, I have a patient to attend to."

I followed him as far as the living-room gates, and glanced in. Betty and Nick were sitting on a rug, not together but near each other. Her body was turned toward him, supported by one straight arm. Nick's face was pressed against his own raised knees.

Neither of them seemed to move, even to breathe. They looked like people lost in space, frozen forever in their separate poses, his of despair, hers of caring.

Dr. Smitheram went and sat down near them on the floor.

10

I DROVE INLAND by way of Anaheim. It was a bad time of day, and in places the traffic crawled like a wounded snake. It took me ninety minutes to get from Chalmers's house to Rawlinson's house in Pasadena.

I parked in front of the place and sat for a minute, letting the freeway tensions drip off my nerve ends. It was one of a block of three-storied frame houses. They were ancient, as time went in California, ornamented with turn-of-the-century gables and cupolas.

Half a block further on, Locust Street came to an end at a black-and-white-striped barricade. Beyond it a deep wooded ravine opened. Twilight was overflowing the ravine, flooding the yards, soaking up into the thick yellow sky.

A light showed in Rawlinson's house as the front door opened and closed. A woman crossed the veranda and came down the steps skipping a broken one.

I saw as she approached my car that she must have been close to sixty. She moved with the confidence of a much younger woman. Her eyes were bright black behind her glasses. Her skin was dark, perhaps with a tincture of Indian or Negro blood. She wore a staid gray dress and a multi-colored Mexican apron.

"Are you the gentleman who wants to see Mr. Rawlinson?"

"Yes. I'm Archer."

"I'm Mrs. Shepherd. He's just sitting down to dinner and he won't mind if you join him. He likes to have some company with his food. I only prepared enough for the two of us, but I'll be glad to pour you a cup of tea."

"I could use a cup of tea, Mrs. Shepherd."

I followed her into the house. The entrance hall was impressive if you didn't look too closely. But the parquetry floor was buckling and loose underfoot, and the walls were dark with mold.

The dining room was more cheerful. Under a yellowing crystal chandelier with one live bulb, a table had been set for one person, with polished silver on a clean white cloth. An old white-headed man in a rusty dinner coat was finishing off what looked like a bowl of beef stew.

The woman introduced me to him. He put his spoon down and struggled to his feet, offering me a gnarled hand. "Take it easy with my arthritis, please. Sit down. Mrs. Shepherd will get you a cup of coffee."

"Tea," she corrected him. "We're out of coffee." But she lingered in the room, waiting to hear what was said.

Rawlinson's eyes had a mica glint. He spoke with impatient directness. "This revolver you telephoned about—I gather it's been used for some illegal purpose?"

"Possibly. I don't know that it has."

"But if it hasn't you've come a long way for nothing."

"In my job everything has to be checked out."

"I understand you're a private detective," he said.

"That's correct."

"Employed by whom?"

"A lawyer named Truttwell in Pacific Point."

"John Truttwell?"

"Yes. Do you know him?"

"I met John two or three times through one of his clients. That was a long time ago, when he was young and I was middle-aged. It must be close to thirty years—Estelle's been dead for nearly twenty-four."

"Estelle?"

"Estelle Chalmers—Judge Chalmers's widow. She was a hell of a woman." The old man smacked his lips like a winetaster.

The woman still lingering by the door was showing signs of distress. "All that is ancient history, Mr. Rawlinson. The gentleman isn't interested in ancient history."

Rawlinson laughed. "It's the only kind of history I know. Where's that tea you were so freely offering, Mrs. Shepherd?" She went out, closing the door with emphasis. He turned to me. "She thinks she owns me. She doesn't, though. If I don't have a right to my memories, there isn't a great deal left at my time of life."

"I'm interested in your memories," I said, "specifically in the Colt revolver you bought in September 1941. It was probably used to shoot a man last night."

"What man?"

"Sidney Harrow was his name."

"I never heard of him," Rawlinson said, as if this cast some doubt on Harrow's reality. "Is he dead?"

"Yes."

"And you're trying to connect my gun with his death?"

"Not exactly. It either is connected or it isn't. I want to know which."

"Wouldn't ballistics show?"

"Possibly. The tests haven't been made yet."

"Then I think I should wait, don't you?"

"You certainly should if you're guilty, Mr. Rawlinson."

He laughed so hard his upper teeth slipped. He pushed them back into place with thumb and forefinger. Mrs. Shepherd appeared in the doorway with a tea tray.

"What's so funny?" she asked him.

"You wouldn't consider it funny, Mrs. Shepherd. Your sense of humor is deficient."

"Your sense of fittingness is. For an eighty-year-old man who used to be the president of a bank—" She set the tea tray down with a slight clash that completed her thought. "Milk or lemon, Mr. Archer?"

"I'll take it black."

She poured our tea in two bone china cups that didn't match. The rundown elegance of the household made me wonder if Rawlinson was a poor man or a miser; and what in hell had happened to his bank.

"Mr. Archer suspects me of committing a murder," he said to the woman in a slightly bragging tone.

She didn't think it was funny at all. Her dark face got darker, grim around the mouth and in the eyes. She turned on Rawlinson fiercely.

"Why don't you tell him the truth then? You know you gave that revolver to your daughter, and you know the exact date."

"Be quiet."

"I will not. You're playing tricks with yourself and I won't let you. You're a smart man but you don't have enough to occupy your mind."

Rawlinson showed no anger. He seemed to be pleased by her almost wifely concern. And his holding back about the gun had been just a game, apparently.

Mrs. Shepherd was the worried one. "Who got shot?"

"A part-time detective named Sidney Harrow."

She shook her head. "I don't know who that would be. Drink up your tea while it's hot. Can I get you a piece of fruitcake, Mr. Archer? There's some left over from Christmas."

"No thanks."

"I'll have some," Rawlinson said. "With a scoop of ice cream."

"We're out of ice cream."

"We seem to be out of everything."

"No, there's enough to eat. But money only stretches so far."

She left the room again. With her warmth and energy subtracted, the room changed. Rawlinson looked around it a little uneasily, as if he was feeling the cold weight of his bones.

"I'm sorry she saw fit to sic you onto my daughter. And I hope you won't go dashing off in her direction now. There'd be no point in it."

"Why?"

"It's true I gave Louise the gun in 1945. But it was stolen from her house some years later, in 1954, to be exact." He recited the dates as if he was proud of his memory. "This is not an *ad hoc* story."

"Who stole the gun?"

"How should we know? My daughter's house was burglarized."

"Why did you give her the gun in the first place?"

"It's an old story and a sad one," he said. "My daughter's husband abandoned her and left her stranded with Jean."

"Jean?"

"My granddaughter Jean. The two helpless females were left alone in the house. Louise wanted the gun for protection." He grinned suddenly. "I think Louise may have been hoping that he would come back."

"That who would come back?"

"Her husband. My egregious son-in-law Eldon Swain. If Eldon had come back, I have no doubt she'd have shot him. With my blessing."

"What did you have against your son-in-law?"

He laughed abruptly. "That's an excellent question. But with your permission I don't think I'll answer it."

Mrs. Shepherd brought us two narrow wedges of cake. She noticed that I wolfed mine.

"You're hungry. I'll make you a sandwich."

"Don't bother. I'm on my way to dinner."

"It wouldn't be any bother."

Her divided attention made Rawlinson uncomfortable. He said with the air of a comedian: "Mr. Archer wants to know what Eldon Swain did to me. Shall I tell him?"

"No. You're talking too much, Mr. Rawlinson."

"Eldon's defalcations are common knowledge."

"Not any more they're not. I say let it lie. We could all be a lot worse off than we are. I told Shepherd the same thing. When you talk about old trouble sometimes you can talk it back to life."

He reacted with jealous irritation. "I thought your husband was living in San Diego."

"Randy Shepherd isn't my husband. He's my ex."

"Have you been seeing him?"

She shrugged. "I can't help it when he comes back for a visit. I do my best to discourage him."

"So that's where the ice cream and coffee have been going!"

"It isn't so. I never give Shepherd a morsel of your food or a cent of your money."

"You're a liar."

"Don't call me that, Mr. Rawlinson. There are things I won't put up with, even from you."

Rawlinson looked quite happy again. He had the woman's attention, and all her heat, focused on him.

I stood up. "I've got to be going."

Neither of them offered any argument. Mrs. Shepherd accompanied me to the front door.

"I hope you got what you came for."

"Part of it, anyway. Do you know where his daughter lives?"

"Yessir." She gave me another address in Pasadena. "Just don't tell her I told you. Mrs. Eldon Swain doesn't approve of me."

"You seem to be bearing up under it," I said. "Is Jean Trask Mrs. Swain's daughter?"

"Yes. Don't tell me Jean's mixed up in all this."

"I'm afraid so."

"That's too bad. I can remember when Jean was an innocent little angel. Jean and my own little girl were best friends for years. Then everything went sour." She heard herself, and sucked her lips inward. "I'm talking too much myself, bringing the past back to life."

11

LOUISE SWAIN LIVED on a poor street off Fair Oaks, between Old Town and the ghetto. A few children of various shades were playing under the light at the corner, islanded in the surrounding darkness.

There was a smaller light on the front porch of Mrs. Swain's stucco cottage, and a Ford sedan standing at the curb in front of it. The Ford was locked. I shone my flashlight into it. It was registered to George Trask, 4545 Bayview Avenue, San Diego.

I made a note of the address, got out my contact mike, and went around to the side of the stucco cottage, following two strips of concrete which made an exigent driveway. An old black Volkswagen with a crumpled fender stood under a rusty carport. I moved into its shadow and leaned on the wall beside a blinded window.

I didn't need my microphone. Inside the house, Jean's voice was raised in anger: "I'm not going back to George—"

An older woman spoke in a more controlled voice: "You better take my advice and go back to him. George still cares about you and he was asking for you early this morning—but it won't last forever."

"Who cares?"

"You ought to care. If you lose him you won't have anybody, and you don't know how that feels until you've tried it. Don't think you're coming back to live with me."

"I wouldn't stay if you begged me on your knees."

"That won't happen," the older woman said dryly. "I've got just enough room and enough money and enough energy left for myself."

"You're a cold woman, Mother."

"Am I? I wasn't always. You and your father made me that way."

"You're jealous!" Jean's voice had changed. A hiss of pleasure underlay her anger and distress. "Jealous of your own daughter and your own husband. It all comes clear. No wonder you gave him Rita Shepherd."

"I didn't give him Rita. She threw herself at his head."

"With a good strong assist from you, Mother. You probably planned the whole thing."

The older woman said: "I suggest you leave here before you say any more. You're nearly forty years old and you're not my responsibility. You're lucky to have a husband willing and able to look after you."

"I can't stand him," Jean said. "Let me stay here with you. I'm scared."

"So am I," her mother said. "I'm afraid for you. You've been drinking again, haven't you?"

"I did a little celebrating."

"What have *you* got to celebrate?"

"Wouldn't you like to know, Mother?" Jean paused. "I'll tell you if you ask me pretty please."

"If you have something to tell me, then tell me. Don't fool around."

"Now I'm not going to tell you." Jean sounded like a child playing a teasing game. "You can find out for yourself."

"There's nothing to find out," her mother said.

"Is that a fact? What would you say if I told you that Daddy's alive?"

"Really alive?"

"You bet he is," Jean said.

"Have you seen him?"

"I soon will. I've picked up his trail."

"Where?"

"That's my little secret, Mother."

"Augh, you've been imagining things again. I'd be crazy to believe you."

Jean made no answer that I could hear. I suspected the two women had exhausted the conversation and each other. I moved from the shadow of the carport into the dim street.

Jean came out onto the lighted porch. The door was slammed behind her. The light went out. I waited for her beside her car.

She backed away from me, stumbling on the broken sidewalk. "What do you want?"

"Give me the gold box, Jean. It isn't yours."

"Yes it is. It's an old family heirloom."

"Come off it."

"It's true," she said. "The box belonged to my Grandmother Rawlinson. She said it would come down to me. And now it has."

I half believed her. "Could we talk a little in your car?"

"That never does any good. The more you talk the more it hurts."

Her face was mournful and her body dragged. She gave off a peculiar feeling, that she was a ghost or cloudy emanation of the actual Jean Trask; her sense of herself was a vacuum, a cold emptiness.

"What's hurting, Jean?"

"My whole life." She spread both hands on her breasts as if the pain was overflowing her fingers. "Daddy ran off to Mexico with Rita. He didn't even send me a birthday card."

"How old were you?"

"Sixteen. I never had any fun after that."

"Is your father alive?"

"I think he is. Nick Chalmers said he saw him in Pacific Point."

"Where in Pacific Point?"

"Down by the railroad yards. That was a long time ago, when Nick was just a child. But he identified Daddy by his picture."

"How did Nick get into this?"

"He's my witness that Daddy is alive." Her voice rose in pitch and amplitude, as if she was speaking to the woman in the house instead of me: "Why shouldn't he be alive? He'd only be—let's see, I'm thirty-nine and Daddy was twenty-four when I was born. That makes him sixty-three, doesn't it?"

"Thirty-nine and twenty-four makes sixty-three."

"And sixty-three isn't old, especially not nowadays. He was always very youthful for his age. He could dive and dance and spin like a top," she said. "He bounced me on his knee."

It sounded like something repeated from her childhood. Her mind was being carried down the stream of memory, swept willy-nilly through subterranean passages toward roaring falls.

"I'm going to find my Daddy," she said. "I'll find him dead or alive. If he's alive I'll cook and keep house for him. And I'll be happier than I ever was in my born days. If he's dead I'll find his grave and do you know what I'll do then? I'll crawl in with him and go to sleep."

She unlocked her car and drove away, turning south onto the boulevard. Perhaps I should have followed her, but I didn't.

12

I KNOCKED ON the front door of the stucco cottage. After an interval, the porch light came on over my head. Then the door was opened about four inches on a chain.

A woman with fading blond hair peered at me through the opening. Her face was set grimly, as if she'd expected to see her daughter again. The atmosphere around her was still charged.

"What is it?"

"I've just been talking to your father," I said. "About a Colt revolver he bought in 1941."

"I don't know anything about a revolver."

"Aren't you Mrs. Eldon Swain?"

"Louise Rawlinson Swain," she corrected me. But then she asked: "Has something come up about my husband?"

"Possibly. Could we talk inside? I'm a private detective."

I handed her my photostat through the crack. She looked it over carefully, and did everything but bite it. Finally she handed it back.

"Who are you working for, Mr. Archer?"

"A lawyer in Pacific Point named John Truttwell. I'm looking into a couple of related crimes—a theft and a murder." I didn't bother adding that her daughter was connected with one of the crimes, possibly both.

She let me in. Her front room was poor and small. As in Rawlinson's house, there were relics of better days. On the mantel over the gas fire a Dresden shepherd and shepherdess exchanged adoring glances. A small Oriental rug lay not on the floor, which was covered with worn matting, but over the back of the chesterfield. Facing the chesterfield was a television set with an electric clock on top of it, and beside it a telephone table with a drawer. Everything was clean and well-dusted, but the room had a musty taint, as if neither it nor the woman in it had been fully used.

Mrs. Swain didn't invite me to sit down. She stood facing me, a large woman like her daughter, with the same kind of heavy good looks.

"Who was murdered?"

"I'll come to that, Mrs. Swain. I wanted to ask you first about a box that was stolen. It's a Florentine gold box with classical figures on the lid, a man and a woman."

"My mother had a box like that," she said. "She used it as a jewel case. I never did know where it disappeared to after Mother died." But her eyes were alive with roving speculation. "What is this all about? Has Eldon been heard from?"

"I don't know."

"You said 'possibly.'"

"I didn't want to rule anything out. I really came here to talk about the revolver your father gave you. But we'll talk about anything you like."

"There's nothing I want to discuss." But after a moment she asked me: "What did Father say?"

"Simply that he gave you the Colt for protection, after your husband left you. The year he mentioned was 1945."

"All that is perfectly true," she said carefully. "Did he mention the circumstances in which Eldon left?"

I threw her a slow curve. "Mrs. Shepherd wouldn't let him."

It jarred her. "Was Mrs. Shepherd present at the conversation?"

"She was in and out of the dining room."

"She would be. What else did my father say in front of her?"

"I don't remember if this was said in front of Mrs. Shepherd. But he told me that your house was burglarized in 1954 and the Colt was taken."

"I see." She looked around the room as if to see how the story fitted into it.

"Did it happen in this house?" I asked her.

She nodded.

"Was the burglar ever caught?"

"I don't know. I don't believe so."

"Did you report the burglary to the police?"

"I don't remember." She wasn't a good liar, and she screwed up her mouth in a kind of self-disgust. "Why is it important?"

"I'm trying to trace possession of the revolver. If you have any idea who the burglar was, Mrs. Swain—" I left the sentence unfinished, and glanced at the electric clock. It was half past eight. "About twenty hours ago, that revolver may have been used to kill a man. A man named Sidney Harrow."

She knew the name. Her whole face caught and held it. The delicate skin around her eyes puckered in distress. After a moment she spoke.

"Jean didn't tell me. No wonder she was frightened." Mrs. Swain wrung her hands and walked away from me as far as the room would let her. "Do you suspect Eldon of killing Sidney Harrow?"

"Possibly. Was it your husband who took the gun in 1954?"

"Yes, it was." She spoke with her head down and her face averted, like a woman in a storm. "I didn't want to tell Father that Eldon had come back, or that I had seen him. So I made up a lie about a burglary."

"Why did you have to tell your father anything?"

"Because he asked me for the gun the very next morning. I believe he'd heard that Eldon had been in town, and he intended to shoot him with the gun. But Eldon already had it. That's quite an irony, isn't it?"

It wasn't the kind I could live on, but I agreed. "How did Eldon get hold of the revolver? You didn't give it to him?"

"No. I wouldn't do that. I kept it at the back of the telephone drawer." Her eyes moved past me to the telephone table. "I got it out when Eldon tapped on the door. I suspected it was Eldon, his knock was so distinctive. Shave and a haircut, two-bits, you know? That was Eldon's speed. He was capable of coming back after spending nine years in Mexico with another girl. After all the other dreadful things he did to me and my family. And expect to smile it all away and charm us as he used to in the old days."

She looked at the door. "I didn't have the chain on the door at that time–I had it put on the following day. The door wasn't locked, and Eldon came in smiling, calling my name. I wanted to shoot him, but I couldn't pull the trigger of the gun. He walked right up and took it away from me."

Mrs. Swain sat down as if her strength had been taken away. She leaned back against the Oriental rug. I sat down beside her tentatively.

"What happened then?"

"Just what you'd expect of Eldon. He denied everything. He hadn't taken the money. He hadn't gone to Mexico with the girl. He ran away because he'd been falsely accused, and had been living in strictest celibacy. He even argued that my family owed him something, because Father publicly called him an embezzler and blackened his reputation."

"What was your husband supposed to have done?"

"There's no supposition about it. He was the cashier of my father's bank, and he embezzled over half a million dollars. You mean Father didn't tell you?"

"No, he didn't. When did all this happen?"

"July the first, 1945—the blackest day of my life. He ruined my father's bank and sold me into slavery."

"I don't quite follow, Mrs. Swain."

"Don't you?" She tapped her knee with her fist like a judge gaveling for order. "In the spring of 1945 I lived in a big house in San Marino. Before the summer was over, I had to move in here. Jean and I could have gone to live with Father on Locust Street, but I wouldn't live in the same house with Mrs. Shepherd. That meant I had to get out and find a job. The only thing I ever learned to do well is sew. For over twenty years now I've been demonstrating sewing machines. That's what I mean by slavery." Her fist clenched on her knee. "Eldon robbed me of all the good things of life, and then tried to deny it to my face."

"I'm sorry."

"So am I. I'm sorry I didn't shoot him. If I had another chance—" She took a deep breath and let it out in a sigh.

"It wouldn't do any good, Mrs. Swain. And there are worse places than this. One of them is the women's prison at Corona."

"I know that. I was just talking." But she leaned toward me intently. "Tell me, has Eldon been seen in Pacific Point?"

"I don't know."

"The reason I ask, Jean claims she found some trace of him. It's why she employed that Harrow person."

"Did you know Harrow?"

"Jean brought him here last week. I didn't think much of him. But Jean was always impulsive about men. Now you tell me that he's dead."

"Yes."

"Shot with the revolver that Eldon took from me," she said dramatically. "Eldon would kill if he had to, you know. He'd kill anyone who tried to drag him back here and put him in jail."

"That wasn't what Jean planned to do, though."

"I know that. She idolized his memory, foolishly. But Sidney Harrow may have had other ideas. Harrow looked like a bum to me. And don't forget Eldon has stacks of money—over half-a-million."

"Provided he hung on to it."

She smiled fiercely. "You don't know Eldon. He wouldn't throw money away. Money was all he ever wanted in life. He went about getting it coldly and methodically. The bank examiners said that he'd been preparing his theft for well over a year. And when he got to Mexico he probably invested the whole thing at ten per cent."

I listened to her, without entirely believing her. According to her own story, she hadn't seen her husband since 1954. Her account of him had the swooping certainty of a mind tracking on fantasy. A woman could do a lot of dreaming in twenty years of demonstrating sewing machines.

"Are you still married to him, Mrs. Swain?"

"Yes, I am. He may have gotten a Mexican divorce but if he did I never heard of it. He's still living in sin with that Shepherd girl. Which is the way I want it."

"You're talking about Mrs. Shepherd's daughter?"

"That's right. Like mother like daughter. I allowed Rita Shepherd into my home and treated her like my own daughter. So she stole my husband."

"Which theft came first?"

She was puzzled for a moment. Then her brow cleared. "I see what you mean. Yes, Eldon was carrying on with Rita before he stole the money. I caught on to them very early in the game. It was during a swimming party at our house—we had a forty-foot pool where we lived in San Marino." Her voice sank almost out of hearing. "I can't bear to think about it."

The woman had been punished severely in the past hour, and I was weary of my part in it. I rose to go, and thanked her. But she wouldn't let me leave.

She got up heavily. "Do detectives ever do things on a contingency basis?"

"What do you have in mind?"

"I don't have the money to pay you. But if I could get back some of the money Eldon took—" Her sentence dangled in the air, hopefully, hopelessly. "We'd all be rich again," she said in a hushed and prayerful voice. "And of course I'd pay you very generously."

"I'm sure you would." I edged toward the door. "I'll keep my eyes open for your husband."

"Do you know what he looks like?"

"No."

"Wait. I'll get a picture of him, if my daughter left me any."

She went into a back room where I could hear her lifting and shoving things around. When she came back she had a dusty photograph in her hand and a smear of grime on her cheek, like a miner. "Jean took all my good family pictures, all my San Marino albums," she complained. "She used to sit and study them the way other young women read movie magazines. George tells me—George is her husband—that she's still watching the home movies we took in San Marino."

I took the photograph from her: a man of thirty-five or so, fair-haired, bold-eyed. He looked like the man whose picture Captain Lackland had found on Sidney Harrow. But the photograph wasn't clear enough to be absolutely certain.

13

I HAD DINNER in Pasadena and drove home to West Los Angeles. The air in my second-floor apartment was warm and stale. I opened a window and a bottle of beer, and sat down with the bottle in the near-darkness of my front room.

I lived in a quiet section, away from the main freeways. Still I could hear them humming, remote yet intimate, like the humming of my own blood in my veins.

Cars went by in the street from time to time, flinging brief lights across the ceiling. The case I was on seemed as hard to hold in the mind as the vanishing lights and the humming city were.

The shape and feeling of the case were changing. They always changed as you moved around in them. Eldon Swain had come into the center, pulling his whole family with him. If he was alive, he could give me some answers I needed. If he was dead, the people who knew his history would have to provide the answers.

I turned on the light and got out my black notebook and put down some notes about the people:

"The Colt .45 I took off Nick Chalmers was bought in September 1941 by Samuel Rawlinson, president of the Pasadena Occidental Bank. Around July 1, 1945, he gave it to his daughter Louise Swain. Her husband, Eldon, cashier of the bank, had just embezzled over half a million and ruined the bank. He ran off, reportedly to Mexico, with Rita Shepherd, daughter of Rawlinson's housekeeper (and onetime 'best friend' of his own daughter, Jean).

"Eldon Swain turned up at his wife's house in 1954 and took the Colt from her. How did it get from Swain to Nick Chalmers? Via Sidney Harrow, or through other people?

"N.B. San Diego: Harrow lived there, ditto Swain's daughter Jean and her husband, George Trask, ditto Mrs. Shepherd's ex-husband."

When I finished writing it was nearly midnight. I called John Truttwell's house in Pacific Point and at his request I read my notes to him, twice. I said it might be a good idea after all to turn the Colt revolver over to Lackland for testing. Truttwell said he already had. I went to bed.

At seven by my radio clock the phone jarred me awake. I picked up the receiver and pronounced my own name with a dry mouth.

"Captain Lackland here. I know it's early to call. But I've been up all night myself, supervising tests on the revolver you turned in to your lawyer."

"Mr. Truttwell isn't my lawyer."

"He's been doing your talking for you. But under present circumstances that isn't good enough."

"What are the circumstances?"

"I don't believe in discussing evidence over the phone. Can you be here in the station in an hour?"

"I can try."

I skipped breakfast and walked into Lackland's office at two minutes to eight by the electric clock on his wall. He nodded curtly. His eyes had sunk deeper into his head. Glinting gray beard had sprouted on his face, like wire growing out from a central steel core.

His desk was cluttered with photographs. The top one was a blown-up microphotograph of a pair of bullets. Lackland waved me into a hard chair opposite him.

"It's time you and I had a meeting of minds."

"You make it sound more like a clash of personalities, Captain."

Lackland didn't smile. "I'm in no mood for wisecracks. I want to know where you got hold of this gun." He pulled the revolver on me suddenly, producing a plywood board to which it had been attached with wire.

"I can't tell you that. The law says I don't have to."

"What do you know about the law?"

"I'm working under a good lawyer. I accept his interpretation."

"I don't."

"You make that clear, Captain. I'm willing to cooperate in any way I can. The fact that you have the gun is proof of that."

"The real proof would be for you to tell me where you got it."

"I can't do that."

"Would it change your mind if I told you we know?"

"I doubt it. Try me."

"Nick Chalmers was known to be carrying a gun yesterday. I have a witness. Another witness places him in the vicinity of the Sunset Motor Hotel at the approximate time of the Harrow killing."

Lackland's voice was dry and official, as if he was already testifying at Nick's trial. He was watching my eyes as he spoke. I tried to keep them unresponsive, as cold as his were.

"No comment," I said.

"You'll have to answer in court."

"That's doubtful. Also, we're not in court."

"We may be sooner than you think. Right now I probably have enough for a Grand Jury indictment." He slapped the pile of photographs on his desk. "I have positive proof that this revolver killed Harrow. The bullets we test-fired from it match up with the slug recovered from his brain. You want to take a look?"

I studied the microphotographs. I was no ballistics expert, but I could see that the slugs matched. The evidence against Nick was piling up.

There was almost too much evidence. Beside it, Nick's confession that he had murdered Harrow in the hobo jungle seemed less and less real.

"You don't waste any time, Captain."

The compliment depressed Lackland. "I wish that that was true. I've been working on this case for fifteen years—nearly all of it wasted." He gave me a long appraising look. "I really could use your help, you know. I like to cooperate as well as the next man."

"So do I. I don't understand what you mean about fifteen years."

"I wish I understood it myself." He lifted his microphotographs out of the way and produced some other pictures from the manila envelope he'd shown me yesterday. "Look here."

The first picture was the cropped one I'd already seen. It was Eldon Swain, all right, flanked by girls' dresses, with the girls cut away.

"Know him?"

"I may."

"You do or you don't," Lackland said.

There was no reason not to tell him. Lackland would trace the Colt revolver to Samuel Rawlinson, if he hadn't already done so. From there it was only a step to Rawlinson's son-in-law. I said:

"His name is Eldon Swain. He used to live in Pasadena."

Lackland smiled and nodded, like a teacher whose backward pupil is making progress. He brought out another picture from his manila envelope. It was a flash picture which showed the weary face of a sleeping man. I blinked, and saw that the sleeping man was dead.

"How about *him?*" Lackland said.

The man's hair had faded almost white. There were smudges of dirt or ashes on his face, and it had been burned by harsh suns. His mouth showed broken teeth and around it the marks of broken hopes.

"It could be the same man, Captain."

"That's my opinion, too. It's why I dug him out of the files."

"Is he dead?"

"For a long time. Fifteen years." Lackland's voice had a certain rough tenderness, which he seemed to reserve for the dead. "He got himself knocked off down in the hobo jungle. That was in 1954—I was a sergeant at the time."

"Was he murdered?"

"Shot through the heart. With this gun." He lifted the revolver on the board. "The same gun that killed Harrow."

"How do you know that?"

"Ballistics again." From a drawer in his desk he got out a labelled box which was lined with cotton, and took out a slug. "This bullet matches the ones we test-fired last night, and it's the one that killed the man in the jungle. I thought of it," he said with careful pride, "because Harrow was carrying this other picture." He tapped the cropped photograph of Eldon Swain. "And I was struck by the resemblance to the dead man in the jungle."

"I think the dead man is Swain," I said. "The timing is right." I told Lackland what I had learned about the passage of the revolver from Rawlinson's hands, into his daughter's, and from her hands into her wandering husband's.

Lackland was deeply interested. "You say Swain had been in Mexico?"

"For eight or nine years, apparently."

"That tends to confirm the identification. The dead man was dressed like a wetback, in Mexican clothes. It's one reason we didn't follow it up like maybe we should have. I used to be a border guard during the war, and I know how hard it is to trace a Mex."

"No fingerprints?"

"That's right, no fingerprints. The body was left with its hands in a fire—the coals of a bonfire." He showed me a hideous picture of the charred hands. "I don't know if it was accidental or not. Some wild things happen in the hobo jungle."

"Did you have any suspects at the time?"

"We rounded up the transients, of course. One of them looked promising at first—an ex-con named Randy Shepherd. He was carrying too much money for a tramp, and he'd been seen with the decedent. But he claimed they'd just met casually on the road and shared a bottle. We couldn't prove otherwise."

He shifted to further questions about Eldon Swain and the revolver, which I answered. Finally he said: "We've covered everything except the essential point. How did you get hold of the gun yesterday?"

"Sorry, Captain. At least you're not trying to pin this old hobo-jungle killing on Nick Chalmers. He was hardly big enough for a cap pistol at the time."

Lackland was as implacable as a chess player: "Children have been known to fire a gun."

"You can't be serious."

Lackland gave me a chilly smile which seemed to say that he knew more than I did, and always would.

14

I STOPPED BY Truttwell's office to report to him. His pink-haired receptionist seemed relieved to see me.

"I've been trying to get you. Mr. Truttwell says it's urgent."

"Is he here?"

"No. He's at Mr. Chalmers's house."

The Chalmerses' servant, Emilio, let me in. Truttwell was sitting with Chalmers and his wife in the living room. The scene looked like a wake with the corpse missing.

"Has something happened to Nick?"

"He ran away," Chalmers said. "I didn't get any sleep last night, and I'm afraid he caught me with my wits down. He locked himself in an upstairs bathroom. It never occurred to me that he could squeeze himself out the window. But he did."

"How long ago?"

"Hardly more than half an hour," Truttwell said.

"That's too damn bad."

"I know it is." Chalmers was taut and anxious. The slow grinding passage of the night had worn flesh from his face. "We were hoping you could help us get him back."

"We can't use the police, you see," his wife said.

"I understand that. How was he dressed, Mr. Chalmers?"

"In the same clothes as he was wearing yesterday—he wouldn't undress last night. He had on a gray suit, a white shirt, and a blue tie. Black shoes."

"Did he take anything else with him?"

Truttwell answered for them: "I'm afraid he did. He took all the sleeping pills in the medicine cabinet."

"At least they're missing," Chalmers said.

"Exactly what is missing?" I asked him.

"Some chloral hydrate capsules, and quite a few ¾-grain Nembutal."

"And a good deal of Nembu-Serpin," his wife added.

"Did he have money?"

"I presume he did," Chalmers said. "I didn't take his money away. I was trying to avoid anything that would upset him."

"Which way did he go?"

"I don't know. It took me a few minutes to realize he was gone. I'm not a very good jailer, I'm afraid."

Irene Chalmers made a clucking noise with her tongue. It was hardly audible, and she made it only once, but it conveyed the idea that she could think of other things he wasn't very good at.

I asked Chalmers to show me Nick's escape route. He took me up a short tile staircase and along a windowless corridor to the bathroom. The rifled medicine cabinet was standing open. The window, set deep in the far wall, was about two feet wide by three feet high. I opened it and leaned out.

In a flower bed about twelve feet below the window I could see deep footprints, toes pointed inward to the house. Nick must have climbed out feet first, I thought, hung from the sill and dropped. There was no other trace of him.

We went downstairs to the living room where Irene Chalmers was waiting with Truttwell. "You're wise," I said, "not to think in terms of the police. I wouldn't tell them, or anyone, that he's gone."

"We haven't, and we don't intend to," Chalmers said.

"What kind of emotional state was he in when he left?"

"Pretty fair, I thought. He didn't sleep much, but we did some quiet talking in the course of the night."

"Do you mind telling me what about?"

"I don't mind. I talked about our need to stick together, our willingness to support him."

"How did he react?"

"Hardly at all, I'm afraid. But at least he didn't get angry."

"Did he mention the shooting of Harrow?"

"No. Nor did I ask him."

"Or the shooting of another man fifteen years ago?"

Chalmers's face lengthened in surprise. "What on earth do you mean?"

"Skip it for now. You've got enough on your mind."

"I prefer not to skip it." Irene Chalmers rose and moved toward me. She had dark circles under her eyes; her skin was yellowish; her lips moved uncertainly. "You can't be accusing my son of another shooting?"

"I simply asked a question."

"It was a terrible question."

"I agree." John Truttwell got to his feet and came over to me. "I think it's time we got out of here. These people have put in a hellish night."

I gave them a semiapologetic salute and followed Truttwell toward the front door. Emilio came running to let us out. But Irene Chalmers intercepted him and us.

"Where did this alleged shooting take place, Mr. Archer?"

"In the local hobo jungle. Apparently it was done with the same gun that killed Harrow."

Chalmers came up behind his wife. "How can you know that?" he said to me.

"The police have ballistic evidence."

"And they suspect Nick? Fifteen years ago he was only eight."

"I pointed that out to Captain Lackland."

Truttwell turned on me in surprise. "You've already discussed this with him?"

"Not in the sense that I answered his questions. He's the source for most of my information about that earlier killing."

"How did it come up between you?" Truttwell said.

"Lackland brought it up. I mentioned it just now because I thought I should."

"I see." Truttwell's manner to me was smooth and neutral. "If you don't mind, I'd like to discuss this in private with Mr. and Mrs. Chalmers."

I waited outside in my car. It was a bright January day, with enough wind to put an edge on its sparkle. But the weight of what had happened in the house, and what had been said, lay heavily on my mind. I was afraid the Chalmerses were going to fire me off the case. It wasn't an easy case, but after a day and a night with the people involved in it, I wanted to finish it.

Truttwell came out eventually and got into the front seat of my car. "They asked me to dismiss you. I talked them out of it."

"I don't know if I should thank you."

"Neither do I. They're not easy people to deal with. They had to be convinced you weren't playing footsie with Lackland."

He meant it as a question, which I answered: "I wasn't. I do have to cooperate with him, though. He's been on this case for fifteen years. I've been on it less than one day."

"Did he specifically accuse Nick of anything?"

"Not quite. He mentioned that a child could fire a gun."

Truttwell's eyes grew small and bright, like little pellets of ice. "Do you think that really happened?"

"Lackland seems to be playing with the idea. Unfortunately, he has a dead man to back him up."

"Do you know who the dead man was?"

"It isn't definitely established. It may have been a wanted man named Eldon Swain."

"Wanted for what?"

"Embezzlement. There's one other thing which I hate to mention but I have to." I paused. I really did hate to mention it. "Before I brought Nick in yesterday he made a sort of confession to a shooting. His confession fits the old shooting, the Swain shooting, better than the shooting of Harrow. Actually he may have been confessing both at once."

Truttwell rapped his fists together several times. "We have to get him back before he talks his life away."

"Is Betty at home?"

Her father glanced sharply at me. "You are not going to use her as a decoy, or a bird dog."

"Or a woman? She is one."

"Before everything else she's my daughter." It was one of Truttwell's more self-revealing statements. "She's not getting mixed up in a murder case."

I didn't bother reminding him that she already was. "Does Nick have any other friends I could talk to?"

"I doubt it. He's always been pretty much of a loner. Which was one of my objections—" Truttwell cut himself short. "Dr. Smitheram may be your best bet, if you can get him to talk. I've been trying to for fifteen years." He added dryly: "He and I suffer from professional incompatibility, I'm afraid."

"When you say fifteen years—?"

Truttwell answered my half-finished question: "I remember that something did happen involving Nick when he was in second or third grade. One day he didn't come home from school. His mother phoned me and asked me what to do. I gave her some standard advice. Whether or not she followed it I still don't know. But the boy was home the following day. And Smitheram's been treating him off and on ever since. Not too successfully, I might add."

"Did Mrs. Chalmers give you any idea of what happened?"

"Nick either ran away or was abducted, I think the latter. And I think—" Truttwell wrinkled his nose as if at a bad smell—"sex was involved."

"So you said yesterday. What kind of sex?"

"Abnormal," he said shortly.

"Did Mrs. Chalmers say so?"

"Not explicitly. It was everyone's deep silence on the subject." His voice trailed off.

"Murder makes for even deeper silence."

Truttwell sniffed. "An eight-year-old boy is incapable of murder, in any real sense."

"I know that. But eight-year-old boys don't know it, especially if the whole thing is hushed up around them."

Truttwell moved uncomfortably in the seat, as if he was being crowded by ugly images. "I'm afraid you're jumping to conclusions, Archer."

"These aren't conclusions. They're hypotheses."

"Aren't we getting rather far afield from your initial assignment?"

"We always expected to, didn't we? Incidentally, I wish you'd reconsider about Betty. She may know where Nick is."

"She doesn't," Truttwell said shortly. "I asked her myself."

15

I DROPPED TRUTTWELL off downtown. He told me how to get to Dr. Smitheram's clinic, which turned out to be a large new building on the fashionable borders of Montevista. "Smitheram Clinic, 1967" was cut in the stone facing over the main door.

A handsome woman with dark-brown hair came out into the windowless waiting room and asked me if I had an appointment.

I said I hadn't. "There's an emergency involving one of Dr. Smitheram's patients."

"Which one?"

Her blue eyes were concerned. There was a slash of grey in her brown hair, as if time had thrust a loving hand through it.

"I'd rather tell the doctor," I said.

"You can discuss it with me. I'm Mrs. Smitheram, and I work professionally with my husband." She gave me a smile which may have been professional but felt real. "Are you a relative?"

"No. My name is Archer—"

"Of course," she said. "The detective. Dr. Smitheram has been expecting you to call." She scanned my face, and frowned a little. "Has something else happened?"

"All hell has been breaking loose. I wish you'd let me talk to the doctor."

She looked at her watch. "I simply can't. He has a patient with him, with half an hour to go. I can't interrupt them except in a serious emergency."

"This is one. Nick's run away again. And I think the police are getting ready to make a move."

She reacted as if she was Nick's co-conspirator: "To arrest him?"

"Yes."

"That's foolish and unfair. He was just a small boy—" She cut the sentence in half, as if a censor had come awake in her head.

"Just a small boy when he did what, Mrs. Smitheram?"

She drew a deep angry breath and let it out in a faint droning sound of resignation. She went through an inner door and closed it behind her.

Eventually Smitheram came out, enormous in a white smock. He looked slightly remote, like a man coming out of a waking dream, and he shook hands with me impatiently.

"Where has Nick gone to, anyway?"

"I have no idea. He just took off."

"Who was looking after him?"

"His father."

"That's preposterous. I warned them that the boy needed security, but Truttwell vetoed that." His anger was running on, finding new objects, as if it was really anger with himself. "If they refuse to take my advice I'll wash my hands of the business."

"You can't do that and you know it," his wife said from the doorway. "The police are after Nick."

"Or soon will be," I said.

"What have they got on him?"

"Suspicion of two killings. You probably know more about the details than I do."

Dr. Smitheram's eyes met mine in a kind of confrontation. I could feel that I was up against a strong devious will.

"You're assuming a good deal."

"Look, doctor. Couldn't we put down the foils and talk like human beings? We both want to bring Nick home safe, keep him out of jail, get his sickness cured—whatever it is."

"That's a large order," he said with a cheerless smile. "And we don't seem to be making much progress, do we?"

"All right. Where would he go?"

"That's hard to say. Three years ago he was gone for several months. He wandered all over the country as far as the east coast."

"We don't have three months, or three days. He took along several batches of sleeping pills and tranquilizers—chloral hydrate, Nembutal, Nembu-Serpin."

Smitheram's eyes wavered and darkened. "That's bad. He's sometimes suicidal, as you undoubtedly know."

"Why is he suicidal?"

"He's had an unfortunate life. He blames himself, as if he was criminally responsible for his misfortunes."

"You mean he isn't?"

"I mean that no one is." He said it as if he believed it. "But you and I shouldn't be standing here talking. In any case, I'm not going to divulge my patient's secrets." He made a move toward the inner door.

"Wait a minute, doctor. Just one minute. Your patient's life may be in danger, you know that."

"Please," Mrs. Smitheram said. "Talk to the man, Ralph."

Dr. Smitheram turned back to me, bowing his head in a slightly exaggerated attitude of service. I didn't ask him the question I wanted to, about the dead man in the hobo jungle; it would only produce widening circles of silence.

"Did Nick talk to you at all last night?" I said.

"He did to some extent. His parents and his fiancée were present most of the time. They were an inhibiting influence, naturally."

"Did he mention any names, of people or places? I'm trying to get a line on where he might have gone."

The doctor nodded. "I'll get my notes."

He left the room and brought back a couple of sheets of paper, illegibly scrawled over. He put on reading glasses and scanned them rapidly.

"He mentioned a woman named Jean Trask whom he's been seeing."

"How did he feel about her?"

"Ambivalent. He seemed to blame her for his troubles—it wasn't clear why. At the same time he seemed rather interested in her."

"Sexually interested?"

"I wouldn't put it that way. His feeling was more fraternal. He also referred to a man named Randy Shepherd. In fact he wanted my help in finding Shepherd."

"Did he say why?"

"Apparently Shepherd was or may have been a witness to something that happened long ago."

Smitheram left me before I could ask any further questions. His wife and I exchanged the numbers of our respective telephone-answering services. But she wouldn't let me go just yet. Her eyes were slightly wilted, as if she'd disappointed herself in some way.

"I know it's exasperating," she said, "not to be given the facts. We operate this way because we have to. My husband's patients hold nothing back, you see. It's essential to treatment."

"I understand that."

"And please believe me when I say that we're very much in Nick's corner. Both Dr. Smitheram and I are very fond of him—of his whole family. They've had more than their share of misfortune, as he said."

Both the Smitherams were masters of the art of talking quite a lot without saying much. But Mrs. Smitheram seemed to be a lively woman who would have liked to talk freely. She followed me to the door, still dissatisfied with what she'd said or left unsaid.

"Believe me, Mr. Archer, there are things in my files you wouldn't want to know."

"And in mine. Someday we'll exchange histories."

"That will be a day," she said with a smile.

There was a public phone in the lobby of the Smitheram building. I called San Diego Information, got George Trask's number, and put in a call to his home. The phone rang many times before the receiver was lifted.

"Hello?" It was Jean Trask's voice, and it sounded scared and dim. "Is that you, George?"

"This is Archer. If Nick Chalmers shows up there—"

"He better not. I don't want anything more to do with him."

"If he does, though, keep him with you. He's carrying a pocketful of barbiturates, and I think he plans to take them."

"I suspected he was psycho," the woman said. "Did he kill Sidney Harrow?"

"I doubt it."

"He did, though, didn't he? Is he after me? Is that why you called?" The quick forced rhythms of fear had entered her voice.

"I have no reason to think so." I changed the subject: "Do you know a Randy Shepherd, Mrs. Trask?"

"It's funny you should ask me that. I was just—" Her voice stopped dead.

"You were just what?"

"Nothing. I was thinking of something else. I don't know anybody by that name."

She was lying. But you can't unravel lies on the telephone. San Diego was an easy trip, and I decided to go there, unannounced.

"Too bad," I said, and hung up.

I tried Information again. Randy Shepherd had no phone listed in the San Diego area. I called Rawlinson's house in Pasadena, and Mrs. Shepherd answered.

"Archer speaking. Remember me?"

"Naturally, I remember you. If it's Mr. Rawlinson you want, he's still in bed."

"It's you I want, Mrs. Shepherd. How can I get in touch with your former husband?"

"You can't through me. Has he done wrong again?"

"Not to my knowledge. A boy I know is carrying a lot of sleeping pills and planning suicide. Shepherd may be able to lead me to him."

"What boy are you talking about?" she said in a guarded tone.

"Nick Chalmers. You wouldn't know him."

"No, I wouldn't. And I can't give you Shepherd's address, I doubt he has one. He lives someplace in the Tijuana River Valley, down by the Mexican border."

16

I GOT TO San Diego shortly before noon. The Trask house on Bayview Avenue stood near the base of Point Loma, overlooking North Island and the bay. It was a solid hillside ranchhouse with a nicely tended lawn and flowerbeds.

I knocked on the front door with an iron knocker shaped like a seahorse. No answer. I knocked and waited, and tried the knob. The door didn't open.

I walked around the outside of the house, peering into the windows, trying to act like a prospective purchaser. The windows were heavily draped. Apart from a glimpse of birch cupboards and a stainless-steel sink pagodaed with dirty dishes, I couldn't see anything. The attached garage was latched on the inside.

I went back to my car, which I'd parked diagonally across the street, and settled down to wait. The house was ordinary enough, but somehow it gripped my attention. The traffic of the harbor and the sky, ferries and fishing boats, planes and gulls, all seemed to move in relation to it.

The waiting minutes were long-drawn-out. Delivery vans went by, and a few carsful of children chauffeured by mothers. The street wasn't much used by the people who lived on it, except for transportation. The people kept to their houses, as if to express a sense of property, and a sense of isolation.

An old car that didn't belong on the street came up the hill trailing oil smoke and preceded by the clatter of a fan belt that needed lubrication. A big rawboned man wearing a dirty gray windbreaker and a dirty gray beard got out and crossed the street, silent in worn sneakers. He was carrying a round Mexican basket under one arm. He knocked, as I had, on the Trask's front door. He tried the knob, as I had.

He looked up and down the street and at me, the movements of his head as quick and instinctive as an old animal's. I was reading a San Diego County road map. When I looked at the man again, he had opened the door and was closing it behind him.

I got out of my car and noted the registration of his: Randolph Shepherd, Conchita's Cabins, Imperial Beach. His keys were in the ignition. I put them in the same pocket as my keys.

A folded copy of the Los Angeles *Times* lay on the right side of the front seat, open at the third page. Under a two-column head there was an account of Sidney Harrow's death and a picture of his young swinger's face, which I had never really seen.

I was named as the discoverer of the body, nothing more. Nick Chalmers wasn't named. But Captain Lackland was quoted as saying that he expected to make an arrest within the next twenty-four hours.

My head was still in Shepherd's car when he opened the door of the Trask house. He came out furtively but rapidly, almost with abandon, as if he'd been pushed out by an explosion in the house. For a moment his eyes were perfectly round, like clouded marbles, and his mouth a round red hole in his beard.

He stopped short when he saw me. He looked up and down the open sunlit street as if he was in a cul-de-sac surrounded by high walls.

"Hello, Randy."

He showed his brown teeth in a grin of puzzlement. With enormous unwillingness, like a man wading into a cold deepening sea, he came across the road toward me. He let his grin become loose and foolish.

"I was just bringing Miss Jean some tomatoes. I used to tend the garden for Miss Jean's daddy. I got a real green thumb, see."

He raised his thumb. It was big and spatulate, grained with dirt, and armed with a jagged dirty nail.

"Do you always pick the lock when you make a delivery, Randy?"

"How come you know my name? Are you a cop?"

"Not exactly."

"How come you know my name?"

"You're famous. I've been wanting to meet you."

"Who are you? A cop?"

"A private cop."

He made a quick bad decision. He had been making them all his life: his scarred face bore the record of them. He jabbed at my eyes with his thumbnail. At the same time he tried to knee me.

I caught his jabbing hand and twisted it. For a moment we were perfectly poised and still. Shepherd's eyes were bright with rage. He couldn't sustain it, though. His face went through a series of transformations, like stop-time pictures of a man growing tired and old. His hand went limp, and I let go of it.

"Listen, boss, is it all right if I go now? I got a lot of other deliveries to make."

"What are you delivering? Trouble?"

"No sir. Not me." He glanced at the Trask house as if its presence on the street had caught him by surprise. "I got a quick temper but I wouldn't hurt nobody. I didn't hurt *you*. You were the one hurt me. I'm the one that's always getting hurt."

"But not the only one."

He winced as if I had made a cruel remark. "What are you getting at, mister?"

"There've been a couple of killings. That isn't news to you." I reached for the newspaper on the seat of his car and showed him Harrow's picture.

"I never saw him in my life," he said.

"You had the paper open at this story."

"Not me. I picked it up that way at the station. I always pick up my papers at the station." He leaned toward me, sweaty and jumpy. "Listen, I got to go now, okay? I got a serious call of nature."

"This is more important."

"Not to me it isn't."

"To you, too. You know a young man named Nick Chalmers?"

"He isn't—" He caught himself, and started over: "What did you say?"

"You heard me. I'm looking for Nick Chalmers. He may be looking for you."

"What for? I never touched him. When I found out that Swain was planning a snatch—" He caught himself again and covered his mouth with his hand, as if he could force the words back in or hide them like birds in his beard.

"Did Swain snatch the Chalmers boy?"

"Why ask me? I'm as clean as a whistle." But he peered up at the sky with narrowed eyes as if he could see a sky hook or a noose descending toward him. "I gotta get out of this sun. It gives me skin cancer."

"It's a nice slow death. Swain died a quicker one."

"You'll never pin it on me, 'bo. Even the cops at the Point turned me loose."

"They wouldn't have if they'd known what I do."

He moved closer to me, cringing on bent knees, making himself look smaller. "I'm clean, honest to God. *Please* let me go now, mister."

"We've barely started."

"But we can't just stand here."

"Why not?"

His head turned on his neck like an automatic mechanism, and he looked at the Trask house once again. My gaze followed his. I noticed that the front door was a few inches ajar.

"You left the front door open. We better go over and shut it."

"You shut it," he said. "I got a bad charley horse in my leg. I gotta sit down or I'll fall down."

He climbed in behind the wheel of his jalopy. He wouldn't get far without an ignition key, I thought, and I crossed the street. Looking through the crack between the door and the lintel, I could see red tomatoes scattered on the floor of the hallway. I went in, stepping carefully to avoid them.

There was a smell of burning from the kitchen. I found that a glass coffeemaker on an electric plate had boiled dry and cracked. Jean Trask was lying near it on the green vinyl floor.

I pulled the plug of the electric plate, and knelt down beside Jean. She had stab wounds in her breast and one great gash in her throat. Her body was clothed in pajamas and a pink nylon robe, and it was still warm.

Even though Jean was dead, I could hear breathing somewhere. It sounded as if the house itself was breathing. An open door led through the back kitchen, past the washer and dryer, into the attached garage.

George Trask's Ford sedan was standing in the garage. Nick Chalmers was lying face up beside it on the concrete floor. I loosened his shirt collar. Then I looked at his eyes: they were turned up. I slapped him hard, once on each side of his face. No response. I heard myself groan.

Three empty drugstore tubes of varying sizes lay near him on the floor. I picked them up and put them in my pocket. There was no time for any further search. I had to get Nick to a stomach pump.

I raised the garage door, crossed the street for my car, and backed it into the driveway. I lifted Nick in my arms—he was a big man and it wasn't easy—and laid him on the back seat. I closed the garage. I pulled the front door of the house shut.

I noticed then that Randy Shepherd and his jalopy had gone. No doubt he was just as good at starting keyless cars as he was at opening locked doors. Under the circumstances, I could hardly blame him for leaving.

17

I DROVE DOWN Rosecrans to Highway 80 and delivered Nick at the ambulance entrance of the hospital. There had been a recent auto accident, and everybody on the emergency ward was busy. Looking for a stretcher, I opened a door and saw a dead man and closed the door again.

I found a wheeled stretcher in another room, took it outside and heaved Nick onto it. I pushed him up to the emergency desk.

"This boy needs a stomach pump. He's full of barbiturates."

"Another one?" the nurse said.

She produced a paper form to be filled out. Then she glanced at Nick's face and I think she was touched by his inert good looks. She dispensed with red tape for the present. She helped me to wheel Nick into a treatment room and called in a young doctor with an Armenian name.

The doctor checked Nick's pulse and respiration, and looked at the pupils of his eyes, which were contracted. He turned to me.

"What did he take, do you know?"

I showed him the drug containers I had picked up in the Trasks' garage. They had Lawrence Chalmers's name on them, and the names and amounts of the three drugs they had contained: chloral hydrate, Nembutal and Nembu-Serpin.

He looked at me inquiringly. "He hasn't taken all of these?"

"I don't know if the prescriptions were full. I don't think they were."

"Let's hope the chloral hydrate wasn't, anyway. Twenty of those capsules are enough to kill two men."

As he spoke, the doctor began to thread a flexible plastic tube into

Nick's nostril. He told the nurse to cover him with a blanket, and prepare a glucose injection. Then he turned to me again.

"How long ago did he swallow the stuff?"

"I don't know exactly. Maybe two hours. What's Nembu-Serpin, by the way?"

"A combination of Nembutal and reserpine. It's a tranquilizer used in treating hypertension, also in psychiatric treatment." His eyes met mine. "Is the boy emotionally disturbed?"

"Somewhat."

"I see. Are you a relative?"

"A friend," I said.

"The reason I ask, he'll have to be admitted. In suicide attempts like this the hospital requires round-the-clock nurses. That costs money."

"It shouldn't be any problem. His father's a millionaire."

"No kidding." He was unimpressed. "Also, his regular doctor should see him before he's admitted. Okay?"

"I'll do my best, doctor."

I found a telephone booth and called the Chalmerses' house in Pacific Point. Irene Chalmers answered.

"This is Archer. May I speak to your husband?"

"Lawrence isn't here. He's out looking for Nick."

"He can stop looking. I found him."

"Is he all right?"

"No. He took the drugs, and he's having his stomach pumped out. I'm calling from the San Diego Hospital. Have you got that?"

"The San Diego Hospital, yes. I know the place, I'll be there as soon as I can."

"Bring Dr. Smitheram with you, and John Truttwell."

"I'm not sure I can do that."

"Tell them it's a major emergency. It really is, Mrs. Chalmers."

"Is he dying?"

"He could die. Let's hope he doesn't. Incidentally you'd better bring a checkbook. He's going to need special nurses."

"Yes, of course. Thank you." Her voice was blank, and I couldn't tell if she had really heard me.

"You'll bring a checkbook, then, or some cash."

"Yes. Certainly. I was just thinking, life is so strange, it seems to go in circles. Nick was born in that same hospital, and now you say he may die there."

"I don't think he will, Mrs. Chalmers."

But she had begun to cry. I listened to her for a little while, until she hung up on me.

Because it wasn't good policy to leave a murder unreported, I called the San Diego Police Department and gave the sergeant on duty George Trask's address on Bayview Avenue. "There's been an accident."

"What kind of an accident?"

"A woman got cut."

The sergeant's voice became louder and more interested: "What is your name, please?"

I hung up and leaned on the wall. My head was empty. I think I almost fainted. Remembering that I'd missed my breakfast, I wandered through the hospital and found the cafeteria. I drank a couple of glasses of milk and had some toast with a soft-boiled egg, like an invalid. The morning's events had hit me in the stomach.

I went back to the emergency ward where Nick was still being worked on.

"How is he?"

"It's hard to tell," the doctor said. "If you'll fill out his form we'll admit him provisionally and put him in a private room. Okay?"

"That's fine. His mother and his psychiatrist should be here within an hour or so."

The doctor raised his eyebrows. "How sick is he?"

"You mean in the head? Sick enough."

"I was wondering." He reached under his white coat and produced a torn scrap of paper. "This fell out of his breast pocket."

He handed it to me. It was a penciled note:

"I am a murderer and deserve to die. Forgive me, Mother and Dad. I love you Betty."

"He isn't a murderer, is he?" the doctor said.

"No."

My denial sounded unconvincing to me, but the doctor accepted it. "Ordinarily the police would want to see that suicide note. But there's no use making further trouble for the guy."

I folded the note and put it in my wallet and got out of there before he changed his mind.

18

I DROVE SOUTH to Imperial Beach. The cashier of a drive-in restaurant told me how to find Conchita's Cabins. "You wouldn't want to stay in them, though," she advised me.

I saw what she meant when I got there. It was a ruined place, as ancient-looking as an archeological digging. A sign on the office said: "One dollar per person. Children free." The cabins were small stucco cubes that had taken a beating from the weather. The largest building, with "Beer and Dancing" inscribed across its front, had long since been boarded up.

The place was redeemed by a soft green cottonwood tree and its soft gray shade. I stood under it for a minute, waiting for somebody to discover me.

A heavy-bodied woman came out of one of the cabins. She wore a sleeveless dress which showed her large brown arms, and a red cloth on her head.

"Conchita?"

"I'm Mrs. Florence Williams. Conchita's been dead for thirty years. Williams and I kept on with her name when we bought the cabins." She looked around her as if she hadn't really seen the place for a long time. "You wouldn't think it, but these cabins were a real moneymaker during the war."

"There's a lot more competition now."

"You're telling me." She joined me in the shadow of the tree. "What can I do for you? If you're selling don't even bother to open your mouth. I just lost my second-to-last roomer." She made a farewell gesture toward the open door of the cabin.

"Randy Shepherd?"

She stepped away from me and looked me up and down. "You're after him, eh? I figured somebody was, the way he took off and left his things. The only trouble is, they're not worth much. They're not worth ten per cent of the money he owes me."

She was looking at me appraisingly, and I returned the look. "How much would that be, Mrs. Williams?"

"It adds up to hundreds of dollars, over the years. After my husband died, he talked me into investing money in his big treasure hunt. That was back around 1950, when he got out of the clink."

"Treasure hunt?"

"For buried money," she said. "Randy rented heavy equipment and dug up most of my place and half the county besides. This place has never been the same since, and neither have I. It was like a hurricane went through."

"I'd like to buy a piece of that treasure hunt."

She countered rapidly: "You can have my share for a hundred dollars, even."

"With Randy Shepherd thrown in?"

"I don't know about *that.*" The talk of money had brightened her dusty eyes. "This wouldn't be blood money that we're talking about?"

"I'm not planning to kill him."

"Then what's he so a-scared of? I never saw him scared like this before. How do I know you won't kill him?"

I told her who I was and showed her my photostat. "Where has he gone, Mrs. Williams?"

"Let's see the hundred dollars."

I got two fifties out of my wallet and gave her one of them. "I'll give you the other after I talk to Shepherd. Where can I find him?"

She pointed south along the road. "He's on his way to the border. He's on foot, and you can't miss him. He only left here about twenty minutes ago."

"What happened to his car?"

"He sold it to a parts dealer up the pike. That's what makes me think he's crossing over to Mexico. I know he's done it before, he's got friends to hide him."

I started for my car. She followed me, moving with surprising speed. "Don't tell him I told you, will you? He'll come back some dark night and take it out of my hide."

"I won't tell him, Mrs. Williams."

With my road map on the seat beside me, I drove due south through farmland. I passed a field where Holstein cattle were grazing. Then the tomato fields began, spreading in every direction. The tomatoes had been harvested, but I could see a few hanging red and wrinkled on the withering vines.

When I had traveled about a mile and a half, the road took a jog and ran through low chaparral. I caught sight of Shepherd. He was tramping along quickly, almost loping, with a bedroll bouncing across his shoulders and a Mexican hat on his head. Not far ahead of him Tijuana sloped against the sky like a gorgeous junk heap.

Shepherd turned and saw my car. He began to run. He plunged off the road into the brush and reappeared in the dry channel of a river. He had lost his floppy Mexican hat but still had his bedroll.

I left my car and went after him. A rattlesnake buzzed at me from under an ocotillo, and focused my attention. When I looked for Shepherd again, he had disappeared.

Making as little noise as possible, and keeping my head down, I moved through the chaparral to the road which ran parallel with the border fence. The road map called it Monument Road. If Shepherd planned to cross the border, he would have to cross Monument Road first. I settled down in the ditch beside it, keeping an alternating watch in both directions.

I waited for nearly an hour. The birds in the brush got used to me, and the insects became familiar. The sun moved very slowly down the sky. I kept looking one way and then the other, like a spectator at a languid tennis match.

When Shepherd made his move, it was far from languid. He came out of the brush about two hundred yards west of me, scuttled across the road with his bedroll bouncing, and headed up the slope toward the high wire fence that marked the border.

The ground between the road and the fence had been cleared. I cut across it and caught Shepherd before he went over. He turned with his back to the fence and said between hard breaths:

"You stay away from me. I'll cut your gizzard."

A knife blade stuck out of his fist. On the hillside beyond the fence a group of small boys and girls appeared as if they had sprouted from the earth.

"Drop the knife," I said a little wearily. "We're attracting a lot of attention."

I pointed up the hill toward the children. Some of them pointed back at me. Some waved. Shepherd was tempted to look, and turned his head a little to one side.

I moved hard on his knife arm and put an armlock on it which forced him to drop the knife. I picked it up and closed it and tossed it over the fence into Mexico. One of the little boys came scrambling down the hill for it.

Further up the hill, where the houses began, an invisible musician began to play bullfight music on a trumpet. I felt as if Mexico was laughing at me. It wasn't a bad feeling.

Shepherd was almost crying. "I'm not going back to a bum murder rap. You put me behind the walls again, it'll kill me."

"I don't think you killed Jean Trask."

He gave me an astonished look, which quickly faded. "You're just saying that."

"No. Let's get out of here, Randy. You don't want the border patrol to pick you up. We'll go some place where we can talk."

"Talk about what?"

"I'm ready to make a deal with you."

"Not me. I allus get the short end of the deals."

He had the cynicism of a small-time thief. I was getting impatient with him.

"Move, con."

I took him by the arm and walked him down the slope toward the road. A child's voice nearly as high as a whistle called to us from Mexico above the sound of the trumpet:

"Adios."

19

SHEPHERD AND I walked east along Monument Road to its intersection with the road that ran north and south. He hung back when he saw my car. It could take him so fast and so far, all the way back to the penitentiary.

"Get it through your head, Randy, I don't want you. I want your information."

"And what do *I* get out of it?"

"What do you want?"

He answered quickly and ardently, like a man who has been defrauded of his rights: "I want a fair shake for once in my life. And enough money to live on. How can a man help breaking the law if he don't have money to live on?"

It was a good question.

"If I had my rights," he went on, "I'd be a rich man. I wouldn't be living on tortillas and chili."

"Are we talking about Eldon Swain's money?"

"It ain't Swain's money. It belongs to anybody who finds it. The statute of limitations ran out years ago," he said in the legalese of a cell-block lawyer, "and the money's up for grabs."

"Where is it?"

"Someplace in this very area." He made a sweeping gesture which took in the dry riverbed and the empty fields beyond. "I been making a study of this place for twenty years, I know it like the back of my hand." He sounded like a prospector who had worn out his wits in the desert looking for gold. "All I need is to get real lucky and find me the coordinates. I'm Eldon Swain's legal heir."

"How so?"

"We made a deal. He was interested in a relative of mine." He probably meant his daughter. "And so we made a deal."

The thought of it lifted his spirits. He got into my car without argument, hoisting his bedroll into the back seat.

"Where do we go from here?" he said.

"We might as well stay where we are for the present."

"And then?"

"We go our separate ways."

He glanced quickly at my face, as if to catch me in a false expression. "You're conning me."

"Wait and see. Let's get one thing out of the way first. Why did you go to Jean Trask's house today?"

"Take her some tomatoes."

"Why did you pick the lock?"

"I thought maybe she was sleeping. Sometimes she sleeps real heavy, when she's been drinking. I didn't know she was dead, man. I wanted to talk to her."

"About Sidney Harrow?"

"That was part of it. I knew the cops would be asking her questions about him. The fact is, I was the one introduced her to Sidney, and I wanted Miss Jean not to mention my name to the cops."

"Because you were a suspect in Swain's death?"

"That was part of it. I knew they'd be opening up that old case. If my name came up and they traced my connection with Swain, I'd be right back on the hooks. Hell, my connection with Swain went back thirty years."

"Which is why you didn't identify his body."

"That's right."

"And you let Jean go on thinking her father was alive, and go on looking for him."

"It made her feel better," he said. "She never found out how he died."

"Who shot him?"

"I don't know. Honest to God. I only know I didn't."

"You mentioned a snatch."

"That's right. It's where him and I parted company. I admit I been a thief in my time, but strong-arm stuff was never for me. When he started to plan this snatch, I backed out on him." Shepherd added meditatively: "When Swain came back from Mexico in 1954, he wasn't the man he used to was. I think he went a little crazy down there."

"Did Swain kidnap Nick Chalmers?"

"That's the one he was talking about. I never saw the boy myself. I was long gone when it happened. And it never came out in the papers. I guess the parents hushed it up."

"Why would a man with a half a million dollars attempt a kidnapping?"

"Ask me another. Swain kept changing his story. Sometimes he claimed he had the half million, sometimes he said he didn't. Sometimes he claimed he had it and lost it. He said once he was highjacked by a border guard. His wildest story was the one about Mr. Rawlinson. Mr. Rawlinson was the president of the bank that Eldon Swain worked for, and he claimed Mr. Rawlinson took the money and framed him for it."

"Could that have happened?"

"I don't see how. Mr. Rawlinson wouldn't ruin his own bank. And he's been on his uppers ever since. I know that for certain because I got a relative works for him."

"Your ex-wife."

"You get around," he said in some surprise. "Did you talk to her?"

"A little."

He leaned toward me, keenly interested. "What did she say about me?"

"We didn't discuss you."

Shepherd seemed disappointed, as if he had been robbed of a dimension. "I see her from time to time. I bear no grudges, even if she did divorce me when I was in the pen. I was kind of glad to make the break," he said dolefully. "She's got mixed blood, you probably noticed that. It kind of hurt my pride to be married to her."

"We were talking about the money," I reminded him. "You're pretty certain that Swain took it and kept it."

"I know he did. He had it with him at Conchita's place. This was right after he lifted it."

"You saw it?"

"I know somebody who did."

"Your daughter?"

"No." He added with a touch of belligerence: "Leave my daughter out of this. She's going straight."

"Where?"

"Mexico. She went to Mexico with him and never came back from there." His answer sounded a little glib, and I wondered if it was true.

"Why did Swain come back?"

"He always planned to, that's my theory. He left the money buried on this side of the border, he told me so himself more than once. He offered me a share of it if I would go partners with him and drive him around and grubstake him. Like I said, he wasn't in very good shape when he came back. Fact is, he needed a keeper."

"And you were his keeper?"

"That's right. I owed him something. He was a pretty good man at one time, Eldon Swain was. When I hit the pavement the first time, on parole, he took me on as a gardener at his place in San Marino. It was a real showplace. I used to grow him roses as big as dahlias. It's a terrible thing when a man like that ends up dead of lead poisoning in a railroad yard."

"Did you drive Swain to Pacific Point in 1954?"

"I admit that much. But that was before he started to talk about snatching the boy. I wouldn't drive him on that caper. I got out of town in a hurry. I wanted no part—"

"You didn't shoot him before you left, by any chance?"

He gave me a shocked look. "No *sir.* You don't know much about me, mister. I'm not a man of violence. I specialize in staying out of trouble, out of jail. And I'm still working at it."

"What were you sent up for?"

"Car theft. Break and enter. But I never carried a gun."

"Maybe somebody else shot Swain and you burned off his fingerprints."

"That's crazy. Why would I do that?"

"So that you wouldn't be traced through him. Let's say you took the ransom money from Swain."

"What ransom money? I never saw any ransom money. I was back here on the border by the time he took the boy."

"Was Eldon Swain a child molester?"

Shepherd squinted at the sky. "Could be. He always liked 'em young, and the older he got the younger he liked 'em. Sex was always his downfall."

I didn't believe Shepherd. I didn't disbelieve him. The mind that looked at me through his eyes was like muddy water continually stirred by fears and fantasies and greeds. He was growing old in the desperate hope of money, and by now he was willing to become whatever the hope suggested.

"Where are you going now, Randy? To Mexico?"

He was quiet for a moment, peering out across the flatland toward the sun, which was halfway down the west. A Navy jet flew over like a swallow towing the noises of a freight train. Shepherd watched it out of sight, as if it represented his last disappearing luck.

"I better not tell you where I'm going, mister. If we need to get in touch again I'll get in touch with you. Just don't try to pull a fast one on me. So you saw me at Miss Jean's house. That puts you on the same spot."

"Not quite. But I won't turn you in unless I find some reason."

"You won't. I'm as clean as soap. And you're a white man," he added, sharing with me his one dubious distinction. "How about a little traveling money?"

I gave him fifty dollars and my name, and he seemed satisfied. He got out of the car with his bedroll and stood waiting by the roadside until I lost sight of him in my rear-view mirror.

I drove back to the cabins and found Mrs. Williams still working in the one that Shepherd had vacated. When I appeared in the doorway, she looked up from her sweeping with pleased surprise.

"I never thought you'd come back," she said. "I guess you didn't find him, eh?"

"I found him. We had a talk."

"Randy's a great talker."

She was stalling, unwilling to ask me outright for the second installment of her money. I gave her the other fifty. She held it daintily in her fingers, as if she had captured some rare specimen of moth or butterfly, then tucked it away in her bosom.

"I thank you kindly. I can use this money. I guess you know how it is."

"I guess I do. Are you willing to help me with more information, Mrs. Williams?"

She smiled. "I'll tell you anything but my age."

She sat down on the stripped mattress of the bed, which creaked and sank under her weight. I took the only chair in the room. A shaft of sunlight fell through the window, swarming with brilliant dust. It laid down a swatch of brightness between us on the worn linoleum floor.

"What do you want to know?"

"How long has Shepherd been staying here?"

"Off and on since the war. He comes and he goes. When he got really hungry he used to travel with the fruit pickers sometimes. Or he'd pick up a dollar or two weeding somebody's garden. He was a gardener at one time."

"He told me that. He worked for a Mr. Swain in San Marino. Did he ever mention Eldon Swain to you?"

The question made her unhappy. She looked down at her knee and began pleating her skirt. "You want me to tell it like it is, like the kids say?"

"Please do."

"It don't make me look good. The trouble is in this business you get so you'll do things for money that you wouldn't start out doing when you're young and fresh. There's nothing people won't do for money."

"I know that. What are you leading up to, Florence?"

She said in a hurried monotone, as if to reduce the size and duration of her guilt: "Eldon Swain stayed here with his girl friend. She was Randy Shepherd's daughter. That's what brought Randy here in the first place."

"When was this?"

"Let's see. It was just before the trouble with the money, when Mr. Swain took off for Mexico. I don't have a good head for dates, but it was sometime along toward the end of the war." She added after a thinking pause: "I remember the Battle of Okinawa was going on. Williams and I used to follow the battles, so many of our roomers were sailor boys, you know."

I brought her back to the subject: "What happened when Shepherd came here?"

"Nothing much. A lot of loud talk mainly. I couldn't help but overhear some of it. Randy wanted to be paid for the loan of his daughter. That was the way his mind worked."

"What kind of a girl was the daughter?"

"She was a beautiful child." Mrs. Williams's eyes grew misty with the quasi-maternal feelings of a procuress. "Dark and tender-looking. It's hard to understand a girl like that, going with a man more than twice her age." She readjusted her position on the bed, and its springs squeaked in tired rhythms. "I don't doubt she was after her share of the money."

"This was before the money, you said."

"Sure, but Swain was already planning to take it."

"How do you know that, Mrs. Williams?"

"The officers said so. This place was swarming with officers the week after he took off. They said that he'd been planning it for at least a year. He picked this place for his final jumping-off place to Mexico."

"How did he cross the border?"

"They never did find out. He may have gone over the border fence, or crossed in the regular way under another name. Some of the officers thought he left the money behind. That's probably where Randy got the idea."

"What happened to the girl?"

"Nobody knows."

"Not even her father?"

"That's right. Randy Shepherd isn't the kind of father a girl would keep in touch with if she had a choice. Randy's wife felt the same way about him. She divorced him while he was in the pen the last time, and when he got out he came back here. He's been here off and on ever since."

We sat in silence for a little while. The rectangle of sunlight on the linoleum was lengthening perceptibly, measuring out the afternoon and the movement of the earth. Finally she asked me:

"Will Randy be coming back here, do you think?"

"I don't know, Mrs. Williams."

"I sort of hope he does. He's got a lot against him. But over the years a woman gets used to seeing a man around. It doesn't even matter what kind of man he is."

"Besides," I said, "he was your second-to-last roomer."

"How do you know that?"

"You told me."

"So I did. I'd sell this place if I could find a buyer."

I got up and moved toward the door. "Who's your last roomer?"

"Nobody you would know."

"Try me."

"A young fellow named Sidney Harrow. And I haven't seen *him* for a week. He's off on one of Randy Shepherd's wild-goose chases."

I produced the copy of Nick's graduation picture. "Did Shepherd give this to Harrow, Mrs. Williams?"

"He may have. I remember Randy showed me that picture. He wanted to know if it reminded me of anybody."

"Did it?"

"Nope. I'm not much good at faces."

20

I WENT BACK to San Diego and drove out Bayview Avenue to George Trask's house. The sun had just set and everything was reddish, as if the blood in the kitchen of the house had formed a weak solution with the light.

A car I had seen before but couldn't remember where—a black Volkswagen with a crumpled fender—stood in the driveway of the Trask house. A San Diego police car was at the curb. I drove on by, and made my way back to the hospital.

Nick was in Room 211 on the second floor, the woman at the information desk told me. "But he's not allowed to have visitors unless you're immediate family."

I went up anyway. In the visitors' lounge across from the elevator Mrs. Smitheram, the psychiatrist's wife, was reading a magazine. A coat folded with the lining turned out was draped across the back of her chair. For some reason I was very glad to see her. I crossed to the lounge and sat down near her.

She wasn't reading after all, just holding the magazine. She was looking right at me, but she didn't see me. Her blue eyes were turned inward on her thoughts, which lent her face a grave beauty. I watched the changes in her eyes as she gradually became aware of me, and finally recognized me.

"Mr. Archer!"

"I wasn't expecting to see you, either."

"I just came along for the ride," she said. "I lived in San Diego County for several years during the war. I haven't been back here since."

"That's a long time."

She inclined her head. "I was just thinking about that long time and how it grew. But you're not interested in my autobiography."

"I am, though. Were you married when you lived here before?"

"In a sense. My husband was overseas most of the time. He was a flight surgeon on an escort carrier." Her voice had a rueful pride which seemed to belong entirely to the past.

"You're older than you look."

"I married young. Too young."

I liked the woman, and it was a pleasure to talk for once about something that had no bearing on my case. But she brought the conversation back to it:

"The latest on Nick is that he's coming out of it. The only question is in what condition."

"What does your husband think?"

"It's too early for Ralph to commit himself. Right now he's in consultation with a neurologist and a brain surgeon."

"They don't do brain surgery for barbiturate poisoning, do they?"

"Unfortunately, that's not the only thing the matter with Nick. He has a concussion. He must have fallen and hit the back of his head."

"Or been hit?"

"That's possible, too. How did he get to San Diego, anyway?"

"I don't know."

"My husband said you brought him here to the hospital."

"That's true. But I didn't bring him to San Diego."

"Where did you find him?"

I didn't answer her.

"Don't you want to tell me?"

"That's right." I changed the subject, not very smoothly. "Are Nick's parents here?"

"His mother's sitting with him. His father is on his way. There's nothing either you or I can do."

I stood up. "We could have dinner."

"Where?"

"The hospital cafeteria if you like. The food is fair."

She made a face. "I've eaten too many hospital-cafeteria dinners."

"I thought you mightn't want to go too far." The phrase had a double meaning that we both heard.

She said: "Why not? Ralph will be tied up for hours. Why don't we got out to La Jolla?"

"Is that where you used to live during the war?"

"You're a good guesser."

I helped her on with her coat. It was silver-blue mink complementing the slash of gray in her hair. In the elevator, she said:

"This is on one condition. You mustn't ask me questions about Nick and his family constellation. I can't answer certain questions, just as you can't, so why spoil things."

"I won't spoil things, Mrs. Smitheram."

"My name is Moira."

She was born in Chicago, she told me at dinner, and trained as a psychiatric social worker in the University of Michigan Hospital. There she met and married Ralph Smitheram, who was completing his residency in psychiatry. When he joined the Navy and was assigned to the San Diego Naval Hospital, she came along to California.

"We lived in a little old hotel here in La Jolla. It was sort of rundown but I loved it. After we finish dinner I want to go and see if it's still there."

"We can do that."

"I'm taking a chance, coming back here. I mean, you can't imagine how beautiful it was. It was my first experience of the ocean. When we went down to the cove in the early morning, I felt like Eve in the garden. Everything was fresh and new and spare. Not like this at all."

With a movement of her hand she dismissed her present surroundings: the thick pseudo-Hawaiian decor, the uniformed black waiters, the piped-in music, all the things that went with the fifteen-dollar Chateaubriand for two.

"This part of the town has changed," I agreed.

"Do you remember La Jolla in the forties?"

"Also the thirties. I lived in Long Beach then. We used to come down for the surf here and at San Onofre."

"Does 'we' refer to you and your wife?"

"Me and my buddies," I said. "My wife wasn't interested in surf."

"Past tense?"

"Historical. She divorced me back in those same forties. I don't blame her. She wanted a settled life, and a husband she could count on to be there."

Moira received my ancient news in silence. After a while she spoke half to herself: "I wish I'd gotten a divorce then." Her eyes came up to mine. "What did *you* want, Archer?"

"This."

"Do you mean being here with me?" I thought she was over-eager for a compliment, then realized she was kidding me a little. "I hardly justify a lifetime of effort."

"The life is its own reward," I countered. "I like to move into people's lives and then move out again. Living with one set of people in one place used to bore me."

"That isn't your real motivation. I know your type. You have a secret passion for justice. Why don't you admit it?"

"I have a secret passion for mercy," I said. "But justice is what keeps happening to people."

She leaned toward me with that female malice which carries some sexual heat. "You know what's going to happen to you? You'll grow old and run out of yourself. Will that be justice?"

"I'll die first. That will be mercy."

"You're terribly immature, do you know that?"

"Terribly."

"Don't I make you angry?"

"Real hostility does. But you're not being hostile. On the contrary. You're off on the usual nurse kick, telling me I better marry again before I get too old, or I won't have anybody to nurse me in my old age."

"You!" She spoke with angry force, which changed into laughter.

After dinner we left my car where it was in the restaurant parking lot, and walked down the main street toward the water. The surf was high and I could hear it roaring and retreating like a sea lion frightened by the sound of his own voice.

We turned right at the top of the last slope and walked past a brand-new multistoried office building, toward a motel which stood on the next corner. Moira stood still and looked it over.

"I thought this was the corner, but it isn't. I don't remember that motel at all." Then she realized what had happened. "This *is* the corner, isn't it? They tore down the old hotel and put up the motel in its place." Her voice was full of emotion, as if a part of her past had been demolished with the old building.

"Wasn't it called the Magnolia Hotel?"

"That's right. The Magnolia. Did you ever stay there?"

"No," I said. "But it seems to have meant quite a lot to you."

"It did and does. I lived on there for two years after Ralph shipped out. I think now it was the realest part of my life. I've never told anyone about it."

"Not even your husband?"

"Certainly not Ralph." Her voice was sharp. "When you try to tell Ralph something, he doesn't hear it. He hears your motive for saying it, or what he thinks is your motive. He hears some of the implications. But he doesn't really hear the obvious meaning. It's an occupational hazard of psychiatrists."

"You're angry with your husband."

"Now you're doing it!" But she went on: "I'm deeply angry with him, and with myself. It's been growing on me for quite a while."

She had begun to walk, drawing me across the lighted corner and away from it downhill toward the sea. Spray hung in luminous clouds around the scattered lights. The green common and the waterfront path were virtually deserted. She began to talk again as we walked along the path.

"At first I was angry with myself for doing what I did. I was only nineteen when it started, and full of normal adolescent guilt. Later I was angry with myself for not following through."

"You're not making yourself entirely clear."

She had raised the collar of her coat against the spray. Now she looked at me over it like a desperado wearing a partial face mask: "I don't intend to, either."

"I think you want to, though."

"What's the use? It's all gone—completely past and gone."

Her voice was desolate. She walked quickly away from me, and I followed her. She was in an uncertain mood, a middle-aging woman groping for a line of continuity in her life. The path was dark and narrow, and it would be easy by accident or design to fall among the rocks in the boiling surf.

I caught up with her at the cove, the physical center of the past she had been talking about. The broken white water streamed up the slope of the beach. She took her shoes off and led me down the steps. We stood just above the reach of the water.

"Come and get me," she said to it or me or someone else.

"Were you in love with a man who died in the war?"

"He wasn't a man. He was just a boy who worked in the post office."

"Was he the one who came down here with you, when you felt like Eve in the garden?"

"He was the one. I still feel guilty about it. I lived here on the beach with another boy while Ralph was overseas defending his country." Her voice flattened sardonically whenever she spoke of her husband. "Ralph used to write me long dutiful letters, but somehow they made no difference. I actually wanted to undercut him, he was so superconfident and know-it-all. Do you think I'm slightly crazy?"

"No."

"Sonny was, you know. More than slightly."

"Sonny?"

"The boy I lived with in the Magnolia. Actually he'd been one of Ralph's patients, which is how I got to know him in the first place. Ralph suggested that I keep an eye on him. There's an irony for you."

"Stop it, Moira. I think you're reaching for trouble."

"Some reach for it," she said. "Others have it thrust upon them. If I could just go back to that time and change a few things—"

"What would you change?"

"I'm not quite sure." She sounded rather dreary. "Let's not talk about it any more now."

She walked away from me. Her naked feet left wasp-waisted impressions in the sand. I admired the grace of her departing movements, but she came back toward me clumsily. She was walking backward, trying to fit her feet again into the prints she had made and not succeeding.

She walked into me and turned, her furred breast against my arm. I put my arm around her and held her. There were tears on her face, or spray. Anyway, it tasted salt.

21

THE MAIN STREET was quiet and bright when we walked back to the car. The stars were all in order, and quite near. I don't remember seeing any other people until I went into the restaurant to phone George Trask.

He answered right away, in a moist, overused voice: "This is the Trask residence."

I said I was a detective and would like to talk to him about his wife.

"My wife is dead."

"I'm sorry. May I come over and ask you a few questions?"

"I guess so." He sounded like a man who had no use for time.

Moira was waiting for me in the car, like a silver-blue cat in a cave.

"Do you want to be dropped at the hospital? I have an errand to do."

"Take me along."

"It's a fairly unpleasant errand."

"I don't care."

"You would if you lost your marriage and ended up with me. I spend a lot of my nights doing this kind of thing."

Her hand pressed my knee. "I know that I could be hurt. I've already made myself vulnerable. But I'm sick of always doing the professional thing for prudential reasons."

I took her along to Bayview Avenue. The police car was gone. The black Volkswagen with the crumpled fender was still in George Trask's driveway. I remembered now where I had seen it before; under Mrs. Swain's rusty carport in Pasadena.

I knocked on the front door and George Trask let us in. His gangling body was carefully dressed in a dark suit and black tie. He had an air of having made himself the servant of the situation, like a mortician. His grief showed only in his reddened eyes, and in the fact that he didn't remember me.

"This is Mrs. Smitheram, Mr. Trask. She's a psychiatric social worker."

"It's nice of you to come," he said to her. "But I don't need that kind of help. Everything's under control. Come into the living room and sit down, won't you? I'd offer to make you some coffee but I'm not allowed to go into the kitchen. And anyway," he went on, as if his voice was being piped in from someplace beyond his control, "the coffeemaker got broken this morning when my wife was murdered."

"I'm sorry," Moira said.

We followed George Trask into the living room and sat down beside each other, facing him. The window drapes were partly open, and I could see the lights of the city wavering on the water. The beauty of the scene and the woman beside me made me more aware of the pain George Trask was suffering, like solitary confinement in the world.

"The company is being very understanding," he said conversationally. "They're giving me a leave of absence, open-ended, with full pay. That will give me a chance to get everything squared away, eh?"

"Do you know who murdered your wife?"

"We have a pretty good suspect—man with a criminal record as long as your arm—he's known Jean all her life. The police asked me not to mention his name."

It had to be Randy Shepherd. "Has he been picked up?"

"They expect to get him tonight. I hope they do, and *when* they do, put him in the gas chamber. You know and I know why crime and murder are rampant. The courts won't convict and when they do convict they won't mete out the death penalty. And even when they do the law is flouted right and left. Convicted murderers walk free, they don't gas anybody any more, no wonder we have a breakdown of law and order." His eyes were wide and staring, as if they were seeing a vision of chaos.

Moira rose and touched his head. "Don't talk so much, Mr. Trask. It makes you upset."

"I know. I've been talking all day."

He put his large hands on his glaring face. I could see his eyes bright as coins between his fingers. His voice went on unmuffled, as if it were independent of his will:

"The dirty old son deserves to be gassed, even if he didn't kill her he's directly responsible for her death. He got her started on this latest mania of looking for her father. He came here to the house last week with his schemes and stories, told her he knew where her father was and she could be with him again. And that's what happened," he added brokenly. "Her father's dead in his grave and Jean is with him."

Trask began to cry. Moira quieted him with small noises more than words.

I noticed after a while that Louise Swain was standing in the hall doorway looking like her daughter's ruined ghost. I got up and went to her:

"How are you, Mrs. Swain?"

"Not very well." She drew a hand across her forehead. "Poor Jean and I could never get along—she was her father's daughter—but we cared about each other. Now I have no one left." She shook her head slowly from side to side. "Jean should have listened to me. I knew she was getting into deep water again, and I tried to stop her."

"What kind of deep water do you mean?"

"All kinds. It wasn't good for her to go wandering off into the past, imagining that her father was alive. And it wasn't safe. Eldon was a criminal and he consorted with criminals. One of them killed her because she found out too much."

"Do you know this, Mrs. Swain?"

"I know it in my bones. There are hundreds of thousands of dollars at stake, remember. For that kind of money anyone would murder anyone else." Her eyes seemed to be squinting against a bright light. "A man would even murder his own daughter."

I maneuvered her into the hallway, out of hearing of the living room. "Could your husband still be alive, in your opinion?"

"He could be. Jean thought so. There has to be a reason for everything that's happened. I've heard of men changing their faces with plastic surgery so they could come and go." Her narrowed gaze swung to my face and stayed on it, as if she was looking for surgical scars that would mark me as Eldon Swain.

And other men, I was thinking, had disappeared and left in their places dead men who resembled them. I said to the woman:

"About fifteen years ago, at the time your husband came back from Mexico, a man was shot dead in Pacific Point. He's been identified as your husband. But the identification has to be tentative: it's based on pictures which aren't the best in the world. One of them is the photograph you gave me last night."

She looked at me in bewilderment. "Was that only last night?"

"Yes. I know how you feel. You mentioned last night that your daughter had all your best family pictures. You also mentioned some home movies. They could be useful in this investigation."

"I see."

"Are they here in this house?"

"Some of them are, anyway. I've just been going through them." She spread her fingers. "It's how I got the dust on my fingers."

"May I have a look at the pictures, Mrs. Swain?"

"That depends."

"On what?"

"Money. Why should I give you anything free?"

"It may be evidence in your daughter's murder."

"I don't *care,*" she cried. "Those pictures are the only things I have left—all I have to show for my life. Whoever gets them has to pay for them, the way I've had to pay for things. And you can go and tell Mr. Truttwell that."

"How did he get into this?"

"You're working for Truttwell, aren't you? I asked my father about him, and he says Truttwell can well afford to pay me!"

"How much are you asking?"

"Let him make a bid," she said. "Incidentally, I found the gold box you were inquiring about—my mother's Florentine box."

"Where was it?"

"That's none of your business. The point is that I have it and it's for sale as well."

"Was it really your mother's?"

"It certainly was. I've found out what happened to it after her death. My father gave it to another woman. He didn't want to admit it when I asked him about it last night. But I forced it out of him."

"Was the other woman Estelle Chalmers?"

"You know about his liaison with her, eh? I guess everyone knows. He had his gall giving her Mother's jewel box. It was supposed to go to Jean, you know."

"What makes it so important, Mrs. Swain?"

She thought for a moment. "I guess it stands for everything that has happened to my family. Our whole life went to pieces. Other people ended up with our money and our furniture and even our little objects of art." She added after another thinking moment: "I remember when Jean was just a small child, my mother used to let her play with the box. She told her the story of Pandora's box—you know?—and Jean and her friends pretended that was what it was. When you lifted the lid you released all the troubles of the world." The image seemed to frighten her into silence.

"May I see the box and the pictures?"

"No you don't! This is my last chance to get a little capital together. Without capital you're nobody, you don't exist. You're not going to cheat me out of my last chance."

She seemed to be full of anger, but it was probably sorrow she was feeling. She'd stepped on a rotten place and fallen through the floor and knew she was trapped in poverty forever. The dream she was defending wasn't a dream for the future. It was a dreaming memory of the past, when she had lived in San Marino with a successful husband and a forty-foot pool.

I told her I would discuss the matter with Truttwell, and advised her to take good care of the box and the pictures. Then Moira and I said good night to George Trask, and went out to my car.

"Poor people."

"You were a help."

"I wish I could have been." Moira paused. "I know that certain questions are out of bounds. But I'm going to ask one anyway. You don't have to answer."

"Go ahead."

"When you found Nick today, was he in this neighborhood?"

I hesitated, but not for long. She was married to another man, and in a profession with different rules from mine. I gave her a flat no.

"Why?"

"Mr. Trask told me his wife was involved with Nick. He didn't know

Nick's name, but his description was accurate. Apparently he saw them together in Pacific Point."

"They spent some time together," I said shortly.

"Were they lovers?"

"I have no reason to think so. The Trasks and Nick make a very unlikely triangle."

"I've seen unliklier," she said.

"Are you trying to tell me Nick may have killed the woman?"

"No, I'm not. If I thought so I wouldn't be talking about it. Nick has been our patient for fifteen years."

"Since 1954?"

"Yes."

"What happened in 1954?"

"Nick became ill," she said levelly. "I can't discuss the nature of his illness. I've already said too much."

We were almost back where we started. Not quite. Driving back to the hospital I could feel her leaning close to me, tentatively, lightly.

22

MOIRA LEFT ME at the hospital entrance to fix her face, as she said. I took the elevator to the second floor and found Nick's parents in the visitors' room. Chalmers was snoring in an armchair with his head thrown back. His wife sat near him, dressed in elegant black.

"Mrs. Chalmers?"

She rose with her finger to her lips, moving toward the door. "This is the first rest Larry's had." She followed me into the corridor. "We're both deeply grateful to you, for finding Nick."

"I hope it wasn't too late."

"It wasn't." She managed a pale smile. "Dr. Smitheram and the other doctors are most encouraging. Apparently Nick regurg–" She stumbled over the word. "He vomited some of the pills before they could take effect."

"What about his concussion?"

"I don't think it's too serious. Do you have any idea how he got it?"

"He fell or was hit," I said.

"Who hit him?"

"I don't know."

"Where did you find him, Mr. Archer?"

"Here in San Diego."

"But where?"

"I'd rather report the details through Mr. Truttwell."

"But he's not here. He refused to come. He said he had other clients to attend to." Her feelings had risen close to the surface, and anger broke through. "If he thinks he can give us the brushoff, he'll be sorry."

"I'm sure he didn't mean that." I changed the subject. "Since Truttwell isn't available, I should probably tell you I've been talking to a Mrs. Swain. She's Jean Trask's mother and she has some family pictures that I'd like to have a look at. But Mrs. Swain wants money for them."

"How much money?"

"Quite a lot. I may be able to get them for a thousand or so."

"That's ridiculous! The woman must be crazy."

I didn't press the point. Nurses were coming and going in the corridor. They already knew Mrs. Chalmers, and they smiled and nodded and looked inquiringly at her hot black eyes. Breathing deeply, she got herself under some control.

"I insist that you tell me where you found Nick. If he was the victim of foul play—"

I cut her short: "I wouldn't get off on that kick, Mrs. Chalmers."

"What do you mean?"

"Let's take a little walk."

We turned a corner and loitered along a hallway past offices that had been closed for the night. I told her in detail where I had found her son, in the garage next to the kitchen where Jean Trask had been murdered. She leaned on the white wall, her head hanging sideways as if I had struck her violently in the face. Without her coloring, her foreshortened shadow looked like that of a hunched old woman.

"You think he killed her, don't you?"

"There are other possibilities. But I haven't reported any of this to the police, for obvious reasons."

"Am I the only one you've told?"

"So far."

She straightened up, using her hands to push herself away from the wall. "Let's keep it that way. Don't tell John Truttwell—he's turned against Nick on account of that girl of his. Don't even tell my husband. His nerves are exhausted as it is, and he can't take it."

"But you can?"

"I have to." She was quiet for a moment, getting her thoughts in order. "You said there were other possibilities."

"One is that your son was framed. Say the murderer found him drugged and put him in the Task garage as a patsy. It would be hard to convince the police of that one."

"Do they have to be brought in?"

"They're in. The question is how much we have to tell them. We'll need legal advice on that. My neck is out a mile as it is."

She wasn't much interested in the state of my neck. "What are the other possibilities?"

"I can think of one other. We'll get to that in a minute." I took out my wallet and produced the suicide note which had fallen from Nick's pocket. "Is this Nick's writing?"

She held it up to the light. "Yes, it is. It means he's guilty, doesn't it?"

I took it back. "It means he feels guilty of something. He may have stumbled across Mrs. Trask's body and had an overwhelming guilt reaction. That's the other possibility that occurred to me. I'm no psychiatrist, and I'd like your permission to talk this over with Dr. Smitheram."

"No! Not even Dr. Smitheram."

"Don't you trust him?"

"He knows too much about my son already." She leaned toward me urgently. "You can't trust anybody, don't you know that?"

"No," I said, "I don't know that. I was hoping we'd reached a point where the people responsible for Nick could do some candid talking with each other. The hush-hush policy hasn't been working too well."

She looked at me with a kind of wary surprise. "Do you like Nick?"

"I've had no chance to like him, or get to know him. I feel responsible for him. I hope you do, too."

"I love him dearly."

"You may love him too damn dearly. I think you and your husband have been giving him a bad break in trying to overprotect him. If he actually killed anyone the facts are going to have to be brought out."

She shook her head resignedly. "You don't know the circumstances."

"Then tell me."

"I can't."

"You might save yourself a lot of time and money, Mrs. Chalmers. You might save your son's sanity, or his life."

"Dr. Smitheram says his life is not in danger."

"Dr. Smitheram hasn't been talking to the people I've been talking to. There have been three killings over a period of fifteen years—"

"Be quiet."

Her voice was low and frantic. She looked up and down the corridor, her gesture mocked and cartooned by her shadow on the wall. In spite of her sex and her elegance I was reminded of Randy Shepherd's furtive sidelong peerings.

"I won't be quiet," I said. "You've lived in fear so long you need a taste of reality. There have been three killings, as I said, and they all seem to be connected. I didn't say that Nick was guilty of all three. He may not have done any of them."

She shook her head despairingly.

I went on: "Even if he killed the man in the railroad yards, it was a far cry from murder. He was protecting himself against a kidnapper, a wanted man named Eldon Swain who was carrying a gun. As I reconstruct the shooting, he made a rough pass at your little boy. The boy got hold of his gun and shot him in the chest."

She looked up in surprise. "How do you know all this?"

"I don't know all of it. It's partly reconstruction from what Nick told me himself. And I had a chance to talk today with an old con named Randy Shepherd. If I can believe him at all, he went to Pacific Point with Eldon Swain but got cold feet when Swain started planning the kidnapping."

"Why did they pick on us?" she said intently.

"That didn't come out. I suspect Randy Shepherd was more deeply involved than he admits. Shepherd seems to be connected with all three killings, at least as a catalyst. Sidney Harrow was a friend of Shepherd's, and Shepherd was the one who got Jean Trask interested in looking for her father."

"Her father?"

"Eldon Swain was her father."

"And you say that this Swain person was carrying a gun?"

"Yes. We know it was the same gun that killed him, and the same gun that killed Sidney Harrow. All of which makes me doubt that Nick killed Harrow. He couldn't very well have kept that gun hidden for the last fifteen years."

"No." Her eyes were wide and bright yet somehow abstract, like a hawk's, looking over the entire span of those years. "I'm sure he didn't," she said finally.

"Did he ever mention the gun to you?"

She nodded. "When he came home—he found his own way home. He said a man picked him up on our street and took him to the railroad yards. He said he grabbed a gun and shot the man. Larry and I didn't believe him—we thought it was little-boy talk—till we saw it in the paper next day, about the body being found in the yards."

"Why didn't you go to the police?"

"By that time it was too late."

"It's not too late even now."

"It is for me—for all of us."

"Why?"

"The police wouldn't understand."

"They'd understand very well if he killed in self-defense. Did he ever tell you why he shot the man?"

"He never did." She paused, and her eyes were suffused with feeling.

"And what happened to the gun?"

"He left it lying there, I guess. The police said in the paper the weapon couldn't be found, and Nicky certainly didn't bring it home with him. Some hobo must have picked it up."

My mind went back to Randy Shepherd. He had been on or near the spot, and he had been very eager to disconnect himself from the kidnapping. I shouldn't have let him go, I thought: a half million dollars was a critical mass of money, enough to convert any thief into a murderer.

23

MRS. CHALMERS AND I walked back to the visitors' room, where Dr. Smitheram and his wife were talking to Larry Chalmers.

The doctor greeted me with a smile that failed to touch his dubious, probing eyes. "Moira tells me you took her to dinner. Thanks very much."

"It was a pleasure. What are my chances of talking to your patient?"

"Minimal. Nonexistent, in fact."

"Even for a minute?"

"It wouldn't be a good idea, for both physical and psychiatric reasons."

"How is he?"

"He has a giant hangover, of course, and he's depressed both physically and emotionally. That's partly the overdose of reserpine. Also he has a bit of a concussion."

"What caused it?"

"I'd say he was hit on the back of the head with a blunt object. But forensic medicine is not my line. Anyway, he's doing surprisingly well. I owe you a vote of thanks for getting him here in time."

"We all do," Chalmers said, and shook hands with me formally. "You saved my son's life."

"We were lucky, both of us. It would be nice if the luck continued."

"What do you mean, exactly?"

"I think Nick's room should be guarded."

"You think he might get away again?" Chalmers said.

"That's a thought. It hadn't occurred to me. What I had in mind was protection for him."

"He has round-the-clock nurses," Dr. Smitheram said.

"He needs an armed guard. There have been several killings; we don't want another." I turned to Chalmers: "I can get you three shifts for about a hundred dollars a day."

"By all means," Chalmers said.

I went downstairs and made a couple of phone calls. The first was to a Los Angeles guard service with a San Diego branch. They said they would have a man named Maclennan on duty in half an hour. Then I called Conchita's Cabins in Imperial Beach. Mrs. Williams answered in a hushed and worried voice.

"This is Archer. Has Randy Shepherd been back?"

"No, and he probably won't be." She lowered her voice even further. "You're not the only one looking for him. They have the place staked out."

I was glad to hear it, because it meant I wouldn't have to stake it out myself.

"Thanks, Mrs. Williams. Take it easy."

"That's easier said than done. Why didn't you tell me Sidney Harrow was dead?"

"It wouldn't have done you any good to know."

"You can say that again. I'm putting this place up for sale as soon as I get *them* out of my hair."

I wished her good luck, and went out the front door for some air. After a while Moira Smitheram came out and joined me.

She lit a cigarette from a fresh pack and smoked it as if she was being timed by a stop watch. "You don't smoke, do you?"

"I gave it up."

"So did I. But I still smoke when I'm angry."

"What are you angry about now?"

"Ralph again. He's going to sleep in the hospital tonight so he can be on call. I might as well be married to a Trappist."

Her anger sounded superficial, as if it was masking some deeper feeling. I waited for that feeling to show itself. She threw her cigarette away and said: "I hate motels. You wouldn't be driving back to the Point tonight?"

"West Los Angeles. I can drop you off on the way."

"You're very kind." Under the formal language I could sense an excitement echoing mine. "Why are you going to West Los Angeles?"

"I live there. I like to sleep in my own apartment. It's just about the only continuity in my life."

"I thought you abhorred continuity. You said at dinner you liked to move in and out of people's lives."

"That's true. Particularly the people I meet in my work."

"People like me?"

"I wasn't thinking of you."

"Oh? I thought you were stating a general policy," she said with some irony, "to which everyone was expected to conform."

A tall, wide young man with a crew cut and wearing a dark suit emerged from the shadows of the parking lot and headed for the hospital entrance. I called to him:

"Maclennan?"

"Yessir."

I told Moira I'd be right back, and took Maclennan up in the elevator. "Don't let anyone in," I told him, "except hospital personnel—doctors and nurses—and the immediate family."

"How do I know who *they* are?"

"I'll get you started with them. The main thing I want you to look for is men, wearing white coats or not. Don't let any man in unless he's vouched for by a nurse or a doctor you know."

"You expecting a murder attempt?"

"It could happen. You're armed?"

Maclennan pulled back his jacket and showed me the butt of the automatic in his armpit. "Who do I look out for?"

"I don't know, unfortunately. You have one other duty. Don't let the boy run away. But don't use a gun on him, or anything else. He's what it's all about."

"Sure, I understand that." He had a large man's calmness.

I took him to the door of Nick's room and asked the private nurse for Smitheram. The doctor opened the door wide as he came out. I caught a glimpse of Nick lying still with his eyes closed, his nose pointed at the ceiling, his parents sitting on either side of him. The three of them looked like something in a frieze, a ritual in which the raised hospital bed served as a kind of sacrificial altar.

The door closed on them silently. I introduced Maclennan to Dr. Smitheram, who gave us both a bored and weary look:

"Are all these alarms and excursions really necessary?"

"I think so."

"I don't. I'm certainly not going to let you plant this man in the room."

"He'd be more effective there."

"Effective against what?"

"A possible murder attempt."

"That's ridiculous. The boy's perfectly safe here. Who would want to murder him?"

"Ask him."

"I will not."

"Will you let me ask him?"

"No. He's in no condition—"

"When will he be?"

"Never, if you plan to bullyrag him."

"'Bullyrag' is a loaded word. Are you trying to make me sore?"

Smitheram let out a clever little laugh. "If I were, I appear to have succeeded."

"What are you sitting on, doctor?"

His eyes narrowed and his mouth talked very rapidly: "I'm standing—standing on my right and duty to protect my patient. And no junior G-men are going to talk to him now or ever, if I can help it. Is that clear?"

"What about me?" Maclennan said. "Am I hired or fired?"

I turned to him, swallowing my anger. "You're hired. Dr. Smitheram wants you to stay outside in the corridor. If anyone questions your right to be here, tell them you're employed by Nick Chalmers's parents to protect him. Dr. Smitheram or one of the nurses will introduce you to the parents when it's convenient."

"I can hardly wait," Maclennan said under his breath.

24

MOIRA WASN'T WAITING downstairs or in my car. I found her eventually in a parking lot reserved for doctors' cars. She was sitting behind the wheel of her husband's Cadillac convertible.

"I got tired of waiting," she said lightly. "I thought I'd test your investigative skills."

"This is a hell of a time to be playing hide-and-seek."

My voice must have been rough. She closed her eyes in reaction. Then she climbed out of the convertible. "I was only kidding. But not really. I wanted to see if you would look for me."

"I looked. Okay?"

She took my arm and shook it gently. "You're still angry."

"I'm not angry at you. It's your goddamn husband."

"What did Ralph do now?"

"He pulled rank on me and called me a junior G-man. That's the personal part. The other part is more serious. He refused to let me talk to Nick, now or ever. If I could have just five minutes with Nick, I could clear up a lot of points."

"I hope you're not asking me to take it up with Ralph?"

"No."

"I don't want to be caught in the middle between you."

"If you don't want that," I said, "you better go and find a better place to hide."

She looked up at me slantwise. I caught a glint of her naked self, shy and mercurial and afraid of being hurt. "Did you mean that? You want me to get lost?"

I took hold of her and answered her without words. After a minute, she broke away.

"I'm ready to go home now. Are you?"

I said I was, but I wasn't quite. My feeling about Smitheram, anger deepened now by suspicion, got in the way of my feeling for his wife. And it started me thinking along less pleasant lines: the possibility that I might use her to get back at him, or get at him. I pushed these thoughts away but they crouched like unwanted children in the shadows, waiting for the lights to be turned out.

We headed north on the highway. Moira noticed my preoccupation. "If you're tired I can drive."

"It's not that kind of tired." I tapped my skull. "I have a few problems to work through, and my computer is a fairly early prebinary model. It doesn't say yes and no. It says mainly maybe."

"About me?"

"About everything."

We rode in silence past San Onofre. The great sphere of the atomic reactor loomed in the darkness like a dead and fallen moon. The actual moon hung in the sky above it.

"Is this computer of yours programmed for questions."

"Some questions. Others put it completely out of whack."

"Okay." Moira's voice became soft and serious. "I think I know what's on your mind, Lew. You gave it away when you said five minutes with Nick could clear up everything."

"Not everything. A lot."

"You think he killed all three of them, don't you? Harrow and poor Mrs. Trask and the man in the railroad yards?"

"Maybe."

"Tell me what you really think."

"What I really think is maybe. I'm reasonably sure he killed the man in the railroad yards. I'm not sure about the others, and I'm getting less sure all the time. Right now I'm going on the assumption that Nick was framed for the others and may know who framed him. Which means he may be next."

"Is that why you didn't want to come with me?"

"I didn't say that."

"I felt it, though. Look, if you feel you have to turn around and go back there, I'll understand." She added: "I can always leave my body to medical science. Or put in an application for equal time."

I laughed.

"It's not so funny," Moira said. "Things keep happening, and the world keeps moving so fast, it's hard for a woman to compete."

"Anyway," I said, "there's no point in going back. Nick is well guarded. He can't get out, and nobody can get in."

"Which takes care of both your maybes, doesn't it?"

We were silent for a long time. I would have liked to question her at length, about both Nick and her husband. But if I started to use the woman and the occasion, I'd be using a part of myself and my life that I tried to keep unused: the part that made the difference between me and a computer, or a spy.

The unasked questions simmered down after a while, and my mind hung loose in silence. The sense of living inside the case, which I sometimes used as a drug to keep me going, slowly left me.

The woman beside me had sensitive antennae. As if I'd withdrawn a protective shield, she moved in close to me. I drove with her warmth all down my right side and spreading through my body.

She lived on the Montevista shore in a rectilinear cliff-top house made of steel and glass and money.

"Put your car in the carport if you like. You will come in for a drink?"

"A short one."

She couldn't unlock the front door.

"You're using your car key," I told her.

She paused to consider. "I wonder what that means?"

"That you probably need glasses."

"I do use glasses for reading."

She let me in and turned on a light in the hall. We went down some steps into an octagonal room which was mostly window. I could see the moon almost close enough to touch, and, far below, the scrawled white lines of the breakers.

"It's a nice place."

"Do you think so?" She seemed surprised. "God knows the place was beautiful before we built on it, and when we were planning it with the architect. But the house never seemed to capture it." She went on after a moment: "Building a house is like putting a bird in a cage. The bird being yourself, I guess."

"Is that what they tell you at the clinic?"

She turned to me with a quick smile. "Am I being terribly talky?"

"You did mention a drink."

She leaned toward me, silver-faced, dark-eyed, and dark-mouthed in the thin light from outside. "What will you have?"

"Scotch." Then her eyes moved and I caught that naked glint of hers again, like a light hidden deep in a building. I said: "May I change my mind?"

She was willing to be taken. We shed our clothes, more or less, and lay down like wrestlers going to the mat under special rules, where pinning and being pinned were equally lucky and meritorious.

She said at one point, between falls, that I was a gentle lover.

"There are some advantages in getting older."

"It isn't that. You remind me of Sonny, and he was only twenty. You make me feel like Eve in the garden again."

"That's pretty fancy talk."

"I don't care." She rose on one elbow, and her silver breast lay heavy on me. "Does it upset you when I mention Sonny?"

"Oddly enough, it doesn't."

"It shouldn't, either. He was a poor little nothing boy. But we were happy together. We lived like silly angels doing things for each other. He'd never been with a girl before, and I'd only been with Ralph."

Her voice changed on her husband's name, and my feeling also changed. "Ralph was always so terribly technical and self-assured. He came on in bed like an army pacifying an undeveloped country. But with Sonny it was different. He was so gentle and nutty. Love was like a game, a fantasy that we lived in, playing house together. Sometimes he pretended to be Ralph. Sometimes I pretended to be his mother. Does that sound sick?" she said with a nervous little laugh.

"Ask Ralph."

"I'm boring you, aren't I?"

"On the contrary. How long did this affair go on?"

"Nearly two years."

"Then Ralph came home?"

"Eventually he did. But I'd already broken with Sonny. The fantasy was running out of control and so was he. Besides, I couldn't just leap from his bed into Ralph's. As it was the guilt nearly killed me."

I looked down along her body. "You don't strike me as the guilt-ridden type."

She answered after a moment. "You're right. It wasn't guilt. It was simple pain. I'd given up my one true love. For what? A hundred-thousand-dollar house and a four-hundred-thousand-dollar clinic. In neither of which I'd be caught dead if I could help it. I'd rather be back in one room at the Magnolia."

"It isn't there any more," I said. "Aren't you building up the past a little large?"

She answered thoughtfully. "Maybe I am exaggerating, especially the good parts. Women do tend to make up stories featuring ourselves."

"I'm glad men never do."

She laughed. "I bet Eve made up the story of the apple."

"And Adam made up the story of the garden."

She crawled close against me. "You're a nut. That's a diagnosis. I'm glad I told you all this. Are you?"

"I can stand it. Why did you?"

"Various reasons. Also you have the advantage of not being my husband."

"That's the finest thing any woman ever said to me."

"I mean it seriously. If I told Ralph what I've told you, it would be the end of me as a person. I'd become just another of his famous psychiatric trophies. He'd probably have me stuffed and hang me up on the office wall with his diplomas." She added: "In a way that's what he has done."

There were questions I wanted to ask her about her husband but the time and place were wrong, and I was still determined not to use them. "Forget about Ralph. Whatever happened to Sonny?"

"He found another girl and married her."

"And you're jealous?"

"No. I'm lonely. I have no one."

We merged our lonelinesses once again, in something less than love but sweeter than self. I didn't get home to West Los Angeles after all.

25

IN THE MORNING I left early without waking Moira. Fog had moved in from the sea, blanketing the cliff-top house and the whole Montevista shore. I drove up the road very slowly between lines of phantom trees.

I came to the end of the fog suddenly. The sky was cloudless except for a couple of smeared jet contrails. I drove downtown and checked in at the police station.

Lackland was in his office. The electric clock on the wall above his head said that it was exactly eight o'clock. It bothered me for a minute. It made me feel as if Lackland had brought me in again at this particular time by the exertion of some occult force.

"Glad you dropped by," he said. "Sit down. I was wondering where everybody was."

"I went to San Diego on a lead."

"And you took your clients with you?"

"Their son had an accident. They went to San Diego to look after him."

"I see." He waited for a while, twisting and biting his lips as if to punish his mouth for asking questions. "What kind of an accident did he have, or is it a family secret?"

"Barbiturate, mainly. He also has a head injury."

"Was it a suicide attempt?"

"Could be."

Lackland leaned forward abruptly, pushing his face toward mine. "After he knocked off Mrs. Trask?"

I wasn't ready for the question, and I avoided answering it directly. "The prime suspect in the Trask killing is Randy Shepherd."

"I know that," Lackland said, making it clear that I hadn't given him anything. "We have an APB on Shepherd from San Diego."

"Does it mention that Shepherd knew Eldon Swain from 'way back?"

Lackland gnawed at his upper lip. "Do you know that for a fact?"

"Yes. I talked to Shepherd yesterday, before he was regarded as a suspect. He told me that Swain ran off with his daughter Rita and half a million dollars. Apparently Shepherd has spent his life trying to latch onto a piece of that money. It's fairly clear, by the way, that Shepherd talked Mrs. Trask into hiring Sidney Harrow and coming here to the Point. He was using them as cat's-paws to find out what he could without the risk of coming here himself."

"So Shepherd had a motive to kill Swain after all." Lackland's voice was low, as if his fifteen years on the case had used up all his energy at last. "And he had a motive to burn off Swain's fingerprints. Where did you talk to him?"

"On the Mexican border near Imperial Beach. He wouldn't be there any more."

"No. As a matter of fact, Shepherd was seen in Hemet last night. He stopped for gas, heading north in a stolen car, a late-model Merc convertible, black."

"Better check Pasadena. Shepherd came from there, and so did Eldon Swain."

I filled Lackland in on the Pasadena end of the case, on Swain and Mrs. Swain and their murdered daughter, and Swain's embezzlement from Rawlinson's bank. "Once you know these facts," I concluded, "you can't seriously go on blaming Nick Chalmers for everything. He wasn't even born when Eldon Swain took the money from the bank. But that was the real beginning of the case."

Lackland was silent for a while. His face in repose was like an eroded landscape in a dry season. "I know some history, too. Rawlinson, the man who owned the bank, used to spend his summers here back in the twenties and thirties. I could tell you more."

"Please do."

Lackland produced one of his rare smiles. It wasn't very different from his mouth-gnawings, except that a shy light flickered in his eyes. "I hate to disappoint you, Archer. But no matter how far back you go, Nick Chalmers is in the picture. Sam Rawlinson had a girl friend here in town, and after her husband died they spent their summers together. You want to know who his girl friend was?"

"Nick's grandmother," I said. "Judge Chalmers's widow."

Lackland was disappointed. He lifted a typed sheet from his in-basket, read it carefully, crushed it up in a ball, and threw it at a trash can in the corner of the office. It missed. I scooped it up and dropped it in.

"How did you find that out?" he asked me finally.

"I've been doing some digging in Pasadena, as I told you. But I still don't see how Nick comes into this. He's not responsible for his grandmother."

For once Lackland failed to offer an argument. But I thought as I left the police station that perhaps the reverse was true, and Nick's dead grandmother was responsible for him. Certainly there had to be a meaning in the old connection between the Rawlinson family and the Chalmers family.

I passed the courthouse on my way downtown. In a cast stone bas-relief above the entrance, a big old Justice with bandaged eyes fumbled at her scales. She needed a seeing-eye man, I told her silently. I was feeling dangerously good.

After a breakfast of steak and eggs I went into a barbershop and had a shave. By this time it was close to ten o'clock, and Truttwell should be in his office.

He wasn't, though. The receptionist told me that he had just left and hadn't said when he'd be back. She was wearing a black wig this morning, and took my troubled stare as a compliment.

"I like to change my personality. I get sick of having the same old personality."

"Me, too." I made a face at her. "Did Mr. Truttwell go home?"

"I don't know. He received a couple of long-distance calls and then he just took off. If he goes on this way, he'll end up losing his practice." The girl smiled intensely up at me, as if she was already looking for a new opening. "Do you think black hair goes well with my complexion? Actually I'm a natural brownette. But I like to keep experimenting with myself."

"You look fine."

"I thought so, too," she said, overconfidently.

"Where did the distance calls come from?"

"The one call came from San Diego—that was Mrs. Chalmers. I don't know who the other one was, she wouldn't give her name. It sounded like an older woman."

"Calling from where?"

"She didn't say, and it was dialed direct."

I asked her to call Truttwell's house for me. He was there, but he wouldn't or couldn't come to the phone. I talked to Betty instead.

"Is your father all right?"

"I guess he is. I hope so." The young woman's voice was serious and subdued.

"Are you?"

"Yes." But she sounded doubtful.

"If I come right over, will he be willing to talk to me?"

"I don't know. You'd better hurry. He's going out of town."

"Where out of town?"

"I don't know," she repeated glumly. "If you do miss him, Mr. Archer, I'd still like to talk to you myself."

Truttwell's Cadillac was standing in front of his house when I got there. Betty opened the front door for me. Her eyes were rather dull and unresponsive. Even her bright hair looked a little tarnished.

"Have you seen Nick?" she said.

"I've seen him. The doctor gave him a fairly good report."

"But what did Nick say?"

"He wasn't talkable."

"He'd talk to me. I wanted so badly to go to San Diego." She raised her fists and pressed them against her breast. "Father wouldn't let me."

"Why not?"

"He's jealous of Nick. I know that's a disloyal thing to say. But Father made it very clear. He said when Mrs. Chalmers dismissed him this morning that I would have to choose between him and Nick."

"Why did Mrs. Chalmers dismiss him?"

"You'll have to ask Father. He and I are not communicating."

Truttwell appeared in the hallway behind her. Though he must have heard what she'd just said, he made no reference to it. But he gave her a hard impatient look that I saw and she didn't.

"What's this, Betty? We don't keep visitors standing in the doorway."

She turned away without speaking, moving into another room and shutting the door behind her. Truttwell spoke in a complaining way, with a thin note of malice running through his complaint:

"She's losing her mind over that sad sack. She wouldn't listen to me. Maybe she will now. But come in, Archer. I have news for you."

Truttwell took me into his study. He was even more carefully dressed and groomed than usual. He wore a fresh sharkskin suit, a button-down shirt with matching silk tie and handkerchief, and the odors of bay rum and masculine scent.

"Betty tells me you're parting company with the Chalmerses. You look as if you're celebrating."

"Betty shouldn't have told you. She's losing all sense of discretion."

His handsome pink face was fretful. He pressed and patted his white hair. Betty had hurt him in his vanity, I thought, and apparently he didn't have much else to fall back on.

I was more disturbed by the change in Truttwell than by the change in his daughter. She was young, and would change again before she settled on a final self.

"She's a good girl," I said.

Truttwell closed the study door and stood against it. "Don't sell her to me. I know what she is. She let that creep get to her and poison her mind against me."

"I don't think so."

"You're not her father," he said, as if paternity conferred the gift of second sight. "She's put herself down on his level. She's even using the same crude Freudian jargon." His face was red now and his voice was choked. "She actually accused me of taking an unhealthy interest in her."

I said to myself: This is a healthy interest?

Truttwell went on: "I know where she picked up those ideas—from Dr. Smitheram via Nick. I also know," he said, "why Irene Chalmers terminated their association with me. She made it quite clear on the telephone that the great and good Dr. Smitheram insisted on it. He was probably standing at her elbow telling her what to say."

"What reason did she give?"

"I'm afraid you were one reason, Archer. I don't mean to be critical," though he did. "I gathered that you asked too many questions to suit Dr. Smitheram. He seems determined to mastermind the entire show, and that could be disastrous. No lawyer can defend Nick without knowing what he's done."

Truttwell gave me a careful look. As our talk moved back onto more familiar ground, he had regained some of his lawyer's poise. "You're better acquainted with the facts than I could possibly be."

It was a question. I didn't answer it right away. My attitude to Truttwell was undergoing an adjustment. It wasn't a radical one, since I had to admit to myself that from the beginning of the case I hadn't wholly understood or trusted his motivations.

It was becoming fairly evident now that Truttwell had been using me and intended to go on using me. In the same way as Harrow had served as Randy Shepherd's cat's-paw, I was Truttwell's. He was waiting now, handsome and quick-eyed and well-groomed as a cat, for me to spill the dirt on his daughter's friend. I said:

"Facts are hard to come by in this case. I don't even know who I'm working for. Or if I'm working."

"Of course you are," he said benevolently. "You'll be paid in full for everything you've done, and I'll guarantee payment through today at least."

"Who will be doing the paying?"

"The Chalmerses, naturally."

"But you don't represent them any more."

"Don't let that worry you. Just submit your bill through me, and they'll pay it. You're not exactly a migratory worker, and I won't let them treat you as one."

His good will was self-serving, I thought, and would probably last only as long as he could use me. I was embarrassed by it, and by the conflict that had risen. In cases like this, I was usually the expendable one.

"Shouldn't I report to the Chalmerses?"

"No. They've already dismissed you. They don't want the truth about Nick."

"How is he?"

Truttwell shrugged. "His mother didn't say."

"Who do I report to now?"

"Report to me. I've represented the Chalmers family for nearly thirty years, and they're going to find that I'm not so very readily dispensable." He made the prediction with a smile, but there was the hint of a threat in it.

"What if they don't?"

"They will, I guarantee it. But if you're concerned about your money, I'll undertake to pay you personally as of today."

"Thanks. I'll give it some thought."

"You'd better think in a hurry," he said smiling. "I'm on my way to Pasadena to meet Mrs. Swain. She phoned me this morning about investing in her family pictures—after Mrs. Chalmers dismissed me. I'd like to have you come along, Archer."

In my trade you don't often have your own way. If I refused to deal with John Truttwell, he could push me off the case and probably close the county to me. I said:

"I'll take my own car and meet you at Mrs. Swain's house. That's where you're going, isn't it?—Pasadena?"

"Yes, I can count on you to follow me then?"

I said he could, but I didn't follow him right away. There was something more to be said between me and his daughter.

26

BETTY CAME TO the front door, as if by prearrangement, and asked me in again. "I have the letters," she said quietly, "the letters that Nick took from his father's safe."

She led me upstairs to her workroom and brought a manila envelope out of a drawer. It was stuffed with airmail letters arranged for the most part in serial order. There must have been a couple of hundred of them.

"How do you know Nick took them from the safe?"

"He told me so himself the night before last. Dr. Smitheram left us alone for awhile. Nick told me where he'd hidden them in his apartment. I went and got them yesterday."

"Did Nick say why he took them?"

"No."

"Do you know why?"

She perched on a large multicolored hassock. "I've had a lot of different thoughts," she said. "It has to do with the whole father-son business, I suppose. In spite of all the trouble, Nick has always had a lot of respect for his father."

"Does that go for you and your father?"

"We aren't talking about me," she said in a stiff-mouthed way. "Anyway, girls are different—we're much more ambiguous. A boy either wants to be like his father or he doesn't. I think Nick does."

"It still doesn't explain why Nick stole the letters."

"I didn't say I could explain it. But maybe he was trying, you know, to steal his father's bravery and so on. The letters were important to him."

"Why?"

"Mr. Chalmers made them important. He used to read them aloud to Nick—parts of them, anyway."

"Recently?"

"No. When Nick was a little boy."

"Eight?"

"It started about that age. I think Mr. Chalmers was trying to indoctrinate him, make a man of him and all like that." Her tone was a little contemptuous, not so much of Nick or his father as of the indoctrination.

"When Nick was eight," I said, "he had a serious accident. Do you know about it, Betty?"

She nodded deeply. Her hair slid forward, covering most of her face. "He shot a man, he told me the other night. But I don't want to talk about it, okay?"

"Just one question. What was Nick's attitude toward that shooting?"

She hugged herself as if she was chilly. Encircled by her arms and masked by her hair, she huddled on the hassock like a gnome. "I don't want to talk about it."

She pulled up her knees and rested her face against them, almost as if she was imitating Nick in his posture of despair.

I carried the letters to a table by a front window. From where I sat I could see the façade of the Chalmerses' house glistening white under its red tile roof. It looked like a building with a history, and I read the first of the letters in the hope of filling in my knowledge of it.

Mrs. Harold Chalmers — *Pearl Harbor*
2124 Pacific Street — *October 9, 1943*
Pacific Point, Calif.

Dear Mother:

All I have time for is a short letter. But I wanted you to know as soon as possible that I have got my exact wish. This letter will be censored for military details, I am told, so I will simply mention the sea and the air, and you will understand what kind of duty I have been assigned to. I feel as if I had just been knighted, Mother. Please tell Mr. Rawlinson my good news.

The trip from the mainland was dull but rather pleasant. A number of my fellow pilots spent their time on the fantail shooting at flying fish. I finally told some of them that they were wasting their time and spoiling the beauty of the day. I thought for a while that I might have to fight four or five of them at once. But they recognized the moral superiority of my view, and retreated from the fantail.

I hope you are well and happy, dear Mother. I have never been happier in my life. Your affectionate son,

Larry

I suppose I had been expecting some further light on the case, and the letter was a disappointment to me. It had evidently been written by an idealistic and rather conceited boy who was unnaturally eager to get into the war. The only remarkable thing about it was the fact that the boy had since become a dry stick of a man like Chalmers.

The second letter from the top had been written about eighteen months after the first. It was longer and more interesting, the work of a more mature personality sobered by the war.

Lt. (j.g.) L. Chalmers
SS Sorrel Bay (CVE 185)
March 15, 1945

Mrs. Harold Chalmers
2124 Pacific Street
Pacific Point, Calif.

Dearest Mother:

Here I am in the forward area again so my letter won't go off for a while. I find it hard to write a letter that I have to hold on to. It's like keeping a diary, which I detest, or carrying on a conversation with a dictaphone. But writing to you, my dearest, is another matter.

Apart from the things that wouldn't get past the censor, the news about me is very much the same. I fly, sleep, read, eat, dream of home. We all do. For a nation that has built up not only the most powerful but the most expert Navy in the world, we Americans are a bunch of awful landlubbers. All we want is to get back to Mother Earth.

This applies to regular Navy men, who constantly look forward to shore duty and retirement, all but the brass hats, who are having a career. It's even true of the British Navy, some of whose officers I met not long ago in a certain port. A rumor of Germany's collapse reached us that night, and it was touching to see the hopeful wishing of those Britishers. The rumor turned out to be premature, as you must know, but Germany may be finished by the time you get this letter. Give Japan one year after that.

I met a couple of fellow pilots who had been over Tokyo and they told me how it felt: pretty good, they said, because none of the planes in their group got hit. (My squadron has not been so lucky.) They were on their way back to the U.S. after completing their missions and they were happy about that. But they were tensed up, their faces were stiff and reacted quite violently to their emotions. There's something about pilots that reminds you of racehorses—developed almost to an unhealthy point. I hope I'm not that way to other eyes.

Our squadron leader Commander Wilson is, though. (He's no longer censoring mail so I can say this.) He's been in for over four years now, but he seems to be exactly the same gentlemanly Yale man he was when he came in. He has, however, a certain air of arrested development. He has given his best to the war, and will never become the man he was meant to be. (He plans to go into the consular service afterwards.)

Apart from one or two rain squalls the weather has been good: bright sun and shining blue sea, which helps with the flying. But there's a fairly strong swell, which doesn't. The old tub lurches and strains along, and every now and then she wiggles like a hula girl and things slide off onto the floor. The cradle of the deep, to coin a phrase. Well, I'm off to bed. Affectionately,

Larry

It was a fairly impressive letter, with a certain sadness running gray through its perceptions. One sentence stayed in my mind—"He has given his best to the war, and will never become the man he was meant to be"—because it seemed to apply to Chalmers himself as well as his squadron commander. The third letter was dated 4 July 1945:

Dearest Mother:

We're fairly near the equator and the heat is pretty bad, though I don't mean to complain. If we're still anchored at this atoll tomorrow I'm going to try to get off the ship for a swim, which I haven't had since we left Pearl months ago. One of my big daily pleasures, though, is the shower I take every night before going to bed. The water isn't cold, because the sea at temperatures around 90 can't cool it, and you're not supposed to use much, because all the water we use on board has to be condensed from seawater. Still, I like my shower.

Other things I would like: fresh eggs for breakfast, a glass of cold milk, a sail off the Point, a chance to sit and chat with you, Mother, in our garden between the mountains and the sea. I'm terribly sorry to hear that you are ill and your sight has failed. Please thank Mrs. Truttwell on my behalf (hi, Mrs. Truttwell!) for reading aloud to you.

You have no cause to worry about me, Mother. After a not-unexciting period (in which our squadron lost Commander Wilson, and too many others) we are fighting a safe war. So safe I feel guilty, but not so guilty that I'm going to jump overboard and swim rapidly in the direction of Japan. Good news from there, eh? —I mean re the destruction of their cities. It's no secret by now that we're going to do to Japan what we've already done to that certain island (which shall be nameless) where I flew so many missions.

Affectionately,
Larry

I put the letters back in the envelope. They seemed to mark points on a curve. The boy or man who had written them had passed from the eager idealism of the first letter into the rather impressive quick maturity of the second, and declined in the third into a kind of tiredness. I wondered what Chalmers himself could see in his letters that made him want to read them aloud to his son.

I turned to the girl, who hadn't moved from her hassock: "Have you read these letters, Betty?"

She raised her head. The look in her eyes was very dark and far. "I beg your pardon? I was thinking."

"Have you read these letters?"

"Some of them. I wanted to see what all the shouting was about. *I* think they're boring. I *hated* the one about bombing Okinawa."

"May I keep the three I've read?"

"Keep them all, why don't you? If Father finds them here, I'll have to explain where I got them. And it will be just another nail in Nick's coffin."

"He isn't in his coffin. It doesn't help matters to talk as if he is."

"Don't fatherize, please, Mr. Archer."

"Why not? I don't believe people know everything at birth and forget it as they get older."

She reacted positively to my sharp tone. "That's the doctrine of Platonic reminiscence. I don't believe it, either." She slid off the hassock and out of her lethargy and came toward me. "Why don't you give the letters to Mr. Chalmers? You wouldn't have to tell him where you got them."

"Is he at home?"

"I'm afraid I have no idea. I don't really spend all my time at this window watching the Chalmers house." She added with a quick wan smile: "Not more than six or eight hours a day, anyway."

"Don't you think it's time you broke the habit?"

She gave me a disappointed look. "Are you against Nick, too?"

"Obviously I'm not. But I hardly know him. You're the one I know. And I hate to see you caught here, between two fairly dismal alternatives."

"You mean Nick and my father, don't you? I'm not caught."

"You are, though, like a maiden in a tower. This low-grade war of attrition with your father may feel like a battle for freedom, but it isn't. You just get more and more deeply engaged with him. Even if you do succeed in breaking away, it won't be into freedom. You've got it arranged so another demanding male will take you over. And I do mean Nick."

"You've got no right to attack him—"

"I'm attacking you," I said. "Or rather the situation you've put yourself in. Why don't you move out of the middle?"

"Where could I go?"

"You shouldn't have to ask me. You're twenty-five."

"But I'm afraid."

"What of?"

"I don't know. I'm just afraid." After a silence she said in a hushed voice: "You know what happened to my mother. I told you, didn't I? She looked out this very window—this used to be her sewing room—and she saw a light in the Chalmers house when there wasn't supposed to be one. She went over there and the burglars chased her out and ran over her and killed her."

"Why did they kill her?"

"I don't know. It may have been just an accident."

"What did the burglars want from the Chalmers house?"

"I don't know."

"When did it happen, Betty?"

"In the summer of 1945."

"You were too young to remember, weren't you?"

"Yes, but my father told me about it. I've been afraid ever since."

"I don't believe you. You didn't act afraid the other night, when Mrs. Trask and Harrow came to Chalmers house."

"I was afraid, though, terribly. And I should never have gone there. They're both dead."

I was beginning to understand the fear that held her. She believed or suspected that Nick had killed both Harrow and Mrs. Trask, and that she herself had acted as a catalyst. Perhaps in some dark place of her mind, back beyond memory and below the level of speech, was the false but guilty knowledge that her infant self had somehow killed her mother in the street.

27

THE MOVEMENT OF a car below the window drew my thoughts out of the past. It was Chalmers's black Rolls. He got out and moved rather uncertainly across the courtyard to his house. He unlocked the front door and went in.

"Now you've got me doing it," I said to Betty.

"Doing what?"

"Watching the Chalmers house. They're not all that interesting."

"Maybe not. But they're special people, the kind other people watch."

"Why don't they watch us?"

She entered into my mood. "Because they're more interested in themselves. They couldn't care less about us." She smiled not very cheerfully. "Okay, I get the message. I have to become more interested in myself."

"Or something. What *are* you interested in?"

"History. I've been offered a traveling fellowship. But I felt I was needed here."

"To pursue a career of house-watching."

"You've made your point, Mr. Archer. Don't spoil it now."

I left her and, after putting the letters in the trunk of my car, crossed the street to the Chalmers house. I was having a delayed reaction to the death of Betty's mother, which seemed now to be an integral part of the case. If Chalmers was willing, he might be able to help me understand it.

He came to the door himself. A worried look had lengthened his bony brown face. His tan looked rather sallow, and his eyes were reddish and tired.

"I wasn't expecting to see *you,* Mr. Archer." His tone was polite and neutral. "I understood my wife had severed diplomatic relations."

"We're still talking to each other, I hope. How is Nick doing?"

"Quite well." He went on in a careful voice: "My wife and I have reason to be grateful for your help. I want you to know that. Unfortunately, you were caught in the middle, between Truttwell and Dr. Smitheram. They can't cooperate, and under the circumstances we have to stay with Smitheram."

"The doctor's assuming a great deal of responsibility."

"I suppose he is. But that's not your affair." Chalmers was getting a little edgy. "And I hope you didn't come here to make an attack on Dr. Smitheram. In a situation like this, a man has to lean on someone. We're not islands, you know," he said surprisingly. "We can't bear the weight of these problems all alone."

His angry sorrow bothered me. "I agree with you, Mr. Chalmers. I'd still like to help if I can."

He looked at me suspiciously. "In what way?"

"I'm getting the feeling of the case. I think it started before Nick was born, and that his part in it is fairly innocent. I can't promise to get him off the hook entirely. But I hope to prove that he's a victim, a patsy."

"I'm not sure I understand you," Chalmers said. "But come inside."

He took me into the study where the case had begun. I felt slightly cramped and smothered, as if everything that had happened in the room was still going on, using up space and air. I was struck by the thought that Chalmers, with family history breathing down his neck, may have felt smothered and cramped most of the time.

"Will you have some sherry, old man?"

"No thanks."

"Then neither will I." He turned the swivel chair in front of the desk and sat facing me across the refectory table. "You were going to give me an overview of the situation, I think."

"I'll try, with your help, Mr. Chalmers."

"How can I help? Events have gone quite beyond me." He made a helpless gesture with his hands.

"With your forbearance, then. I've just been talking to Betty Truttwell about her mother's death."

"That was a tragic accident."

"I think it may have been more than an accident. I understood Mrs. Truttwell was your mother's closest friend."

"She was indeed. Mrs. Truttwell was wonderfully kind to my mother in her last days. If I have any criticism at all, it has to do with her failure to tell me how bad things were with Mother. I was still overseas that summer, and I had no idea that Mother was close to death. You can imagine my feelings when my ship came back to the West Coast in mid-July, and I found that both of them were dead." His troubled blue gaze came up to mine. "Now you tell me Mrs. Truttwell's death may not have been an accident."

"I'm raising the question, anyway. The question of accident versus murder isn't crucial, really. When someone is killed in the course of a felony, it's murder under the law, in any case. But I'm beginning to suspect Mrs. Truttwell was intentionally killed. She was your mother's closest friend, she must have known all her secrets."

"My mother had no secrets. The whole community looked up to her."

Chalmers rose angrily, spinning the creaky swivel chair. He took up a stance with his back to me, which reminded me oddly of a stubborn boy. Facing him was the primitive picture that concealed the door of the safe: the sailing ship, the naked Indians, the Spanish soldiers marching in the sky.

"If the Truttwells have been maligning my mother," he said, "I'll sue them for slander."

"Nothing like that happened, Mr. Chalmers. Nothing's been said against your mother by anyone. I'm trying to get at who the people were that broke into the house in 1945."

He turned. "They certainly wouldn't have been known to my mother. Her friends were the best people in California."

"I don't doubt it. But your mother was probably known to the burglars, and they probably knew what was in the house that made it worth breaking into."

"I can answer that," Chalmers said. "My mother kept her money in the house. It was a habit she inherited from my father, along with the money itself. I repeatedly urged her to put it in the bank, but she wouldn't."

"Did the burglars get it?"

"No. The money was intact when I got home from overseas. But Mother was dead. And Mrs. Truttwell, too."

"Was there very much money involved?"

"Quite a sum, yes. Several hundred thousand."

"Where did it come from?"

"I told you: Mother inherited it from my father." He gave me a pale suspicious look, as if I was planning to insult her again. "Are you suggesting the money wasn't hers?"

"Certainly not. Couldn't we forget her for a bit?"

"I can't." He added in a kind of gloomy pride: "I live with the thought of my mother constantly."

I waited, and tried again: "What I'm trying to get at is this. Two burglaries or at least two thefts occurred in this house, in this very room, over twenty-three years apart. I think they were connected."

"In what way?"

"Through the people involved."

Chalmers's eyes were puzzled. He sat down opposite me again. "I'm afraid you've lost me."

"I'm simply trying to say that some of the same people, with the same motives, may have been involved in both these burglaries. We know who did the recent one. It was your son Nick, acting under pressure from a couple of other people, Jean Trask and Sidney Harrow."

Chalmers leaned forward, resting his forehead on his hand. His bald spot gleamed, defenseless as a tonsure.

"Did he kill those people?"

"I doubt it, as you know, but I can't prove he didn't. Yet. Let's stick to the burglaries for now. Nick took a gold box which had your letters in it." I was being careful not to name his mother. "The letters were probably incidental. The gold box was the main thing: Mrs. Trask wanted it. Do you know why?"

"Presumably because she was a thief."

"She didn't think so, though. She was quite open about the box. Apparently, it had belonged to Mrs. Trask's grandmother, and after her grandmother's death it was given to your mother by her grandfather."

Chalmers's head sank lower. The fingers supporting it raked up through his hair. "You're talking about Mr. Rawlinson, aren't you?"

"I'm afraid I am."

"This is infinitely depressing to me," he said. "You're twisting a harmless relationship between an elderly man and a mature woman—"

"Let's forget about the relationship."

"I can't," he said. "I can't forget about it." His head had sunk closer to the table, guarded by his hands and arms.

"I'm not judging anyone, Mr. Chalmers, certainly not your mother. The point is simply that there was a connection between her and Samuel Rawlinson. Rawlinson ran a bank, the Pasadena Occidental, and it was ruined by embezzlement around the time of the burglary. His son-in-law, Eldon Swain, was blamed for the embezzlement, perhaps correctly. But it's been suggested to me that Mr. Rawlinson may have looted his own bank."

Chalmers sat up rigidly. "Who suggested that, for heaven's sake?"

"Another figure in the case—a convicted burglar named Randy Shepherd."

"And you'd take the word of a man like that, and let him blacken my mother's name?"

"Who said anything about your mother?"

"Aren't you about to offer me the precious theory that my mother took stolen money from that whoremaster? Isn't that what you have on your rotten mind?"

Hot wet rage had flooded his eyes. He stood up blinking and swung an open hand at my face. It was a feeble attempt. I caught his arm by the wrist and handed it back to him.

"I'm afraid we can't talk, Mr. Chalmers. I'm sorry."

I went out to my car and turned downhill toward the freeway. Fog still lay in a grey drift across the foot of the town.

28

INLAND IN PASADENA the sun was hot. Children were playing in the road in front of Mrs. Swain's house. Truttwell's Cadillac, which stood at the curb, acted like a magnet on the children.

Truttwell was sitting in the front seat, engrossed in business papers. He glanced up impatiently at me.

"You took your time about getting here."

"Something came up. Also, I can't afford a Cadillac."

"*I* can't afford to waste hours waiting for people. The woman said she'd be here at twelve."

It was twelve thirty by my wristwatch. "Is Mrs. Swain driving from San Diego?"

"I presume so. I'll give her until one o'clock to get here."

"Maybe her car broke down, it's pretty old. I hope nothing's happened to her."

"I'm sure nothing has."

"I wish I could be sure. The leading suspect in her daughter's death was seen in Hemet last night. Apparently, he was heading this way in a stolen car."

"Who are you talking about?"

"Randy Shepherd. He's the ex-con who used to work for Mrs. Swain and her husband."

Truttwell didn't seem much interested. He turned to his papers, and rattled them at me. From what I could see of them, they were Xeroxed copies of the articles of incorporation of something called the Smitheram Foundation.

I asked Truttwell what it was. He didn't answer me, or even look up. Irritated by his bad manners, I went and got the envelope of letters out of the trunk of my car.

"Have I mentioned," I said in a casual voice, "that I recovered the letters?"

"Chalmers's letters? You know very well you haven't. Where did you get hold of them?"

"They were in Nick's apartment."

"I'm not surprised," he said. "Let's have a look at them."

I slid into the front seat beside him and handed him the envelope. He opened it and peered at its contents:

"God, but this brings back the past. Estelle Chalmers lived for these letters, you know. The early ones were nothing much, as I recall. But Larry's epistolary style improved with practice."

"You've read them?"

"Some of them. Estelle gave me no choice. She was so proud of her young hero." His tone was just faintly ironic. "Toward the end, when her sight failed completely, she asked us—my wife and me—to read them aloud to her as they came. We tried to persuade her to hire a nurse-companion, but she refused. Estelle had a very strong sense of privacy, and it got stronger as she got older. The main burden of looking after her fell on my wife." He added in quiet regret: "I shouldn't have let it happen to my young wife."

He fell into a silence, which I finally broke: "What was the matter with Mrs. Chalmers?"

"I believe she had glaucoma."

"She didn't die of glaucoma."

"No. I think she died of grief—grief for my wife. She gave up eating, she gave up everything. I took the liberty of calling a doctor, very much against her wishes. She lay in bed with her face to the wall and wouldn't let the doctor examine her, or even look at her. And she wouldn't let me try to get Larry home from overseas."

"Why not?"

"She claimed to be perfectly well, though obviously she wasn't. She wanted to die alone and unseen, I think. Estelle had been a real beauty, and some of it lasted almost to the end. Also, as she grew older, she became a bit of a miser. You'd be surprised how many older women do. The idea of having a doctor come to the house, or hiring a nurse, seemed like a horrible extravagance to Estelle. Her poor-mouthing actually had me convinced. But of course she'd been quite wealthy all along.

"I'll never forget the day following her funeral. Larry was finally en route home after the usual snafu, and in fact he arrived a couple of days later. But the County Administrator didn't want to wait to check the house and its contents. As a member of the courthouse crowd he'd known Estelle all his life. I think he knew or suspected that she kept her money in the house, as Judge Chalmers had before her. And of course there had been the attempted burglary. If I had been in full possession of my faculties, I'd have checked the safe the morning after the break-in. But I had troubles of my own."

"You mean your wife's death?"

"The loss of my wife was the main disaster, of course. It left me with full responsibility for an infant girl." He looked at me with painful candor. "A responsibility I haven't handled too well."

"The point is that it's over. Betty's grown up. She has to make her own choices."

"But I can't let her marry Nick Chalmers."

"She will if you keep saying that."

Truttwell went into another of his silences. He seemed to be catching up at last with great stretches of lost time. When his eyes changed back to present time, I said:

"Do you have any idea who killed your wife?"

He shook his white head. "The police failed to come up with a single suspect."

"What was the date of her death?"

"July 3, 1945."

"Exactly how did it happen?"

"I'm afraid I don't really know. Estelle Chalmers was the only surviving witness, and she was blind and saw nothing. Apparently my wife noticed something wrong at the Chalmers house and went over there to investigate. The thieves chased her out into the road and ran her down with their car. Actually it wasn't their car—it had been stolen. The police recovered it in the tules below San Diego. There were—physical evidences on the bumper that proved it had been used to murder my wife. The murderers probably escaped over the border."

Truttwell's forehead was shining with sweat. He wiped it with a silk handkerchief.

"I'm afraid I can't tell you anything more about the events of that night. I was in Los Angeles on business. I got home in the small hours and found my wife in the morgue and my little girl being cared for by a policewoman."

His voice broke, and for once I saw through Truttwell's surface into his hidden self. He lived with a grief so central and consuming that it drained the energy from his external life, and made him seem a smaller man than he was, or had once been.

"I'm sorry, Mr. Truttwell. I had to ask you these questions."

"I don't quite see their relevance."

"Neither do I, yet. When I interrupted you, you were telling me about the County Administrator checking the house."

"So I was. As the representative of the Chalmers family I opened the house for him. I also turned over the combination of the safe, which Estelle had given me some time before. It turned out to be stuffed with money, of course."

"How much?"

"I don't recall the exact figure. Certainly it was up in the hundreds of thousands. It took the Administrator most of the day to count it, even though some of the notes were in large denominations, up to ten thousand."

"Where did it all come from, do you know?"

"Her husband probably left her some of it. But Estelle was widowed when she was still quite young, and it's not exactly a secret that there were other men in her life. One or two of them were very successful men. I suppose they gave her money, or told her how to make it."

"And how to avoid taxes on it?"

Truttwell shifted uneasily in the car seat. "It hardly seems necessary to raise that question. All this is far away and long ago."

"It seems here and now to me."

"If you must know," he said impatiently, "the tax issue is dead. I persuaded the government to settle for inheritance taxes on the full amount. They had no way of proving the source of the money."

"The source is what interests me. I understand the Pasadena banker Rawlinson was one of the men in Mrs. Chalmers's life."

"He was, for many years. But that was a long time before her death."

"Not so very," I said. "In one of these letters, written in the fall of 1943, Larry asked to be remembered to him. Which means that his mother was still seeing Rawlinson."

"Really? How did Larry feel about Rawlinson?"

"The letter was noncommittal."

I could have given Truttwell a fuller answer, but I had decided to suppress my interview with Chalmers, at least for the present. I knew that Truttwell wouldn't approve of it.

"What are you getting at, Archer? You're not suggesting that Rawlinson was the source of Mrs. Chalmers's money?"

As if he had pushed a significant button which closed a circuit, the phone began to ring in Mrs. Swain's front room. It rang ten times, and stopped.

"It was your idea," I said.

"But I was speaking generally about the men in Estelle's life. I didn't single out Samuel Rawlinson. As you perfectly well know, he was ruined by the embezzlement."

"His bank was."

Truttwell's face twisted in surprise. "You can't mean he embezzled the money himself."

"The idea has come up."

"Seriously?"

"I hardly know. I got it from Randy Shepherd. It originated with Eldon Swain. Which doesn't help to make it true."

"I should think not. We *know* that Swain ran off with the money."

"We know that he ran off. But the truth isn't always so obvious; in fact, it's usually just as complex as the people who make it. Consider the possibility that Swain took some of the bank's money and Rawlinson caught him at it and took a great deal more. He used Mrs. Chalmers's safe to cache the money, but she died before he could recover it."

Truttwell gave me a look of appalled interest. "You have a tortuous imagination, Archer." But he added: "What was the date of the embezzlement?"

I consulted my black notebook. "July 1, 1945."

"That was just a couple of weeks before Estelle Chalmers died. It rules out the possibility you suggest."

"Does it? Rawlinson didn't know she was going to die. They may have been planning to use the money, go someplace and live together."

"An old man and a blind woman? It's ridiculous!"

"That still doesn't rule it out. People are always doing ridiculous things. Anyway, Rawlinson wasn't so very old in 1945. He was about the age that you are now."

Truttwell flushed. He was self-conscious about his age. "You'd better not mention this wild idea of yours to anyone else. He'd slap a libel suit on you." He turned and gave me another curious look. "You don't think much of bankers, do you?"

"They're no different from anyone else. But you can't help noticing that a high proportion of embezzlers are bankers."

"That's a simple matter of opportunity."

"Exactly."

The phone in Mrs. Swain's house began to ring again. I counted fourteen rings before it stopped. At the moment my sensibility was pretty highly keyed, and I felt as if the house had been trying to say something to me.

It was one o'clock. Truttwell climbed out of the car and began to pace the broken sidewalk. A clownish youngster walked behind him, aping his movements, until Truttwell shooed him away. I got the envelope of letters out of the front seat and locked them in a metal evidence case in the trunk of my car.

When I looked up, Mrs. Swain's old black Volkswagen had entered the little street. It turned onto the strips of concrete that formed her driveway. Some of the children lifted their hands to her and said: "Hi."

Mrs. Swain got out and walked toward us across the brown January grass. She moved awkwardly in her high heels and tight black dress. I introduced her to Truttwell and they shook hands stiffly.

"I'm awfully sorry to keep you waiting," she said. "A policeman came to my son-in-law's house just as I was about to leave. He asked me questions for over an hour."

"What about?" I asked her.

"Several matters. He wanted a full history of Randy Shepherd from the time he was our gardener in San Marino. He seemed to think that Randy might come after me next. But I'm not afraid of Randy, and I don't believe he killed Jean."

"Who do you suspect?" I said.

"My husband is capable of it, if he's alive."

"It's pretty definite that he's dead, Mrs. Swain."

"What happened to the money, if he's dead?" She leaned toward me, both hands out, like a starving beggar.

"Nobody knows."

She shook my arm. "We've got to find the money. I'll give you half if you find it for me."

There was a high shrieking in my head. I thought I was having a bad reaction to poor old Mrs. Swain. Then I realized that the shrieking wasn't in me.

It came from a siren whirling its whip of sound over the city. The sound grew louder but it was still far away and irrelevant.

On the boulevard there was another, nearer, sound of tires shuddering and squealing. An open black Mercury convertible turned into the little street. It skidded wide on the turn and scattered the children like confetti, nearly running some of them down.

The man at the wheel had a beardless face and bright red synthetic-looking hair. In spite of it I recognized Randy Shepherd. And he recognized me. He kept on going past us to the end of the block, and turned north out of sight. At the other end of the block a police car appeared for an instant. Without turning or pausing, it fled on up the boulevard.

I followed Shepherd, but it was a hopeless chase. He was on home territory, and his stolen convertible had more speed than my almost-paid-for car. Once I caught a glimpse of it crossing a bridge far ahead, with Shepherd's bright red hair like artificial fire in the front seat.

29

I FOUND MYSELF in a blind street ending in a barricade. Beyond it a deep ravine opened. I turned off my engine and sat getting my bearings.

At just about my level, a red-tailed hawk was circling over the treetops in the ravine. There were scrub oak and sycamores along the hidden watercourse. I realized after a while that this was the same ravine that cut across Locust Street, where Rawlinson lived. But I was on the other side of it, facing west.

I drove the long way around to Locust Street. The first thing I saw when I entered it was an open black Mercury convertible standing at the curb half a block from Rawlinson's house. The keys were in the ignition. I put them in my pocket.

I let my own car in front of Rawlinson's house and mounted the veranda uneasily, tripping on the broken step. Mrs. Shepherd opened the door with her finger to her lips. Her eyes were deeply troubled.

"Be quiet," she whispered. "Mr. Rawlinson is taking his nap."

"Can I talk to you for a minute?"

"Not right now. I'm busy."

"I've come all the way from Pacific Point."

This information seemed to fascinate her. Without removing her gaze from my face, she closed the front door quietly behind her and stepped out onto the veranda.

"What's going on in Pacific Point?"

It sounded like a routine question, but it probably stood for questions she was afraid to ask in detail. She gave the impression that in her age she had stumbled back into all the desperate uncertainties of youth.

"More of the same," I said. "Trouble for everybody. I think it all started with this."

I showed her the copy of Nick's graduation picture that I'd taken from Sidney Harrow. She shook her head over it:

"I don't know who it would be."

"Are you sure?"

"I'm sure." She added solemnly: "I never saw that young man in my life."

I almost believed her. But she had neglected to ask me who he was.

"His name is Nick Chalmers. This was supposed to be his graduation picture. But Nick won't be graduating."

She didn't say, "Why not?" But her eyes said it.

"Nick's in the hospital recovering from a suicide attempt. The trouble started, as I said, when a man named Sidney Harrow came to town and began hounding Nick. He brought this picture with him."

"Where did he get it?"

"From Randy Shepherd," I said.

Her face had taken on an underlying pallor which made it almost gray. "Why are you telling me these things?"

"You're obviously interested." I went on in the same quiet tone: "Is Randy in the house now?"

Her uncontrolled upward glance probably meant that Shepherd was upstairs. She didn't speak.

"I'm pretty sure he's in there, Mrs. Shepherd. If I were you I wouldn't try to hide him. The police are after him, and they'll be arriving any time now."

"What do they want him for this time?"

"Murder. The murder of Jean Trask."

She moaned. "He didn't tell me."

"Is he armed?"

"He has a knife."

"No gun?"

"I didn't see one." She reached out and touched my chest. "Are you certain Randy gave that picture to the other man—the man who went to the Point?"

"I'm sure now, Mrs. Shepherd."

"Then he can burn in hell." She started down the steps.

"Where are you going?"

"The neighbors' to phone the police."

"I wouldn't do that, Mrs. Shepherd."

"Maybe you wouldn't. But I've suffered enough in my life on his account. I'm not going to jail for him."

"Let me go in and talk to him."

"No. It's *my* neck. And I'm calling the police." She turned away again.

"Don't be in such a hurry. We have to get Mr. Rawlinson out of there first. Where *is* Randy?"

"In the attic. Mr. Rawlinson's in the front parlor."

She went in and helped the old man to walk out. He was limping and yawning, and blinking against the sun. I put him in the front seat of my car and drove him to the barricade at the end of the street. The police used a lot of firepower nowadays.

The old man turned to me impatiently. "I'm afraid I don't understand what we're doing here."

"It would take a long time to explain. Briefly, we're wrapping up the case that started in July 1945."

"When Eldon Swain robbed me blind?"

"If it was Eldon."

Rawlinson turned his head to look at me, the flesh of his neck twisting in stringy folds. "Is there some doubt that Eldon was responsible?"

"The question has been raised."

"Nonsense. He was the cashier. Who else could have embezzled all that money?"

"You could have, Mr. Rawlinson."

His eyes grew small and bright in their nests of wrinkles. "You must be joking."

"No. I admit the question is partly hypothetical."

"And pretty damn insulting," he said without much real heat. "Do I look like the kind of man who would ruin his own bank?"

"Not unless you had a powerful reason."

"What possible reason could I have?"

"A woman."

"What woman?"

"Estelle Chalmers. She died rich."

He manufactured a quick small rage. "You're throwing dirt on the memory of a fine woman."

"I don't think so."

"I do. If you persist in following this line, I refuse to talk with you." He made a move to get out of my car.

"You better stay here, Mr. Rawlinson. Your house isn't safe. Randy Shepherd's in the attic, and the police will be here soon."

"Is this Mrs. Shepherd's doing? Did she let him in?"

"He probably didn't give her any choice." I brought out my picture of Nick again, and showed it to Rawlinson. "Do you know who this is?"

He took the picture in his swollen arthritic fingers. "I'm afraid I don't know his name. I could guess who the boy is, but you don't want that."

"Go ahead and guess."

"It's someone near and dear to Mrs. Shepherd. I saw this in her room early last week. Then it disappeared, and she blamed me for it."

"She should have blamed Randy Shepherd. He was the one who took it." I lifted the picture out of his hands and replaced it in the inside pocket of my jacket.

"That's what she gets for letting him into my house!" His eyes were moist, leaking away his old-man's anger. "The police are coming, you say. What's Randy been up to now?"

"He's wanted for murder, Mr. Rawlinson. The murder of your granddaughter Jean."

He made no response, except that he sank a little lower in the seat. I felt sorry for the man. He had had everything and bit by bit lost nearly all of it. Now he had outlived his own granddaughter.

I looked out over the ravine, hoping to lose my borrowed pain in its deep green spaces. The red-tailed hawk I had seen from the other side was visible from this side, too. He turned, and his ruddy wedge of tail flashed in the sun.

"You knew about Jean, Mr. Rawlinson?"

"Yes. My daughter Louise phoned me yesterday. But she didn't say that Shepherd was responsible."

"I don't think he is."

"Then what is this all about?"

"The police think he is."

Almost as if he could hear us talking about him, Randy Shepherd appeared at the side of Rawlinson's house and looked in our direction. He was wearing a wide-brimmed Panama hat with a striped band, and a moth-eaten tan polo coat.

"Hold on there, that's my hat!" Rawlinson cried. "By God, that's my coat, too!"

He started to get out of the car. I told him to stay where he was, in a tone which he obeyed.

Shepherd sauntered up the street like a gentleman out for a stroll. Then he scampered across to the black convertible, holding the loose hat on his head with one hand. He sat in the car for a frantic minute, looking for the keys, then got out and headed for the parkway.

By this time the sirens were rising in the distance, curdling the daylight at the edges. Shepherd stopped dead and stood perfectly still in a listening attitude. He turned and started back in our direction, pausing for an instant at the Rawlinson house as if he was thinking of going back in.

Mrs. Shepherd came out on the front porch. By this time two patrol cars were in the street and rolling toward Shepherd. He looked at them over his shoulder, and all around at the long Victorian faces of the houses. Then he ran in my direction. His Panama hat flew off. His coat billowed out behind.

I got out of the car to head him off. It was an unconsidered reflex. The patrol cars stopped abruptly, ejecting four policemen who began to fire their revolvers at Shepherd.

He went down flat on his face and slid a little. Then splashes on the back of his neck and down the back of his light coat were darker and realer than his slipping red wig.

A bullet ripped into my shoulder. I fell sideways against the open door of my car. Then I lay down and pretended to be as dead as Shepherd was.

30

I ENDED UP high on pentothal in a Pasadena hospital room. A surgeon had had to dig for the slug, and my arm and shoulder would be immobilized for some time.

Fortunately, it was the left shoulder. This was pointed out more than once by the police and D.A.'s men who came to visit me late that afternoon. The police apologized for the incident, while managing to suggest at the same time that I had collided with the bullet, not it with me. They offered to do what they could for me, and agreed at my suggestion to have my car brought to the hospital parking lot.

Still, their visit made me angry and concerned. I felt as if my case had run away and left me lying. I had a bedside phone, and I used it to make a call to Truttwell's house. The housekeeper said he wasn't at home, and neither was Betty. I put in a call to Truttwell's office and left my name and number with his answering service.

Later, as night was coming on, I got out of bed and opened the door of the closet. I was feeling a little lightheaded but I was worried about my black notebook. My jacket was hanging in the closet with my other clothes and in spite of the blood and the bullet hole the notebook was in the pocket where I'd put it. So was Nick's picture.

As I was on my way back to bed the floor tilted up and smacked me on the right side of the face. I blacked out for a while. Then I sat up with my back against a leg of the bed.

The night nurse looked in. She was pretty and dedicated and wore a Los Angeles General cap. Her name was Miss Cowan.

"What in the world are you doing?"

"Sitting on the floor."

"You can't do *that.*" She helped me to get to my feet and into bed. "I hope you weren't trying to get out of here."

"No, but it's a good idea. When do you think I'll be sprung?"

"It's up to the doctor. He may be able to tell you in the morning. Now do you feel up to a visitor?"

"It depends on who it is."

"She's an elderly woman. Her name is Shepherd. Is that the same Shepherd—?" Delicately, she left the question unfinished.

"Same Shepherd." My pentothal high had changed to a pentothal low, but I told the nurse to send the woman in.

"You're not afraid she'll try to pull something on you?"

"No. She's not the type."

Miss Cowan went away. Shortly afterwards, Mrs. Shepherd came in. Gray pallor seemed to have become her permanent color. Her dark eyes were very large, as if they had been distended by the events they'd witnessed.

"I'm sorry you were injured, Mr. Archer."

"I'll survive. It's too bad about Randy."

"Shepherd was no loss to anybody," she said. "I just finished telling that to the police and now I'm telling you. He was a bad husband and a bad father, and he came to a bad end."

"That's a lot of badness."

"I know whereof I speak." Her voice was solemn. "Whether he killed Miss Jean or not, I know what Shepherd did to his own daughter. He ruined her life and drove her to her death."

"Is Rita dead?"

My use of the name stopped her. "How do you know my daughter's name?"

"Somebody mentioned it. Mrs. Swain, I think."

"Mrs. Swain was no friend of Rita's. She blamed my daughter for everything that happened. It wasn't fair. Rita was beneath the age of consent when Mr. Swain got interested in her. And her own father pandered to Mr. Swain and took money from him for her."

The words came pouring out of her under pressure, as if Shepherd's death had opened a deep volcanic fissure in her life.

"Did Rita go to Mexico with Swain?"

"Yes."

"And died there?"

"Yes. She died there."

"How do you know that, Mrs. Shepherd?"

"Mr. Swain told me himself. Shepherd brought him to see me when he came back from Mexico. He said she died and was buried in Guadalajara."

"Did she leave any children?"

Her dark eyes wavered and then held firm, meeting mine. "No. I have no grandchildren of any kind."

"Who's the boy in the picture?"

"The picture?" she said with a show of puzzlement.

"If you want to refresh your memory, it's in my jacket in the closet."

She glanced at the closet door. I said:

"I mean the one Randy Shepherd stole from your room."

Her puzzlement became real. "How do you know that? How come you're digging so deep in my family affairs?"

"You know why, Mrs. Shepherd. I'm trying to wrap up a case that started nearly a quarter of a century ago. On July 1, 1945."

She blinked. Apart from this tiny movement of her eyelids, her face had recovered its immobility. "That was the date that Mr. Swain robbed Mr. Rawlinson's bank."

"Is that what really happened?"

"What other story did you hear?"

"I've found a few bits and pieces of evidence pointing another way. And I'm beginning to wonder if Eldon Swain ever got the money."

"Who else could have taken it?"

"Your daughter Rita, for one."

She reacted angrily, but not as angrily as she should have. "Rita was sixteen years old in 1945. Children don't plan bank robberies. You *know* it had to be somebody in the bank."

"Like Mr. Rawlinson?"

"That's just plain silly, and you know it."

"I thought I'd try it on you."

"You'll have to try harder than that. I don't know why you're straining so hard to make Mr. Swain into a whited sepulchre. I know he took that money, and I know Mr. Rawlinson didn't. Why, the poor man lost everything. He's lived from hand to mouth ever since."

"On what?"

She answered quietly: "He has a little pension, and I have my savings. For a long time I worked as a nurse's aide. That helped to keep him going."

What she said sounded like the truth. Anyway, I couldn't help believing her.

Mrs. Shepherd was looking at me more kindly, as if she sensed a change in our relations. Very gently, she touched my bandaged shoulder with her fingers. "Poor man, you need a rest. You oughtn't to be troubling your head with all these questions. Aren't you tired?"

I admitted that I was.

"Then why don't you get some sleep?" Her voice was soporific. She laid her palm on my forehead. "I'll stay in the room and watch for a while if you don't mind. I like the smell of hospitals. I used to work in this very hospital."

She sat down in the armchair between the closet and the window. The imitation-leather cushions creaked under her weight.

I closed my eyes and slowed down my breathing. But I was very far from going to sleep. I lay and listened to Mrs. Shepherd. She was completely still. Sounds drifted in through the window: the sounds of cars, a mockingbird tuning up for a night song. He kept postponing his song until the sense of something about to happen had screwed my nerves up tight.

The imitation-leather cushions of the chair emitted a tiny noise. There was the faintest possible sibilance from Mrs. Shepherd's feet sliding across the composition floor, the rattle of a doorknob, the paired whispers of a door opening and closing.

I opened my eyes. Mrs. Shepherd wasn't visible. Apparently she had shut herself up in the closet. Then its door began to open slowly again. She came out sideways, and held the picture of Nick up to the light. Her face was full of love and longing.

She glanced at me, and saw that my eyes were open. But she thrust the picture under her coat and left the room quietly, without a word.

I didn't say anything to her, or do anything. After all, it was her picture.

I turned out the light and lay listening to the mockingbird. He was singing all-out now, and still singing when I went to sleep. I dreamed that I was Nick and that Mrs. Shepherd was my grandmother who used to live with birds in the garden in Contra Costa County.

31

IN THE MORNING, as I was eating a poached egg on a damp piece of toast, the resident surgeon came in.

"How are you feeling?"

"Fine," I lied. "But I'll never build up my strength on this kind of rations. When can I get out of here?"

"Don't be in such a hurry. I'm going to have to ask you to take it easy for at least a week."

"I can't stay here for a week."

"I didn't say you had to. You're going to have to look after yourself, though. Regular hours, mild exercise followed by rest, no rough stuff."

"Sure," I said.

I rested very carefully all morning. Truttwell failed to return my call, and the waiting began to get in the way of the resting and finally displaced it.

Shortly before noon I called his office again. The switchboard girl informed me that he wasn't there.

"*Really* not there?"

"Really. I don't know where he is."

I did some more resting and waiting. A Pasadena motorcycle officer brought me the keys to my car and told me where to find it in the hospital parking lot. I took this as an omen.

After an early lunch I got out of bed and to a certain extent put on my clothes. By the time I had on underwear, trousers, and shoes I was wet and shaking. I sort of draped my bloody shirt over my chest and shoulders and covered it with my jacket.

In the corridor, the nurses and nurses' aides were still busy with lunch. I crossed the corridor to a gray metal door that opened on the fire stairs and walked down three stories to the ground floor.

A side exit let me out into the parking lot. I found my car and got in and sat for a while. Mild exercise followed by rest.

The freeway was crowded and slow. Even with all the concentration I was giving it, my driving wasn't too good. My attention kept slipping away from the traffic I was moving in. Once I had to burn rubber to avoid running into the rear end of another car.

I'd originally intended to drive to Pacific Point. I barely made it to West Los Angeles. In the last block of the trip, on my home street, I caught a glimpse in the rear-view mirror of a bearded man carrying a bedroll. But when I turned to look at him directly he wasn't there.

I left my car at the curb and climbed the outside stairs to my apartment. The phone started to ring, like an aural boobytrap, just as I opened the door. I picked it up and carried it to my armchair.

"Mr. Archer? This is Helen at the answering service. You've had a couple of urgent calls, from a Mr. Truttwell and a Miss Truttwell. I've been ringing your office."

I looked at the electric clock. It was just two o'clock. Helen gave me the number of Truttwell's office, and the less familiar number his daughter had left.

"Anything else?"

"Yes, but there must be some mistake about this call, Mr. Archer. A hospital in Pasadena claims that you owe them a hundred and seventy dollars. That includes the cost of the operating room, they said."

"It's no mistake. If they call again, tell them I'm putting a check in the mail."

"Yessir."

I got out my checkbook and looked at the balance and decided to call Truttwell first. Before I did, I went out to the kitchen and put a frozen steak in the gas broiler. I tasted the milk in the refrigerator, found that it was still sweet, and drank half of the remaining quart. I wanted a shot of whisky as a chaser, but it was exactly what I didn't need.

My call to Truttwell's office was taken by a junior member of the firm named Eddie Sutherland. Truttwell wasn't in at the moment, he said, but he had set up an appointment for me at four thirty. It was very important that I should be there, though Sutherland didn't seem to know why.

I remembered as I was dialing the number Betty had left that it belonged to the phone in Nick's apartment.

Betty answered. "Hello?"

"This is Archer speaking."

She drew in her breath. "I've been trying to get you all day."

"Is Nick with you?"

"No. I only wish he were. I'm very concerned about him. I went to San Diego yesterday afternoon to try and see him. They wouldn't let me into his room."

"Who wouldn't?"

"The guard on the door, backed up by Dr. Smitheram. They seemed to think I was spying for my father. I did manage to get a glimpse of Nick, and let him see me. He asked me to get him out. He said they were holding him against his will."

" 'They'?"

"I think he meant Dr. Smitheram. Anyway, it was Dr. Smitheram who ordered him to be moved last night."

"Moved where?"

"I don't know for certain, Mr. Archer. I think they're holding him prisoner in the Smitheram Clinic. That's where the ambulance took him."

"And you seriously believe that he's a prisoner?"

"I don't know what I believe. But I'm afraid. Will you help me?"

I said that she would have to help me first, since I wasn't up to driving. She agreed to pick me up in an hour.

I went out to the kitchen and turned my steak. It was hot and sizzling on one side, frozen solid on the other, like schizophrenic people I had known. I wondered just how crazy Nick Chalmers was.

The immediate problem was clothes. My not very extensive wardrobe included a stretchable nylon shirt that I managed to get into without putting the left arm in the armhole. I completed my costume with a soft cardigan jacket.

By this time my schizoid steak was brown on both sides and red in the center. It bled on the plate when I stabbed it. I let it cool and ate it with my fingers.

I finished the quart of milk. Then I went back to the armchair in the front room and rested. For just about the first time in my life I knew how it must feel to get old. My body was demanding special privileges and offering not much in return.

The yelp of Betty's horn brought me out of a half-sleep. She gave me a hard look as I climbed rather awkwardly into her car.

"Are you sick, Mr. Archer?"

"Not exactly. I took a slug in the shoulder."

"Why didn't you tell me?"

"You mightn't have come. I want to be in at the end of this thing."

"Even if it kills you?"

"It won't."

If I was looking worse, she was looking better. She had decided after all not to be a gnome who lived in the gray underground.

"Who on earth shot you?"

"A Pasadena cop. He was aiming at another man. I got in the way. Didn't your father tell you any of this?"

"I haven't seen my father since yesterday." She spoke these words rather formally, as if they constituted an announcement.

"Are you leaving home?"

"Yes, I am. Father said I had to choose between him and Nick."

"I'm sure he didn't mean it."

"Yes, he did."

She made her engine roar. At the last moment I remembered that Chalmers's war letters were still in the trunk of my ear. I went back to get them, and looked over the top ones again as Betty drove me to the freeway.

The heading of the second letter stopped me:

Lt. (j.g.) L. Chalmers
USS Sorrel Bay (CVE 185)
March 15, 1945

I turned to Betty. "You mentioned Nick's birthday the other day. Didn't you say it was in December?"

"December 14," she said.

"And what year was he born?"

"Nineteen forty-five. He was twenty-three last month. Is it important?"

"It could be. Did Nick rearrange these letters, with certain ones up front and out of chronological order?"

"He may have. I think he had been reading them. Why?"

"Mr. Chalmers wrote a letter at sea in the forward area, dated March 15, 1945."

"I'm not too good at arithmetic, especially when I'm driving. Is it nine months from March 15 to December 14?"

"Exactly."

"Isn't that strange? Nick always suspected that his fa—that Mr. Chalmers wasn't his real father. He used to think he was adopted."

"Maybe he was."

I put the three top letters in my wallet. The girl turned up the on-ramp to the freeway. She drove with angry speed under a brown firmament of smog.

32

SOUTHWARD ALONG THE coast it was a bright, windy day. From the mesa above Pacific Point I could see occasional whitecaps on the water, and a few sails leaning far over.

Betty took me directly to the Smitheram Clinic. The well-groomed, rather formal young woman who presided over the reception desk said that Dr. Smitheram was with a patient and couldn't possibly see us. He would be with patients all the rest of the day, including the evening.

"What about a week from Tuesday at midnight?"

The young woman looked me over disapprovingly. "Are you sure you don't want the emergency ward at the hospital?"

"I'm sure. Is Nicholas Chalmers a patient here?"

"I'm not authorized to answer questions like that."

"Can I see Mrs. Smitheram?"

The young woman didn't answer for a while. She pretended to be busy with her papers. Finally she said:

"I'll see. What did you say your name was, again?"

I told her. She opened an inner door. Before she closed it behind her, I heard a flash of noise that made the back of my neck bristle. It was a high yell; someone crying out wordlessly in pain and desolation.

Betty and I looked at each other. "That may be Nick," she said. "What are they doing to him?"

"Nothing. You shouldn't be here."

"Where should I be?"

"At home reading a book."

"Dostoevsky?" she said sharply.

"Something lighter than that."

"Like *Little Women*? I'm afraid you don't understand me, Mr. Archer. You're fatherizing again."

"You're daughterizing."

Moira and the receptionist opened the inner door and came out unaccompanied by any sound. Moira gave me a look of surprise and Betty a more complex look which seemed to combine both envy and contempt. Betty was younger, Moira's look seemed to say, but she herself had survived longer.

She moved toward me. "What on earth's been happening, Mr. Archer?"

"I was accidentally shot, if you mean this." I touched my left arm. "Is Nick Chalmers here?"

"Yes. He is."

"Was that him yelling?"

"Yelling? I don't believe so." She was flustered. "We have several patients in the closed wing. Nick isn't one of the more disturbed ones."

"Then you won't object if we see him. Miss Truttwell is his fiancée—"

"I know that."

"—and she's quite concerned about him."

"There's no need to feel that way." But she herself seemed deeply concerned. "I'm sorry I can't let you see him. Dr. Smitheram makes these decisions. He evidently thinks that Nick needs seclusion."

Her mouth twisted sideways. The strain of keeping up her public face and voice was telling on Moira.

"Could we discuss this in private, Mrs. Smitheram?"

"Yes. Come into my office, please."

The invitation excluded Betty. I followed Moira into an office which was partly sitting room and partly file room. The room was windowless but hung with abstract paintings, like inward windows replacing the outward ones. Moira closed the door and locked it and stood against it.

"Am I your prisoner?" I said.

She answered without trying to be light: "I'm the prisoner. I wish I could get out of this." A slight upward movement of her hands and shoulders suggested the almost insupportable weight of the building. "But I can't."

"Won't your husband let you?"

"It's a little more complicated than that. I'm the prisoner of all my past mistakes—I'm feeling sententious today—and Ralph is one of them. You're a more recent one."

"What did I do wrong?"

"Nothing. I thought you liked me, is all." She had dropped her public face and voice entirely. "I acted on that assumption the other night."

"So did I. It was a true assumption."

"Then why are you giving me a bad time?"

"I didn't mean to. But we seem to be ending up on different sides."

She shook her head. "I don't believe it. All I want is a decent life, a possible life, for the people concerned." She added: "Including me."

"What does your husband want?"

"The same thing, according to his lights. We don't agree about everything, of course. And I made the mistake of going along with all his large ideas." Once again the movement of her arms referred to the entire building. "As if we could save our marriage by giving birth to a clinic." She added wryly: "We should have rented one."

She was a complex woman, spinning off ambiguities, talking too much. I moved solidly against her, held her not very masterfully with one arm, and silenced her mouth.

The wound in my shoulder was beating like an auxiliary heart.

As if she could sense the pain directly, Moira said:

"I'm sorry you're hurt."

"I'm sorry *you're* hurt, Moira."

"Don't waste your sympathy on me." Her tone reminded me that she was or had been a kind of nurse. "I'll survive. But it isn't going to be much fun, I'm afraid."

"You're losing me again. What are we talking about?"

"Disaster. I can feel it in my bones. I'm partly Irish, you know."

"Disaster for Nick Chalmers?"

"For all of us. He's part of it, of course."

"Why don't you let me take him out of here?"

"I can't."

"Is his life in danger?"

"Not as long as he stays here."

"Will you let me see him?"

"I can't. My husband won't allow it."

"Are you afraid of him?"

"No. But he's a doctor and I'm just a technician. I simply can't second-guess him."

"How long is he proposing to keep Nick here?"

"Until the danger is over."

"Who's the source of the danger?"

"I can't tell you that. Please don't ask any more questions, Lew. The questions spoil everything."

We stood and held each other for a while, leaning against the locked door. The warmth of her body and her mouth revived me, even though our minds were at odds and part of my mind was keeping track of the time.

She said in a low voice, "I wish we could walk out of here this minute, you and I, and never come back."

"You have a marriage."

"It isn't going to last."

"On account of me?"

"Of course not. Will you promise me one thing, though?"

"After I know what it is."

"Don't tell anyone about Sonny. You know, my little La Jolla postal clerk. I made a mistake in talking about him to you."

"Has Sonny cropped up again?"

She nodded. Her eyes were somber. "You won't tell anyone, will you?"

"I have no reason to."

I was hedging a little, and she sensed this. "Lew? I know you're a powerful man, and a very one-way man. Promise me you won't do anything to us. Give Ralph and me a chance to work this thing out."

I stepped away from her. "I can't make a blind commitment. And you're not being clear, as you bloody well know."

She made an anguished monkey-face which wiped out her good looks. "I can't be clear. This is a problem that won't be solved by talking. There are too many people involved, and too many years of life."

"Who are the people involved?"

"Ralph and I and the Chalmerses and the Truttwells—"

"And Sonny?"

"Yes. He's in it." The focus of her eyes shifted to something beyond my knowledge. "That's why you mustn't tell anyone what I told you."

"Why did you tell me?"

"I thought you might be able to advise me, that we might become better friends than we have."

"Give it more time."

"That's what I'm asking you for."

33

BETTY WAS WAITING impatiently in the parking lot. Her gaze narrowed on the lower part of my face.

"There's lipstick on you. Wait." She got a piece of tissue out of her bag and dabbed at me quite hard. "There. That looks better."

In her car, she spoke to me in a neutral voice: "Are you having an affair with Mrs. Smitheram?"

"We're friends."

She said in the same neutral tone: "No wonder I can't trust anybody, or do anything for Nick." She turned to me: "If you're such a good friend of Mrs. Smitheram's, why won't she let me see Nick?"

"Her husband is the doctor. She's only a technician, she says."

"Why won't her husband let him go?"

"They're holding Nick for his protection. Against what or who isn't clear, but I agree he needs protection. It shouldn't be handled entirely by his doctor, though. He needs legal counsel."

"If you're trying to bring my father into this—" Her knuckles struck the wheel of her car in a sharp blow that must have hurt her.

"He is in it, Betty. There's not much use arguing about it. And you're not really helping Nick by turning against your father."

"He's the one who turned against *us*—against Nick and me."

"Maybe so. But we need his help."

"*I* don't," she said loudly and indecisively.

"Anyway, I need yours. Will you drive me to his office?"

"All right. But I'm not going in."

She took me to the parking lot behind her father's building. A polished black Rolls was standing in one of the Reserved slots.

"That's the Chalmerses' car," Betty said. "I thought they'd had a falling-out with father."

"Maybe they're falling back in. What time is it?"

She looked at her wristwatch. "Four thirty-five. I'll wait out here for you."

I was interested in the Rolls. I went and looked it over, admiring its deep leather upholstery and walnut trim. The whole car was immaculate, except for a yellow spillage on a plaid traveling rug in the back seat. It looked like a dried froth of vomit.

I scraped some of it up with the edge of a plastic credit card. When I looked up a thin man in a dark suit and a chauffeur's cap was coming toward me across the parking lot. It was the Chalmerses' houseman, Emilio.

"Get away from that car," he said.

"All right."

I slammed the rear door of the Rolls and stepped away from it. Emilio's black eyes focused on the card in my hand. He made a grab for it. I pulled it out of his reach.

"Give me that."

"The hell I will. Who's been sick in the car, Emilio?"

The question worried him. I asked it again. His anger evaporated suddenly. He turned away from me and climbed in behind the wheel of the Rolls, raising the automatic window on my side.

"What was all that about?" Betty said as we walked away.

"I'm not sure. What kind of a character is he?"

"Emilio? He's pretty dour."

"Is he honest?"

"He must be. He's been with the Chalmerses for over twenty years."

"What sort of life does he lead?"

"A very quiet bachelor life, I believe. But I'm no great authority on Emilio. What's that yellow stuff on the card?"

"That's a good question. Do you have an envelope?"

"No. But I'll get one."

She entered the building through the back door and came out right away with one of her father's business envelopes. I put my findings in it, with her help, sealed and initialed it.

"What laboratory does your father use?"

"Barnard's. It's between here and the courthouse."

I handed her the envelope. "I want this tested for chloral hydrate and Nembutal. They're fairly simple tests, I believe, and they can be done right now if you tell them your father says it's urgent. And tell them to take good care of the sample, will you?"

"Yes sir."

"Will you bring me the results? I'll probably still be in your father's office. You can wear a disguise or something."

She refused to smile. But she trotted dutifully away on the errand. I could feel new adrenalin in my own veins, making me feel stronger and more aggressive. If my hunch was good, the froth of vomit in the envelope could break the case.

I went into Truttwell's building and started along the corridor to the waiting room at the front. I was stopped at an open door by Truttwell's voice:

"Archer? I'd just about given up on you."

He drew me into his law library, which was completely lined with shelves of reference books. A young man in an Ivy League suit was working over a film projector. A screen had already been set up at the far end of the room.

Truttwell surveyed me with not very sympathetic eyes. "Where have you been?"

I told him, and dropped the subject. "I gather you bought Mrs. Swain's home movies."

"No money changed hands," he said with satisfaction. "I persuaded Mrs. Swain it was her duty to serve the truth. Also I let her keep the Florentine box, which was her mother's. In return she gave me some film. Unfortunately, the reel I'm about to show you is nearly twenty-six years old and in rather poor condition. It broke as I was running it through just now." He turned to the young man at the projector. "How are you doing, Eddie?"

"I'm splicing it. It should be ready in a minute."

Truttwell said to me: "Do me a favor, Archer. Irene Chalmers is in the waiting room."

"Is she back in the fold?"

"She will be," he said with a glint of teeth. "At the moment she's here rather against her will. Just go and make sure she doesn't run away."

"What are you planning to spring on her?"

"You'll see."

"That her maiden name was really Rita Shepherd?"

Truttwell's satisfied look fell apart. A kind of rivalry had been growing between us, perhaps rising from the fact that Betty had trusted me.

"How long have you known that?" he said in a prosecutor's voice.

"About five seconds. I've suspected it since last night." It wouldn't have been a good idea to tell him that the idea had come to me in a dream about my grandmother.

As I moved along the corridor, the dream came back into my mind and blunted my aggression. Mrs. Shepherd merged with the memories of my grandmother long since buried in Martinez. The passion with which Mrs. Shepherd had guarded her daughter's secret gave it some value.

Irene Chalmers lifted her face to me as I entered the waiting room. She didn't seem to know me right away. The switchboard girl spoke to me in a whisper, like someone speaking in the presence of illness or mental retardation:

"I didn't think you were going to make it. Mr. Truttwell is in the library. He said to send you right in."

"I've just been talking to him."

"I see."

I sat next to Irene Chalmers. She turned and looked at me with slow recognition, almost like a woman coming awake from a dream. As if the dream had been frightening, her mood was apologetic and subdued:

"I'm sorry, my mind's been wandering. You're Mr. Archer. But I thought you weren't with us any more."

"I'm still on the case, Mrs. Chalmers. By the way, I've recovered your husband's letters."

She said without much interest: "Do you have them with you?"

"Just a few of them. I'll return them through Mr. Truttwell."

"But he isn't our lawyer any longer."

"I'm sure you can trust him to give you the letters, anyway."

"I don't know." She looked around the little room with a kind of primitive suspicion. "We all used to be the best of friends. But we aren't any more."

"On account of Nick and Betty?"

"I guess that was the last straw," she said. "But we had our real trouble some time ago, over money. It always seems to be over money, doesn't it? Sometimes I almost wish I was poor again."

"You say you had trouble over money?"

"Yes, when Larry and I set up the Smitheram Foundation. John Truttwell refused to draw the papers for us. He said we were being taken by Dr. Smitheram, setting him up in a free clinic. But Larry wanted to do it, and I thought it was a nice idea myself. I don't know where we'd be without Dr. Smitheram."

"He's done a lot for you, has he?"

"You know he has. He saved Nick from—you know what. I think John Truttwell is jealous of Dr. Smitheram. Anyway, he isn't our friend any more. I only came here this afternoon because he threatened me."

I wanted to ask her what she meant, but the girl at the switchboard was listening openly. I said to the girl:

"Go and ask Mr. Truttwell if he's ready for us, please."

Unwillingly, she went. I turned back to Mrs. Chalmers.

"What did he threaten you with?"

She didn't respond defensively. She was acting as if a numbing blow had knocked all discretion out of her:

"It was Nick again. Truttwell went to San Diego today and dug up some new dirt. I don't think I should tell you what it was."

"Did it have to do with Nick's birth?"

"He told you, then."

"No, but I read some of your husband's letters. Apparently he was overseas when Nick was conceived. Is that true, Mrs. Chalmers?"

She looked at me in confusion and then with hard disdain. "You have no right to ask me that. You're trying to strip me naked, aren't you?"

Even in her anger there was an ambiguous erotic underplay, which seemed to ask for my complicity. I offered her a smile which felt strange from inside.

The switchboard girl came back and said that Mr. Truttwell was waiting for us. We found him alone in the library, standing behind the projector.

Irene Chalmers reacted to the machine as if it was a complex weapon pointed at her. Her fearful gaze moved from Truttwell to me, standing between her and the door. I closed the door. Her face and body froze.

"You didn't say anything about movies," she complained to Truttwell. "You said you wanted to review the case with me."

He answered smoothly, very much in command of the situation. "This film is a part of the case. It was taken at a swimming party in San Marino in the summer of 1943. Eldon Swain, who gave the party, shot most of it himself. The bit at the end, where he appears, was taken by Mrs. Swain."

"Have you talked to Mrs. Swain?"

"Somewhat. Frankly, I'm much more interested in your reaction." He tapped the back of an armchair near the projector. "Come and sit down and be comfortable, Irene."

She remained stubbornly unmoving. Truttwell approached her smiling and took her arm. She moved slowly and heavily like a statue thawing reluctantly into flesh.

He settled her in the armchair, leaning over her from behind, withdrawing his hands lingeringly from her upper arms.

"Turn off the lights, will you, Archer?"

I flicked the switch and sat down beside Irene Chalmers. The projector whirred. Its quiet shotgun blast of light filled the screen with images. A large rectangular pool with a diving board and a slide reflected a blue old-fashioned sky.

A young blond girl with a mature figure and an immature face climbed onto the diving board. She waved at the camera, bounced excessively, and did a comic dive with her legs apart and kicking like a frog's. She came up with a mouthful of water and spurted it at the camera. Jean Trask, young.

Irene Chalmers, née Rita Shepherd, was next on the diving board. She walked to the end of it gravely, as if the eye of the camera was judging her. The black rubber helmet in which her hair was hidden made her look oddly archaic.

She stood for quite a while with the camera on her, not once returning its stare. Then she bounced and did a swan dive, cutting the water without much splash. It wasn't until she disappeared from sight that I realized how beautiful she had been.

The camera caught her coming up, and she smiled and turned onto her back directly under it. Jean came up behind and ducked her, shouting or laughing, splashing water at the camera with her hands.

A third young person, a boy of eighteen or so whom I didn't immediately recognize, climbed up onto the board. Slowly, he walked to the forward end, with many backward looks, as if there were pirates behind him. There was one. Jean rushed him and shoved him into the water, laughing or shouting. He came up floundering, his eyes closed. A woman wearing a wide-brimmed hat held out a padded hook to him at the end of a long pole. She used it to tow him to the shallow end. He stood there, in water up to his waist, with his narrow back turned to the camera. His rescuer took off her floppy hat and bowed toward unseen spectators.

The woman was Mrs. Swain, but Swain's camera failed to linger on her. It shifted to the spectators, a handsome older couple who were sitting together on a shaded swing. In spite of the shadow falling across him, I recognized Samuel Rawlinson and guessed that the woman beside him was Estelle Chalmers. The camera moved again before I had a chance to study her thin, passionate face.

Rita and Jean went down the slide, singly and together. They raced the length of the pool, with Jean coming out ahead. She splashed the hydrophobic boy still standing as if rooted in waist-deep water. Then she splashed Rita.

I caught a fuzzy background glimpse of Randy Shepherd, redheaded and red-bearded in gardener's dungarees, looking over a hedge at his daughter taking her place in the sun. I glanced sideways at Irene Chalmers's face, which was fitfully lit by the flickering inexact colors reflected from the screen. She looked as if she were dying under the soft bombardment of the past.

When my eyes returned to the screen, Eldon Swain was on the diving board. He was a man of middle size with a large handsome head. He bounced and did a swan dive. The camera met him coming up and followed him back onto the diving board. He performed flips, front and back.

Next came a double dive with Jean on his shoulders, and finally a double dive with Rita. As if controlled by a documentary interest, the camera followed the pair as Rita stood spraddled on the diving board, and Eldon Swain inserted his head between her legs and lifted her. Tottering slightly, he carried her out to the end of the board and stood for a long moment with his head projecting from between her thighs like the head of a giant smiling baby being born again.

The two fell off the board together and stayed underwater for what seemed a long time. The eye of the camera looked for them but caught only sparkling surfaces netted with light and underlaid by colored shadows dissolving in the water.

34

AFTER THE REEL ended, none of us spoke for a while. I turned on the lights. Irene Chalmers stirred and roused herself. I could sense her fear, so powerful it seemed to make her drowsy.

She said in an effort to throw it off: "I was pretty in those days, wasn't I?"

"More than pretty," Truttwell said. "The word is beautiful."

"A lot of good it ever did me." Her voice and language were changing, as if she was falling back on her earlier self. "Where did you get this movie—from Mrs. Swain?"

"Yes. She gave me others."

"She would. She's always hated me."

"Because you took up with her husband?" I said.

"She hated me long before that. It was almost as if she knew it was going to happen. Or maybe she *made* it happen, I don't know. She sat around and watched Eldon, waiting for him to jump. If you do that to a man, sooner or later he's going to jump."

"What made you jump?" I said.

"We won't talk about me." She looked at me and then at Truttwell and then at nothing. "I'm taking the fifth."

Truttwell moved closer to her, gentle and suave as a lover. "Don't be foolish, Irene. You're among friends here."

"I bet."

"It's true," he said. "I went to enormous trouble, and so did Mr. Archer, to get hold of this evidence, get it out of the hands of potential enemies. In my hands it can't be used against you. I think I can guarantee it never will be."

She sat up straight, meeting him eye to eye. "What is this? Blackmail?"

Truttwell smiled. "You're getting me confused with Dr. Smitheram, I'm afraid. I don't want anything from you at all, Irene. I do think we should have a free and frank discussion."

She looked in my direction. "What about him?"

"Mr. Archer knows this case better than I do. I rely completely on his discretion."

Truttwell's praise made me uneasy: I wasn't prepared to say the same things about him.

"I don't trust his discretion," the woman said. "Why should I? I hardly know him."

"You know me, Irene. As your attorney—"

"So you're our lawyer again?"

"I never ceased to be, really. It must be clear to you by now that you need my help, and Mr. Archer's help. Everything we've learned about the past is strictly in confidence among the three of us."

"That is," she said, "if I go along. What if I don't?"

"I'm ethically bound to keep your secrets."

"But they'd slip out anyway, is that the idea?"

"Not through me or Archer. Perhaps through Dr. Smitheram. Obviously I can't protect your interests unless you let me."

She considered Truttwell's proposition. "I didn't want to break with you myself. Especially not at this time. But I can't speak for my husband."

"Where is he?"

"I left him at home. These last few days have been awfully hard on Larry. He doesn't look it, but he's the nervous type."

Her words touched a closed place in my mind. "Was that your husband in the film? The boy who got pushed into the water?"

"Yes it was. It was the first day I met Larry. And his last free weekend before he went into the Navy. I could tell that he was interested in me, but I didn't get to know him that day, not really. I wish I had."

"When did you get to know him?"

"A couple of years later. He grew up in the meantime."

"What happened to you in the meantime?"

She turned away from me abruptly, her white neck ridged with strain. "I'm not going to answer that," she said to Truttwell. "I didn't hire a lawyer and a detective to dig up all the dirt in my own life. What kind of sense would that make?"

He answered her in a quiet careful voice: "It makes more sense than trying to keep it secret. It's time the dirt, as you call it, was laid out on the table, among the three of us. I needn't remind you there have been several murders."

"*I* didn't kill anybody."

"Your son did," I reminded her. "We've already discussed that death in the hobo jungle."

She turned back to me. "It was a kidnapping. He killed in self-defense. You said yourself the police would understand."

"I may have to take that back, now that I know more about it. You held back part of the story—all the really important parts. For example, when I told you that Randy Shepherd was involved in the kidnapping you didn't mention that Randy was your father."

"A woman doesn't have to tell on her husband," she said. "Isn't it the same for a girl and her father?"

"No, but it doesn't matter now. Your father was shot dead in Pasadena yesterday afternoon."

Her head came up. "Who shot him?"

"The police. Your mother called them."

"My mother did?" She was silent for a while. "That doesn't really surprise me. The first thing I remember in my life is the two of them fighting like animals. I had to get away from that kind of life, even if it meant—" Our eyes met, and the sentence died under the impact.

I continued it for her: "Even if it meant running off to Mexico with an embezzler."

She shook her head. Her black hair fluffed out a little, and made her look both younger and cheaper.

"I never did."

"You never ran off with Eldon Swain?"

She was silent.

"What did happen, Mrs. Chalmers?"

"I can't tell you—not even at this late date. There are other people involved."

"Eldon Swain?"

"He's the most important one."

"You don't have to worry about protecting him, as you very well know. He's as safe as your father, and for the same reason."

She gave me a lost look, as if her game with time had failed for a moment and she was caught in the limbo between her two lives. "Is Eldon really dead?"

"You know he is, Mrs. Chalmers. He was the dead man in the railroad yards. You must have known or suspected it at the time."

Her eyes darkened. "I swear to God I didn't."

"You had to know. The body was left with its hands in the fire so that the fingerprints would be erased. No eight-year-old boy did that."

"That doesn't mean it was me."

"You were the one with the motivation," I said. "If the dead man was identified as Swain, your whole life would collapse. You'd lose your house and your husband and your social standing. You'd be Rita Shepherd again, back on your uppers."

She was silent, her face working with thought. "You said my father was involved with Eldon. It must have been my father who burned the body—did you say he burned the body?"

"The fingers."

She nodded. "It must have been my father. He was always talking about getting rid of his own fingerprints. He was a nut on the subject."

Her voice was unreflective, almost casual. It stopped suddenly. Perhaps she had heard herself as Rita Shepherd, daughter of an ex-con, trapped again in that identity without any possible escape.

The knowledge of her predicament seemed to be striking down into her body and penetrating her mind through layers of indifference, years of forgetfulness. It struck a vital place and crumpled her in the chair, her face in her hands. Her hair fell forward from her nape and sifted over her fingers like black water.

Truttwell stood over her looking down with an intensity that didn't seem to include any kind of love. Perhaps it was pity he felt, laced with possession. She had passed through several hands and been slightly scorched by felony, but she was still very beautiful.

Forgetful of me, and of himself, Truttwell put his hands on her. He stroked her head very gently, and then her long tapering back. His caresses weren't sexual in any ordinary sense. Perhaps, I thought, his main feeling was an abstract legal passion which satisfied itself by having her as a client. Or a widower's underground desire held in check by the undead past.

Mrs. Chalmers recovered after a while, and asked for water. Truttwell went to another room to fetch it. She spoke to me in an urgent whisper:

"Why did my mother call the police on Randy? She must have had a reason."

"She had. He stole her picture of Nick."

"The graduation picture I sent her?"

"Yes."

"I shouldn't have sent it. But I thought for once in my life I could act like a normal human being."

"You couldn't, though. Your father took it to Jean Trask and talked her into hiring Sidney Harrow. That's how the whole thing started."

"What did the old man want?"

"Your husband's money, just like everyone else."

"But not you, eh?" Her voice was sardonic.

"Not me," I said. "Money costs too much."

Truttwell brought her a paper cup of water and watched her drink it. "Are you feeling up to a little drive?"

Her body jerked in alarm. "Where to?"

"The Smitheram Clinic. It's time we had a chat with Nick."

She looked profoundly unwilling. "Dr. Smitheram won't let you in."

"I think he will. You're Nick's mother. I'm his attorney. If Dr. Smitheram won't cooperate, I'll slap a writ of *habeas corpus* on him."

Truttwell wasn't entirely serious, but her mood of alarm persisted. "No. Please, don't do anything like that. I'll talk to Dr. Smitheram."

On the way out I asked the switchboard girl if Betty had come back with the lab report. She hadn't. I left word for her that I'd be at the clinic.

35

IRENE CHALMERS DISMISSED Emilio. She rode between Truttwell and me in the front seat of his Cadillac. When she got out of the car in the parking lot of the clinic she moved like a drugged woman. Truttwell gave her his arm and guided her into the reception room.

Moira Smitheram was behind the desk, as she had been the day I met her. It seemed like a long time ago. Her face had aged and deepened, or maybe I could see more deeply into her. She looked from Truttwell to me.

"You didn't give me much time."

"We're running out of time."

Truttwell said: "It's very important that we talk to Nick Chalmers. Mrs. Chalmers agrees."

"You'll have to take that up with Dr. Smitheram."

Moira went and got her husband. He came through the inner door, striding angrily in his white smock.

"You don't give up easily, do you?" he said to Truttwell.

"I don't give up at all, old man. We're here to see Nick, and I'm very much afraid that you can't stop us."

Smitheram turned his back on Truttwell and said to Mrs. Chalmers: "How do you feel about this?"

"You better let us in, doctor," she said without raising her eyes.

"Have you re-engaged Mr. Truttwell as your attorney?"

"Yes I have."

"And has Mr. Chalmers concurred?"

"He will."

Dr. Smitheram gave her a probing look. "What sort of pressure are you under, anyway?"

Truttwell said: "You're wasting time, doctor. We're here to talk to your patient, not to you."

Smitheram swallowed his anger. "Very well."

He and his wife conducted us through the inner door, along a corridor to a second door which had to be unlocked and relocked. The wing beyond it contained eight or ten rooms beginning with a suicide room in which a woman sat on the padded floor looking out at us through thick glass.

Nick had a bed-sitting room with an open door. He sat in an armchair holding an open textbook. In his light wool robe he looked almost like any other young man interrupted at his studies. He stood up when he saw his mother, his black eyes large and bright in his pale face. His dark glasses were on the desk beside him.

"Hello, Mother, Mr. Truttwell." His glance traveled across our faces without pausing. "Where's Dad? Where's Betty?"

"This isn't a social occasion," Truttwell said, "though it's good to see you. We have some questions to ask you."

"Keep them as brief as possible," Smitheram said. "Sit down, Nick."

Moira took his book and put a marker in it; then stood beside her husband in the doorway. Irene Chalmers sat in the other chair, Truttwell and I on the single bed facing Nick.

"I'm not going to beat around the bush," Truttwell said. "About fifteen years ago, when you were a small boy, you shot a man in the railroad yards."

Nick raised his eyes to Smitheram's and said in a flat disappointed tone: "You told him."

"No, I did not," Smitheram said.

Truttwell said to the doctor: "You took on quite a responsibility when you kept that shooting quiet."

"I know that. I acted in the best interests of an eight-year-old who was threatened with autism. The law isn't the only guide to the conduct of human affairs. Even if it were, the homicide was justifiable or accidental."

Truttwell said wearily: "I didn't come here to argue law or ethics with you, doctor."

"Then don't attack my motives."

"Which are, of course, as pure as the driven snow."

The doctor's large body made a small threatening move in Truttwell's direction. It was inhibited by Moira's hand on his elbow.

Truttwell turned back to Nick. "Tell me about that shooting down by the tracks. Was it an accident?"

"I don't know."

"Then just tell me how it happened. How did you get to the railroad yards in the first place?"

Nick answered haltingly as if his memory operated by fits and starts like a teletype ticker. "I was on my way home from school when the man picked me up in his car. I know I shouldn't have got in. But he seemed terribly serious. And I felt sorry for him. He was sick and old.

"He asked me a lot of questions about who my mother was, and who my father was, and when and where I was born. Then he said that he was my father. I didn't exactly believe him, but I was interested enough to go along to the hobo jungle with him.

"He took me to a place behind the old roundhouse. Someone had left a fire burning and we added some wood and sat beside it. He got out a pint of whisky and took a pull and gave me a taste of it. It burned my mouth. But he drank it down like water, and finished the bottle.

"It made him foolish. He sang some old songs, and then he got sentimental. He said I was his darling boy and when he came into his rights he'd assume his true position and look after me. He started to paw me and kiss me, and that was when I shot him. He had a gun in the waistband of his trousers. I pulled it out and shot him, and he died."

Nick's pale face was still composed. But I could hear his rapid breathing.

"What did you do with the gun?" I said.

"I didn't do anything with it. I left it lying there and walked home. Later I told my parents what I'd done. They didn't believe me at first. Then it came out in the paper, about the dead man, and they believed me. They brought me to Dr. Smitheram. And," he added with wry bitterness, "I've been with him ever since. I wish I'd gone to the police in the first place." His eyes were on his mother's half-averted face.

"It wasn't your decision," I said. "Now let's get on to the Sidney Harrow killing."

"Good Lord, do you think I killed him, too?"

"You thought so, remember?"

His gaze turned inward. "I was pretty confused, wasn't I? The trouble was I really felt like killing Harrow. I went to his motel room that night to have a showdown with him. Jean told me where he was staying. He wasn't there, but I found him in his car on the beach."

"Alive or dead?"

"He was dead. The gun that killed him was lying beside his car. I picked it up to look at it and something clicked in my head. And the ground literally shifted under my feet. I thought at first it was an earthquake. Then I realized it was in me. I was confused for a long time, and suicidal." He added: "The gun seemed to want me to do something with it."

"You already had done something with it," I said. "It was the same gun that you left in the railroad yards."

"How could that be?"

"I don't know how it could be. But it was the same gun. The police have ballistic records that prove it. Are you sure you left the gun beside the body?"

Nick was confused again. His eyes looked at our faces in naked helplessness. He reached for his dark glasses and put them on. "Harrow's body?"

"Eldon Swain's body. The man in the railroad yards who said he was your father. Did you leave the gun there beside him, Nick?"

"Yes. I know I didn't take it home with me."

"Then someone else picked it up and kept it for fifteen years and used it on Harrow. Who would that be?"

"I don't know." The young man shook his head slowly from side to side.

Smitheram stepped forward. "He's had enough. And you're not learning anything." His eyes were full of anxiety, but whether it was for Nick I couldn't tell.

"I'm learning a good deal, doctor. So is Nick."

"Yes." The young man looked up. "Was the man in the railroad yards really my father as he said?"

"You'll have to ask your mother."

"Was he, mother?"

Irene Chalmers looked around the room as if another trap had closed on her. The pressure of our silence forced words out of her:

"I don't have to answer that and I'm not going to."

"That means he was my father."

She didn't answer Nick or look at him. She sat with her head bowed. Truttwell stood up and put a hand on her shoulder. She inclined her head sideways so that her cheek rested against his knuckles. In contrast with her flawless skin, his hand was spotted with age.

Nick said insistently: "I knew that Lawrence Chalmers couldn't be my father."

"How did you know that?" I asked him.

"The letters he wrote from overseas—I don't remember the dates exactly, but the timing wasn't right."

"Is that why you took the letters out of the safe?"

"Not really. I stumbled onto that aspect of it. Sidney Harrow and Jean Trask came to me with a wild story that my father—that Lawrence Chalmers had committed a crime. I took the letters to prove to them that they were mistaken. He was overseas at the time the theft occurred."

"What theft?"

"Jean said he stole some money from her family—from her father—actually an enormous amount of money, half a million or so. But his letters proved that Jean and Harrow were wrong. On the day of the alleged theft—I think it was July 1, 1945—my fa—Mr. Chalmers was at sea aboard his carrier." He added with a look of sad irony: "In proving that I also proved that he couldn't be my father. I was born on December 14, 1945, and nine months before, when I must have been—" He looked at his mother, and couldn't find the word.

"Conceived?" I said.

"When I must have been conceived, he was aboard his ship in the forward area. Do you hear that, Mother?"

"I hear you."

"Haven't you any other comment?"

"You don't have to turn against me," she said in a low tone. "I'm your mother. What does it matter who your father was?"

"It matters to me."

"Forget it. Why don't you forget it?"

"I have some of the letters here." I brought out my wallet and showed Nick the three letters. "I think these are the ones you were particularly interested in."

"Yes. Where did you get them?"

"From your apartment," I said.

"May I have them for a minute?"

I handed him the letters. He went through them quickly.

"This is the one he wrote on March 15, 1945: 'Dearest Mother: Here I am in the forward area again so my letter won't go off for a while.' That would seem to prove conclusively that whoever my father was, he wasn't and isn't Lieutenant (j.g.) L. Chalmers." He looked at his mother again in murky speculation: "Was it the man in the railroad yards, Mother? The man I killed?"

"You don't want an answer," she said.

"That means the answer is yes," he said in bleak satisfaction. "At least I know that much for certain. What did you say his name was? My father's name?"

She didn't answer.

"Eldon Swain," I said. "He was Jean Trask's father."

"She *said* we were brother and sister. You mean it's really true?"

"I don't have the answers. You're the one who seems to have them." I paused, and went on: "There's one very important answer I have to ask you for, Nick. What took you to Jean Trask's house in San Diego?"

He shook his head. "I don't recall. The whole thing is a blank. I don't even remember *going* to San Diego."

Dr. Smitheram came forward again. "I have to call a halt now. I'm not going to let you undo what we've done for Nick in the last couple of days."

"Let's finish it off," Truttwell said. "After all, it's been dragging on now for most of Nick's young life."

"I want to finish it, too," Nick said, "if I can."

"And so do I." It was Moira coming out of a long silence.

The doctor turned on her coldly. "I don't remember asking for your opinion."

"You have it, anyway. Let's get it over with."

Moira's voice had overtones of weary guilt. The two of them confronted each other for a moment as if they were the only ones in the room.

I said to Nick: "When did you start remembering in San Diego?"

"When I woke up in the hospital that night. I was missing the whole day."

"And what was the last you remembered before that?"

"When I got up that morning. I'd been awake all night, with one thing and another, and I was feeling awfully depressed. That horrible scene in the railroad yards kept coming back. I could smell the fire and the whisky.

"I decided to turn off my mind with a sleeping pill or two, and I got up and went into the bathroom where they kept them. When I saw the red and yellow capsules in the bottles I changed my mind. I decided to take a lot of them and turn off my mind for good."

"Was that when you wrote your suicide note?"

He considered my question. "I wrote it just before I took the pills. Yes."

"How many did you take?"

"I didn't count them. A couple of handfuls, I guess, enough to kill me. But I couldn't just sit in the bathroom and wait. I was afraid they'd find me and not let me die. I climbed out the bathroom window and dropped to the ground. I must have fallen and hit my head on something." He balanced the letters on his knee and touched the side of his head tenderly. "Next thing I knew I was in the San Diego hospital. I've already told Dr. Smitheram all this."

I glanced at Smitheram. He wasn't listening. He was talking in intense, low tones to his wife.

"Dr. Smitheram?"

He turned abruptly, but not in response to me. He reached for the letters in Nick's lap. "Let's have a look at these, eh?"

Smitheram riffled through the flimsy pages and began to read aloud to his wife: " 'There's something about pilots that reminds you of race horses–developed almost to an unhealthy point. I hope I'm not that way to other eyes.

" 'Commander Wilson is, though. (He's no longer censoring mail so I can say this.) He's been in for over four years now, but he seems to be exactly the same gentlemanly Yale man he was when he came in. He has, however, a certain air of arrested development. He has given his best to the war–' "

Truttwell said dryly: "You read beautifully, doctor, but this is hardly the occasion."

Smitheram acted as if he hadn't heard Truttwell. He said to his wife: "What was the name of my squadron leader on the Sorrel Bay?"

"Wilson," she said in a small voice.

"Do you remember I made this comment about him in a letter I wrote you in March 1945?"

"Vaguely. I'll take your word for it."

Smitheram wasn't satisfied. He went through the pages again, his furious fingers almost tearing them. "Listen to this, Moira: 'We're very near the equator and the heat is pretty bad, though I don't mean to complain. If we're still anchored at this atoll tomorrow I'm going to try to get off the ship for a swim, which I haven't had since we left Pearl months ago. One of my big daily pleasures, though, is the shower

I take every night before going to bed.' And so on. Later, the letter mentions that Wilson was shot down over Okinawa. Now I distinctly remember writing this to you in the summer of 1945. How do you account for that, Moira?"

"I don't," she said with her eyes down. "I won't attempt to account for it."

Truttwell stood up and looked past Smitheram's shoulder at the letter. "I take it this isn't your writing. No, I see it's not." He added after a pause: "It's Lawrence Chalmers' writing, isn't it?" And after a further pause: "Does this mean his war letters to his mother were all a fake?"

"They certainly were." Smitheram shook the documents in his fist. His eyes were on his wife's downcast face. "I still don't understand how these letters got written."

"Was Chalmers ever a Navy pilot?" Truttwell said.

"No. He did make an attempt to get into the pilot training program. But he was hopelessly unqualified. In fact, he was given a general discharge by the Navy a few months after he enlisted."

"Why was he discharged?" I said.

"For reasons of mental health. He broke down in boot camp. It happened to quite a few schizoid boys when they tried to assume a military role. Particularly those whose mothers were the dominant parent, as in Larry's case."

"How do you know so much about his case, doctor?"

"I was assigned to it, in the Navy Hospital in San Diego. Before we turned him loose on the world, we gave him a few weeks of treatment. He's been my patient ever since—except for my two years' sea duty."

"Was he the reason you settled here in the Point?"

"One of the reasons. He was grateful to me and he offered to help set me up in practice. His mother had died and left him a good deal of money."

"One thing I don't understand," Truttwell said, "is how he could fool us with these phony letters. He must have had to fake Fleet Post Office envelopes and markings. And how could he receive answers if he wasn't in the Navy?"

"He had a job in the Post Office," Smitheram said. "I got him that job myself before I shipped out. I suppose he set up a special box for his own mail." As if his head was being wrenched around by an external force, Smitheram looked at his wife again. "What *I* don't understand, Moira, is how he got a chance—repeated chances—to copy my letters to you."

"He must have taken them," she said.

"Did you know he was taking them?"

She nodded glumly. "Actually, he borrowed them to read, or so he said. But I can understand why he copied them. He hero-worshipped you. He wanted to be like you."

"How did he feel about you?"

"He was fond of me. He made no secret of it, even before you left."

"After I left, did you see him regularly?"

"I could hardly help it. He lived next door."

"Next door in the Magnolia Hotel? You mean you lived in adjoining rooms?"

"You asked me to keep an eye on him," she said.

"I didn't tell you to live with him. Did you live with him?" He was speaking in the hectoring voice of a man who was hurting himself and knew it but kept on doing it.

"I lived with him," his wife said. "I'm not ashamed of it. He needed someone. I may have had just as much to do with saving his mind as you had."

"So it was therapy, was it? That's why you wanted to come here after the war. That's why he's—"

She cut him short: "You're off the track, Ralph. You usually are where I'm concerned. I quit with him before you ever came home."

Irene Chalmers lifted her head. "That's true. He married me in July—"

Truttwell leaned toward her and touched her mouth with his finger. "Don't volunteer any information, Irene."

She lapsed into silence, and I could hear Moira's intense low voice.

"You knew about my relationship with him," she was saying to her husband. "You can't treat a patient for twenty-five years without knowing that much about him. But you chose to act as if you hadn't known."

"If I did," he said—"I'm not admitting anything but if I did, I was acting in my patient's interest, not my own."

"You really believe that, don't you, Ralph?"

"It's true."

"You're fooling yourself. But you're not fooling anyone else. You knew Larry Chalmers was a fake, just as I did. We conspired with his fantasy and went on taking his money."

"I'm afraid you're fantasying, Moira."

"You know I'm not." He looked around at our faces to see if we were judging him. His wife brushed past him and left the room. I followed her down the corridor.

36

I CAUGHT MOIRA at the locked door beside the suicide room. For the second time in our acquaintance she was having trouble unlocking a door. I mentioned this.

She turned on me with hard bright eyes. "We won't talk about the other night. It's all in the past—so long ago I hardly remember your name."

"I thought we were friends."

"So did I. But you broke that."

She flung one arm out toward Nick's room. The woman in the suicide room began to moan and cry.

Moira unlocked the door which let us out of the wing and took me to her office. The first thing she did there was to take her handbag out of a drawer and set it on top of the desk, ready to go.

"I'm leaving Ralph. And don't say anything, please, about my going with you. You don't like me well enough."

"Do you always think people's thoughts for them?"

"All right—I don't like *myself* well enough." She paused and looked around her office. The glowing paintings on the walls seemed to reflect her anger with herself, like subtle mirrors. "I don't like making money from other people's suffering. Do you know what I mean?"

"I ought to. It's how I live."

"But you don't do it for the money, do you?"

"I try not to," I said. "When your income passes a certain point you lose touch. All of a sudden the other people look like geeks or gooks, expendables."

"That happened to Ralph. I won't let it happen to me." She sounded like a woman in flight, but more hopeful than afraid. "I'm going back to social work. It's what I really love. I was never happier than when I lived in La Jolla in one room."

"Next door to Sonny."

"Yes."

"Sonny was Lawrence Chalmers, of course."

She nodded.

"And the other girl he took up with was Irene Chalmers?"

"Yes. She called herself Rita Shepherd in those days."

"How do you know?"

"Sonny told me about her. He'd met her at a swimming party in San Marino a couple of years before. Then one day she walked into the post office where he worked. He was terribly upset by the meeting at first, and now I can understand why. He was afraid his secret would leak out, and his mother would learn he was just a postal clerk instead of a Navy pilot."

"Did you know about the deception?"

"Naturally I knew he was living a fantasy life. He used to dress up in officers' clothes and walk the streets at night. But I didn't know about his mother—there were some things he didn't talk about, even to me."

"How much did he tell you about Rita Shepherd?"

"Enough. She was living with an older man who kept her stashed in Imperial Beach."

"Eldon Swain."

"Was that his name?" She added after a thinking pause: "It all comes together, doesn't it? I didn't realize how much life, and death, I was involved with. I guess we never do until afterwards. Anyway, Rita shifted to Sonny and I moved to the sidelines. By then I didn't much care. It was pretty wearing, looking after Sonny, and I was willing to pass him on to the next girl."

"What I don't understand is how you could stay interested in him for over two years. Or why a woman like his wife would fall for him."

"Women don't always go for the solid virtues," she said. "Sonny had a wild psychotic streak. He would try almost anything once."

"I'll have to cultivate my wild psychotic streak. But I must say Chalmers keeps his pretty well hidden."

"He's older now, and under tranquilizers all the time."

"Tranquilizers like Nembu-Serpin?"

"I see you've been boning up."

"Just how sick is he?"

"Without supportive therapy, and drugs, he'd probably have to be hospitalized. But with these things he manages to lead a fairly well adjusted life." She sounded like a salesman who didn't quite believe in her product.

"Is he dangerous, Moira?"

"He *could* be dangerous, under certain circumstances."

"If somebody found out that he was a fake, for example?"

"Perhaps."

"You're very perhapsy all of a sudden. He's been your husband's patient for twenty-five years, as you pointed out. You must know something about him."

"We know a good deal. But the doctor-patient relationship involves a right to privacy."

"Don't lean too heavily on that. It doesn't apply to a patient's crimes, or potential crimes. I want to know if you and Dr. Smitheram considered him a threat to Nick."

She sidestepped the question. "What kind of a threat?"

"A mortal threat," I said. "You and your husband knew that he was dangerous to Nick, didn't you?"

Moira didn't answer me in words. She moved around her office and began to take the pictures down from the walls and pile them on the desk. In a token way she seemed to be trying to dismantle the clinic and her place in it.

A knock on the door interrupted her work. It was the young receptionist. "Miss Truttwell wants to speak to Mr. Archer. Shall I send her in?"

"I'll go out," I said.

The receptionist looked around in dismay at the empty walls. "What happened to all your pictures?"

"I'm moving out. You could help me."

"I'll be glad to, Mrs. Smitheram," the young woman said brightly.

Betty was standing in the middle of the outer room. She looked windblown and excited.

"The lab said there was quite a lot of Nembutal in the sample. Also some chloral hydrate, but they couldn't tell how much without further testing."

"I'm not surprised."

"What does it mean, Mr. Archer?"

"It means that Nick was in the back of the family Rolls some time after he took his overdose of pills. He vomited some of them up, and that may have saved his life."

"How is he?"

"Doing quite well. I had a talk with him just now."

"Can I see him?"

"That isn't up to me. His mother, and your father, are with him right now."

"I'll wait."

I waited with her, each of us thinking his own thoughts. I needed quiet. The case was coming together in my mind, constructing itself in inner space like a movie of a falling building reversed.

The inner door opened, and Irene Chalmers came through on Truttwell's arm, leaning on him heavily, like a survivor. She had shifted her weight from Chalmers to Truttwell, I thought, as she had once shifted it from Eldon Swain to Chalmers.

Truttwell became aware of his daughter. His eyes moved nervously, but he didn't try to disengage himself from Irene Chalmers. Betty gave them a so-that's-how-it-is look.

"Hello, Dad. Hello, Mrs. Chalmers. I hear Nick is much better."

"Yes, he is," her father said.

"Can I talk with him for a minute?"

He hesitated for a thoughtful moment. His gaze flicked across my face, and back to his daughter's. He answered her in a careful, gentle voice: "We'll take it up with Dr. Smitheram."

He led Betty through the inner door and closed it carefully behind them.

I was alone in the reception room with Irene Chalmers. As she knew. She looked at me with a kind of dull formality, in the hope that nothing real would be said between us.

"I'd like to ask you a few questions, Mrs. Chalmers."

"That doesn't mean I have to answer them."

"Once and for all, now, was Eldon Swain Nick's father?"

She faced me in passive stubbornness. "Probably. Anyway he thought he was. But you can't expect me to tell Nick he killed his own natural father—"

"He knows it now," I said. "And you can't go on using Nick to hide behind."

"I don't understand what you mean."

"You suppressed the facts about Eldon Swain and his death for your own sake, not for Nick's. You let him carry the burden of the guilt, and take the rap for you."

"There isn't any rap. We kept everything quiet."

"And let Nick live in mental torment for fifteen years. It was a lousy trick to pull on your own son, or anybody's son."

She bowed her head as if in shame. But what she said was: "I'm not admitting anything."

"You don't have to. I've got enough physical evidence, and enough witnesses, to make a case against you. I've talked to your father and your mother, and Mr. Rawlinson, and Mrs. Swain. I've talked to Florence Williams."

"Who in hell is she?"

"She owns Conchita's Cabins, in Imperial Beach."

Mrs. Chalmers raised her head and swept her fingers across her face, as if there was dust or cobwebs in her eyes. "I'm sorry I ever set foot in that dump, I can tell you. But you can't make anything out of it, not at this late date. I was just a juvenile at the time. And anything I did away back then—the statute of limitations ran out on it long ago."

"What did you do away back then?"

"I'm not going to testify against myself. I said before that I was taking the fifth." She added in a stronger voice: "John Truttwell will be back in a minute, and this is his department. If you want to get rough, he can get rougher."

I knew I was on uncertain ground. But this might be the only chance I would have to reach Mrs. Chalmers. And both her responses to my accusations, and her failures to respond, had tended to confirm my picture of her. I said:

"If John Truttwell knew what I know about you, he wouldn't touch you with a sterilized stick."

She had no answer this time. She moved to a chair near the inner door and sat down inexactly and abruptly. I followed and stood over her.

"What happened to the money?"

She twisted sideways away from me. "Which money do you mean?"

"The money Eldon Swain embezzled from the bank."

"He took it across the Mexican border with him. I stayed behind in Dago. He said he'd send for me but he never did. So I married Larry Chalmers. That's the whole story."

"What did Eldon do with the money in Mexico?"

"I heard he lost it. He ran into a couple of bandits in Baja and they took it off him and that was that."

"What were the bandits' names, Rita?"

"How should I know? It was just a rumor I heard."

"I'll tell you a better rumor. The bandits' names were Larry and Rita, and they didn't steal the money in Mexico. Eldon Swain never got it across the border. You set him up for a highjacking, and fingered him for Larry. And the two bandits lived happily ever after. Until now."

"You'll never prove that! You can't!"

She was almost shouting, as if she hoped to drown out the sound of my voice and the rumors of the past. Truttwell opened the inner door.

"What's going on?" He gave me a stern look. What are you trying to prove?"

"We were discussing what happened to Swain's half million. Mrs. Chalmers claims that Mexican bandits got it. But I'm fairly certain she and Chalmers highjacked it from Swain. It must have happened a day or two after Swain embezzled the money and brought it to San Diego, where she was waiting for him."

Mrs. Chalmers glanced up, as if my freewheeling reconstruction had touched on a factual detail. Truttwell noticed the giveaway movement of her eyes. His whole face opened and closed like a grasping hand.

"They stole a car," I went on, "and brought the money here to Pacific Point, to his mother's house. This was July 3, 1945. Larry and Rita staged a burglary in reverse. It wasn't hard, since Larry's mother was blind and Larry must have had keys to the house, as well as the combination of the safe. They put the money in the safe and left it."

Mrs. Chalmers got to her feet and went to Truttwell and took hold of his arm. "Don't believe him. I wasn't within fifty miles of here that night."

"Was Larry?" Truttwell said.

"Yes! It was all Larry's doing. His mother never used the safe after she lost her sight and he figured it was a perfect place to stash—I mean—"

Truttwell took her by the shoulders with both hands and held her at arm's length.

"You were here with Larry that night. Weren't you?"

"He forced me to come along. He held a gun on me."

"That means you were driving," Truttwell said. "You killed my wife."

The woman hung her head. "It was Larry's fault. She recognized him, see. He twisted the wheel and stomped on my foot and speeded up the car. I couldn't stop it. It went right over her. He wouldn't let me stop till we got back to Dago."

Truttwell shook her. "I don't want to hear that. Where is your husband now?"

"At home. I already told you he isn't feeling well. He's just sitting around in a daze."

"He's still dangerous," I said to Truttwell. "Don't you think we better call Lackland?"

"Not until I've had a chance to talk to Chalmers. You come along with me, eh? You too, Mrs. Chalmers."

Once again she sat between us in the front seat of Truttwell's car. She peered far ahead along the freeway like an accident-prone subject living in dread of still further disasters.

"The other morning," I said, "when Nick took all those sleeping pills and tranquilizers, where were you?"

"In bed asleep. I took a couple of chloral hydrates myself the night before."

"Was your husband in bed asleep?"

"I wouldn't know. We have separate rooms."

"When did he take off to look for Nick?"

"Right after you left that morning."

"Driving the Rolls?"

"That's right."

"Where did he go?"

"All over the place, I guess. When he gets excited he runs around like a maniac. Then he sits around like a dummy for a week."

"He went to San Diego, Mrs. Chalmers. And there's evidence that Nick rode along with him, lying unconscious under a rug in the back seat."

"That doesn't make sense."

"I'm afraid it did to your husband. When Nick climbed out the bathroom window, your husband intercepted him in the garden. He knocked him out with a spade or some other tool and hid him in the Rolls until he was ready to leave for San Diego."

"Why would he do a thing like that to his own son?"

"Nick wasn't his son. He was Eldon Swain's son, and your husband knew it. You're forgetting your own life history, Mrs. Chalmers."

She gave me a quick sideways look. "Yeah, I wish I could."

"Nick knew or suspected whose son he was," I said. "In any case, he was trying to get at the truth about Eldon Swain's death. And he was getting closer all the time."

"Nick shot Eldon himself."

"We all know that now. But Nick didn't drag the dead man into the fire to burn off his fingerprints. That took adult strength, and adult motives. Nick didn't keep Swain's gun, to use it on Sidney Harrow fifteen years later. Nick didn't kill Jean Trask, though your husband did his best to frame him for it. That was why he took Nick to San Diego."

The woman said in a kind of awe: "Did Larry kill all those people?"

"I'm afraid he did."

"But why?"

"They knew too much about him. He was a sick man protecting his fantasy."

"Fantasy?"

"The pretend world he lived in."

"Yeah, I see what you mean."

We left the freeway at Pacific Street and drove up the long slope. Behind us at the foot of the town the low red sun was glaring on the water. In the queer, late light the Chalmers mansion looked insubstantial and dreamlike, a castle in Spain referring to a past that had never existed.

The front door was unlocked, and we went in. Mrs. Chalmers called her husband—"Larry!"—and got no answer.

Emilio appeared laggingly in the corridor that led to the back of the house. Mrs. Chalmers rushed toward him.

"Where is he?"

"I don't know, ma'am. He ordered me to stay in the kitchen."

"Did you tell him I searched the Rolls?" I said.

Emilio's black eyes slid away from mine. He didn't answer me.

The woman had climbed the short flight of stairs to the study. She pounded with her fist on the carved oak door, sucked her bleeding knuckles, and pounded again.

"He's in there!" she cried. "You've got to get him out. He'll do away with himself."

I pushed her to one side and tried the door. It was locked. The room beyond it was terribly still.

Emilio went back to the kitchen for a screwdriver and a hammer. He used them to unhinge the door of the study.

Chalmers was sitting in the judge's swivel chair, his head inclined rather oddly to one side. He had on a blue naval uniform with a full commander's three gold stripes. Blood from his cut throat had run down over his row of battle ribbons, making them all one color. An old straight razor lay open beside his dangling hand.

His wife stood back from his body as if it gave off mortal laser rays.

"I knew he was going to do it. He wanted to do it the day they came to the front door."

"Who came to the front door?" I said.

"Jean Trask and that muscle boy she traveled with. Sidney Harrow. I slammed the door in their faces, but I knew they'd be coming back. So did Larry. He got out Eldon's gun that he'd kept in the safe all those years. What he had in mind was a suicide pact. He wanted to shoot me and then himself. Dr. Smitheram and I talked him into a trip to Palm Springs instead."

"You should have let him shoot himself," Truttwell said.

"And me too? Not on your life. I wasn't ready to die. I'm still not ready."

She still had passion, if only for herself. Truttwell and I were silent. She said to him:

"Look, are you still my lawyer? You said you were."

He shook his head. His eyes seemed to be looking through and beyond her, into a sad past or a cold future.

"You can't go back on me now," she said. "You think I haven't suffered enough? I'm *sorry* about your wife. I still wake up in the middle of the night and see her in the road, poor woman, lying there like a bundle of old clothes."

Truttwell struck her face with the back of his hand. A little blood spilled from her mouth, drawing a line across her chin like a crack in marble.

I stepped between them so that he couldn't hit her again. It wasn't the sort of thing that Truttwell should be doing.

She took some courage from my gesture. "You don't have to hurt me, John. I feel bad enough without that. My whole time here, it's been like living in a haunted house. I mean it. The very first night we came, when we were here in the study, putting the packages of money in the safe—Larry's blind old mother came down in the dark. She said: 'Is that you, Sonny?' I don't know how she knew who it was. It was creepy."

"What happened then?" I said.

"He took her back to her room and talked to her. He wouldn't tell me what he said to her, but she didn't bother us after that."

"Estelle never mentioned it," Truttwell said to me. "She died without mentioning it to anyone."

"Now we know what she died of," I said. "She found out what had become of her son."

As though he had overheard me, the dead man seemed to have cocked his head in an attitude of stiff embarrassment. His widow moved toward him like a sleepwalker and stood beside him. She touched his hair.

I stayed with her while Truttwell phoned the police.